ESHKOL NEVO

Eshkol Nevo was born in Jerusalem in 1971. His novels are bestsellers in Israel and have received prizes in several countries – his first, *Homesick*, was longlisted for the Independent Foreign Fiction Prize. He is an Israel Cultural Excellence Foundation chosen artist – one of Israel's highest recognitions for excellence in the arts.

ALSO BY ESHKOL NEVO

Homesick
World Cup Wishes

ESHKOL NEVO

Neuland

TRANSLATED FROM THE HEBREW BY
Sondra Silverston

VINTAGE

1 3 5 7 9 10 8 6 4 2

Vintage
20 Vauxhall Bridge Road,
London SW1V 2SA

Vintage is part of the Penguin Random House group of companies
whose addresses can be found at global.penguinrandomhouse.com.

Penguin
Random House
UK

Published by arrangement with The Institute for the
Translation of Hebrew Literature

Eshkol Nevo has asserted his right to be identified as the author
of this Work in accordance with the Copyright, Designs
and Patents Act 1988

First published in Vintage in 2016
First published in Great Britain in 2014 by Chatto & Windus
First published in Israel in 2011 by Zmora-Bitan

www.vintage-books.co.uk

A CIP catalogue record for this book is available
from the British Library

ISBN 9780099578550

This book has been selected to receive financial assistance from
English PEN's 'PEN Translates!' programme, supported by Arts
Council England. English PEN exists to promote literature and our
understanding of it, to uphold writers' freedoms around the world,
to campaign against the persecution and imprisonment of writers
for stating their views, and to promote the friendly co-operation of
writers and the free exchange of ideas. www.englishpen.org

Supported using public funding by

ARTS COUNCIL
ENGLAND

Typeset by Palimpsest Book Production Ltd, Falkirk, Stirlingshire

Printed and bound in Great Britain by Clays Ltd, St Ives plc

For my grandmother, Pracha Frishberg (1916–2010). If she hadn't made the journey from there, I would not be here.

Inbar and Dori. Missiles

To: Dori
From: Inbar
Subject: Worried about you
I found your email address on your school's website. I know
we said we wouldn't write, but I also know that you were
supposed to go on active reserve duty. And that makes my
heart climb up into my mouth. So I just want to hear that
everything's okay with you.

After that I promise not to bother you again.

To: Inbar
From: Dori
Re: Worried about you
Hi,

I'm fine. I hate to ruin the heroic image, but in the end
they didn't call me up. I showed up at my unit the morning
after we got home. They kept me waiting all day for the
liaison officer who was supposed to decide what to do with
me. Turns out that nothing's changed in the canteen. Even
the drinks machine is still broken.

They sent me home in the evening and told me to be
ready to be called up at any time. They've already filled their
quota of spotters, but I might have to go up north later on.

How's your grandmother? Is she back to her old self?

It's a real madhouse here. My in-laws came running from
the kibbutz to stay with us after a rocket landed in the dining

hall, and from the minute they got here, this place turned into Neuland. General meetings, daily schedules, procedures. My sister and her kids come over a lot too because she's afraid to sleep on her own. There are mattresses in every corner like there used to be at my aunt and uncle's place in Arad during the music festival, and last night, on the way to the bathroom, I stepped on someone and I still have no idea who it was. Maybe a total stranger who took advantage of the chaos to crash here for the night. Or maybe I'm actually the stranger in this house.

It's probably pretty crowded at your place too, right?

Write to me. Even though I'm not sure it's such a good idea for us to be in touch.

Dori

To: Dori
From: Inbar
Re: Worried about you
Hi,

Did you hear my sigh of relief? Did it manage to climb over the Castel mountains and reach Jerusalem?

It's great that you replied. And it's so good that you're not there, at the front. I mean, I'm sure you're the best spotter in the army, but from my narrow and worried point of view, I hope the quota stays filled.

My place is a madhouse too!

My grandmother, to answer your question, shifts from being absolutely clear-minded to being totally confused, and in both states, she fights constantly with my mother. This is more or less what they sound like: You won't tell me what to do/I will tell you what to do/It's hot, I'm turning on the air conditioning/Air conditioning isn't healthy, Hana/ Actually, it is/As healthy as living in Germany?/My boyfriend happens to be German/What did he do in the

Holocaust?/I told you Mum, he was a child./So what did his father do?

And as if that isn't enough, my father suddenly showed up. They bought non-refundable tickets in advance, and the way he saw it, from Australia, 'This isn't a real war, just an operation that'll take a few days.' So they flew over, he, his new wife and my half-brother, and rented a hotel room. They come here at prearranged times so my mother can leave before they arrive. Get the picture? And I'm the one they hired to produce a radio show about family problems.

And that's not all. Yesterday we all sat down in front of the TV and tried to figure out what Nasrallah meant when he said they would attack places 'beyond Haifa' and 'beyond beyond Haifa', and Eitan asked if it would be okay – if the rockets reached Yokneam – for us to take in his family too, so I said, five people more, five people less, what's the difference.

Do you remember that only a few days ago we were in Neuland, Dori? 'Suddenly it seems so far away' – people always say that, don't they? But it's not true. At least not for me. I still speak Spanish to people sometimes, I still see images of the countryside in my mind, the rhythm of the journey is still in my body. And so are you, to be perfectly honest: you still flow in my blood.

Will you write to me again?

Yours,

Señorita Inbar

PS The business with my grandmother is actually pretty sad. It's really hard for me to see her like this. She was always my anchor.

PPS This war, there's something so unreal about it. Don't you think? Maybe Mr Neuland was right after all?

To: Inbar

From: Dori

Re: Worried about you

Señorita Inbar,

These emails remind me — towards the end of our stint in the army they took us on a tour of the Intelligence Corps research division. They already had computers but they still weren't totally secure, so they sent highly classified information to section chiefs through a system of chutes that opened into boxes in every office. They called those pages of classified information 'missiles' because a vacuum mechanism delivered them, rolled up like scrolls, to the personal box of whoever was authorised to read them. You've received a missile! the deputy section chief would announce to the chief—

And that's how I feel when I see your name in my inbox. I hope you're keeping my emails to yourself, by the way. One forward and I'm dead.

I have to admit that, for me, our trip does seem a bit distant. There's something about children that doesn't leave you any choice but to live in the moment. Even more so with mine (we never talked much about him, did we?). He's been showing me who's boss since I came back. For the first two days he wouldn't even let me hug him. Then he did, but informed me that he wouldn't hug me back. And the nights were horrible. Little Oedipus got used to sleeping with his mum and didn't like the idea of my taking his place. So at about three in the morning, he gets out of his bed, comes into ours and starts kicking me out. And this is a boy — I have no other words to describe it — that I love like mad. We've always had a very strong connection. He's a wonderful child (objectively speaking, of course . . .). Clever and sensitive and beautiful. But before my trip, he had a lot of problems. Morning farewells at nursery were unbearable. Other kids didn't want to come to our house and we couldn't figure out why. And he did other things we

6

didn't know what to make of. Like claiming there was a terrible smell in the house and no matter what we did to air the place, he kept crying about it. He cried constantly before I left on my trip. And then it turned out that my trip did what a year's worth of family therapy hadn't. He stopped crying and he's a happy camper now, as if I or maybe my relationship with him had been the problem all along.

I hope it's okay with you that I'm writing about him. It just seems strange to write about other things when he's really all I think about.

Just so you understand how deeply connected he and I are – yesterday I was giving him his bath and he suddenly looked up at me with those eyes that are as blue as my father's, and said: Daddy, who's Inbar?

I swear, that's what he said.

I don't know, I said. Maybe a girl at nursery?

No, he said firmly, there's no Inbar at nursery. Then he asked me to bring him his bath crayons and forgot the whole thing.

But I didn't. Nothing like you has ever happened to me before, Inbar. And I have no idea how to get my head around it. Maybe because it's something you can't get your head around and the road not taken has to remain not taken. Which means that we have to stop writing. Immediately. In fact, I shouldn't even send this email.

Dori

PS It really is so sad to see a person you love fade away right before your eyes. I remember it with my mother. Towards the end, I actually wanted her to die.

PPS This war gets weirder every day. I don't know whether Mr Neuland was right, but one good thing has definitely come out of my time there. Yesterday I asked a music teacher at our school if he would give me some refresher trumpet lessons, and we're meeting next week. Nice, isn't it?

To: Dori
From: Inbar
Re: Anyone who really wants to end a correspondence shouldn't end his emails with a question mark

I'm happy to tell you that our place is now a mattress madhouse too. A Grad rocket landed 50 metres from Eitan's family's house in Yokneam and they've escaped to our place. My father and Eitan cleared out all the mess that was on the balcony, cleaned it up, closed it off with canvas and installed lighting and an overhead fan, and all of a sudden we have four rooms.

Even the smell of the house has changed over these last few days. Every house has its own smell, and ours used to be a combination of Eitan's aftershave, my shampoo, the fabric softener we both like and the fairly mouldy aroma of the large, old living room carpet.

Now there are so many new smells: my grandmother's old-age smell. The smell of the German perfume my mother seems to be using these days. The smell of chocolate that Reuven leaves behind. The smell of the embarrassment my father leaves behind. And the strongest of all: the smell of Eitan's teenaged brothers' sweat. Or to be more exact: the smell of the cheap deodorant they spray on their underarms *when* they're already sweaty.

Don't get me wrong. I love Eitan's family. But it's weird being with them when I know I'll probably be leaving him soon.

I think that deep inside, if I stop trying to persuade myself otherwise, I've known for quite a while that that's what I have to do. But two encounters helped me admit it to myself.

One, with you. And the other, with Reuven. My brother. What you said, it's absolutely right, that children force you to live in the moment. The minute he walks in the door – I'm totally his. For the few hours he's with me I don't think about anything (not even you!) but how to make him happy. We play whatever he wants: Lego, hide-and-seek, chasing. I even taught him Go Fish, and every time he says it with that Australian accent of his, I completely crack up. I love being with him. And he loves being with me. And it's because of him that I realise I made a mistake: it's not that I don't want to have children, I don't want to have them with Eitan.

So why don't you leave him? I hear your deep voice asking me from beyond the Judaean Hills.

Because, Mr Dori, it still takes strength to leave someone who loves you so much.

I'm building it now, my strength. Day after day. Hour after hour. And I'm also waiting for the war to end so I can have a normal breaking-up conversation in this house.

Yours,

Inbar

PS How great that you're going back to playing. You were fantastic on the drums in Neuland. As if they were actually part of your body. So I'm sure you'll be a star with the trumpet too. And when you appear with David Broza in bomb shelters during the next war, I can say that I was there when it all began. Anyway, let me know how the lesson goes. I, by the way, have finally started to write. Not the great novel yet, just a short story about a Jewish girl from Buenos Aires who falls in love with the son of a Nazi who fled to Argentina (for some reason, I've been preoccupied recently with impossible loves . . .).

PPS Don't worry about my forwarding your emails. I don't want you to die.

PPPS Don't worry about your son either. When I found out that my father had a new family, I was furious with him. But you can't stay angry at a parent for too long when the ties that bind you are stronger than your anger. It's a fact — he's here now and I don't bear him any ill feelings. Almost.

To: Dori
From: Inbar
Re: An idea
Hi,

I know I'm supposed to wait till you answer. But I suddenly thought I'd toss you a note over the wall that says: maybe we could meet?

I know it's daring, but (1) Don Anjel has already said that I'm daring by nature. (2) I'm sick and tired of writing prim and proper emails to hide the fact that I'm dying to see you. And (3) I'll be in Jerusalem next week, on Monday.

To: Inbar
From: Dori
Re: An idea
I don't think so, Inbar. I mean, it's tempting. Very tempting. I really miss our conversations. And when I heard on the news that the home front is strong enough to handle everything it has on its shoulders, I remembered your hand stroking my shoulders when we were on the way to Neuland. But I can't see you. Not now. And probably not later either. Even this emailing is difficult for me. I'm not the type, you see. I never knew how to hide things. I'm happy for you (really) that you've made your decision. But things are a little more complicated for me. I don't think it's right to involve you in it — but let's just say that I've been asking myself a few questions too after what happened to my father — and after meeting you. But in my case, we're talking about three people, and how did Don Anjel put it? The geometry of a triangle is a complex matter.

My grandfather Pima once told me: just don't make the

same mistake I did – spending your whole life thinking about another woman. So I think I'll refuse your invitation because even now, without seeing you, I think about you quite a bit. Please, try to understand.

Dori

PS The nights here can be cold, so if you're coming to Jerusalem, bring a *jacketito*.

To: Dori
From: Inbar
Re: Pima?
My grandmother had a shipboard romance with a man named Pima. She met him on the way to Israel and I have no idea if anything even happened between them, but afterwards she dreamed about him all the time, and in the morning she'd tell my grandfather her dreams. If I'd been my grandfather, I'd have been jealous – some of those dreams were very detailed, but he'd just listen to her and stroke her hand patiently while she spoke.

After he died, I took over his role. I'd call her on my way to work and we'd tell each other what we'd dreamed at night. Including the most embarrassing things.

Her condition has got worse over the last few days. If before, the ratio of clear-minded moments to confused moments was 50–50, now it's 20–80. For example, she can't remember Eitan's name. She calls him by my old boyfriends' names – all of them except his. He's not offended because he's not the type to take offence. But when she calls my mother by one of her friends' names, she does take offence. My mother still takes care of her, but every time my grandmother makes a mistake with her name, my mother gets another white hair.

But my grandmother always recognises me. Always. *Tsipke feuer*, she calls me. Firebird. And also Inbari, sometimes.

Every morning she sits down at the window on the chair she brought from her apartment, then asks me to put the fan in front of her face, turn it on full blast and make her a cup of ordinary tea, 'not all those new kinds with the funny names'. When I hand her the steamy cup, she takes a small sip, then asks me to leave the room because she has something to do. Yesterday, I couldn't control myself any longer and asked her what she does when she's alone. She didn't say anything for a minute, took another sip, then said, 'What's left for a woman my age to do? I remember.'

In the end I didn't go to Jerusalem. I didn't really have an appointment. I'm Yossi Benbenisti's daughter, you see. I lie to the world and to myself all the time. With you I tried to do it as little as possible, but a scorpion always stings in the end.

Yours sincerely, Señorita Inbar

PS There was a direct hit on my grandmother's house yesterday. So that's it, she has no home left to go back to. There are thousands of people across the border who don't have homes any more either. And the craziest thing is that all of this is actually a repeat of the first Lebanon war. Do you think that from now on all the wars will start to repeat themselves in reverse order? That we'll have a second Yom Kippur War? A second Six Day War? Do you see why there's something to be said for what Mr Neuland is trying to do? True, his means are radical, but maybe only radical means can work when everything else is at a statemate?

To: Inbar
From: Dori
Re: *Tsipke feuer*
That nickname, it really suits you.

Yesterday − you asked me to tell you − I had my first lesson. So first of all, we're not the only people whose homes are in chaos. My teacher's house is upside down because he's turned it into a refugee camp for dogs. There's a golden retriever from Kiryat Shmona, a dachshund from Acre and an Irish setter from Kfar Netter (I swear, not because of the rhyme). They were abandoned by their owners, who took off for the centre of the country, and he went up north to bring them home with him. When I walked in, all these displaced dogs jumped on me and I couldn't really imagine having a lesson with all that commotion. But he took me into an acoustic room where the ceiling was covered with egg cartons, closed the door behind us and said: play. Play what? I asked him. Whatever you want, he said. So I wiped the dust off Grandpa Pima's trumpet and played a piece he taught me once. I have no idea what it's called. Something Jewish, melancholy. While I was playing I thought of my grandfather, how he used to sit with me so patiently for hours. And how he took me to his performances, always sure that lots of people would attend, though only a few ever showed up. But it doesn't matter, he always said, I play because apart from love, music is the only thing that helps me get through life.

I remembered that as I played. And when I finished, my teacher said, okay, you made seven mistakes a minute, but you have the soul of a musician. Let's start working. And as we worked, I thought how long it's been since I was the one being taught, the one on the receiving end – since university, actually, and how nice it would be if I could believe that my grandfather and my mother, who always said it was a shame I didn't play an instrument, could look down and see me now.

Dori

PS My sister has started talking about going to Neuland too, after the war. I don't know what to say to her about that.
PPS What's your grandmother's name?

To: Inbar

From: Dori

Re: Later (not too late, I hope)

I know that it's your turn now, but I can't sleep. I tossed and turned in bed for two hours and finally came back to the computer. Suddenly, with a two-week delay (I'm slow, I know), my head is flooded with images from the journey. Voices, sounds, people. For example — I don't think I told you this — Alfredo and I stopped at a kind of small shop on the way to the market in Otavalo to get out of the rain. It was before we met you. In short, when the owner heard that I was from 'Jerusalén' he insisted on giving me a note to put in the Western Wall for him. I'd completely forgotten about it, but yesterday I put on the trousers I'd worn that day and the note was there. In the pocket. Amazingly, the trousers have been washed at least once since then, but somehow the note didn't crumble or fade. So I feel that I have to put it in the Wall, or else I'll suffer dire consequences. And . . . I thought I'd ask you to join me.

Not now, of course, after the war. When there are no more guests in our houses or fighter planes in the air.

What do you say? I know this is exactly the opposite of what I said before. And the last thing I want is to drive you crazy, but I have conversations with you in my mind all day long, Inbar, and these emails, they're becoming less and less connected to reality, and they create a separate, utopian world, and maybe if we stop writing and really see each other — one meeting, no more — it would help us to really let go of each other. And finally put an end to our journey.

I'll understand if you refuse, Señorita. But still —

Yours, Dori

Dori. One Month Earlier

IT'S A GOOD THING IT'S AT NIGHT, HE THINKS, standing at the door to Netta's room. If the flight were during the day, he'd have to forcibly tear the boy off his waist. There had been so many times when he'd stayed at home just because he couldn't bear his crying. And other times, when he was leaving the house, the child would climb on to the plastic highchair and open the window that faces the street and cry, so the entire world could hear, don't go, Daddy, don't go, as if his father were leaving home for ever, not just going out to play basketball.

For the entire time he was preparing for the trip, Dori hoped with all his heart that he wouldn't have to go. That at the last minute his sister Tse'ela and her ex, Aviram, would get their act together. That they'd find a way to put aside for a few weeks the anger and hurt that had accumulated between them during their ugly separation so that she could go herself. After all, she'd always been daddy's little girl and he'd been mummy's little boy in that unspoken division that occurs in all families, and she was also the one who'd kept in constant touch with their father since he'd left on his trip.

But it didn't happen. And his suitcase is waiting for him at the door. And the taxi driver called to say he would be a bit early because there was a traffic jam at the entrance to the airport.

He goes into the room. On the floor are Netta's small shoes, a stray red Lego piece and *Bob the Man in the Moon*, the book he read to his son at bedtime. When he finished, they closed the book and Dori lay down next to him, his long body beside Netta's short one. Don't forget that I'm going away tomorrow, he said. Will you be here for my birthday? Netta asked. I'll try, he answered. Promise me you will! Netta demanded. I promise that I'll try to be there, he said cautiously, although he thought that Tse'ela's concern was over the top and that his trip wouldn't be long.

Da-a-a-ddy! Netta said, and Dori tensed for the expected outburst, for the legs kicking at the cover, the small fists pounding on the pillow, the eyes peering out from the spaces between his fingers . . .

But Netta, apparently more tired than angry, thank God, closed his eyes and Dori stroked his head through his fine hair in a slow, spiral movement until he heard Netta's breathing settle into the even breathing of sleep.

He looks at him again now. How beautiful the boy is. And the position he's lying in — how misleading. On his back. Arms spread to the sides. Generously. You might really think he was a happy child.

He leans over and kisses him on the forehead — a light kiss so as not to wake him. And another one on his cheek. And another on the other cheek.

He doesn't feel like going. Not in the slightest. He wants to bury his nose deeper and deeper into Netta's smell, the smell of no-tears shampoo and the pyjamas still redolent of fabric softener even though he's already slept in them for a few days, and the warm milk with a teaspoon of brown sugar he drinks at bedtime, and a dash of Roni's perfume that stuck to him when she kissed him goodnight.

The driver calls again. He's already in the car park outside. And in the meantime, he's found out the reason for the traffic jam at the airport. Seems there's a terrorist attack alert and every car is being stopped for a thorough security check. So they really should get going. Another minute, Dori promises.

He moves from Netta's room into the light and takes out of

his pocket the list Roni prepared for him in her neat handwriting. He's crossed out all the items that are already packed in his suitcase or his hand luggage, but he still has the feeling that something is missing. He rechecks the usual suspects: passport, ticket, vaccination card, sunglasses, history book, the set of pictures of his father. Then he goes into the bedroom and finds Roni completely buried under her blanket, only a single curl visible. When they slept together the first few times in the apartment in Nahalot, he was afraid that she'd suffocate and he'd uncover her face when she'd fallen asleep. With time, it didn't worry him any more.

He traces the lock of hair with his finger till he reaches her head, and then Roni turns to him, reaches out and pulls him to her for a hug that surprises him. For the whole of the last week, she'd seemed to be anxious for him to leave. She spent the evenings locked in her study, claiming that 'those emails just create more and more work!' And once, when he tried to touch her under cover of darkness after they'd turned off their reading lamps, her body tensed and shrank back. Take care of yourself there, she says now. Her eyes are still closed, and he wonders whether she's really half asleep or whether she's pretending, avoiding meeting his eyes, as she's been doing all week. Maybe even all year.

Take care of Netta, he says and covers her again, thinking, I'm really going. It's really happening. Then he takes off his wedding ring and puts it on the dresser because where he's going, you don't walk around flashing gold jewellery, then goes back and turns off the lights, except in the bathroom – Netta screams if they don't leave it on. He takes in his last breath of the house, again thinking, what did I forget, what did I forget, what did I forget, damn it, then double-locks the door and leaves the key in the fuse box next to a dead cockroach that has been lying there on its back for a month because no one has removed it.

Night air enters his nostrils, but quickly turns into the cigarette smoke being exhaled by the driver, who offers to put his suitcase into the car for him. The driver looks about his father's age, so Dori does it himself, then gets into the back seat and drops his hand luggage next to him.

So, catching a flight, are we? the driver asks.

Yes, Dori says. Briefly. Curtly. As matter-of-fact as possible.

Business or pleasure? the driver continues his interrogation.

Neither, Dori admits.

*

It isn't until he sees the mobile phone company logo that he remembers. His mobile. Shit. That's what he forgot. Lucky they have a branch here, he thinks. But when he gets closer, he sees the sign on the door of the shop: A service stand opening here soon. Soon isn't good. How can he get in touch with Tse'ela? How will he let Roni know he's arrived safely? He looks at his watch. Fifty minutes to take-off. There's no way he can make it back home. Besides, he's already passed the point of no return for passport checks.

A girl with a mobile pressed to her ear walks past him. Suddenly he's seized by a criminal urge of the kind he's felt too often lately: to bump into the young girl, as if accidentally, and snatch her phone. He takes a deep breath, lets the urge pass, and walks over to the café. In the queue, he's approached by two guys and a girl who ask him to take a picture of them. What is there to photograph? he thinks, you haven't done anything yet, but he agrees and waits for them to choose a pose – arms out to the sides, as if they were an aeroplane – and, focusing on the girl's cleavage, he clicks the button, returns the camera and asks them where they're going. Quito, one of the guys says, with a connection in Barcelona, and Dori takes a closer look at them, wondering about the makeup of the group, two guys and a girl – it would clearly end in tears – and says: me too. They ask how long he's planning to be in South America and he says he doesn't know, for the time being he doesn't have a return ticket, and the girl smiles at him, exposing a crooked tooth, and says to the guy standing furthest from her, you see, Tuvy, I told you, that's the way to travel, and he says, but we bought return tickets because of you, sunshine, and the other guy, who's standing next to her, explains, Noya's starting her Master's degree in international relations.

Dori nods, as if in confirmation, but still can't figure out the relationships in this threesome, and thinks momentarily of a world in which everyone lives in threesomes, how many problems it would solve and how many new problems it would create, and he thinks that he, in fact, lives in a threesome too, with Netta and Roni. If you need anything – Noya touches his arm, interrupting his thoughts – just say the word. We're hooked up. Hotels, treks, prices.

Thanks, see you on the plane, he says in a tone much cooler than he intended, and they draw back, as if he'd pushed them, and go off on their way. Recently, he thinks regretfully, this has been happening to him quite a bit: speaking in a tone that's inappropriate to the circumstances and to what he's actually feeling. As if he's already forgotten how to act with people who aren't his students. As if he's lost the simple ability to engage in a sincere conversation, to search for the common denominator, to move closer.

From his table, he continues to watch the three as they go in and out of the duty free shops without buying anything. There is such exuberance in their movements, the way they walk, the way they stand still, the way Noya pushes her beautiful black hair from side to side every few seconds. They tease each other, clink tall glasses of the red wine they buy and take another picture beside the fountain.

The departure board is above the fountain. Written next to their flight is: ON TIME.

Dori's former friends – all of his friends became 'former' after they became parents – also went travelling after the army. They learned Spanish before they went. They attended lectures for travellers. They worked at all sorts of odd jobs to pay for their tickets. He didn't go. His most burning need when he left the army was not to go away, but to find something he was good at, something that would help rebuild his confidence, his identity, which had become shaky during his three years of reconnoitring Lebanese villages along the security strip. On the Mount Scopus campus he met Roni, who stated with her usual conviction that 'all those trips are one big escape, an attempt to postpone real life', thus putting an end to the possibility that he would be a backpacker, because from the moment he met Roni and joined his fate to hers, he felt a pit of longing open instantly beneath him whenever he was without her. His friends, for their part, returned from their long holidays with tasteless gifts and an unlimited supply of in-jokes. Years later, recalling a Brazilian drag queen they met in the carnival, or some disastrous sandboarding they'd done in Peru, they'd convulse with laughter. And he'd convulse right along with them. He'd heard those stories so many times that he felt as if he'd been there himself. Now, with a slight delay of fifteen years, he really would be there. Light ripples of the thrill of the journey pass through him, and immediately, to subdue them and remind himself of the real reason he's at the airport, he puts down his coffee, takes three pictures of his father out of his bag and spreads them on the table.

The first is a 'mug shot' that his sister Tse'ela found tossed in their father's document drawer. He looks startled. The lighting is unflattering. The close-up is cruel. And yet, even in the mug shot his father looks handsome. Soft eyes. Strong nose. Intelligent forehead. Women always smiled broadly at his father. As a child, Dori didn't understand why, but when he got a bit older and the girls at school used to whisper and gather around them on parents' day, he began to realise that his father looked good. And he hoped that some of that would rub off on him. If not right away, at least in the future.

The second picture was cut from a photo found in Tse'ela's wedding album. The original showed Tse'ela, her hair braided in the elaborate style so many brides seem to have, beside Aviram, her former husband, and on either side of them their parents glowing like two moons, each with a hand hugging the one closest to them and the other hand holding a drink: Mum orange punch and Dad his usual sparkling water.

The piece cut from the photo shows his father's head and the very edge of his neck. His hair, not yet dotted with islands of white, is brushed into a giant crest that juts out of the frame. He has a protruding Adam's apple, as do all the men in the family (did you swallow a spoon, Dori, or are you just happy to see me? Roni once asked him as he approached her in Rachel's cafeteria).

The third picture was too old to really help, but he took it anyway. It was the only one in all the albums in which both he and his father appear. Tse'ela must already have been in the army. His mother, as usual, took the picture. And they, the two of them, are standing on their skis on Mount Hermon, wearing woollen hats. His father's is black, his white. They are almost the same height. He might have been a little taller than his father, though he probably didn't feel that way because he was only fifteen and his height was new to him.

Cold. You can tell that it's cold from their jackets, which are zipped all the way up. Even the touch of that picture, Dori thinks, is colder than the others. And yet, even though it is so cold, they're not hugging, just standing next to each other. They never really hugged. Not all the way. Even when Dori would come back from Lebanon, even at his mother's funeral, their hugs were always tentative – his father would tap his back lightly with one hand, and with the other he'd already be pushing him away. When I see him this time, Dori promises himself now, I'll throw my arms around him and hold him so tightly that he won't have any choice but to hug me back.

There are dozens of other pictures of his father in his suitcase, carefully packed. Alfredo, his contact in Quito, wasn't too keen on pictures, saying that he didn't believe in them, only in information, but that Dori could bring a few, just in case. So last Saturday, he and Tse'ela took the albums off the shelf and went through them, sharing the memories each picture summoned up as they removed it from its clingy plastic cover. Here's the trip to Nahal Yehudia, when Mum sprained her foot and Dad carried her to the car. Here's that visit to the amusement park when Dori realised for the first time that his father wasn't omnipotent: he suffered from motion sickness and couldn't go on the roller coaster. Here's the house in Mevasseret that Dad built for ten years and they never lived in because Mum didn't want to. Look, Tse'ela pointed to their father wearing a hard hat and standing near a scaffold. Here he is at your age, she said. Can you see how much he looks like you? What are you talking about, Tsel, he objected, he doesn't look like any of us. Maybe a bit like Aviram. You are evil, she said, giving him a look, even though she knew he was right. The physical resemblance between Aviram and their father had always been so striking that Dori had to stop himself from laughing the first time Aviram came to their house for dinner.

Tse'ela put the bar mitzvah album back on the pile. Sorry, Dori apologised quickly. I didn't mean to pour salt on your . . . Aviram. And she said, it's not because of him . . . it's just . . . I'm worried about Dad.

I'd like to remind you, Tsel, that this is our father, Dori said. He survived the toughest battle of the Yom Kippur War, so what's South America for him?

That's exactly why I'm worried, Tse'ela insisted. This whole business just isn't like him.

Dori reaches into his back pocket now for his mobile to write a short, optimistic text message to his sister –

His pocket is empty. Never mind, he reassures himself. When

we land in Barcelona I'll find an Internet café and write to her. *Let's make a deal*, he writes the message in his head. *I'll find Dad and you find a new love. Why? Because you deserve it. True, you always stole my toys when we were little, and you always have to stick your nose into everything, but I think you're awfully brave for getting up and leaving Aviram, and you're a fantastic mother to your kids. Yes, fantastic. So you deserve only good things. And don't worry about Dad. I mean, worry. It's impossible not to. But I promise to leave no stone unturned, as if I were you.*

'Will passengers on flight 256 to Barcelona please proceed to the boarding gate'. The announcement interrupts his thoughts and he puts the pictures back in his bag. Fastens the buckle. Gets up. And goes.

*

These earphones they give you on planes – he tries again to fit them into his ears so they'll hurt less, and remembers that the film that's about to start, *Before Sunset*, played at the Smadar a few months ago and he asked Roni if she wanted to go. She said she wasn't sure she could handle all that romantic blab-bering. Do you remember where . . . ? He tried to kindle a flame in the dying coals. Of course I remember where we saw *Before Sunrise*, she answered with the fatigue that follows a day of battling at work, that cinema, you know, the one near the beach in Tel Aviv, after you threw me out. I didn't throw you out, he said, playing his part in the familiar dialogue, I just wanted a few days' break.

Two days, to be exact. A little less than forty-eight hours without her was enough to break him, even though none of the reasons he asked for that break, none of the foreboding he felt, had disappeared. He was still upset about her past history with love – from the age of sixteen she'd never been alone, and even when she first met him, at Shlomo Barr's drumming workshop, she had a boyfriend and they actually lived together, which didn't stop her from breaking up with him in cold blood, via a note on the fridge, the minute she decided she wanted Dori. That coldness she sometimes had scared him. The speed with which she became bored by the subject of a conversation. Or by people. The efficiency with which she advanced towards her goals, not all of which he approved of. There was no harmony between them, no serenity. Even back then. They argued quite a bit. Much more than his parents, for example. And she won most of the time. And when they walked together on the street, her small, rapid steps created a gap between them and he always had to ask her to slow down. One day she'll just refuse, the thought crossed his mind, one day she'll keep walking and I'll be left behind. And sometimes, when they were having sex, he had the feeling that it would be the last time. That after she came, she'd get up and leave him. So to prevent that, he got up and went himself. Told her he had 'to think', but his thoughts quickly sank into the bubbling swamp of yearning and of fear that grew into terror that he might lose her, the first woman he'd let touch the bitter kernel of his loneliness, the first woman he could tell, without being afraid she'd laugh, that Kissinger and de Gaulle were permanent characters in his dreams, the first woman whose sharp intelligence and way of thinking turned him on, the first woman who told him, your body is like a Greek statue, and said: I can only be strong when I face the world if I know there's a place where I can be weak, the first woman he allowed himself to trust completely, to lean on, to become addicted to.

So after two days of withdrawal symptoms, he called her and said: let's go to the cinema. She asked, does that mean you've finished thinking? And he said, I guess so, and she waited for him on the promenade wearing the green skirt she knew he couldn't resist, and they kissed and rubbed against each other on the sand, fully clothed, like a pair of school kids (how easily she came then), and then they went to see *Before Sunrise* together, their fingers intertwined in the darkness as if they'd made a pact to be together for ever, and the touch of her fingers, still a bit hesitant, gave him chills all the way to the top of his head, and he thought, you can never know what'll happen anyway, and every decision is a bit of a gamble, so he moved his lips close to her ear and said, I love you so much, Roni, you have no idea. She put her hand between his legs and her mouth to his ear and sang in a hoarse voice, to the tune of an old folk song, *Crazy 'bout me, can't live without me, crazy 'bout me, can't live without me . . .*

And from that day till this morning – ten whole years – he has never left her, on his own initiative, for more than a day.

Ten years had also passed for Ethan Hawke and Julie Delpy between the two films, and it showed. Ethan Hawke – Jesse in the film – has crow's feet when he laughs. And Julie Delpy looks sadder and paler. Or had she been pale before too? They walk out of a bookshop, go into a café, leave the café, walk along the streets of Paris, and very slowly, wound by wound, the ten years between the two films is revealed to Dori, the ten years between their first promise-filled night, before sunrise, and what they might salvage of those promises now, before sunset.

The picture freezes for a moment, and the pilot's voice announces that there's an air pocket ahead and passengers are requested to return to their seats. The flight attendants urge the passengers standing in the aisles to sit down and fasten their seatbelts, as if a seatbelt can help anyone if the plane spirals down into the ocean.

Maybe that's what happened to Dad? The possibility suddenly strikes Dori. Maybe a small plane he took to avoid a tortuous bus journey crashed and he plummeted, along with his special Dr Gav backrests, down, down, splash, to his death. Dori saw it clearly in his mind: his father lying on the ocean floor, eyes open wide, like a fish's mouth, the grey Dr Gav backrest he was never without lying beside him, and he, Dori, leading a group of divers, gas tanks strapped to their backs, through the fish and coral until he finds him and gives him a real hug, for the first time. And the last. Does the backrest float or sink? The minor question occurs to him, pulling him up out of the imaginary deep. The plane has stopped shuddering, and the woman next to him closes her small book of psalms. Alfredo said that he'd made initial enquiries at all the hospitals and all the companies that operated light aircraft, and his father's name hadn't appeared anywhere. But there was also the possibility that he'd flown in some unregistered private plane and crashed, right? You're right, Mister Dorrri, Alfredo elongated the r, but I've been doing this job for twenty years now. I learned to listen to my gut feelings. And my gut feeling tells me that your father is alive.

The last email Tse'ela received from their father was two months ago, from Ecuador. It said that he was going to be out of touch for two or three weeks and she shouldn't worry about him. Before that, they'd had a few phone conversations that Tse'ela described as 'weird'. In one of them, he told her that her whole lifestyle was wrong. That she didn't really want to be happy. When she began arguing with him, he cut her off and told her that there were things she wouldn't understand until she set out on a true journey. And in another conversation, he sent her and Dori regards from their mother. He'd seen her there.

That might have been all right if their mother hadn't died the previous year. And if the speaker hadn't been their father. Menny Peleg. The cool, level-headed, war hero. One of Israel's most successful strategy consultants for the management of business crises.

The insurance company refused to take it seriously. We're not talking about some kid, here, the man in charge said. Wait another two or three weeks before you get hysterical. He didn't take out a rescue policy, so if you get us involved, you'll have to pay the expenses. Also, he explained, take into account that the minute you put the process in motion you can't keep anything secret.

This is a small country. Your father is a well-known figure in his field. You both need to think long and hard about whether he would want that kind of exposure. You might find him in a day or two lounging on the beach in Peru, but there's no way you'll be able to repair the damage to his reputation.

I feel that he's in danger, Tse'ela said to Dori. I feel it in my body. He said that he wouldn't be in touch with us for two or three weeks, not two months. And Dad is always precise about things like that.

Go to him, Roni said, without looking up from her laptop, that's the only solution. Tse'ela really can't travel because of the kids. And anyway, you never know what to do with yourself at the beginning of the summer holidays. Plus you'll never forgive yourselves if it turns out that he really is in trouble.

What kind of trouble? he almost shouted. So now you're as hysterical as Tse'ela? Now you've started to 'feel things in your body' too?

The truth is – Roni lowered the screen of her laptop so she could look at him – that I think everything is fine with him and he's just enjoying his trip. But what would happen if you find him there after two days and travel together for a while? Maybe it would be an opportunity for you . . . to get closer? After all, only last week you told the psychologist that you'd both missed out on a real relationship.

That isn't what I said. I said that it makes me sad that I've *reconciled* myself to the kind of relationship we have.

So, maybe you *shouldn't* reconcile yourself to it.

I don't know. And what about Netta? He's terrified. I mean, when I held him in my arms in the delivery room, I promised to be a strong father to him. Never to disappoint him.

Netta will be fine, Roni replied. He has a mother, you know. But – she went back to looking at the computer – you need a local person to help you. Someone who specialises in finding people. You can't just land at the airport in Ecuador, out of the

29

blue. You can't even speak Spanish. Here, look, I found you a few options.

Options? . . . What? . . . When did you have the time? Where? On Google, Dori, of course. Sit here next to me for a minute.

I DON'T SEARCH. I FIND. That was the name of Alfredo's site, which was undoubtedly the most impressive of all the sites Roni showed him. Under the name was a picture: a short, older man, slightly bald, with a small pot belly, wearing a too-large suit. He didn't look especially daring, not Che Guevara or Simon Bolivar, but there was something fierce, almost wild, in his gaze. His face was tilted slightly forward, like a bull about to gore a red cloth, and the top buttons of his shirt were wide open. Next to that picture were others that showed him hugging the people he'd rescued. In those, he was dressed differently, more appropriately: large sunglasses reminiscent of the ones worn by Carlos the famous terrorist, khaki trousers, and a shirt with the sleeves cut off that showed his strong shoulders. And in all those pictures he wore a broad, surprisingly vulnerable smile.

Among the thank-you letters and newspaper articles that filled the site was a clip from a TV story about him broadcast on the Israeli news programme, *Roim Olam*. 'Twenty per cent of my clients are Israelis,' he said as he rubbed his chest hair through the opening in his shirt. 'Sometimes I have the feeling that you Israelis really want to get lost.'

He'd never had a son looking for his father, he told Dori during one of their phone conversations before Dori's trip. I had a mother looking for her daughter. A brother looking for his sister. A husband looking for his wife. A wife looking for her husband. But someone like you, I never had.

What do I care who you had or didn't have? But Dori chose his words carefully because reading the site had made him realise that Alfredo was flooded with requests from all over the world and agreed to take on only the cases he found interesting.

The plane stops shaking completely now and the fasten-seatbelts sign goes off. His screen comes back to life, but instead of a continuation of *Before Sunset*, it's showing an episode of *Married with Children*. He calls the flight attendant and tells her that the film was stopped in the middle. She says she'll check it and get back to him, but she doesn't come back, not even after ten minutes. Shame Roni isn't here, he thinks. She would know how to ask the flight attendant to get the film back in a way that would leave her no choice. He gets up to organise a wider coalition of protesters and discovers that most of the passengers are sleeping. Even Noya's threesome is dozing. She's sitting in the window seat, a black sleep mask over her eyes. Her knees are drawn up to her body and her small feet are pressed against the seat in front of her. Her socks don't match. One is red and the other is yellow.

One morning, he suddenly remembers, he complained to his father that he had no more matching pairs of socks in his drawer and his father said: so wear socks that don't match, son. No one will notice. That surprised him – it wasn't like his father to suggest such a subversive act, and he wondered whether, for all those years, his father had gone to work wearing highly polished shoes and unmatched socks.

One morning – this too he suddenly remembered – they were listening to a radio interview of someone named Yaakov Hasdai, a major-general in the reserves, and his mother said, just imagine, if Hasdai had got five mandates in the election, you'd be sitting in the Knesset today. And his father said, five? He didn't even get one. And Dori, surprised, asked, you mean you were once on a Knesset ticket, Dad? I didn't know. His father smiled and said in a different, unfamiliar voice, there are a few other things you don't know, Dorinyu.

*

When he opens his eyes, he doesn't know where he is. It takes him only a few seconds to remember, but the feeling is strange because after all, you can't ask the flight attendant: excuse me, can you please tell me where this flight is going? Quito, the answer finally pops into his mind, connecting flight to Quito, and along with it the realisation that his lower back is killing him. He tries to get up and out: to pass over the sleeping passenger next to him without waking him by placing his feet on the armrests, first his own, then his neighbour's. The manoeuvre works, but makes his back worse. Fuck it, he curses silently. In the narrow aisle, he tries to loosen his muscles by swivelling his hips. From the corner of his eye he catches a glimpse of Noya looking at him, and that makes his movements more self-conscious, more restrained. Until the flight attendant asks him politely but firmly to sit down so as not to block the approaching food trolley. Which meal is it, he wonders and looks at the trolley. Breakfast? Dinner? Actually, what difference does it make? He climbs back to his seat with his back hurting even more – the pain has already spread to his shoulders and knees – and thinks that, silly as it might be, it wouldn't hurt to have one of his father's special Dr Gav backrests now.

His father had four different orthopaedic back supports. One in his office, one in his car, one in his study at home and one – just in case. When he and Tse'ela went to say goodbye to him before his trip, they found him pushing his 'just in case' backrest, the grey one, into his backpack.

Doesn't that take up too much space? Tse'ela wondered. And he said yes, but even two days without his special Dr Gav backrests and he'd start having pains again.

I plan to do some trekking, not to lie around in a hammock all day, he said proudly. He pronounced the word as if it were spelled 'treeking', but they didn't have the heart to correct him.

The first time he told them about his travel plans was when they'd come from the memorial service thirty days after their mother's death. The house was no longer filled with visitors as it had been during the six days of mourning – his impatient father's abridged version of the traditional seven days – and only the hard core of people who loved his mother was in the living room drinking coffee. Or tea. Without pretty saucers under their cups. With only one kind of biscuit.

I want to close the office and go to South America, he said. And they took the announcement to be just one more instance of the strange behaviour he'd been exhibiting since she died: his horrifying, total breakdown at the funeral; his attack of rage when he saw that Tse'ela had changed the sheets on her parents' bed, thus stealing their mother's scent from him; his shortening of the traditional seven days of mourning to six because 'your mother was good at this, it came naturally to her', and without her, having guests, 'this trying to be pleasant all the time', annoyed him.

A few weeks after he'd announced his trip, his study was already full of maps, Spanish-language textbooks, pages of touring recommendations he'd printed out from the Internet, and notebooks in which he'd summarised the lectures he'd been to at the Lametayel travel shop in Dizengoff Center.

You probably drove the lecturers mad there, Tse'ela laughed at him (only she had the privilege of laughing at him. Dori never did. Not that he was afraid to, but it just never seemed to fit their relationship). They probably regretted the moment they agreed to give a lecture!

Just the opposite, his father smiled, but answered with total seriousness, I think they were glad I asked my questions. After all, if the currency changes when you go from Peru to Bolivia, you should know where in the border town you can get the best exchange rate, right?

Peru . . . Bolivia . . . Tse'ela muttered. Why are you even talking about . . . Tell me, Dad, what's wrong with travelling in Israel? Why do you have to go so far?

Travelling in Israel is nice, but I've already walked most of its trails. Usually with your mother. And anyway, it would be too short a trip for my needs.

Too short? What needs? I don't understand: how long are you planning to be in South America?

I don't know, little girl, I really don't know. That's why I bought a one-way ticket.

You do know that it's dangerous there, Dad, don't you? I read that they cut off people's fingers for their wedding rings.

I won't take my ring with me.

But they steal kidneys in the middle of the street, Dad! They just put a person to sleep, remove his kidney and sell it!

Oh come on, Tse'elonit, it isn't any more dangerous there than it is here.

But why South America, of all places, Dad? I don't understand.

Do you know what they called that continent when it was discovered? 'The New World'. That's what I need now. A new place that doesn't remind me of anything.

He won't go, Tse'ela had predicted after they said goodbye to him at the door – she with a tight hug, Dori with a light pat on the back – and when they'd walked far enough away for him not to hear. Two months later, she was still sure: he won't pass the medical tests, you'll see. At his age, the insurance companies won't give him a policy, and you know Dad, he won't go without health insurance. Five months later, she decided: he won't be able to leave his clients. He's too committed to them.

Dori didn't say anything. Whether she was right or not, he knew that Tse'ela needed to believe that their father would always be at her side.

So you're really going, are you? she said six months later, and rubbed the grey fabric of his Dr Gav backrest. The grandchildren were running from the bedrooms to the living room, playing catch, hide-and-seek, forging alliances of two against one – the one was always Netta, and Dori tried as hard as he could not to interfere. Not to try and rescue him. The psychologist said that Netta had to learn by himself how to act with

34

children his own age, and that Dori's over-protection would only get in the way.

You see these shoes? his father asked, lifting two tanks with soles. Believe it or not, these are the most expensive items in my bag.

Not the camera? Dori asked.

I'm taking a cheap camera because they say the expensive ones attract thieves. And I'm not that keen on taking pictures, anyway. It was always your mother who thought it was important to document everything.

Their mother observed them from her framed picture on the TV table, and Dori had the feeling that her eyes were gazing directly at him, still keeping the secret pact the two of them had made in their family of four. Only after she died did they notice that because she was the family photographer, she herself almost never appeared in their pictures, and they were embarrassed to have to ask her friends to look for photos of her that they could use to put together an album.

And tell me – what about your clients, how will they feel about your trip? Tse'ela asked, her voice filled with the hope that they might be the ones to come to the rescue.

You'd be surprised how many of them told me they wanted to join me, his father said.

And do I? Dori asked himself silently. But a glance at Netta, looking glum beside his happy-go-lucky cousins, was enough for him to know that he didn't.

I'll miss you terribly, you know, Dad. Tse'ela suddenly threw her arms around him and began to cry. The children left Netta alone and hurried over to see this amazing event: 'Mum, are you crying?' the older one asked. Tse'ela wiped away her tears with the sleeve of her shirt, pulled the two of them towards her, sat them on her knees, put a forced smile on her face and continued talking to her father, in English now: it's just . . . it's a very difficult time for me. First Mum. Also — things at home are really bad. And now — you're going away.

Enough of that emotional blackmail of yours, Dori thought, moving his chair slightly away from them. And the thing is — he thought bitterly — that it always works for her. That's the way to do it with his father. Be weak — get love. He might cancel his trip for her even now.

To his surprise, his father just put his hand on Tse'ela's shoulder and said in Hebrew, I'm sorry, Tse'elonit, that my trip comes at a bad time for you, but I have to go. I have no choice. What did Begin say about Lebanon? 'I can no longer carry on.'

Strange, Dori thinks now. Strange that he used that remark of Begin's. He always called Begin a demagogue, and he hadn't shed any tears when he resigned as prime minister after the war in Lebanon.

They said goodbye at the door, where their mother's name still appeared on the nameplate. I'm leaving a key with Hanita and Elisha if you need it, his father said casually, not knowing that in less than a month Tse'ela would pack up her children and some clothes and drive there in the middle of the night, ring Hanita and Elisha's bell with her elbow because she wouldn't have a free hand. She'd press it and press it, five short rings and one long one, like a car alarm blaring after an accident, until Elisha finally opened the door wearing a Beitar Jerusalem team tracksuit, took one look at her and the stunned children in her arms and, without a word, grabbed the key off the hook and handed it to her.

Come here, my little ones, and give your grandfather a last hug, his father said when all the words had been used up. Tse'ela's kids jumped into his arms while Netta waited submissively for his turn, and Dori kept himself from urging him to be more assertive. Kids, it's Netta's turn now, his father said. And Netta approached him somewhat hesitantly. A panpipe? Is that all you want? his father asked again to make sure. And Netta nodded.

He'll miss you a lot, Dori said after Netta had climbed down from his grandfather's arms and he himself stood in front of his father, exposed. Try to call as often as you can and email us pictures. Absolutely, his father said, and patted him on the shoulder, four times instead of the usual once.

There was no way he could have imagined at that moment, at the door, that a few months later he would be tracing his father's steps and find himself between sky and sea, on a connecting flight to Ecuador, sitting in front of a meal that tasted like cling film, his lower back screaming with pain, as if he were the one who had been wounded in the Yom Kippur War, or as if those back pains weren't the result of an injury at all, but a dubious genetic inheritance that had just been waiting for the right moment to appear.

Alfredo

The good thing about Israelis, Alfredo thinks on the way to the airport, is that you don't have to wear costumes for them. With North Americans, you can't get by without a suit and tie. They just won't give you any respect without it. It doesn't matter to them that suits are wrong for the weather here and ties make people on the street think you're a fucking banker. Anyway, he can't stand those North Americans. They talk like they have potatoes in their mouth. Think they're masters of the world. Correct his English like he's their student. True, he didn't go to school, but that doesn't make him less smart than anyone else, eh? Is a fact that with all their schools and their colleges and the money that pours out of them like Iguazu, they never understand how it happened. But my daughter sang in the church choir! they whine when they see the picture of her in the jungle, topless. But my son, he was on the baseball team! they say when the kid stares at them with peyote eyes and doesn't even recognise them. Baseball, such a stupid sport. Once, a client showed her thanks by flying him to a game in Minnesota. So boring. Watching cows sleep is more interesting. Once an hour someone manages to hit the ugly ball and the crowd goes wild, like who knows what just happened. He left during the seventh inning break, of course. Walked out of the stadium and went looking for whores. What kind of city doesn't have whores? There's something fucked up about those North Americans, completely fucked up. The Israelis are fucked up too, he thinks now, but different. With them, it has to do with the wars. And that he can understand. He was never a soldier, but his mother, may God save her soul, was shot in the civil war. A stray bullet, but it goes straight into her heart like it was aimed to hit her. He is there when it happens. Helping her hang laundry on the line in the yard, handing her the wet clothes from one tub and putting the dry clothes in another one, and then, all of a sudden, she falls down. In the movies, people who get shot fall down slowly, grab on to all kinds of things on the way, but his mother just folds up into herself, like an umbrella. And that is that. He can't do anything. The minute he bends down and sees that her beautiful eyes have no more light, he knows that there is no way he can save her. So Alfredo, he knows what pain is too, eh? Don't think he doesn't. And he also knows a few words in Hebrew. That always softens up the Israelis. You throw them a few words in that weird language of theirs, which no one speaks but them, and already they open up a little. Not that they really trust you. They're very suspicious, those people. Okay, is understandable after what the Germans did to them in World War II. Is funny that he didn't even know about that. A Jew from South Africa whose son disappeared rafting told him. At first it seemed exaggerated – six million? It sounded like a number somebody threw out so they could compromise on less later on – but he went and asked Marcello from the watch store who used to be a high school history teacher before one of his students broke a chair over his head, and Marcello said yes, it's true, it's written in books. Only then did he, Alfredo, suddenly remember that in the city where he grew up, Granada, there really was an old German who had a bakery, and people said that once he killed Jews for Hitler, but no one wanted to believe it or know about it because that German was a nice man. At the end of every day, he always handed out the bread that no one bought to the orphans who slept on the benches in the Plaza de Armas.

Another good thing with the Israelis – Alfredo thinks as he turns towards the terminal – is that they like to eat. Most of them have no problem polishing off a steak first thing in the morning. Even though the last Israeli woman he had was a vegetarian. Is so stupid to be a vegetarian. Man, when he was still a monkey, ate meat. Is what is natural for us to do. Is it any wonder that woman was so pale? It took them less than a week to find her drugged-up daughter. But then the mother, who didn't eat anything all week because the food wasn't healthy enough for her, collapsed because she was so weak and was in the hospital in Lima for a month. Which straightened out her daughter completely, by the way. Is funny: the minute the mother collapsed, the daughter threw her pills into the trash, got up on her feet and started taking care of her. He wouldn't have minded fucking her, the daughter. The mother too, in fact. That's something he never had, a mother and daughter, one after the other. Or together. Even though he doesn't think they would have agreed to do it together. Is always that awkwardness between parents and children. He wouldn't care, let's say, if other people saw him jack off, but when his mother, God rest her soul, once walked in when he was in the middle – he wanted to die. But not really. He's just saying 'I wanted to die.' Maybe he was embarrassed, maybe he turned red with shame, but he never wanted to die. He always had a very strong desire to live. Otherwise, how did he manage to escape from Nicaragua to Costa Rica in a boat after his mother died and he had no one else in the world? How did he go from being a shoeshine boy to a boss of shoeshine boys? How did he build his search and rescue business from nothing to the number one on the continent, eh?

He did his first rescue job almost for free. A tall old Dutchman came to him. Very tall, those Dutch people. He showed him a picture of his son and asked if he could help him. So he said to him: come with me. They went to a shop that photocopied documents and made fifty copies of the picture. Then they went back to the plaza and handed them out to all the shoeshine boys. Anyone who brings me information about this boy will get a week's wages! he promised them. And in a few hours, they already had a lead. A week earlier, someone who shined shoes at the airport saw the Dutchman's son get on a plane to Belize. Fly now to Belize, he told the father. But the father insisted that he go with him. I'll pay all your expenses, he said. And he had that look in his eyes that parents have when they think something has happened to their children. Okay, I'm with you, he said to the Dutchman. And flew to Belize with him. It turned out that the kid had fallen in love with a black girl from Isla Mujeres and had cut off all communication with his family so they couldn't tell him to leave her. She really was classy, that black girl of his. One of those women you get hard just thinking about. You don't have to touch. You don't even have to stand next to them. Just think about licking their chocolate. Excuse me, she wasn't black. Afro-American. That's what you have to say nowadays. If you want your clients not to think you're an ass. That's another good thing about the Israelis — you don't have to follow those rules. And you can even laugh with them sometimes. After all, you

can't do this kind of work without some laughs. Because it's all
so fateful, because when you're looking for someone, hope can
turn into despair as quickly as you can whip out a knife; that's
why you have to tell a few jokes. Drink together. Eat well and
pass gas after your meals. Is a shame that not everyone understands this. Is a shame that some people think that if they let
themselves enjoy something, even for a minute, they will have
less of a chance to find whoever they're looking for. People,
they're fucked up. They'd rather suffer instead of being happy.
Even this Israeli whose father broke off contact. He, Alfredo,
tried to explain to him that after two days of flights, he should
go from the airport to his hotel, eat, shower and rest, and start
searching the next day. But no. I'm not coming for a holiday, I'm
coming to work, the Israeli said on the phone, so I want to go
straight from the airport to the first stop on our route. Okay,
you're the boss, he told him. Even though he knew that after
the flight, he'd sing a different tune.

Dori

He's standing with Noya and her pals at the luggage carousel
in Quito. He's been standing with Noya and her pals at the
luggage carousel in Quito for an hour and a half. He's been
standing with Noya and her pals at the luggage carousel in
Quito for an hour and a half, and only one beige suitcase is
circling round and round. And no one picks it up.

Welcome to South America, one of them says.

I actually think it's fun, Noya says. That they're already kind
of getting us into the rhythm of the trip.

Okay, enough, I'm dying to get to the hostel. One of the others sticks a pin into the balloon of her attempts at self-persuasion, and the three of them laugh the same laugh. Dori laughs along with them. Throws his body into the laughter, like them.

So, like all the Israelis, are you staying at the Iguana too? Noya asks him. Her long black hair is pulled back in a ponytail, a single rebellious curl lying on her cheek.

Actually I don't know where I'm staying, Dori says. Someone's picking me up.

Ah . . . Noya's confused. But I thought you said . . . that you . . . wait a minute . . . you work here?

Udi, his friend — that is, Udi who used to be his friend — would probably lie now, Dori thinks. When they drove his parents' car to the army base on Sundays and didn't feel like picking up any hitch-hikers, Udi would pull up at the stops on the outskirts of the city where soldiers waited for rides and shout: Jenin! — chasing them all away. At the club, he would loudly regale all the girls with stories about his flights into enemy territory piloting a drone, and after the army he fabricated a CV for himself that got him hired for any job he wanted. It's not that I'm against the truth, he always claimed. It's just that it's so boring. 'I'm an advisor to the President of Ecuador on how to suppress the Maoist underground' he'd probably say to Noya now. Or: 'I was summoned urgently by the Minister of the Treasury to stop the spiralling inflation!'

I'm searching for my father, Dori says.

The threesome crowded around him like an audience around a group of South American Indian musicians in the Ben Yehuda pedestrian zone in Jerusalem. What do you mean, searching for your father?

He gives them a quick, rough outline of the story, like a police composite sketch.

Hold on a minute, when was the last time you heard from him? Noya asks.

Two months ago, Dori explains. He emailed my sister. From here. I mean he told her that he was in Quito. And he hasn't been in touch since then. That's why we're starting our search here.

And what did his email say?

That he'd learned all kinds of things during his journey. That he thinks she should take this kind of journey if she wants to make changes in her life. And that he wouldn't be in touch with us for a while.

Do you have a picture of him?

Yes, here.

He takes the pictures out of his bag and shows them to the three.

Good-looking, Noya says, and her eyes glitter at him, as if she means him, not his father.

He looks very familiar to me. Is he famous or something? one of her friends asks.

A bit, Dori says. Mostly in the business world.

So that's where I know him from! the other one crows. I only shit with the financial news in my hand!

You idiot, the first one admonishes him. This guy here is looking for his father. Get serious.

Do you have copies of the pictures? Noya asks.

Yes, but they're in my suitcase, Dori says and points to the circling carousel.

We'll make copies then, Noya says firmly. And without hesitating, unties her ponytail, goes over to the local policeman, stands slightly too close to him, moves her hair from side to side, swishes attractively, and a few minutes later comes back with some copies he's made for her. Give us your email address, she tells Dori, in case we bump into your dad, and he writes down for her the special address he created for the trip, findfather@gmail.com. She lowers her gaze to the paper, and when she raises it again the look in her eyes embarrasses him, so he stares at his knees.

Then the carousel begins spitting out all the suitcases. Except for his. Great, he thinks. I have no phone and now my suitcase is gone. Noya suggests that they stay with him till it arrives, but he urges them to go to their hostel. My suitcase might have flown somewhere else, and then I'll have to fill out forms, he says. Anyway, we'll most probably meet again down the road. Okay, Noya seems desolate at first, then stands on tiptoe and gives him a surprising kiss on the cheek. For a moment, only a moment, he feels like running his hand through her beautiful hair, but she's a young girl and he's already a father. So he just holds out his hand for a brief, correct handshake. And says bye, enjoy your trip, to her and her two friends. Then they walk away from him, the three of them, forging a path with their trolley to the New World, like Columbus.

*

Dorrri, *hay problema?* A warm hand grasps his shoulder. Dori turns in surprise and sees a short, muscular man smiling kindly at him, as if they've known each other for ages. *Shalom*, Mister Dori, the man says and suddenly hugs him, I am Alfredo, and before Dori can decide what to do with that ardent hug, Alfredo is already pulling away and turning to the Lost Property desk. *Que pasa?* he reprimands the clerk firmly, takes a note out of his shiny leather wallet and hands it to him as he asks Dori where his connecting flight came from. Barcelona, Dori replies, and the clerk writes it down along with the rest of the details on a form which, until a minute before, he'd insisted that Dori fill out himself, in Spanish. Fucking bureaucracy, Alfredo says as they walk towards the exit. Not to worry, your suitcase will be here within forty-eight hours. That imbecile now has a personal interest in tracking it down for you. Meanwhile, we'll buy you a *mochila*. A suitcase won't be much good anyway. We'll also buy you some clothes. A full outfit here costs the same as a pair of underpants in Tel Aviv. Sorry, in Jerusalén. You are from Jerusalén, yes? I'd like to go there sometime. Follow the path of Jesus. He was a good guy, Jesus. A little bit of a sucker, a *freier*, like you say in Hebrew, but a good guy. There is something important in your suitcase that didn't come? Yes, Dori nods, most of the pictures of my father. *Hijo de puta!* Alfredo says angrily, and Dori feels the chill of a screw-up run down his spine. But it seems that Alfredo is angry because a tall policeman standing next to his red Ford Fiesta is writing a parking ticket. Hey *muchacho*, he yells, goes over to the uniform and exchanges a few words with him that lead to the rapid cancellation of the ticket, then opens the car door for Dori. Don't get the wrong idea, he says, starting the car, Ecuador is a law-abiding country. But that policeman, his father works for me as an informant, so you see that it's worth his while to treat me right. You're hungry? Thirsty? Horny? I'm kidding. I picked up on the sunburn lines on your finger. How? My job is to pick up on details like that, little ones. But really, you should get that white band of skin sunburned as fast as you can. Because it'll send the *chicas* running. Just kidding again. Where's your sense of humour, Mister Dori?! Is excellent that you came without the ring. Here they can cut off your finger for something like that. Even though, you should know, Quito is okay, a beautiful city. Quiet, more or less. No more than eight or nine murders a day. You want some of those peanut snacks from Israel, Bamba? I have a whole supply of Bamba in my office, not that other stuff, that Bissli. Bissli is junk, he says, and hands Dori a bag. No? So I'll eat them, if you don't mind. That way I'll stop talking so much and you can take a look at the city yourself, eh, Mister Dori? Don't worry about the pictures, amigo, we'll manage with what we have. Look, we'll stop here. You have a specially good view from this spot. Oops, watch your ass. I forgot that you're still not used to the way I brake. You are alive? Good! Now get out on your side, yes, like that, and take a deep breath because you're going to see a *panorama fantastica* now.

For the first few seconds in a new place, Dori's spotter's eyes always search for potential threats: rooftop snipers; suspicious movements in alleyways; a drawn-back curtain; a glint of reflected light that means someone is observing them with binoculars. Even as he does it, he knows that it's totally unnecessary, but he can't not do it. That's how it's been since his reconnaissance course: his first look around is always aimed at thwarting enemy action.

His instinctive reaction fades in a few seconds, and he gives his full attention to the breathtaking view spread out before him: cradled in an expansive valley between high, red-hued mountains is a vast city that appears as serene as a small village. And from the highest summit, a merciful, golden Madonna looks out over all that human diversity. 'There's a majesty about Quito that's hard to describe in words' – he suddenly recalls what his father wrote in the last email he sent from here.

That is our Virgin, and the mountains all around are the eternal Andes, Alfredo says in a different, respectful voice. He lets Dori take in the panoramic view for another few seconds, then leads him back to the car. And the road. Buses taken out of use in Israel in the 1970s move towards them on their way out of the city. Their roofs are loaded with gear and sometimes people too. Peddlers sit on the narrow pavements, their wares spread on colourful mats, the kind that once used to hang on his friends' walls. The peddlers' faces have a different shape. Not Israeli or American. Slightly reminiscent of Japanese faces, but not exactly. The men are short, except for one giant who is sitting in the doorway of a tyre repair shop. The women have wide hips and very black hair. Even the older ones. Two blond tourists stick out in the crowd, drawing looks. They go into a shop that has a sign saying FOTOCOPIA. Next to it is a pharmacy with a sign that says FARMACIA. Maybe it really is easy to learn Spanish, as his father claimed in one of his early emails when you could still understand what he wrote. A large, unfamiliar kind of tree stands at the side of the road. Its leaves are serrated. How do you say tree in Spanish? he almost asks Alfredo. But if he starts asking how to say every single thing, there'll be no end to it. And here's a school. Students wearing uniforms burst out of the gate. An excellent idea, uniforms. Equalisers. It's a shame his school stopped requiring them. Now, in summer, the girls come to school in tank tops that barely reach their belly buttons, and he usually feels like covering them up, but sometimes, when Netta wakes him up a few times during the night and the next morning he comes into class tired and susceptible, as if a taut wire inside him might break at any moment, and a girl in a tank top comes up to him after class, to ask a question . . .

More and more students flood the street, like ants escaping from a nest under attack. More and more schoolbags. The way the bags dance on the children's backs, he notices, is no different on this side of the planet.

And suddenly – brakes.

A man in a suit signals for them to stop and Alfredo's brakes squeal.

A number of men in suits stand around a coffin. Leading them is a man carrying a red and yellow flag, followed by a group of musicians. Behind that cluster – the women. The drummers beat their drums. The trumpeters blow their trumpets. A song rises from the throats of the mourners as the funeral procession moves forward. It doesn't sound like a dirge, more like a song. Happy, bouncy. The crowd on the street splits into two to let them pass. The coffin isn't large. Maybe a woman's? This is how it is with us, Alfredo explains. This is how we say goodbye to someone who has died. And Dori thinks, it's a very nice way. Dignified. And remembers his mother's funeral. Almost a year has passed since then, and he hasn't thought of it even once. He's covered it completely with the ashes of oblivion. Now an image of it flashes into his mind so quickly that he can't fight it: the way Tse'ela stood so confidently beside his father, and he didn't know where to stand; that is, he knew that he had to stand with them, but he found it hard to leave Roni, to relinquish her support at that moment, and he remained stuck in the middle, till they called him to help with the stretcher, to tilt it so that the body fell into the grave. His father held one of the wooden poles, he held another, and the gravediggers held the two remaining ones. His father looked okay at this point, he looked fine. Even when the very small body – he had never thought of his mother as a small woman – landed in the grave, his father looked okay.

Who would have imagined – even now it seems incredible – that then, when it was almost over and Zvi Mandolina began to play, would be the moment his father fell apart, collapsed to the ground and began a series of wails that created a strange and terrible duet with the melody Zvi Mandolina was strumming.

Your father is not in the city, Alfredo says after the last of the funeral procession has passed and the road is open before them once again. I did some preliminary work these last few days, and according to all the signs, and after my last phone conversation with your sister, I think he went to the outdoor market in Otavalo. So let's go there now, Dori suggests – the memory of his father's sobs crowding his mind, choking him – what are we waiting for? *Tranquilo*, Alfredo pats his knee, Mister Dori, this is Ecuador. You must get used to waiting. But I don't understand, Dori says angrily. The market won't open till the day after tomorrow, Alfredo explains, on Saturday, and before Friday there isn't anyone there to talk to. First you need to eat well, to sleep in the good hotel room I booked for you, shower with hot water, because you won't have it every place we go, and tomorrow morning we'll be on our way. You know what *churrasco* is, Mister Dori? Alfredo will take you to the best *churrascaria* in Quito.

*

Dori has no logical explanation for the feeling that overcomes him the minute Alfredo parks the car and they begin to walk the narrow streets of the old city of Quito. As far as he knows, there is no hidden South American branch on his family tree. He was never drawn to the salsa classes that cropped up everywhere in Jerusalem when he was a student, was never wowed when his friends showed him their photo albums after the 'big trip', didn't think that Machu Picchu was such a big deal. And the seminars he attended at university were on the origins of Zionism, not on Latin America.

Nonetheless, he feels comfortable in Quito. Not at home – because only Jerusalem is home – but comfortable. Very. Maybe it's the high altitude that's making him slightly dizzy, filling him with a pleasant kind of fuzziness. On the plane, he read in the tour guide that Quito's altitude is 2,850 metres and that many tourists report feeling a lack of oxygen during their first few hours in the city. Or maybe it has to do with the music: every city has its own rhythm, and while in Tel Aviv, for example, he always feels the rhythm of the city clashing with his own internal rhythm, from his very first minutes in Quito he feels no need to make a special effort to fit in. As if he and the city were matched in advance.

Alfredo doesn't speak much on the way to the restaurant. Experienced in leading people around, he lets the person with him absorb the sights and sounds of the street. And the smells. So many smells assail Dori's nostrils – fried rice, chicken, incense, shoe polish. Shoeshine boys line the pavement. Roni sometimes polishes her shoes too, when clients come from abroad. The kibbutz girl who went to university classes in her All Star trainers today polishes high-heeled shoes. Women wearing flats pass by carrying on their back red sacks with yellow strings that are larger than they are. A bus stops and lets the women with sacks cross. Slowly. Strange, Dori thinks. The street is bustling, but slowly. Like in the old days. Bustling and slow. A line from a song came to mind: *They say that life here was great before I was born.* Maybe this is where I was before I was born? Here, in this city, is where I was before I was? And maybe my father walked down this same street and I am walking in his footsteps, the way I used to do on the beach during our summer holiday, walking back to our bungalow?

A policeman blows his whistle. Tries to get the world back to its senses. He looks like a basketball referee at a Hapoel game. Does Netta still sing the Hapoel song he loves so much? What's he doing now? How's he managing? Who was mean to him at nursery school? Did he eat lunch or go back to his hunger strike? I'm hungry too, how long has it been since I ate, I'm not just hungry, I'm starving . . . Excuse me, Alfredo, didn't you say something about a restaurant?

*

Here, read this while I bring our food. Alfredo takes a thick loose-leaf folder out of his bag and puts it on the table between the fork and spoon. So you won't think I'm all talk, he says.

Dori's seat faces the street. His eyes have not yet had their fill of the city sights. Occasionally he raises them to absorb more of the passing colour, then returns them to the black-and-white of the folder.

It's filled with thank-you letters. More and more thank-you letters. Each one in a separate plastic sleeve. In English, Hebrew, Chinese. Or maybe that's Japanese? He's never sure which of those languages is written vertically.

Dori takes one that's written from right to left out of its sleeve and reads it:

We hadn't heard from our Yaroni for three months. We were beyond hopeless. We tried looking for him with the help of the official authorities and came up with nothing. Until someone

told us about Alfredo. The minute we met him, we knew there
was a chance. He just wasn't willing to give up hope, and for
two weeks he took us to places that don't appear in guidebooks
or even on maps. In one of those places we finally found our
Yaroni, severely undernourished. The doctors said that if, God
forbid, we'd found him a week later, he wouldn't have been alive.

We warmly recommend Alfredo to anyone who is unwilling
not to find their loved one. He may seem a little rough, but he
has a huge heart. And most important of all – he's a highly
qualified professional.

Sincerely,
The finally reunited Aviv family

And another one, immediately following it and in similar
handwriting (maybe someone had forged all the letters for him,
Dori suspects, then feels embarrassed for his suspicious mind).

To Everyone Who is Undecided about Hiring Alfredo!
My screwed-up brother got into trouble with a whole lot of
criminals in Colombia that the police didn't have the guts to
touch. It was only through Alfredo's connections that we got to their
camp in the jungle and started to negotiate with them. We had
to sell half our house in Israel to release my brother from those
shits. But we never even thought twice about it. Alfredo was with
us through the whole process and explained what was happening
and let us make our own decisions. He's expensive, that mamzer
(and he understands Hebrew, so watch out when you talk around
him) – but worth every dollar.

Sincerely,
Omer Barzilai, his brother

There's also a picture in that sleeve: two young guys hugging.
Smiling. They both have long hair, like guitarists in a rock
band. The one on the right looks older, but he has a vague look

in his eyes. The one on the left seems more physically relaxed, but his eyes are more alert. It's hard to know which one rescued the other.

A heavy body plops down beside Dori, causing him to look up from the letters. A broad-faced, broad-shouldered Indian woman wearing a wide skirt, her legs spread like a man's, pushes him against the wall. More and more people come into the restaurant. Some in business suits, some in rags. There are no chairs in this restaurant, only benches. And when you finish eating, you get up to leave room for the people standing and waiting. Just like the Pinati restaurant at home, Dori thinks, and for a moment imagines that he's hearing the 'don't chew, just swallow' of the Jerusalem waiter who simultaneously made him laugh and pressured him the first time his father took him there.

That was one of their three rituals. Pinati, once every few months. A Hapoel basketball game against one of the strong teams. And a James Bond movie every time a new one came out.

They didn't talk a lot during those meetings. Pinati was too noisy. The basketball games were too nerve-racking. And at the James Bond movie, all they had was the interval.

So how's school? his father would ask when they were sitting alone in the cinema (and as the years passed: how's teaching? then: how are things with Netta?), and Dori would say, fine. And he'd know that his father thought he could do a lot more with himself than teach. You like it there? the seemingly interested father would ask, and Dori would say, yes. All things considered, yes. Knowing he had to save the bitter complaints for his mother, who was a better listener and would pass on a concise summary to his father before they went to sleep anyway. Need any help, son? came the next question on the list. And Dori would say, no, thanks. We're managing. It was because he'd chosen a low-paying job that he felt he had to prove he could support his family on his own. Work after school hours. Give lectures to adults. To tourists. Pick up a few more teaching hours at another school. Okay, but if you need anything, just let me know, his father would say, and then they'd be saved by the bell calling the audience back from the foyer.

But the last time they went to the cinema, Dori recalls, it was different. During the interval his father didn't ask him anything, just sighed and said, these James Bonds, they get worse every time. Dori said nothing. He actually thought the film had been fine up to then, that the new actor playing Bond was better than the previous one. Then his father said, you know, every time I came back from the cinema, your mother would interrogate me. She always started with the film, asked me to tell her the plot. But while I was describing it, she would throw in questions about what really interested her. Her son. How is he? What did he tell you? How does he look? His father sighed, rubbed the corner of his eye with his little finger as if he were trying to wipe away a tear and said, who can I talk to about the film when I go home? The walls?

Dori didn't know how to answer him. He'd never had to cheer up his father, had no idea how to do it. He felt that this was a rare opportunity for a frank conversation between them, but he didn't know how to begin. And before he could find the words and choose the right way to put them together, the bell rang. His father quickly straightened up in his seat. And the film began again.

When I find him, Dori swears to himself now, we'll sit down and talk, really talk, the way normal people do.

Okay, Dor-r-r-i. Here's your *churrasco*. Alfredo returns in a flurry and puts an oval plate down in front of him. Sorry for the delay, amigo. I asked them to fry the *lomito* a little more for you because a gringo's stomach can be sensitive the first few days. And we don't want you to get sick on us, eh?

Dori looks at his plate. Squeezed together, some actually climbing on top of each other, are a paper-thin steak, a sunny-side-up egg, avocado wedges, black beans and tiny potatoes that still show smudges of soil. It's really an odd combination, but he's too hungry to be choosy.

Bon appétit, Alfredo says and when he begins eating, Dori notices that he uses his knife like a fork: spears the centre of a potato with it and puts it into his mouth. When he's finished stabbing all the pieces of his steak, this time with his fork, Alfredo returns the large folder to his bag and takes out a small one. There are a few things you have to sign, he says, handing Dori several printed pages. Take them to the hotel and read them so you know what you're signing, eh? Meanwhile I'll explain to you a little about our method of work. I say 'our' because you and me, as far as I am concerned, are a team. After all, I could have looked for your father alone, right? Or I could have sent my informants. So why do I bring you all the way here, Mister Dori? Because a journey, amigo, does two big things: it stirs your appetite and it stirs your memory. For your appetite, I'll be responsible – and for your memory, you. What does that mean? That everything you think of related to your father, you tell me. Even if you don't think it's related. Everything! For example, your sister S-e-e-la called me in my office today and asked me what our plans are. I told her that today you are resting and tomorrow morning we go to the Otavolo market. And what does she say to me? That in her last conversation with your father he said something about buying himself a sweater in the market because it was getting a little cold. Now, we – me and her – already went over her conversation with him maybe ten times, no? So how come she remembers a new detail all of a sudden? Because of the journey. Our journey, *mine and yours*, opened her channels of information. And only complete and exact information helps us find people, believe me, Mister Dori.

He loves James Bond movies, my father, Dori hears himself say.

Sero-sero-siete? Alfredo lights up, Double-O-Seven?

Yes, Dori says. We go together to see every one.

Very important! Alfredo pulls out a notepad and writes it down.

But how can that help? Dori asks.

In Quito, there are five movie houses. By tomorrow I'll find out if any of them is showing a James Bond movie now. That could interest him to go there, yes?

Yes, but—

Of course, Alfredo interrupts him, the chance is small. But what does it cost to give the cashier his description and promise a reward if he gives us information? You see, every detail you can give me might lead us to him.

Dori nods and finishes eating the last bits of avocado left on his plate. The heavy Indian woman sitting next to him hauls herself slowly to her feet, and a young mother, her tiny baby tied to her body with a brightly coloured cloth, sits down in her place. The baby fixes its black eyes on Dori and gurgles at him in the international language of babies, and Dori remembers that, when Netta was born, they bought a fabric baby carrier that was so complicated they couldn't tie it properly, not even after watching the instruction tape twice, and in the end, after a night of frustration, they wound it around each other, laughing at their failure and kissing, laughing and kissing and winding the cloth around their bodies.

And women he loves, your father? Like James Bond? Alfredo suddenly asks.

Women? Dori says, almost alarmed. No . . . What do you mean? Why are you asking? My father loved . . . my mother.

That's what your sister said too. But I thought that you . . . as a man . . . maybe you could come up with a different angle.

No. Dori felt the anger forcing his hands into fists. My father was a member of the conservative party of people who have only one great love in their lives. They were — both of them — you should have seen them. Her. She was an amazing woman, my mother, he adored her.

Si, si, sure, Alfredo says with blatant impatience. You are finished eating, Dor-r-r-ri? *Vamos*, we'll take you to the hotel.

The hotel is in a different city. That is, it's still called Quito, but it's so different from the old city: suddenly, banks. And bars. And hotels with neon signs. Suddenly, the English of tourists tickles the ears, settling momentarily on the earlobe, then rolling onward. And maybe — the idea pops into Dori's mind as they walk — the new city is really the authentic one and the old city is just an empty display for tourists? There are no roast pigs or stray dogs here, but there's a McDonald's. And a shop with a poster of Madonna in the window. Roni loves Madonna. She went to her concert in Hayarkon Park, with a friend. She asked him first if he wanted to go, but he heard in her voice that she'd rather he didn't. She came back from it giddy with excitement. She puts on such an amazing show! she enthused as she floated around the living room. And what a body. It's unbelievable that she's fifty!

But it's crap music, he said instead of keeping his mouth shut.

In *your* opinion.

You're telling me that, in *your* opinion, it's good music?

First of all, yes. And second, it's a good thing I went to the concert with Limor and not you. You probably would have stood there and whinged the whole time.

Here's your hotel, Alfredo pulled up by a wide pavement. Everything's arranged for you, amigo. The room is clean, waiting for you. Go to sleep early because tomorrow I pick you up at 5.30 in the morning. Anyway, you shouldn't walk around the streets here at night. It's too dangerous. They can take your head off. And then what will I tell Se'ela? How will I explain to her that I didn't take good care of her brother?

Dori nods, unconsciously probing beneath his shirt, checking to see that the money belt shoved under it is still there. And if you decide to go out for a drink after all, because at the end of the day, you're still a man – Alfredo smiles broadly, exposing a gold tooth he's been hiding till now – then take a taxi, Mister Dori, okay?

I didn't come here to drink in bars, Dori feels the need to remind Alfredo out loud, maybe because, for the last hour, he's been much more carried away by the joy of discovering the city than he thought he could be.

Alfredo says, *claro*. Of course. He pats him on the shoulder. And pushes him lightly toward the hotel.

*

He wakes up in the middle of the night. The clock shows 2.30, local time. His body apparently thinks it's already morning and refuses to fall back asleep. He misses Roni. When he gets into bed at home, he always winds himself around her, that is, around the blanket she's buried under, or says into her exposed ear, 'Come to me,' and she, even if she's been cool to him all evening, all week, all month, all year, she turns towards him in her sleep, presses her thighs against his legs and rests her head in the deep hollow between his chest and right shoulder, and her exhaustion, the exhaustion of a senior manager, drains from her body into his. Slowly, like a drug.

He no longer knows how to sleep without her. That's the truth.

When she travelled to Barcelona a few months earlier, he read books in their bed. Finished one and immediately began the next. He went to the kitchen to make tea and put the cup on a saucer. And tried to fall asleep with a pillow. And without. On his side. On her side. Her side smelled of fresh rolls. Her smell. So he stayed there and tried to picture what she was doing now in Barcelona. Then he called her, even though it was late. She didn't answer. And suddenly he thought that she might be with someone else. From work. That thought aroused him. His prick stiffened when he thought of her having sex with someone else. And the more he thought about it, the clearer it became that it was really happening. Right now. That his years-long connection to Roni was so strong and deep, so fraught with emotion that he could feel it happening despite the thousands of kilometres separating them. She called again a few minutes later, drowsy. Did you call me? Yes, where were you? Sleeping. Alone? What do mean, Dori? she said in a voice that sounded forced to him: of course alone.

He takes the book he brought with him out of his bag. History always puts things into perspective.

It turns out that the Incas ruled Ecuador till 1535, when the Spanish wiped them out. Then the continent's liberator, Simon Bolivar, wiped them out. Which led, in 1830, to the establishment of the independent country of Ecuador.

He thinks about his brief tour of the city. Based on what he has seen in the old city, the Incas haven't been wiped out at all. And the Spaniards are still here too. In their language and their colonial buildings. But on the other hand, based on what he's seen in the new city, Ecuador is not an independent country at all, but an additional state of the United States of America, where the residents pay each other in dollars, wear Levis and listen to Madonna.

He loves to widen these cracks in official history for his students so that through them they can catch a glimpse of what is beyond the material they have to learn for their exams. I don't teach history, he always explains to them in their first lesson, I teach histories. The Middle Ages? Not everything was dark then. World War II? The question is not why the US joined the war, but why it joined so late. The Holocaust? Not just ours. Other nations had holocausts too. Even though they're not included in the syllabus. The War of Independence?

If you check the numbers, it wasn't really a few against the many. Yes, it's important to notice, kids, that the victor is usually the one who writes the story, so it's always a good idea to be suspicious of him.

A week has gone by since the last day of school. Funny, he remembers, it was his year 12 class – the group that refused to warm to him, so he had dragged his feet on the way to his classroom – that gave him the best summer send-off. They bought him Yuval Banai's latest CD (how did they know? It wasn't till he got home that he remembered playing one of Banai's songs – 'Can't Stop It' – when they talked about World War I, as a way of helping them to empathise with the experience of a soldier at war). Then Roi Yakobi came up to the front, asked him to sit down and 'adjust the focus button', as Dori always said, and then went on to do a pretty good imitation of him, including dramatic hand-waving that made the cover of the erasable Magic Marker fly off when he got carried away during a lesson, and his demand 'to listen to the wheels of your brain turning' after tough questions, and the basketball metaphors that didn't always work, and his obsessive aversion to mobile phones and text messages, and the way his voice went all soft and squishy when he spoke to Netta on his own phone, and the good coffee he went out to buy during breaks because the staffroom coffee was tasteless, and the way he stood at the window while they wrote in their exercise books, slowly stroking his non-beard, staring unseeingly at the car park as if he were pondering the new *Altneuland*, when all he was thinking about was whether Dror Hajaj should be one of the opening five at the Hapoel game. Even though they all laughed hard, he felt that their laughter contained more affection than mockery, and he laughed too, and applauded, and when Roi finished he even extended his hands forward and bowed his head the way the basketball fans at Malha do. Then they gave him the farewell card they'd made for him, a framed Photoshop picture of him alongside Churchill, Roosevelt and Stalin in the famous portrait taken at the Yalta Conference, and at the bottom they wrote: *To Dori, a teacher for life, thank you for putting us into history*.

He held the framed picture in his hand and didn't go into the staffroom so as not to absorb its smell of bitterness, but went straight to the bus stop instead and thought with a rare sense of satisfaction that he had chosen correctly ten years earlier. Until the disastrous stampede at the Arad music festival and the Rabin assassination he'd been sure he'd stay at university, but after those two events, coming within a few months of each other, he felt a powerful urge to get close to life, to have an impact on it, not only to observe it from the ivory tower, through its bibliography. And now it's really happening, and yes, at these moments of feeling that he has truly touched life and children, that he has shifted something in their souls, he knows that it's been worth everything he's had to put up with: the salary that forces him to work three evenings a week giving lectures to adults; the meagre curriculum he's always trying to circumvent; the idiot, former colonel, petty tyrant headmaster; the two wild kids in every year's batch of students; the fact that you actually spend twenty minutes teaching what, on paper, should take only five; the impossible Hebrew calendar, with all its holidays, that doesn't let you create any momentum with a class; the profound misgivings of today's youth about the need to study the past and the constant struggle to convince them that their present is just a thin shell; the collective eyebrow-raising everywhere, from the garage to the doctors' surgery, that he gets when he says he's a teacher; and the subtle condescension of Roni's colleagues at the ostentatious parties thrown by her employers on a section of the beach that they illegally close off, the condescension that had begun to trickle down to her – at least that's how he'd been feeling lately, and maybe that's why, when he got home, he didn't show her the card his students had given him but went and put it in his bookcase.

He closes the book, turns off the reading lamp and tries to fall asleep again. Just don't look at the clock, he tells himself. Just don't look at the clock. If he looks at the clock, he'll see how much time has passed and that'll only stress him out more and keep him awake.

He looks at the clock. A quarter past three. The time when Netta wakes up and calls him: Da-a-addy! Da-a-addy, come here! The boy has already learned that his mother is buried so deeply under her blankets that there's no way she'll hear him. So Dori gets up quickly and goes to him, dragging his blanket behind him. Chalking up a small victory in the covert battle between him and Roni for the boy's heart. Netta is already sitting up in bed, his legs crossed, his hair standing up like a fright wig. Sleep next to me, he says. And Dori pulls out the other mattress from under Netta's bed and lies down. Give me your hand! Netta demands. And Dori puts his hand under the wooden safety rail and grasps his son's small, damp hand. Sing the Hapoel song, he demands. And Dori sings it, slowly, the unplugged version, several times. There's a smell in my room, he always says when Dori finishes singing. There's no smell, Dori replies as usual. Why did you wake up? I had a bad dream. What was in the dream? They were being mean to me. Who was being mean to you? Children. Which children?

Silence. The same conversation for a year. And the same silence when it's over.

Sometimes Netta falls asleep in a few seconds, and Dori goes back to sleep with Roni. And sometimes the boy refuses to let go of his hand, and he falls asleep in his room and wakes up in the morning with a stiff neck, not knowing where he is for the first few seconds. Just like on the plane.

He wonders what's happening now, when he's not there. Does Netta still call him? Still complain about the smell? Still wake up crying in the morning for no obvious reason? Suddenly he has to know. Has to talk to him. To them. He doesn't understand why he hasn't called until now. Doesn't understand why there's no phone in the room. What kind of hotel doesn't have phones in its rooms? He goes downstairs to the reception desk in his tracksuit bottoms and white vest, wakes up the dozing clerk who is enclosed in a barred cage and asks him how much a call costs. The price is scandalous. He's better off waiting till tomorrow and calling from Alfredo's office. And how much does it cost to send an email? Okay, that's more reasonable. And Roni constantly checks her email anyway. She'll see it at once. The clerk opens the cage and lets him sit at the computer.

> *Hi my love,*
>
> He writes, then deletes it and writes:
>
> *Hi love,*
>
> *I'm here in Ecuador. Quito is so colourful that I'm beginning to understand why my father was so excited by this continent.*
>
> *Alfredo is fine. Talks a little too much, but seems to know his job.*
>
> *It's night here now. I can't fall asleep, because of the jet lag or because I miss home.*
>
> *As you've probably noticed, I very cleverly forgot my phone. So I'm writing.*
>
> *How's Netta? How's nursery? Is he waking up in the night?*
>
> *Hug him and kiss him for me. And tell him that Daddy misses him. Say it in exactly those words, okay? Fuck the psychologist.*
>
> *I'll try to call you tomorrow from Alfredo's office.*

*

Welcome to my office, Alfredo says and points to the trailer. The first stripes of morning sun illuminate the quiet street.

Dori climbs up after him, slightly disappointed – he'd pictured a spacious office located in a tall building, the kind they saw on their way here – but when they enter, his disappointment turns to astonishment. Two laptops, one white, the other black, sit on a long, spotlessly clean desk. Two mobiles. A satellite phone. Over the desk, a large compass and six clocks showing the time in New York, Tokyo, Bangkok, London, Sydney and Quito. The right wall is lined with maps, like in a war room. On the wall above the desk are framed thank-you letters and chummy photos of Alfredo with clients: the slight awkwardness of people who have never had their picture taken together; the dim, neon lighting. Alfredo hugging the women, the men, the young people, the elderly. Alfredo hugging an important-looking man. The important-looking man is leaning against him more than hugging him, his eyes sad. John Moving, Alfredo says, noticing Dori linger at the photo. Senator from Arizona. His daughter went rafting on the Chicamocha River in Colombia and fell off the boat into the rapids. Two months he looked for her and found nothing. It took me exactly two days to understand the river. You know what it means to understand a river, Mister Dori? To know every bend, every rock. To understand where the water wants to flow. At every moment. To know that every part of the river flows with a different force and reflects a different flash of the sun. After two days, I stood at a certain spot on the bank and told them: Look here, under this rock. They said, it can't be, this is nowhere near where she fell. I told them: Check it. What can you lose? They found her body there. Of course.

How coldly he says the word 'body', Dori thinks.

One of the computers pings. The mail icon appears on the screen – then goes up in flames. Alfredo ignores it.

Tell me, isn't this . . . all this equipment . . . expensive? Dori asks. Is someone here at night to guard it for you?

Instead of answering, Alfredo takes down a small remote from a hook on the wall where it's hanging next to the compass. And presses it.

A large box slides forward on tracks from under the desk. Then it opens all at once, like a gift, into a single bed.

I don't like hotel rooms, Alfredo says and asks: are you ready to get moving, Dori? The *mochila* I bought you is on the back seat. You'll find some clothes there too. Your suitcase, I believe, will arrive by the end of the day.

Just before he starts the engine, when they're already sitting in the cabin, Alfredo gets a call and spends the next few minutes calming down a Jeremy from Australia: psychotic episode. Still don't know. Probably peyote. Is very strong stuff. He's being treated, of course he is. Zyprexa. I'm in touch with them all the time. Plus, I have someone sitting in the emergency room. Me? I don't recommend it. Because it could make his condition worse. Seeing you. Yes. Exactly. I hope to get him on a British plane tomorrow. No, for the time being they don't want to discharge him. But my people are working on it. Right now, let's be happy we found him. You want to come? Again, I'm telling you . . . okay. Fine. You're the boss, Jeremy.

Alfredo closes the phone and says: another Jew. Will you please explain to me what is it with you people, you Jews, Dori? Listen to what I'm telling you: most regular people have five senses, but you, you Jews have a sixth sense. Of worry.

Dori doesn't answer. Considers whether this is an anti-Semitic remark. Alfredo starts the trailer, then suddenly turns off the engine and curses, *la concha*. He pats down his body, looking for something. Then the top of his head. His shirt pockets. His trousers. Then curses again.

What have you lost? Dori asks, quite familiar with the situation: at home, he's the one who finds everything that falls off Roni because of the frantic rush she's always in. Keys, wallet, TV remote.

Sunglasses, Alfredo complains.

Dori closes his eyes, retraces their morning movements in

his mind and says: they're in the hotel, on the reception desk. Next to the bell. I can run in and get them if you want.

Alfredo

Poor guy, Mister Dori. Asked for my phone to call home, and before I finished the call I'd just taken – he fell asleep. That's how it is with the gringos. Their whole body is messed up for the first few days. And sometimes their minds. Sleep a little, Mister Dori, I'll turn down the music for you. Here, like this. People are like little children when they sleep. Even the sluttiest looking whore looks like a little girl. Sometimes I pay them for another hour just to watch them sleep.

Mister Dori, he has long lashes. Like a girl's. And thin eyebrows like a girl's. But his forehead is strong like a man's. And a little bit under his hair, he has a wrinkle that I know *excellente*. The wrinkle that you get when the parent you really love dies on you. Is not long, that wrinkle, but is deep. Like a slit. Drops of sweat can flow through it like through a river bed.

A year ago his mother died. From cancer. That's what his sister told me, Se'ela. She told me also that there were *mucho* people at the funeral, in Jerusalén. That it was a very hot day. That a woman from the mother's work started to read from the speech she wrote, but she couldn't go on. That in the cemetery at the same time there was the funeral of someone who died when a bus exploded, and that fucked-up husband of Se'ela's, I mean the one who used to be her fucked-up husband then, came late because he had to stay late at work and at first he went to the other funeral by mistake. I don't know why she told me all that. But that's how every conversation with that Se'ela is. At first she always tries to bring my price down, to argue with me about clauses in the contract. And then, very slowly, she starts talking about her life. Then you can't get a word in edgewise. That's the problem with lonely people. If you're already listening to them, they won't stop chewing your ears off. Ever since our mother left this world, Se'ela told me, everyone has been leaving everyone else. My father left his office and went travelling in South America, like he's some kid just out of the army. I left my husband. And even at the museum, everyone's left. After six months, there was no one left of the original staff. My brother Dori is the only one who hasn't left anything. I'm not sure he even cried over our mother. I certainly never saw him cry over her. And that's the reason, Se'ela's tone got more serious, that's why I'm worried about him, Señor Alfredo. I'm his big sister, I can't help it. Worrying is part of being a big sister. I would be there instead of him if I could. I mean, if my ex wasn't such a shit. You'll see when you meet him. Not my ex, Dori. Don't be misled by him. He looks serious and responsible and a little square. The type you can depend on. But inside, he's fire. Believe me. At school once, he over-turned a desk. They wouldn't let him read aloud from the Israeli history textbook because he read really well, and the teacher wanted someone who had trouble reading to do it. And another time, a teacher accused him of copying and he was so insulted that he didn't even defend himself. He just got up and walked out. I remember that very well because they took me out of my lesson to help look for him. We finally found him up in a tree. And he said that he wouldn't come down until that teacher apologised to him. A nine-year-old boy, remember. And when he was sixteen, he fell in love with the leader of his youth group. Aviva was her name. Three years older than him. Pretty. With curls. Looked a bit like his wife, actually. All of Jerusalem was talking about it. Even people my age. Why? Because after she told him that a leader going out with a member of her group was against the rules of the youth movement, he sprayed graffiti on the walls of the shed at the Russian compound: LOVE HAS NO RULES, AVIVA. Everyone thought he'd lost his mind. Except for my mum. Even when he farted, she thought it was wonderful. Dori and my mum had a special relationship. They loved each other without even trying. In the army, Dori used to call her when he was on night duty and they'd talk till morning. When I tried to tell her something, she'd put me off with a wave of her hand: not now. Dori had a tough time in the army. Only men were allowed to go into Lebanon, so he had no one to fall in love with. Also, there are a lot of stupid people in the army. And he's clever, my brother. A lot cleverer than me. You'll see when you talk to him. His students worship the ground he walks on.

Si, claro, I said and sliced an apple for dessert. While that Se'ela is talking, you can eat a nine-course meal.

To cut a long story short, she continues, our mother was Dori's lifeline when he was in Lebanon. And afterwards too, for years, they had their rituals. Do you see? That's why I'm worried about him. Up till now, his work has kept him going, it stopped him from falling apart when she died. Work and Netta. When you have a child like that to deal with, there's no room for self-pity. No, Netta's not autistic. Just the opposite. He wants to communicate. But he can't manage it. It's hard to explain. He cries all the time. No, he's not the least bit spoilt. It's as if he was born sad. Children aren't supposed to be sad. They still don't know that life is an ongoing heartache with rare interludes of happiness. I have my own theory about him. Anyway, don't worry, I'm telling you too much as it is. Of course you're thinking I'm banging on. Of course you're saying to yourself, I see why this woman doesn't have a man — she won't shut up.

No, what are you talking about, Se'ela. I said what she expected me to say.

In any case, Alfredo – she went on – what I wanted to tell you is that in another few days, when Dori reaches you, he won't have the safety net of work and family any more to keep him from crashing to the ground. I'm not saying you'll have to look for him too, Alfredo, I'm just saying that while you're both looking, keep an eye on Dori, and if you notice anything out of the ordinary, call me.

Don't worry, I'll take care of him as if he was my son, I promised her at the end of the call.

I don't have a son. Someone like me, who gets up in a different place every morning, can't be a good father, and is better not to be a father at all than to be a shitty one – but Se'ela doesn't know all this, so what difference does it make.

Dori

Opens his eyes. He only fell asleep for a few minutes because of the stupefying rhythm of the moving trailer, but a dream still managed to flash through his brain. In Israel, he never remembers his dreams, but here, he remembers clearly that in this fleeting dream he was looking for Netta – yes, it was Netta, not his father, who was lost – and he and Tse'ela hung a picture of him in the Napoleon costume he wore for Purim on the neighbourhood noticeboard. And he was worried about him, terribly worried.

Look to your right, Mister Dori, Alfredo says. Through the window he sees a breathtaking view: an immense lake of crystal clear water that reflects the clouds, surrounded by mountains. Mountain ridges that stretch to infinity. And the panorama is undisturbed by motorway junctions. Or the skyscrapers of a new city. Or a long line of SUVs.

I have to come back here with Netta, Dori thinks (before, when visiting beautiful places, he used to think: I have to come back here with a woman I love). The child doesn't know what open spaces are. Over the last few years, all the green places in Jerusalem have been covered over by asphalt: a road now winds through Emek Ha'arezim; a flyover was built above the village of Lifta; they hadn't touched Emek Ha'tsvaim, but they built the Holyland apartment complex above it. Only the ancient village of Sataf remains. But even on weekdays, there's a queue to get into the tunnel that leads to the springs. At one stage they had tried to take Netta to places further away, in the Galilee, or the Negev. They packed on Friday night, got up at six on Saturday morning to beat the traffic. They avoided the main road, Roni's work-Mazda rattling along dirt roads. But always, a few minutes after they spread their picnic blanket in a place that was as isolated as possible, another family would pull up behind them. With its own picnic blanket. And its own coolboxes. And a portable disk player blasting music so loud that it rustled the leaves.

Whereas now their huge vehicle looks like a grasshopper in comparison with the tall trees and high mountains and the deep wadis through which fresh water, not sewage, flows. And the sun shines through the clouds, its golden beams shimmering on the lake. What is that colour? Not exactly blue, not exactly green. Purplish. There are no waves in this lake, nothing foams. A small rowing boat cuts slowly through the water, its bow drawing a question mark.

When was the last time his pulse had pounded at the sight of sheer beauty? In the Sinai, probably. The last time he was at Sayyid's, in Ras al-Satan. The taxi slid towards the central hut and his breath caught at the sight of the shoreline, with the small sand mushroom at its tip. But they killed the Sinai for him too. Two years ago. When the first pictures of the terrorist attack arrived and he realised that it had happened on 'his' beach, he began to cry. Funny. Even at his mother's funeral he didn't cry. But when he saw the pictures of the destruction at Ras al-Satan – the beach huts that had collapsed, the shattered plates – his shoulders began to shake. At first, the tears welled up in the living room, but then he decided it wouldn't be good for Netta to see his father cry like that, so he went into the bedroom, where his restrained crying turned into racking sobs. Netta wanted to follow him, but Roni stopped him. Daddy just wants to be on his own for a minute, she explained.

Later, after Netta had fallen asleep, she asked him with the old gentleness: what was that?

And he said, I don't know.

Did you see someone you recognise?

No.

So what, then?

I don't know.

Maybe it's an accumulation, you know, of stress.

Maybe. But it's also—

What?

I had a place, Roni, you see? One place I could escape to. I haven't been there in years. But I knew that if I needed them, the mountains would always be there. And the water.

They'll still be there, you know.

But it won't be the same. It's enough for something like that to happen once, and that's it, the place has been contaminated by fear.

I have to come back here with Netta, he thinks now. If everything turns out okay – he's already promised himself, his thoughts serious now – I'll fly to uncontaminated South America with him next summer. (Roni will probably be too busy to come. So it'll be just the two of us. Compensation for having abandoned him now.)

In the meantime, while all of nature – leaves, dewdrops on the leaves, rocks, dewdrops on the rocks – glitters into a new morning, Alfredo speaks constantly on the phone.

A British girl caught with hashish in Bolivia was jailed. There's no choice, he tries to convince the parents. If we want her to have a chance of getting out, you have to open your wallet and contribute to the local police. That's how it works in Bolivia. How much? the parents on the other end of the line try to find out, and Alfredo pauses, maybe to mentally translate from the Bolivian currency to pounds sterling, maybe to calculate his profits from the deal—

And suddenly, he brakes. A short line of cars in front of us. Alfredo apologises to the person he's talking to on the other side of the planet, closes his phone and curses. What happened? He has an idea. He gets out of the trailer to find out and comes back a minute later. A demonstration, he explains to Dori. The government wants to build a dam on one of the rivers here to generate electricity, and the villagers who make their living fishing in that river are against it. So they stop the traffic. Until the government says that it is cancelling the dam – they're building a dam of cars.

So what do we do? Dori asks.

Is up to you, Alfredo says. We can wait till the demonstration ends or we can take another road. The other road is a little less *simpatico*, but it will get us to Otavalo in time.

How long will it take for the authorities to get them off the road? Dori points to the demonstrators.

Between two hours and a week, Alfredo says.

The other road has crumbling shoulders. A few minutes after they veer on to it, it starts to rain. Dori is used to the rain in

Israel, which has to accumulate in the sky for a few hours before it dares to fall, so the first drops that come through the open window catch him unprepared and wet his shirt. He closes the window, and in seconds the drizzle turns into a real downpour. In a few minutes, the soil that makes up the edges of the road crumbles so badly that the trailer's tyres spray it to the sides.

Alfredo, he says, isn't this dangerous?

Not to worry, Mister Dori, Alfredo says, and actually drives faster.

Dori has the feeling that they are driving on a thin rope, that only a narrow strip of earth is still hard enough to bear the weight of the trailer, and everything on either side of it is dropping into the abyss.

As a child, he loved dangerous situations like this: climbing trees he couldn't get down from; being the first to jump over the waterfall in Nahal Yehudia. And in Lebanon, when mortar shells landed in their position, he hadn't feared for his life even for a second. But since he's become a father, everything frightens him, and every mild threat to his life now stirs a fear of death in him. Is almost a prophecy of death. It's enough for a taxi driver to go through a yellow light, or his temperature to climb above thirty-eight for a picture of his funeral to flash before his eyes. And it's always the same picture: they're burying him beside his mother, in the empty grave originally intended for his father. Tse'ela sobs as the rabbi cries 'God full of mercy', but not Roni. She's not crying. Roni is restrained, refined. She's wearing a black dress that shows off her lovely body, and is supported on either side by two men he doesn't know, but who remind him of Svirsh and Tenzer, the suitors waiting to pounce on the newly divorced heroine of Agnon's story, *Panim Acherot*. And Netta is standing in front of her, his head reaching her waist, watching as his father is covered with earth, looking lost, abandoned, fatherless . . .

Alfredo slows down. The road bends sharply and there's a van coming at them. There isn't room for two vehicles on the crumbling road that has become almost a goat path, so Alfredo shifts into reverse. Tries to shift into reverse. To Dori, the manoeuvre looks dangerous, almost impossible, and chills – this is it, this is really the end – cut through his bowels. But somehow the van manages to pass without scraping them and without leaping suicidally into the wadi.

Listen, Alfredo, Dori says, maybe—

We make a stop in a minute, Alfredo says.

They pull up in front of a cabin that has a red Coca-Cola sign over its door.

The owner knows Alfredo. Everyone knows Alfredo. Though the owner has a very wrinkled face, his hair is as black as a young boy's and he's wearing a jumper that looks like the ones Amos Oz wears in photographs. Dori asks for a Coke, but they only have Inca Cola. Drink up, Alfredo says, is delicious. Dori drinks. It's not delicious. And it's almost flat. He asks for water. They give him fizzy water. But he feels uncomfortable about giving it back, so now he's drinking sparkling water, just like his father. And to his surprise, he actually likes the saltiness.

A large old radio of the kind that broadcast the UN vote on the establishment of the State of Israel, is standing on a shelf, broadcasting in mono something that sounds like the Ecuadorian version of Israel's weekend football programme. Empty beer bottles labelled CERVESA flank the radio on both sides. A few more days will go by before Dori understands that that isn't the name of the manufacturer, but the Spanish word for beer. Any kind of beer.

Alfredo and the owner are talking. Quite seriously. He understands a few words here and there. *Padre*, Otavalo, Jerusalén. Jerusalén? The owner's mouth drops open in astonishment, revealing rotten teeth. Suddenly the words are pouring out of him and his eyes keep shifting from Alfredo to Dori and back again.

Alfredo translates for him: he says that you have a wall in

73

Jerusalem, and in the . . . slots between the . . . stones, you can put notes with requests for God.

Dori nods.

Then he asks if Dori will take his note and put it in . . . that wall, when he goes back to Jerusalem.

Unbelievable, Dori thinks, and says: no problem.

But there is a problem. It seems that the man doesn't know how to write and he has to send his young son to summon his older son, who went to school in Quito for a few years.

Alfredo, maybe you can write it for him? Dori suggests.

But Alfredo explains that it is very important to Jesus that his son himself writes the requests, and suggests that, in the meantime, Dori show his father's pictures to him. Dori takes the pictures out of his bag and puts them on the table next to the bottle of Inca Cola. Jesus picks them up, looks at them for a long time, looks at Dori for a long time, and mumbles *sí, sí, sí.*

Hope stirs in Dori. *Sí* means yes! But when Alfredo translates the next few sentences to him, it turns out that all Jesus said is that Dori looks like the man in the pictures.

Did he ever come across him?

No, never.

That doesn't mean anything, Alfredo puts his hand on Dori's shoulder, quick to comfort him. This road is very out of the way. Few people take it.

So why did you even suggest that I show him the pictures? Dori is angry and Alfredo doesn't reply, but takes his hand off his shoulder.

The boy who once went to school arrives an eternity later with a maths notebook and the father dictates the note to him. The boy's hair falls into his eyes and every once in a while, he pushes it away quickly. He writes slowly, every letter an effort, and Dori thinks that the boy could actually be writing *his own* request to God, say, 'to get the hell out of this shit hole', without Jesus ever knowing: that's how dependent the father is on him.

The boy finishes writing and hands the page to Jesus, who looks at it for a long time, as if he can read, then folds it carefully, the way you fold an ironed shirt, kisses the paper and gives it to Dori.

Gracias, he says to him with glistening eyes.

Por favor, Dori tries.

No *por favor*, Alfredo corrects him. *Por favor* is please. Say: *de nada*.

De nada, Dori tries again, and Jesus nods and waits expectantly to see what Dori does with the note.

He puts it into his money belt. Then changes his mind and puts it into the small pocket of his jeans. Jesus confirms with a look that the pocket is a respectable enough place and offers him another Inca Cola. On the house. Dori refuses. Anything but that syrupy stuff again. Meanwhile, the rain has stopped, the sun is reappearing with amazing speed, and he wants to get moving.

A rainbow arcs across the sky and they say *chiao* to Jesus and his sons and drive towards it.

How long it's been since I've seen a rainbow like this one, with all its colours separate and distinct from one another, Dori thinks and leans back into a memory of their last family holiday in Beit Lehem Ha'Glilit. The weekend that broke the camel's back.

He and Roni fought from the minute they got into the car. Actually, even before then. They argued while they were packing, which they started late because she was late getting home from work, and went on until nine that night. What's the point? we'll leave tomorrow, he suggested. But she insisted: we've already paid for tonight. Do you want to throw away a thousand shekels? And Netta, of course, fell asleep the second they started driving, and later, when they reached the B&B – which was much smaller than the pictures on the website and had no divider between Netta's room and theirs, which destroyed the possibility, faint at any rate, that they would have sex – Netta woke up and didn't let them get a moment's sleep the entire night. The next day he was tired and cried endlessly over the slightest thing, and, as usual, drove a wedge between them when he asked that 'only Daddy' carry him and 'only Mummy' take him to the loo, and insisted on asking for more and more Bamba, which was the 'snack of contention' between them at home because Roni thought it was the least of all evils and Dori thought it the greatest. Later, he embarrassed them at dinner in the Galilean restaurant, with its low tables, where they stood out a mile among the fresh young couples who exuded *shanti* when they spoke and wore sharwals and looked as if they'd just finished fucking three times in a row and now were chilling out with their chai, and feeling sorry for that family at the isolated table whose child was eating his snot and drumming his knife and fork on his plate and ripping packs of sugar in two, spreading the grains all over the place. He must have some kind of problem, they were saying to themselves, something in the brain, maybe hereditary, because his parents looked a bit disturbed too, their eyes wild, their nerves shot to hell.

They left the B&B right after breakfast the next morning, skipped the walking tour, ostensibly to beat the traffic but in fact to minimise damage. They were approaching Zikhron Yaakov when it began to rain, which they were happy about because look, they weren't really losing out on anything, and then a breathtaking rainbow stretched from the edge of the sky to the end of the mountain. Can you see it? they asked Netta, and he nodded and listed the colours, and his beautiful smile spread across his beautiful face, and a little while later he fell asleep peacefully, and until the Havazelet Junction, they were a functional family.

But at the Havazelet Junction, Yaheli's mother called to say that her son wouldn't be coming to play with Netta as planned – what the excuse was, he no longer remembers, a stomach bug, a grandmother with a broken leg. Parents made Herculean efforts not to tell them the bitter truth: their kids didn't want to play with Netta.

Something about Netta's neediness puts them off, he said out loud after Roni put the phone down.

Don't be ridiculous, Roni said.

Then what is it?

I don't know. He runs us ragged. So maybe he runs them ragged too. I don't know.

Then maybe we need to talk to someone professional, he suggested, knowing full well she'd say no. The one and only time she'd gone to a psychologist she'd had the feeling (probably justified) that he was coming on to her, and ever since, she'd distrusted the entire profession.

Okay, she said, to his surprise. On condition that it's a woman. And let me talk to her about the payment. So she won't rip us off.

Picturing the first session in his mind, he was sure that Roni would be late and that from there, the discussion would naturally segue into the fact that she didn't spend enough time at home, and that was hurting their son – and he could relax in his armchair, probably black leather, the relaxation of 'I told you so.' But Roni actually arrived on time, and the discussion, which began with a general survey of their lifestyle – because the psychologist said, 'I want to learn about your daily life before I offer an opinion' – then went on to focus somehow on him, on his and Netta's sleep rituals, which the psychologist thought were 'exaggerated for a child his age' and 'utterly without boundaries'.

Psychologists are most annoying when they're right. Netta really wasn't outside him, on the other side of some boundary. He was inside him, beating like a second heart. Friends had warned him that the bond doesn't happen right at the beginning. It took me a whole year before I felt something for my son, one of them had said, oddly proud. But it took Dori less than an hour. True, he'd dreamed of that child on many nights. Amazingly enough, his paternal instinct had matured even before his marital instinct. Years before Roni had broken through the clouds of his loneliness, he would imagine himself rolling down a grassy hill with his future son, or playing basketball in the garden with him, or reading him *King Matt the First*. What he never imagined was that his son would be so beautiful. More beautiful than either of them. Dark eyes, fair hair and skin.

Here, love, Roni had handed Netta to him after having held him at her breast for a long time. He's yours too. She never called him love: not before then and not after. Like the word 'island', which appears only once in the Bible. And Dori hesitated. Afraid he'd drop him. Afraid Netta would slip out of his hands like a dolphin in a pool. You'll see, it'll be great, Roni encouraged him, her face shining with that special afterglow.

There are mothers who exclude the man, keep the child for themselves. But Roni was generous, even during the early days. And in everything. Five months later, she went back to her senior position in the company and left Netta in his hands. She'd planned that in advance, of course. Became pregnant at a time that would allow her to return to work when he began his summer break from school. And so it was. He and Netta entered into a covenant. They learned about each other on the rug. Went out for short walks with the buggy in the mummies' park. Came back and listened to King Crimson and Genesis (the boy loves good music! Not all that kids' rubbish, he told Roni proudly). And rested in each other's arms as the slow, lazy hum of the Hapoel basketball team song rocked them into their long afternoon nap, from which they awoke tense and expectant − Netta would cry and Dori would devour apricots − for the door to open and their love to come in.

The child is definitely attached to you, but I have the impression that he also has good communication with his mother, the psychologist said when they talked to her about the trip. It won't be easy for him, considering that he's going through a bad time at nursery at the moment, but he'll adjust. Children are naturally able to adjust. What I'm asking myself – she added, the hint of a thin smile on her lips – is how you will get through it.

Roni laughed. And the sisterhood that had been present covertly in the room since the first session finally solidified right before his eyes.

*

La puta que te parió, Alfredo swears now. He thinks he left his sunglasses in Jesus's shop and now they'll have to go back to get them.

Your sunglasses are in your coat pocket, Dori says. You put them there when the rain started.

Alfredo sticks a hand into his coat pocket and laughs. We're a good team, eh? he says to Dori and punches his shoulder.

A few moderate bends in the road later, the town of Otavalo appears before them, nestled in a small valley like a bit of fluff in a belly button. Dori looks at his watch: despite everything, they'll manage to get there before the market opens.

Alfredo

He keeps looking at his watch all the time, Mister Dori. Nothing is so unnecessary as looking at your watch when you're travelling, if you think about it. After all, you'll get there when you get there. These gringos. They think that time is theirs. That they can control it. Such a shame. Here, already on the first day of school you realise it isn't like that, because your teacher comes two hours late. His car got stuck in the mud. Or he just drank a little too much the night before and didn't wake up. And is a very good thing he doesn't wake up. Because that way he teaches his pupils a very important lesson: for most of your life, you are going to wait. So don't make a big deal out of it, eh?

This Mister Dori, he probably never keeps his students waiting. He probably prepares the lesson well and gives difficult homework, but not too difficult. Is probably also a good father to his son. And faithful to his wife. And never hungry enough to steal. A cigarette? I offer him before the last hill down to Otavalo. Don't be silly. He doesn't smoke. Drink? A little, sometimes. Gamble? Of course not. But then again, there was . . . one time.

Tell me, tell me, I say, excited. Maybe now the little boy who turned over a desk in school will come out. The one Se'ela told me about.

Before I got married, he says, my friends organised a kind of stag party for me. We went to a casino in Jericho. It doesn't exist any more, the casino. It was bombed during one of my country's wars. And my friends aren't exactly my friends any more, to be honest.

So then . . .

I bought a few chips so they'd be happy. And I put them on number four on the roulette wheel. That's my lucky number.

Don't tell me, you won.

How'd you know?

Is the worst thing, to win the first time.

I just couldn't stop after that. You could buy chips there with a credit card. So I kept buying and buying. I was already down two thousand dollars. And I couldn't stop. Until my friends grabbed me under the arms and dragged me out of there to the car park, kicking and screaming. I didn't want to go with them. I tried like mad to break loose.

That is the smartest thing in life, I tell him: knowing when to stop. Most of the people I look for didn't know when to stop. With the drugs. With the women. With the path that ends, and they still decide to keep going into the bushes.

Is that what happened to my father, you think? he asks.

I knew he'd ask. Maybe, I answer. But he's a grown man. So maybe the story here is different.

*

You should have seen how the women played up to him during the shivah, Se'ela told me in one of our last conversations. Before that, she tried to argue with me about the Argentina clause of the contract. What do you mean that if the search happens to reach Argentina, you aren't obligated to accompany Dori there?! Forget it, I told her. Is in all my contracts. There's nothing much to say about it. But — she tried. Take it or leave it, I told her. But why? Not your business. I thought we were open with each other, Alfredo. Yes, we are open, Se'ela. So tell me a little more about your father. You said he's a handsome man. Was he involved with any women after your mother died? No, of course not. How do you know? He's not . . . he's not like that. I mean, there were a lot of women who wanted him. You should have seen what went on during the shivah. What's a shivah? It's how the Jews mourn. They sit at home for seven days and people come to extend condolences and eat pastries. With us, it was only six days because, towards the end, my father couldn't take it any more. Women came with pots of food. And the top button of their blouse undone. Married women, widows, single women. They would all bend over with their plunging necklines, kiss his stubbly cheeks and sit down on a chair next to him. Too close. But there's no way anything happened. He was in complete shock when my mum died. You know, Alfredo, people use the word love, but there are all kinds of love in the world. I, for example, loved my ex-husband, the shit. But not like that. I, for example, had no problem going out with other men a week after we separated. I'd go out with you too, Alfredo, if you weren't so far away. You sound okay to me. A little too hefty for my taste, from the pictures on your site. But nothing that a diet couldn't cure. No, no, the way my dad loved my mum, it was a completely different kind of love. It's all a question of trust, you know. If you truly believe that your partner will never leave you, you'll be prepared to leave larger pieces of your soul with him.

No. I can't imagine that my dad is with another woman now. I just can't picture it. What can I picture? Him slipping and falling off a cliff. A snake biting him in the middle of the jungle and no one there to take care of him. The Colombian underground holding him prisoner. Yes. In a pit covered with iron bars, like in the films about Vietnam. How do you know that's not true, Alfredo? A gut feeling? If you said a spleen feeling, a pancreas feeling, a liver feeling, I'd believe it. But what is a gut feeling? It's terribly general.

So you know what, I told her, a heart feeling. My heart tells me that your brother and me, we'll find your father alive. And you and me, we go for a weekend in Paris to celebrate, okay.

Is very lucky that they still have not invented a machine that reads minds because when we enter Otavalo, I put on a serious face and bite my bottom lip so I look professional. And really, I do want to find Mister Dori's father for him. For a long time I haven't wanted so much to find someone for someone – but the only thing I have in my head when we pull up in front of the market square is a picture of Se'ela, his sister, and me fucking against the wall of a hotel in Paris. That fucking on a wall, in real life, it doesn't work out so good, but in my imagination, Dori's sister winds her legs around my waist and I love her so hard that she forgets what her shitty husband did to her and forgets also to talk so much, only syllables come rushing out of her mouth, first in Hebrew, then in Spanish, then in French, and later in the international language women use when a man makes their body happy, and then I don't pay her and she doesn't go. She stays. And we lie next to each other quietly, and I tell her about all my searches that ended with nothing, the ones I don't tell anyone about, and she holds my hand and I hold hers till I have the strength for another go.

Dori

Holds the binoculars that Alfredo gave him and looks around for his father's shock of silver hair. Or for his special gait – bent slightly because of his war injury, proud because of his personality – or for his brown jacket, or a very pronounced Adam's apple in profile –

His heart gives an occasional leap when he thinks that maybe . . .

But it's only a passing illusion. A Father Morgana.

The Otavalo market square, almost empty when they climbed up to the observation balcony, has filled with hundreds of crowded stalls within two hours. The streets around it have been closed off to lorries, and the entire world – locals with baskets alongside tourists with cameras alongside policemen – is trying to navigate its way through the narrow aisles between the stalls, making Dori's search difficult.

Let's go down there, Alfredo says.

I don't understand. Dori lowers the binoculars. You don't want us to stay up here and try to spot my father in the market?

Your father is gone from here a long time, Alfredo says.

He was here two months ago, and Otavalo, it is not a place where people stay for more than a few days.

So what the fuck are we doing here? Dori feels his blood rise to the back of his neck.

Trying to understand the river, Alfredo answers serenely. I want to see you walk around the market. I want to look at you. What interests you. What stalls you stop at. I want you to think about your father walking around the market. And tell me everything that comes into your mind.

So why the hell did you give me the binoculars?

Ah, yes. Alfredo again exposes a gold tooth: is for you to look at the breasts of the women tourists.

Listen . . . ah . . . Señor Alfredo — Dori can barely restrain his urge to punch Alfredo and knock that gold tooth, and others, right out of his mouth — I didn't come here to look at breasts. I came to find my father. And I don't understand why, instead of walking around the market like a couple of morons, we're not doing something simple, like checking the hotels to see if his name is in a register.

Look, Dori — Alfredo remains calm — I tell you something. One year ago a French guy got lost in the forests here. His parents had a fat wallet, so they hired a whole team to search the area, a metre at a time. For a month. And they find nothing. In the end, they took me, as a consultant. I went down there and found his body for them in two days. Why? Because they tried in an organised way. And I tried to get lost. I looked at the last place he was seen, and from there, I tried to continue like someone who doesn't know where he's going. Like someone who thinks that every opening in the bushes is — a path.

I'm getting fed up with this guy's boasting, Dori thinks and says, so you're saying what?

That the world is not really organised, Dori. Is just what we tell ourselves so we can keep on living. The world is one big *kilombo*. You think I didn't send people to check the hotels? I did. Your father's name is not in the registers, but still I tell you that he was here.

But . . .

Look, Dori. This is how I work. If you don't like it, if you don't trust me – say it now. I had three other searches I could have taken. But I picked you, because your story . . . touched my soul. But if you are not interested, just say it. And I pack up myself and my office and leave without charging you a peso.

Bastard, Dori thinks. And holds back his answer, even though he already knows in his heart what it is.

Come to the market, amigo, Alfredo puts a hand on his shoulder. Come, before the prices go up.

And they go down and are swept away into the eye of the storm in the square, walking down the narrow aisles between the stalls. Dori tastes unfamiliar yellow seeds, squeezes watermelon-size pears, eats a watermelon that tastes like a pear, pushes his way among long-braided Indians, smells their sweat, smells the aroma of the pungent spices wafting from the spice stalls, sneezes on a pumpkin and imagines for a moment that he's in the Mahane Yehuda market in Jerusalem listening to the stall-holders selling their wares. He buys himself a few pairs of socks, a white T-shirt with an Incan calendar drawn on it, and a woollen sweater with a rectangular pattern, all at ridiculous prices, and stands stunned in front of a stall that sells masks, dozens of masks in vibrant colours arranged on poles, a kind of theatre without a play – masks with horns, masks with protruding tongues in red, orange, turquoise. He almost buys one for Netta, but is afraid it might frighten him, and moves on to the fabric stalls. The guy spreads the fabrics out for them, and they really are beautiful. Tse'ela loves stuff like this, but it seems weird to buy presents on this kind of trip. The market is bustling now, but calm; teeming with activity, but languid. A row of people wearing proper button-down shirts are sitting behind old typewriters, under cream-coloured umbrellas, and Alfredo explains that they are professional letter writers. They usually write formal letters for people, but they do personal ones too. Maybe I'll go over there, Dori thinks, maybe they'll be able to write a letter to Roni for me — a letter that begins with 'My Love', and goes on to say in a clear voice all the things I've been feeling this last year and can't put into words myself. But here's a stall that sells erotic wooden statues, a man and a woman intertwined in impossible positions, the man's prick huge. The stallholder is a dwarf and she offers them a necklace made of green stones. Alfredo haggles with her, lowers the price, and in the end, doesn't buy it. Dori checks that his money belt is still on him, then checks the stall of pirated CDs to see whether it has Western music and finds a Bob Marley collection. That's funny, there's not a single song on it that he knows. A stall selling hammocks tempts him into lying down for a minute, he still hasn't slept well since he left Israel, maybe that's why he lashed out like that at Alfredo, who is now walking beside him, and says *ola* to the hammock man too. Only once in her life has Roni been in a hammock; the only time she went to Ras al-Satan with him she decided that all those flies were not for her. Come: Alfredo pulls him away from the hammocks and the stench of the fish stalls further down the aisle, then to the area of electrical appliances, mixers, toasters, all looking broken, dozens of Rubik's cubes — what, did they only just get here? I could never figure out that cube, Dori thinks and looks for an alarm clock, something simple; after all, he can't ask receptionists to wake him up every time during this whole trip—

And then he sees his father's watch.

At first, he doesn't think it really is his watch, and he just admires the quality of the imitation. It looks almost like a genuine gold watch, he says to himself. And the strap — how did they manage to find such a wide one? They haven't been manufacturing them for years. But then, when he asks if he can have a closer look, he sees the engraving on the rim of the watch: *To Menny, with admiration, from your buddies in 162.*

What the hell is his watch doing here?

Frightening scenarios begin to inhabit his mind.

Robbers killed him and took his watch. His kidney and his watch. He had to sell the watch after all his money was stolen. At knifepoint.

A beautiful watch. Your father's? Alfredo moves closer to him. There's not a drop of alarm in his voice.

Alfredo moves closer still, violating his personal space. They don't make watches like this any more, he says. Is true art!

But how . . .

He probably had his pocket picked, Alfredo says in a perfectly calm voice. Someone pushed into him and removed his watch without his noticing it. This market is full of pickpockets, Mister Dori, you didn't read about it in Lonely Planet?

Bullshit, Dori says, refusing to accept the collapse of his armed robbery theory, I don't believe you can nick someone's watch so easily if he's awake.

You don't believe? Alfredo smiles sadly. So tell me, Mister Dori, where is your watch?

Dori extends his right hand to touch where his watch is supposed to be. There's only his left wrist. Bare.

I started like that too, Alfredo says, returning his watch. This whole area – he makes a sweeping gesture to include the large area of stalls – is called Thieves' Market. All the items you see here, they are really stolen merchandise being resold. Sometimes to the same person it was stolen from. By the way, you want to buy back your father's watch?

Dori nods and Alfredo haggles a bit and buys the watch. Put it in your money belt so they don't pick your pocket too, he suggests. And adds: I need a few minutes with the stall holder. I'll find out where he got this watch, and that way we'll know where your father spent the night when he was here. If you stay here, it might make the man keep his mouth shut. *Vamos*, keep walking around without me for a little while and we will meet in twenty minutes at the Bolívar café at the far end of the square. Okay?

Dori tries to walk around the stalls a bit more, but the market, which had looked so colourful until a few minutes ago, now seemed pathetic and artificial. A forced show for tourists. With their phallic cameras. And why do all the mask stalls sell the same masks? What happened to originality? No wonder they live in such abject poverty. They have no initiative. This isn't serenity, it's criminal indolence. And how the hell do you get out of this place? One alleyway after another, and all of them seem to lead inward. Maybe his father got so dizzy from walking around in circles that they were able to take off his clothes, his shoes, his underwear. Who knows what else of his is being sold here. Grey hair? A kidney? A Dr Gav backrest? And what's with the Bob Marley? Why does there have to be a Bob Marley CD at every hammock stall? There's nothing more annoying than Bob Marley when you're terrified about what might have happened to your father.

*

He puts his cup of coffee down on the table and picks up his father's watch, turning it in every direction. He puts it on. Takes it off. Perhaps he'll find another clue.

From the little he knows, this watch was in his father's possession before the war, but it took on the special status of a lucky charm during the war (when they said 'the war' at home, it was clear that they meant the Yom Kippur War). His father never spoke about what had happened then. In the Sinai. And on Yom Kippur itself he locked himself in his study and allowed no one in except Grandpa Pima, who used to come with his harmonica two hours before the fast ended. Every once in a while there was a film on TV about the war, and his father would be trapped in front of it like a moth in front of a flame, and Mum would sit down next to him and hold his hand, to keep it from burning. The bookcase in the sitting room had an entire shelf of books on other heroes of that war, men like Avigdor Kahalani or Yanosh Ben-Gal, and Dori read them in the desperate hope that he would find some mention of Major Menny Peleg (Pimstein) that would lift the fog surrounding what happened to his father, who didn't want to tell them how he was wounded or why he was considered a hero or why he didn't keep in touch with his buddies from the company. When one of them called, he gave his wife the usual signal — two fingers on his lips, like a smoker taking a cigarette out of his mouth — after which she said in her convincing voice that 'Menny's at work'. He wasn't willing to tell them the story of the watch either. Except for the remark, 'It watched over me, so I watch over it,' he once made to his mother, when she asked about an especially expensive spray he bought to clean the glass with, Dori managed to gather no more intelligence on the subject. His father took off the watch only when he showered. He slept with it on, got up with it on, went to work with it on, and at the beach he put it in a special case with a silk cloth, and only then went into the water. When every now and then the watch's mechanism would break, he'd sit down with his set of tools and invite Dori to come and learn how to repair it. And every time, Dori would try his best to follow the rapid movements of his father's hands, the switching of the tools, the precise explanations, but, despite himself, his thoughts would wander to the book he'd left in his room or the girl in his class he'd fallen in love with, and when his father finished and closed the case and said 'Next time, you can do it by yourself, okay?' they both knew that the next time Dori would have to ask him to 'show me' again.

He constantly disappointed his father. By not staying in his Hapoel Yerushalayim Youth Group. By choosing to study history and literature instead of maths and physics. By not having a girlfriend until he was older. And when he finally did have one after his army service, she wasn't pretty and didn't know how to answer his father when, at a Friday night dinner, he asked her what she wanted to be when she grew up. He disappointed his father by going into the Intelligence Corps and not into a combat unit. By not taking the officers' training course when it was offered to him. His father only said one word: But . . . Then he was silent and averted his eyes. Perhaps because his mother nudged him under the table, and perhaps because at that point he had already begun to understand, to digest the fact that Dori was not the son he had dreamed of.

Nonetheless, Dori had managed to utterly astound him when he decided to become a teacher. Go into the staffroom, his father said, and see if you can find even one teacher who's happy with what he's doing. Go into a classroom, Dori wanted to answer, and see if you can find one child there who isn't hungry for a good teacher. But he didn't answer him because he felt that the gap in their understanding of each other was so huge that there was no point in trying to bridge it.

He's not disappointed in you, he's just worried about you, his mother tried to explain.

He's looking for ways to get closer to you and you don't even notice, Roni said after his mother died.

And he knew that, as always, she was right. After all, he and his father both missed the same woman. And really, in the mourning period, there was something more vulnerable in his father, something that, for instance, enabled Dori to invite him to give a guest lecture on 'crisis situations' during career week at school. The boys were fascinated by him. No, hypnotised. At the age of thirty-six, for the first time in his life, Dori watched his father give a talk and was surprised to discover how similar their hand movements were when they spoke, and how his father managed to speak clearly and cogently without talking down to his audience — a balance so difficult to achieve — and how he used his computer presentation sparingly enough to keep the students' eyes from glazing over with boredom, and how patient and attentive he was to the questions flying at him from every corner of the auditorium, and how the older women teachers undressed him with their eyes and went up to him after the lecture to compliment him and give the new widower the once-over up close. His father was polite but didn't flirt, not even for a second; after all, he was a member of the conservative party of one great love in life, maybe even the chairman of that party.

When everyone had gone, leaving only the two of them and lots of empty chairs, his father said, thank you very much for asking me here, Dori, it was a refreshing change from the cynics I usually speak to. I hope they enjoyed it. What do you mean, 'enjoy it,' Dori said. It was fantastic! And he was already beginning to plan joint programmes in his mind. Yes, maybe this is the way to get close: to do things together. To combine business and educational projects. To use knowledge from the business world to help youth at risk. To put CEOs together with head teachers and show them what they can learn from each other. And at the centre of it all, the two of them as the moving force behind the entire project. Meeting. Writing emails. Finding a common language.

And then his father went away.

Just like I thought, Dorrri, your father was here. Alfredo suddenly turns up, and pulls Dori after him, almost tearing him out of his chair and making for the street. We found the boy who picked his pocket, he explains on the way. He told us what street he was on when he deliberately ran into him on his bicycle, and that led us to the hostel. His name wasn't in the guest book because he didn't pay. But the owner remembers him very well.

Wait a minute, why didn't he pay?

Tranquilo, Dori. You'll hear in a minute.

The Atahualpa hostel was relatively far from the market square, and the closer they got to it, the more distant the voices of the stallholders grew, as the air filled with a sleepy, lazy silence.

The door of the hostel looks as if it belongs to an ordinary house, but when they open it they see a spacious inner courtyard surrounded by several guest rooms. In the middle of the courtyard stands a burbling fountain ringed by a tangle of wild ferns. At the edge of the courtyard is a sink for hand washing, and beside it are a few clotheslines covered completely with clothes held in place by pegs. And even though there's no one wandering around outside the rooms, the place seems to be breathing.

The owner finally comes out to them, an erect old man wearing pristine white, cropped trousers, a blue poncho with a grey pattern and rope sandals. *Ola*, he greets them, and then adds something directed at Alfredo.

He says that you look like your father, Alfredo translates.

Dori nods. He doesn't know if he should say thank you. And he doesn't know how to say thank you.

Edgar, the old man says, reaching out and grasping Dori's hand very firmly. (Roni told him not too long ago that she enjoys shocking business people with a crushing handshake. They don't expect it from a woman, she laughed, and it's great seeing them try to hide their pain.)

Edgar leads them to his home, which is adjacent to the hostel. A courtyard full of split logs. A small house. Two cold rooms. My wife – he gestures towards a picture hanging in the main room, as if he's introducing them to a living person and now they have to shake her hand. The woman in the picture has a hint of moustache and a lovely smile, and she's wearing a brightly coloured beret folded on her head in a triangle that reminds Dori of the pastry known as Haman's ears, eaten on Purim.

He says a few words in Spanish and points to a small table. Alfredo translates for him: he says that this is where your father used to sit.

There are four chairs around the table, and Dori sees that one of them has a backrest similar to the Dr Gav backrests his father uses. Edgar offers them food his wife has cooked. It seems that she had a stall of home-cooked food in the market. A week before she died, she cooked him enough food for a few months and put it in two freezers: one that they had, and the other, a huge one, that she bought specially.

Dori declines. Politely. Even though he's hungry. He usually likes elderly people, listening to their stories, their slow memories. But now he wants information. And quickly.

Then at least drink some *chicha*, Edgar insists, in a tone which makes it clear that this time he will not take no for an answer, and puts three bottles filled with an unknown liquid on the table. Alfredo sips from his bottle. Edgar sips from his bottle. Dori has no choice. It tastes like corn. Like the liquid you pour out of a can of corn before you eat it on your annual school field trip.

So, how's business? Alfredo asks Edgar in Spanish. Dori doesn't understand a word, but from the tone, it's clearly a question.

Business is good, thanks to your father, Alfredo translates Edgar's answer for Dori.

It turns out that his father stayed here a week, and he and Edgar became fast friends. It isn't every day that someone who has more years than teeth comes here. Most of the guests in the hostel are young people who want to suck the honey then fly off to the next flower. And right at the beginning, he noticed that strange board that Señor Menny sat on when he was outside his room. How do you say it? . . . Doctor . . . ? *Si*, Doctor Gav. So they began to talk and found that they had back pain in common, and Edgar tried sitting on that Dr Gav and when he saw that it really did ease the pain a little, he asked Señor Menny if he could take the backrest to his carpentry workshop for a few hours because he wanted to try to build a Doctor like that for himself. Señor Menny said okay, but only if Edgar would let him see how he made it, and Edgar said that he liked to work alone, quietly, and he was too old to change his habits, but if the Señor would like, he is invited to eat his defrosted dinner with him, at exactly 6.30. And so they began to eat two meals a day together, dinner and breakfast, and Edgar told Señor Menny what he hadn't even told his children, because he was an outsider: that his wallet has been empty lately because Felicia's stall in Modesto Jaramillo closed and the hotel is only full the night before the market, and that he's thinking about closing it because the upkeep costs money too. Señor Menny said, what you're describing now is a business crisis, and in such a situation you have to be creative, change direction. Edgar didn't understand what he was talking about, so Señor Menny said, by tomorrow morning, I'll come back to you with a plan, and it'll help if you can give me all the material you have on your area.

The next morning, Señor Menny explained to him – your hotel is fine. Your problem is that people only come here for the market and don't know about all the other wonderful things they can do in the area. You have to tell every person who comes here that he has to stay at least a week to truly experience Otavalo. And you have to offer tours. For money, of course. Ah, and you need a website too. That's how older tourists look for accommodation these days. And they're the tourists you want here, because they have money to spend. But how . . . what . . . tours? . . . Website? . . . Edgar was at a loss. Your children, Señor Menny said, could any of them provide transport? Yes, Edgar admitted. My youngest son just finished school and does nothing but drive around in his van and bother the female tourists. So see to it that he's available to work for you next week, Señor Menny said. And I'll take care of the website.

There are people in Israel who owe me . . . a favour or two. They'll design a site for you. And also an attractive schedule of activities you can hand out to all your guests. And . . . how much do you want for this? How much is your fee? Edgar asked because time had already taught him that no one gives you anything for free. *Nada*, Señor Menny said and explained that for years he'd been helping rich people out of business crises so they could continue taking money from poor people. For once, he wanted to do the opposite.

Your father even insisted on paying for his room, Edgar said. And I wouldn't let him. He pushed the money into my shirt pocket and I threw it back at him and made a scary face, like he was insulting me. And your father . . . it was . . . my face . . . it really did scare him . . . Edgar laughs out loud, his whole body shakes with laughter, which slowly turns into a hacking cough. Alfredo hands him the bottle of *chicha*, and Edgar drinks from it until the coughing subsides.

There's a knock at the door and a couple of Vikings stoop their way into the room. They're leaving today and want to pay their bill. Edgar gives them a page he tears out of his bill pad and they pay him and leave. Five nights, he waves all five fingers of one hand proudly in the air. They found out about us on the Internet. They went out in the van with Manuel to tour Lagunas de Mojanda and Cotacachi. Just like your father said.

Ask him if my father told him where he planned to go from here, Dori requests, and Alfredo translates.

Edgar closes his eyes as if trying to recall, but after a few seconds of closed eyes, his mouth opens slightly and gentle snoring emerges. Alfredo touches his elbow lightly, then shakes his shoulder harder, and Edgar wakes up. And immediately begins speaking. His voice is slightly different, there's a dream in his eyes, and Dori isn't sure he's completely awake.

Your father – Alfredo translates simultaneously – your father is a very strong man, but he loved your mother very much, and she died, eh? So he has to speak to her. But that's impossible. Because she's dead, right? Wrong. I speak to Felicia in my dreams. She comes to me and speaks. And I answer. But your father doesn't dream. That is his problem. He needs some help to dream.

Alfredo nods in understanding. Dori understands nothing. Alfredo asks Edgar a question that ends with the word 'Guatemala', and Edgar nods.

Then he asks him another question, and Edgar mumbles something.

Dori is sorry that he never learned Spanish like his father did. Because actually, Alfredo can make up anything he wants to. And now Alfredo says, there are substances in Guatemala . . . special substances . . . that help you dream. And your father asked Edgar if there were any in Ecuador, and Edgar told him that in Ecuador there was only one area of farms where you can get stuff like that.

Edgar speaks again, and raises a warning finger. Your father didn't tell him specifically that he was going there, Alfredo translates. And Edgar warned him that it was not a good idea to use stuff like that without a shaman to guide you. That's what they call the man who knows the paths to the world of the dead. But your father said that he only wanted one more time . . . to rise high, to the place where the souls are, because there are a few more things he wants to ask her about. Your mother.

Okay. Dori gets up and says to Alfredo, we've heard enough, don't you think? Thank him nicely and let's get going.

Tranquilo, Mister Dorrri. Alfredo doesn't move.

Tranquilo, tranquilo. I've had enough of this *tranquilo*! Dori says, unconsciously clenching his hand into a fist.

Dorrrri, calm down. Right now we have no indication that your father is in danger. On the contrary, what we do know is that he went to the farms with a specific purpose in mind. He didn't go there to get high or to howl at the moon at night, but to dream about your mother. Is a good chance that is what he did, then went on his way.

But . . .

Besides — Alfredo takes a leisurely sip of the *chicha* — the road to the farm area is as narrow as the waist of a Thai whore, and is open only until one in the afternoon. From one in the afternoon, is open only for people who want to come back from there. I say we should sleep here and leave at sunrise tomorrow.

Edgar excitedly waves the key that the Vikings left on the table and speaks in a torrent of words.

Look at this, Alfredo translates. By chance, the room that the Swedes left is number 3, the room where your father slept. Edgar says that this is a sign from the gods that your voyage will come to a good end.

*

His parents met at school. That much they agreed on. But about what happened after that, their two histories diverge. She claimed that he asked her if she wanted to study with him for their final maths exam, and that before then, she hadn't noticed him at all. He claimed that she'd been making eyes at him all through their last year and in the end he had no choice but to go up to her and ask if she wanted to go to the Edison cinema with him. Study for an exam? What are you talking about? He didn't remember anything like that. He never had to study for his exams.

From that point on, the two streams of the story again flowed onward as one, in mutual agreement: during their first year in the army, she left him. She did it in a letter. There were no mobile phones or text messages then, so she wrote to him and told him that she loved him but that she couldn't handle the fact that he came home on leave only once every few weeks. Later on, she understood that it wasn't just that. She simply wasn't ready yet for how sure he was that he loved her. He already knew, but she still needed to check. He'd already found, and she was still looking.

So she looked. For five years. And he waited for her, for five years. Occasionally he would send her messages through mutual friends. And once a year, on her birthday, he'd call her and ask how she was, heroically enduring stories of her boyfriends while remaining silent about what he himself had been up to, even though she knew everything, because Jerusalem was and still is a small town, not to say a shtetl, and at the end of the conversation he would always say: happy birthday, Nurit. And you know that I'm waiting for you, right?

They met again during their first year at the Hebrew University. She was studying psychology and art and he, economics and business administration. Her girlfriends didn't understand why she ignored that gorgeous man who was pursuing her with such persistent gentleness, and told her with laughter that had more than a dash of seriousness that they gave her until the end of the term to decide whether she wanted him or not.

By the end of the term they were living together in a small apartment in Beit Ha'Kerem, and two years later they got married. Three years later, Tse'ela was born. And for all the years that followed, his father continued to court his mother as if she were still undecided about him.

Separations are not always a bad thing, his mother tried to comfort him during those two awful days when he tried to separate from Roni. Look at what it did for your father and me. It brought us closer together than anything else ever did.

His parents didn't touch each other a lot. Sometimes, though not often, sitting in front of the TV, she would put her head on his chest, and when he came home from a business trip abroad, they would come together for a longer embrace in the airport arrivals hall, one of his arms around her, the other on his luggage trolley. That was the sum total of their public, physical displays of love. Nonetheless, despite the few overt gestures, a great, unequivocal love flowed consistently between them, like the waters of a hidden spring.

A year or two before he left school, Dori spent his first weekend as a guest in another family's home. A friend, a fellow student, invited him to stay for a weekend of parties to be held at homes close to his. Without any preparation, Dori was thrown straight into a totally different family world, with different codes, different table manners, a different sense of humour. But he was especially stunned by the almost open loathing between the parents which, despite their desperate attempts to conceal it from their young guest, kept rearing its ugly head. In the aggressive, dismissive tone of the father's voice in response to everything the mother said. In the ostensibly innocent barbs about the father's pot belly, which the mother unleashed only to get back at him.

And how did his parents' love make itself known? There were the old-fashioned pet names. She called him Mentsch, he called her Nurik. There was the private, trilling whistle they used to locate each other in the house when a fuse blew because once again she had forgotten that you couldn't turn on the dryer and the boiler at the same time. And there were also those quiet evening conversations in the sitting room after the nine o'clock news: he talked and she listened with her usual patience and restraint, as if nothing in the world existed but him. At times she would express her opinion and he would listen intently. Then they would switch roles again. And there was also their dynamic division of labour: she remembered for him everything that had happened to them since their marriage – names, places, dates. He took care of Grandma Simona's funeral arrangements for her because she was too sad to do it. She rinsed the dishes before she put them in the dishwasher. He took them out of the dishwasher and put them into the cupboard. She ordered a new kitchen because there was mould in the cupboard. He haggled about prices. She came in after the negotiations blew up and suggested a compromise. With astonishing naturalness, they slid into each other's domains so often that it became impossible to know who was the Yin and who was the Yang.

And there was their constant concern for each other's health, of course. Even before she became ill. Mentsch, don't bend down like that, it's not good for your back. Nurik, put on a coat, you'll catch cold. And his small acts of chivalry: Nurik, I'll take your bag, I'll open the door, I'll go out and get the milk. And the compliments he showered on her: look at your mother, isn't she gorgeous, he'd say when she was being critical of her reflection in the mirror. A real teen beauty queen, she'd reply, but she couldn't hide her delight at the compliment. And he continued to compliment her even when she grew older, when she got heavier, when her illness reached its final stages and she began to wither away. And once, when he and Tse'ela were little, she went to a conference in Tiberias and he suddenly went mad with missing her, so he asked Grandpa Pima to come and look after them so that he could go to Tiberias, to the hotel. Just to see her for a few minutes. And they had their in-jokes. So many in-jokes. He would make her laugh, and she had the most beautiful laugh in the world: her two dimples deepened, her green eyes shone, her large nose danced, her glasses slid slightly down. At first, he and Tse'ela would ask them to explain: what's so funny? With time, they learned that even after the explanation, they didn't understand. And he went dancing for her, folk dances. Even though he couldn't stand them. And even though he was a terrible dancer. Once a week, he'd go to the community centre with her just so she'd have a partner for the dances, albeit a partner who would tread on her feet. The main thing was that no one snatched her away from him because — as he always said — that whole folk dancing group is one big adulterers' club.

He continued to be afraid that she'd be snatched away from

him even when she was sixty. Because of that look that he claimed she had in her eye; the look of an adventuress, he called it. And she'd get angry, saying it was all in his mind. Then they'd go into their bedroom. And there, only there, was where they had their arguments. Which, as a child, Dori thought was natural. But when he became a father, it seemed superhuman to him. Or, at the very least, admirable. Roni and he fought endlessly during Netta's first year. Right before his eyes. Before his ears. While he cried. And as they shouted, Dori would say to himself: stop it. Don't answer her. It's not good for the baby. But he couldn't stop.

What did his parents argue about? Who knows? The ground falls away under his memories – how much can a child really know his parents? If his father is using 'substances', surely anything could be true?

Nevertheless, when he pressed his ear against the closed door, he heard, or thought he heard, that they were arguing a lot about them. The children. He claimed that she was raising Dori like a girl. She claimed that he spoiled Tse'ela in a way that would harm her for life. 'I want to hear you say "no!" to her just once' was the comment they heard quite a few times through the door. During the last year, they also fought about his mother's illness. He claimed that she was giving up. That she wasn't fighting hard enough. That they could emerge from the crisis stronger than ever. She told him to stop using his strategies on her. And that if he once had to undergo chemo himself, he wouldn't talk that way. He fell silent after that remark. But he didn't let her give up. And he didn't give up, either.

Dori and Tse'ela often went to visit their mother in the oncology department. His father, on the other hand, didn't have to visit her – he was simply there. Day and night. Until the final silence.

Bitter waves of longing rise up in Dori's throat, and he gets out of bed to drink something. Then he begins to walk around the room, diagonally, like a snooker ball. Suddenly, an idea seizes him: his father slept here. In this room. Maybe he left something behind? Maybe he dropped a note? A museum ticket? A bus ticket?

He begins searching. Feverishly. Moving chairs, opening desk drawers, taking pictures off the wall, moving the small TV. He lies down on the floor to see if there's anything in the dark cave under the bed, and continues to crawl, looking for loose floor tiles, hidden buttons. He sniffs the room – maybe he'll catch a whiff of the aroma of the pipe his father smoked when the mood was upon him. He sniffs in the bathroom: maybe there's a vestige of his father's Old Spice there. He opens all the drawers in the stand under the mirror, and in one of them he finds a square of toilet paper. In his first year of secondary school, Tali Haran wrote on a piece of toilet paper that he had beautiful eyes. But he was in love with Ruthie Gadish. And this piece of toilet paper has nothing written on it. He throws it into the loo and flushes. He shoves his hand into every fold of the shower curtain, then pulls it open and sees a soap dish behind the tap. A soap dish! An excellent place to leave a message. Quickly he reaches for it. But the soap dish is empty. There isn't even any soap in it. The entire room is empty: empty of his father's presence. Maybe he's never been here at all? Dori sits down on the bed, defeated. Maybe Edgar and Alfredo made up the whole story? Maybe he should get rid of Alfredo and turn to the Embassy for help? To hell with secrecy, his father is using psychedelic drugs! Although . . . even that detail could be part of the fairy tale Edgar and Alfredo have concocted to con him out of his money. Come off it – Menny Peleg using drugs?

Dori feels an intense need to consult with the oracle at 6 Kobobi Street, where he grew up. But she's no longer among the living.

His mother had the rare ability to listen. Few people really do. Many are formulating their next sentence even before you've finished yours – and it's only at the end of a sentence, the very end, that the truly important things are said. Other people – their thoughts wander. Their eyes continue to stare at you, but the spark of attentiveness is already lost. And then there are the hmm'ers. They nod with such frequency that you can only suspect that, like burglars in a museum, they keep projecting the same tape on the monitoring screen while they are actually somewhere else more exciting than your chatter, stealing a Picasso.

Dori's mother would take off her glasses and put them on the table, 'because then all the distractions around me are blurred and I can focus on the person with me'. Her friends always told her that she was a psychologist manqué and she would reply that she liked it better that way, being the head curator of the Museum of the Golden Age as a profession and listening to people she loves out of choice. Even though Dori sought her advice often, she never lectured him 'from her own life experience' and never began a sentence with 'When I was your age' or 'If you ask my opinion'. She just helped him uproot the weeds and see his indecision for what it was, with all its true motives. When he couldn't decide between law school and history, she helped him see that all the reasons in favour of law stemmed from fear (the fear of not making a living, the fear of losing his grasp on the present), while all his reasons in favour of history stemmed from passion. When he suddenly lost interest in teaching, during the first year after Netta was born, she helped him to see that it wasn't because he was sick of his students, but because fatherhood was having such an impact on him that it dulled everything else. If you were a woman, no one would be surprised, she said. They would meet in the 'café' – her code for a corner of the kitchen, under the window, which she'd marked off with a plasterboard divider she painted in autumn colours so it would look like a Parisian café. She put up two bookshelves there, one for her favourite books and the other for new ones (his mother read with such passion that when she was in the middle of a really good book, her temperature rose), and she hung a special ceiling light she bought from someone named Eitan in the Netanya industrial area, one that shed new light on everything. Dori would come to the 'café' late because those were her hours, the time she read, prepared catalogues for exhibitions, spoke to Grandma Simona, her mother, when she was still alive. All the while eating cheese she bought from Abu Daoud in the market, washing it down with a cup of hot tea that had a quarter of a teaspoon of sugar in it.

When he was a child, it was the same: his father and Tse'ela loved going to bed early, and he and his mother loved stretching their tea-and-cheese talks late into the night. And no matter what they talked about, or even if she was critical of him, he was always left with the feeling that his choices were fine and he was fine and, whatever happened, he always had himself.

(When Roni was in Barcelona, Netta kept complaining about mysterious pains. But where exactly does it hurt? Dori tried again and again to find out. In your leg? No. Your stomach? No. Your head? No. So where? It hurts in my mummy, he finally said. In my mummy.)

What he would give for a time machine, a time–place machine, actually, that would take him to his mother now. To his mother before her illness. But wait a minute – understanding cuts through the fog of his sorrow – my father found the time and place machine I was just wishing for. So what the hell am I supposed to do? Deny it to him?

He can't talk it over with Tse'ela. No. The word 'drugs' would be enough to make her hysterical. He leaves his room and heads over to Alfredo's trailer to ask if he can use his phone. And call Roni. Forget the cost. But as he reaches out to knock on the door, he hears the unmistakable sigh of a woman very close to planting a flag on the summit of her orgasm. What a bastard! he curses out loud and pounds the door with his fist. What is this supposed to be? How can Alfredo indulge himself like this when he's supposed to be looking for his father? He stops pounding and starts kicking. Hard. Until Alfredo has no choice but to open the door. He stands there, decked out in a tycoon's red silk robe, and asks *que tal*, amigo? I am a little . . . ah . . . busy here.

I'm glad you're having a good time, Dori says. Without smiling. And asks for the satellite phone, if possible, and when he receives it he doesn't say thank you in order to make it crystal clear to Alfredo who's the boss and who's the employee. He walks a little way from the trailer and calls Roni, praying the line isn't engaged, and she answers. Suddenly, he feels like asking her, of all things, why she doesn't come hard, the way she used to, but instead he says how good it is to hear her voice, and she asks, whose number is this? Alfredo's, he replies, I forgot my phone . . . At home, she says finishing his sentence, on the sitting room table. Do you want me to FedEx it to you? The truth is . . . you could – he's amazed yet again by her practicality – but at the moment I can't tell you where to send it. Tomorrow we won't be here any more. And I haven't the slightest idea where we'll be the day after tomorrow. So what's happening? she wants to know. Come on, tell me. And he gives her a summary of everything that has happened and also tells her the sensational news about his father. Wow, she says in a totally wow-less voice. Who would have believed it. He waits for her to say something else, but the silence on the other end of the delay lingers on the line. So he asks her what she thinks he should do; after all, maybe his father is in real danger, and she – he thinks he hears her typing on her keyboard, he thinks she's working while she's talking to him – tells him that if she were him, she'd let Alfredo stay in the lead, he's supposed to be an excellent professional, and the truth is that, so far, his instincts have been spot on, which doesn't mean that Dori shouldn't keep a close eye on him, and under no circumstances should he be naïve, because he sometimes has that tendency –

If there's a word Dori despises, that's it. Ever since Roni became head of her department, she thinks everyone has become naïve, especially him, with 'that bubble he creates for himself at school', where they try to implement principles of mutual respect and courtesy and attentiveness and far too much seriousness. It's not naïvety, he always throws back at her, a naïve person is a fool cut off from reality. I, on the other hand, know exactly what's happening out there and try to show my students that another way is possible.

Can I talk to Netta? He changes the subject to rescue the conversation from the danger of the argument that began hovering over it from the minute she uttered the word naïve.

He's at my mother's.

On the kibbutz?

Yes. I have a big presentation on Thursday, so I asked her to take him for a few days.

How stupid of me, Dori thinks, how naïve of me to believe that she'd use my absence to spend more time with him. And how is he at night? Is he waking up a lot? he asks.

They're suddenly disconnected and an engaged tone fills his ear.

He tries unsuccessfully to call again. Then waits a few more minutes in the street; maybe she'll call him.

That doesn't happen, and he goes back to his room. At the door is his lost suitcase. Less than forty-eight hours and it's here. Just as Alfredo promised. Maybe he really should trust him more?

*

He spends a long time moving his clothes from the suitcase to the *mochila*, then gets into bed and shoves the second, orphaned pillow under his head too and closes his eyes, and opens his eyes, and looks at the ceiling fan spinning round and round, and closes his eyes and tries to fall asleep, and again, like the first night, he can't fall asleep even though he's so terribly tired . . .

And slowly he fills up with a quiet panic.

It's been a long time since he felt that panic, which is something like the dizziness you feel before jumping from a high place, a sort of fear of falling that contains within it a desire to fall. The first time he felt it was when he became separated from his family in the Tel Aviv central bus station. It returned on his annual school trips, during too-long nights with his binoculars in Lebanon, during his trial separation from Roni. It was difficult to put a finger on it: at some moment, the loneliness turns into fear. Since Netta was born, he hasn't gone anywhere near that part of his mind, he just hasn't had the time, and now, as he stares at the ceiling fan spinning above him, he feels that panic returning, growing stronger and trying to convince him: you're completely exposed now, Dori, stripped naked, you have no defence, that fan might break off its axis and pierce your heart, your father might die before you find him—

He turns on the TV. Maybe a little channel-hopping will stop the rapid beating of his heart. It's not a good sign when you can hear the beating of your heart. Floods in Bangladesh. Murder in Somalia. A sex scandal in England. There's nothing like other people's troubles to numb you. A local channel is broadcasting an item about a shaman who was apparently asked to perform ceremonies on the football fields where Ecuador's national team will play in the next World Cup games. Dori doesn't understand what the presenter is saying, but the picture fills him with a strange sense of peace and calms his pounding heart: a shaman, clad surprisingly in jeans and a West Indian white T-shirt, is standing in the centre circle of the Allianz Arena in Munich, scattering incense you can almost smell through the screen, mumbling a prayer, waving leaves and feathers, and at the end, spreading his fingers like a fan to bless the turf.

When the adverts come on, he opens his Lonely Planet and scans the index for 'shaman' or 'shamanism'. He expects to find a lot of references. But to his surprise, there isn't even one.

Alfredo

What exactly is a shaman? Mister Dori asks when we start driving.

I don't say anything. Go and explain a dolphin to an alpaca.

That . . . shaman . . . he's actually a doctor? he persists.

Also.

And what else?

All kinds of things.

For example?

You won't understand.

Try me.

You won't understand.

*

He won't understand. It goes against his gringo mind.

Alfredo? He won't give up.

Si, Mister Dori.

Do you . . . go to a shaman sometimes?

Yes.

When was the last time you went?

A year ago.

Why?

I had what your mother had, may she rest in peace. A tumour.

You had a cancerous tumour?

Yes.

And the shaman helped you?

He cured me *totalmente.*

What? How?

He explained to me that I don't live healthy. That I see too many dead people every month. And death is catching. He said: you personally should only handle cases where you believe there is a chance, even a small one, of finding a live person. The ones that are corpses for sure, leave for your assistants.

And that's what cured your cancer?

Yes.

I don't believe that.

I told you that you wouldn't believe it, Mister Dori.

But . . .

Look how beautiful that is, I say, because this conversation is getting too heavy for me, and I point to a schoolgirl walking towards us in a skirt down to her socks. Socks up to her knees. A white blouse with buttons you can imagine tearing off with pleasure.

Come on, Alfredo, you're a paedophile, Mister Dori says.

Que paedophile? You want to tell me that you never have a hard-on in the middle of a lesson?

No, he tells me. I don't feel things like that when I'm teaching.

I don't believe you, I say. When the girls come up to you after class with their boobs hanging out, I can't believe you don't feel like taking them apart like a chicken.

No, he tells me, I don't. They're girls. In principle, girls don't arouse anything in me but . . . paternal feelings.

So what does do it for you – I'm almost yelling – sheep, donkeys, men?

My wife, he answers calmly. My wife does it for me.

You have a picture? I ask. Now I really want to see who is this woman that twists him around like that, on her finger.

Yes. I have a picture of the three of us together. But there are things you can't see in a picture. Personality, character, an interesting mind.

What is all that compared to a beautiful ass? I laugh. And to my surprise, he laughs with me. No, really – I take advantage of the fact that he is with me for a minute – explain what you mean when you say 'personality'.

Intelligence, for example. I find intelligence sexy, he says. And assertiveness. And complexity. Many contradictory forces acting against each other in the same woman.

Come on, show me the picture already.

You're driving now.

Show the picture, amigo. Or else I will think you are lying to me and that . . . is not good for the trust between us.

Mister Dori takes a picture out of his money belt, slowly, like he's doing me a favour, and I put one eye on the road and the other on his wife.

Look at the road, he says.

Don't you worry – I keep looking at the picture – Alfredo doesn't need more than a few seconds to know everything he needs to know.

She's really beautiful, his wife. The kind of beauty that gringos like. Thin like a boy, not like a mother. No ass. Small, beautiful breasts. You can see that they're beautiful from the way the folds of her blouse are spread out. Long, brown curls. Slanted green eyes, almost Chinese. Not tall. But strong. Knows something you don't know. Her eyes are hard, not soft. Her body is slender and her eyes are hard. Even though she's laughing in the picture. Even though her little boy is standing next to her, between her and Mister Dori. Her eyes are hard. And beautiful. She probably likes to be on top. In bed. She doesn't fuck a lot. She always has more important things to do.

But when she does fuck, she's in it all the way and blows your mind. I also take a quick look at their boy, and give Mister Dori back the picture.

So, did you see what you need to see? he asks. There is contempt in his tone, thin, like a tortilla. Yes, I say. I saw that your wife – is better to be with her than against her. And I am willing to bet you up to twenty llamas that you fell in love with her because of her eyes.

(I don't tell him that I also saw that he and his wife, they are both trying to pull the boy, each one holding an arm and pulling him towards them, and he is torn between them. The boy's expression is not good, not happy. I don't say it because there is a limit to what clients are prepared to hear about themselves.)

Not bad, he says, and puts the picture back into his money belt, not bad at all, Señor Alfredo.

Once a day he takes my satellite phone and calls his green-eyes. Usually I charge my clients for things like that, write everything down in my notepad, but this Dori makes me feel like I want to open my whole hand for him. I have no idea why. She has a young voice, his wife. Roni is her name. A young, beautiful voice, but not a nice one. But he's very nice to her, he envelops her with warmth through the phone. And she talks to him like he's a good friend from a long time ago. I don't understand all the words she says, but I do understand women's tones, and this one, she has the tone of someone who doesn't miss her man, and I don't like that, I don't like it all, the way she treats him. I see that after they talk on the phone, he's not happy. But I don't say a word to him. He and his father belong to the party of people who have only one great love in their lives, that's what he told me. He repeated that a few times. And I am not in politics. So I just give him some Bamba when he hands me my phone and ask him what the head of the party said. He looks out the window, takes a deep breath and says:

she thinks you're right, Alfredo, that we have to keep going patiently from farm to farm. Until we pick up his trail.

Dori

The deeper they go into the farm area, the fewer signs of the world there are. Every once in a while a riderless horse peers out from among the bushes. Every once in a while, a phone booth with the receiver torn off makes an appearance on the side of the road. The roads are full of potholes, like the surface of the moon. And sometimes, they end suddenly – with a barrier or a tangle of bushes – and you have to continue on foot to the farm itself. Alfredo cocks his gun every time they're about to step out of the trailer. There are gangs here that rob drugged-out gringos blind, he says, and immediately adds: but they do not kill here. There has not been a killing here for twenty years. They just steal here. Well, that's comforting, Dori says, and Alfredo doesn't pick up on the irony in his voice. The showers on the farms don't usually have hot water. And if they do, it stops running in the middle of your shower. That bothers Dori at first – that hair-raising moment when the freezing water touches his shoulders – but he gets used to it after a few days. He stops shaving. He doesn't have the energy, and somehow, it seems more appropriate to the unshaven area they're in. The bushes and trees are rampant with thousands of branches and leaves on which the frequent rain plays concertos for raindrops. The sound of drops hitting a leaf – he notices after a few days – is different from the sound of drops splattering on a branch, which is different from the sound of drops hitting a jacket, which is different from the sound of drops falling into the small puddles that form between the trees. The water flows constantly, everywhere, until you can't differentiate between the river and the tributaries. It's not exactly a jungle, not according to the biological definition. There are no monkeys or alligators here, and there's no Tarzan or Mowgli. But there are butterflies in dazzling colours, and there is something wild and frightening in the air. Even the farms themselves are fairly wild. A few straw huts around a central hut with a kitchen, and a food tent next to it. Everything is made of natural materials: the tables are wood, the night lights are candles, the hammocks are braided rope. Clothes are washed with hard soap in a rushing stream and hung to dry on bamboo chairs outside the huts. This doesn't always work. Because of the rain. After a while, you learn to guess when it's going to rain, other tourists tell him. After a while, you learn to distinguish between the various colours of the clouds.

He sits with the other tourists, talks to them, shows them the pictures of his father. And always, in the seconds that pass before they finish looking at them, buds of hope form in his chest. No, they haven't seen him, they always say in the end. A drug that helps you dream? There is some talk about it. You can get some if you go further, deeper into the tangled vegetation. No, they haven't tried it. Maybe they will in the future. On the one hand, you only live once. On the other, there are stories about people who got so screwed up by it that they never recovered. And it'd be a shame to ruin the whole trip because of such a stupid thing. Anyway, what's wrong with good old marijuana? You want some? No thanks, he says, feeling ancient. But he remains sitting around the wooden table with them, listening to their conversations, rarely speaking. And when he does, he's sure that he's said something idiotic. That he's of a totally different generation. That there's a gaping chasm between him and them. That he knows too much. Or maybe the opposite, too little.

Most of them are in their twenties, consumed by self-doubt and full of life, the two traits not clashing. And none of them lives in the place where he was born. The Australians live in London. The Brits work in Spain. The Spaniards work in Switzerland. The French work in China. Or Singapore. And the Swiss have fallen in love with Ecuador and are already checking out the possibility of buying land near Quito and setting up an ecological farm on it. The Israelis – there aren't that many of them. It's not on the hummus road, a guy named Miron from Kfar Saba explained to Dori. The hummus road, how can you not know what that is? The Israelis move from place to place in groups, along a well-trodden route based on recommendations passed on by word of mouth. And the farm area is not on that route. Why? It's not clear. Maybe because there's not enough action there?

The Australians (who live in London) laugh a lot. Dori doesn't always understand the joke but he enjoys being with people who drink and are funny and play a daring version of musical chairs in which the girls can sit on the boys if there are no empty chairs.

And he enjoys going back to his hut at some point during the night. He still can't fall asleep. But the fear of falling that consumed him in the room in Otavalo hasn't returned. It's as if he had to experience a full, heart-pounding attack once so that he could leave it behind and then lie in bed with open eyes till morning, just listening to the clouds move. Alfredo goes back to his trailer at night, usually in the company of one of the female tourists, and Dori stays on the farm, in the company of his thoughts, which grow increasingly free, more scattered and weirder: I could have enjoyed myself here, if not for . . . What do you mean, if not for? Admit it, you're enjoying yourself. I'm enjoying myself. A tiny bit. But then I remember why I'm here. And the ones I left there. Hot. Rainy and hot. Rainy and hot and stars. What'll happen if? What'll happen if? Lose—lose. The holes in this mosquito net are too big. Or the mosquitoes have made themselves smaller. Otherwise how did I get bitten? Maybe my dad slept here too? Under this same mosquito net? I used to put my feet into his shoes and walk across the sitting room in them. And Tse'ela would take my mum's shoes. That was when we were little and they'd leave us on our own at home. How old were we when they left us alone? Tse'ela was ten. I was seven. They used to go out a lot, for parents. They had a life. Roni and I hardly ever go out. It's not her, it's me. I can't leave Netta with a babysitter. I mean, I can. But I can't really enjoy myself when I'm worried about him. It's fucked. No two ways about it. That's one of the things I'll change when I get back. As if it'll help. So what will? A bird. Another bird. And another bird. That means it'll be light soon. And maybe I'll go out of the hut and my dad will just be standing there. In the sun. Maybe we'll hug. And I'll tell him that Hapoel won the cup, and maybe we'll keep travelling together for another few days. From farm to farm. I have to admit that this part of Ecuador is fantastic. Another few days like this and I'll be addicted, move away from the mother ship, break away, give up, drop into the atmosphere. Wake up. I have to wake up. Pull myself out of this lethargy and move on to the next farm. There is no choice.

*

First it's Manuel's farm. And then Rafael's. Like the classrooms he enters, each farm has its own unique magic, but there's always a stream within walking distance, most of the dishes on the menu have bananas in them, the night sky is strewn with hope, and people take out guitars, bongos, Persian flutes and a didgeridoo, an instrument with such a hypnotic sound that one night he walks out of his hut to the circle of people and asks how it's played.

It's not easy, they tell him, and demonstrate. You have to inhale and exhale at the same time in order to maintain the long, continuous sound. Cyclical breathing, it's called. He tries, and fails and fails and fails, to the sound of everyone's laughter, until suddenly – after all, he is still Pima's grandson, and he did play the trumpet for two years – he succeeds, and the buzzing sound bursts from the long instrument. He continues to ride the wave he's found for quite a while, forgetting everything: the tension of the school year that has just ended, the search for his father, his yearning to see Netta, Roni's coldness on the phone – that's how it is with him, only when he plays music or fucks can he devote himself completely to the present until all thought is obliterated. A few Australian girls get up to dance, and he accompanies their writhing movements, inhales and exhales, inhales and exhales, inhales and holds it until the dance dies on its own and the generator turns off and the stars fall without leaving a tail behind them, and even though they don't tell him to stop playing, he knows that it's enough.

What did his father do here? he wonders later, alone once again in his hut, what exactly did he do when they played the didgeridoo and raised their dilated pupils to the stars – drink soda water and offer them strategic consultation?

I don't think we're on the right track, he complains to Alfredo the next day. He's beginning to be really afraid that another few nights of cyclical breathing on the didgeridoo and he'll sink so deeply into the sound that he won't have enough willpower to get out of his hammock. To search. To rescue.

Tranquilo, Mister Dori, Alfredo insists. We have to penetrate deep into the forest. Make connections. Gather clues. I'm not sure we'll find your father here, he says. But I am almost positive that he passed through here. I smell him around us all the time.

What is all that crap? Dori thinks. You don't even know what my father's smell is (a mixture of pipe tobacco, Old Spice fumes, a pinch of the plastic of a basketball, my mum's shampoo, the toner of a laser printer, and car seats).

But Tse'ela says that he sounds trustworthy – Alfredo sends her daily email reports on their search efforts – and Roni says that she saw an article on the British *Independent* site about a girl whose body Alfredo helped find a month ago in Colombia after the official searchers had given up.

I don't need him to find a body.

Yes . . . right . . . that's not what I'm talking about. What I'm saying is that they called him the number one in the search and rescue field. No one else comes close. And that's the *Independent*, Dori.

So what's he been doing with me for a whole week? Dori is suspicious. If he's such a shark, why is he wasting his time on a little silverfish like me?

I have no idea, Roni shrugs telephonically. Ask him. Maybe your story touches some personal story in him.

I miss you, he says.

And Roni is silent. Right at the beginning, during their first months together, she told him that she didn't know how to miss anyone. And that he shouldn't be hurt by it. That's how it is with kibbutz survivors. When you cry for your mother all night in the children's house and no one comes to you . . . I don't know . . . my missing mechanism must have got screwed up, she tried to explain once. And he said, but I *do* miss people. For me it's an inseparable part of loving and I don't want to suppress it. Then don't, she said. Say whatever you feel like. Just don't be hurt if I don't say it back.

Fine, he said then. The basic conditions, the major clauses in all relationship contracts, are written in the first months, and later on it's so hard to change them. Like their names, which they'd written in the wet cement being used in the renovation of the entrance to the first building they'd lived in together, on Shabazi Street, and were still there. Even though that entire area had become ultra-Orthodox, and that declaration of love, complete with a heart and arrows, must seem very inappropriate to the yeshiva boys who look at it now.

Is Netta there? he asks.

Yes, she says, but . . .

Try, he almost pleads.

And then there's a few seconds' silence, and some muffled voices too far away to hear, and then—

He doesn't want to.

Dori feels a stab of pain in his stomach. Tell him that I just want to ask him something about his present.

Drop it, Dori.

Tell him.

Silence again, shorter this time. And again: I'm sorry, he doesn't . . . he's watching TV now.

TV in the morning?

Oh really, Dori, you left me alone here with him, so don't start telling me what to do.

Netta has been refusing to talk to him for a few days now. Actually, they've only spoken twice since he left. The first time, he asked: Daddy? in pre-crying surprise, then gave the phone to his mother. The second time he asked: When are you coming back, Daddy? I drew you a picture! And when Dori said, soon, I don't know exactly when, he hung up. Since then, he hasn't wanted to come to the phone. The psychologist told Roni that it's completely natural. That this is how children cope with separation. But it's driving Dori crazy. What if he's messing the boy up? What if he causes irreparable damage, and from now on, all his life, Netta won't dare to get close to anyone out of the fear that, one day, they'll go away and leave him? And what if this trip stretches out – a different, more selfish fear grows in him – and Netta just forgets about him, wipes him out of his mind? (When Dori's father came back from the Yom Kippur

War, family legend has it that when that strange man with the thick beard suddenly appeared at their front door, Dori ran away crying and hid under his blanket.)

Listen, amigo – he interrupts Alfredo's flirtation with an American girl who looks ten – I . . . I've had it. With all due respect to . . . your sense of smell, I'm paying for this trip and I say that we've been wasting our time for almost a whole week now.

No hay problema, Alfredo surprisingly agrees. But let's go to one more farm, with your permission. El Loco's farm. It's at the foot of the White River. We can leave tomorrow morning if you want.

Loco's farm is accessible only by boat. They leave the trailer on the riverbank under the watchful eyes of another two locals who know Alfredo.

A bare-chested boy in Bermuda-length jeans sails them downstream in a small rubber boat. There's no way my father would get on a boat like this, Dori thinks. He gets seasick. Every now and then, they come upon a small waterfall but the boat glides smoothly through it. The current isn't very strong. The water is thick, heavy. There's an occasional wooden hut on one of the banks. Smoke rises from invisible campfires. Trees extend long arms to them. Brightly coloured fruit, in new shapes, grow on some of them. A hairy, long-tailed animal that Dori has never seen in any zoo scampers away between the trunks. He asks Alfredo to ask the boat boy what animal it is, but the boy's only response is an enigmatic smile. His face is pretty strange: one eye is wide open and the other is narrowed to a slit, as if his face froze into a grimace of fear when he was a child. But he knows how to row. They move further and further inward, to the innards of inward. The river grows narrower, the air more humid. They seem to be passing slowly into a different climate zone. A huge tree with twisted limbs appears on their left. Netta would really enjoy climbing a tree like that, Dori thinks. He climbs every tree he sees, that boy. Fearlessly. It scares Dori, who was a pretty good climber himself when he was a child. He sees the fall coming. Calm down, Roni says. Let him experience the feeling.

Since there's no point in asking the boat boy the name of the enormous tree, Dori invents one himself: *popa*, after the giant basketball player, Constantin Popa. And he calls the small, iguana-like lizard sitting on a low branch, Iguanita. And if his father did get into this boat – he wonders, perplexed – did he insist on sitting on his Dr Gav? And what exactly did he prop it up against?

Drink something, Alfredo hands him a bottle of water. Is important to drink.

He gulps down a whole litre. He had no idea that he was so thirsty. 'El Loco' means crazy in Spanish, Alfredo explains. But he's American, the guy. He came here forty years ago, after Vietnam. He bought a huge piece of land and surrounded it with a fence of cactus plants. You can only get into his farm through the main gate. And it is always locked.

What do you mean? So how *do* you get in?

You press a button near the door, and then he looks at you through his cameras. If he likes you, he lets you in. If not – and he doesn't like most people – the gate stays closed.

So probably nobody comes here.

Just the opposite. People love to be treated like garbage, Mister Dori. And besides, they say that inside is *un paraiso*, a paradise. And that El Loco cooks nine-course meals for his guests. So people come down here on the boat, try their luck over and over again, maybe this time he'll let them in.

As soon as the boat boy slows down and ties the boat to a small dock, the mosquitoes swoop down on them. Dozens, maybe hundreds of them. In a matter of seconds, Dori has bites every-where. Even on his arse. How the hell did a mosquito's proboscis get to his arse? Alfredo hands him the lotion. It stinks. A lot. But he has no choice. He rubs it over all the exposed parts of his body. And on his arse. The boat boy waits patiently for them, the same enigmatic smile on his lips. His chest is still bare. Not a single mosquito has bitten him, as if he and the mosquitoes had forged an alliance. He leads them along a narrow path among banana trees, which ends in a silver, electric gate more suited to a villa in the exclusive Jerusalem neighbourhood of Talbieh than to Ecuador.

The boat boy rings the bell for them and retreats, waiting for their sentence to be pronounced. Would he go back with a full boat or an empty one this time? With surprising speed – even the boat boy himself is surprised – the gate opens. And Joe Cocker wearing a white vest, a red bandana and a crooked smile appears behind it.

Iguanita is sitting on his naked right shoulder. Welcome aboard, you're Menny Peleg's son, right? he asks Dori in a scorched voice.

*

They're sitting under a huge, white mosquito net that covers the farm's restaurant like a chuppah. El Loco hands them glasses of iced tea that he brewed in their honour, filled with ice cubes. Dori takes a long sip, then bends forward to place his glass on the table. Nooooooo! El Loco yells, and with horrified eyes leaps forward and places cork coasters on the table, then breathes heavily, as if he's just prevented a terrible disaster.

But apart from that, he seems quite nice. A burn covers his left cheek, and his pet iguana sits on his right shoulder, but he's far from the image Alfredo painted of him.

The glass of tea arrives after a nine-course meal he prepared and brought to their table himself. After the first course, Dori was ready to ask the questions that were burning inside him, but Alfredo signalled him with a finger on his mouth to shut up. Too bad that the stuck-up chef of the cooking workshop Roni dragged him to isn't here, Dori thinks as he eats. He could learn something from El Loco about using natural products, and about modesty. Cucumber salad with llama yogurt, leek soup, fish in spicy sauce, duck in honey, fruit ice cream – all served on small plates, with no attempts to jazz up the dish.

So how did you know that I'm the son of . . . my father? he asks, and sips his tea.

Ah, I believe that it's enough to look at a person once, El Loco replies and lights cigars for Alfredo and himself. If it's a good look, if it's focused, you know everything you need to know right away. You, for example, prefer your artichoke with mayonnaise, not sea salt. You prefer basketball to football. You like strong, independent women. And you haven't had a really good fuck in a long time. Am I right or am I right?

Before Dori has a chance to reply (he calculates quickly that El Loco has scored three bullseyes and one hit), a bell plays the first three notes of the Doors' 'Riders on the Storm', the little iguana raises its head and El Loco apologises to them. Potential guests are at the gate and he has to go and see whether they're right for the farm or not.

He comes back a minute later. The gate remains closed.

Your father is a very special person, he tells Dori. He stood here outside the gate with that backrest of his . . . What's it called?

Dr Gav?

Yes, that's it. He stood outside and I could see right away that he was a member of the club.

The club? What club? Dori doesn't understand. The only clubs his father belongs to are the bank and credit card clubs of preferred customers.

Ah – El Loco pats his red bandana – I forgot. He told me that his children have no idea.

*

Under his mosquito net, that night, like an archaeologist of the memory, Dori wants to dig and find at least one bit of evidence that will support the story El Loco told him after their meal. There was the fact that his father sequestered himself on Yom Kippur, and there was that business with the watch, but it couldn't be, it just couldn't be that, apart from those two things, there was nothing. His friend Udi's father was wounded in the Golan Heights and he used to wake up screaming every night because of his nightmares. His own father, on the other hand, slept so soundly and deeply that even the Friday morning leaf blowers didn't wake him up. Okay, so it's not the nights. But there has to be something. A sign. How could he hide something like that from everyone for so many years?

Dori mulls over bits of family history for hours. Memories and more memories drift out of his mind, through the holes in the netting, into the night, and he waits for one of them to grow large enough to be caught.

It isn't until the next night, at 5 a.m., to be exact, when he hears the mooing of an early-rising cow, that it finally comes.

*

They stopped at the Yotvata cafeteria for a break. Five families of his mother's colleagues, on the way to the Sinai. Lital, Ashkenazi's daughter, looked at him as she sipped a mocha drink from a small carton. Or so he thought. A few drops fell from the corners of her mouth and down her neck. They were barely visible because her skin was mocha-coloured too. She was a young girl, and he was just a kid, but there were already a few hairs on his balls and he thought that this time, it would happen. For several years now there'd been a kind of sweet awkwardness between them at their families' picnics. His father, of course, made fun of him; he turned everything into a joke. At least try, he'd always tell him on the way home. Nothing ever came of just staring, Dori. At least try! And his mother hurried to defend him. We all do things at our own pace, Menny. And some girls actually like shy boys.

This time it'll happen, he thought. He still didn't know exactly what would happen, but he was sure that in the Sinai, he'd have the courage. The Sinai was far away. In the Sinai, they slept in tents. In the Sinai they'd lie around on the beach all day. Go snorkelling with masks. His parents had never agreed to go to the Sinai before. But Israel would soon be returning the Sinai to Egypt, so this was their last chance.

On the way from Yotvata to Eilat, they played their family pass-the-time game in the car: Twenty Questions. Tse'ela knew many more famous people than he did, and she'd always guess the name of the chosen person long before he did. So when it was his mother's turn to choose, she'd try to pick someone Dori knew, let's say a basketball player. But it was so obvious that it didn't make him feel any better.

His father acted as usual. There was no sign of what would come later. When Tse'ela announced that she needed to pee, ten minutes after they left Yotvata — she always needed to pee — he immediately pulled over to the side of the road. But Dad, Dori protested, we'll lose everybody else. Tse'ela can hold it in for a few more minutes. And his father said, don't worry, son. Then smiled and added, Lital will wait for us.

When Tse'ela came back, she asked them to put on a Michael Jackson CD, and so, to the sound of the frightening laughter at the end of 'Thriller', they entered Eilat.

You know, it would've been really cool to sleep in a five-star hotel, Tse'ela grumbled.

You can get out, Dori teased her. We'll manage without you, brat. She kicked him with her fancy shoe — who goes to the Sinai in fancy shoes? — and his father intervened, as usual, a second before he could kick her back. We're going to a million-star hotel, he said. The tent I bought has a transparent ceiling. You'll have all the stars you want.

They were now in Eilat, had already passed the cranes in the port – and he was still talking about the tent he bought. Unbelievable.

The other families were waiting for them in Taba, near a snack van. A southern wind played with Lital Ashkenazi's honey-coloured hair. She'd changed from her trousers into a breathtaking beach outfit – when did she have time to do that? – and was leaning on her parents' Subaru, looking at him.

And then it happened.

Instead of signalling everyone to keep driving, his father stopped the car with an unnecessary squeal of the brakes. Unbuckled his safety belt. And ran. He didn't walk; he got out of the car and actually started to run. After a few dozen metres, he stopped next to another snack van, circled it and disappeared behind it. They wanted to run after him with their mother, but she wouldn't let them. Stay in the car! she said in a chilling voice she'd never used before.

A few minutes later, Lital Ashkenazi came over to his window and asked, what happened to your father?

Nothing, Tse'ela answered for him. He went to pee. Don't worry. He'll be back in a minute.

Not long after, his father returned. His eyes were weird. Expressionless. His mother held his hand the way you hold a little boy's hand.

She sat him down in the passenger seat and went to talk to the other families. You keep going, she told them. Menny doesn't feel well. We'll catch up with you later.

Bye, see you soon, Lital Ashkenazi said. And before getting into her parents' car, she gave him one last look that held the spark of a promise.

Then there was a waiting period. They sat in the car for a long while, silent, waiting for something. Tse'ela asked if she could play her music and their mother said it wasn't the right time. His father was taking long, heavy breaths, as if he were trying to subdue some kind of anger. Even though he didn't look angry at all. If anything, he looked disappointed. His hand rested on their mother's lap and his throat glistened with sweat, despite the completely dry air. It's okay, Menny, she said, took her glasses off and put them in her lap, whatever you decide is fine with me. Drive, he said. And she asked, you're sure? He nodded in a way that seemed too slow to Dori. She put her glasses back on and started the car. Then he said, wait, wait a minute, and was silent. And then: It's been ten years; I never imagined that . . . My heart is going to explode. He unbuttoned his shirt, took her hand and placed it on his chest.

Dori didn't understand. What happened? He looked at Tse'ela. She was the older one. She should know. But Tse'ela's eyes reflected only fear.

I don't think I can, Nurik, his father finally said. Let's go back.

At least try! Dori wanted to shout. At least try! But he had the feeling that an invisible divider separated the front and back seats, a divider that precluded any possibility of words passing from the children's world to the world of the grown-ups.

They turned around. And rented a hotel room in Eilat. With a jacuzzi.

Tse'ela was ecstatic. Dori wandered around the hotel and saw all kinds of girls, but none of them had the promising look in their eyes that Lital Ashkenazi had, and he was angry and very disappointed; he couldn't even masturbate undisturbed because of that infuriating sister of his who went in and out of the room without warning. And he had three new, unsqueezable spots on his forehead. And twice a day, his father played basketball on the hotel court, bursting with energy – racing forward to attack and falling back quickly to defend – and in the evenings he danced with his mother in the club, hands up baby, hands up, till morning, and didn't look the least bit like someone with heart problems, which was the explanation their mother had given them for the sudden cancellation of their trip to the Sinai. When they went to the underwater observatory on their last day, Dori took advantage of a moment when his father and Tse'ela went up to the snack bar for Cokes, leaving him and his mother behind at the big glass wall, to ask her in the voice he used for their intimate conversations, Mum, what happened to Dad? What's the real reason we didn't go to the Sinai? She said nothing for a long minute, and just when he thought she'd never answer, she said, it's amazing, absolutely amazing. There's another world under the water that's just as rich as our world, and we don't know a thing about it. Look! She pointed to a pair of long, narrow flute-fish that were approaching them. They followed the flutefish with their eyes until they disappeared behind some yellow coral, and then his mother stroked his head and said, in a tone that left no room for argument, let's go up to the snack bar too.

*

Incredible. Dori didn't say the word aloud, but his sense of how incredible it was stretched his forehead and raised his lashes. It was incredible how memory, just like the Intelligence Corps before the Yom Kippur War, rejected details that don't fit in with a preconceived idea. He remembered Lital Ashkenazi very well; she'd starred in his fantasies for years. But what happened on the way to the Sinai . . .

And now *another* moment – where had *this* been hiding? – in the '80s. He is about ten or eleven. All the kids have an Atari computer game, so he asks his parents to buy him one too. After long negotiations, plus his success finding the afikomen at the Passover Seder, they do. In the sitting room he plays Pong, Pac-Man and Battle Zone. His father plays with the Atari too. For hours on end. But only Tank Battle. Every night, when his mother calls him to come to bed, he says: in a minute. But doesn't go. In the morning, he's bleary-eyed, stubble-cheeked and jumpy. And then, a day before all Dori's classmates are supposed to come over to play, the Atari disappears. His mother claims that she took it back to the shop because it kept him, Dori, from concentrating on his homework. But whenever she lies, a flush spreads over her neck.

El Loco

Your father came out of his hut and starting running around the farm, yelling: MiGs! MiGs! So I had to calm him down. There was no choice. The horses would have run off. I tried to get close to him, and he pointed to the sky and said something in your language. His hands shook and his whole body was sweating. He was covered in sweat. I came even closer to him. I was going to hug him. A hug sometimes helps. But your father's a strong man. He grabbed me by the arm, pulled me behind a bush and threw me on to the ground. MiGs! he screamed, and gestured for me to put my hands on the back of my neck. So I put my hands on the back of my neck. That, you should know, is the first rule of the club: you don't argue with your buddy's imaginings. Because no one can guarantee that what the system calls 'reality' is more real. So we lay under the bush for twenty minutes. Maybe half an hour. Every time I tried to raise my head, your father smacked me hard, like this, on the back of the neck and pushed my nose back into the ground. At eleven at night, the farm generator turned off. It always stops working at exactly that time. Then your father picked himself up, and after checking that there were no more MiGs on the horizon, he signalled for me to follow him quickly. I asked him, where are we going? And he screamed at me that there are wounded men and we have to evacuate them. Okay, man, I said, I'm with you. You should know that that's another rule: you don't leave a buddy in the middle of a flashback. We started running through the farm, in the dark, looking for his wounded buddies. He ran in a zigzag so that the enemy's bullets wouldn't hit him, and I ran behind him. Also in a zigzag. And he cursed the whole time. Fell, got up, and cursed. Fuck. Shit. And curses in Hebrew, which I don't understand. And between one curse and the next, he yelled the names of soldiers. I remember them well because he kept repeating those names. Rafi! Yedidiya! Elida! Elida! Yedidiya! Rafi! He wanted us to shoot flares so we could see the field better and find them. I told him I had no flares. We'd run out. Then he suddenly stopped, straightened up and ordered me: okay, soldier, get me General Gorodish. All of a sudden, he sounded like a commander. Calm. Authoritative. Someone you want to obey. My phone happened to be in my pocket, so I took it out and pretended to be calling, then pretended I was waiting for someone to answer, then listening to someone telling me that more troops were on the way. He screamed at me that I was a liar. Liar! Liar! Liar! He repeated that accusation maybe twenty times. At first in a rage, then as if he was stating a fact. Then as if he was pleading: please be a liar.

The twenty-first time, he broke down, fell into my arms like a baby and began to cry. Real tears. From his eyes to his cheeks, to my shirt, to my undershirt. And between sobs and gasps, he kept saying the same thing over and over again: it's my fault it's my fault it's my fault it's my fault.

So I brought him home with me and took care of him. What do I mean, took care of him? Listen, kid, your father is very lucky that all that happened on my farm. If it had happened in Jerusalem or New York or Willford, Tennessee, they would've put him away. Just like that, without thinking. Just like they did to me. And then they would've stuffed him full of those yellow pills, and you wouldn't recognise your father any more, believe me. That's another rule of our club: a member doesn't give his buddy pills because pills are the system's way of silencing our cry. How did I take care of him? I have my methods. Mainly healthy food. Special things I grow here, on the farm. For my own problems. When did it first start with me? Five years after Nam. In my parents' town. When I came back, they didn't want to hear what happened there. No one wanted to hear. Not them, not my friends, not women. So, hell yes, they were surprised when one day I walked stark naked into the public library and asked for a book by Kerouac. The librarian called the police, and that same night, they put me away in a hospital. I was there for a year, with all the cuckoos, till I ran away from the nest. I travelled and travelled, and I died and was resurrected and came here. To the flowing water and the quiet and the natural substances that helped me. It's none of your business what substances. But they helped your father too. It's a fact that three days later, he got out of bed and started talking. He talked and I listened. No, we didn't sit here, in the restaurant. We sat in his place. Everything came back to him all at once. In chronological order. It's like that with a lot of people. He told me what happened in '73, hour by hour. From the minute they told him he'd been called up till the final battle and what happened to him there. We sat together like that for a week. He sat on his Dr Gav and talked. Every once in a while, his throat went dry and I brought him some tea so he'd have something to wet it with. I didn't do anything for a whole week except make him tea and listen to him. Anyone who buzzed at the gate, I sent back to the river. When it got to be too much for me — every one of your father's stories reignited my own pain — I'd say to him, Mister Menny, I'm going now to chill out a little with my iguana, and in the meantime, you write. He filled up two notebooks. Maybe more. I have no idea where they are. He wrote with a fountain pen he brought with him from Israel. Yes, exactly. Brown with a black nib. I told you, I have no idea where the notebooks are. He most probably took them with him. You want some iced tea? You don't look so good, Mister Dori, you look pale. And your hands are shaking like crazy. Is that a family thing with you? I hope you're not about to run outside and start screaming MiGs, MiGs, eh? I'm kidding, man. I know it's not funny. I know it's a big fucking shock for you. I have no idea why he didn't tell any of you what happened in the war. You'll have to ask him that. I think you should go to sleep now. We talked enough for one day. Everyone has a limited number of words that he gets from the gods, and words shouldn't be wasted, or else when you really need them, they won't be there for you. Your hut is ready. Number three. The same one your father slept in. I hope that's okay with you.

Dori

Tell me, did my father mention my mother, he asks. Did he tell you anything about her?

It's their fourth day on El Loco's farm, and the owner seems to want them to leave. But he won't tell them where Dori's father has gone. In general, Dori's dialogue with him is slightly reminiscent of his phone conversations with Netta: sometimes El Loco just doesn't answer. Sometimes his responses are unnecessarily expansive and he digresses to marginal subjects. Then he suddenly remembers that the gods have granted each of us a limited number of words, and he stops speaking in the middle of a sentence.

At first, he doesn't answer Dori's question about his mother either, just strokes Iguanita, who's perched on his shoulder. Then, after a long silence – Dori has already imagined himself choking El Loco with that stupid bandana of his – he suddenly says, yeah, sure. Your father said that your mother was his guardian angel. That she reassembled the pieces of his puzzle after the war. That thanks to her, he kept things together all those years. And only after she died . . .

Iguanita crawls slowly off El Loco's shoulder and down his arm, coming to rest in his lap.

Sometimes I wonder, he says, whether everything would have been different if I'd had someone like that in Willford. Shirley didn't want to see me when I came back. She said I changed. Of course I changed, *putana*. There was a war.

Putana, Alfredo says, empathetically.

Since they've been on the farm, Alfredo hasn't been speaking much. The young daughter of wealthy parents in Lima has run away from their villa in Miraflores after a fight with her mother, and he's sent out his people to find her. At night, he paces around restlessly outside his hut, number two. With no trailer. But he doesn't give up.

We will not leave this place until that character tells us where your father went, Mister Dori, he says. I know people like him. He is checking us out. Until he trusts us, he will not say a word.

Do you know that he summoned her to come into his dreams? El Loco says after a long time during which the birds chirp to each other in a rhythm Dori is already beginning to recognise.

So we heard, Dori nods. Even though he doesn't know exactly what 'summon into dreams' means.

That's the reason why . . . it all came bursting out. The stuff he took . . . if you don't take it the right way, the gods can get angry and turn their power against you.

Gods? Power? What kind of bullshit is this? Dori thinks. He doesn't understand.

But it's okay. After I took care of him for a week and he pulled it together, I taught him how to respect the gods, and then she came into his dreams again.

You're telling me that after he lost it because of . . . that drug, you helped him take it again? Dori raises his voice.

The iguana leans forward, as if preparing to leap on him, and gives him a hard, threatening look.

Alfredo places a restraining hand on Dori's shoulder and asks El Loco: and what did she tell him in the dream? Where did she send him?

To the Island of the Sun in Lake Titicaca, El Loco says. To the place where everything began.

Ah . . . *naturalmente*, Alfred nods in satisfaction, like a detective who has just solved a mystery. They exchange another few words in Spanish, which only infuriates Dori more and makes him feel that they are plotting something behind his back. Then Alfredo takes him outside.

Calm down, he says. Then go into the restaurant and thank him. The information he just gave you can get him into trouble. That is why he waited a few days to tell us. You do not understand: the drug that your father took is illegal. Our shamans used it to get answers from the gods about matters that troubled them. But the government wants to suck up to the North Americans now. So it calls that holy substance 'a dangerous drug', and hunts down the people who distribute it.

If that substance is so dangerous, how come Edgar from Otavalo talked about it freely? A suspicion nags at Dori, and he asks: so what do you suggest we do now? Go all the way to Titicaca just because he told us to? And what if El Loco is lying? Or if he himself is high?

First of all, it is not such a long way. The border with Peru is not far from here. A two-hour, maybe four-hour drive to the town called Tumbes. That is all. From there, two days, maybe four, and we're on the Bolivian side of the lake. Secondly—

Listen, Alfredo, Dori interrupts him. His sudden longing to see Netta is a sharp pain in his stomach. He usually feels it in his chest or his neck, but this stab of longing comes straight from the depths of his stomach: at this rate, he'll miss Netta's birthday party at nursery. They'll lift him up in his chair and Dori won't be there. He'll blow out the candles and Dori won't be there. The other children will be mean to him and Dori won't be there.

This whole business, he tells Alfredo — gods, holy substance — it seems so far-fetched to me. It just doesn't sound like my father. And a trip to Titicaca, it's another expense ... more time ... I want ... I have to talk to my sister before I make a decision.

No hay problema, Alfredo says, unfazed. And hands him the phone.

*

So, did you see it? his sister asks him before he has a chance to speak.

See what?

The email. I thought that was why you were calling.

No, there's no Internet here. I'm in the middle of an area where—

Dad sent me an email.

What?

Yes, he said that he's sorry he didn't write to me sooner. But there were things he had to work out by himself.

That's what he wrote, in those words?

Wait, it gets even weirder. Then he said that he was at Lake Titicaca and found all the answers there, and now he's setting up something that we'll all be proud of, but he can't talk about it.

What?

That's what he said.

And what else?

That's it.

What do you mean, that's it?

At the end, he said he didn't know when he'd be in touch again and we shouldn't worry about him.

That sounds worrying.

Yes. Would you ever have believed this . . . ? It's just so not like him.

He doesn't say anything, momentarily picturing his sister at the other end of the phone. She's probably wearing her new tracksuit now, the purple one she bought after her divorce, when she was determined to go running, but it very quickly became just another outfit she wore at home. She's probably holding the phone in one hand, a cigarette in the other, and one of the children in her third hand, the one that only parents have.

He hesitates about telling her what he's heard these last few days; after all, her home has fallen apart around her this last year, and Menny is the only stable man left in her life. But, he thinks, this is what has always driven him mad about their father's relationship with her: protect, protect, protect and minimise.

Are you there? she asks. I said that that email just doesn't sound like the father we know.

Yes, he says, but how well do people really know their parents, Ts'el?

*

After his mother died, all sorts of people he didn't know came to offer their condolences during the not-quite-seven days of mourning. They brushed the stubble on his father's cheeks with their lips, told him they hoped 'this would be the last sorrow you ever know' or 'the Almighty will comfort you', and told stories about her. Some of them, he'd already heard. Like the one about how, during the siege of Jerusalem in the War of Independence, his mother was so hungry that she ate orange peel. Or the one about the time, on a youth movement hike, she fell from a rope slide over the Kaziv stream and broke a rib.

But some of the stories surprised him. They didn't shock him, but they definitely surprised him. Like when they said that she sang at youth movement ceremonies. His mother? With that cracked voice of hers? She sang? Or that towards the end of her army service, she lost vision in her right eye and the doctors couldn't explain why; nor could they explain why it returned later. And there was that distant aunt, or close cousin, who let something slip about a miscarriage, between Tse'ela and him, and when he asked Tse'ela whether she knew anything about it, she said no in a hesitant voice that suggested perhaps she did . . .

*

The road to the border has as many holes as a vegetable grater, the trailer lurches along, rocking and rattling, but Dori still has to believe in something, to cling to solid facts, so he continues to read the chapter about Lake Titicaca in his guidebook. It turns out that it is the highest lake in the world, and according to Incan tradition it really is where 'everything began'. The ruins of the temple on Isla del Sol, which is in the middle of the lake, symbolise the place where, according to the Incan faith, the children of the sun god descended to earth, the Adam and Eve of the Incan dynasty, Manco Cápac and Mama Ocllo.

In 1968 – Dori continues to read as he strokes the growing stubble on his cheeks – the diver Jacques Cousteau conducted a search of the lake for eight weeks trying to locate the Incan gold treasure which, according to legend, had been buried in the water because the Incas feared it would be taken by the Spanish conquerors. The treasure wasn't found. Every once in a while, another team of searchers tries its luck. To this day, without success.

*

He asks Alfredo to stop at the first Internet café they pass. He has to see his father's email with his own eyes. He pays, receives a card, opens findfather@gmail.com, types in his password, netaaaaa — and his inbox opens in front of him. His sister has forwarded an email from Noya Green with the subject: somebody saw your father.

Hi Dori — Noya writes — *how are you?*

You won't believe this. We're here in Banios, an absolutely gorgeous little town. And last night we're sitting at the bar with some other Israelis. So we're talking, and I tell one of the girls about you (truth is that we were complaining that there were no good-looking guys in South America, and I said that when you finally find one, he's married. But never mind. Let's pretend I didn't just write that) — anyway, she saw your dad! I mean, I told her you're looking for him and I showed her the picture we took, and she said he was with them some time in April, in the hostel on the Island of the Sun in Bolivia in Lake Titicaca, and he almost never came out of his room. They were sure he was German and the joke was going around that maybe he's a Nazi hiding there from the Mossad, but one day she saw him typing on the hostel computer and saw that the letters were going from right to left. So she went up to him and said shalom. But he didn't answer her. Weird, isn't it? Oh — and on the last day there, she saw him walking around the ancient temple on the island, talking to himself and writing things down in a small, grey notebook.

And that's it. That's all she knows. I hope it helps you find him (maybe you already have?) and I also hope (secretly, in parentheses) that maybe we'll meet again down the road.

Yours,
Noya

Look, a voice erupts inside Dori — its power is proof of how long it's been suppressed — now there are two sources indicating that his father is alive and well, and alive and well is more than enough, right? He wants to play hide-and-seek? Let him play alone. Waiting for me at home are a sad little boy and a woman who doesn't look me in the eye, so why do I have to chase after him, running around like some kind of Crocodile Dori from one shit-hole to another, with all this lower back pain he bequeathed me. Let him go and look for his friends. Oops, a problem, he never had any friends, just clients. So let him go and look for himself and leave me alone. Leave me alone to leave him alone. Lake Titicaca? What is this madness? I'm giving up. I'm going home. I can already see the picture Netta will draw for me which Roni will tape to the door, and the hot water flowing in the shower.

He reads Noya's email again and lingers on the words: 'She went up to him and said shalom. But he didn't answer her. Weird, isn't it?'

No, Noya, he answers silently. Not weird at all. When he was a child and he asked his father things — let's say, on the way to school — something like why the buses in Israel aren't double-deckers like in England, he would wait in vain for an answer. A minute, two minutes. Like a dog. What kind of behaviour is that, not to answer your child? Dad is very preoccupied now because of the business he's setting up, his mother would try to translate his father's silence for him. But even in the years that followed, he found it unforgivable. So what? Wasn't he preoccupied when he was preparing a lesson? But there was no way that Netta would ever ask him something and not get an answer on the spot. Besides, how come his father always answered Tse'ela no matter what he was doing at that moment?

Listen carefully. You're closing the computer now, getting up on your feet and asking Alfredo to drive you to the airport. Enough, Dori, you've done all you can, he tells himself out loud, and remains sitting in front of the open computer.

A few minutes later, he gets up. And walks to the cabin of the trailer without saying a word to Alfredo.

Beneath the anger – he can't help it – he's still very worried. What does that mean, 'your Dad talks to himself'?

And beneath the worry is an even deeper issue, as basic as an instinct: that damned habit that had become ingrained in him, absorbed from his father during the countless times they'd done trigonometry homework together.

You don't take on a job and not finish it.

*

I'm in Tumbes now, he tells Roni after two days of back-breaking travelling. It's a border town. In Peru, yes. We're continuing on from here for a few more hours. When the road opens. Do you know what Tumbes means in Spanish? Graves. My room here is like a grave too. The same size. So I came up to the roof of the hostel. There's a kind of sitting area here, two old sofas with torn upholstery. Is Netta home? At a friend's? That's great. The second time this week? Wow. Maybe I should stay in South America. I see that my trip is doing you both good.

This is when you're supposed to say no, what are you talking about, come home, we miss you.

Roni?

Roni?

With this delay, I can't tell whether you're not saying anything or it just takes time for your words to reach me.

Where were we? Never mind. How's work? It was stressful before too, wasn't it? Yes. Of course. Listen, I'll see my father, and if he isn't a danger to himself, I'll give him a hug, let him talk to Tse'ela on the phone – and then I'll come home. I have no intention of staying here for even one day after I see him, Roni. I'll get on the first plane to Israel. And then you can work late every night, just the way you like it. I'm not being sarcastic. You can't see my face, so you can't see that I'm not being sarcastic. I'm serious. And I'm so anxious to get back to you both. And I'm so worried about my father. Where are we going from here? Lake Titicaca. Titicaca. It's on the border between Peru and Bolivia. There's an island there where maybe . . . Yes, of course. No, go. Why should you be late picking him up because of me? Will you tell him I miss him?

*

Do you love me at all? he wanted to ask. And didn't.

Because it doesn't sound like you do, he wanted to say. And didn't.

He stayed on the roof. Put Alfredo's phone in his pocket. Supported his lower back with his hand and went to the railing to look at the city, to draw beauty from it.

But he saw only ugliness. Decrepit houses, scrawny horses, futureless beggars, sewage overflowing and running along the pavement, an unlovely, perhaps unused church, a drunk shouting at the little kids hassling him, big kids hassling the little kids who are hassling the drunk, a policeman going over to the big kids who are hassling the little kids who are hassling the drunk.

He went back to the sofa.

He felt empty. Not empty, tired. Not tired. Despondent. Not despondent. Back pain. Just fucking back pain. Not just fucking back pain. Despondent. The desire to put down his walking stick. Not the desire to put down his walking stick. The desire to break it. He tried to define the feeling precisely – maybe precision would save him. But before he could be precise, the feeling passed. And became tense expectation.

He heard footsteps on the stairs leading to the roof. And

then, a woman. He still hadn't seen her, but he already knew it was a woman.

Nice-looking. He saw now. Not his type at all, but nice-looking.

She didn't look like the other female tourists he'd seen in the markets and on the road. She wasn't as young as the young ones, nor as old as the older ones. Somewhere in the middle. Like him. At the age when you don't go to South America unless you have a special reason.

She walked past him without saying a word, leaned on the railing and looked down at the city. He saw her in profile.

She was wearing wide, loose trousers. With a lot of pockets. And a tight-fitting top. Her trousers looked like the ones all the female tourists wore. But the top was something else.

He couldn't decide whether she was Israeli or not.

On the one hand, she had a healthy tan. And solid walking shoes. And the backpack she put on the floor near her feet had the kind of plastic rain cover Israelis really like. On the other hand, there was her cheery, red-blue-and-yellow checked cap with a small visor, which didn't manage to keep her brown hair from spilling out with elegant impishness. French impishness. Perhaps Spanish?

And as he tried to decide—

She turned and smiled at him in Hebrew. How do you do, I'm Inbar. How do you do, he said and extended his hand: Dori (and immediately rebuked himself: why a handshake? What is this, a business meeting?).

What an ugly city, hey? She turned away from him and pointed beyond the railing.

Totally, he agreed. And said nothing else, afraid. What to say? What the hell do tourists say to each other? Or people?

So what . . . ah . . . Inbar . . . he finally asked, where . . . where did you come here from?

Inbar. One Month Earlier

EITAN INSISTED ON DRIVING HER, BECAUSE 'IN MY family, there's no such thing as going to the airport alone', and she protested weakly before finally agreeing.

This is for you, he said when he pulled up at the airport drop-off and took a present out of the glove compartment.

What's this? she ran her fingers over the long object. You've got me a vibrator?!

Yeah, right, he laughed with those beautiful dimples of his.

That's good, she said, and put a hand on his knee. I'm not exchanging the original so fast. And with her other hand, she tore off the paper to reveal an elegant box that contained two pens.

They're for the journal you want to write, he said, explaining, as usual, what required no explanation.

This is so nice, she said (and thought: this is so nice). They'll definitely make me want to write (and thought: these pens are too expensive; they'll probably turn me off writing).

He leaned over and kissed her. He was definitely the best kisser she'd ever had, but her soul had already taken off for somewhere else. Or at least was warming its engines in preparation for take-off. So she moved away from him after two kisses and said: have a good time while I'm gone. Mess up the house, just the way you like it. Leave wet towels everywhere.

You have a good time, he said.

I'll try, she said. You know, my mother and I together, we're not exactly a winning combination.

Who knows, he said, maybe you'll be pleasantly surprised.

He helped her put her bag on a trolley, said goodbye with a crushing hug, and then she walked through the automatic doors, not looking back even once. First, she went through the security and passport checks – once again, the rapid pounding of her heart when the policewoman looked at her passport. It had been like that for five years now, ever since she'd scratched Professor Hoffman's Honda with a nail file, and he'd shouted that he knew it was her and he was going to complain to the police, and she'd screamed back that he'd better not, but didn't know whether he had or hadn't in the end, she hoped not, she really hoped not; no, he probably hadn't. Then she went to duty-free to look for a cheap pen, one she wouldn't be afraid of losing, and found one in the chemist's, of all places, next to the colourful packs of condoms. After buying herself some chocolate milk that was two-thirds water and one-third milk, she sat down at a table where a tray strewn with the crumbs of an almond croissant still rested, opened her journal and took the cheap pen out of her bag, intending to write something short about the stamps on a passport or a passport that had no more room left for stamps, or about the croissant crumbs of the person who'd sat at the table before her, crumbs that were like an arcane mathematical formula left on the blackboard from a previous lesson in a classroom she'd just entered. But before she could put pen to paper, her phone buzzed, and without even looking at the message she knew it was from Eitan and it would say, *I miss you already*, and wondered when she'd start missing him, if at all, and what was wrong with her. She texted back, *me too*, and put down her phone, intending to return to her journal, but the inspiration had gone and left her far behind.

She picked up her phone again and texted her mother: *boarding plane soon.* She tried to imagine what her Bruno looked like. Probably like all the others, a version of Leonard Cohen, but with glasses. Or maybe not, maybe this time her mother would surprise her with a broad-shouldered, chubby geek you could actually depend on – who knows, maybe this time she'd arrive on time to pick her up from the airport and not make her wait there, remembering all the other, hurtful times she'd waited for her like a waif, outside nursery, outside school, outside ballet class, outside the army basic training camp.

Look, if you want to get away for a few days, come here, her mother had said. You'll adore Berlin. We'll walk around, and we can visit anywhere in Europe from here. If you want.

But what will Grandma Lily say?

She doesn't have to know.

And Bruno . . . it won't bother him?

There's a small studio with a separate entrance here, where his son used to live – you could stay there. Anyway, he's always travelling or out at meetings.

You're sure you're both okay with it? she asked (and really meant to ask: are you sure it's a good idea for you and me to be together for more than two hours?).

Yes, her mother said. And the very next day, she checked which airlines offered the cheapest flight.

Flight 525 to Berlin is now boarding at Gate D7, came the loudspeaker announcement. But Inbar stayed where she was. And continued sipping her chocolate drink. She'd already learned that it was better to wait for the last call and gain a few more minutes outside the aeroplane-cage. It wouldn't hurt them to wait for her once, would it?

She looked around. A fountain. Duty-free bags. Rapid steps. People talking. *How joyfully people leave this country*, she began the first sentence of her journal, *and how relieved they look. Two thousand years of longing to kiss the ground here, and turning to face east three times a day at prayer, but the minute they arrive, all they want is to go west.*

A guy with slumped shoulders sitting at the opposite end of the café caught her attention. She saw him in profile, examining some pictures that were spread out on his table. His hair was clipped short, shot through with grey at the temples. His lips were tight, as if he were holding back something that might erupt from inside him. His Adam's apple was very prominent, and the one arm she could see was quite muscular. Occasionally, he ran two fingers over his temple with a gentle, almost feminine movement. She was sitting too far away to see what was in the pictures, but there was something disturbing about the way he was looking at them. Like a Mossad agent studying pictures of an escaped Nazi he's supposed to eliminate, she thought. And before she could stop it, a plot began taking shape in her mind: her mother's Bruno is the Nazi marked to die, but instead of breaking into Bruno's house, the agent mistakenly enters the studio in the middle of the night, and she's lying alone in bed there, wearing a very short nightdress she doesn't actually own, and which she would never have dared to wear.

This is the last call for passengers on flight 525 to Berlin. Please go immediately to gate D7 for boarding – the announcement urged.

She waited another few seconds to see whether her Mossad agent – he must have a deep, beautiful voice, she thought, he looks like a man with a beautiful voice – would also respond to the call. She moved the ends of her hair to her nose and smelled them, a gesture she always made unconsciously when she liked someone. Then she took a final sip. Closed her journal. Put it into her bag. Got up. And left.

Grandma Lily

Her father, wearing a karakul hat, escorted her to the hotel where all the members of the Chalutz youth group had assembled, and left her at the foot of the stairs. I'll stay here until it gets dark, he said. Come outside again, if you can. But Papa, she protested. Only if you can, he hushed her, and if not – that's all right too. We'll meet again in a few months in Eretz Yisrael anyway, won't we?

And for that, I'll never forgive myself, she always says. The pain that story brings her has not dulled with the years. On the contrary, it has only grown sharper. My father stood outside – she says, holding her wine glass without drinking a drop from it – and standing outside there is not like it is here, there it's cold at night, there, the rain is angry even in summer. I'm not sure he even had an umbrella. But he stood there and waited for me. Just for the chance that he might see me again.

But you couldn't know, Grandma! No one knew then that . . . Inbar always tries to convince her.

It doesn't matter, she says, refusing to make it easier for herself. I went into that hotel and met up with all the other Chalutz members. We drank. And danced. And laughed. And I forgot that my father was waiting for me outside. The next day, we got on the train that took us to the port. And I never saw my father again.

She tells that story at every Passover Seder, and Aunt Nira, who isn't really an aunt at all, but Grandpa's unmarried sister, talks about her escape from a British prison. And Uncle Simo tells about the great day on which he was liberated from a Syrian prison camp in the deal that was struck after the Yom Kippur War. Only she, almost despite herself, has to ruin the happy mood of those family stories of 'the exodus from Egypt' with the story about her father who waited in vain outside the hotel in that karakul hat. In his last letter to her before the letters stopped coming altogether, he described how some thugs yanked it off his head in the middle of Warsaw and didn't give it back.

When she finishes the story, the emptiness of the Prophet Elijah's chair seems more present, and someone always begins to sing in an effort to lighten the oppressive atmosphere, and everyone joins in, shouting with the raspy voices of people drunk on grape juice. Only she remains silent, her thoughts wandering to that journey.

Inbar

They should have a separate section on planes for babies, she thought. The first airline to do it will make millions – a separate section with a totally soundproof divider cutting it off from the rest of the plane. The tickets would cost more, a lot more, but there'd also be nappy-changing areas, special films for babies, and of course, special baby food that would shut their mouths for a while.

Coffee or tea? An eager-to-please flight attendant leaned towards her.

Neither, she replied.

Would you like something else? The flight attendant didn't move.

Can you please strangle that baby?

Excuse me? What did you say?

I asked if you have something sweet, maybe.

The portly matron sitting next to her shot her an accusing look. When you have children of your own, you won't talk that way, the look said. I don't know if I'll have children of my own, Inbar thought. One of the reasons I'm going away is to try and figure that out. And I can tell you that all those screams — they're not actually individual screams, but one long shriek — are not tipping the scales towards 'yes'.

She looked through the window at the ocean. From that height, no waves or foam were visible, only a large expanse of blue carpet. With a single ship on its edge, like a shoe forgotten in the sitting room at the end of a day. Who sailed on ships these days? Modern pirates? Illegal fisherman? Here you are: the flight attendant came back and placed a chocolate bar on her small table. They're really only for business class, but we want you to be happy.

This, Inbar thought, is exactly why I was never a good waitress. That relentless need to please. I could never hack it.

Her first job in Tel Aviv was as a waitress. She was fired after a week because she tried to organise the other waitresses to mutiny, demanding a higher percentage of the tips. She was fired from her second waitressing job after only two days because she refused to wear the café's ugly uniform. And then she started writing 'Serially Sacked'. At first, she wrote it for herself, then she sent a few chapters to friends, and then — the assistant editor of a local paper was on a friend's mailing list — it appeared as a weekly column for a year and a half in that lowly local paper, earning her a pittance and making no great impact. Every week, a few amusing letters rife with spelling errors arrived in her inbox (she included her email address at the end of every column), except the week when her column entitled 'Veiled Sexual Harassment at Work' was published. Then she received a torrent of emotional letters from women who offered her their own stories as support, or suggested that she join a support group, or offered to support her over dinner because all men were shits. And there's nothing like a woman's love.

In the end, she had to stop writing 'Serially Sacked' because she found a proper job.

A local radio station manager called and offered her the job of editing a new, call-in advice programme that was about to be launched. But I don't know a thing about radio, she told him in surprise. He laughed on the other end of the line and said, you see, this is exactly why I thought of you. Other people would immediately start blabbing about their wealth of experience in the field. But what I love about you and your columns is your directness. Your incisiveness. And you know how to read people. That's the quality the editor of a programme like this needs to have more than any other. You have to be able to recognise who's right for the programme and who isn't in a few seconds. All the rest is just technical stuff we can teach you.

Who's presenting the show? she asked. Who's the advisor?

A few days later, in a busy café, Dr Adrian Levine sat across from her, stroked his beard in long, slow movements, then took off his watch, placed it on the table and asked her to tell him about her family.

My family? she repeated, trying to buy time. This is not what she imagined the first question in her job interview would be.

Yes, Dr Adrian said. The programme deals with everything related to family life. Everything that happens in the family unit. So I'm interested in knowing a little about the family you come from.

Familology, the word slipped out.

What? Dr Adrian's beard shot up.

We could call the programme Familology, she explained. And Dr Adrian gave a long nod (in time, she'd get to know his nods and learn that the longer the nod, the less he liked the idea).

There was a long silence. Dr Adrian put his watch back on. Then took it off again. I hate it when psychologists don't talk I hate it when psychologists don't talk I hate it when psychologists don't talk how I hate that psychologists don't talk, she thought. Then she thought: let him be the one to break the silence let him be the one to break the silence let him be the one to break the silence. And then she said: I don't really have a family. I mean, I have one. Had one. But it split apart. Scattered.

Dr Adrian asked what she meant, and she lowered her voice because she thought the woman sitting at the next table with a laptop was eavesdropping on their conversation, perhaps hoping to add some of it to the book she was writing at that very moment, and Inbar wasn't too thrilled at the idea of finding words she'd spoken in someone else's book rather than in her own, which didn't yet exist but would one day, when her heart wasn't so homeless and she could make herself sit down and write—

Dr Adrian leaned slightly towards her so he could hear her hesitant voice. He smelled of pipe tobacco, even though he didn't have a pipe, and when she finished giving him a summary of her family history, he thanked her for her frankness and said, Yizhar will be in touch with you. She was sure that that was it, there was no way that Yizhar would be in touch, no way that Dr Adrian would believe that a screwed-up girl like her could edit anything, but the next day Yizhar sent her a contract to sign, a humiliating one, of course, and she succeeded only partially when she tried to improve the terms. A month later she was sitting in a small office adjoining the studio, listening to voices through headphones, male voices, female voices, voices they sometimes distorted later on in the broadcast to conceal the speakers' identities. But she always heard the originals, all of which sounded basically upset and contained other timbres she learned to distinguish between: a hint of suppressed violence or falsehood. An intimation of tears, which were sure to erupt during the conversation with Dr Adrian. Voices that sounded desperately defeated. Or desperately protesting. Or desperately hostile. And of course, there were those that hinted at mental illness (with time, she could differentiate, based only on the tone of voice, between depression, schizophrenia, and anxiety).

'When does the film start?' the portly matron sitting next to her asked the head flight attendant, and her voice, slightly hoarse and containing vestiges of a foreign accent, vaguely Eastern European, sounded familiar to Inbar. That happened to her sometimes: suddenly emerging from the hustle and bustle of the world was a voice she'd already heard on the programme. She closed her eyes and tried to recall what that voice had wanted to tell Dr Adrian. Burns? Was it something about burns? That her daughter burned herself? No. It was air. She had no air. She would wake up at night unable to breathe, and the medical tests she'd had indicated that her lungs were fine. Do you sleep with your husband? Dr Adrian had asked her. She replied in the affirmative. Try moving to a different room in the house, he suggested. Sometimes, at a certain age, people feel a powerful urge to sleep alone again. And they don't do it, because it doesn't seem fitting. But the matron had said, I'm not sure my husband would take it very well. You won't know until you try, Adrian told her.

Now the matron was alone. She was wearing a large, surprisingly daring, purple earring in her left ear, the one Inbar could see. Had she taken Dr Adrian's advice, and had her husband left her as a result? That could definitely be the case. They never did follow-ups on the people he counselled. And sometimes, especially after what had happened the month before – dammit, how nice it had been not to think about that for the last hour – she was surprised that Dr Adrian could fall asleep, with all the responsibility he took upon himself. How come he didn't wake up in the night, unable to breathe?

The film started. She inserted the headphones and found

the channel. Ethan Hawke was reading aloud in a Parisian bookshop. Julie Delpy suddenly walked in. Isn't this? . . . It is . . . *Before Sunset*. She knew that a sequel to *Before Sunrise* had come out, but she deliberately hadn't gone to see it so she wouldn't be disappointed. She'd loved the first one so much. In it, Julie Delpy meets Ethan Hawke on a European train, he persuades her to get off at his station even though she's supposed to continue on to somewhere else, and they spend a long night of frank talk and sweet sexual tension in Vienna.

She once broke up with a guy because he didn't like *Before Sunrise* enough. They watched it together in her apartment, and she saw his eyes wander away from the screen every few minutes, and in the middle, at the most beautiful moment, when they squeeze together in the small listening booth of a record shop and, both very embarrassed, listen to Kath Bloom sing, that guy – Yoav Krau was his name – had the nerve to answer his phone, and right then she knew he didn't have a chance with her. You must have a heart of stone not to be moved by that film! she pounced on him when it ended, with all the intensity of a twenty-year-old, and he said, we're all moved by different things, and had the gall to try and touch her, to stroke her hair – they always wanted to stroke her hair then – but in her mind, she'd already broken up with him.

Ethan Hawke finishes reading. And Julie Delpy – in the films she's called Celine – walks over to him. They had planned to meet at the train station in Vienna six months after that once-in-a-lifetime night. That reunion, we learn now, never happened. But he's written a book about the night they spent together. How many years had passed since their night in Vienna? Inbar calculated. Ten. Ten years in the life of the characters. Ten years in the lives of the actors. Ten years in her life. And she still hadn't written the book she wanted to write. Time was dribbling through her fingers, the thought

wafted across her mind, but she made a supreme effort to postpone the self-flagellation till later. And abandon herself to Paris
and the film now.

Lily

They left in the middle of the night. The group leaders woke
them up. An unfamiliar hand shook her shoulder. She was in
the middle of a dream in which she was having sex with Natan
on a raft that was too small. Their legs kept falling over the
edges into the water. The water was green. Natan laughed. A
cold, fluorescent light illuminated the hotel room and froze his
laughter. She didn't jump out of bed immediately, as she had
thought she would. She pretended to be asleep, stole a few more
seconds to remain in her inner world. Finally, she got up reluctantly and washed her face in the dirty sink. Their group leader
opened the door a crack and urged them to hurry. She dressed
in the clothes she'd laid out in advance on the chair near the
bed. Tourist's clothes, as they'd been asked to wear. Her suitcase
was also ready. A small one containing some underwear, wool
gloves, a wide-brimmed yellow hat to protect her from the sun
in her new country. Freud's *Interpretation of Dreams*. Mapu's
Love of Zion. A photo of her and her father, well wrapped to
safeguard it from water and dampness. The only letter that had
arrived from Natan. A notebook, two pencils, a rubber, and a
sharpener.

When she put her nightgown into the suitcase, the zip didn't
close. She took out the thick wool gloves, shoved them into her
jacket pockets and tried the zip again. This time she was able

to close it. She went outside, relieved to see that she wasn't the last one. There were others still not there yet, mainly girls. Henia, Regina, Ruth. Combing their hair. Putting on make-up. Unwilling to forgo seductiveness, even at a moment like this. 'You look like you're wearing makeup even when you're not. That's because of the fascinating contrast between your black hair and porcelain complexion,' Natan once told her as his fingers, like a paintbrush, glided from her hair to her neck, from her neck to her shoulder. She's making this journey to meet him. She no longer has to seduce anyone. He'll be waiting for her on the beach and he'll take her into his arms, now probably tanned by a year's worth of sun.

A truck was waiting in front of the hotel. Trucks like this, she thought, usually transport furniture, not people. If you were a piece of furniture — what would you be? she imagined Natan asking her as she waited in the short queue that had formed. A reading lamp, she replied.

First the suitcase, the group leader said, standing near the luggage compartment. Now put your foot here. She turned around for a last look — her father might still be waiting for her under a streetlamp — then she placed her foot on the group leader's hands, cupped together to form a step, and pressed down. The momentum propelled her into the back of the truck. Some boys from the group were already inside. Rejoicing. Singing. It was too soon for her to be singing, but slowly, their joy infected her. The other girls got into the truck and joined in. She doesn't remember what they sang. She remembers the smell of canvas and one of the boys who took advantage of a sharp turn to press up too close to her. He smelled of canvas too. The grey canvas enclosed them, hid them, and also hid things from them. They couldn't see the route they were taking. But how many routes could there be? There was only one road from the hotel to the station, and it passed by her house. She was sorely tempted to lift the canvas and take a last look at the home she was leaving, and felt a bit ashamed for the small thoughts she was thinking at such a great moment.

The station was deserted. No conductors, no gypsies, no people running late, bumping into each other and losing their last chance to catch their trains. When her mother was alive, they would travel from here to visit her sister, Aunt Mina. Lily's heart would always beat faster when they entered the large station. So many voices. *Tzeitung! Tzeitung!* Smells, frankfurters with mustard, tastes, iron on her tongue. So many temptations. She always wanted to try this. And this. And this. And this too. But her mother would never stop. We'll miss the train because of you! She'd pull her along angrily, almost tearing her arm out of its socket.

In the end, they'd be early, of course. And they'd sit alone in the cold, empty car. Platform number 3. Yes, that was the platform of the train to Aunt Mina's. The group leader was walking past it now, and past platforms 4, 5 and 6. Then he opened a small door in the gate and led them to a side platform. Small, concealed behind the management office.

Their train stood there. Dark, sleepy. It was supposed to take them from Warsaw to the port of Constanța in Romania, where the ship was waiting for them. But no destination appeared on the front of the first carriages, as it usually did, and there were no small lights at the doors to the cars, as were required. Lily found it hard to believe that this ghost train would actually get them to their destination.

Please stay in carriage number five, the leader told their group a short time after the train woke from its slumber, with surprising speed, and set off, but Lily had already been called to handle an emergency in another carriage.

Our comrade here . . . she hasn't stopped crying since we left, they explained to her, pointing to a girl her own age who was sitting with her face glued to the dark window. Lily sat down next to her, and a circle of curious onlookers gathered around them. They wanted to see if Lily would live up to her reputation as someone who knew how to draw people out. Could we have a little privacy? she asked, and someone teased her: we're all partners in everything here, that's how it is in a kibbutz, right? But when she asked again, this time in her resolute tone, they gave in and drifted away.

What's your name? she asked the girl pressed up against the window.

She didn't answer. She only reached up distractedly to touch her hair, which was pulled back in a bun, as if checking to see that it hadn't come undone.

Where are you from, comrade? Lily tried. And again, silence.

You know – she began speaking about herself – before every one of the group's trips I went on, even the short ones, I always felt a twinge of worry: maybe I should stay? What's wrong with being at home? And even now, when they woke us up at the hotel, I stayed in bed for a little while. If I hadn't been afraid that they'd make fun of me, I probably would have stayed there much longer.

But in the end, you got up, the girl hissed without turning her head, and the words shot back at Lily like a view from the window.

Because I want to live in a place where it's not shameful to be me, Lily said, sounding to herself as pompous and hollow as the propaganda pamphlets sent to them from Eretz Yisrael (no, she thought, this is not the road this conversation should go down!).

But – the girl turned to her, her bun still tightly coiled, her eyes still hard – what will happen to humanity if everyone wants to run away all the time? To move all the time? If we want to maintain the world's balance, maybe what we need to do is stay where we are. Where we grew up. Where we know the shopkeeper. The doctor. The dentist. To stay! Maybe that's true courage!

Someone sitting behind them clapped. For a moment, they thought he was applauding the girl's words, but then it turned out that the clapping belonged to a more cheerful conversation going on two rows behind them.

What world are you talking about? What balance do you want to maintain? Hitler, the German Chancellor is bal— Lily began to say, but stopped herself. Her experience in drawing people out had taught her that concealed beneath every well-phrased ideology there was almost always a personal, emotional motive. That was what she had to unearth if she wanted to help this girl.

The train continued to move forward. Clattering along like a horse-drawn carriage. The girl with the bun turned back to the window. A bald man suddenly burst into their car. His Adam's apple was too prominent. A harmonica holder hung around his neck. We're organising a klezmer orchestra! he announced. Anyone who knows how to play is invited! He put the harmonica in his mouth and played a short étude that fitted right in with the clattering rhythm of the train. After bowing deeply – he almost stabbed his own chest with his Adam's apple – he looked expectantly at Lily.

I . . . don't . . . play, Lily apologised. When she was ten, she tried to play the violin. She loved holding it under her chin, loved to feel the touch of the wood on her skin, but never managed to coax even one clear note out of the instrument.

I know how to play the piano, the girl with the bun said. She stretched one long, beautiful leg forward as if the pedals that lengthened the sound were located under the seat in front of her. The bald man with the Adam's apple laughed: We don't have a piano here, but we have pots, pans, forks. Your choice, Miss. Maybe later, the girl said, we're in the middle of a conversation now, in case you hadn't noticed. Oh, yes, certainly, certainly, I would never interrupt your important conversation. Heaven forbid. If you wish to play, please go to the next carriage and ask for Yitzhak Pimstein, okay?

He spoke to the girl, but he was looking at Lily with blazing eyes, and she lowered her glance to her shoes.

You know him? the girl with the bun asked when the bald man and his Adam's apple continued on to another car. He looks at you as if you've already been introduced.

There are brazen men in the world, Lily said, and thought about her Natan, who'd asked her permission before he kissed her for the first time.

His manners must have fallen out with his hair, the girl said. And they both laughed.

So you play? Lily asked quickly, before the rapport created by their laughter could evaporate.

A little. My mother is the real pianist in the house, the girl said, but since she fell ill, she hasn't had the strength for it.

The picture is starting to become clear, Lily thought. And didn't say anything.

An emaciated girl walked down the aisle — how had they let her get on the train? Lily wondered. She won't survive the hardships of the voyage! — and handed out squares of bitter chocolate to the passengers. Lily and the girl with the bun declined with a thank-you.

I won't see Mama any more, the girl with the bun said when the girl handing out the chocolate was out of earshot, and from the angry tone — not a sorrowful one — that had taken over her voice Lily sensed, guessed, that she was like her. When Lily's mother died of heart failure, sorrow at her death had been pushed aside by an intense feeling of missed opportunity.

I'm just afraid that . . . that was the last time I . . . The girl's voice died in mid-sentence and she crossed her arms over her chest as if she were trying to cover herself up against the chill of her words.

Lily didn't know what to say to her. At the start of their training in the movement, the idea of aliyah, immigration to Eretz Yisrael, was presented to them as self-fulfilment. But the news coming from Germany this last year gave their voyage the urgency of an escape from a snow avalanche growing more powerful as it thundered down a mountain. No one talked about it. Everyone, including Lily, preferred to think of himself as the pioneer who would make future immigrations possible, not as someone leaving their family behind.

And for what? the girl continued, what am I leaving Mama for? Eretz Yisrael? What do we know about it? What does it have to do with us? Before they used all that propaganda on us in the training camp, we had no desire to go to that country. Who's waiting for us there? The British? The Arabs?

Natan, Lily thought. But she knew that if she mentioned his name it would only make the girl envious. Since she had never envied others, she had tended in the past to believe that others didn't envy her. No more. In the past year, her best friends had distanced themselves from her through no fault of her own. And she realised that if she wanted them to be close to her, she had to stop telling them about the special love that she and Natan had for each other. And begin to complain. About him. About physical pain. About nightmares. The important thing was not to be too happy when she was with them.

Pale light rose in the window and shapes began to appear in the darkness. Trees, shacks. An early-rising ploughman. Lone farmers in the cornfields watching with surprise as the train passed them: a train had never steamed across their land at such an hour.

Look, look at how long our train is! the girl cried out in amazement and gestured for Lily to move closer to the window. Lily bent over, to avoid touching the girl. Every touch reminded her of Natan; every accidental touch heightened the yearning of her skin for an intentional touch.

The train had reached a sharp turn, and now it was curved

into a semicircle, so she could see all the way to the end of it: there were many carriages, so many carriages.

What do you think, comrade? Lily asked the girl: that all those carriages are because of Eretz Yisrael? and shifted back to her seat.

Then what are they for? The girl looked at her expectantly, ready to be persuaded.

They are for people being given the chance to start fresh from the beginning! Lily said passionately. To build a new society. A better society. To establish new ways for people to live together. For couples. For mothers . . . and daughters. Every generation makes the same mistakes as the generation that came before it, and our generation says – enough! Let us create something new!

The girl nodded slowly, as if to say: I'm not sure you're right, but let's agree on it for now.

And Lily thought: I'm not sure I'm right either. I'm consumed by questions too. But encouraging others distracts me.

Then, lulled by the rhythmic clatter of the train, they fell asleep on each other's shoulders.

Inbar

For the first few seconds in the arrival hall of the Berlin airport, when all she saw were unfamiliar faces, the ancient affront of her mother's lateness rose in her throat, and a pre-tantrum tingling began to spread over her scalp. But then she noticed that the woman waving at her with barely controlled excitement from the far end of the hall had a figure that reminded her of her mother's, except that this woman's hair was . . . so white. Inbar! The white-haired woman spread her arms, and Inbar abandoned herself to the embrace, which was longer than she'd expected and shorter than she needed. You look wonderful, her mother said, but her eyes, quickly scanning her body, said something different. You too, Inbar said. And wasn't lying. Even with the white hair, her mother was still undeniably attractive. Something about the combination of the aristocratic nose, the high cheekbones and the large eyes. Come on, large eyes said, Bruno is waiting outside with the car. So how come you arrived on time? The spiteful remark was on the tip of Inbar's tongue, but she reminded herself of Eitan's 'maybe you'll be pleasantly surprised' and said nothing.

The German Leonard Cohen, wearing a black polo shirt, pressed her hand and took her suitcase.

How was the flight? he asked in heavily German-accented English as they drove off, looking at her somewhat uneasily through the rearview mirror. What had her mother told him about her? A cool wind blew in through Inbar's window. The Partisans' forests were visible on the horizon. The flight was okay, there was a great film, she said. And waited for her mother to ask what film it was. But all she asked was, are you hungry? Because we can stop at a restaurant if you want.

They passed a murky grey industrial area, the kind that heralds a big city. She looked for swastikas on the walls of the factories. Or the words *Juden raus*. But there was only graffiti in fat, illegible letters and the logos of international companies. Coca-Cola. Toys Я Us.

There's an excellent restaurant at the petrol station here, her mother said. They also have a diet menu.

To be honest – Inbar restrained herself – what I'd like most is a shower.

*

The shower in Bruno's studio was the electric kind that has a very elusive G-spot between the cold and hot water. As soon as you cross that spot, the water gets boiling hot, and if you cross back over it — freezing cold. Inbar played with the handle for a few seconds till she found the desired spot, which disappeared again when she adjusted the shower head and tried to increase the water pressure. Atmor, she remembered. That's what they call those showers in Israel. Her father had installed an Atmor for her in the basement after they decided to exile her there.

The bitter arguments between her and her mother had grown worse during that period. All her friends argued with their mothers then, as part of adolescence. But with Inbar and her mother it was uglier, more confrontational, more unbridled. It could begin over something small, like why did you leave your shoes in the sitting room? and in seconds, they would both lose it completely and stand there, their hoarse voices screaming things at each other that burned into their flesh. What did I ever do to deserve a daughter like you as punishment? You're *my* punishment, Mum, I'm not yours. Nothing good will ever come of you. As if anything good came of *you*. Stop answering me back all the time. So stop getting on my case all the time. You're not pretty enough to be so insolent. And you won't get university tenure in your next life either.

Once, little Yoavi stood between them and started crying and pleading, stop it, why are you so mean to each other, and her mother hurried to hug and soothe him, of course, all the while blaming Inbar for ruining him, her innocent little brother, and told her to go to her room this minute. I don't want to go to my room. I told you to go to your room this minute. You don't tell me what to do. What did I ever do to deserve a daughter like this? Try to remember, maybe you really did do something bad.

Her father would come home in the evening and mediate, running from one to the other like an American peace broker in the Middle East, with compromise proposals and implied threats.

The mediator's strength ran out in the end, and he initiated a separation of forces between the disputing sides. He installed a roll-up cover at the entrance to the staircase leading from the sitting room down to the basement, which had been his study, and the transportation books he removed from the shelves were replaced with her clothes. She loved her 'submarine' from the first minute. She had a separate entrance from the garden, which allowed her to invite over whomever she wanted without having to walk past her mother's disapproving eyes. A week after she moved to the submarine, she parted with her virginity with the help of her private maths tutor, a student who came three seconds after entering her, and was stupid enough to ask if it was good for her. After that, less hasty partners came to the submarine, and so did a lot of girlfriends, who loved sitting there, coughing over their first cigarettes, talking about *Catcher in the Rye* and the hot history teacher Ami Gur-Arieh, and telling her over and over again how cool it was that she had a submarine like this.

She totally agreed with them, and missed only the bath of the 'upper world', where the hot water flowed strong and steady. Only very rarely – when she came home from annual school trips, or broke up with her first serious boyfriend, or there was a regional power cut that neutralised the Atmor – did she receive special dispensation to shower upstairs. But the rest of the time, her mother made it clear to her that she didn't belong there. When Yoavi replaced her in the submarine, after she left for Tel Aviv, he called it a bunker and showered upstairs whenever he felt like it, of course. Without any comments from her mother.

The water in Bruno's Atmor grew colder every minute. She tried to play with the handle, but it didn't help. That's another thing about these Atmors, she remembered. The supply of hot water runs out very quickly.

She wrapped herself in a large towel. She used to wrap her dripping hair in a towel too, but with her new haircut, there was no point. As she was about to turn the handle of the door that separated the bathroom from the sitting room, a sudden fear chilled her: the Mossad agent from the airport would be there, a silenced pistol in his hands. She opened the door slowly, gingerly, and stuck out one bare foot. The room was empty, of course. And rather dark. She thrust her feet into her slippers and flicked a switch, turning on a small light fitting. She'd never seen such a small, adorable light fitting. She had to tell Eitan about it. They would sell really well in Israel now that rents were going up and everyone was moving into small apartments. She dried herself for a long time, till the last drop of water was gone, then stood naked in front of the mirror that hung on the inside of one of the wardrobe doors. She thought that from certain angles she looked plump, and from others, curvy and feminine. From certain angles, her new haircut was flattering, emphasising her long neck, and from others, it looked too masculine. Her legs looked short when she stood directly in front of the mirror. But in profile, they suddenly looked great. Her lips were full. Fleshy. From every angle. Guys always complimented her on them, said she had lips that begged to be kissed. But today they looked cheap. Too swollen. As if they'd been injected with silicone. Funny, as long as she was at Eitan's side and illuminated by his look of love, she felt absolutely fine about her body. Less than ten hours without him – and she was already having doubts.

She moved away from the mirror, took her phone out of her bag and texted him: *I'm naked and thinking about you.*

His reply came in less than a minute: *I'm dressed and thinking about you naked.*

That's too clever for him, she thought. And checked that she'd really sent the message to him and not to the name that came before his in her list of contacts – Adrian. It might be amusing to see the doctor's face when he read it, she thought. And immediately opened her travel journal and wrote: *A story that begins with a text message sent by mistake to the wrong person*, but as she wrote, she was already berating herself for having such a small idea. It could be a side story in the sprawling novel she wanted to write, but nothing more.

She lay down on the bed and covered herself with a thin blanket. There were two Holocaust novels in her bag that she'd brought along to offset her betrayal of Grandma Lily – one about a boy who hides in a wine cellar near Toulouse for the entire war, and the other about a sister and brother who join the Partisans in the forests. But she didn't have the strength to open them. Somewhere in the back of her mind, she dimly recalled that there were urgent questions she was supposed to ponder. But post-flight fatigue spread from her feet to her knees, up to her hips, her neck and her eyelids. Even that very specific place in her chest, which always flickered Yoavi, Yoavi, like a lighthouse beacon flashing in the darkness, grew faint.

Inbar! her mother's voice came from behind the door, are you ready?

Oof, she muttered, and looked at the time on her phone. What is this new, German habit of hers, being on time?

*

I just listened to your programme, her mother said.

They were walking side by side towards the train.

I listen to it every day. On the Internet. It was boring today. Your absence was felt.

That's ridiculous, Inbar said. I'm not that important. No, really, her mother persisted. The people they put on the air . . . it was as if no one had screened them properly. And Dr Adrian, too . . . I don't know. He sounded a bit lacklustre without you. There was only one interesting conversation, with a mother whose son hasn't spoken to her for fifteen years, and now he suddenly wants money from her for—

Mum! – Inbar interrupted her – I don't want to hear. That's one of the reasons I'm here. All those stories . . . all those people on the air . . . I wanted to get away from them.

Okay, fine, I didn't mean . . . I just wanted you to know that at the end of the programme, they mentioned your name. Even though you weren't even there. 'Chief Editor – Inbar Benbenisti.' That's what Dr Adrian said.

Where are we going? Inbar changed the subject. If she kept talking, she might tell her mother what had happened on the programme a few weeks ago, and she couldn't handle being judged by her. Her mother's voice, the one she'd internalised as if it were one of those chips inserted under the skin of slaves in science fiction stories, hadn't given her any peace for a month as it was.

They stood on the platform. She was on her mother's right, next to her good ear. The other ear had become blocked after Yoavi. A man carrying a dog came up to them and asked if they wanted to buy a newspaper, and her mother took out money and bought one. It's the homeless people's newspaper, she explained to Inbar in an admiring tone. They don't want to beg, so they put together a newspaper for themselves. A good idea, don't you think?

Inbar thought that the dog was too well groomed to be a homeless person's pet. But she didn't say anything. Then she thought that actually, her favourite way to sightsee in a new city was alone, with no particular destination in mind.

A rumbling came from the tunnel, announcing the arrival of the train. I think we'll start with the major places, her mother said after they got on. The Brandenburg Gate, Alexanderplatz, the Reichstag building. And then maybe we'll take the Hau-Bahn to Kreuzberg. That's where Turkish workers and artists live. I think you'll like it. We can have coffee there.

Have coffee, Inbar thought. That means we'll have to talk. Talking means that she'll ask me difficult questions. Difficult questions means that I'll have to give answers.

All the train windows had fat letters scratched into them. Another type of graffiti, apparently. No colours, just letters scratched on glass. What could they possibly have to protest about here? Inbar wondered.

A very long announcement in German came over the loud-speaker, and Inbar wanted to ask her mother whether, by chance, it was asking all the Jews to change trains at the next station, to Theresienstadt. But she restrained herself. As the announcement kept giving instructions, an image flashed through her mind of a scene in a porn film in which Bruno and her mother are in bed together (with her on top), and he's whispering terms of endearment in that language into her ear. That gross image made her feel slightly nauseous, a feeling intensified by the rapid swaying of the train.

Come, her mother said, to her relief. We get off here.

This is the new central train station, the Hauptbahnhof, she explained as they crossed the sprawling terminal. They opened it a year ago. Before the Wall fell, there were two stations, one in the East and one in the West. After the unification, they built a new one. That's what they did with all the important buildings, Inbar. You'll see in a minute. The Chancellor's building, the Bundestag, all of it was rebuilt on the seam to create the feeling that the country had set out on a new, joint path.

How is it that her mother had never been a tour guide? Inbar thought. It suits her so well. She truly loves to show off her knowledge.

They began walking through the city's major tourist sites, with her mother spicing the tour with anecdotes that made the places – Inbar had to admit – more vivid. Look at that fountain. The students who demonstrated in the '60s threw soap into it, and the foam would overflow into the square and stop traffic. Can you picture it? . . . Have a good look at the television tower. Under the antennas. The onion, yes. Can you see the shape formed by the sun's rays when they're broken? (Inbar couldn't see anything, but didn't want to say.) You can imagine how embarrassing it was for the East German Communists to discover that on sunny days, sprouting from their most important monument was a Christian cross!

As her mother flowed on down the river of knowledge, Inbar looked up at the tops of the buildings to find the angels. Wim Wenders' angels. She'd seen *Angels in the Skies of Berlin* when she was seventeen, and fell asleep in the middle, on the too-comfortable seats in the Haifa Cinematheque. Boring, she enjoyed complaining to her fellow students on her course, but a year ago, she came across it again on one of the film channels and found it hypnotic (or maybe the passing years had turned her into someone more in need of the kindness of angels?). Her mother chatted away about the wonderful Impressionist collection in the old National Gallery, which they were approaching, and she remembered that in Wenders' film, the characters' thoughts appeared in parentheses, and the idea popped into her head to write an entire story in parentheses, that is, the first and last sentences would be outside the parentheses and describe actual events, but between them, in parentheses, are ten pages of memories, free association, and erotic fantasies. She unzipped her bag to take out her travel journal and write down the idea, but then changed her mind because she knew that her mother would ask her what she was writing, and a single critical remark from her was liable to crush the crisp desire to write she'd been feeling since the trip began, just as a single critical remark from her ('it's just a shame, sweetie, that you swallow your words a little') at the end of the Purim school play destroyed her dreams of becoming an actress.

Are you even listening? Her mother stemmed the flow of knowledge for a moment.

Ah . . . yes . . . sure . . . That's very interesting, she said.

Because if you're not interested, we can go on to the next place.

Actually I'm wondering where the building is that the angel in *Angels in the Skies of Berlin* stood on?

In the opening scene?

Yes.

The Victory Column, her mother said. The Berliners call it The Goldelse. Bismarck built it, and the Nazi architect Albert Speer moved it. It's scheduled for later on our tour, she said, as if they'd agreed in advance on a specific route, and after a few seconds of silence, corrected herself: we can go there now, if you want. There's a lovely path through the park.

*

A double buggy was coming towards them, and Inbar prepared an answer in case her mother couldn't stop herself and made a remark that contained the words 'biological clock'. Her mother controlled herself. You could hear the effort in the deep breath, close to a sigh, that escaped from her. Then some young people on bicycles passed them on the path. Without children. Relaxed. As if they were in no hurry to get anywhere.

On Saturdays, she remembered, her father used to take her to the university car park, one of the only flat places on the Carmel, and teach her to ride her bike. First with stabilisers, then without anything. Mum would stay at home, doing crossword puzzles with Yoavi and working on her eternal thesis.

You know, Bruno was a partner in the production of *Angels in the Skies of Berlin*, she said now.

Which Bruno? Your Bruno?

Yes, he had a large production company then. And that was one of the films they produced. He actually sat in the editing room with Wim Wenders. Ask him about it, if you're interested.

And what did he do during the Holocaust?

What? . . . How did you get to the . . . He was a child. He was three.

And his father? Which camp did he serve in?

His father died from an illness when he was two. And his mother was a shoemaker. The only female shoemaker in Berlin. Not all the Germans were . . . Nazis, Inbar.

But they were all here when the Nazis ruled, weren't they? Inbar persisted.

Her mother bit her lip. The water in the river flowed extremely slowly. Inbar's eyes followed a wooden beam that was barely moving. Both she and her mother were thinking about the same woman, but refrained from mentioning her, like people careful not to enter the less desirable parts of a city, and continued walking in silence to the Victory Column.

Her mother took a picture of her with the statue in the background. Try to get me and Else, Inbar asked. Her mother backed away, moved forward, and backed away again, held the camera vertically and horizontally, then vertically again, until she found the angle her daughter wanted. Then, with a slight motion of her hand, she stopped a young Japanese girl with an assertive nose and asked her to photograph them together. And stood beside her daughter. Without touching her.

He fell in love with a circus trapeze artist, Inbar remembered. That's why Wim Wenders' angel decided to leave his job. He wanted to touch and be touched.

The Japanese girl handed back the camera along with a flyer: an invitation to a performance by the New-York-based group, the Klezmatics, at a church in Kreuzberg: 'klezmer music with a touch of modern jazz − in their Berlin debut.'

In Israel, there's no way I'd buy a ticket to something like that, Inbar thought. But I'm not in Israel now. Let's go to it, she said to her mother.

But it's *today*. Her mother pointed reprovingly to the date and hour printed on the bottom of the flyer.

So what?

So we won't have time . . . We have to go back home . . . freshen up and change. Aren't you tired?

A little bit — but so what? And why do you need freshening up? You look completely fresh right now.

But what you're wearing won't be enough for the evening, sweetie. This isn't Tel Aviv. You'll be cold.

How maddening that is, Inbar thought, that subtle selfishness of hers disguised as concern for someone else.

If you don't feel like going, she said, then say it, Mum. Don't pretend it's because you're worried about me.

*

The church was small, but the brightly illuminated dome could be seen from a distance, and people stood on the steps holding glasses of beer. Over the church door hung a banner with the name of a radio station: Multi Kulti. That's the government-funded station, her mother replied to Inbar's unasked question, they promote multiculturalism throughout Germany. Inside were long, wooden church benches, and in front of them a small, raised stage had been built. Jesus looked down on everything from above, close to the ceiling, and Inbar could see a certain satisfaction in his eyes. Where's the box office? her mother asked an usher. You pay at the end of the performance, based on how much you enjoyed it, explained the usher, who looked like a musician himself. Sounds like an excuse for an amateur performance, Inbar thought. But during the Klezmatics's first number she realised her mistake. A bearded clarinettist wearing a yarmulke came onstage first and filled the church with a sound that was both bright and sad, and also very Jewish. Then the rest of the musicians joined him, and the wailing slowly became more subdued. Inbar looked around and saw that the pews had filled up. Only yesterday, Eitan and I spent forty minutes looking for a parking place in Tel Aviv, she thought, and today I'm here. At a performance of Jewish music. In Berlin. With my mother. What a crazy world. And a fantastic one. Freedom! Her body was suddenly awash with intense joy (she'd forgotten how extreme her feelings always were when she was abroad: when she was happy, she was ecstatic; when she was lonely, she was utterly forlorn).

The first numbers the Klezmatics played were mostly subdued and moving. Then the bass, guitar and drums grew stronger, and the clarinet, which until then had been mostly crying, began to laugh. To roar with laughter. Her mother drummed her long fingers gently on her knees, as if she were accompanying the clarinet on the piano. A few young Berliners stood up and danced in the wide aisle between the rows of benches. Inbar danced too. In her seat. It was impossible not to. A klezmer group from Brooklyn. In a church. In Berlin. Liberty, equality and rhythm. She moved her hips, slightly shaking the pew she was sitting on. And during the next number, which was totally, wildly exuberant, she really shook it.

An older woman sitting on her left suddenly turned around and screamed at her in German.

It wasn't a shout. It was a shriek. The blood-curdling shriek of a storm trooper.

The people sitting around them ignored what was going on. You could see their neck muscles straining not to turn around.

Her mother leaned over and whispered in her ear that the woman was asking her to stop moving the bench.

She stopped. And then she turned her head and stared right into the storm trooper's eyes. I won't go like a sheep to the slaughter, she thought. I'm willing to stop moving the bench, but no German is going to scream at me without getting an appropriate response.

A staring war broke out between her and the storm trooper. At school, they did that a lot in the winter. They couldn't go outside because of the rain, so they sat facing each other in the classroom, staring into each other's eyes and waiting to see who would be the first to look away.

The storm trooper was the first to break. She dropped her blue-grey eyes, muttered a series of complaints to her husband and swapped places with him.

That would never happen in Israel, Inbar said to her mother after the three encores were over and they went out into the street. When her mother didn't respond, Inbar remembered and walked around to her mother's good ear. That would never happen in Israel, she repeated.

You're right, her mother said. The openness they have here in Berlin is really extraordinary. Did you see how the minister sang the last encore with them?

That's not what I meant, Mum. She stopped walking. I meant that woman's screeching. What was that all about?

To be honest, Inbar, you . . . were jiggling the bench.

I don't believe it. You're siding with her? Inbar's voice was already slightly broken around the edges (how quick her mother always was to save Yoavi and be furious at her without checking first to see who'd been the instigator; how he learned to exploit that and cry even when she hadn't touched him just so their mother would be angry at her; how she always oohed and aahed over the silly presents he gave her and the infantile pictures he drew for her, but never bothered to respond to any of Inbar's calls, silent though they were; how her face would light up with joy when he came home, and she'd always run to the door as if she didn't have bad knees, but when Inbar came in, she'd say hello from wherever she was sitting; how she travelled to every shit-hole he was stationed at when he was in the army to bring him shop-bought food because she didn't know how to cook, but hardly ever visited her, and if she did, her lips would always twist with disappointment that her daughter was a lowly NCO in the Education Corps and not an officer or a spy or a programmer in the computer centre, something that she could tell her colleagues at the university, proudly, loudly, not half-heartedly, because after all, she couldn't know then what would happen, it wasn't as if she knew then what would happen, she just—).

I'm not – her mother began speaking in a controlled voice, but the storm clouds were already gathering at the edges – siding with her . . . I'm just saying . . . I think . . . that you could have danced in the aisle like all the other young . . .

Yes, but what was that Nazi shrieking?

Inbari, you can't stick the word Nazi on to everything. If the same thing happened to you in . . . Barcelona, let's say, would you say 'Nazi' then?

But we're not in Barcelona, Mum, we're in Germany! It might be convenient for you to push that fact aside. Of course it's convenient for you to push it aside. Because you're living here on their money. That's exactly what Grandma Lily said – they buy us off so we'll forget.

That's what Grandma thinks. She has the right to think it. But I think differently.

But Grandma's right, Inbar said, feeling the pleasant surge of electricity through her body that you feel when you're about to attack someone's Achilles heel – and she's also right about Bruno.

Bruno? What did she say about Bruno?

She said that, knowing you, he's probably as rich as Croesus.

With all due respect, neither one of you can judge me! I have the right to be happy! her mother said, suddenly raising her voice.

Her mother could shift all at once from speaking with the

calm control of an academic to screeching like a fishwife. Her voice would suddenly skyrocket, and Inbar hated it when that happened, hated the chills that ran through her, and hated the fact that no one in the outside world knew that her mother could carry on like that; everyone thought she was a gentle, affable person. Once Inbar went out with a man who, on their third date, suddenly raised his voice – she was driving her white Fiat Punto and when she stopped at a green light, he roared: what are you doing?! – and again those chills had run through her from the tips of her toes to the top of her head. She'd stopped the car and said to him: Out. Now. And neither his pleading, nor his broad chest nor his strong arms could help him.

Okay, Mum, she said in a voice as cool as night, I've been shouted at enough for one day. I think I want to walk around by myself now.

But you have no idea where you are – her mother pleaded.

Inbar looked around. A row of buildings. New ones alongside old ones. And a demolished building that looked as if it had just been bombed by the Allies. A man stuck his shaved head out of a passing car and laughed derisively. At them? At someone standing behind them?

I'm in Kreuzberg, aren't I? Inbar said. Give me Bruno's address, and I can take a taxi back if I have to.

I'll worry about you. You know me. I won't be able to go to sleep until you're back. That would be a shame. Let's go back together. The studio is completely separate from the house. How will I know when you're back? Let's go back together, Inbari. It would be a shame to end our first day like this.

I'll send you a text message when I come in, Inbar said, and was momentarily choked with sorrow. Her mother was trying so hard, why couldn't she try back? Look, she leaned over and pecked her on the cheek, we've ended our first day together differently.

*

During her partying years, she and her mother decided that she'd raise the cover that separated her submarine from the rest of the house before she went out clubbing at Second City or Vertigo, and when she came back in the early morning, she'd loosen the clip that held it open and let it slam down hard so that her mother would hear that she'd arrived home in one piece. When her brother replaced her in the basement, the arrangement was still in place, and when he didn't come back from the army, the cover remained raised for long months and no one dared to loosen the clip.

Inbar walked through the streets of night-time Berlin, and as always when she thought about her brother — it almost never happened in Israel, she didn't let it — the surroundings blurred for her. It took more than an hour for her to rise up from the dark depths of longing to notice that she was walking in a lovely area.

Small local pubs were overflowing on to the pavements. A powerful yellow glow poured from streetlights on to the people's faces. There were neither too many nor too few of them outside. Just the right number. Against her will, this city was slowly growing on her as she walked. A night-time flea market consisting of three small shops, one next to the other, drew her to its dusty furniture. She saw an Israeli in the third shop, who knew immediately that she was Israeli too. Yossi, he introduced himself and shook her hand limply. Something about his soft chin made her like him even before they spoke. How long have you been here? she asked. Since the '80s. Before the Wall fell? she asked. Yeah, sure, I came here after Lebanon, he explained, as if the word Lebanon was enough to explain everything. And how's life here? *Wunderbar*, easy and cheap, he said, sounding like a computer-generated announcement. Can I help you?

She walked around the shop, Yossi following her at a considerable distance, not breathing down her neck the way salespeople in Israel do. There was a floor lamp there, slightly scratched, slightly crooked, that might interest Eitan, but she could hear her grandmother reminding her 'we don't buy German products!' and even if she got around that by telling herself that the salesman was named Yossi, like her father, how would she shlep the lamp all the way back to Israel?

Thank you, she said. You have some terrific things here, she apologised, but I don't have any money on me. Maybe another time . . .

No problem, Yossi said and handed her a card he took from behind the cash register: Israelink, it said in Hebrew and English.

That's our community, he explained. We meet once a month. Lots of Israelis come. We have singalongs. And every three months, we have a meeting with a writer from Israel. You're invited.

I'm only here . . . on a visit, she said.

So 'maybe another time,' he mimicked her. And she suddenly thought that she heard a German accent in his Hebrew.

She went outside to the street. An ambulance passed. It had a fairly subdued siren, not hysterical, not like the ones in Israel. Three girls were walking down the steps leading to the subway. Giggling. She noticed that there weren't a lot of cars on the road, and the ones that passed weren't luxurious, and suddenly she realised what it was that she liked about this damn city, what distinguished it from London or Paris, let's say: the modesty. There was nothing fancy or attention-grabbing about the clothes people wore. The furniture in the cafés was from the small flea market she'd just walked through. And the bicycles looked like the ones on a kibbutz. *Every large city* – she took out her journal and, standing under a streetlight, wrote in it – *has a brief golden age in which it is successful, but not too successful. Effervescent, but not overflowing. In demand, but not so much in demand that only wealthy people can live in it.*

What do you know about it anyway? she berated herself, and immediately shoved the journal into the depths of her bag. Half a day in Berlin, and you're already presuming to have insights about it?

She took her phone out of her jacket pocket – and called Eitan.

He answered after two rings.

Hi, gorgeous. I was just thinking about you. Good things? Of course good things. What, for example? Oh, nothing. Why nothing? You won't like it. What, picturing what our son would look like again? More or less. Why more or less? This time it was a girl. Let it go, Eitan, let it go. I've already told you that it has to come from me. You see, that's why I didn't want to tell you what I was thinking.

Silence. Heavy. Silence that meant that the conversation had reached a dead end and now they had to backpedal. They'd had a lot of silences like that before she left. Only this time, against the background of the familiar way he breathed during silences, she also heard a voice. Female. Chattering. In their apartment. Is there a girl with you?! In the apartment.

Yes, he admitted in a guilt-free voice. The sports presenter on the TV. A great girl.

Ah, she said, her sense of relief mixed with a sense of missed opportunity. (The day after it happened, Dr Adrian told her he 'didn't feel 100%', and Yizhar decided to broadcast a selection of conversations from old programmes instead, and let her go home earlier. Back in their building, on the staircase, she could hear a girl's voice coming from their apartment, and to her surprise, she was neither shocked nor angry. When she opened the door and discovered that the girl was conducting a survey for the Central Bureau of Statistics and Eitan was answering her questions with bored patience, she was almost disappointed, as if deep down she wanted the jealous scene, or the revenge of a fuck for a fuck that would follow it, and that was something else she intended to check out with herself on this trip, yes, that too.)

So how's it going with your mother? Eitan asked. So-so, she replied. You mean you've already had time to have an argument? Yes. I mean, no. I mean, she's actually trying . . . Forget it, I don't have the energy to talk about it (I mean, she thought, I don't have the energy to go into the nuances of my complicated relationship with my mother and to be disappointed again because you come from a super-normal family and are too healthy to understand it).

Give her a chance, he said.

You're right, she said, I'll try.

Where are you, anyway?

I don't know. Somewhere in the eastern part of the city, I think.

I'd come to pick you up if I could.

Thanks, sweetie. I think I'll just get a taxi.

Good. But if the driver's bald and he has a swastika tattooed on his scalp, don't get in, okay?

Lily

And then – she was dreaming that she was having sex with Natan, this time in a luxurious sleeping-car – the train lurched to a stop. They were asked not to get off. Or open the curtains. When no one explained what was going on, rumour after rumour began to fly through the carriage. Lily tried to close her ears. After so much training and waiting, they surely wouldn't send them back. She wondered whether that clever girl – whose name, it turned out, was Esther – was happy about the sudden possibility that she might return to her parents, or whether, in her heart, she was already reconciled to the parting. Lily wanted to see her again, to talk to her, but when they stopped, they were told not to move through the train under any circumstances.

After her mother died, Lily's father told her that she'd be going to live with her grandmother in the village for a while. She hated the idea, but she was too young to raise the flag of rebellion, so she parted sorrowfully from all her classmates and wrote each one a letter. She kissed her close friends on the cheek, a long, hard kiss, as if she were branding them. And then, out of the blue, her father told her that in the end, 'it hadn't worked out' with Grandma, and she'd be staying with him. I thought you'd be happy, he said when he saw the disappointment on her face, but she was too young to explain to him or to herself that her heart had already reconciled itself.

The train remained motionless for several hours, causing much concern. She took *The Interpretation of Dreams* out of her suitcase and tried to read it. 'Wish fulfilment' . . . 'Distortion of dreams' . . . She read the same sentence again and again, the words unconnected, the meaning fragmented. So she put the book back in her suitcase, took out her coat, balled it into a pillow, rested her head on it and tried to go to sleep. Someone behind her said: Those idiots, they put too many people on the train. Someone else explained with barely contained hysteria: There's a problem with the tracks. That's all. I'm telling you. The tracks. That's all. Finally, a group leader came into their car and admitted that the problem was more serious. The British had found out about their train and its destination, and they were pressuring the Romanians to deny it entrance to the port of Constanta, where the ship was anchored. The Haganah people are working hard to solve the problem! And I'm positive that it will all turn out fine! he cried, but his raised voice revealed how worried he was. And why shouldn't he be worried? How much older was he than they? Two years? Three?

No one was allowed to get off. One young fellow, who disobeyed the order and went out to the platform, was beaten by the Romanian policemen. They saw it happen through the train window, saw his arm twisted behind his back, saw a foot kick his stomach, saw his body fold like a centipede after the kick – and there was nothing they could do. After they'd thrown the boy back into the train as if he were a sack of potatoes, the policemen walked through all the cars, shouting: *Vesos la vagon! Vesos la vagon!*

Only in the carriage.

The passengers panicked. Lily had always believed that moods – not only substances – were made up of particles, and now she could actually see them fill the aisle and the narrow spaces between the seats.

Until the klezmorim arrived.

They burst into the carriage with a trumpet call, and everyone turned to look at them. In addition to the trumpet, the makeshift orchestra consisted of a mandolin, a clarinet, a triangle and a large variety of percussion instruments, from a hand-held Miriam drum to a stew pot. And conducting them all was the bald harmonica player, Yitzhak Pimstein. He was the one who led the players into the carriage, signalled them to begin, gave them quick glances to indicate when to move on to the next piece, and gestured to the audience when it was time to sing along. He was wearing long cloth trousers and a grey, work vest with a bow tie pinned to it. He looked ridiculous, but he couldn't have cared less. Despite herself, Lily found herself mesmerised by his mimicry. His large Adam's apple rose and fell to the rhythm of the music, and the nostrils of his large nose alternately widened and narrowed. When they played an upbeat piece, his thick lower lip vibrated with joy.

When they played a sad piece, his thick eyebrows contracted with exaggerated seriousness, and when he wanted to signal to the audience to stop applauding and listen to the mandolin player – who was actually the only professional musician in the orchestra – he closed his eyes in gentle concentration and leaned slightly forward, as if he were about to kiss a girl.

'The hora lights a fire in my heart,' the entire carriage sang. Then, 'If I had the strength, if I had the strength, I would take to the streets and shout: salvation is on the way!' then 'The train has a whistle so loud and clear, down below water flows, and up above, smoke blows.' When the particles of dejection had completely evaporated from the air, Yitzhak Pimstein allowed himself to lead the orchestra in an especially sentimental waltz, and when it ended, he bent low towards Henia, a member of Lily's training group, and handed her an imaginary flower.

He handed the flower to Henia, but looked directly into Lily's eyes. She wondered whether anyone else had noticed.

After the applause, the orchestra proceeded to the next carriage, and Lily stood up and followed them. Quietly. She wanted to see how Esther was and thought that if the orchestra was allowed to move from one carriage to another, then why couldn't she? Maybe you just want to feel strong again alongside someone weak, she rebuked herself as she walked, and in the space between the carriages, where they were exposed to the gusting wind, she stumbled and fell against the mandolin player in front of her, but pulled away from him the minute she regained her balance. The spot on her shoulder that had touched him burned, and waves of shame spread through her body, but the mandolin player gallantly ignored the incident and she continued walking.

Esther was glad to see her. I wanted to come and find you too, she said. But they said we couldn't. Come here, she invited: sit next to me. Lily squeezed beside her, their hips touching, and listened to the performance again. The songs were the same, but Yitzhak Pimstein's mimicry continued to fascinate her. She noticed now that even his bald head took part in the show — furrowing and smoothing out to the rhythm of the percussion pots. Wow, he said after one of the songs, and looked straight into her eyes, I see that we already have a loyal fan.

No . . . What are you talking about . . . she stammered and pointed at Esther. I . . . just came to see how she was.

Yes, of course, he nodded, smiled an infuriating smile, and signalled that the players should go on to another piece. They began the waltz they'd played in the previous car, and Lily was already wondering who would receive the imaginary flower —

And then a group leader came in and asked the orchestra to stop. They can hear you outside, he warned, and it's attracting unnecessary attention. We need to maintain complete silence until the problem is solved.

Yitzhak Pimstein broke the silence by exhaling one final time, an exhalation of protest, into his harmonica. The group leader glared at him and said: Enough, Pima, this is no time for your foolishness. Anyone who doesn't belong in this carriage should return to his own, and that includes the klezmorim.

Pima — that nickname suits him, Lily thought, as she parted from Esther with an overly cheerful wave.

The difficult hours began at noon. The heat became unbearable. Sweat dripped down Lily's back and was absorbed by the band of her pants. A powerful stench came from the toilet, its radius widening with each additional person who entered it. Flies circled the cars, searching for the source of the smell. Some of them came in through the window and annoyed the passengers. The young men in Lily's carriage began a fly-swatting competition. Who could kill more? But there was no fun in that. Several girls took off their blouses and sat there in short camisoles. Lily thought that unseemly, even though her own blouse was too thick for the humidity. She could change into a thinner one, she thought, but where? The smell from the toilet made her feel mildly but constantly nauseous, and she was afraid that if she went in there, the nausea would rise up and overflow. In the afternoon, some young Romanian fellows knocked on the window and offered to bring them water from the station taps. Containers of all kinds were passed through the window, along with some coins, and were returned full of rust-coloured water. But they were too thirsty to be fussy. The Romanians continued to supply them with water all night, but in the morning they had a sudden change of mind. Someone had apparently told them that the passengers were Jews, and they shouted: Jews, go home! And threw rocks at the windows. One hit the window Lily was sitting next to, leaving a spiderweb of cracks on the glass. The Romanian policemen took their time removing the rock-throwers, and Lily thought: What home are they talking about? Exactly how can I go home now?

Every few hours, the group leaders came in and gave them the latest update – which was that there was no update. Yanek, a disturbed young man from her training camp, began banging his head on a window frame, and his friends hurried to stop him. She knew that they'd soon ask her to get him talking, to calm him down, and she used the few seconds she had left to gather emotional strength for the task. She closed her eyes and pictured a scene that always filled her with serenity: she and Natan in their new home in Eretz Yisrael. She didn't really know what Eretz Yisrael looked like, but in her imagination, their home was surrounded by greenery, a small stream burbled beside it, and the inside of the house was painted in bright colours. Natan, wearing shorts and a vest, brought one of his wonderful omelettes from the kitchen, and the sun shone through the window. She sat cross-legged on a soft carpet and beside her, napping on a bed of soft blankets, was their little baby girl, whose name she already knew.

Hana

They took Inbar away from her right after the birth. She remembered that every time they argued. Once, she used to try and fight that memory, smash it on the head, so that it would return to the depths from which it had come. So it would drown. She no longer fights it now, but knowingly abandons herself to the torment. Like a nail scratching a wound created by a different nail that had scratched a bite. She was haemorrhaging and they had to stop it, so they took Inbar from her. The baby had been at Hana's breast for only a few seconds of quiet joy when the midwife grabbed her and handed her to Yossi, who was sitting on her right. He cradled her in his arms, extolling her beauty, which was already evident, and then they grabbed her from him as well – why the hell did he let them? Because they asked, he always said – and then they took Hana to the recovery room, and she didn't hold Inbar again until eighteen hours later.

Sometimes, that is, when she's feeling hopeless, that is, after one of their battles, she tells herself that everything was decided there and nothing can be done about it. Everything she'd tried to change and fix stemmed from those first fateful seconds. That's crap, Yossi told her. It's crap, the psychology books told her. It's crap, she knew in her clear moments. Nonetheless, when Yoavi was born, she took no chances: Even if I'm dying, don't let them take him away from me, she reminded Yossi, and refused to take painkillers so that they couldn't take advantage of her temporary wooziness to whisk him away, and she warned the midwife that if she did, she'd sue her. She held Yoavi close to her body, and only two hours later did she agree to let Yossi hold him, just for a moment, before she snatched him back quickly, almost violently.

Bruno shifts on to his other side, turning his back to her. As if he senses in his sleep that her thoughts have become ugly and he's distancing himself from them. Before they fell asleep, she told him everything that happened that day. You know, she told him, now that I finally feel I have something to give, she won't accept it. Patience, he said, and stroked her head, which was resting on his chest, patience. But maybe it's too late already, Bruno, she persisted. Maybe there's a point after which it can't be fixed. Look at us, Hana, he says, do you think there's such a thing as a point after which it can't be fixed?

He's sleeping now, with that quiet, European breathing of his. His face is relaxed, free of anxiety. Maybe he's dreaming one of those dreams he'll present her with in the morning, the way a child presents his parents with a beautiful drawing. (For her entire childhood, she was forced to listen to every detail of her mother's dreams at breakfast, and she slowly developed an almost Joseph-like ability to interpret them.)

Twenty-five minutes past midnight. And the child hasn't sent a text message.

She's doing this deliberately, to drive me crazy. Like those miniskirts she used to wear to school. Or that time she ran away to Eilat. Or that boyfriend from the Air Force she'd bring in through the separate entrance to the basement, but never came upstairs with him to say hello.

She gets out of bed and goes to the study Bruno set up for her. She especially loves the dark oak desk he built, whose charm derives mainly from its gentle lines and whorls, which make it look more like a perked ear than a rectangle. Above the desk is a glass-doored cabinet that holds all the books by her favourite writer, Stefan Zweig, in the original language. One look at them before beginning her work is usually enough to give her the humility needed by anyone who wishes to write down a new idea.

She turns on the computer and brings up her doctorate file: 'The Representation of Jews in Early Contemporary European Folk Literature: Between Romanticism and Anti-Semitism (working title).' As a mental warm-up before writing, she begins to read the opening paragraphs of the chapter on the Wandering Jew.

The first pamphlet in German was published in 1602, describing the encounter between the Bishop of Schleswig, a region in northern Germany, and a man who revealed to him that he was Ahasuerus, the wandering Jewish shoemaker from Jerusalem. Legend has it that when Jesus was carrying the cross on his way to Golgotha, that same Ahasuerus prevented him from leaning on the wall of a house to rest for a while – and the Wandering Jew was cursed for this sin, condemned to live until the end of days –

She scrolls down to the passage that deals with Richard Wagner's, 'Judaism in Music', the passage she hasn't been able to make up her mind about for several months now.

Wagner claimed that Ahasuerus the Shoemaker symbolises the entire Jewish people: a people of eternal ghosts that has survived among mortal peoples. Other peoples are born, mature, age, and finally pass from this world. But the Jews do not know this cycle of life because they have been cut off from the roots of their tradition and are forced to live as parasites on the bodies of others and suck out their vitality. Their salvation will come only

if Ahasuerus's concealed, true wish is realised: to completely
disappear.

Perceptive readers, people of the radical intelligentsia,
understood Wagner's call for the Jews to disappear completely
as a call to eradicate their self-identity as part of the general
struggle for the liberation of man. Other readers interpreted
this as a call for murder, a call to destroy them physically.

But what do *you* think? Hana asks herself as she places the
flashing cursor at the end of the last passage. How do you prefer
to interpret Wagner's suggestion? Against the background of
previous events, the Romantic perceptions of the nineteenth
century, which saw the Wandering Jew as a type of universal
traveller traversing wide expanses and eras, symbolising the hardships of humanity as it treads the path of progress? Against the
background of the blatant anti-Semitism sprinkled throughout
the article, or against the background of what came after it – the
twentieth century, Nazi Germany, Wagner's compositions
performed at Hitler's rallies? A sudden understanding blossoms
in her mind: your true difficulty has nothing to do with deciding
between the nineteenth and twentieth centuries; it has to do with
the twenty-first century. Your true difficulty is reading that legend
of the Wandering Jew in the Berlin of today. From within the
good life you are living. After all, you enjoy life so much here
that even your daughter's visit arouses no longing for there. And
perhaps, in the culture of the new millennium, there is no 'there'
or 'here', perhaps those concepts have become obsolete. She
hastens to type, in 16 point font, several key words so that in the
morning she'll be able to continue to develop the new idea:

The 21st century. Here and now. Multi Kulti.
Multi Guilty. Wandering as punishment ('40
years in the desert'). Wandering as survival
('Go down to Egypt to escape the famine')

She wants to write a few more reminders — but then her phone buzzes.

I'm back. Inbar writes. *Who's the guy sleeping in my bed?*

Inbar

For a second, she thought it was the man from the airport. The Mossad assassin. Help! a cry escaped her lips. If the bear-person sleeping in her bed hadn't been snoring, she would even have run. But there was something about his snoring — only Grandma Lily snored so loudly, and Grandpa Natan made her and Yoavi swear that when they stayed during the summer holidays, they wouldn't say a word about it because Grandma was a lady and if she knew, she'd feel uncomfortable. There was something about the strange man's snores that added a comic element to the whole business.

She sidled over to the bed. She saw now that it wasn't the Mossad agent, but someone else. With lighter skin. For a moment, she amused herself with the idea of undressing, putting on her red nightgown and lying down next to this Aryan guy. She wondered whether he'd get a hard-on even when he was unconscious. And maybe — she was writing a scene in her mind more than she was seriously weighing the option — maybe she'd even sleep with him when he was unconscious, the way Garp's mother does with the pilot in *The World According to Garp*. But wait a minute, she remembered, in the book, that got her pregnant!

She sat down on a chair, and the squeak of the wood made the figure in the bed sigh and turn over.

It's Bruno's son, she guessed. He both resembles him and doesn't resemble him. The same nose and haircut, but there was a small, pouty line on his lower lip. There was an earring in his exposed ear, and a wedding band as wide as a bracelet on his finger. The widest she'd ever seen on a man.

Who's the guy sleeping in my bed? she texted her mother. She could have said that Bruno's son was in her bed – but she wanted her mother to be frightened. She was thirty-two years old, a mature, independent person, and she still wanted her mother to come running in a panic, clad in a nightgown, her hair unkempt, from her lavish home into the cold night, to the stairs leading to the studio.

Bruno arrived first. I apologise, he said. That's my son. I told him the studio was occupied, but he must have had too much to drink and forgot. He still has a key, you understand.

Now her mother appeared at the door. With every hair in place. Come on, sweetie, come upstairs with us. We'll open the sofa bed. When Hans drinks – she pointed to the bed – it's not easy to wake him. Even pouring water on his face might not help.

(Once, on a youth movement group tour of the Ramon Crater, one of the boys poured cold water from his canteen on her face. G-o-o-d morning! Inbar, he said, and she woke with a start, so furious that she chased him – his name was Itamar – and slapped him, hitting his nose instead of his cheek. That was the first time she'd hit anyone except her brother. The group leader came running to separate them, then assembled the whole group around the embers of the previous night's campfire and gave them a talk about mutual responsibility and verbal violence.)

Don't worry, don't wake him, she said. Let me just get a few things together and I'll be right up.

*

Before dawn, she was running after that boy again, this time up the emergency stairs to the Azrieli Tower in Tel Aviv. He was faster than she was, and younger, and in the dream she decided she had to start working out. In the end, they reached the roof. A large radio antenna rose up from behind one of the many solar panels there. Give me a reason! the boy said, and climbed on to the railing that encircled the roof. She was still trying to catch her breath, which she'd lost with the exertion of the climb. She couldn't speak. Give me a reason, or else — he said and leaned forward. Leonard Cohen, she said quickly. The boy hesitated for a moment, then said, don't know him. And jumped.

She pulled herself out of the dream (heavy lids refuse to open heavy lids refuse to open heavy lids — cut). For the first few seconds, out of habit, she reached for Eitan, until she remembered where she was. European light came through the window shutters. The faint aroma of coffee tickled her nostrils. She reached for her bag, took out her journal and wrote down every detail of the dream. As she closed the journal to put it back, she suddenly heard her mother's voice behind her: I didn't know you wrote.

She turned around. How long have you been sitting here, Mum?

A few minutes. You know, when you were little, your temperature would go up when you were reading a book that gripped you. With *Anne of Green Gables*, it went up to 38.1. With *Little Women*, it went past 39. And you were reading both of them at the same time. You always loved to read two books at the same time. Do you remember that?

How could I forget, Inbar said (adding in her mind: when you always remind me).

They could always talk about books. That's how they would grope their way towards each other, emotionally wounded after the bitter arguments of adolescence. 'So what did you think of the latest . . .' 'Me too. Though the end was a little weird, wasn't it?'

Sometimes, after a fight, her mother would buy her a book as a peace offering and place it on the armchair near the steps down to the submarine. But for the last two years, it had been Inbar who bought her mother books and sent them from Israel to Berlin. Later they would talk about them on the phone. Usually, her mother's taste was suspiciously similar to that of the literary critics for *Haaretz*.

Bruno has a wonderful library here. She pointed to the long shelves and the metal ladder standing halfway across them.

What good is it, Inbar thought but didn't say. It's all in German.

So . . . You write? her mother dared once again.

Inbar closed the notebook and placed her hand on it, the way a witness places his hand on the Bible in court and swears to tell the truth.

No, she lied. I mean, I only write down my dreams. So I won't forget them.

So, was it . . . an interesting dream?

Nu shoin, she said, imitating her grandmother's Yiddish, I saw Pima in my dream again, and they both laughed.

Grandma Lily remembered her dreams perfectly and was happy to tell them in great detail to anyone prepared to listen. It was a real ritual. You drank pale coffee with lots of milk, nibbled biscuits and listened to Grandma Lily's dream. When he was alive, even Grandpa Natan used to sit with them and listen patiently, accepting, with no particular agitation or resentment, the frequent presence of another man named Pima in his wife's dreams. Then suddenly I see Pima! Grandma Lily says, surprised, as if she hadn't seen him dozens of times already in other dreams. Once, he appeared in a cowshed, riding a cow that gave no milk. Once he was sprawled on the floor of the supermarket. Once he was driving a car without tyres. And sometimes he made do with a brief cameo appearance in dreams on other subjects ('and then I'm standing in front of Pinhas

Sapir telling him that tomatoes can't possibly cost twelve shekels a kilo, and Pima is standing behind him with his big Adam's apple and writing everything I say in a black notepad, and then Sapir answers me, my dear madam, tomatoes may have become more expensive, but marrow is now quite a bit cheaper').

So what was your dream *really* about? her mother asked, as if sensing that it was a point worth pursuing. Come on, we'll make you some coffee. If you wrote it down in a notebook, it must have been important, mustn't it?

Not necessarily, Inbar said, and followed her mother into the kitchen. A drying rack from Ikea stood next to the sink. Just like in my kitchen, she thought, and felt on the verge of breaking. One more of her mother's questions and she'd give in. And tell her (she'd told Eitan about it the day it happened, and he was appropriately shocked, but was also quick to tell her not to feel responsible, it wasn't her fault, no court would find her guilty, and she'd thought, you can't tell older siblings not to feel responsible for something, it's in their nature, and she'd told him that he was right, of course, and was grateful for the broom he'd given her, and she tried to use it to sweep the whole business into the corners of her mind. But the next day, and the week after that, she couldn't stop thinking about it, and when she tried to talk to him about it again, the words stuck in her throat because it wasn't just the episode itself, but also the Yoavi memories it stirred in her).

Guten Morgen! Bruno's son came into the kitchen. Bathed. Perfumed. A wreck. I'm sorry about yesterday, he said to her in accent-free English. My wife changed the lock, and when I came home I couldn't get in. So I came here. I have a key . . . and forgot that my father said . . . He did tell me . . . I'm really very sorry.

It's okay. Inbar tried to be polite. It happens.

It's because she's angry with me, Bruno's son continued. He said 'angry with me' indifferently, as if the words were clothes pegs he was hanging laundry with. Then he made himself a cup of coffee, and put down next to it a square of bitter chocolate he'd broken off from a bar that was in the fridge.

She and her mother sat down next to each other at the small kitchen table, and gave him a waiting-for-details look, the way they used to when her father came back from one of his conferences and said at the door, 'People are the most interesting things in the world,' and they'd know that in another minute, he'd give them the usual warning, 'Whatever I tell you is in strictest confidence,' followed by her mother's acerbic response, 'Anyone would think you're about to reveal state secrets', followed by a good story.

The problem is that her father was a drinker, Hans began in the middle. He spoke mainly to Inbar's mother, but every once in a while gave her a quick, searching glance as well. He gestured wildly with his hands, like a rock singer in the middle of a performance.

Her father was a heavy drinker, he said. Not like me. He'd come home and hassle her mother. He'd pinch her waist too hard and sing vulgar songs. So she thinks I'm like him. And that's not true. I'm not the least bit like him. Just the opposite. When I drink, I love my family more. Because it's as if I've come home after a long trip. How much can a person be himself? So once a week I drink instead of going to prostitutes or running off and travelling round Australia alone in a camper van. Isn't that better? Tell me, as women, what do you think?

Inbar scraped the coffee-flavoured sugar from the bottom of her cup with her finger and put it in her mouth. Her mother mixed the air that was in her cup with a spoon. It was obvious to both that he didn't really want an answer.

This whole business with family, he went on, I knew from the beginning that it wasn't for me. But I loved her so much that I agreed. She wanted to get married and I wanted her. So I agreed. And then she wanted children and I wanted her.

So I agreed. And that's how I found myself running a nursery. Hans' Nursery School. People in this city live with two partners, or three, and couldn't care less about the family and kids thing, they do what they feel like. But I don't care about that — you know what, I don't care about anything. As long as I can be with her.

And . . . drink, her mother added in a tone sympathetic and mocking at the same time.

Every once in a while, only every once in a while, Hans pleaded with them, as if he were pleading with his wife now.

And then his father walked into the kitchen — and Hans' metamorphosis was astonishing. He straightened up in his chair and threw back his shoulders. His bleary look became suddenly focused. For a moment, it looked as if the stubble on his face had shaved itself.

Bruno said something brief to him in German, and Hans replied (it sounded to Inbar like a demand and submission to a demand). Then they discussed business (money talk has an international tone — Inbar knew that from overhearing Eitan on work calls). Hans was authoritative throughout the conversation. And to the point. His gestures were deliberate and balanced. His right hand divided a sum into payments on the table. His left proposed three stages, finger after finger. The first stage: gathering all the Jews into ghettos. The second stage: transporting them to camps. The final stage: extermination. That wasn't what he said, but Inbar couldn't stop the association.

They're talking about a partner they have, her mother translated. An *Ossie*, a former East German. They're saying that they don't trust him, that he has no work ethic. All the *Ossies* are still considered parasites here. Economically, that is.

I apologise from the bottom of my heart for what happened, Hans said to them when he had finished planning the upcoming *Aktions* with his father. I promise you that tonight you'll be able to sleep in your bed without any worries.

Maybe, just to be on the safe side, I'll change the lock, she said. There was a silence that went on for too long. After which, Hans burst into a wild, hiccuping laugh, and, pointing alternately to her and her mother, said, you really look alike — has anyone ever told you that?

Lily

That's new, Lily thinks after her brief conversation with Eitan. Inbar going to bed at nine at night? Strange. She never goes to sleep before eleven, twelve. And it's also suspicious that Inbar hasn't called back after she left her two messages over the last couple of days. She usually returns her calls quickly and happily, and always begins her conversation with that beautiful, warm 'Hi Grams'.

She misses her granddaughter. With her daughter, things are so tense and full of anger — Hana was always Natan's girl. *Nu*. Natan's dead. And Lily's not like her friends, who go to the cemetery and tell their life stories to the worms. What a bunch. And the ones who are still alive only want to talk about their diseases. Or their Filipino carers. Or politics. Some of them have started talking like lunatics this past year. (I feel the Germans coming closer, Elza told her in their last phone conversation. I smell the frozen-potato-smell of their uniforms.) When *she* starts losing her marbles, Lily knows, she'll take her leave. Sleeping pills or a noose, she still hasn't decided. The main thing is not to turn into a joke. An anecdote on a chat show. Last Friday, she saw an Alzheimer expert on the health channel telling jokes about his patients. What kind of insane world is it when a doctor talks that way in public and isn't ashamed?

For the time being, her brain is fine – usually. And that brain tells her that something is going on with Inbar. Mothers always say that they can feel their children in their bodies. With Hana, that never happened: from the day she was born, there was a clear, stubborn separateness about her only daughter that only a hug from her father could dissolve. And it didn't happen to her with her grandson Yoavi either. Before the tragedy, she had no physical presentiment of what was going to happen. And when she received the terrible news – by phone, on a Saturday morning, three rings before she picked up – she grew dizzy and collapsed into a chair, like everyone else.

Only with Inbar does she always sense something. Years ago, she remembers, on the day the Berlin Wall fell, she'd just finished snipping the headlines out of the newspapers and putting the cuttings in her archive when she was suddenly filled with a strong, clear feeling that not too far away from her, someone was causing Inbar pain, and immediately went into the kitchen to bake the honey cake she loved. When she finished, she went to rest so she'd have the strength to tend to her granddaughter's wounded heart. To lighten her disappointment. Again. For the unpteenth time.

Even as a child, a really small child, Inbari was too brave. She remembers one occasion: Yossi, Inbar's father, was at a conference. Of course. Another conference. And Hana asked her to come away to a hotel with them on a holiday organised by her employers, to help with the children. Adjoining the lobby, behind a glass door, was a games room. The glass was so clean that it looked to Inbar as if the door wasn't there. That nothing separated her from the games. So she got up and ran – she didn't actually walk until she was older; she only ran – straight into the glass. She didn't cry from the blow, didn't shed a single tear. But a huge red bruise blossomed on her forehead almost immediately. Hana asked the hotel restaurant for ice cubes, and up in the room, held a bag of them to Inbar's forehead for quite a while, until the swelling went down. But the next day, the glass was too well cleaned again. And again, they sat in the hotel lobby in the evening. And again: Inbar. A look. A sprint. A blow.

What's going to become of you, Hana shouted at her, will you ever learn?

It's not true that she doesn't learn – Lily hastened to defend her granddaughter – she just doesn't give up!

Lily always defended her. She couldn't bear it when Hana raised her voice to her daughter and so obviously preferred Yoavi. Look at how much she eats, Hana would say, and Lily would reply: Do you want her to be all skin and bone like you? Look at the way her breasts stick out, Hana would complain. Leave her alone, Lily would reply, she has lovely breasts, why should she be ashamed of them? Inbar, for her part, continued to dare. Continued, without her mother's knowledge, to send poems to the teen magazine, *Maariv Lanoar*, in the hope that one day they'd stop rejecting them. Continued to go out with that fellow from the Air Force, even though she knew he'd break her heart. Organised the other girls in her basic training course to rebel against their commander, even though she knew she'd be punished.

It went on like that until Yoavi. And then, all at once, she buried that audacity. Something froze in her. Or matured. Or just became sadder. Anyway, she stopped racing headfirst into clear glass.

Something is going on with Inbar, Lily feels now. She's been feeling it for a few days, waiting for them to stop keeping it from her so she can start baking the honey cake.

And meanwhile . . .

She sits on her memory chair every evening. There's one chair, an ordinary one, really, a kitchen chair, and when she sits on it in the evening, facing the window at a very specific angle, and turns the fan up to the second speed, not the first or the third, and holds a glass of regular Wissotzky tea, not any of those new kinds with those ridiculous names – then the memories of that voyage come to her, as clear as the ocean waters.

Inbar

She was never good with dates, but the date the Berlin Wall fell was one she remembered very well: 9 November 1987. On that day, she was being interviewed in Tel Aviv for acceptance into a Jewish Agency youth delegation. The members of the delegation were supposed to live in the States for six months, each in a different city, and give lectures to the Jewish community there. The screening process was very stringent. After a year of tests and interviews held throughout the country, the list had shrunk to twenty teenaged boys and girls, ten of whom would be chosen by the acceptance committee. The representative of the American Jewish community had come especially to participate in the last stage of the selection process; the secretary stressed this in her phone call, and told her that the interview would be conducted – Oh no! – in English.

On the night before the interview, she consulted her mother about what to wear, and as always, they ended up arguing. Her mother didn't think she needed to dress like a mature woman because it was a delegation of teenagers. So what do you want me to do, show up in a miniskirt and a tank top? Inbar snapped. Look, her mother said, landing the first blow, as far as a miniskirt is concerned . . . you know what I think . . . I'm not sure they suit you. But I think dark jeans and a smart shirt would do the trick. Just tell me you don't want to lend me your skirt and that's that! she hit back at her mother. Have I ever lent you a piece of clothing that didn't come back stained or torn? her mother raised her voice—

Shut up, would you, I can't concentrate with you both shouting like that, Yoavi said. He was holding a guitar and trying for the thousandth time to play 'Nothing Else Matters'.

Do what you want. Her mother ended the fight with her usual zinger, which was always spoken in a tone that contradicted its meaning. And Inbar thought that what she wanted was to get the hell away from that house. Especially from her mother.

On the train to Tel Aviv, a little past Benyamina, she panicked, suddenly afraid she'd made a mistake about the day. That the interviews had actually been the day before. She rummaged around in her bag to find the invitation and opened it with trembling hands. Thursday, 9 November. Today. Yes. Yes. Yes. With half an ear, she heard someone speaking English and turned her head – sitting on the seats diagonally opposite her was a couple of older American tourists. Determined to practise her English before the interview, she took her things and went to sit across from them. The seat did not face the direction the train was travelling in, which she didn't like, but she had a goal.

So, how long have you been in Israel? she asked the moment there was silence between them.

Two weeks, the woman replied.

And how do you find my country? she went on.

Well, replied the man, who was wearing a hat with a sun visor even though it was winter.

It turned out that they weren't just ordinary tourists. They were American Jews considering immigrating to Israel.

But why? Inbar wondered.

Well, the man said again . . .

Jeffrey always says, the woman continued his sentence, that your Israel is the greatest experiment of the twentieth century. Jews with their own territory! That's something! So we thought we'd stop looking at the experiment from a distance and try to be part of it ourselves. To be honest, the woman pulled at some fluff on her woollen jumper, this visit is really a preliminary tour. We wanted mainly to see whether there are enough nudists here.

Excuse me? Inbar wasn't sure she'd heard right.

It turned out that they were members of the American Nudist Association, and it was a very important part of their lives. So before they took the big step, they wanted to find out whether they would have a community here that would accept them. And they discovered that there are two. In Haifa, near Atlit. And in Kibbutz Ga'ash. But there are very few people in each community. And the privacy at the beaches is nothing to write home about.

Actually, we're more confused now than we were before we came, the woman concluded.

The constant dilemma between change and stability, the man finally spoke. He took out a business card and handed it to her. If you ever come to Miami, you're invited to spend Shabbat with us, he said. Our children don't live at home any more . . . their rooms are empty and . . . we also welcome fully clothed guests.

If that's the case, there's a chance I might come, Inbar laughed and told them about the delegation and the last interview she was on her way to now, which unfortunately was going to be conducted in English. They encouraged her, saying that her English was absolutely fine and she had nothing to worry about; they'd spoken to her throughout as if she were a grown-up and not a young girl with shaky self-confidence. Then they asked her advice about what they should do for their last two days. See Jerusalem, she told them. Jerusalem. If I only had a week in Israel, I'd spent at least five days in Jerusalem. Even though there's no sea there? the man asked sceptically. And she said — later, she didn't understand where this had come from; maybe she'd read it somewhere? — that's just it, there really is a sea there. But not everyone notices it. It's a sea of memories. From every high point in the city, you can see that sea. Wow, the woman laughed, if you're capable of saying that there's a sea in Jerusalem and sound convincing, I'm sure you'll be accepted into that delegation, and the man took a green note out of his pocket and said, here's five dollars, buy yourself something nice. Don't be silly, Inbar refused to take the money, but the man insisted and shoved the note into the outside pocket of her bag. Before she got off the woman said, we'll keep our fingers crossed, and the man said, as if she'd already been accepted, call us when you arrive. Inbar smiled and waved the business card he'd given her earlier and, filled with hope, strode quickly all the way from the station to the Jewish Agency office in the Kirya as if there were a wind at her back.

But when she reached the floor where the meetings were being held, it turned out that they were not personal interviews, as she'd thought, but group interviews. Five candidates at a time were called in. As youth delegates, you'll be working mainly with groups, so we want to see you in this kind of setting as well, the committee chairwoman explained, and at that moment Inbar knew that her fate was sealed — groups always made her either too shy or too conspicuous; she was never able to find the middle ground and feel comfortable in it. With the speed of sound, she always developed the feeling that she was different from everyone else, that all the others had so much in common that she didn't share. And it happened there too.

The other four sitting in the room with her looked like Tel Avivians, seasoned and relaxed, speaking English as if it were their mother tongue, and they had so many interesting hobbies to talk about. When it was finally her turn – you should have volunteered to go first, she berated herself – she'd already lost all the confidence she'd built up on the train and stammered a few words about what a great Zionist she was, and about why it was important to her to be in the delegation, and suddenly she heard herself say that her hobby was tennis (she'd never even *touched* a racket, *ever*), and that one of the reasons she wanted to be in the delegation was so she could see the great women tennis players play in a real stadium and not just on TV. The committee members averted their eyes in embarrassment, and later she didn't have to wait for the page with the list of names to know that she wasn't on it. But she waited anyway. She looked up at the noticeboard and shrugged off a girl from Ramat Aviv who'd been accepted and tried to put a hand on her shoulder with infuriating condescension. Then she walked slowly to the station, the wind in her face now, and on the train sitting on the seat across from her was a man reading the paper. When he folded it so he could feast his eyes on a well-built girl soldier who'd just come into the carriage Inbar saw the main headline: BERLIN WALL FALLS.

Grandma Lily – she could only go to her in this situation – also welcomed her with the headline. Finally! she said and kissed her granddaughter's cheek. She was wearing the dress she wore for guests. Her bluish hair was combed, her eyes were lightly made up, and her pearl necklace rested on her chest. Why are you all dressed up, Grandma? Are you going out today? And Grandma Lily laughed: Going out? Where exactly? To do the twist in a nightclub? I'm all dressed up because today is a holiday. Today, finally, the war really ended, Inbar.

For her grandmother, there was only one war, World War II, the war in which she lost her entire family. The war she was saved from at the last minute. All the Israeli wars that came later, the ones she actually experienced, were provincial in her eyes: worrying, but not anxiety provoking. They required preparation, but not flight. In general, Grandma Lily was the queen of keeping things in perspective: for her, every misfortune was always compared to a more dire misfortune, thereby diminishing its severity. A leaky ceiling? There were days when we lived in a shack. A kidney transplant? What's that compared to a heart transplant. Your heart is broken? Nu, you're lucky you two are not married; otherwise you'd have to start dealing with lawyers now.

With another grandmother, all that perspective might have been annoying, but Grandma Lily knew how to do it elegantly. First, she'd show interest – why do you look so glum, Inbari? Then she'd make a cup of tea and put a slice of honey cake on a separate glass plate – so that the moisture from the tea would not stick to the cake, because wet cake is like a kiss with too much saliva – and then she'd carry the cup and the plate to the sitting room with hands that shook more with each passing year, place them on the small table in front of the sofa and say, drink it while it's hot. Look, *tsipke feuer*, my little fire bird, she'd say, it really is disappointing. I know how much you wanted to be in that delegation. But it doesn't say anything about you. It only says something about them, that they're stupid.

But I wanted to go so much, Grandma – a tear fell from her lashes and salted her tea. I can't take it with her any more, she added. And they both knew who she meant.

Nu, Inbarinke, imagine if you were accepted and your plane was hijacked by terrorists? There's a warning about that on page three of the paper. Here, look.

Grandma Lily didn't like travelling. The long, exhausting voyage to Israel 'was enough to last a lifetime'. Tell me, don't you think that the Jews have wandered more than enough? At family dinners, she would always rebuke Aunt Kati, who was a travel agent. And Aunt Kati would lower her gaze in response. Once she tried to stammer out something about the convenient working hours for a mother – and that ended badly. Ever since, she'd accepted Grandma Lily's admonishments submissively. For at least ten generations, we have to hold on to this land and not move, Grandma Lily would tell her. Ten generations at least!

When Grandpa Natan was alive they used to go to a hotel by the Dead Sea once a year, and after he died, she stopped doing that too. She tried to talk Hana and Yossi out of their family trips to Europe, and always checked to make sure that they weren't going to pass through Germany by accident. They took down all the borders there, so be careful you don't end up there by mistake! she warned them after the European Union was established. And when her daughter announced that she was going to spend her sabbatical year in Berlin, living with her new German boyfriend, and asked her to sign forms that would help her get a Polish passport, because she'd have an easier time with the academic bureaucracy—

Well! Neither honey cake, nor tea, nor sweet carrots were put out on the table. Go out for a walk, Inbar, Grandma Lily said. Your mother and I need to have words.

I'm a big girl, Grandma. Come on.

Her grandmother didn't even answer her. She just opened the door. And waited beside it till Inbar walked past her.

So she left the building and walked along the streets of the Remez neighbourhood in Haifa till she reached the youth movement camp she used to attend. It was closed, and she looked through the fence at the small building and the playground adjoining it. The broken windows, overgrown weeds and torn netting of the baskets, made it clear that there hadn't been any activity there for a long time. The sign above the door was still there, but the E had fallen, so it read VER UPWARD, instead of EVER UPWARD. Once, years ago, she'd repainted that sign with her own hands. And when Guy, the group leader, wanted to show her how to use the brush – his hand had touched hers. Accidentally. Once, she had passionately defended principles here which, unknown to her, she'd violate time and time again in the future. Once, she saw *The Blues Brothers* here, but only the first and third reels, because she fell asleep on her open sleeping bag during the second. And many times, she'd felt lonely here. Of all places. Many times, she'd felt that there was not a single person in the group who was close to her. And as she stood in front of the closed gate, the smell that filled her nostrils was the smell of loneliness. And the taste on her lips was the bitter taste of the longing to finally be understood. Not desired or admired. Understood. By one person, at least.

Soon, they'd probably sell the lot to someone who'd build an apartment block on it with a lobby and doorman, she thought, and felt a pang in her heart. Despite everything. A pang. How illusory everything is. She continued to the shopping centre, bought herself a pink grapefruit drink in a pizzeria, sat down on a bench and observed the conversation between her mother and her grandmother. She didn't *imagine* that conversation. She actually *saw* it and *heard* it in her mind, down to the smallest detail. As if she were there. It was obvious that her grandmother wouldn't begin talking straight away, she'd tidy up the sitting room, and then she'd get a wet cloth and wipe the dust off the picture of Grandpa Natan that stood on the TV – consulting him about how to act with 'his' rebellious daughter – and it was obvious that her mother, with her short fuse, would break first and say, Bruno loves me, he makes me happy, Mama, and Grandma would shake her head disdainfully and say, Heidegger loved Hannah Arendt. Then she'd add, so why can't he come to Israel if he can't live without you, and her mother would reply, it's not as simple as that, his businesses are there. Then Grandma would shout, what do I ever ask of you, I give and give and give to you my whole life, and what do I ask? and her mother would shout, you ask for an awful lot. All those years, you made us be Second Generation Holocaust, even though . . . you and Papa weren't there. Grandma would bite her lower lip and hiss, they murdered my father and three sisters, is that not enough Holocaust for you? What do you want, a number on my arm? Fine, Hana, look – she'd reach out and take the black marker that was always next to the phone, and write on her arm, 46, that was my father's age, and these are the ages of my sisters, 17, 15 and 12. Look, you have a number. Are you happy now? And Mum would freeze for a minute and look at Grandma's arm, then she'd take the marker and write a huge number 19 on her own arm, and say loudly, I want to remind you that I have my own dead, okay? But that doesn't mean I don't deserve to live! Grandma would yank the marker out of her hand, and for a few deceptive minutes there'd seem to be a pause in the battle, but then Grandma would say, you . . . you never stopped living after what happened, the only thing you stopped doing was being a mother to your daughter, and now you're asking me to help you get a Polish passport, *cholera*, and for what, so you can move even further away from your daughter, abandon her like her father did, she's still a child, Hana, she still needs you both—

And that would be too much for Mum, because the most annoying thing anyone can do in an argument is tell you the devastating truth. Between clenched teeth, she'd say that she didn't need any favours, and she'd sweep her keys and phone into her small red handbag, go out and slam the door hard behind her, so all the neighbours would hear. She'd get into her car and listen to the classical music station to calm herself, and when the announcer said, 'We've just heard the Double Concerto in A Minor by Brahms', she'd start the car, and drive around looking for her daughter, first at the youth movement camp, then in the shopping centre, because where else could she go in this sleepy neighbourhood . . . there—

A car horn roused Inbar from her reverie. Her mother pulled up at the pavement and Inbar got into the back seat. So, she asked, did you convince her? Her mother shook her head and changed gears. And when she returned her right hand to the wheel, Inbar saw the large number 19 written on her arm.

*

They're together now too. This time, on a train. To the Berlin Wall. To what remains of it. Several Germans are reading the *Bild.* Above their heads, a wallpaper of adverts for a holiday in the Bahamas – coconut trees and a turquoise sea. Where do the Bahamians go on holiday? Inbar wonders. And why can't they set up a circular arrangement? One month a year, the world can satisfy its travel lust by moving one country to the left. Her mother is reading the travel guide she has in her hand. There are brown age spots on her arms. Incredible, Inbar thinks, even her age spots are beautiful. Symmetrical. Almost artistic.

Look, her mother whispers, as if anyone could understand their Hebrew, and moves her head in the direction of an older woman with thick glasses. She's an original Easterner, she says. How do you know? Inbar asks. You can smell it, her mother says. And there's something about the way they dress. Either it's too gaudy or too faded. And their English, it's absolutely hilarious. Did you know that, after Communist rule collapsed, all the Russian teachers in the Eastern schools instantly became English teachers? So you can imagine what a disaster it is.

They get off at the Warschauer Strasse station. A long section, a very long section, of what remained of the Wall stands before them. Completely covered in graffiti. The contrast between the greyness of the Wall and the bright colours of the paintings draws Inbar closer. The Wall itself is surprisingly low. Nothing like as high as the separation wall you can see on Route 6, for example. And it has cracks – quite a number of cracks, through which you can see the other side. The Eastern side? The Western side? Inbar wasn't sure any more. This is the largest street gallery in the world! her mother says with the pride of a native, and explains that after the Wall fell, the Germans decided to leave this section and asked artists from all over the world to paint on it. They walk slowly along the length of the wall, from painting to painting. Her mother reads from the guidebook. Usually, Inbar doesn't like being read to from guidebooks, but this time it's actually interesting, because some of the paintings have non-English texts, and she wants to understand.

'The Wall must fall when the meteor of love arrives,' is written next to a painting of a large object crashing into the world. Irina Dubrovskaya, her mother says, that's the artist's name. Inbar nods. She never remembers those names later. She'd even forgotten the name of the Soviet leader shown in the next painting. Andropov? Brezhnev, her mother reads. Here he's French-kissing Erich Honecker, who was the President of East Germany when the Wall fell. And what's written next to it? Inbar asks. 'God, help me to survive this deadly love,' her mother says. Deadly love, Inbar thinks. What a perfect phrase. 'Anyone who wants the world to remain as it is doesn't want the world to remain,' says the next painting, suddenly in English. The painting after that is concealed by plastic sheeting. They're restoring it, her mother explains, refreshing the colours. And look, the next one, a truly amazing mural. Totally abstract. Rows of thimbles in warm and cold colours, straight and bent, sometimes facing each other and sometimes not, looking a bit like headstones and a bit like hand puppets, spread across a long stretch of the Wall. This painting . . . her mother begins to read, but Inbar stops her. That's not necessary, I don't want to know what's written, I just want to look at it. Let's stay here for a while. Here's a bench.

They sit down. Close to each other, because the bench is small and they have no choice. They continue to look at the painting, and now they have the feeling that the thimbles are looking back at them.

You're right, her mother says and closes the guidebook and puts it into her handbag, it really speaks for itself.

Two kids pass the Wall on skateboards, not giving them a second glance. Is the Second Generation recognisable? Inbar wonders, can you tell that someone's *parents* are from the East just by looking at them? What difference does it make, she thinks, suddenly surprised at herself. Easterner, Westerner — since when does she even care about that *selektzia*?

How happy Grandma was when this Wall fell, she says, then immediately regrets it: after all, the last mention of her grandmother on this visit led to an argument.

One of the thimbles on the wall perks its ears up in surprise. Really? her mother is also surprised, her voice free of resentment. Why does Grandma care about the Berlin Wall?

I was at her place the day it fell. She said that finally, the war was really over. She has a kind of theory that great wars continue for many years after they're over, echoing forward into the lives of the people who took part in them, and into the lives of their children and their children's children. It's like when you shout in front of a mountain, she told me. It echoes and echoes, but in the end, there's quiet. The Cold War was an echo of World War II, and now that that echo has died—

I can actually imagine her saying that, her mother says.

She was really happy, Mum. I never saw her like that. She got all dressed up and played music and danced a bit.

Danced?!

Not really danced, but moved her feet in time to the music.

One of the thimbles on the Wall moves its feet too, as if it is about to climb up and jump over to the other side, to freedom, Inbar thinks. And she also thinks that the heat is beginning to affect her. And she's thirsty.

Did you tell her you were coming here in the end? Her mother takes out a bottle of water and gives it to her.

No, Inbar admits. I told Eitan to say I wasn't in. It's only three days, you know.

So why was it suddenly so urgent for you to come? What happened? Her mother takes the bottle back. You don't have to tell me . . . only if you want to.

With surprising ease, as if she hadn't tormented herself for long weeks before this moment, Inbar begins to confess. And she stops after a few sentences and says, I have a weird feeling that those thimbles are giving me accusing looks. Let's go and sit somewhere, okay?

Lily

The permit from the Romanians was slow in coming. Stubborn rumours claimed that it was a matter of money, that the agency was trying to raise the necessary funds to bribe the clerks. Even more stubborn rumours claimed that it had to do with the threats of war coming from Germany, and no amount of bribery could help them. The train, in any case, did not move on its tracks for three days. The water ran out. The Romanians who sold drinks through the windows disappeared. Many women fainted. Lily didn't, but her throat was dry. How can you explain thirst like that to someone who can, at any time, turn on a kitchen tap and drink? How can you explain thirst like that to someone who has both a water purifier and a filtered water dispenser in his home? A desert in her throat. Lips split like the Red Sea, but no one passed through to the parched land. Temples pounding as if they wanted to be hydrated directly through the skin, not through the mouth. Mind confused.

Unreliable. Packed with coloured sand like a bottle from the Ramon Crater. Confusing faces and names. Seeing flashing purple stars. Raising dead mothers from the grave. And amidst all that, he suddenly appeared. Itzhak Pimstein. Pima. Entered their carriage, the harmonica still dangling from his neck. The Adam's apple still prominent. As if a spoon were stuck there. Don't think about a spoon. Water is cupped in a spoon. Does she want to go with him? he asks, his bald head bending towards her. His smile bending towards her. His lips bending towards her. He has something to give her. Go where? she asks weakly, where is there to go? He takes her arm and leads her to the space between the carriages. The toilet's stench. Dizziness. Just don't lean on him. Just don't lean. A random touch would arouse a desire for an intentional touch. Suddenly, he takes a small bottle of whisky from his pocket. She doesn't understand, does he want to get drunk now? And almost laughs. You're crazy, she says, and he shakes his head. It's not whisky, it's water. Water he got for her. But who asked you to do that? she says, suddenly angry, her strength suddenly restored (she'd collapse later). No one asked me, I wanted to, he said, moving the mouth of the bottle to her lips. His Adam's apple rose and fell as if he were the one drinking. The smell of the water reached her nostrils before the mouth of the bottle reached her lips. She'd never noticed that water had a smell.

No, she pushed the bottle away. And thought, this isn't right. It's not right. I have a boyfriend. My love. He'll fill my mouth with kisses when I reach him.

Wait a minute, Lily, he protested and took her arm. How did he know her name? Sand poured through her mind, filled it. She wanted to pull her arm from his grip, but didn't have the strength.

And then, at precisely that moment, there was a toot. Of the steam engine. A long toot, an indisputable signal that the train was about to move. But where to? For several seconds, neither of them could tell what direction the train would take: back to Poland or forward, to the Constanta port. For several seconds, Lily wasn't sure which she preferred. For several seconds, his eyes (blue, dammit) tried to catch hers, to engrave them on his heart.

The train began to move. Forward. Yes, forward. Joyous singing burst from all the cars. And blood began to course along the tracks of Lily's body.

Give the water to Esther, she said, disengaging her arm from Pima's grip and moving away from him. She needs it more than I do.

Inbar

What a story, her mother said.

One more small nudge at the sticky centre of my pain, Inbar thought, and it'll all come pouring out of me.

They were sitting on the riverbank on the other side of the Wall, in a café with umbrellas, where most of the customers were drinking beer. In an attempt to make the place look like a Caribbean beach, sand had been spread on the ground among the chairs. Two large palm trees with a hammock strung between them also tried to give the place an air of tranquillity. Inbar took off her shoes and buried her feet in the damp sand. The Spree flowed languidly beneath them, its water made golden by the sun's rays.

But they seemed to be surrounded by an aura of gloom.

Inbar tore open a packet of sugar and poured its contents into her cappuccino. The sugar sank slowly into the whipped milk.

Blackmail? That's what Dr Adrian told her? Her mother shook her head in disbelief.

Yes, Inbar confirmed, the woman said that she was afraid of what her son would do to himself if she told him to leave the house, and Dr Adrian said that the boy was blackmailing her. And she shouldn't go along with it. And what probably happened the next day is that she took his advice. She threw her son out of the house and changed the lock.

So how did he get in?

Through the kitchen window.

And you're absolutely sure that . . . ?

Absolutely. When they call me, they give their real names. Later, we give them false names and distort their voices, if they want us to.

And Dr Adrian . . . the producer I can understand . . . but Dr Adrian didn't . . . ?

I showed them both the article and told them that it was her. From Sunday's show. And that was her son. The producer said I was just assuming, and there was no way to actually prove it. I told him that her name was written in my records, and he said it was a common name. I told him that I understood he was glad the boy had shot his mother before he killed himself, because that way, no one could blame the programme. And he said that if I'm right, then I should also be glad that the mother is unconscious.

And what about Dr Adrian?

He said that he needed some time to digest it. And the next day, he called half an hour before the programme and said he was 'not feeling 100 per cent'. So Yizhar re-broadcast conversations from previous shows. He came back two days later. As if nothing had happened. You know how much they pay him?

Her mother nodded. A slow nod.

Inbar shuddered. So why isn't she having a go at her yet? After all, her inner mother, the one who talks to her non-stop from inside her head, has been tormenting her with whips and scorpions ever since it happened. Collaborator, her inner mother calls her. And passes judgement: you are just as responsible for what happened as they are.

No wonder you took it hard, her mother said to her now. It's totally clear . . . why.

Yes, Inbar said, took a breath, and encouraged, continued: I don't know if I can keep working there. I mean, it's been five weeks since then, and it's as if we're back to normal, but—

Leave, her mother said. There's no reason for you to keep working in a place like that.

But it's a great job, Mum.

There'll be other jobs, Inbari. You're talented. And hard working. There'll be other jobs.

You think so?

I know so.

But my inner mother tells me something else, Inbar wanted to say. My inner mother claims that I have to be a hard worker because talented, I'm not. And that I have to lose weight because no eligible man would want me the way I am. And that there's no way my dream of writing will ever—

Her mother put her hand on hers (her mother! put her hand on hers!). A waiter approached, obviously concerned, and asked if they wanted anything else. They didn't say yes and they didn't say no. A strong wind churned ocean waves in the river. The waiter walked away in silence.

You know, Inbar said in a breaking voice what she still hadn't said to another living soul, I . . . dream about that boy almost every night. I always try to save him in the dreams. But I don't. I don't manage to save him, Mum.

Her mother didn't say anything, She just squeezed her hand gently.

The last time she'd touched her that way was on the first night after the shiva. The plastic chairs and the trays of pastries were already gone from the sitting room, the photo albums had been returned to their shelves, and the samovar to the kitchen. The cups had been washed sloppily, leaving small coffee stains on every one of them, and they'd all gone to their rooms. Her parents were still sleeping in their double bed. Grandma Lily slept on a single bed in the study. And she, who hadn't dared to go down to her submarine, which had become Yoavi's bunker, spread a sheet on the living room sofa. And couldn't fall asleep.

The sofa was too narrow to contain her, and she was too narrow to contain her sorrow. At three in the morning, she gave up trying to fall asleep on her stomach, on her back, with a pillow, without a pillow, and turned on the TV and watched a DVD, *The Best of The Simpsons*. Yoavi's favourite show. Even as a teenager, he had posters of Bart, Lisa, Homer and Marge on the walls. And even though the posters came down at a certain stage, he remained a fan. The older I get, he explained more than once, the more I realise how brilliant that show is. Brilliant — another one of his words that no one would ever say the way he did. Barely able to hold back a wave of pain, she pressed Play. A few seconds later she heard the scuffle of slippers approaching and reached out for the remote to turn off the DVD, but her mother's voice said: Don't turn it off. The white clouds heralding the beginning of an episode scattered to the sides, and her mother sat down close to her and put a hand on hers. They watched six episodes back-to-back, and cried the entire time. At dawn, her mother stood up and said, Yoavi was right, that is really a very entertaining show. And went to her room. Inbar turned off the TV and then closed the shutters and drew the curtains so all that damned light would stop coming in. There was something offensive about a new day dawning, despite everything.

In Berlin, the day was about to end, and her mother still hadn't taken her hand off hers (her mother! hadn't taken her hand off hers!) They sat like that for a long while, in silence.

A man at the next table was writing a letter, and every few minutes, he raised his glance from the pages and looked at the river. A bee circled her mother's glass of juice, drawn to the liquid, and banged into the sides of the glass at risk of drowning, and then, at the very last moment, took off, saved.

Neither of them said the word 'Yoavi', but he was so very present there. As if at some point in their conversation he'd opened the door of the café and come over to them with his swaying gait, had run a hand through his long hair – she refused to remember his clipped, army haircut – pulled out a chair without permission and sat down next to them, his legs spread to the sides. Hi, Mum, she could almost hear him say. What's happening, Sis?

Zusammen oder getrennt? The waiter, standing at their table with his order pad in his hand, finally put an end to their silence.

*

Thanks to the Yiddish that Grandma Lily had sometimes spoken with Grandpa Natan, she understood that, before giving them the bill, he was trying to find out whether she and her mother were 'together or separate'.

*

When she got back to the studio, she called Eitan. He answered after too many – to her taste – rings, but immediately said, 'Hey beautiful, I'm so happy you called.'

I wanted to hear your voice, she said.

Here's my voice, he said.

Tell me something nice, she said, and with the hand that wasn't holding the phone, she stroked her inner thigh.

Something nice? he hesitated. And that delay there always

is during an international call only lengthened and underscored his hesitation. Today . . . Today, I realised that I've been turning on more and more lights in the house because without you, everything here is darker.

Wow, she said in amazement, and from beneath the amazement still came the whisper of that secret prosecutor, who had claimed from their first meeting that he wasn't—

Hey, she said, I think it might be worth my while to stay here a bit longer. You're getting more poetic by the day!

How's it going with your mother? he asked.

You know, you have a beautiful voice, she said.

Thanks, he said matter-of-factly, missing the opportunity (once, when he was in Italy at one of his exhibitions, she tried to seduce him into telephone sex, but he burst out laughing in the middle, ruining it, and said that he was sorry, his imagination wasn't as highly developed as hers, but he promised he'd do whatever she wanted him to do to her when he got back. Even in the terminal car park, if she wanted).

We actually had a good day today, my mum and I, she said. We had coffee and I told her about what happened on the programme, and she was really good about it. Naturally, on the way back here, she pissed me off, because she started saying that it was no accident that things like that happened. That Israeli society is being stripped of all its values. Worshipping the golden calf. You know those speeches of hers. And they're even more annoying when she gives them in Berlin. But I kept a lid on it. I didn't scream at her. I'm doing what you told me to do, giving her a chance.

Good, he said. How much more time do you have left together? A day? If you manage to get through it without a blow-up, then you're ahead of the game, aren't you?

Yes, we're ahead of the game, she said, holding back the angry words she really wanted to say: This is no game, it's my life. Tell me . . . Tani, she slowly said into the phone the words she'd really wanted to say throughout the conversation, would it be terrible if I decided not to go back to the programme?

What do you mean, not go back, he asked. I don't get it.

If I left, she said.

Li-s-ten, he said. I don't know. It's a terrific job. That you're really good at. I wouldn't give it up so easily.

Maybe you're right, she said. You're probably right. She was so anxious for him to just say, ya'allah, go for it, do what makes you happy. But why are you even asking him? — a totally different, rebellious voice spoke in her mind — after all, it's not a joint decision, it's your decision, your life. And *you* have to choose how to live it.

When they'd finished talking, she put the phone down on the heavy table next to the bed. First she stared at the small, pretty light fitting, and then her gaze dropped and began to wander over the furniture. A no-nonsense desk. A small bookcase with books whose faded spines did nothing to tempt you to take them out and read them. A wardrobe with heavy doors. It was a room that cried out to have colourful pictures hung on its walls to offset the gloom, but instead they were adorned with portraits of grim-looking people. Who were those people? And what was she doing here with them? And how was it that every attempt she made to belong ended with her feeling exiled? She closed her eyes, pulled the duvet up over her waist and put a finger under the elastic of her pants, yearning for a brief surge of pleasure to drive away the intense loneliness that was suddenly choking her.

Her fantasies had permanent visitors. Ofer, Eitan's loyal best friend from Yokneam, with whom nothing had ever happened, except for one kiss on the cheek that missed and touched the corner of her lips. A waiter in the café near their apartment who always looked at her with lust in his eyes. And a colleague of her father's, who once gave her a lift from Haifa to Tel Aviv and didn't try anything or say anything, but even so, just before the Ga'ash exit, she was positive he'd pull off the motorway on to a dirt road, and wasn't sure whether she'd scream for help or try to enjoy it, but suddenly—

Suddenly, a new visitor burst into the space of her private lust. The Mossad agent from the airport. The man with the photos on the table. Weird, she thought during the first few seconds of his appearance; after all, she'd already forgotten him – and immediately got busy developing a new plot.

At Carni's hen party – which depressed her because that was when she found out that Carni was four months pregnant, making her the only not-yet girl in the room, and that made her feel like she'd come last in a race – they played a version of poker in which every loser had to describe her sexual fantasy, and that's when she realised that she was the only one whose fantasies had plots. Girls who had once been her closest friends, before they started dropping babies, laughed at her as she went on and on, and they complained: t-o-o l-o-ng, where's Brad Pitt? But it never worked that way with her. She had to believe the fantasy in order to get satisfaction from it. Her protagonists were real people, people she knew, and she had to find a convincing reason for her encounter with them, and a place, of course.

So where would she meet her Mossad agent? In her imagination, she led them both to a small bar in the Berlin airport, where Nick Cave's 'Into My Arms' was playing in the background. Their flight was delayed because of the heavy fog over the city, and after a clever dialogue, during which he touched her arm once, as if by accident, and her hair (which, in the fantasy, was long) brushed his face as if by mistake, they went to a VIP room that had been reserved for him. At first, the images changed slowly: the Mossad agent with the sad shoulders was gentle, very gentle with her on the purple sofa in the VIP room, in contrast to what she would have expected from a professional killer, and took his time simply stroking her face with his hands, looking at her as if she were the most beautiful thing in the world. Then he slowly reached down to her neck and her shoulders, and only after she'd pressed her nails into his back and pulled him close, between her legs, did he kiss her in the small delta between the arteries of her neck, and from there began to descend with kisses and bites, stopping slightly below her belly button. Deliberately. To drive her crazy.

*

The boy lay on the railway tracks. He resembled the newspaper photo, but he had Yoavi's green eyes. When she noticed him from the small hill of cyclamens where she was strolling, she began to run towards him, careful not to tread on the cyclamens, because the cyclamen is a protected flower. She ran and ran and slid – at one point, she seemed to be skiing – veering to the right and to the left to avoid stepping on the cyclamens, which were suddenly as tall as flagpoles. When she reached the tracks, the boy was still lying there. She put her hand on the track and felt the increasing vibration. The train is coming, she told him. But he didn't move. She looked at the tunnel, terrified, and tried to grab his arm and pull him away from there. He was as heavy as a boulder, and she couldn't move him even a millimetre. She heard the long, unequivocal blast of the train engine coming from the tunnel. Tomato soup in winter, she said to him. But he didn't move. Beautiful Hebrew words, a good conversation with a friend, bike riding! she continued, already despairing. The boy kept lying there. His Yoavi eyes were open to the sky. And he didn't seem to be listening to her any more. But she still kept trying, pleading, the Meshushim Pool in the Golan, the dolphin reef in Eilat at sunset, The Simpsons, your mother, your sister – the train came out of the tunnel towards them, and then she lay down beside him on the tracks. Maybe that would shake him up enough.

A moment before the train ran over them both, she woke

up. The initial sense of relief — while it was still spreading through her body — turned into bitter disappointment.

She had believed that after she told her mother the whole story the nightmares would end. She took out her journal and wrote down all the details she could remember of the dream, and also wrote: *Pouring out your heart is sometimes just pouring out your heart. And the returns it brings are short term.*

She threw off the duvet and shivered slightly. July, and the air here is cool. Eitan is probably showering now, she thought. Washing away the sweat of the night. How he sweats in the summer! Shame they can't desalinate sweat. From his body alone, they could irrigate the entire city of Ramat Gan. Shame you can't live half a year here and half a year there. Six months in the Middle East and six months in enlightened Europe. Forget there was a Holocaust. Forget we were driven out of this continent by the storm troopers' whips. But really, why not? — she took two tops out of the wardrobe and tried to decide between them — sixty years have passed, Grandma Lily, and maybe the flood waters have subsided and we're allowed to be like birds migrating to a more comfortable place every few months.

*

So where would you like to go on your last day? her mother asked after she'd gone up to the apartment and they were drinking their morning coffee. Two tourist guidebooks and a huge map were already spread on the table.

Let's just wander. With no specific plan, she said. And she was suddenly filled with sorrow that this was her last day. It was too soon for her. She still felt that invisible bars were keeping her from getting to the heart of the questions that had brought her here.

(She was once walking through Central Carmel with her

father, and a one lira coin fell out of her hand and through the grate of an air vent is the street, and no matter how much she wanted it back or how much she stamped her foot, there was no way to retrieve it — the bars were very close together and the hole was so deep that even her father's long, omnipotent hand couldn't reach it.)

What do you mean, without a plan? her mother said, taken aback.

Let's take the S-Bahn and get off wherever. Maybe we'll rent bikes.

But . . . Inbari . . . That way you won't . . . I mean . . . There are still so many things we haven't seen . . . Look — her mother continued to run one of her long, manicured nails along the map — we can start at the Jewish Museum, go on to the Broniatowski Monument, and then to platform 17. After all, you can't be in Berlin without going to platform 17. The transports to the camps left from there.

Like that famous Israeli comedy sketch, Inbar thought. Three memorial sites for the price of one.

So what do you think? her mother asked, her finger still on the map.

I think that today we shouldn't take the guidebook with us, Inbar said. And began to fold up the map. I think that I want us to rent bikes today, and except for that, we shouldn't decide on anything in advance. Okay?

*

They almost made it. Only two more hours to spend together in the city. And then the train journey home. Shower. Pack. And drive to the airport.

The spontaneous bike ride went off without a hitch. They even accidentally ended up at a less well known memorial site. A schoolteacher from the Bavarian quarter, which had once been a Jewish neighbourhood – her mother told her – had initiated a project in which all the school children in the area adopted a Jewish family that had lived there in the past and learned about it in depth. At the end of the school year, each child wrote on a brick, 'I think about the Hartmann family' or 'I think about the Schwartz family', and then placed the brick in the playground.

They stood in front of the small, heartbreaking wall for quite a few very Jewish moments, and then pedalled, more slowly, to a street lined with ice cream parlours.

If only there hadn't been a children's clothes shop tucked in among the ice cream parlours. If only her mother hadn't insisted that they stop and get off their bikes in front of the shop window. If only—

Bullshit, Inbar knew in her heart, the ugly fight between them had begun the minute she landed. There was no way they could be together without an ugly fight. For them, the ugly fight was the sure, familiar way to go.

Look – how sweet! her mother said. And pointed to a pair of tiny, pink dungarees.

Not relevant – Inbar shot the words at her. And continued walking.

They have wonderful things for children here, and the prices are much lower than in Israel, she said, and remained where she was.

I'm glad to hear it. Can we get going now? Inbar put her foot on the pedal.

In the end, it really won't be relevant, her mother said, refusing to move from the shop window. In the end, you'll want to have children – but you won't be able to.

And maybe I won't want to? She felt her foot begin to tremble on the pedal, that's how angry she was. Who says I have to? Is there some law about it?

It's a natural urge in most women, her mother said. And at

that moment, as if to reinforce her words, two women with buggies went into the shop and the sound of music from a mobile momentarily drifted over to them, then stopped when the door closed again.

That really kills me, Hana, Inbar said – she deliberately used her name the way she used to during her great rebellion when she was sixteen, which culminated in her flight to Eilat – it kills me that, even with that whole doctorate of yours, you can still be so primitive sometimes. Half the women in Europe don't have children. Are you going to tell me that they're all doing something unnatural?

First of all, it's not half, her mother said (oh that academic precision! Inbar thought, the coil of her mind growing red hot; even at the most painful moments, she has to be exact about her research data!) and anyway, all I'm saying is that you need to examine your real reasons for not wanting children.

Why can't you just respect it and back off?! Now Inbar's entire body tensed, not just her legs, and she didn't care, maybe she was even glad, that a man in a suit talking on a phone as he walked turned to look at them.

Speak quietly, Inbar. Have some respect for me too.

I don't want to! she continued shouting – now the shouting didn't come from her frustration and anger but from her desire to embarrass her mother – why does Dad always accept my choices and you always criticise them? Why?

Oh yes, your father, he's sacred, her mother muttered.

That muttering of hers, Inbar thought. There's nothing more infuriating. As if she's talking to herself, but not really.

Dad isn't sacred, but at least he loves me, she said.

Yes, he loves you so much that he hasn't made an effort to see you for two years.

You know what, Hana? Even if I do have a baby, I won't let you see it. So you won't be able to destroy its self-confidence the way you destroyed mine. With those comments of yours.

But Inbari, all I ever wanted . . . all I ever wanted was for you . . .

I'm going, she interrupted her mother and bore down on the pedal. You can keep looking at those baby clothes if it makes you feel good. We'll meet at the station in an hour.

*

Raus, Inbar, *raus*, a beautiful day in Berlin, and she's riding a bike, escaping, coasting past parks and rivers, obeying road signs, crossing bridges, the outer scenery passing with the speed of her pedalling, the inner scenery moving more quickly, first blind rage at her mother, linked to a childhood memory: Saturday morning, everyone's going to the beach, and at six years old, she's already waving the flag of separatism, doesn't want to go with them, wants to stay at home. Absolutely not, her mother says, a girl your age, at home on her own, and though her father tries to smooth things over – but Hana, Inbari's a very responsible child – her mother stands firm: don't be silly, what if there's a burglary? And she makes Inbar go with them to the beach, where Inbar tries to get lost on purpose to teach them a lesson, taking refuge under another family's umbrella, very far from them, and pretends to be building a sandcastle, but after a few minutes she panics and when she tries to get back to them, can't see them, suddenly they've disappeared into all the naked chests and sun cream smell and slaps of the bats and balls. She wanders among the umbrellas and towels spread like carpets, who do you belong to, little girl? and her feet burn in the blazing sand, and her eyes sting from the sweat that's dripping into them, and there's no sign of them, no sign, no sign, until finally her name is called over the loudspeaker, and her father stands waiting for her at the lifeguards' station, his pot belly, still small then, protruding over old-fashioned swimming trunks, and his strong arms swing her up into the air and he runs with her straight into the water. Where are you now, Daddy – she turns her bike into a small park – why don't you call me to the lifeguards' station now? Look at what happens when you're not around, there's no one here to step between her and me, no one to make peace between us after we argue and explain us to each other. Maybe that's a good thing, her father answers in her mind, this way, you'll both learn to manage without me. But we don't manage, Daddy, she answers him, and pedals faster, I don't manage without you, and how long are you planning to stay there, in Australia? Isn't four years enough? Yes, you explained that you had to start again, that it was either that or end it all, that Vivian and Reuven saved you, and yes, you wrote me the most beautiful love letters I've ever had from anyone, and it suddenly occurred to me that maybe the urge to write comes from you, not her, maybe it's *your* secret wish that I want to make come true. You ended every letter with 'I believe in you, my little girl', and you also paid half our rent this year, when I mentioned that Eitan and I were having money problems – but Daddy, if you came to visit, you'd see that I'm not sure about him, that my hidden prosecutor is constantly making speeches in my ear, but no, you can't come to visit because you have a new family and a new son who needs you more than I do, and you're still angry with everyone, and I understand, Daddy, I totally understand that it's easier to be angry than to be sad, but the bottom line is that you left me alone, and now I'm imprisoned in my life, my memories are the bars and my guilt is the jailer, and I don't know how to escape. Maybe I'll just keep riding this bike for ever, like in Sivan Shavit's song, she's another great singer you'd know about if you weren't stuck with your '60s musical taste, maybe I'll just keep riding, out of this park, which looks like the perfect place to assemble Jews before transporting them to the camps, and slice through summer puddles with my front wheel, all the way to Vienna, to Paris, to Ethan Hawke, to anywhere. What do you think, Daddy?

*

So, were you really on the production team for *Angels in the Skies of Berlin*? she asks Bruno on the way to the airport. More than she wants to know the answer, she wants to break the tense silence that has been filling the car from the moment they set off.

Is that what they called the film in Israel? He gives her a quick glance through the rearview mirror.

Yeah. In German that isn't . . . ?

The Sky over Berlin originally, *Wings of Desire* in English, he explains.

Our title is the nicest, Inbar thinks. But she doesn't say it, to avoid sounding provincial.

Yes, I took part in the production of the movie, Bruno says. And of the sequel, by the way.

Sequel? Inbar says in surprise. I didn't know there was one.

Oh, certainly, Bruno straightens up slightly in his seat. It's called, *So Close, So Far*. But you're not the only one who's never heard of it. The movie was a flop, compared to the first.

Yes, sequels are always a problem. Especially when the first one is so good.

Oh no, Bruno says. In this case, the second movie was better than the first, in my opinion.

They stop at a light. Men who look like Turkish workers are drilling on the nearby pavement. Her mother remains silent. Inbar wants to reach out and touch her shoulder, but doesn't dare.

So what was the problem? she asks. As long as she keeps talking, she won't cry.

I think that . . . the second movie is more sombre. Casiel,

the second angel, comes down to earth. He becomes an alcoholic and goes to prison, where he gets into trouble with criminals. It's a bleak movie. And people prefer art to smooth the rough edges of life.

Inbar nods. It seems that this Bruno isn't such a loser. How like her to discover this only on the way to the airport. For the few days she's been here, she hasn't really taken an interest in him. Or in her mother, really. She never even asked her how her doctorate was going, or the Hebrew course she'd started teaching this year at the university. And now it's too late.

Her gaze moves to the window again. Weird. She usually knows very quickly whether or not she likes a particular city. Haifa — no. Tel Aviv — yes. Madrid — no. But she still hasn't decided about Berlin. Maybe because its past is constantly humming, like a subway, beneath the present. And maybe because the city itself is still . . . unsure about itself. No longer divided, but still not united. No longer in the East, but not completely in the West either. A city that is coming together. Creating itself from day to day. Ruins among the buildings. Construction cranes in the clouds. A city on the way to somewhere. Not there yet. Wait — she wonders — was there a city like this one in Calvino's *Invisible Cities*? Doomed to be a connection for ever?

Her mother must know.

Her mother and Bruno are now discussing which road will have less traffic at this hour. Their voices are quiet, pleasant, warm. Her parents always fought when they were driving, each trying to impose his opinion on the other. Sometimes, she and Yoavi would start fighting just to put a stop to their parents' argument before it got out of hand. No, she tells Grandma Lily in her mind, she's not with a German for his money. She loves him. They're really good together. For the first time since Yoavi, there's light in her mother's eyes. Still dim, but light. A flash of envy shoots through Inbar. She wants that kind of light in her eyes too. Or another kind of light. As long as something finally lights up in her. Bruno glances at her through the mirror again. His glance is watery, sliding away quickly. So different from her father's intense, penetrating gaze that might have been frightening if it hadn't always been accompanied by his amused smile.

So what do you think of Berlin? Bruno asks, turning off on to a road with a sign above it showing a picture of a plane.

She can feel her mother tense expectantly in her seat.

I wasn't here long enough to reach any conclusions, Inbar says. Seems like I'll have to come back.

You're always welcome, Bruno says. And next time, I'll see to it that you don't find Hans in your bed.

She and her mother laugh at the same instant. In the same way. Suddenly, she's very aware of that.

The car pulls up at the drop-off and they all get out. Her bottom still hurts from the rapid, frantic bike ride, and she tries to relax the muscles a bit. Bruno takes her bag out of the boot and throws it on to a trolley. Then he shakes her hand formally and gets back into the car, giving them space for their farewells.

I'm sorry about . . . this morning . . . her mother says. I shouldn't have . . .

No, I'm sorry, she says. You tried so hard the whole time. And I . . . I just . . . I haven't been feeling great lately. And I came here to find out why. I mean, also to be with you . . . But also to try and understand myself . . . and I haven't really managed to do that. I mean, I have, but maybe I'm afraid to admit it. And all this . . . this confusion . . . spilled over on to you in the end. And you're the last person who deserves it.

What do you mean, the last person who deserves it? I'm your mother. That's a mother's job, isn't it? To absorb and contain. It's just a shame that I was never really . . . good at it.

But you're progressing! Inbar says, and they both smile at the memory of the story of Grandma Lily, who one day looked at her daughter Hana's school report and wondered: 'Next to every subject, it says "progressing". May I ask exactly where you're progressing to, little girl?'

Her mother once had the most beautiful laugh in the world, Inbar thinks and looks at her. Wrinkles would flare out from the corners of her eyes like fireworks. Her mother once had the most beautiful hair in the world. On family trips, Inbar used to sit in the back and stroke it through the space between the two front seats.

Now the wrinkles have turned into furrows. And the laughter is etching them into her face. And that hair is diluted by white. But the way she stands, her posture, is still that of a woman who knows she's beautiful.

She leans over to her and they hug, a longer hug than usual. And shorter than she needs.

*

After going through security, Inbar went to sit in a small bar. And waited for her Mossad agent. Waited for him to come, like in her fantasy, to save her from herself straight to the purple sofa in the VIP room. Meanwhile, she drank. One pineapple cocktail after another. And looked at the fake flames on the large plasma screen in a corner of the bar. After her fifth glass, the barman hinted gently that because of the sweetness of the pineapple, people don't always notice, but those cocktails are very strong. *Zuper!* she said in an exaggerated German accent. And ordered another one.

The bar overlooked the airport, and she saw an Air Jamaica plane moving slowly along the width of the picture in the window frame. The plane was painted in happy colours. Pothead colours, she said out loud to herself. Look, she drew the barman's attention to it, aeroplane of junkies, she said in English. But the barman followed the movement of her finger, puzzled, and went back to what he was doing. Where are the barmen of the good old days that I could talk to? she thought. If this barman were a bit more attentive to her, she'd tell him — what would she tell him? That she isn't sure she wants to go home. That there's nothing waiting for her in Israel. In fact, that she's afraid that when she gets back, gravitational pull will make her fall back into a job she can't do any more without feeling corrupt, and to a house empty of excitement. I don't miss my boyfriend enough, she'd tell the barman, and he'd nod his head in understanding. And then, what would happen? Pouring out your heart is just pouring out your heart. Where had she read that sentence? Ah yes, she's the one who wrote it. In her journal. Writing in a journal is sometimes just writing in a journal.

An announcement called passengers on the Lufthansa flight to Tel Aviv to proceed to the departure gate. She didn't move. Let them call my name — she thought, and ordered another drink — I want to hear my Jewish name reverberate in the air of Berlin airport. Ten minutes later, it happened: Miss Benbenisti. Miss Benbenisti. Please go immediately to the lifeguards' station. She knew that the Mossad agent wouldn't be coming today. She knew that she should get down off her barstool. But couldn't. Her limbs were leaden and her head was spinning. Last call for Miss Benbenisti, the loudspeaker boomed, last call for Miss Benbenisti—

And the realisation suddenly penetrated her alcoholic haze: it was right. The announcement was right. This was her last call before she went back to the treadmill of work, home, work, home, a quick fuck in the middle of the week, a more earnest one on Friday morning, which would probably get her pregnant, and she'd be happy, not because of the baby, but because it would be her ejector seat from the radio and everyone's nagging. And nine months later she'd give birth, and then that indefatigable fatigue and distraction she saw in her girlfriends, and the endless talk about wanting to open her own business — a children's clothing shop, or maybe a gymboree – talk that would never go beyond her and the other mothers in the playground, where she'd lift her child on to the slide over and over again in a sort of mind-numbing ritual, occasionally broken by the intense urge to break a vase or stick a pin into the pad of her finger and watch the blood flow, or let go of the buggy with the screaming baby in it a minute before the steep drop on the way home.

Quite a while later, she ordered a large espresso, downed it, went to the Lufthansa desk, shook off the alcoholic haze and explained to the staff that she'd fallen asleep and missed her flight, and now she wanted to exchange her ticket for a ticket to a different destination. The next flight to Tel Aviv isn't until tomorrow, the woman said, and we're sorry, but you'll only be credited for a third of the original price of the ticket. I don't want Tel Aviv, she explained again. I want to fly out on your next flight, to wherever it's going. Whatever the price. But isn't your suitcase already on the plane? I don't have a suitcase, just this, Inbar said, and pointed to her bag. Okay, the woman said slowly, inspecting her with the wary eyes of an admissions nurse in a mental hospital, our next flight is to Teheran. We have a few empty seats on it. And the one after that? Inbar asked. Peru, the clerk replied.

Lily

Peru, the Mossad representative briefed them on the pier – because back then, the Mossad was for aliyah, not espionage – if anyone asks you where you're going for, tell them that the ship is sailing to Peru. He gestured with his head in the direction of the flag.

Even in the dim moonlight, Lily could make out the red-and-white flag on the mast and the name of the ship: *Futuro*.

Now — the group leader said — I want you all to take out your passports.

Lily had known that the moment would come. After all, they'd been told they'd have to give up their old citizenship if they wanted to be absorbed into Eretz Yisrael. As long as you have a Polish passport, they can return you to Poland, they'd explained.

Nonetheless, her hands refused to give it up, and her fingers slid over the picture on the first page: a young girl who still didn't know what danger was, smiled into the camera. One Saturday, in central Warsaw. The wind had blown a single strand of hair across her cheek, but the photographer said that it was a very modern look and there was no need to take another picture. Her father was glad because he didn't want to pay any more than he already had.

Several months after the picture was taken, she met Natan. How easily you can see on a woman's face whether or not she has already known a man, Lily thought. She closed her passport and reluctantly handed it to the fellow who was collecting them from her group.

Then all those who had collected the passports took several steps forward, and at a prearranged signal, threw them into the water. They heard the quick slaps of leather hitting water, then silence. No one cheered. No one began dancing a joyous hora. They weren't in the mood and they didn't have the time. The group leaders, perhaps to keep final regrets from floating to the surface, hurried them all on to the ship. Each person received a piece of paper with his section and shelf numbers. Lily thought it was nice that she'd have a shelf for the books she'd brought. But when they went down into the hold, it turned out that shelves were really boards on which they would sleep — three tiers of boards filled the space between the deck and the ceiling in the sleeping quarters. Lily put her bags on one of the boards at the bottom and looked around. She breathed in the air, which smelled of bags being opened, shoes being removed and hats being taken off sweaty hair—

And immediately wanted to run out of there. To go up. To break out. To escape. But the instructions were to stay in the hold of the ship until it was a safe distance from the Romanian coast. Only those who fainted were taken up to the deck, and Lily had never been the swooning type. (On her fourth date with Natan, when she'd begun to fear that he wouldn't work up the courage to touch her this time either, she decided to take things into her own hands and staged a minor collapse in a public park, leaning on his arm for support and complaining weakly of a sudden attack of *halushes*, nausea. It worked: at the end of that date, he asked permission to kiss her. But later on in their relationship, when they'd begun speaking less, he told her that he'd known she was pretending then. In the park. It just isn't like you to faint, he'd laughed.)

Only much later were the non-fainters allowed to go up on deck. The queue of people waiting to climb the stairs was long, and she decided to give up on it. Mild seasickness churned inside her and something in her body pulled her towards sleep. But then Esther came to her bed and shook her shoulder gently. Come with me, she said. I don't want to be alone there.

Most of the illegal immigrants were gathered in the prow of the ship. The klezmorim, led by Pima, were there too, playing *Eine Kleine Nachtmusik*. They heard a mishmash of languages. Yiddish and Polish of course, but many other, unfamiliar languages as well. Some people were dancing between the ropes on the deck. Come on, Esther pulled her in another direction, all this cheerfulness is not for us. Lily followed her. After Pima had offered her stolen water on the train and she'd been on the brink, she thought it would be better, in every way, to keep her distance from him.

She and Esther rested their forearms on the railing and looked out into the night. The lights of the port of Constanța were already quite distant. Like the glittering of small, nameless stars. They stood like that for a long while, swallowing the salt air, getting slightly wet from stray drops and listening to the sound of the waves beating gently, as if in a languid dream, against the sides of the ship, and Lily thought how rare it was to enjoy such a comfortable, unforced silence with another person after such a brief acquaintance.

When the last of the glittering had faded, Esther raised her hand and waved goodbye to the darkness. A small wave, not the dramatic gesture of a stage actress. A wave in which the hand remains close to the heart.

Lily did the same. And for a deceptive moment felt as if the deck were stationary and it was her previous life that was sailing onward, away from her.

Inbar

Their plane is circling the airport in Lima, Peru. Due to the weather, we don't have clearance to land, the pilot explained, and announced that there would be a fifteen-minute delay. Then twenty minutes. Then he stopped announcing. Maybe it's like the legend of the Flying Dutchman, Inbar thinks. Our pilot is cursed, we're going to stay in the clouds for ever and ever, and we'll never touch solid ground, never land.

Even though the safety belt sign is on, which means that

you have to stay in your seat, two men are standing in the aisle. Israelis, of course. Their chutzpah and the Velcro on their watches give them away. One of them looks familiar. Maybe a friend of Yoavi's? He senses that she's staring at him and returns an inquiring glance. No, not a friend of Yoavi's, she decides. Even though the age is right. If Yoavi were alive, he'd already be out of the army and heading off on a trip. A long trip. Not like his sister, who made do with three weeks in Europe. He'd do some serious travelling. With his guitar. Maybe even pay for it all by busking. There are people who need to have the order of things changed for them, she thinks. First they should do their post-army travelling, and then their military service. If he'd gone travelling − she knows that the sweetness of 'if' thoughts is deceptive, but all this circling in the air has weakened her ability to resist them − if he'd gone travelling, she believes, he would have grown stronger. Would have learned to believe in himself. To close the gap between what he felt and what he showed the world.

On the Saturday before the disastrous news − it's incredible that she hasn't thought about this for so long − she didn't go back to Haifa because at the end of the week Professor Hoffman took her to their corner at the end of the corridor in the Institute for Islamic Studies, now closed by budget cuts, kissed her on the mouth and grabbed her bottom, and said, good God, do you know that I'm in love with you? And added that he thought he could escape for a few hours on Saturday morning − he always used the word 'escape', as if he lived in a prison and not in a refurbished penthouse in luxurious north Tel Aviv − and she called her parents to tell them that she wouldn't be home for Friday night dinner because she was loaded with work, and her mother said, but Yoavi's coming home! And she − if only we could click Undo for things we say − said sarcastically, so we all have to jump to attention and salute? Her mother sighed the sigh of despair she reserved for her and, as usual, sent her father to try and persuade her, and, as usual, he said the right thing in his soft voice, that they missed her too and wanted to see her very much, and if it would help, he was ready to drive her back to Tel Aviv after dinner. She almost told him about Professor Hoffman, but swallowed the story as if it were saliva, because she knew that the minute she told him, it would be over. And not only that. He'd go to Hoffman's home and make a scene in front of his wife and kids, the way he did when she was at school and made a comment about a rough kid from the wrong side of the tracks who waited for her in the pizzeria after her youth movement meetings and hassled her. He asked, what do you mean, hassle? She got a bit carried away with her description, and on Tuesday he showed up at the pizzeria and asked her, who? Already she regretted the whole business, but he wouldn't drop it till she pointed out the boy. Her father went over and told him to stand up and come outside with him. She had no idea what he said or did to him outside, but that boy never showed his face in the pizzeria again.

No, she didn't want Professor Hoffman out of her life, even though the first time he asked her to see him after class and looked at her lips while she was speaking she knew it would end badly, but she still walked headfirst into the glass, just so she would finally feel something. She slept with him in his office at the university, in his car, in an adulterers' cheap B&B, and in her apartment, when her room-mate was off visiting her family in Ashkelon, and came like she'd never come before in her life. She dug her nails into his back to leave some kind of mark on him, and they had discussions on literature and morality, from which she learned a great deal. She stroked the white hair on his chest, and became addicted to the pain she felt while waiting for the next time, and didn't want it to stop, not yet, she still needed to suffer a little.

Thanks for the offer, Dad. But I don't think it'll work out this time. Tell Yoavi that I love him, she said on that Friday morning, and on Saturday she waited and waited, but Hoffman didn't come. It wasn't until five in the afternoon that he sent her a text message, *couldn't manage it*. His academic articles were long and full of endless, Yaakov Shabtai sentences that began on one page and ended on another, but his text messages were always insanely short. For revenge, she called the guy from Introduction to Psychology who'd sort of come on to her a few weeks earlier, and arranged to go to the cinema with him the next day, even though she knew that nothing would come of it, just as nothing had come of all the dates she'd had since Hoffman began to chip away at her heart.

In the end, she never made it to the cinema because half an hour before she was supposed to leave, the phone call from Haifa came.

Of course she was thunderstruck. Of course, like everyone else, she immediately accepted the accident version of events, but when versions of a different sort began to emerge from under the army camouflage, she wasn't as surprised as she would have liked, because on the Friday before last she had gone to Haifa, and she had seen Yoavi. When she came in, he was just waking up from his long soldier's sleep, and when she hugged him, he still smelled of sleep, his smell of sleep, which she knew so well from the time they'd shared a room. Sis, you look fantastic! he said, examining her from head to toe. Did you lose weight or something? Yes, she admitted. I haven't had much of an appetite lately. What about you? How's it going in the Israel Defense Forces? Shit, he said in a tone that clearly discouraged further discussion. Shit? she smiled to herself. Who would've believed that this mummy's boy would talk that way. Good at maths. Good at literature. Good at sports. Good at music. Never really outstanding, but always good. And sensitive to others. Sometimes too much so. Sometimes he'd torment himself for weeks about some silly little thing. Sometimes he didn't sleep all night, for no reason. But everyone loved him.

So did she. How could they not? Big green eyes. Almost skeletally thin. Wild humour. And that ability of younger brothers to flow around things instead of banging their head against the wall. To unashamedly let others spoil them and not pretend to be independent. To wait for someone else to take responsibility for a situation and save them the effort.

Yoavi, come and have coffee, their mother said, stealing him away. Inbar was supposedly invited to take part in their conversations, but she always felt superfluous, as if she were with a pair of lovers, and preferred to watch sitcom repeats in the sitting room. There was something comforting about it: hers wasn't the only life stuck on replay. Later on, her father came home with the Chinese takeaway, and the four of them sat down to eat. Her mother never cooked. Not every woman likes to spend hours in the kitchen, she always said. And her father once confided in her that it was her response to Grandma Lily's obsession with cooking.

But no one ever made an issue of it. Sometimes her father would prepare one of the four things he knew how to cook — spaghetti with cream and mushrooms, stir-fried chicken, meatballs with mashed potatoes, or a tuna casserole — and sometimes he'd go out and bring food home. They'd place the aluminium trays in the middle of the table on a lazy Susan her father had bought for that purpose, and they each put whatever they wanted on their plate.

There was nothing unusual about that last supper. That is, in retrospect, you might consider Yoavi's refusal to imitate his squad commander a portent, or the fact that he didn't eat any lychees a portent, or that he went back to bed straight after the meal instead of going out with his friends a portent. But only in retrospect.

He woke up at midday on Saturday but didn't come upstairs to eat lunch with everyone. They knew from the sounds of his guitar coming from his room that he was awake, and they knew that they weren't allowed to disturb him when he was playing. Then he called up to her. That wasn't unusual either. He always called her when he needed help with the words.

Come in, he said after she'd already done so, I still need one more rhyme.

She sat down on his beanbag chair and listened.

He was wearing blue tracksuit bottoms with yellow stripes down the sides and a plain white T-shirt. His cheeks were covered with morning stubble. That's what she remembers. If she had known it was the last time she'd see him, she would have burned more details into her memory. Definitely.

She didn't remember the words either. He never recorded his songs or wrote them down. He just remembered them. Dozens of songs. Everything's here, he'd say and tap his head every time she said what a shame it was and she knew someone in Tel Aviv who was a soundman in a studio and could set something up for him there. Anyway, he said, putting his fingers back on the strings, it still isn't good enough to record.

The first lines were a kind of description of a soldier's life, something like: *Night duty again, lying* (or lonely?) *stars again. Shlomo Artzi songs on the radio again, love the words but not the refrain* (or vice versa?).

Then came two lines that she'd completely forgotten. And then the chorus –

> *And nobody knows how I feel*
> *And nobody knows how I feel*
> *Na na na na na na na*
> *Nobody knows how I feel*

Good song, she said. One of your best. Include it on the album? He grinned without conviction. Of course it'll be on the album, she tried wholeheartedly to cheer him up. So where do you need a rhyme – where you have the *na na na na na na na?* He nodded, and she asked him to play it again. By the third time, she was already tossing out suggestions: *How will I ever heal? Is it really such a big deal? Is any of this really real?* Only the last one fitted the melody, but he wasn't satisfied with what it said. Maybe something related to time, he threw out the idea. She asked him to play it again, and just as he reached the missing line, the right words popped into her head and she sang –

> *Time rolls on like a spinning wheel*
> *And nobody knows how I feel*

We've got it, he said. There was no trace of the happiness his voice usually held at such moments. Nor did he sing the entire song again, adding the new line, as he liked to do. He put the guitar down on the bed and stretched his skinny body out beside it. And closed his eyes. In the dozens of times she'd re-imagined that moment, she sat down in the small space left by his body and asked, so really, how *do* you feel, bro? But in reality, she waited a few seconds, and when she saw that he wasn't opening his eyes, she assumed that he wanted to doze off again and left. And began to pack her things.

She wanted to be in Tel Aviv early. In case Hoffman managed to escape in the evening.

Even during the seven days of mourning, in the midst of all the grief, she wondered when he would finally show up at the door. After all, she'd sent him a message, and he must have read about it in the newspaper. For the first two days, she told herself that he was probably waiting for the stream of visitors to thin out. For the next three days, she thought that those were the days when he taught until late, so the drive to Haifa would probably be too hard for him. And for the final two days, every time someone came into the house she raised her head in the hope, diluted by the anticipation of disappointment, that it was him.

But I sent you an email every day! he claimed in his defence on the seventh day, when she finally phoned him from the path outside her parents' house, and yelled, terrifying butterflies off their perches, fuck emails! You think I was in the mood to surf the Net during the shiva?! And he said, but Inbar, you must realise the awkwardness of the situation. My sudden appearance at your parents' house would lead to all sorts of whispered speculations, and neither of us wants that, do we?

My brother is dead! I don't know what I want or don't want any more! Her voice cracked, and she hung up because she didn't want him to hear her at a moment of weakness, and she ignored his next two attempts to reach her (why only two? why not six? why doesn't he persist? she thought furiously). That night, she crept into her father's study, opened her emails and found three messages from him, only three, and even these were full of literary quotes from Kafka and Brecht and Yaakov Shabtai, of course, but contained only a few terms of endearment, which were forced, making it clear that none of it moved even a single hair on his balls, as he liked to say when his department colleagues criticised the articles he published.

So, Inbar, you've been humiliated till it hurts, she told herself. That's what you wanted, isn't it? But on the drive from Haifa back to her apartment in Tel Aviv, the stabbing humiliation was replaced by fury. During all the months of her relationship with him, she'd fluctuated between two stories. The first, the one she wanted to believe, was that he really was in love with her because, as he said, the connection between them was rare, went beyond the age difference, was a meeting of kindred spirits; and the second − that in the end, she was nothing but a fuck for him. And all his talk about kindred spirits was just a cover for his itch to screw a student twenty years younger than he was. What a bastard, she said to herself as she was nearing Netanya. What a bastard, she said out loud, further south at Herzlyia. And at the Namir-Rokach junction in north

Tel Aviv, instead of continuing straight into the city she turned left, towards his neighbourhood. She found his Honda, in which her pants had been pulled down too many times, and scratched a line across the doors with a nail file, and the next day she bought black spray paint and wrote ADULTERER on the door to his apartment, and CHARLATAN on the door to his office in the university, and forwarded to his department office a few of his juicier emails, which she'd saved despite his demand that she delete everything she received from him.

After the restrained sadness of the shiva, there was something liberating in all that rage. Unlike her father, who was angry in general at institutions like 'the government' or 'the military establishment', her anger was focused and personal. And therefore more satisfying. If Hoffman hadn't called and threatened to complain to the police, she would have continued on her rampage of revenge. No problem, Yoram, she said coolly. Complain. Just remember that I can counter your complaint with one of my own: exploiting your authority over me as my teacher, you know.

Nonetheless, she stopped.

She didn't want to add to her parents' sorrow. They were crumbling like dry earth as it was.

She was filled with sadness every time she went to see them. They had never really been a good couple, her parents. And they actually did love each other. That is, he loved her very much and she loved him back, as much as she could. Maybe they could have lived in peace together if her father had been a submissive type, the kind who was always trying too hard to please. But he wasn't. He tried to be, but it always came bursting out of him. His lust for life, his unwillingness to reconcile himself to the fact that she was so un-giving to the world and to him. As a child, Inbar hadn't known how to formulate it that way for herself, and even now she wasn't sure that she wasn't projecting her own complaints about her mother on to her father, but with a child's intuition, she always knew that there was a kind of extortion in her parents' marriage. And once, when she was very small – she was almost sure that this was a memory, a real memory, not an imagined one – after her parents had argued in the sitting room, her father came into her room, and instead of giving her a kiss on the forehead, he lay down beside her and sighed heavily, and she said, don't worry Daddy, everything'll be okay, and stroked his head, and he laughed joylessly and said, of course everything'll be okay, Inbarina, I have you, and you have me, no matter what happens.

And yet, the possibility that her parents might not stay together never entered her mind when she was a child. Simply because in the Haifa of the '70s, no one got divorced.

It wasn't until she was about eleven, when the parents of Rakefet Bild, the class queen, separated that the idea dawned on Inbar for the first time. She knew quite well who she'd go with if they split up, and it really bothered her that in TV shows judges tended to award custody automatically to the mother, unless she was insane. She wasn't sure that the sum total of her mother's weirdnesses would make the jury think she was insane, and to be on the safe side she wrote a list of them in her diary so that she'd have it ready if the judge asked for it:

1. Doesn't like to hug, and is generally repulsed by physical contact.
2. Treats literary characters as if they're real people (!)
3. Shouts at her daughter for stupid little things like the noise that she (the daughter) makes when she drinks milk.
4. Every once in a while, doesn't fall asleep for a whole night.
5. Eats like a bird. And sometimes doesn't eat at all.
6. Clearly prefers one of her children to the other, even though all the psychology books say that's really not a healthy thing to do (!)

Before he went into the army, the preferred son came to visit Inbar in her Tel Aviv apartment. As always, he complained about the noise and the dirt in the big city. As always, he brought her unshelled pine nuts from the pine trees that grew on the path below their parents' house. And as always, he hugged her twice: the first time at the door, and the second time a few minutes after they'd sat down on the balcony, adding his usual: Sis, I'm so happy to see you.

So are you excited about the army? she asked him. And he sipped the Sprite she'd bought especially for him and said, mainly I'm just dying to get the hell out of that house.

She looked at him in surprise – what could possibly be bad for the golden boy? – and he said, you escaped in time. They're arguing all the time now. All the time! Once they used to fight and make up. Now they fight and fight and fight. Without the peaceful breaks in between.

But you're in the submarine, what do you care? she asked.

First of all, it's a bunker, he reminded her. And anyway, you can hear them shouting all the way downstairs. Never mind the shouting. It's the energy. The bad energy that percolates down through the floor to me by some kind of osmosis.

Percolates down? Osmosis? Refresh your vocabulary, Bro.

When I'm with you, Sis, I keep using language like that. Words like that.

Don't correct me, you snob.

Okay, of course they argue. Mum is pretty hard to live with.

Dad isn't . . . such an angel either, Yoav said, abiding by coalition discipline.

What does that mean? she said, angered.

Forget it, he said. I didn't come here to talk about them. Are we going to the gig or not?

What did you say the name of the band is?

Seroxat. And if you've never heard of them, that's your screw-up.

Your screw-up – hey there, man. Nice one with the military slang.

She went to the gig with him, of course. And suffered greatly from the music. But enjoyed watching him carry on and scream the words – all in English – with the soloists, and as far as she could hear through the curtain of noise, it was all about the futility of love, career, and life in general.

Yes, that was a portent too. In retrospect. The way he identified with those songs. But who was looking for portents then? The only thought she had about him that night was that he was still a boy, absolutely a boy, and how the hell could they take kids like him and put them in uniform? Does anyone seriously think that uniforms will turn them into adults? She watched him dancing and thought that more than anything, she wanted to cover him in bubble wrap and write on it in large, clear letters: FRAGILE.

On the morning he was inducted, she drove to Tel Hashomer, parked her car close to the gates of the induction centre, and stood there and waited. At 12.31, she reported to her parents that the operation had been completed: the bus on which the golden boy was travelling slowed down at the gate. The golden boy was sitting at the window on the right-hand side. She waved at him and he waved back, even blew a kiss.

Wonderful! her father said.

You're the best! her mother added in a weaker voice from the bedroom extension.

So they were still doing it. Both on the line at the same time, for a kind of conference call. After Yoavi was gone, they dropped that custom. Along with a few others.

The first time she noticed that a single bed with a sheet and pillow had been added to her father's study, she stood rooted to the spot. She'd gone there for a Sifria La'am book, one of the many dozens of literary works in that series that took up four long shelves. (Her mother maintained a strict borrowing policy: Inbar had to write down the name of every borrowed book on a piece of paper and paste it to the bookcase, and she had to return the book the next time she came over. If she hadn't managed to finish it, she had to request an extension. By phone. Or email.)

As she was trying to decide between the dubiously titled *Doctor Fischer of Geneva or The Bomb Party* and *Travels with my Aunt*, which she'd made a failed attempt to read when she was a child – she saw the made-up bed. And her father's eternal, light blue pyjamas lying folded on it.

And froze.

Even during their bad times, even when they'd held grudges for days, they'd go to sleep together every night in their large, royal bed – the only piece of furniture in the house that deviated from the norm in the workers' city of Haifa. A four-poster bed. Carvings and openwork on the front of the frame. Expensive, solid mahogany. A remote control that allowed them to play with the angles of the mattress.

Children were not welcome in that kingdom. If Inbar woke up before her parents, she had to knock on the door and wait for one of them to come out. On Saturday mornings the door was always locked, and she had to be in charge of Yoavi until her father woke up, tore himself away from the thick duvet used only on their bed, and got up to make them a cheese omelette.

The bed in the study, on the other hand, had only a thin blanket that looked more like a bedspread. And the small, colourful pillow, which had no case on it, had once been a scatter cushion in the sitting room.

Her mother and father reacted to what happened to Yoavi in totally different ways. Her father launched a crusade to uncover the truth. We have to know what really happened there before we can . . . he said to Inbar when the shiva ended, then fell silent. After Yoavi, his sentences died in the middle before he could finish them. He used all his connections in the academic world and the corridors of government to get the incident investigated on the General Staff level, not the regimental level. He refused to accept the Military Police inquiry, and met personally with Yoavi's commanders and buddies, and with the current and former mental health officers. His study, usually full of folders of transportation plans, now filled up with folders of witness statements. If those shits dare . . . they'll have to deal with the . . . he threatened.

Her mother didn't understand why he was running around from one office to the next. Bureautherapy, she called it behind his back. For her part, she had already reached her own conclusion. My son didn't play with guns, she explained to everyone. He just wasn't like that. So what if he didn't leave a letter? They crushed him there. That's what it was. They must have crushed his soul so hard that he didn't have enough strength left even to write a letter. And we didn't see a thing. That's what hurts the most. We had a dead man walking here at home and I didn't notice (that's what she said: *I* didn't notice). You don't have to be a professor in the Technion to understand that.

A few months before the first anniversary of his death, her mother organised a competition for young rock bands in Yoavi's name. She obtained funding from the council, found a lighting crew and sound people who agreed to volunteer their services, and mobilised the support of *Kolbo*, the local Haifa newspaper, which gave her free advertising space. Come on, she said to Inbar, I need your help. Someone has to take charge of the musical side. I don't know a thing about that. And you love music so much.

I'll find you someone to do it, Mum, she said. I'm sorry, I just can't.

Because, while her father tried to throw the stun grenade that had landed in the middle of their sitting room back into the world, and her mother tried to lie on top of it, Inbar chose to run as far away from it as she could. The pain was too terrible to bear, so she tried to cut-and-paste it to the future, to better days when she'd be strong enough to cope with it. She hardly ever went to Haifa. And a month after it happened, she left her apartment in the heart of the city because she couldn't stand her flatmate's smoking for even one more day, and rented an unfurnished place for herself in the southern part of the city. She wanted to stay in Tel Aviv. Now that everything inside her was turned off, she needed to be surrounded by life and movement. For the first few months, she slept on a single mattress she'd found on the street, and except for that — and a stereo she placed beside her — she left the apartment empty of furniture for a long time. She didn't have the strength for guests, so there was no point in putting a sofa in the sitting room. Her sex drive had dried up, so there was no need for seduction accessories. She made do with one bottle of perfume and one of shampoo, which she placed under the bathroom mirror. Pictures looked either too happy or too sad to her, so the walls remained bare too.

It took her almost a year to hang the first picture, on the wall of the hallway between the bedroom and the sitting room. A Modigliani reproduction.

Then she bought a new tablecloth for the kitchen table.

Then a double mattress. And new sheets. Then she dyed her hair. And in a panic, went back to her original colour a week later.

Then she added chairs and sofas that she found in the street and did up herself. She drove to the Netanya industrial area because she heard that some guy there named Eitan designed amazing light fixtures at student prices.

Six months later, she and that some-guy-named-Eitan moved in together. He knew about Yoavi, of course. But he also knew that she didn't like to talk about it. And that the few times that she did talk to him about it, his reaction disappointed her.

He went with her to the second competition in Yoavi's memory. He stroked her thigh all the way there and told her that finding her was like winning the lottery.

Together with her, he saw how her father refused to shake hands with the army representatives who'd come to the event. And how her mother broke down in the middle of her speech and left the stage without finishing it. And how the house in which Inbar had grown up had become dark, even though all the lights were turned on. And how the entrance to the bunker was still wide open and cold air was flowing, against all the laws of physics, from downstairs to the upper floor of the house. And how Inbar's parents, instead of supporting each other, offering each other comfort, were stabbing at each other where it hurt. Constantly. And how Inbar herself, who was all defiance with him, kept fading, growing more defeated with every passing hour she spent in her parents' home.

He seems like a good man, that new boyfriend of yours, her father told her on the phone the next day. I feel as if I'm leaving you in good hands.

Leaving me? What does that mean?

I've had a job offer in Australia, Inbari. They're about to re-plan all the transportation in Sydney. And they . . . want me as a consultant. I've never been involved in such a large project. And it's an offer I can't refuse. I mean – the professor from the Technion inside him felt the need to be precise – there's no such thing as an offer you can't refuse, but this one is very tempting.

And what about Mum?

She . . . isn't interested in coming along. And I thought . . . we both thought that it would be good, in every sense, to have some space. Do you understand?

She understood. And after the separation anxiety died down, she thought that actually it wasn't a bad idea for him to go off and vent his rage somewhere else. She called him a week later to wish him a safe trip.

Thank you, he said. I really wanted to hear you say that, because you know that . . . and she said yes, I know, Dad, never imagining that three months later her parents would be exchanging divorce papers, and that he would stay in Australia for four straight years, and for the first two, he'd shrug off all her offers to visit him with lame excuses, and then, out of the blue, he'd send her a plane ticket to Hong Kong, along with a note saying, 'Let's meet halfway, Inbari. There's something I have to tell you', and she never imagined he'd be waiting for her at the Hong Kong airport with Vivian, his new wife, beside him, and a little boy in his arms, and say with a broad smile, Inbar, meet your brother.

*

The first moment she saw Reuven, she couldn't breathe – he looked so much like Yoavi. The second moment, she already loved him. And the third moment, she was enraged at her father for hiding him from her like that. And so it was for four days in Hong Kong: rage and love, love and rage, her father's attempts to explain and her attempts to understand.

The plane continues to circle above Lima, and she remembers – she just can't stop the memories tonight – a conversation they had. Vivian stayed in the room with Reuven, and she and her father went down to have a drink at the hotel bar. In the hope that alcohol would break the tension.

I'm so glad you're getting on with each other, he said. You and Reuven.

He's a lovely boy, she said. And after a brief pause, added: doesn't he look so much like Yoavi?

So much, her father agreed. He sometimes makes this little movement – with his nose.

Exactly. And doesn't it drive you mad, Dad?

Yes, it does, but it makes me more mad being in the house

where Yoavi grew up and walking past his room, hoping every time that maybe, in spite of everything, he's still there. And more mad, Inbari, shopping in the supermarket and putting tubs of vanilla pudding in my basket and then remembering that there's no one to buy it for. Do you remember how much he—

Yes.

And it makes me even madder to see his friends walking around Haifa. So . . . alive. I once stopped to get petrol and the attendant looked familiar to me from somewhere, so I asked him from where, thinking that maybe he'd been a student of mine. And he said, you're Yoavi's father, then added, 'may he rest in peace'. Suddenly I couldn't bear it, Inbari. Suddenly I had no air. Even now, when I think about it, I can't breathe. Do you remember when we used to go to the beach and I'd take a very deep breath and dive, and you and Yoavi had to pull me out of the water?

She nodded. She'd never liked that game. She was always too afraid for her father to enjoy it.

There was no more air for me in Israel, Inbari. I had to leave. It was either that or . . . He stopped in the middle of the sentence. As if he were waiting for her to finish it for him.

But she didn't finish it, and her hand, which had almost reached out to stroke his cheek, remained close to her body. Which made him despair even more. Do you understand? Do you? he asked, and when she maintained her silence, he ordered another gin, gulped it down in one swallow and tossed all his engineer's caution to the wind.

Before Reuven was born, I walked through my life like a guest, he said. There was a kind of . . . transparent wall. Emotions were far away, in a place I couldn't reach. And it isn't just Reuven, he continued. It's Australia too. It taught me how to be happy again. Australians' happiness is the happiness of people who know that life is full of pain, and yet they choose to be happy. To live in the present. Not in the past. In retrospect, he added, I know I was in a bad way, emotionally. But I want you to know that my relationship with your mother wasn't . . . good . . . even before Yoavi. You're a smart girl. You must have felt it.

So why didn't you separate? she asked silently. And he answered out loud: We didn't separate because we didn't want to upset your world. We were afraid that it wouldn't be good for either of you.

Then it's a good thing Yoavi died. It gave you courage, she said, sticking a pin in the unbearable calm he exuded all the time, even when he said 'I was in a bad way, emotionally.' He put down the glass he was about to drink from. He turned very white, and for a moment she thought he was going to pass out. He took a few long breaths, then put his hands under his thighs and said, I had no choice. It was either that, or give up completely. Can you understand that?

She didn't give him the nod of understanding he was expecting, because overshadowing all of it was the lie. It wasn't that her father had always been a knight of truth. Definitely not. But his lies had always been small and stupid, like telling her that he had no money in his wallet instead of just saying that he didn't want to buy something, or telling her that he was late because of traffic when he was really late because he forgot that it was his turn to pick her up from school, and she let all those lies go because she felt that his love for her was pure. But to hide from her the fact that he had a child? That was no lie. That was genuine deceit.

Nonetheless, at the end of that evening, there was a smile, before she got out of the lift at her floor, because she couldn't help herself, she loved him from the bottom of her heart, that habitual liar of a father. At the very end, they parted at the airport very early in the morning. Reuven pressed up against her and refused to let her go, and her father cried – she'd never seen him cry before – the tears falling from his eyes to his cheeks, which had turned grey, and from there to his neck, which was ridged with small wrinkles, and he promised her, hand on his heart, that the three of them would visit Israel within a few months. She no longer believed a single word he said. But she nodded as if she did.

*

The pilot announces that they have finally received permission to land in Lima, and apologises for the delay in three languages.

She can see through her window that it's already totally dark outside. It's weird that in such a big city there are no lights at all. Your flight lands in the daytime, the airline assistant who sold her the ticket in Berlin said. And added: Better that way. It's not a good idea to arrive at night. Why not? she asked. Never mind, the assistant said, just go straight from the airport to a good hotel and put all your money in the safe the minute you walk into your room.

*

As she watches the taxi that brought her from the airport drive away, she realises that she's been had. She asked the driver to take her to a good hotel, and he took her to one that was probably owned by his friends.

It's dark everywhere. And there's no one in the street. And she's a woman.

Idiot. You should have gone with the two Israeli guys who offered you a lift. So what if they reminded you of Yoavi.

The receptionist in the Paraiso Hotel, a grim-looking Japanese guy wearing huge, black-framed glasses, explains to her in broken English that they don't have a safe and that she must pay for the room by the hour. But I need to stay here until the morning! Don't you have a night rate? she asks angrily. Her clothes are sticking to her body after so many hours of flying and she's dying to peel them off. Just a minute, he tells her, and turns to talk to a young couple who have just walked in. They shove a few notes into his hand and get a key from him. The woman puts her hand on the man's arse as they walk up the squeaky steps to the room. She's wearing heels and he's in flip-flops. Ah — Inbar protests to the Japanese guy — this is a hotel for prostitutes? No, no. He denies this firmly, and explains that the young couples in this city don't have a place . . . to meet. Intimate meetings, if she catches his drift. Because they all live with their families.

So this is hotel for fucking? Inbar asks. Well, the receptionist says, leaving it at that.

Me not fucking today, okay? So please give me nice room. Good price.

Aahh . . . not fucking, the receptionist says sympathetically. I give you room for one, good for tourist, okay?

The single room contains one bed, one window that looks out on to another building, and one picture of a huge water-fall, with the word Iguazu written under it. Aluminium arms sprout from the wall opposite the bed, but there's no TV on them. In the bathroom, instead of a bath, there's a shower stall with its door torn off, and lying in the small bin next to the lid-less toilet is a long, snaky hair. The lighting in the room is sick. Even when she turns on all the lights at once, it's still dim. Eitan would find a solution, she thinks. On their first holiday together, at Lake Kinneret, they ended up in a room with lighting like this and she had said, don't bother, it's just for three nights, but he played with the wires and turned a few screws while she was asleep, and then there was light.

She undresses and lies down on the narrow bed, her face to the ceiling, feeling too tired and screwed over to have a shower. 'Morrissey mood', she used to call it once, after the melancholy soloist of the Smiths. Screw Peru screw Peru screw Peru, she chants to herself, and closes her eyes with a strong sense of having made a terrible mistake.

When she opens them again, she notices the writing. It covers the ceiling and slides down to the walls. More and more writing, in many languages. Mainly English. Someone wrote all the words of 'California Dreaming' from beginning to end. Someone else quoted Nietzsche. There's even a comic strip near the window. Twelve squares depicting the heartbreaking story of a tourist who gets such a bad case of the runs in Rio de Janeiro, during Carnival, that he can't leave the bathroom. Next to the reading lamp, someone has written an abridged guide with a long title: 'Ten ways to cope with an anxiety attack that overpowers you in a single room in Lima'. Some of the ideas aren't bad. For example, 'Keep thinking about a girl you always wanted to sleep with. In many cases, horniness conquers anxiety.' Or, 'Breathe through your ass.' Or, 'Read an academic article on industrial and administrative engineering.' The final suggestion, number 10, says in summary, 'If everything you've tried up to now hasn't helped, then get the hell out of the room, you idiot.'

She stands in front of the wall with her pen and wants to add something in Hebrew, but can't manage to think of anything clever enough. Maybe tomorrow, she tells herself. But then again, maybe I'll change hotels tomorrow. She takes out her phone to call Eitan, to explain the laconic text message she sent him from the airport in Berlin, but the battery's dead and she doesn't have an adaptor for the plug. Maybe it's better this way, she thinks. I don't have a good enough explanation now anyway.

As she closes her eyes, the sound of a woman on the brink of orgasm comes through the wall. She's moaning in a very thin voice. Thin, rhythmic moans.

That arouses her envy, and she covers herself with the thin blanket, closes her eyes and tries to picture a gang of Peruvian bandits kidnapping her, and the Mossad agent, the one with the prominent Adam's apple and the strands of grey at his temples, is sent by the Israeli government to rescue her, but just as he begins to undo the ropes they used to tie her to a tree and runs his finger along one of the marks left on her skin by the tight knots, the moans of the woman in the next room grow louder, invading her imagination and suddenly sounding like moans of sorrow, not pleasure. When she tries to close her eyes again and get on with her fantasy, despite the fear, she can't do it. The story is still there, but not the desire, and she already knows that you can't push things like that. So she lets it go and gets up. Checks that the door is locked. Closes the window. Draws the curtain. And then turns on to her stomach and tries to breathe through her ass.

Lily

Knowing, however infuriating it can be, is better than not knowing. For more than a day now, her head has been full of scenarios that grow more frightening with each passing hour: Inbari was fired, and that's why they didn't mention her name on her radio programme today (how many adverts they have between one listener and the next, and how loud they all are!); Inbari has cancer (all those conversations on that damn mobile, she knew it would end badly!); Inbari has disappeared and she's on her way to do what Yoavi did to himself, after all, there is something genetic about that tendency — it's like a time bomb in her psyche waiting to be detonated, and maybe Yoavi was the detonator, a remote detonator; or maybe Hana's the one something has happened to, something that both of them are hiding from her, taking advantage of her age to form an alliance, to plot against her . . .

Inbar went to see her mother in Berlin and now she's decided to go travelling in Peru, Eitan said.

And she breathed a sigh of relief, but her voice, faithful to her role, grumbled: so in the end, she took reparation money from them like her mother.

You should know that it was very hard for her to go there, Eitan hurried to defend her. That's why she didn't want you—

You should know, she interrupted Eitan, that her great-grandfather, my father, was sent to the gas chambers by those people. You should know that there is no such thing as a different Germany. Behind that cultured façade of theirs, they're still exactly the same. Only now they don't hate Jews, but Turks or East Germans. Yes, they write poetry, go to concerts. They're just as enlightened as they were then, in the '30s. But you should know that today, like then, they don't have a drop of compassion in their hearts.

Uhhhm . . . okay . . . Inbar'll probably call you from there, from Peru, Eitan said, ignoring her speech.

Good, but I might not be home, she said, and a different voice immediately spoke in her mind: Where exactly will you go, an old woman like you? How far can your aching legs carry you? To the bedroom? The lift? The shop?

She got as far as her memory chair. Shifted it so that the sunbeams would fall on her at exactly the right angle. Turned the fan on to the second speed. Sat down.

And couldn't remember a thing. The image of Inbar filled her mind and refused to leave. Peru? Why Peru, of all places?

It's all because of that father of hers. How can a person get up and leave his wife and daughter like that: how? And then, for two years, hide from them the fact that he has a new family. He must have had an affair with that Vivian before then. He probably met her at one of his conferences abroad. Otherwise, how did it happen so quickly? And how can you leave your little girl like that? It doesn't matter that she was thirty. A father's little girl remains a father's little girl even when she's thirty. And she needs her father at the age of thirty too. And Inbari, instead of being angry with him, understands him. 'He had no choice.' 'He was having a very hard time.'

'Hard.' Life is hard. It's hard for everyone. But when you have children, you don't have the privilege of indulging yourself.

She didn't like Inbar's father from the first minute she saw him. No, that's not exactly true. How can you not like a man like Yossi Benbenisti? Always jumps up to clear the table after a family meal and goes straight to the sink. Rinses the dishes badly, as if his mind is elsewhere. Leaves crumbs, but is full of good intentions. Brings small presents every time he comes: flowers for her; special watercolours for Natan. He hugs and kisses, laughs with all his teeth. Tells stories that have a thin thread of untruth running through them. Twirls his moustache around his finger. Asks her before he goes if they need him to do anything in the house. He doesn't ask that when Natan's there, to avoid wounding his self-respect. And if she says yes, there is something, he stays for as long as it takes. He hammers. Drills. Placates a recalcitrant shutter. There's no getting away from it, Yossi Benbenisti brought new life into their home, added the fourth leg to a family table that had always wobbled on three—

But no. She never trusted him.

If he were a Goldberg, not a Benbenisti, you'd definitely trust him, Gita had mocked when Lily told her about her fears before the wedding.

But she knew that was rubbish. Three weeks on a ship with Ashkenazim like herself had taught her that superior, they were not. And in some way, she was pleased that the man her daughter had chosen was Benbenisti and not Goldberg.

What she didn't like was simply his look. Stupidly, she had hinted at that to Hana after one of their dinners ('It's nice that he's studying to be an engineer, but watch out that he doesn't engineer you, God forbid') – which guaranteed once and for all that Hana would marry him just to prove her wrong. But it's hard to be wrong about the look of men like him. No, Yossi Benbenisti was no Clark Gable. Even at the time of the wedding, he had a tiny pot belly, which swelled with every trip he took to those endless conferences abroad. But neither was he ugly. And he had that yearning look in his eye, a look that he bestowed on any woman – even a worn-out old mother-in-law – who held his eyes for more than a few seconds, a look that said: you have something I need. Something I'm hungry for. And to get it, I'll flatter you as much as I have to.

Her Natan didn't have that look. When she arrived at the kibbutz, her friends told her: Every time a girl tried something with him, he'd begin talking about you. We were starting to think that we weren't good enough for him and that he was making up 'his Lily' as an excuse.

Pima, on the other hand, had exactly that look. She sensed it whenever she walked around the ship's deck. She sensed that look as if it were burning the skin on a different part of her body each time: on her bottom, her neck, her thighs. At first, she turned quickly to catch him in the act. Then she settled for the burning alone, fearing that she might meet his eyes. There was something unpleasant, unsavoury in those looks of his. But since he made do with the looks and never approached her, she could do nothing but voice her complaint to Esther.

They leaned against the rail as evening fell and watched the pod of dolphins that had been swimming alongside the ship for several hours. The dolphins circled the lifeboats in varying formations, and occasionally, when someone threw something to them from the deck – an empty onion sack, maybe – they competed to be the first to grab it in its mouth. The winner would leap up in victory, but when it landed and discovered that the victory had been an empty one, it would let the sack go and, reconciled, return to circling around with its pals.

What the dolphin realised, Pima will also realise in the end, Esther said.

What do you mean? Lily asked.

If you keep on ignoring him, he'll realise that you're not easy prey and he'll leave you alone, Esther explained. And Lily thought that she was clever and right.

But even at Tsippora Roth's sad funeral, Pima kept giving her those looks.

She had been called to the clinic in the middle of the night and recognised the deceased immediately: the emaciated girl from the train. The one who had handed out squares of bitter chocolate to the passengers. Even then, she had looked too weak. Too pale. She was ill when she boarded the ship, the doctor told the people in the clinic. She hid her illness because she wanted to make aliyah to Eretz Yisrael. His words seemed muffled, as if they were moving through water. That was the first time she'd ever seen a dead person. When her mother died, Lily had been a little girl and they wouldn't let her anywhere near her mother's bed or her grave. Now she'd come face to face with that final absolute paleness. It left her weak and trembling. For the first few days, like many of the ship's passengers, she'd suffered from seasickness, and learned that sucking lemon slices made her feel better, but no lemon slice could settle the dizziness she felt in the presence of Tsippora Roth's body. Other people entered the small clinic, including Pima, damn it, with his harmonica dangling from his neck, grazing his Adam's apple. She straightened up to keep him from noticing her attack of weakness.

The commander of the journey spoke: the deceased had no friends or acquaintances on the ship, he said. That is why you, as heads of the culture committees of the various groups of immigrants, have been asked to come here and take part in the funeral. It will take place soon, under cover of darkness. And since you will certainly want to know why the funeral is not being held immediately, this is the reason: sailors believe that the death of a passenger in the first few days of sailing is a bad omen for the fate of the entire ship. We are afraid that if the Greek sailors employed on this ship were to know about the death, they would become alarmed and leave the ship at the first opportunity.

Later that night, a small cluster of people walked on the deck in silence, holding a stretcher above them. When they came close to the rail, they tried to lower it. The wind was strong, and one of the people carrying it did not hear the command. For a moment, Lily thought the stretcher would overturn and the wrapped body would slide off it, but in the end the four of them managed to steady themselves and place Tsippora on the deck.

The commander of the journey gave a eulogy filled with restrained pathos. 'Like Moses, on Mount Nevo,' he waxed poetic, 'Tsippora did not see the Land of Israel with her own eyes, nor will she enter it.' Then he spoke of how brave the deceased had been. She hadn't allowed her illness to prevent her from making this journey. The rest of her training camp were on a different ship and she didn't know anyone on this ship, but that did not prevent her from trying to fulfil her dream of making aliyah to Eretz Yisrael.

I knew her, I saw her passing out squares of chocolate, sweetening for others the bitter pill of leaving home, Lily wanted to say. But one of the comrades, wearing a yarmulke, had already begun to recite the Kaddish.

And then someone – perhaps Pima? – said 'May you rest in peace.' The signal was given, the stretcher was lifted over the rail and the body slid into the water. They heard a muted blow, like a fist hitting a bag.

In the ensuing silence, she felt Pima's glance burning the back of her neck and wanted to turn around and slap him: now? Have you no respect? Our comrade is dead and you keep giving me those indecent looks of yours? We're lucky you're not playing the harmonica and dancing now. A comedian, that's what you are. Why are you even making aliyah to Eretz Yisrael? Clowns like you have no place there. There it's all working the land, ploughing and planting and picking, and the blazing sun beating down on your head. You should have stayed in Warsaw, Pima. Entertaining the *curvas*, the whores. That suits you much better —

That's what she wanted to say to him. But she kept silent and didn't turn her head, lest she turn into a pillar of salt. She walked very quickly, heading the group, her neck thrust forward, to escape from Pima and the muted slap of the body on the water, which, though it had no echo, continued to resonate in her mind.

When she reached the hold, she lay down on her pallet without taking her shoes off.

All the others in her group were also sprawled on their pallets, deeply asleep. Oblivious sleep. Every now and then someone turned and a board squeaked softly. Every now and then someone muttered in his sleep, stray words that did not join together into a sentence. She pulled up her thin blanket and closed her eyes, but her heart was awake: and if I knew — she couldn't help thinking — that the sailors' superstition was correct, and the fate of this journey has been sealed, if I knew that tomorrow was my last day, that I had one final chance to live out all my dreams before they drowned along with me, would I keep on running from Pima even then?

Inbar

She dreams at night about slugs. Those slimy shell-less creatures, climbing up her body, and she tries to brush them off gently. But every time she manages to get rid of one, two new ones replace it. She knows that in order to really remove them she has to kill them, and in order to kill them, she has to sprinkle salt over them, but she doesn't have the heart to do it.

During the day, Lima closes in on her even more than it did at night. We haven't seen the sun for three months now, a waitress in the restaurant next to the hotel tells her. Because of the smog. The clouds here mix with the pollution from the factories, and not even a single ray gets through it. If I were you, I'd get the hell out of here as fast as I could. Where to? Inbar asks. Cuzco, the waitress suggests. There's sun there. And that's where all the gringos are. Is there a night bus that goes there? Inbar asks. Yes, the waitress says, but it's not recommended for women travelling alone, you know. There have been incidents.

Inbar buys a ticket for the morning bus to Cuzco, and then walks around the streets for a while. There are police on every corner. A chemist dispenses medications through bars. A gang of men with empty beer bottles ogle her with rapists' eyes. What a mistake it was to wear a low-cut top.

She remembers that once, after a woman on Dr Adrian's programme talked about her boss sexually harassing her, the women in the production crew began talking about the subject, and it turned out that every one of them – there were six in the room – had experienced sexual harassment at least once.

If I were here with Eitan, she thinks, I'd feel a lot safer.

There are adaptors for sale in an improvised open market near the bus station. She knows she should buy one and call him, but instead, she buys herself some pepper spray. Maybe she'll spray it into the eyes of a Peruvian rapist. Or maybe she'll spray it into her own eyes. And then the tears will finally come.

She retreats from the men's glances, back to the hotel, and remembers that she wanted to move to a different one. But she no longer has the energy.

The smell of mildew assails her nostrils when she enters the lobby. What is she doing in this hole? This entire trip suddenly seems wildly unrealistic. Weird. Inappropriate for someone her age.

No packing today? the receptionist says, and smiles at her.

Without smiling back, she takes the key to her tiny room.

She lies down on the bed. She has smog in her heart. She looks at the writing that covers the ceiling. Words she didn't notice yesterday now catch her eye. Written diagonally across from number 10 of The Guide to Coping with Anxiety Attacks, and in the same handwriting, is: THE WANDERING JEW TOUR.

Slightly below that is the drawing of a violin. And under the violin, as on rock band T-shirts, is a list of cities and dates: Florence 1411, Toledo 1457, Munich 1606, Paris 1777, London 1934, Rio de Janeiro 2004, Lima 2006.

She takes her journal out of her bag and copies the dates. It'll be interesting to see whether it's just a lot of nonsense or whether it's actually based on something. She can call her mother, she would know. But she doesn't have an adaptor. Why didn't she buy an adaptor? Why doesn't she call Eitan? It's so not right. What's going on with her?

And what about the Wandering Jewess? she writes in her notebook. Why is it always the men who are wandering? Cain, Odysseus, Marco Polo, Don Quixote? Is the gene for wandering missing from women's DNA? Or is the wandering dangerous for them because they're too easily hurt, and that's why they're doomed to remain for ever in the tent, at home, in Ithaca?

And maybe — her hand trembles slightly as she writes in her notebook — the Wandering Jew had a hidden female partner on his journey. Nessia was her name. Derived from the Hebrew verb meaning 'to flee'. Nessia had no fear of being hurt, and she was the one who cheered up the Wandering Jew in his low moments, when he broke down and stopped believing that he would ever finish serving his punishment and return home.

*

At night, the slugs come to her again. But this time it's more frightening. They climb from her chest to her shoulders, on their way to her neck, and from there, her face, at least seven or eight of them on her face, and then they slide into her mouth, she tries to spit them out, but can't, and they slither into her throat, one after the other, till they block it, and all at once she can't breathe can't breathe can't breathe

When she wakes up, her heart is pounding so hard that she thinks it'll break through her skin. Her hands are trembling, her teeth are chattering and her left eyelid is twitching. She knows, she knows that she has to get up and leave this room, but she's paralysed, and anyway, she has nowhere to go. For people who have no place, the journey will be their place, she'll write before dawn, in Nessia's name. But at such moments, she's all panic, plunging downward with nothing to grab on to; anyone she could have grabbed on to is out of reach now — her father has moved, Eitan has changed, Yoavi is gone. What would Dr Adrian say now if she called the programme? The thought flashes through her mind. What difference does it make? What does he even understand? She searches the wall for The Guide to Coping with Anxiety Attacks. That seems to be what she's having now. An anxiety attack. But the Guide has vanished.

How can that be? It was here two hours ago! Her eyes keep searching for it, but it looks as if the entire wall is covered with the Wandering Jew's road trip, which, by popular request, has been extended to other cities. You won't be here tomorrow, she thinks, trying to calm herself down, but how will she get through the night, how? She feels as if an old-fashioned metal clothes peg is squeezing her windpipe shut, her heart is beating faster, faster, if she doesn't do something to stop it, it'll just explode. She pulls her journal out of her bag, uncaps her pen feverishly, and begins to write Nessia. She doesn't plan to write Nessia, just the opposite: ever since Yoavi, she's decided that it's pretentious of writers to believe that they know the depths of their characters' psyches. Who can even guess what's going on in someone else's mind if there are areas in the minds of the people closest to you in real life, let's say younger brothers in the army, that remain invisible to you – but Nessia doesn't wait. Nessia simply creates herself. Line after line. All night.

Nessia

Maybe Nessia is a bird that has lost her flock. And maybe she lost it deliberately: at some point, she grew sick and tired of that whole business of maintaining formation, so she stopped to scratch her wing, and when the flock had gone far enough away – she changed direction.

When Nessia's on the road, her favourite word is: maybe.

It's not that she doesn't look at her watch (after all, sometimes she has to catch a train. Or check out of a hotel room by a certain time).

But when Nessia arrives at a new place, she doesn't hurry to look for somewhere to spend the night. She knows that, first of all, she has to sit down on a bench under a tree (there's at least one bench like that everywhere), close her eyes and listen to the history of the place that the leaves are whispering in her ears.

For Nessia, being on the road (sometimes it takes a few days until she feels it) is like it was when she was a child rolling down a grassy hill – at some point, your body begins to turn itself without any effort on your part.

It's not as if Nessia doesn't sometimes ask herself, 'What are you doing here?' – but she doesn't ask it to reprimand herself, she says it simply to remind herself of the real reasons for her journey.

Nessia is a difficult character on which to base a novel. She doesn't undergo a process. Her dialogues aren't clever enough. And she's too uninhibited from the very beginning to require any loosening up. Actually, she should have a song written about her, but she's always moving.

A writer she once met told her that. He lived in a camper van and had a driver who took him from one place to another on the continent. He can only write when he's moving, he explained to her. Only when the scenery is changing in the window above his desk do the words flow from him.

That writer wanted to sleep with her. He whispered in her ear that she smelled like the days right before spring bursts forth, and Nessia said, thank you, really, thank you, but moved slightly away from him and explained that for her, there's something very unattractive about writers. They all take on the shape of a chair after a while, and you're always afraid that they're sleeping with you as part of their research.

Inbar

As soon as she leaves Lima for the open road, her windpipe opens too. She tries to convince herself that if she survived the explosion of Yoavi memories on the plane and the heart-pounding night in the hotel, then she can survive anything. She's on a special tourist bus with seats that tilt back, air conditioning, and small TV screens, just like on a plane. The ticket costs the equivalent of a few months' salary for a Peruvian.

None of the tourists are her age. They're either younger or older. She's in the middle, in the decade when people put down roots and don't make big changes or forge new paths or leave a good job or travel alone, without a boyfriend, without friends, to South America.

The seat beside her is empty. And the people who get on at the next stops don't sit down next to her. Maybe she looks too old to the younger ones. And to the older ones – too young.

Eitan could be sitting beside her now, she thinks. She'd rest her head on his shoulder and he'd stroke her hair and everything would grow dim and pleasant, and she'd fall asleep and not dream about slugs or be afraid that the bus was going to fall into an abyss or crash into one of the trucks coming too quickly at them from the opposite direction.

After all, she's nothing like as fearless as the character she's writing about.

Nessia

She doesn't sleep with the writer. But she does sleep with his driver. No, she's not the kind who separates the physical from the emotional, she simply develops the emotion quickly. Very quickly. It's enough for her to hear the driver cheering up a friend on the phone for her heart to open to him completely, and she'll move to the cabin and put her hand on the inside of his thigh and tell him to pull over to the side of the road.

How does Nessia make love? Unashamedly. Wholeheartedly. Impartially. Wow, the driver says after the third time. Where did you come from? Nowhere in particular, she explains. I'm always wandering. And what's that like, he asks, getting off her, lying down by her side and staring at her with eyes genuinely eager to understand (now she knows she hasn't made a mistake with him).

When you wander, she says, caressing his biceps as she explains, the letters that make up your name wander with you. But sometimes one of them gets tired and stays behind to rest in a hotel, and you spend a whole day without an N, for example. When you wander, your childhood memories are so tangible that one of them can suddenly sit down next to you in a bus. When you wander, the laces of your shoes and your soul come untied more often. When you wander, you're the letter in the carrier pigeon's beak, as well as the pigeon itself. Do you understand?

Not completely, he smiles. But go on. It turns me on.

When you wander – she kisses his chin, his chest, and lower – your falling-in-love zone is turned on, and you're in danger of falling in love even with a city. When you wander, your dreams are explicit and too full of magic wands to ignore. When you wander, loneliness is as intense as an orgasm, and many things that usually seem important suddenly seem unimportant, such as the question: what's your name?

Inbar

She finally buys an adaptor in Cuzco, the morning after a dance party she spent pressed up against the wall because she felt she was dressed wrongly, and because she thought the music was terrible, and because she never dances because she doesn't feel comfortable enough with her body. The only reason she went to the club was because some Dutch girl she met near the laundry dragged her along, and because she hoped it would be a good way to meet real people, not fictitious ones. But the ones in the club were all children, really children, and the Dutch girl, who, at second glance, looked like a child too, buggered off with some Dutch guy, and no one chatted her up, even though she did try to smile a bit and move away from the wall. And men seem wicked when you're unwanted.

Inbari? Eitan says when she calls. His voice is a little shaky.

Yes.

I . . . you . . . I was starting to think that you . . . I've been so worried about you. Are you okay, Inbari? What happened?

Nothing.

What do you mean, nothing?

Nothing happened. Everything's fine.

Everything's fine???

Yes.

So why . . . so what . . . Half an hour before your flight back you text me — text me! — that you're not coming back. And then you disappear. Do you have any idea . . . Hey, I'm going completely mad here . . .

I'm sorry, Tani. I should have called sooner. I know.

Where are you anyway? I don't have the slightest idea where you are!

Cuzco.

Where the hell is that?

Peru.

Did you meet someone in Berlin, Inbar? Is that it?

No. Of course not. Where'd you get an idea like that?

So what happened? I don't understand. Just like that, on the spot, you decided not to come back?

Not on the spot. I've been toying with the idea for a long time now.

What idea, a trip to Peru?

No. Of course not.

What, then? I don't understand.

She's silent. At first, she waits. Maybe after the delay he'll have something to add. Then she just doesn't know what to say.

So what do you want me to tell the radio? He diverts the conversation to a more practical track, one that's more comfortable for him. They're hounding me—

Don't tell them, she says. I'll call them myself and tell them I'm leaving.

Leaving? Sweetie, wouldn't it be better if you tell them that you're extending your holiday? . . . You know, in case you change your mind.

I have to leave it behind me, she says.

But, sweetie—

Drop it. I've already decided. It's my decision, she says, and thinks: actually, I don't like it when he calls me sweetie.

Tell me, why, all of a sudden . . . What did you do, exchange your ticket for another? Isn't that, like, seriously expensive?

It is, so what? I've already thought about that. I'll take it out of my last month's pay. I want to get rid of that dirty money.

But what . . . How does spending it make it less dirty? I don't know. Inbar, I can't really understand what's going on in your head.

That's the problem – Inbar thinks, but doesn't say: that I have to explain everything to you. That you don't understand on your own. That you don't see that I've been lost for a long time now. That you don't get the connection between what happened on the programme and what happened to Yoavi. That you don't accept the idea that you can both hate and love a person, especially if he's your dead brother. That you don't understand anything complicated or dark, because for you, everything's illuminated.

Okay, never mind, he gives up. When are you coming back?

I don't know. She tells him the truth. And to allay his fears, she says quickly: how're things in the store?

Fine, he says. I sold five chandeliers this week.

Wow. That's a world record, isn't it?

Yes, he says, but somehow, when you're not here, I can't get excited about it.

I'm sorry it turned out like this, Tani. She takes pity on him, despite everything.

Don't be sorry if you're not really sorry, he says.

I really am sorry.

So come home as fast as you can. I'm waiting for you.

Really?

Just don't disappear like that. Send me a sign of life every once in a while, so I don't lose it, okay.

Okay, she says, But the delay is so long that he doesn't hear her okay, and asks again, okay? And she answers again, okay. And saying okay twice makes her feel that nothing is okay.

Do you need anything? he asks towards the end of the call. Do you want me to FedEx you anything?

No, she says. I'm managing.

*

Managing? Not only are the clothes she took to Berlin not enough now, they're wrong for this kind of trip. There aren't really any shopping centres in the places she's passing through, so she begins collecting bits and pieces while she's on the move. A shirt from a market stall, a colourful waistcoat from a man who boards the bus, trousers that give her the waist of a Canadian student on her way home who doesn't want to be charged for going over her luggage allowance.

Who's she dressing for? Hmmm . . . it's not clear. For herself, maybe. And maybe for the Mossad agent too.

But meanwhile, she isn't meeting anyone. And she barely speaks to people. They all look so . . . not.

After the fiasco in Cuzco, she doesn't go out at night either. Neither to drink nor to dance. She just goes back to her room and lies down and writes and writes and lies down.

Nessia

She's never in another country. Even when she's in Kathmandu or Timbuktu, she's not in another country, because to be in another country, you have to have your own country, and

Nessia has never had land. Gravity pulls her forward, not downward.

Always, on all of her journeys, she carries with her two copies of the *Tao* book by Lao Tzu. One for her and one that she can give to the first guy she likes, after they've slept together, and ask him to choose a sentence from it, and then – after he chooses – to write it with his finger, letter after letter, on her arse. And based on the sentence he chooses and the way his finger feels on her skin, she decides whether she likes him enough to spend another night with him.

The writer's driver chooses the sentence, 'Since he has no ambitions, he is able to practise love to its fullest.' And while he's writing on one of her buttocks, he gently bites the other one. So she spends another night with him, in the cabin of the camper van. And only on the next day does she ask him to drop her off in the middle of the road. What?! he protests after he stops, I thought that something real was starting to happen between us. Sorry, she says. Wait a minute – he tries to grab her coat, how . . . I mean . . . when . . . can we see each other again?

But she's already outside, waving goodbye from the edge of the road.

The writer looks up from his typewriter and blows her a kiss. Maybe he's been eavesdropping on them while they were doing it? Or watching them? She doesn't really care. If he wants to stand on the periphery of life and not step into it, that's his problem.

She keeps on going, and a few minutes later, comes to a junction. The road splits into two – one paved, the other not.

She begins to walk on the dirt road. Her steps are light. Relaxed. As if she were walking in a sitting room in her slippers.

Inbar

She's walking on a path that begins on the left of the church, in Pisac, in the Sacred Valley. She's wearing a red-blue-and-yellow checked cap made of thin cloth. The minute she laid eyes on it yesterday in the Cuzco thieves' market, it made her happy. She wouldn't have bought it in Israel because only religious women wear hats there, but here, as soon as she put it on, she felt (she knew it was stupid, but this was her feeling) that her journey (and not just Nessia's) could truly begin.

It's late, most of the tourists are making their way down the path, and she's walking in the opposite direction, up towards the Inca fortress on the top of the hill. She's wearing thick-soled walking shoes, the kind real hikers wear. In her money belt is a raincoat shoved into its own sleeve, a special snack called Alto for places where the air is thin, and a map they gave her at the hostel reception desk. The steep, terraced path looks out over other hills. There are occasional white steps embedded in the ground, also steep, the kind you have to press your hands on before you can steady yourself. Every now and then, the path becomes very narrow and you have to be careful not to slide into the abyss. She's really not ready to slide into an abyss now that her heart has finally begun to beat.

She stops for a moment to get her breath back. She hears the Urubamba River flowing in the valley below, but can't see it. Maybe she'll be able to see it from the fortress.

She enters a rock tunnel and emerges close to the entrance to the site. She takes her *Boleto Turistico* out of her money belt, and the guard lets her inside. We close at six, he warns her, and she's proud of herself: after only two weeks in Peru, she's picked up enough Spanish to understand what he says. Just as everyone is born with two ears and two legs — she develops a new theory as she climbs — everyone is also born with two mother tongues. One takes effect when you're born, and your stepmother language takes over only if your life leads you to places where it's spoken.

Awaiting her at the end of her climb, at the top of the terraces, is the area where rites were held, and the Intihuatana stone, the altar. It's surrounded by canals filled with present-day, not ancient water, and interspersed among the canals are small temples and basins for ablution, all admirably well kept.

It's amazing how rooted Peruvians are in their past, she thinks. The Inca kingdom was conquered by the Spanish five hundred years ago, but it still rules over the hearts of the people. At first, she suspected that it was just an empty show for tourists, but day by day, the understanding crystallised: the Inca period is the source of their pride. It's the source of their bold facial expression and the reason why they never bow and scrape in their dealings with foreigners.

She wanders among the ancient ruins for several minutes, almost alone, trying to imagine what it was like there once, and then has a powerful urge to see the river. After all, it can't be hidden from sight everywhere.

An unmarked path leads to the cliff behind the fortress. She walks along it, even though it's almost closing time. Strange alcoves gape on both sides of the path, and she opens her guidebook to see if it says anything about them. Yes, it says that those alcoves are ancient Inca graves that were looted by grave-robbers. How charming. She walks a bit faster, until she reaches the top of the cliff, and several metres before the summit, the river is glistening below: yes, you can — you can see the river from here.

The Urubamba is wide and slopes gently as it crosses the entire Sacred Valley. Inbar sits down, her back against a large rock. The strong wind cuts through her clothing and reaches her soul. She takes off her cap and her hair dances in the air. Clouds sail quickly through the sky, like in that Kate Bush video. The sun behind them must be setting.

Voices coming from the group that was there earlier with a German-speaking guide fade away.

The water of the river looks clear and pure. Good air rises from the Sacred Valley.

Everything is forgiven now.

She knows that it's only a moment, and that the soul-searching continues to live inside you until you die –

But at the sight of that calm river, that's what she feels. That loneliness is no longer fear. And that everything, everything is forgiven.

*

An hour later, she even forgives the gang of Israelis that comes into the only bar in the small city and talks too loudly –

So I tell the driver . . . so he tells me . . . I really wanted to do Machu Picchu, but they closed the route, so I did Huarez instead. That's where I met Osnat. I did her, yeah I did her. It took a couple of nights of deep conversation, because she grew up religious. But in the end, I did her like a stud. What's on for tomorrow, bro?

And she forgives the hostel shower, which not only doesn't have hot water, but has hardly any pressure.

And looking in the mirror, she forgives her body for a moment. She's not a skeleton. True. So what?

She lies down naked on the bed and pictures the Mossad agent with the clenched lips coming into the city bar. He's hot on the trail of his Nazi, who, it turns out, has managed to escape his grasp, and is here now. He plans only to stop for a drink in the bar and get back to the chase, but he sees her and sends her a drink, and then sits down next to her. His knees press up against hers and he smells so unbelievably good and he tells her that the man he's hunting is not far from here, two kilometres, but suddenly he's not sure that he wants to kill him, and she asks, why not? He looks around at all the Israelis sitting in the bar and says, this is not the place to have this conversation, and they go to her room. The minute he closes the door behind them, there is no more dialogue, her hands on him and his hands on her and his tongue in her ear, deep, the way she likes it.

It isn't until she opens her eyes that she notices the drawing of a violin and the familiar handwriting on the ceiling: THE WANDERING JEW TOUR. And under it, the details: Florence 1411, Toledo 1457, Munich 1606, Paris 1777, London 1934, Rio de Janeiro 2004, Lima 2006, Pisac 2006. Now that's weird. That Wandering Jew, is he following her? Or is she following him?

The next day, at one of the computers located in a crumbling colonial building in the city, she turns to the only person she can think of who might know something on the subject:

Dear Mum,

    How are you?

    I've come across something a few times that might interest you: some graffiti about the Wandering Jew. Isn't that weird? I'm sending you two pictures I took in Lima and Pisac, both cities in Peru. Maybe it's just some idiot who likes to scribble on walls. But maybe it's really the eternal, Wandering Jew, and he's wandered from Europe to South America? What do you think, Mum? Could it be? Your doctorate is about something like this, isn't it? Reply to this email, I'll log on every now and then. And please don't think that I'm mad for coming here ('Has she completely lost it?' I can hear you saying to Grandma, who probably told you about my trip. ('It's just like her, to run away instead of facing things'). I know it's hard for you to understand, Mum, but try to see that it's just the opposite. I've been lost since Yoavi, and here, I finally feel that I have a (small) chance of finding myself.

Hana

Thank you for sending me the pictures, she replies to her daughter. *I'm really happy that you thought of me.*

There are bigger experts on the subject than I, but if you want my opinion, the appearance or disappearance of the Wandering Jew is never just a 'scribble'.

Since we're talking about a myth, a legend, and not the objective truth – is there really such a person? Did he really appear in those places on those dates? – that's what's interesting. The use of that myth at certain periods of history.

Most researchers agree that since the establishment of the State of Israel, there has been a sharp decrease in the number of 'appearances' of the Wandering Jew throughout the world. As if, with the establishment of the national home of the Jews, they no longer need that story to explain their eternal wandering to the world. But academia has always lagged a bit behind actual events (it takes time to write an article, send it to a journal, receive comments, make corrections, and even more: the academic world tends not to follow the groundbreakers, but rather those who stay on the trodden path), and yes, there are quite a few records of sightings from the continent where you are now, which indicate that the Wandering Jew has been resurrected over the last decade.

Why now, of all times?

Conservative interpretations will focus on the fact that most of the new sightings come from remote areas of the globe, and they will claim that this is the natural pace at which folk tales are diffused.

I, personally, have a different view. I think that as more time passes, it becomes clearer to the world that the State of Israel has failed in its mission: it hasn't solved the Jewish problem. Though the Jews have a home now, thank God, they're still annoying the world in many ways. Annoyance number one: they never stop making noise. They control the news media and never give the world any rest from their troubles and the troubles they cause—

(I can hear you saying, 'Mum, enough of that self-hate', but nevertheless, here is annoyance number two.)

And they, meaning Israeli Jews, wander endlessly. They pop out of their shells like snails, or like a brigadier-general out of the bunker in military headquarters. Activating the gene for wandering that is embedded in their DNA, even though they already have a home. There are thousands of Israelis in Berlin. There are thousands of Israelis in Paris. There's a huge colony of them in New York. And in Toronto. But why speak of 'them'? Look at our family. I'm here, you're in Peru (maybe in a different country now?), your father is in Australia with a new family (seems a bit ridiculous to me for a man his age to have a child, but never mind. I know that you experience every criticism of him as a criticism of you. And his egoism has long since ceased to upset me).

My guess, by the way, is that your writer is Israeli. That is the new Wandering Jew. His choice to write in English is also one of the manifestations of this trend: I, says the writer, do not belong to a particular, small nation of people, I am part of the large, enlightened world.

It would be interesting to know whether I'm right. Let me know if you meet him.

I'm glad that you wrote to me. After you left, everyone here commented on how alike we are, and I felt a special pride. Yes, Inbari, pride.

I don't think that you've 'lost it' (is that how I speak? Really?).

I think that you're trying to find your way. That's hard to do as it is, and our family's special circumstances make it even harder. Only now, five years later, do I understand that I will never return to being the person I was before what happened. That you can never again be what you were after something like that. And you can never really start over.

If only I could help you, Inbar. Mark the path to the treasure of psychological calm with arrows and notes. But whatever I say – even if I'm completely right, as I am about your biological clock – I'd only make you angry. The way everything your grandmother told me when I was your age only made me angry.

Nevertheless, maybe one thing ('I knew you wouldn't be able to control yourself,' I hear you saying in that sharp tone you use with me): write.

You always had the propensity. I tried to write after what happened, but couldn't. All the years of writing research papers had dried up the fountain. Even this letter, which I've just read from beginning to end, is tainted by academic dryness. I know that, but like a scorpion that has to sting, I'm unable to avoid it.

I hope you take this in the spirit in which I wrote it.

Yours,

Mum

PS I'm worried about your grandmother. The last time we talked, she didn't remember where she lived or what day it was. I asked her if she wanted me to hire someone to help her, and she began to shout at me saying she doesn't need my German money. Call her every once in a while, Inbar. She'll listen to you.

Lily

When Inbar called, Lily wanted to tell her about the conversation she'd had with her boyfriend, but she suddenly forgot his name. Arik? No. Amnon? Oshik? And while Inbar was telling her that, in a few hours, she'd be crossing from Peru into Ecuador, she tried to fish the name from the depths of her memory. Alon? Arnon? Everything's very cheap here, Inbar said. You can buy lunch on the street for two shekels. It's not good to eat on the street, Lily said, focusing on the conversation again. Who knows what kind of bacteria they have there, Inbari. Home-cooked food is better for you. And the best food is what you cook in your own home. Here in Israel.

Okay, Grandma, Inbar said.

And don't take drugs, all right? I saw an article in the paper that said all the young Israelis travelling around smoke dope. Drugs are like the food in the street. Nice at first, but you pay the price later, with interest.

O-o-k-a-a-y, Inbar said. And from the way she stretched the 'okay', Lily knew that she was treating her like an old lady again, so she added: and if you do take drugs, and they're good, bring back some for your grandmother.

Inbar laughed and said, no problem. And asked: how do you feel, Grams?

Fine, she replied, considering my age and the weather and the fact that my granddaughter went to Germany without telling me.

I'm sorry, Grandma, Inbar said. I was afraid of how you'd react.

Rightly so, she said. We'll have it out when you come back. Meanwhile, I took you out of my will.

Oy, Inbar laughed and asked, is it hot there now?

Khamsin, she replied. And suddenly, because of the final 'n', she remembered the name that had escaped her, and said, Eitan called.

*

Yesterday, when she got to the shop, the name of something she wanted to buy also escaped her. Milk? Haim asked. Eggs? Margarine?

Ah, yes, butter.

And last Thursday, she missed her weekly gin rummy game because for some reason she was sure it was Wednesday. Her friends called to see why she hadn't come, and she was ashamed to tell them the real reason, so she said she hadn't felt well, and the next day, she was punished for the lie and came down with a real case of the flu. If she had a Filipina carer, she could send her to the chemist's, but she didn't. If there's no love, she believes, it's better to be alone. So she dragged herself to the chemist's, sweating profusely, and bought some cold pills, sweating profusely on the way back too. She took the pills with a glass of water. And because she took the cold pills, she forgot to take her cholesterol pills. In the evening, she saw Shimon Peres on TV, and couldn't decide whether he was Prime Minister or President now, or if he was just trying to discredit one of them.

Like the hairnet she puts around her bun – that's how her memory is now. Or like the box for playing the apricot-stone game that Inbar made at school, which had holes so big that the children could easily throw their stones through them. At the end of breaktime, Inbar owed them stones, and after school, her eyes filled with tears, she ran to her grandmother's house because she knew that there, in the summer, she could always find a bowlful of apricots.

Funny – she takes an apricot out of the fridge, slices it in two and takes out the stone – she remembers Inbar's apricot-stone box perfectly. And also everything that happened on that journey – in the last century! – down to the last detail.

For example – she sits down on her special chair, takes a bit of the apricot and keeps the juice in her mouth for a while – she remembers the name of the ghost ship that came sailing towards them in the second week of their voyage, when they were approaching the Turkish port. *Tziona*.

First, the ship's masts appeared on the horizon, and a wave of conjecture washed over the passengers: was it a ship coming to drive them away? Or a ship whose route had crossed theirs by accident?

As the unknown ship came closer and closer, more and more passengers came on to the deck to see it up close. The seasick came up from the sleeping quarters in the hold. The queue of people waiting to receive rusty water thinned out all of a sudden, as did the queue for the clinic. Lily acceded to the demand of the members of the Newsletter Committee and called a temporary break from their work so that they too could witness the unusual, newsworthy event. Together with the others, she squeezed into the crowd at the far end of the ship and shaded her eyes to help her see the approaching vessel. But then, owing to the weight of the huge crowd massed together on one side of the ship, it listed to that side, and the commander had to shout over the loudspeakers: four steps back, everyone! Four steps back, immediately!

They stepped back and the unknown ship sailed forward, coming to a stop a short distance from them. There was a long, stunned silence: a group of pitiful people wearing faded, salty-looking trousers, stood on the deck before them, their hair unkempt, their bodies skeletal, their necks burnt by the sun, their skin peeling, haunted by a dream—

Just like them.

The realisation that they were looking at their doubles dawned slowly on the crowd standing on the deck. It wasn't that the passengers didn't have mirrors – some of the women had small make-up mirrors, and there was a mirror in the bathroom for the men who wanted to use a razor, but even so . . .

There was no sound but the hum of the ships' engines. No hand waved in greeting, no hat was lifted. Two ships of illegal immigrants stood facing each other in tense silence, as if a battle were about to break out between them and everyone was waiting for the first shot.

And then they heard the sound of Pima's harmonica.

Every song has a moment when it dovetails perfectly with the tone of the person singing it. Lily had sung 'Hatikvah' dozens of times before, but she had never really listened carefully to the words, never truly understood the meaning of the stipulation contained in the line, 'As long as the Jewish spirit yearns in our hearts', or the despair beyond the horizon in the words 'Our hope is not yet lost' – as she did at that moment, when hundreds of people on both ships burst into tumultuous song. At first, the sister ship lagged a line behind Lily's ship, as if singing the second voice. But towards the second repetition of 'To be a free nation', they joined together to become a single choir that demanded in a loud, strong voice: 'The land of Zi-yon, Ye-ru-sha-la-a-yim.'

And then, before each of the vessels continued on its way, something else happened.

In the ship's logs, which were filed in the Haganah archives, that event, for some reason, is not mentioned. But Lily remembers clearly that after they'd finished singing the anthem, a man suddenly leaped from the deck of the *Tziona* into the water. And right after him, someone jumped from their ship. The vessels moved closer for a long moment, which felt like hours. Lily recalls that the person from their ship did the breaststroke, while the one from the other ship did the back-stroke, so they met not halfway but closer to the *Tziona*. The rumour was already spreading on both decks that the two were brothers who had been separated by events on land. But after they'd been hauled on deck, salty to the bone, and wrapped in towels, and after they'd eaten the greasy vegetable soup sent by the kitchen, it turned out that they didn't know each other at all. They didn't even have a common language: one spoke Polish and the other Romanian.

So why did you jump into the water to get to each other? the curious onlookers asked. I don't know, each gave the same answer in his own language: I suddenly had an uncontrollable urge.

Inbar

She recognised him by the sad shoulders, but it seemed so impossible. So she leaned on the rail and pretended to be looking at the city, all the while giving him quick, sidelong looks.

His hair, which had been clipped short when she saw him in the airport, was a little longer now, and the small crest that had grown on the top of his head made Inbar feel like wetting it and combing it down. The shot-with-grey hair had become grey hair that made him look older. And there was a beard on his chin, not a manicured, intellectual beard, but random, unkempt stubble, like grass after a drought. His jeans drooped, there was dried mud on his shoes . . .

But judging by the shoulders and the prominent Adam's apple, it was probably him. Maybe his Nazi really had escaped

him and come here, she thought. After all, at the end of the
Second World War, there had been Nazis who tried to put an
ocean between them and their past.

He folded the map he'd been poring over, put it into his bag
and zipped it up. Now he'll get up and go, she thought, and I
won't talk to him this time either. And I probably won't see
him again. He'll find his Nazi and kill him, and then he'll
disappear, change his name, identity, face. Never mind, she tried
to persuade herself, I can still fantasise about him. Maybe it's
better this way. No complications.

But Nessia refused to accept that, and moved her towards
him.

Only when she was standing really close to him did he look
at her, his expression somewhat surprised, but not enthusiastic.
As if she had interrupted a very private thought.

Shalom, she said anyway, and in the long seconds that passed
before he responded, she rebuked herself for not even knowing
whether he spoke Hebrew, and what a disaster it would be if
he didn't and why in the world was she approaching him like
this, what was she looking for, what did she actually want, this
isn't a story she's making up this is reality, and in reality people
don't—

Shalom, he said, and extended his hand. How do you do,
she said ('How do you do?' Do people even say that any more?
Is her hand sweaty? A little, or a lot?). I'm Inbar.

How do you do, he said. Dori.

Inbar, Dori and Alfredo

Dori

HEBREW. THAT'S ALL THERE WAS BETWEEN THEM,
at first.

He was happy to speak Hebrew with her. That's all. Have
a conversation with her in his native language.

It's been a long time since I met anyone from Israel, he told
her.

We could pretend we never met, she said and smiled. To be
honest, I understand people who prefer . . . you know . . . not
to spoil the magic.

She had a pleasant smile. Open. And she used the word 'magic'.

Just the opposite, he said. How much English can a person
speak? The English muscle in my mouth is hurting already.

The English muscle, brilliant! she laughed. Where exactly
is it located, this muscle?

Well, let me see, he said in English, opening his mouth wide
– it's hard to tell, he continued in that language. Somewhere
. . . hmmm . . . in the suburbs of the tongue.

Well, what do you know, she said, that's right. The tongue
is actually a muscle.

He didn't say anything. An image rose in his mind of his
tongue moving between Roni's legs. And then the word 'oral'
came to mind, which led to another image, in which he's sucking
a fruit-flavoured yogurt, and his father tells him to eat it with a
spoon.

She didn't speak either. She pulled the ends of her hair to
her nose and smelled them.

He opened the map of Peru and folded it and opened it and folded it, and thought, I don't know how to talk to people any more. Even when there's something to talk about.

Try speaking Spanish, she finally said, to his relief.

Spanish?

It's a lot less painful on the tongue.

You know Spanish?

I'm . . . trying to learn it here, while I'm travelling around. Some of the words are similar to the English words; both languages come from Latin. And the words that aren't similar – their melody is so lovely that it's easy to remember them: *corazón*, let's say, which means heart, and resembles a croissant. And *tranquilo*, which means calm, and if you say that word a few times, you really do calm down straight away. And *catarata*, which is a waterfall, and you can actually hear the consonants fall on to one other. *ca-ta-ra-ta.*

You're making me regret not having studied Spanish. There was a beginners' course in the History Department. But at the time, it seemed too difficult.

You studied history? There was a touch of surprise in her voice.

Yes.

And you work in it?

More or less.

What does that mean?

(What *does* it mean, he berated himself silently. Tell her what you do, don't be ashamed of it –) I'm a history teacher.

A teacher! What a tough, important job! she said, without the slightest hint of sarcasm. And after a brief pause: It's funny, I was sure you were a Mossad agent.

Inbar

So if he's not a Mossad agent, she wondered, why had those pictures been spread on the table in Ben Gurion airport?

Tell me – she said quickly, because he wasn't saying anything, just folding his map and looking as if he were about to get up and go – do you have any books you want to swap? I'm stuck with two Holocaust books here. I went to Berlin and wanted to get some perspective. But never mind that. I didn't know I'd be coming here. And for the past few weeks, I've been looking for someone I could swap books with. And the Israeli kids here, just out of the army . . . not all of them read.

Sorry, he said. I didn't bring any novels with me.

Tell me, she tried a different tack, are you hungry, by any chance?

Actually, I am. I haven't eaten anything since this morning.

I thought I'd walk around town, get something to eat. Feel like coming with me?

He looked at his watch and said in a voice devoid of happiness: I'd be happy to. And added: But I don't have a lot of time. We're supposed to head south in three hours, when the road opens . . .

No worries, she says. *Tranquilo.*

So I'll just leave a note for Alfredo, he said. And touched his right temple with two fingers, in the gentle movement she remembered from the airport in Israel.

He's not on an ordinary trip, she thought. He seems too troubled. Too distracted. Maybe he's not a Mossad agent, but . . .

Dori

I'm looking for my father, he finally told her. Before she asked.

They'd already eaten some very bad pizza they bought at a stand in the centre of the city, and she'd said: Why do the newspapers always run stories on 'the best hummus' or 'the best falafel'? They should compile a list of the worst in all categories.

The same goes for Lonely Planet – he replied to her clever remark, surprising himself: why don't they list the ugliest places alongside the most beautiful?

Places Not to Go, she suggested as an English name for the new category.

A gang of teenaged boys sat down at a table on their right. You could almost hear the hormones leaping out of them. On their left sat a group of young girls, also chattering loudly in fluent Spanish. And the two of them sat on once-white chairs, in the middle, between the two groups, like an island.

Are you cold? he asked, because he noticed the slight paleness spreading across her cheeks.

Well, a little bit, yes, she admitted.

Here. He took off his jacket and handed it to her.

What about you?

I'm fine.

Seguro?

What?

That's 'are you sure' in Spanish. It's easy to remember

because it sounds like the Hebrew word for closed, *sagur*. *Seguro* that you're not cold?

Absolutely.

She draped the jacket over her shoulders and let the sleeves drop on either side.

The olives aren't too bad, you know, she said after a moment of grimacing.

And he laughed.

What? I'm serious! she protested, touching his arm lightly. But then she laughed too.

And then, as if he were removing a heavy backpack whose straps were hurting him, he told her.

Nessia

She fell in love with him during that conversation. In the middle of 'the history of the search for my father', which he recounted methodically to Inbar, like a teacher explaining to a student, there was a moment when he spoke about his son, Netta.

Tomorrow's his birthday, he said, shifting his glance to the street. And I'm here. And that's not . . . not right. It's a bit like playing the didgeridoo, he added after a brief pause. I try to inhale and exhale at the same time, worry about my father and worry about my son too.

She noticed the band of white skin on his un-ringed finger, and she noticed that he was rooted deeply in his fatherhood. And tightly bound to his wife. He mentioned her name three times. Men who want to flirt can build bypass roads dozens of words long just to avoid passing directly through their wife's name.

So she said to herself: Eitan.

And said to herself: This is the moment to put a full stop (there is always a moment, she believed, when you can still put a full stop).

Nonetheless, she told him about her new brother, who had been waiting for her at the Hong Kong airport. And as she spoke, she heard herself sounding the way people who called the studio would sound, embellishing their stories in order to get on the air.

After a brief silence, she said: I don't sound believable.

And he said simply, I believe you.

Then he asked her a frighteningly perceptive question: your brother, Reuven, is he your father's first son?

And she replied, no, he's not, and said quickly: How about a walk? She didn't feel like getting into that subject, and she did feel like seeing that walk of his again, which was – she'd noticed in the pizzeria – so very different from the rigid way he sat: a happy, swaying, almost dancing gait. As if his body spoke two languages.

Dori

Where can you walk in a godforsaken border town with a name that means 'graves'?

Back and forth. The important thing is to be moving. That way, the ugliness bothers you less. And we can keep talking in our own little bubble.

They'd been walking for several minutes before he noticed that he was on Inbar's left. When he walked with Roni, he was always on her right. It was more comfortable to put his arm around her waist from that side. And now, with Inbar, he was on the left. His arm not around her waist. Just the opposite. He stayed out of touching distance, like a yeshiva student.

So you've come from Ecuador? she said. What's it like there? They say it's gorgeous.

Could be, he said.

And she aimed her surprise straight at the heart of his self-deception: You mean you don't have any moments when you . . . enjoy yourself?

I do, he said, but then I remember my father. And it passes.

Tell me about one moment like that, she asked. And then made fun of herself out loud: Wow, I sound like Dr Adrian. From the programme I edit . . . edited.

He nodded politely. To his shame, he wasn't familiar with the programme she was talking about. But that didn't seem to disappoint her. On the contrary.

So tell me, she persisted, you didn't have a single moment like that, one you really managed to live in?

And he thought, surprised: Now. With you. This is a moment like that.

But said: In the old city of Quito, just after I landed. I walked around and felt as if I'd already been there, in a previous life. Has anything like that ever happened to you?

Inbar

Yes, she said. In Jerusalem. I've always felt very much at home in Jerusalem, even though I have no Jerusalem past or even family there. From when I was sixteen until two years ago, I used to treat myself to a day in Jerusalem every year on my birthday.

Alone?

I never felt alone in Jerusalem, I felt as if the city . . . embraced me.

Like that song . . .

Yes, the Red Hot Chili Peppers' song – 'Under the Bridge'. Exactly like that.

I'm from Jerusalem, by the way.

Aha! That explains a few things.

Really? What, for example?

It explains why your walk is a bit weird, and why you're a bit repressed, and why there's a kind of involuntary serious-ness about you even when you try to be light-hearted, and why I can imagine you as a boy, wearing dark jeans that your mother folded and hemmed on the outside, and why our conversation is almost embarrassingly personal and direct – she thought.

But said: The fact that you're not cold now, for example.

That's true. Nothing else seems cold after you've walked around Zion Square at night, in January.

A local bus, full to bursting, slowed down as it passed them, in case they wanted to get on. Then its engine sputtered – like

the engines of the buses climbing the Carmel, she thought —
and went on its way.

So where to now? she asked Dori. I mean, what's the next
stop in your search?

Lake Titicaca, he said and sighed lightly, as if he'd rather not
think about the next stop. That's where my father was last seen.

Nessia

She stopped, feigning amazement, and said: I don't believe it!
I was thinking about going there too.

And shushed Inbar, who said: Not believable! Not believable!
How can you be thinking about going back to Peru when you've
just come from Peru?

Nessia's voyages had taught her that lying sometimes means
telling a deeper truth. After all, who chooses one particular lie
out of the thousands of possible lies? She does. Based on her
truest preferences.

Dori

Why don't you come with us, he said. I mean — the words shot
out before he could stop them — we'll give you a lift. If you
were thinking of going there anyway.

Inbar grew silent, as if someone else, not she, had mentioned the possibility. And she suddenly looked pensive, distant, as if lost in deep thought now, and a minute later she stopped in front of a tall building and said, look, there's a cinema here. A cinema in the city of graves. I wonder what's playing now.

James Bond, he knew even before they reached the window where the poster was displayed. He'd recognised the 007 from a distance.

My dad loves James Bond, he said as they approached. That's one of the things we used to do together. I mean, he hastened to correct himself, that we do together.

(And an image rose in his mind: he's a teenager, standing in the queue at the drinks counter, holding the fifty shekel note his dad had given him, and when it was his turn, he bought a Coke for himself, sparkling water for his dad, and a medium-sized popcorn for them both, because the medium-sized container – his dad had calculated – gave you the best value for money.

*

Over the next few days, as he and Inbar became more and more involved, more and more things emerged from parentheses into speech, but meanwhile . . .)

*

I went to the cinema in Cuzco to see *Lord of the Rings*, she said. It was a totally different experience than it would have been in Israel. People kept coming in and out, drinking, eating. There's no interval. They have their own interval whenever they feel like it. People shout to their friends at the other end of the cinema. Applaud when the good guys win.

And that didn't annoy you?

At first, it did. But then, I don't know . . . there was something about it — that mix of what was happening on the screen and what was happening in the room. Blurring the boundaries.

Like in *The Purple Rose of Cairo*, he said, but the opposite.

Exactly. She gave him an admiring, sidelong glance.

They turned away from the poster and continued walking, separated only by the empty, dangling sleeve of the jacket he'd given her.

If she hasn't said anything yet, he thinks, she probably doesn't want a lift.

I used to go the cinema with my dad too, she said. He didn't like going with my mum. He complained that the minute the final credits started rolling, she already had a blistering critique to deliver.

My wife can be like that, he wanted to say. But he didn't think it was the time or place to speak ill of Roni.

The film's probably wildly chauvinistic, like all the others in the series, she said. And several seconds later, she laughed and said: Hey, I'm just like my mum. No, wait a minute, I'm part of the more progressive generation! I'm criticising even *before* I see the film!

They continued walking, and he noticed that she kept smelling her own hair and wondered if the scent was so wonderful that it justified that constant sniffing. It began to rain, and they didn't duck into the nearest shelter, the way people in Israel do when it rains, but kept strolling along till they came to the door of the hostel. And stopped. He'd already prepared himself to say goodbye, ask for his jacket back and exchange email addresses with her, out of politeness—

When she suddenly asked: are you sure it won't bother Alfredo if I come along?

Alfredo

Why not? I said. A little bit of woman smell in the cabin will be good, because honestly, my nose is a little tired of your smell, Mister Dori. O-o-k-a-y, great, he said slowly. Like he really wanted me to say she can't come with us. And half an hour later, I'm already offering her some Bamba snacks from a bag I take out of its hiding place. Bamba! she said, just what the doctor ordered! And took the bag from me and offered some to Dori, who said no, so she finished the whole bag herself, and when she was done, she turned to me and said, Alfredo, you're the best. And then she asked, so this is what you do in life? Fish for people? What an interesting profession. How did you get into it in the first place? So I told her about the Dutch guy. And added a few details that never really happened, that is how I am around beautiful women. One hour turns into three hours. A streetlight turns into a star. A valley turns into an abyss. She listened *excelente*, with her whole body, not just her ears. And Dori listened too, even though he pretended not to. Two weeks we are together, and he never asks me anything. Doesn't take an interest. Like he's mad at me. And I am on his side. It has been a long time since I was so much on a client's side. A long time since I wanted so much to find a live person and not a body. So what does he have against me?

An hour later, the señorita asks me to make a toilet stop. I didn't get mad. In fact, it made me happy. That Dori, to him, every stop seems like a waste of time, and it is just the opposite. The most important things happen on those stops. I also knew that, if we stopped, I could get a better look at her. She had climbed into the cabin before I could see much. And now, when she went to the toilet and came back, I could look at her without shame, and see that she is *exactamente* my taste. Beautiful, full lips. Large, honey-coloured eyes. Soft, round chin. Wonderful cheeks. Cheeks, they can really turn me on, if they're like that, like hers. And the way she walked was hot, a little bit slow, a little bit flirtatious. But with her head high. Maybe there are gringos who will say she is a little too round, and convince her to eat lettuce. But I never understood that thing gringos have about women with lots of curves. No, really, what is more interesting, a flat plain or hills and valleys?

Someone should publish a guide with details and ratings of all the toilets in every country, including the ones like they have here, which nobody should ever go into. *Lonely Toilet*, that's what the guide should be called, she said, and sat down in her seat. Her ass almost spread over to me. The visor on her strange hat almost touched my shoulder. Dori laughed. The first time I hear him laugh out loud since we started looking for his father. I pulled on to the road and they began to think together about the sections in that guide of theirs. Places to Pee. Off the Beaten Places to Pee. To tell you the truth, that gringo talk of theirs annoyed me a little. Who cares if the toilets in, let's say Paris, are clean, if the people there are shitty?

Your family is from South America, Inbar? I asked her just to change the subject. No, she answered. My family is from Israel. And before that, from Turkey and Poland. Why do you ask, Alfredo? Because you are a little . . . you have – I wanted to tell her that her body is like our women's, like a pear, but I once insulted a Yaela from Tel Aviv when I said that to her –

Energy, you have South American energy, I said.

I wish, she said. But I saw that she liked it, what I said.

The phone rang. Morales, one of my people, had found the rich people's daughter from Miraflores, dancing at the Arequipa fiesta, three hundred kilometres from home, wearing a bull face mask so no one would recognise her. Now he doesn't know what to do. Let her keep dancing? Give her a phone so she can call her parents and reassure them? Or snatch her, mask and all, and put her in the car before one of the drunks at the fiesta starts manhandling her?

I could hear in Morales' voice that he was dying to snatch her right off the dance floor. That he was dying to grab her hard and hurt her arms, payback for all the times the rich people in Miraflores humiliated his mother when she cleaned their houses. How's the weather? I asked him. *Mucho calor*, Morales said. So wait till she takes off the mask. She's a spoilt brat from Miraflores; soon it'll be too hot for her. Then take a picture of her and send it to my office. There's an Internet café on the north side of the plaza, next to the laundromat —

But Señor Alfredo — Morales tried.

We'll look at her face and then decide, I cut him off.

Twenty minutes later, we heard the computer ding that meant an email had arrived. I asked Inbar if she could go to the office, print the picture that opened on the screen, and bring it back to me. What office? She didn't understand. I didn't show it to her before, on purpose. I love the moment of shock when they turn the key and the door opens —

Wow — she came back and sat down a little closer to me — it looks like the CNN situation room in there.

I looked at the picture she brought me. The spoilt brat's eyes showed no signs of drugs. I told Morales to wait till the fiesta was over, and then approach her quietly, without attracting attention. Especially not the police's. Five years ago, I told him, I had a case like this of a young girl who ran away to Arequipa, and the idiot police commander put her in jail for a week because that's the procedure in the district.

Tell me, Alfredo, Inbar asked me after I put down the phone, how many . . . searches like this . . . do you work on at the same time?

I could hear in her voice that she had respect for me.

Three, four, seven, depending on the season, I said. And put my arm on the ledge of the open window.

And how many people are working for you right now?

A hundred, I said. The real number was half of that.

In how many countries?

Ah . . . at least eight.

And how do you decide which case to handle personally?

I didn't say anything. All of a sudden, I realised where her questions were going. Bad girl.

Why did you decide, for example – she persisted – that you'd go with Dori? You had lots of other options, right?

Dori

Instantly alert. Before that question, he'd actually been trying to stay as far removed from their conversation as he could. When Inbar started playing with the idea of the Lonely Toilet, he was momentarily energised and he laughed, but very quickly lost interest. Moved closer to the window. Looked out at the mountains. Almost nodded off. Let the two of them talk. Truthfully, the longer they travelled, the less he liked Inbar. People with too large a gap between the way they act one-on-one and the way they act in groups always made him draw back. And that flirtatiousness of hers – that also made him angry. Roni, for example, had never been a flirt (as far as he knew – the qualification crossed his mind). What he did know for sure was that she had her line. And she didn't cross it every minute so that people would like her. Netta had inherited that trait from her. When he was enjoying a show – he said so. When it was too loud – he said so. When his dad's stubble scratched him – he complained. And when his dad got carried away with his hugs, he said: No more hugging.

Alfredo continued to boast to Inbar, and Dori felt like a stranger with them. Different from them in the most basic way.

This is not my threesome, he thought. And sang Ehud Banai's song silently, '*This isn't our party*.' His father hadn't liked it when he sang songs to himself on family trips. He'd claimed that you can't listen to the car radio and the Dori radio at the same time. So Dori had learned to sing silently. Inbar asked Alfredo all sorts of technical details. But she's not really interested, Dori thought. She's just afraid of silences. '*I won't leave till the side ends . . . it's a great song*,' he sang to himself without moving his lips—

When suddenly, Inbar asked Alfredo why he'd decided to go with Dori on the search.

Alfredo didn't answer at first. He seemed to be considering how forthcoming he could be with her.

A large truck passed them, sending feathers flying in the air.

Well? Dori turned away from the window, abruptly giving up his pretence of not listening.

Well what? What do you both want? Alfredo spoke in the plural, but looked at him. An explanation? A reason? That is exactly your problem, you know. All you smart people.

What's the problem? Dori asked.

You always look for reasons. You try to understand the world that way. Cause. Effect. Effect. Cause. Instead of looking at the Nasca Lines, for example, and saying how beautiful, what a dream, you make up all kinds of crap about people from another planet who came and painted them. Just so you have an explanation. There is no way we will ever know the real reasons for our actions, so there is no point in searching for them. We should dance instead.

Dance?

You dance sometimes, Mister Dori?

Yeah, his friend Udi would reply now, I tear up the dance floor every week at the Oman 17 club.

Actually I haven't danced in a while, Dori admits. (When his friends were still really his friends, he liked to go dancing with them. The first time Roni saw him was at a party celebrating the first anniversary of a club. I knew from the way you dance that it would be great to sleep with you, she told him when they started telling each other things like that.)

Anyone who dances knows, Alfredo said. And shifted his glance to the road.

That it is the gods who play the music of the world. And it is left for us to choose how to dance to it.

What?

Never mind, Mister Dori. There is no way you will understand. But you, Señorita, you understand me, no?

Inbar

She told Dori, later that night, about her flight over the Nasca Lines.

Before the flight, she'd called her father from her room. She'd actually planned to call Eitan, but she suddenly missed her new brother terribly, and she remembered how, on their last night in the Hong Kong hotel, the boy had asked her to sleep with him.

What . . . what do you mean, sleep with you? she asked, alarmed.

Read him a story, then lie down next to him in the dark and sing to him, her father reassured her. That's all.

But what story can I read to him?

It seemed that the boy liked falling asleep to the sound of children's stories in Hebrew. He didn't understand the words, but their melody made him drowsy. She read him 'Raspberry Juice' (what a long story it is! she thought. It could've been cut in half) and 'The Lion That Loved Strawberries'. Then she turned off the large lamp, turned on the small one and lay down beside him on the mattress they'd pulled out from under his bed. She felt his small hand reaching out from under the bed rail, and held it, and sang him gibberish based on the Brazilian theme song of a radio programme: *Nao posso fica, nao posso fica, nem mai un minuto con joze.* Then she sang him Yonatan Gefen's 'A Song for Shira,' which had just come out in a new version in Israel: '*A brave new world I'll give you/To feast your blue gaze upon/How lovely to see a half-moon/ Winking yellow, yellow before the dawn –*'

She heard his breathing become rhythmic, and stayed in the bed another minute or two to make sure he'd really fallen asleep. And another minute or two to make sure that it had really happened, that she had really put a little boy to sleep and had enjoyed it.

Inbari! Her father was pleased to hear her voice on the phone now. Dad, she replied coolly and asked, if it was possible, to talk to Reuven. It turned out that the minute he heard her name, the boy ran to the phone and demanded to be handed the receiver. And a minute later, he was talking gibberish to her in his thick Australian accent, which her father translated.

He asked when he's finally going to see you.

Soon, yes?

Yes. We'll be in Israel in two weeks. We have tickets. This time it's final.

Wonderful.

He says he has a new game he wants to show you.

Great. Tell him I miss him.

That's it, her father said. He's gone to watch TV. But I want you to know that was a really long conversation for him. How's the weather in Tel Aviv?

I'm not in Tel Aviv, Dad. I'm in Peru.

Peru?

Yes . . . I went to see Mum in Germany and then I didn't feel . . . like going back.

So you just went to Peru. Great.

Great? You're not worried about me?

No. I trust you, little girl. Just don't hitch-hike under any circumstances, otherwise . . . I'll have to send Gadi after you, eh?

She smiled, despite herself. When she was sixteen, she ran away from home after a terrible fight with her mother and left a note on the fridge saying that she was hitch-hiking to Eilat. So her father sent Gadi, his friend from Ashdod, after her, and he found her at the stop at the Bnei Darom junction, where hitch-hikers thumb rides, and drove her to Eilat. It wasn't until they reached the city that he told her who'd sent him.

See you in Israel, her father said.

Terrific, she said. But still didn't believe him.

*

After she hung up, she had a long shower, luxuriating in the water, which was hot for a change, and then rubbed on some body lotion, sprayed perfume on her neck, and applied some light make-up. For me, she told herself. Certainly not for him. One Hoffman in my life is enough.

She was leaving her room on the way to the lobby just as Dori came out of his room. As if their internal clocks were ticking in the same rhythm. They sat on straw chairs under the canvas covering, far from each other, but not too far. She noticed that he'd shaved for her. The smell of his aftershave — different from Eitan's — tickled her nostrils and then touched the tip of her tongue. The air around them was as thick as milk. Bright clouds sailed very low in the sky. She really had the feeling that if drops fell from them, they'd be drops of milk.

A few minutes after we took off from the small Nasca airport — she told him — the helicopter steadied itself over the desert and the pilot said to us: Look. At first, I couldn't see anything. Just sand. But then the forms started to take shape. The monkey, the spider, the astronaut. Who, by the way, looked like an ultra-Orthodox guy from Mea Shearim and not like an astronaut. And suddenly, I realised that all the explanations for those lines were wrong. They were made for the sheer wonder of it. Someone, maybe one of their shamans, had a dream one night, and when he got up, he decided to draw it. On a large scale. And then that became his dream: to draw gigantic figures in the sand. The fact that he could never see the drawings, because you can only see them from the air, doesn't seem at all strange to me. It's part of the whole thing! Because a dream always has to be impossible, unachievable. Does that make sense, or am I just babbling?

Dori gave a small, almost imperceptible nod. And yet — even though he didn't say a word — it was obvious to her that he understood. She basked in that understanding as if it were a light, velvety breeze.

Then everyone started puking, she continued the story. I mean everyone! Into bags, out the window, on each other. The planes there are awfully small, and the wind is strong. It was exactly like the eating contest scene in *Stand by Me*. An orgy of vomiting. Remember that scene?

Of course.

We landed within five minutes. The flight was supposed to last half an hour, but everyone on the plane pleaded with the pilot to cut it short. No lines and no Nasca. People wanted solid ground.

Wait a minute, Dori said. There's something I don't understand. The Nasca Lines are in Peru . . . and you came to Tombes from the direction of Peru . . . So now you're going backwards? Where's the logic in that?

Oh, Mister Dorrrri – she imitated Alfredo – that is your *problema*. That you try to understand the world like that. Cause. Effect. Effect. Cause.

But—

The gods play the music of the worrrrld and it is left forrrrr us only to decide how to dance to it.

He laughed at her imitation. His laugh was deep, throaty, and surprising, and that made her want to tell him about the moment she asked the woman at the airport where the next flight was going, and she said Teheran. But she didn't tell him, because she knew it would lead to other questions, like why she didn't want to go back to Israel, questions she'd have to answer, because he'd answered hers in detail, and then she'd once again be the bereaved sister and she didn't want to be that, not with him, not now . . .

Tell me – he asked after a long, interstellar silence – didn't you think Alfredo was giving us a load of crap with that answer of his? Don't you think he's hiding something?

I don't know, she said. In the two weeks that I've been here, I've noticed that the locals have a slightly . . . different take on the concept of truth.

You're implying that they're liars?

I prefer flexible. They bend their truth to fit a changing reality.

I don't know – he shifted in his chair as if he were in pain, as if his back hurt – I'm supposed to trust Alfredo. He's supposed to help me find my dad. And I always have the maddening feeling that he's hiding something from me.

But we all hide things, all the time, she said with conviction. And to keep the conversation from ending with that unsettling remark, she added: Don't you think?

Dori

He didn't say anything for a while and thought, how long it's been since I've had a conversation as expansive as this. Conversations with Roni are quick, brief, because of all the things we have to do, because her phone vibrates, and also because of the idea that we understand each other so well that there's no need for details, headlines are enough. And he hasn't seen his friends since their children were born. Moving away from them, which at first he thought was a temporary break in a relationship that had lasted years, went on week after week, until calling them became awkward because he hadn't called for so long. And with his students . . . he had to be careful with them. Even if there was an interesting one every now and then, he had to watch himself, or it confused them. Not to mention conversations with an interesting girl in his class, because that was totally unacceptable. And the other teachers required a different kind of caution. He couldn't arouse their jealousy by telling them about what he earned on the side, or by showing off the excellent student feedback he received. They'd stand him in the corner. Several years ago, he had some conversations with a literature teacher who had a sense of humour, but in the end she got sick and tired of the pathetic salary she earned, and she and her husband relocated to San Francisco, leaving him with the important words trapped in his throat. He used to be able to get them out with his mother, but now . . . And so it was that the only person he'd been able to talk to for the last year — he was embarrassed to admit — was his son Netta, but even though he was a sensitive child and mature for his age (and creative! and kind! and honest! How can it be that no one else sees it?), there were still nuances that he couldn't understand and things you couldn't say to him. And maybe people just can't say anything significant to each other any more, maybe those conversations are a thing of the past, leaving only text messages, and he's the only one who persists, like a dinosaur on the verge of extinction, in hoping for them.

Ah . . . he shook himself out of his reverie to keep from losing the thread, yes, you're right about the fact that we all . . . hide things. Take my dad. It turns out that even he had a secret he kept to himself for years.

Nessia

She doesn't know what day it is. In the Tuesday-or-Wednesday sense. But she can tell you whether it's a good day for fishing, or for shooting arrows into apples placed on farmers' heads, or for sex with married men who have one child.

There's no mistaking this about Nessia: she's anything but wistful. There's nothing pensive about her look. She doesn't walk on air. And she doesn't wear lacy dresses. All her senses are as taut as an archer's bow, waiting to be released to the next moment of pleasure.

Of all the zodiac signs, Nessia is a Virgo. But on the horoscope wheel, she faces Pisces. Because what it says about Pisces suits her better.

Nessia loves water. Just let her stand in the space between Iguazu and a rock to watch the bubbling foam. Just give her a small pool among the rocks on the Ga'ash beach. Or in the Bahamas.

Some people claim that Nessia has gills under her clothes.

Some people claim she has a criminal past.

Criminal past or not — if it were up to her, she'd put her hand on Dori's now, as he tells her about his visit to El Loco's farm and his father's secret, which was revealed to him there. And then she'd lead him tenderly to her room. And remove his shirt, his trousers and his sadness, and make him happy in her bed. With no delays or hesitations. Because why be frightened of the past or the future when only the present is present?

Inbar

She lies to Dori, saying that she's tired, and goes to her room. Then she lies to Eitan, saying in a text message that she misses him. Then she opens her journal and continues Nessia, because writing about falling in love is much less dangerous than falling in love. Then she lies down on the single bed and suddenly sees the violin drawing on the ceiling, the one she'd already seen in the hotel in Lima and in the hostel in the Sacred Valley. Under it, the cities and dates are listed again:

Florence 1411, Toledo 1457, Munich 1606, Paris 1777, London 1934, Rio de Janeiro 2004, Lima 2006, Pisac 2006, Ica 2006.

Ica is here – she remembers the name of the town that appeared on a road sign they passed. And 2006 is now. He must be really close, the man with the violin. Tomorrow morning, I'll ask Dori to come to my room to see the writing, she thinks. Morning is less dangerous than night. At night, she might tempt him or be tempted herself, and she knows herself, Samantha from *Sex and the City* she's not, and when she sleeps with someone, she immediately wants him to be hers alone. No, she resigns herself, morning is definitely safer.

*

Just before she woke up, she dreamed about the boy. He'd climbed on to the railing of a bridge and was going to jump into a river that looked like the Urubamba. But then Reuven, her new brother, came and put his hand on the boy's shoulder. In real life, that couldn't have happened because the boy was tall and he was standing on a bridge railing, and Reuven is four, but in the dream, Reuven's arm was long enough for him to place his hand on the boy's shoulder and persuade him to come down. Then they walked away, close to each other, like two best friends, and after they passed Pima, who tucked a violin under his chin and played the sad violin part of the song, 'Children are Joy', they asked the woman in the colourful cap who was walking towards them on the bridge to take their picture as a souvenir, even though they didn't have a camera. And neither did she.

Lily

In the dream, she's standing in front of a newspaper kiosk, reading the first page of the weekend paper. I don't understand, she says to Pima, who's standing close to the back of her neck, I don't understand why they don't write about the new medication for loneliness. What they print is up to the editor, Pima says, and pulls the arts and culture supplement from inside the thick, folded newspaper. That's not nice, she scolds him. You might at least buy it before you open it. Tell me, he laughs, will you try to correct me when I'm in my grave too? Then he bought a new kind of ice cream called Magnum. She doesn't feel right about telling him, in the dream, that he's been in his grave for quite a few years now. She doesn't want to take a bite of that Magnum of his because she's afraid her teeth won't be up to it. Look, he says, accepting her refusal, and points to a small headline on an inside page, 'Israeli Girl Disappears in South America'.

She wakes up in her bed, uncovered. She must have unconsciously thrown off her blanket again. That's probably why she was cold in the dream.

She gets up, puts in her false teeth, and makes herself a cup of tea and some crackers with margarine. For years, she loathed crackers because they reminded her of her seasickness on that journey, but since Natan died, normal bread has been too soft for her.

When Natan was here, she'd tell him every detail of her dreams. Even the ones that Pima was in. The first few times, she asked him: Doesn't it bother you hearing that there's another man in my dreams? He just shrugged. But when she insisted on an answer, he put his hand on hers and said: Of the two choices, being the man in your dreams or the man who eats breakfast with you and puts his hand on yours, I prefer the second.

He wasn't a man of words, Natan. But sometimes, unintentionally, he spoke poetry.

After he died, she'd tell her dreams to Inbar. In the morning, before she forgot, she'd call her mobile, and they'd exchange dreams. But now Inbar was far away and incoming calls to her phone were blocked. It's good that she's gone, Lily thinks. Not good for her worried grandmother, but good for her. She's been sad for too long, her granddaughter. She's had that yearning-for-other-places look in her eyes for too long. I don't know where I was in my dream, but it wasn't in this country, she'd said more than once, and also: I don't know who the man in my dream was, but he wasn't Eitan.

If, during the signing of the lease, there had been a moment when the lawyer asked the witnesses if anyone had any objections, she would have stood up and said: I do. Inbar shouldn't live with Eitan because she doesn't really—

And maybe not — she takes a bite of a cracker — maybe she wouldn't say anything because it was enough that she'd pushed away her daughter with her big mouth; she didn't have to do it to her granddaughter too.

She sighs and sits down on her memory chair. When she was young, she never thought she'd ever sigh like that, like an old lady. When she was young, she never thought her daughter would want only to get away from her. When she was young, she never thought she'd live to this age. When she was young, she didn't understand that beauty is a gift with an expiration date. When she was young, she didn't believe she'd ever eat pork. And not feel the slightest twinge of guilt. When she was young—

The ship's captain called her to his office and asked her to edit a daily newsletter (aha! That's why she'd dreamed about a newspaper kiosk last night). Rumours were spreading among the passengers, he said. There was a great deal of misinformation. And I think that we would do well to issue a newsletter every day with short updates. Of course, he added, all the languages spoken here on the ship must be represented. Of course, she thought, all the political movements found here on the ship must be represented.

You can use my office, he said. And that very night, Lily called a meeting of the heads of culture committees in all the groups. And Pima was among them.

Oy, just not that *comediant*, she thought as he walked in with his harmonica hanging around his neck. In a minute, he'll start playing a hora and make a joke of the whole thing.

But, surprisingly, Pima proved to be an excellent partner in setting up the newsletter. First of all, he liked the idea. And while other culture-committee heads smirked and grumbled that the newsletter would be biased, and anyway, who has the strength to read a newsletter when he's hungry and thirsty?, he thought that a newsletter was just what they needed now.

I myself have no problem with uncertainty, he said, looked at her, and then turned to look at the others in the room. But most of our comrades find it difficult not knowing where they're heading. And as far as 'biased' is concerned – that depends on us. On how we shape it. Anyone who decides from the beginning that it'll be biased – they must be talking about their own tendencies. Why, for example – he turned to the representative of the religious youth movement – can't we print something learned about the weekly Torah portion, or an article about topical things, and things relevant to the life of the young, new immigrant?

Yes, the representative's eyes lit up, that's not a bad idea. For example, this week, the Torah portion is *Miketz*, in which

322

Jacob's sons go down to Egypt to escape the famine, and our ship has been trying to escape famine for the last few days, and maybe there's an analogy there?

That's what I said, Pima concluded. And with a slight, almost imperceptible gesture of his hand, signalled that she could continue running the meeting.

With time, a clear division of labour developed between them. She was in charge of the day-to-day running of the newsletter: collecting the columns in the various languages on time; editing them; adding last-minute announcements and updates; and hanging a copy at the entrance to the sleeping quarters. After the first days' massive crowding around the only copy, she decided to produce another one and hang it near the stairs leading up to the deck.

Pima was in charge of the daring ideas. Some of them – like his idea to publish a collection of jokes that the members of the various youth movements had told about each other, to defuse the tension between them with laughter – she had to reject. But in other cases, he actually managed to infect her with his enthusiasm. We have to remind our readers of the great goal! he told her. It's very easy to forget why we set out on our journey in the first place and where we want to go, and who better to remind us than Benjamin Zeev Herzl?

In every newsletter, they published a short passage from Herzl's book *Altneuland*, his utopian vision of a Jewish state. Naturally, they began with the passage that described the *Futuro*, the ship that leaves Europe with dozens of intellectuals and visionaries on board, their only purpose, in addition to enjoying the sun-drenched pleasure cruise, being to imagine together what they could create in Palestine. Then they published additional passages in the newsletter. Pima chose them and Lily abridged them.

Why don't you pick shorter ones to begin with? she asked him a week later.

Because I rely on you, he replied, and his Adam's apple was suddenly swallowed up into his throat, as if it had been rounded out.

As the days went by, she began to rely on him more and more where the newsletter was concerned, and sought his advice when she had problems making decisions on matters of principle.

About the stealing, for example. Hunger was growing more intense on the ship, and whenever they tried to anchor at a port and purchase supplies, they were driven away. Their food supply dwindled, as did the water. One morning, they passed a mountain with two waterfalls flowing between the rocks, two waterfalls of sweet water, an abundance of sweet water, and some of the passengers went down to the hold because the sight scorched their throats.

Then things began disappearing. From the storage rooms. From the clinic. From their suitcases. People began whispering and pointing fingers, and Lily didn't know whether to write about this in the newsletter or not. (On the fortieth anniversary of the journey, she suddenly remembered, those who had survived it met at Kibbutz Gal-On. And even forty years later, they hadn't forgiven Asher Eisenbaum, who'd been caught with a bottle of wine in his possession. No one went over to hug him.)

I don't know whether to write a few words about the stealing in the newsletter or ignore it, she admitted to Pima. If we do mention it, it might give others ideas. If we don't, then we're burying our head in the sand. We'll write something about stealing, Pima suggested, but we'll also mention the sanctions to be imposed on the thief. And we'll add a few words from the religious representative. 'Thou shalt not steal' and all that.

That's a good idea, Lily thought. She looked at Pima with new eyes. You've learned a lesson, Lily Freud, she berated herself. You've already begun to believe what they say about you, that you can see inside people's minds. That you have special abilities. So maybe it's good that this Pima has come along and proved to you that even you can be mistaken. And that a person can be a total clown and sharp-witted at the same time.

Furthermore: throughout the long hours they worked together on the newsletter, Pima never tried anything with her. He kept his body away from hers, and his breath far from her nose. Lily thought that Esther had been right, and as soon as he realised that she wasn't easy prey, he stopped. She felt relieved that she didn't have to keep her guard up with him any longer, and while they were working she let herself talk to him about personal things. For example, that she loved to write, and had never imagined that her first opportunity to write for a newspaper would come on a ship of illegal immigrants, of all places. He didn't make fun of her for calling their shabby newsletter a newspaper, and told her about his father, who'd been angry with him for choosing music over Torah studies. If it hadn't been for his grandfather, who was a cantor in the synagogue and encouraged him to continue playing, and gave him the money he needed to pay his various teachers, he would never have been able to play the way he did, which admittedly wasn't exceptional, but at least it made people happy.

And what about your mother? she asked. What does she think about your playing?

My mother's dead, he replied. And from the way he said the word 'dead', and the way he averted his glance, it was obvious that he didn't want to talk about it.

So, really, why haven't you been playing for the last few days? she changed the subject. Pessia, he explained, the clarinet player, is depressed and won't get out of bed, and without a clarinet, there's no klezmer music. Why is he depressed? she asked. No one knows, Pima said. He refuses to speak to us. I can try to get him to talk, she offered quickly. We all miss your music.

Pessia, it turned out, missed his mother's *Cremeschnitte*. When he said the word '*Cremeschnitte*,' Lily's mouth filled with saliva. I miss the sweet carrot salad my father used to make for us, she admitted, and told him — knowing that for Jews, talking about food was often a substitute for talking about the weather, an appetiser before the real conversation — how each of her sisters had a favourite dessert, and her father would try to please them all.

Apple sauce, all my brothers and I get apple sauce during the week, and *Cremeschnitte* on Shabbat. Pessia used the present tense, but unconsciously took his clarinet out from under his blanket and held it loosely, noncommittally.

Tell me, she asked — she was genuinely curious about this, and had already learned that if her question was authentic, her attempt to channel the conversation remained hidden — why the clarinet . . . I mean, how did the clarinet happen to become identified with us, with our people?

Because of the wandering, of course, Pessia replied; how can you wander with a piano? Or a cello? The clarinet and the violin are instruments you can move easily from place to place.

She nodded.

He was silent, his glance moving quickly around the room, his eyes blinking, a look that was familiar to her: the gaze of someone who wants to confess, but needs to be sure that only the person he's confessing to will hear what he's about to say. There were always people in the sleeping quarters. Seasickness claimed victims every day. Fortunately, at that moment, no one was lying in bed near them.

But what's going to happen there, in the new land we're going to? Pessia said, exhaling a long breath, as if he were exhaling into his clarinet. Everyone says that all our hopes will be realised there, and our wandering will come to an end. And who will guarantee that there, they won't demand that I use my clarinet as a hoe, heaven help us? And what will they do with me there? he wondered in a grim voice. Pima is strong. Itzhak is stubborn. Avraham has good fists. All of them will fit into the new land. But what will they do with a Pessia like me there?

Exactly what they do with you here, Lily reassured him. Do you know how important your music is to our comrades? How much they long to hear you again?

A barely visible tremor crossed Pessia's face. Lily knew that tremor from Natan, and thought of it as 'the tremor of an artist who has received a compliment'. A sort of quick, internal straightening of the backbone of pride.

And you? Are you one of those who longs to hear me play? he asked, looking at her with hopeful eyes.

Yes, I want to hear you too – she formulated her response carefully, so as not to give him false hope – just as everyone else does.

The item appeared in that day's newsletter: A festive performance of the klezmer orchestra will he held on deck tomorrow.

In the name of the orchestra's management, I thank you sincerely for what you have done, Pima told her with shining eyes that evening, among the ropes on the deck, and suddenly, before she could respond, bent down and planted a lingering kiss on her hand. We'll save you a place of honour tomorrow, in the front row! he said, and once again, just when she was sure that he had reconciled himself to her rejection, she saw a flash of desire in his eyes.

Dori

And it came to pass that they drove. And parked. And drove. And parked. And showered in hot water. And listened to salsa music on Alfredo's radio. And it came to pass that Dori hated the salsa. And grew used to it. And it came to pass that he swayed his hips to the rhythm in his seat. And Inbar laughed at him. And swayed hers too.

Sometimes, when they're on the Pan-American Highway at night and Alfredo speeds up, Dori feels as if they're on a plane about to take off.

And sometimes, when they're on a side road and rain pours down on to the windows, and waterfalls gush on either side of the road, and the tyres can barely make it through the flooded road, Dori feels as if they're sailing on a ship. A ship of illegal immigrants.

Every now and then, they stop and buy *agua mineral sin gas, hamburguesa con tomate.* Inbar insists on ordering for herself, to show off her tourist Spanish, and he's mildly embarrassed that he can barely distinguish between *gracias* and *por favor*: that's how much he's let himself rely on Alfredo till now.

Every few hours they pass a sign with the name of a place that Inbar has already visited, and she tells him about it. He loves listening to her talk. Everything is a story for her: with a beginning, a middle, and at least one end. And a lot of small, colourful details, accompanied by passionate gesticulation. When she describes walking up the path to the Inca fortress and looking for a place where she could see the river, her fingers make a climbing movement, and he feels that he is walking beside her, panting with her in the thin air. When she describes walking into a party at a club in Cuzco and feeling old, he's embarrassed along with her, and presses up against the wall with her. When she describes seeing a pelican in Islas Ballestas diving for its prey, he feels as if he himself has been trapped inside the bird's pouch, and when, eyes closed with pleasure, she describes immersing herself in the warm springs of Paracas, he can actually feel his lower back pain ease — and all of it makes him very curious, and at the same time intensifies his underlying sense of missed opportunity, of having to see this spectacular continent through the murky glass of his concern for his father.

She's stopped flirting with Alfredo, to his great relief. Yesterday, before they climbed into the trailer, she told Dori that he'd knocked on the door of her room in the hostel and asked her, just like that, without a hint of shame, whether she wanted to sleep in the pull-out bed in his office. You, he said in his *macho de la shmatte* voice, look like a woman who knows how to have a good time. She explained to him that she didn't want to have a good time with *him*, and also hinted that he should take a shower before he propositioned women. I don't think he took it too hard; he seems like the kind of man who takes things as they come, but still — she says to Dori — I'd like it if you'd get into the cabin before me today and sit between us.

Of course, Dori says. And is glad that she trusts him.

They sit a safe distance from each other. She and Dori. Knees not touching. Her sock-clad foot (she takes off her shoes the minute they start driving) not touching his shod foot. She has very high arches. He's never seen such high arches, and his fingers are drawn to them. Drawn to slide slowly down from the soft underside up to the hill of her heel, and perhaps also to encircle her thin ankles. But what is he thinking? Even when she asked him to come and see the Wandering Jew's grafitti on the wall of her room she left the door open and kept her body as far away as she could from his. Occasionally, while they're driving and he passes her the bag of Bamba Alfredo keeps taking from his hidden supply especially for her, his little finger touches hers. And when the wind gusts through the window, her hair brushes lightly against his face. And that's it.

She almost never speaks about her life in Israel. She apparently has some guy named Eitan. And a newly discovered brother in Australia. And a father who made her angry, but you can tell that, under the anger, she loves him very much. And there's a Yoavi, and every time she mentions his name, the small wrinkle above her lip deepens and a rain-filled cloud darkens her eyes. He doesn't ask her about Yoavi. Or the others. Because something about her seems to say: When I'm ready, I'll tell you.

But on the other hand, she expects him to answer all her questions. Immediately. After all, they're sleuthing together and she needs to know as much as possible if she's going to help.

You really do have a detective's hat. He tries to be evasive at first.

What, isn't it pretty? She gives him a hurt look in advance.

Just the opposite, it suits you perfectly, he says truthfully.

Good – she's determined to keep probing – where were we? Your father loved your mother very much.

Yes.

Give me an example of how it showed.

There were . . . lots of small things.

Tell me one.

It took him ten years to build a house in Mevasseret Zion, and in the end, we didn't move into it because he saw how sad the thought of leaving Jerusalem made her.

What?! That's a small thing?! Explain. Elucidate. Expound.

He built the house slowly – he explains, trying to linger on the details, to repay her in kind, to tell her a story with a beginning, middle and at least one end – and did some of the simple work himself. Every once in a while, he'd hire contractors and then fire them soon after, because they didn't treat his dream house with the proper awe and respect. Sometimes he paid them. But they always disappeared in the middle of the job. A few times, he stopped the construction altogether – when the stock market fell, he lost a great deal of money—

So did my dad.

Yes, that stopped the work for at least two years – but once a month, as regular as a metronome, he'd take my sister Tse'ela to visit the frame of the house in Mevasseret. My mother didn't go with them. For her, that house didn't exist. She'd say, I love Jerusalem with all my heart and soul, and Mevasseret . . . It's not Jerusalem, it's the epitome of suburbia. And he'd say, exactly which Jerusalem are you talking about? All that's left of your Jerusalem is a small ghetto of secular people concentrated in a few neighbourhoods. And she'd say, that's exactly why we can't leave. And she'd quote him: I won't give up on her until she sees the light!

Wait, what about you? Did he ever ask you to go there?

He did. I didn't want to.

Why not? Weren't you curious?

The thing is . . . in retrospect, it seems a bit strange to me too, but as a child it was perfectly clear to me: if my mum and dad were disagreeing on something, I was on her side.

So, wait a minute, how did he manage to finish the house in the end?

He had no choice. His partner in the two-family building finished and pressured him to finish too. Because you can't have a house joined to the frame of a house. So he took out a loan and put all the money into the build and finished the house in three months. Then he took my mum to see it. She said she wasn't committing herself to anything, and he said, as far as

I'm concerned, Nurik, you can think of it as a visit to a museum. My sister also went with them.

And you?

I said I had better things to do, and waited for them to come home so I could see . . . what they'd decided.

So . . .

My mum came home and walked around the house like a ghost for a few days, till he gave in and said, okay, Nurik, I can't bear to see you like this. We don't have to decide now. We'll rent it out for the time being, okay?

And that was that. That 'for the time being' has been going on for thirty years now.

Did you ever get to see the house?

Only recently, after he left for South America. I went there to collect the rent from the tenants.

So, how does it look?

Beautiful. Really, it's special. Hand-crafted. I stood there for a few minutes, checked the address twice. I couldn't believe that he'd been willing to create something like that and give it up for her.

It seems like . . . they really did have an amazing relationship, your parents. Maybe that's why it was so hard for him . . . I mean, after she . . .

Died. It's okay, you can say it.

They're quiet for a few minutes. The salsa sounds booming from the radio fill the space of the cabin. Totally inappropriate to the moment, and yet, somehow, appropriate.

You know, she finally says, when people talk about losing someone close to them, they say that they feel as if an organ has been removed from their body. But it's just the opposite: an organ has been added. The sorrow gland, near the diaphragm. I'm sure it really exists, that gland. I'm sure that X-rays haven't revealed it yet because it's hiding really well between the bones.

She suddenly sounds like a child, and looks like one too,

with those lips puckering for a kiss or clenching to ward off an affront. And he still isn't sure if he's allowed to ask about her sorrow. As he tries to make up his mind whether a non-question is worse than a question, or vice versa, she closes her eyes and falls asleep.

A few minutes later, her head falls on to his shoulder. All his muscles tense as if he's been hit and doesn't know what to do. For eleven years, it's only been Roni's head resting on his shoulder. And suddenly, different hair, a different neck. Different weight.

He takes a sidelong glance at Alfredo, to see whether he's noticed what's happened. But Alfredo is busy with another phone call.

Which, in itself, doesn't cancel my membership of the party, he says to himself. And thinks that easing her head off his shoulder now would be rude of him.

The curled end of a strand of her hair falls on to his chest. He wants to take it in his fingers and bring it to his nose, but makes do with a long-distance sniff. The fragrance is delicate, almost imperceptible. But pleasant. Very different from Roni's fragrance. Not better, just different.

It's a good thing she's not my type, he thinks.

And also thinks that he deleted Netta from the story he told. When he went to see the disputed house, he took him along because he'd noticed that even the most onerous tasks take on meaning if he does them with Netta. On the way, they listened to the CD of Passover songs – which Netta refused to part from, even though months had gone by since the Seder night – and he explained that Zion is Jerusalem in the Bible, and Mevasseret Zion is called that because *mevasser* means to announce and the town comes before Jerusalem: it 'announces' it. Netta said, but it's the other way round, first comes Jerusalem, and then Mevasseret, so they should really call Jerusalem Mevasseret-Mevasseret Zion. Dori laughed and explained that it depends on which direction you're coming from, and thought, how can they not see, all those children who don't want to play with him, and the nursery staff who treat him as if he's a burden, how do they not see that he's a magical child? He drove into Mevasseret and continued straight, in the direction of the new neighbourhoods, and looked again at the address he'd written on a piece of paper. Roni had offered to print out a map for him, but he told her he didn't need it, never taking into account how much the town had grown, and how winding it had become. And there was no one on the streets he could ask about the address – just like his mother had said, as suburban as a suburb could get – and Netta was already beginning to lose his patience. D-a-a-ddy! When are we going to get there?! D-a-a-ddy!?! in the whining tone that always drove Dori mad and aroused violent urges. Afterwards, he would feel a profound sense of shame for having entertained thoughts of hitting his child. And then, completely by accident, he saw a sign with the name of the street he'd been looking for and breathed a sigh of relief, because Netta's series of monotonic questions, like a well-orchestrated piece of music, was always followed by a total flip-out, which included – and not always in this order – kicking the back of the seat in front of him as hard as he could, tearing at his ears, screaming at the top of his lungs, banging his fists against the window, opening his safety belt while they were still driving, sinking his teeth into it, biting his tongue by mistake, screaming even louder.

But now, he was saved from the flip-out. There it was, number 24. On the right-hand side of the street.

Welcome, said the woman who opened the door, wearing an apron over her clothes. You're Menny's son? You look like him, I swear, just like him. And this is the grandson? I mean, your son. Yes, this is Netta, Dori said, and tried to pull Netta's face from his thigh, where it was buried, and turn him towards her. How old are you, Netta? she asked, and Netta responded by pressing even harder against Dori. Four and a half, Dori replied for him. Imagine that! the woman cried enthusiastically. Exactly the same age as my little one! They can play together! A-a-m-i-i-ti-i, come downstairs, she called. Dori's refusal was on the tip of his tongue — we only came, he intended to say, to collect the rent and go — but before he could speak, Amit skipped down the beautiful stairs, took Netta's hand and led him confidently to his room.

So, how does the house look? We're taking good care of it, aren't we? the woman asked. Dori gulped, ah . . . to be honest, I've never been here before. Really?! she said with the same enthusiasm — so that Dori began to wonder whether it was fake — so come in and I'll give you a tour.

She took him on a tour around rooms that were too numerous to count, in one of which he found Netta and Amit building a Lego bridge in marvellous harmony. Then she took him out into the huge garden and spoke at great length about each tree and bush, mentioning which ones his father had planted and which ones they had added. Then she offered him coffee and cake in the highly polished kitchen and chattered on about nurseries and classes, and every time there was a momentary silence, which he thought he'd take advantage of to raise the subject of the rent, she quickly filled it with more trivia, and so, between this and that, two hours passed. Dori looked at his watch and said, it's late, and the woman with the apron said, you can stay for dinner, and Dori said, no, no, Netta's mum will be home from work soon, and thought: better leave while things are still good, before Netta hits his bad time and starts making a scene. He stood up and went to the room where Netta was and said, time to go. No! Amit protested, and began crying, and Netta looked at him in amazement — that had never happened to him before. No other child had ever wanted to be with him so much. And Dori was so excited that it had finally happened, that Netta had finally had a positive experience with a child his age, that he gave them another few minutes, and in the end almost forgot to ask for the rent. It wasn't until they were at the front door that he remembered, and said, about the rent . . . and the woman said, my husband and I had a misunderstanding. We each thought the other had a chequebook, but you can drop in next week, and bring your son with you, if that's okay?

*

He misses his son so much that it hurts, and resting on his shoulder is the head of a woman, wearing a cap, who is not his wife.

Resting on his shoulder is the head of a woman wearing a cap who is not his wife, and he misses his son so much that it hurts.

In the background, salsa music trills lightly. And in the more distant background is his father. Lost. Worrying. Deceiving.

He misses Roni too. Yes, he misses her. And his back aches. But he doesn't want to move. It might wake up Inbar.

Alfredo is on the phone to a client. Relax, he tells him. Let's look at the facts: Your daughter was supposed to go down to the jungle on the Death Road, and she hasn't contacted you for a few days now. O-o-kay. There can be all kind of reasons for that. For example? That she's in the jungle and there's no Internet or telephones there. Or that in the end, she didn't go down to the jungle at all, but met people in La Paz who convinced her to go to Salar. Give me twenty-four hours — you know what, give me twelve hours, Mr Cooper, and I'll get back to you with an update. Okay? I know it's hard. But that's how it is. Sometimes you just have to take a deep breath before the picture becomes clear.

Lily

Before bad days came, there were good days: they were permitted to enter the port of Beirut to stock up on supplies. Small fishermen's boats surrounded their ship and offered them merchandise. Sacks of fruit and vegetables – fresh! – were loaded on to the ship. Fresh meat. And pitta bread. Endless pitta bread. She ate some for the first time in her life, and it tasted strange to her. Too doughy. As if the baker hadn't done his work properly. But Pima – where had he learned all those things? – suggested that she eat it with an onion. Cut the onion into thick slices, he said, dip it into oil and then put it into the bread.

And that – she had to admit wholeheartedly – was a true delicacy.

Later that evening, Esther almost choked to death trying to eat an unpeeled banana. I didn't know, she explained when she revived. It's the first time I've ever seen that crooked fruit.

After consulting Pima, she decided to devote the daily newsletter to food: instructions, recipes, serving suggestions. The religious representative added some *kashruth* rules.

People stood at the entrance to the sleeping quarters and read the newsletter. They smiled. They had always read it with serious expressions on their faces, open-mouthed, hungry for news that would ease their worries. That evening, holding their glasses calmly (the amount of water allowed per person had been doubled in the morning, and the water was no longer brown with rust), they caressed the letters with their eyes in satisfaction and smiled.

The moon was full that night, and the klezmer orchestra played especially upbeat music on the deck.

She took her pretty dress with the blue collar out of her suitcase (I'm not getting dressed up for him, she told herself, but for me!). The dress was creased from having been in the suitcase for so long, and she tried to smooth out the wrinkles by applying her mother's method: she rubbed her hands together till they were warm. Then placed them like an iron on the dress.

It didn't work for her the way it had for her mother . . .

But her body was already arched in anticipation of putting on the dress, so she slipped into it. She put on a matching necklace. Walked up to the deck. And danced.

She felt Pima's gaze on her body, but it no longer burned. On the contrary, it felt good. Men came over and asked her to dance. She refused. Instead, she danced with Esther as if they were husband and wife. What she would do if Pima stopped playing and asked her to dance a waltz with him, she didn't know. How can you ever know anything for sure? So she closed her eyes and abandoned herself to the music. Especially to the rippling sound of the harmonica. She'd forgotten how much she loved dancing. How simple and possible everything is when you dance, how airy your thoughts are when you dance, how everything spins when you dance, and you almost stumble and fall, but you don't.

*

And now she stands up in her kitchen, in her apartment on the third floor of a building in the Ramot Remez neighbourhood in the port city of Haifa – and dances. The music from the ship is still playing in her head, and she moves her feet on one floor tile, not moving off it, and imagines Pima's arms around her waist, twirling her around. It goes on for only a few seconds – her

338

knees can't take more – but she keeps her eyes closed even after she sits back down on her memory chair.

Two days after the 'ball', they tried to dock for the first time. A large motorboat was tied to their ship and pulled along behind it to be used as a ferry. When they were close enough to shore – the hills of the Promised Land had begun to materialise on the horizon – the signal was given and the passengers began to board the boat.

The first boatload consisted mainly of the sick and the frail, and children.

Each group was asked to give the names of their comrades who had to reach land as soon as possible. Arguments broke out, as well as one fist fight, and Pima had to separate the combatants.

A list was finally compiled. Itzhak Pessia, along with his clarinet, was on it. Although he returned to playing in the orchestra after his talk with Lily, not only did his depression persist, but it deepened. One night, Pima caught him near the ship's clinic with two packets of sleeping pills in his possession, and even though he firmly denied that he had any intention of harming himself, Pima had persuaded all the members of their group not to take any chances.

Lily and Pima watched him now, as he found a place in the boat. He held his clarinet case close, cradling it in his arms the way the young mothers in the boat were cradling their babies.

The boat's skipper pulled a rope and the motor hummed. The boat began to move away, and Lily's muddled emotions roiled inside her, like the churning trail left in the water by the propeller: envy was there, of course. Those people were going to set foot on the land of Eretz Yisrael before her. Guilt about the envy was there too. And concern that Itzhak Pessia might jump into the water prematurely, that his clarinet might fall in. And also surprise about the the hills of Zion, which were emerging on the horizon: how could they look like any other, ordinary hills? There was supposed to be something unique about them, something that would justify the difficult journey they had endured to reach them.

When the boat disappeared from view, a spark of cautious joy finally ignited inside her: she would be in one of the next boatloads. Yes, maybe her wandering and nausea would come to an end, at long last, tonight.

Several minutes later, a rumour began to spread: the boat's officers sent a radio report that a great deal of water was leaking into the boat from the cracks caused by the sun and wind while it had been tied to the mother ship, and now the officers were undecided: continue or return? The water level keeps rising, said the reports from the communications room, and it's already reached people's knees. They should continue, Pima said, either to her or to himself, it's never good to go back.

A large crowd had gathered on the deck and was watching with growing anxiety as the boat reappeared on the horizon. Returning. Approaching. Sinking. Suddenly it looked more like a walnut shell than a boat. The passengers on it were standing, eyes gaping in terror, legs immersed in water. The crowd on the deck watched it as if it were a play, as if the sea were a stage set made of aluminium foil, as if the sound of crashing waves were coming from a gramophone. Lily felt a powerful urge to break the divider between the play and the audience. To fire a shot into the air, to pull down the curtain. To scream at her comrades to stop staring. But they could do nothing: only wait until the boat was close enough to return the passengers to the ship. When the boat was alongside, Itzhak Pessia fainted. Pima left Lily and ran down to the lower deck, then climbed aboard the boat to rescue Pessia. He tried to get his hands under Pessia's arms, but even unconscious, Pessia clutched his clarinet case as tightly as a vice and Pima couldn't get a comfortable grip. The boat began to tilt into the sea. They were the only two people left on it. A chill ran down Lily's spine. This is exactly how she felt when they walked past amputees in the square of the Warsaw market — she wanted to look away, but couldn't. Her heart beat Pima. Pima. Pima. Pima wrenched Pessia's clarinet away from him and threw it into the sea. Then he hauled him on to his back, as if he were a sheep, and carried him up the rope ladder that had been tossed down to him from the ship.

A few seconds later, with a soft murmur, the boat sank into the depths, and along with it, their hope of reaching the desired destination that night. Shortly afterwards, they received an order to sail quickly away from the coast or risk discovery by the British Coastguard. And if that weren't enough, the communications people picked up some very upsetting broadcasts: The Germans were concentrating large forces on the Polish border. Hitler denied intentions to invade. But who could believe that hateful enemy. And their families were there, across the border — brothers, sisters, her father, who had waited for her, wearing his karakul hat, on the pavement in front of the hotel until night fell, and had said before parting from her, don't worry if you can't come out to see me, we'll see each other again in a few months in Eretz Yisrael anyway. Then he had leaned over and kissed her on the forehead, and laughed, once I had to bend down to kiss you on the forehead, and now look, Lilinka, I have to stand on my tiptoes—

None of the members of the newsletter committee came to the meeting that night. Lily was feeling weak, especially in the fingers she used to hold a pen. What in God's name could she write on a day like this?

Nonetheless, she forced herself to describe the day's events and find a bright spot: the boat might have sunk with all the passengers on it, she wrote. It was a miracle, she wrote. Then rubbed it out. Then tore up the page and started again. And tore up the second page as well. So it went until the middle of the night, when she finally found a reasonable version that didn't make things look better than they were, on the one hand, or cause complete despair on the other. But she still felt she was disappointing her readers. Because what's the point. What's the point of words on days like this, when everything drowns?

She hung the page at the entrance to the hold, and with rubbery legs stumbled down the stairs to the sleeping quarters.

The sour smell assailed her nostrils more powerfully than usual: tonight, she thought, the strong smell of fear had been added to that of sweat and vomit. She planned to go to her bed and take the photograph of her father out of her suitcase, but halfway there her legs changed their mind and took her to Pima's bed.

He had put up a sort of curtain – a sheet – that separated him from the others and could be opened and closed like a normal curtain. So she opened it slowly and found him sleeping on his back (Natan always slept on his side). Beads of sweat dotted his bald head. Or were they drops from the sea that still hadn't dried? If she tasted them she'd know.

She took off her shoes and lay down in the small space left by his body. He turned on his side in his sleep, facing her, making his body concave to give her more room. Her back against his stomach, her head on his chest – she felt his heartbeat accelerate and his blood slowly awaken towards her. A moment later, his hand began to caress her body. In long strokes . . . that became bolder and bolder.

Nor arumnehmen, she said in Yiddish, taking his hand and placing it around her waist. Just hold me.

Nor arumnehmen, he repeated. His breath, she remembers, made the back of her neck tingle.

Nessia

Usually, she likes men who navigate without a compass. Men who don't think too much. With large, rough hands. Men who'd been to Tuichi and returned. With long legs. And a broad back. And fresh sweat. And light-coloured eyes. Fearless wanderers like her, with at least two passports.

Dori didn't have all of that . . .

But still (maybe she'd picked up a vibe from him, a kind of subliminal wildness), she was the one who pushed Inbar's head on to his shoulder. In her sleep. On purpose.

Inbar

Wakes up, embarrassed and not embarrassed, moves away from Dori slowly. First her head, then her body, point of contact after point of contact – until their thighs separate too. She takes off her hat. Finger-combs her hair. Looks out of the window. Brushes non-existent crumbs off her shirt. Pulls it up to her nose and finds that a man smell is clinging to it. A ripple of guilt passes through her torso. What's happening here isn't fair to Eitan. *Maybe it's good that you went to Peru. It's probably what you need now. Just take care of yourself there, okay*? his lovely last email said. And what about her? A ripple of guilt, that's all. That's all she feels for him. Not a wave, definitely not a tsunami. A ripple that passes. That dissipates. It was so nice to rest my head on another man's shoulder, she thinks in alarm. Does that mean something? Or is it just the journey that's deceiving her? Where is she anyway? On the road to Haifa, for example, she can open her eyes at any given moment and know exactly where she is and how much longer, down to the second, it will take to reach Hadera. But here? Alfredo's talking on the phone, his voice more lively than usual. She tries to understand something of his rapid Spanish. *Computador* means computer. *Claro* means clear. *Hijo de puta* is *hijo de puta*.

Wake him up, he tells her after he ends the phone conversation, and gestures towards Dori with his head. Hey – she touches his sad shoulder – wake up (if she knew his nickname, Dori'keh or Dori'le maybe, she'd use it now). She shakes him a little harder, but still tries to be gentle. Finally, he opens his eyes. Rolls them. Runs a hand over his cheek. His neck. Lightly strokes the spot where her head had rested – what? Has something happened?

Good news, Mister Dori, Alfredo says, and lowers the volume of the salsa. My people found the hostel where your father slept in Isla del Sol. And not only that. It turns out that he left a file on the computer there.

A file?

With something that he wrote.

Everyone writes, the inappropriate thought passes through Inbar's mind, all of a sudden, everyone writes.

So come on, Dori says, tell them to send it to us here, to your office.

The hostel owner says that he cannot do this. It violates the privacy of his customers. In Spanish, that means he wants money. But that is okay. After the next turn in the road, look

344

out of the window and you will see Lake Titicaca. We will get up tomorrow and cross the border to Bolivia. We will take a boat to Isla del Sol and I will take care of the file then, *bueno*?

Dori

Jumps into the boat first and holds out a hand to Inbar. She ignores it and jumps over the space between the pier and the boat, and almost loses her balance when she lands, almost falls into his chest, but manages to steady herself without any help. There's a large tourist ferry next to them, also sailing to the Island of the Sun. Alfredo had warned them that it spends quite a while at several of the Straw Islands, so they rented a private motorboat. Their backpacks are at one end of the boat, and they're at the other. There's also a lifebuoy, and the captain, a man with a furrowed brow who looks like one of the Incan gods, asks them to put on the yellow life jackets. They set off with a gentle hum of the motor. The water is clear, the sun turns everything golden and the snow-capped mountains frame everything in white. When their boat passes through a very narrow strait between two tiny, verdant islands, he glances sidelong at Inbar. To his surprise, she seems unimpressed. This is the highest lake in the world! Alfredo announces, but she remains indifferent. The motor sprays two drops of water on her face, and one hangs from each eyelash.

So, Dori asks her, don't you think Lake Titicaca is beautiful?

She wipes the drop off her left eyelash – it's beautiful, very beautiful, but – then says nothing.

But what? he asks her loudly, trying to be heard over the sound of the motor. Beautiful but what?

To be honest, I . . . want you to find your father, she shouts. That's more important to me now than . . . the scenery.

He bends over her, his cheek grazing her hair, and then says into her ear, as if whispering a secret, that's not good, you won't enjoy your trip that way.

It's not a matter of good or not good, she says sharply, looking him straight in the eye but drawing back slightly, it's how I feel.

*

What the torch does to the bowl of oil during the opening ceremony of the Olympics—

That's what her words do to him.

*

He wants to get up and hug her, but the balance of the boat and of life is too delicate. So he stays where he is, and to make it up to her somehow he says: My father has motion sickness. I didn't find that out until I was pretty much grown up. We went to a fairground and when I asked if he'd go on the roller coaster with me, he said he couldn't. I was very angry. I thought he didn't want to. That he'd rather be with my sister. I just could not believe that there was something he couldn't do.

He didn't explain it to you?

He tried. But it wasn't in him . . . to admit a weakness. The man received a medal of valour after the Yom Kippur War.

So how do you know that he— who told you?

My mother. In the end, she went on the roller coaster with me, and after we survived that drop when everyone screams, she told me he had motion sickness.

346

Hang on . . . If he has motion sickness, how did he get to the Island of the Sun by boat? Something doesn't make sense here.

Only one thing doesn't make sense? he says. Nothing makes sense here!

Maybe now that computer file will explain it for us, Inbar hopes.

Her use of the plural makes him both happy and embarrassed, and he restrains a sudden urge to reach out and wipe away the bead of water still hanging on her right eyelash. And lick it off his finger.

*

A steep staircase leads from the dock to the dry part of the island, on the hill. They're called the Inca Steps or the Yumani Steps, and according to Lonely Planet, there are 1,396 of them, and according to Alfredo, 1,500.

In any case, there are a lot of them. But they have no choice, so they buy a bottle of mineral water and start climbing.

Alfredo excuses himself — he wants to settle things with the hostel owner — and skips up the steps like an alpaca on an urgent mission, two at a time. Then suddenly stops and searches his pockets.

You left them in the boat, Dori shouts up at him.

He goes back to the boat, skips past them lightly again, this time with his sunglasses on.

His lungs must have adapted to these heights, Dori says to Inbar as they watch him climb the hill. The very act of speaking robs him of precious oxygen. Now he has to stop. He's dizzy. His temple pulses with a dull ache and slight nausea begins to roil in the bottom of his stomach.

How did my father do this? he wonders. A sixty-year-old man. How did he escape having a heart attack in the middle?

Inbar stops one step above him. Breathing easily.

You don't find this hard going? he says in surprise.

I'm from Haifa. Every morning, just to get to the top of the street from my house, I had to walk up 123 steps. Look at my calves — they're like a football player's.

She raises her trouser legs, revealing Roman calf muscles and those ankles of hers.

She sees his glance lingering slightly too long, but her hand is in no hurry to lower the fabric.

Shall we sit for a while? she finally says, drops her trouser legs and comes down one step. They sit. Dori dips his hand in the water flowing in the narrow aqueduct beside the steps and wets his face. Only after he does this three times can he get his breath back and really focus on the beauty of the scene.

The water of the lake is still, very still, and the colour is a spectacular bluer-than-blue. The mountains that encircle the blue are tiered with well-tended agricultural terraces that reach almost to the shoreline. A tourist-packed motorboat leaves the dock, drawing a resolute arrow in the water: move forward, move forward.

These first moments in Isla del Sol, like his first moments in Quito, fill Dori with an intoxicating sense of familiarity. As if he and the place fit together. Or as if he's been there in a previous life. But in Quito, he had no one to share this with, and now . . .

Your brain isn't getting enough oxygen, so it can't distinguish between familiar and unfamiliar, Inbar says with a smile when he shares his thoughts with her.

But I felt the same way in Quito.

So maybe there's a hidden South American branch in your family?

My grandparents came from Poland and Jerusalem, so I don't see how . . .

What do you mean, Jerusalem?

My mother is ninth generation Israeli, from a long line of Sephardic Jews.

So that's it – Inbar jumps up as if she's found a treasure – her family's originally from Spain. And Spain ruled here for hundreds of years. And Poland too—

What do you mean, Poland?

Wasn't there something about Jews who came here to escape the pogroms? I have a vague memory of that from history at school.

They didn't come here, exactly. It was Argentina. Baron Hirsch bought a lot of land there because he thought it was the best place to establish a national home for the Jews. And not only Baron Hirsch – Dori inhales oxygen and continues, and unconsciously begins moving his hands as if he's lecturing in front of a class. Herzl himself considered two territories for his vision of the Jewish state: Palestine and Argentina.

Not Uganda?

The truth is that the possibility of Uganda was forced on him. It wasn't something he really wanted. But he seriously considered Argentina. He devoted an entire page in his book to comparing the two options and points out that Argentina is 'a very spacious land with a small population and mild climate'.

And they never really persecuted Jews there, did they? Sounds perfect. So why did he finally go for Palestine anyway?

Because he believed that the myth of the return to Zion had a better chance of persuading a critical mass of people to leave their homes for the unknown.

You don't say!

A couple of tourists are coming up the steps towards them, and Dori thinks: they're my father's age. The woman stops; the lace of her right shoe has come undone. Without a word being said, the man, seeing the untied lace, bends down and ties it. As they approach, Dori moves closer to Inbar to let them pass. And after they've gone, he remains very close to her.

I wonder what would've happened if we'd taken the Argentinian road, the road untaken, she says in a slightly hoarse voice, rubbing her chin with her hand as if Herzl's beard were growing there.

'The road not taken' — what's that poet's name?

Shame on you, Mister Teacher — she teases him — Robert Frost! Didn't you learn that poem by heart at school?

Yeah. Two roads diverged in a yellow wood . . . ahem . . . etc., etc.

And sorry I could not travel both. No, really, imagine if the Jewish state were in South America. The big trip after the army would be to Eretz Yisrael.

And maybe . . . maybe there wouldn't *be* an army.

Yes, Inbar sighs sorrowfully, then moves slightly away from him and shakes her head as if her thoughts were plant stalks you could shake, and stood up and asked, can you go on?

I'm not sure I can, but I want to, he smiles at her.

And she holds out a hand and pulls him forward, up the steps.

People pass them on their way down from the hill to the dock, to sail back to land:

A large, noisy groups of Israelis.

A woman trying to take pictures as she walks.

And a little boy of Netta's age, alone. Barefoot. Maybe an orphan.

Alfredo is waiting at the top of the steps. It is all taken care of, Mister, he says, and places his hand on Dori's shoulder. The file is open on the monitor, the computer room is at your disposal. The owner and I agreed that no one would enter the room while you are reading. I will not go in either, amigo. But if there is something disturbing written there, I want you to tell me immediately.

What do you mean, disturbing? Dori tenses. What do you call disturbing?

Alfredo hesitates briefly before he says, if your father writes that he wants to die, *por ejemplo*.

Menny

to write now to write in order to slow the beating of my heart if you think about how fast your heart is beating it beats faster so it's better now to write faster than your heart is beating better not to use words like better they're the words of a strategic advisor but i no longer have advice or strategy and there is no balance and only a step separates me from

when i came back from the inferno i was sure i had a piece of shrapnel stuck in my body so i went to the family doctor he said it didn't seem likely but he still sent me for an x-ray which didn't show anything but i demanded to see a specialist and i went to four or five doctors and nurit came with me to all of them and didn't say a word to me or the doctors and the last one of them asked her to stay in the consulting room after i went out and i didn't understand what that was about i was no boy i was a war hero i had a medal but i went out anyway there's something intimidating about doctors and i was already thinking that he was flirting with her that he'd picked up on that adventurous look in her eyes and he'd take her away from me now when I need her the most but in the end he just told her that they shouldn't dismiss out of hand the possibility that there's something emotional going on here what kind of language is that dismiss out of hand that's exactly how they started to cover their arses in intelligence after the war post trauma the doctor said it has strange ways of manifesting itself and maybe the shrapnel here is metaphoric metaphoric my arse i told nurit and she said it's no shame mentsch there are a lot of people who and i cut her off I think that was one of the only times i ever shouted at her i'm not people just be with me and everything will be fine and she said of course i'll be with you i'm not going anywhere but i still thought that one day she'd leave me for someone else it was in her eyes or at least that's what i thought and in the end she really did leave me but not for someone else and the pain of her going of her not being never leaves me even writing about it doesn't alleviate it

the keyboard has hebrew letters that's a fantastic marketing idea even in the hurricane state of my brain i can see that there are so many israeli kids on this continent so many kids with shrapnel in their bodies not only the boys but also some of the girls are like that they're restless and need drugs to forget men from other countries our young people they travel for no reason run away escape i already said restless but sometimes one word leads to another one thing leads to another an internal domino knocks over an internal domino and you find yourself on the roof of a hostel on the Island of the Sun looking at the sunset and seeing blood spilled on the sky look at the snow-capped summits of the cordillera real and see the pale faces of people who died thirty years ago in the desert look at the boats and notice that one of them draws a question mark in the water where do you go to from here after all going back is impossible

my father used to come on yom kippur afternoon walk the whole long way from armon hanatziv with his harmonica around his neck happy for the chance to be without mum without her driving him crazy he'd give a rhythmical knock on the door kiss nurit on both cheeks because she taught him that that's how the sephardim do it and he'd ask her for a glass of water and make fun of her for fasting who are you fasting for nuritke god left the earth in 1939 didn't they tell you and she'd laugh they got along well from the first minute those two an adventurer had found his adventuress he'd ask if i was in my room and she wouldn't say a word but i could imagine her nodding with her chin she always nodded with her beautiful chin and then he'd come in and sit down and play his harmonica continuously till the meal that broke the fast and i'd listen we barely spoke a word here and there my father only talked with women actually only with beautiful women every now and then he'd disappear for a few days saying he had a performance

and i wrote in a diary every day not on a computer like now but in a real notebook with a yellow binding and white pages without lines our teacher asked us to write about what we did on our summer holiday and i wrote with spelling mistakes about fairgrounds and bungalows and four flavours of ice cream and a sea you could float on but it burns terribly and about a father who packed a large suitcase and said he was going to america and maybe I'd go to see him in america after he got settled he said there are huge fairgrounds there don't cry son don't cry he said and kissed me on the forehead and came back a week later in the middle of the night and came into my bed instead of theirs and tossed and turned till morning and I pretended to be sleeping but I heard every single sigh

to write now never stop writing so that maybe finally i'll reach the heart of the artichoke so that maybe finally i'll be calm so that maybe finally

he tried to teach me how to play what a humiliating failure that was we tried everything piano recorder guitar harmonica xylophone flute nothing worked and he'd say what a shame you don't know what you're missing and my mother would say leave the boy alone what do you want from him and it would turn into a big argument which usually ended with her saying no one's keeping you here pima the door is always open you can always go to your lily and i swore to myself that i'd never argue like that with my nurik and really i never did argue with my nurik at least not around tse'ela or dori with him my father did succeed from the first minute from the first time he touched the trumpet he received for his bar mitzvah it was clear that the musicality in our family had simply skipped a generation like eye colour there were years when they were very close because of the music there were trumpet duets there were performances and later when dori said he wanted drums he bought him a set he just went out and bought him the most expensive set of drums in the shop that miser and i wasn't jealous i was glad that he had a grandfather figure if not a father figure

to write now and spill out every bit of it here for example what I wrote about that grandfather figure is something i never dared to think about when you shuffle the deck you have no idea what you'll pull out of it when i came back from the inferno i didn't feel anything as if all my feelings had been blunted blocked barricaded what difference does it make how you say it i felt nothing and dori was a year old and cried when i came in the door because he didn't recognise me and i wasn't sad that he cried i couldn't care less that he cried tse'ela was four she fought for my love until she got it and dori was too young to fight so he just gave up on me and i immersed myself in my strategic consultant work what would you say now about what's happening to you menny peleg what in your opinion is the streategy for getting out of the crisis

if only it were a crisis it's like a dam collapsing and all at once everything

i saw it happen to someone else ra'anan rom was his name a pilot in the reserves a senior director who fell in love with a woman 20 years younger than him and she toyed with him for a few months till she threw him over for someone her own age we talked about his business for five meetings until he got to that until he cracked suddenly i can't stop thinking about her he said and took off his glasses i'm sitting at a directors meeting and i imagine her coming into the room my heart he said has been beating too rapidly lately he said i'm afraid i'm going to lose it he said and stood up and wanted me to hug him so i hugged him he was a big, unpleasant man and it was hard to put my arms all the way around him but i hugged him as tight as i could to calm his trembling and asked myself as i was doing it whether i should charge him for it or not

slowly after the war i started feeling again nurik taught me feelings all over again the way you teach a child to tie his shoelaces but there was still a terrible awkwardness between me and dori why terrible who wrote that word whose are these fingers playing do re mi fa sol la enter on the keyboard you see dad i finally found myself an instrument

last night i saw nurik again on the roof of the hostel you can see the lake from there and the moon that illuminates it like god's huge torch it's not like in hamlet a ghost that pulls me to a hidden place in a castle and talks to me after midnight and telling me to take revenge it's something different like a screening in my head she wears a different outfit each time today she had on a crimson jacket that i didn't like but she never used to dress according to what I liked dori cried at nursery once because someone took his crimson marker he cried all day crimson crimson until the teacher called us to take him and i was ashamed that my son was such a crybaby you're allowed nurik told me on the roof of the hostel tonight after so many years of being strong you're allowed to be weak and fall apart a bit so you can put yourself back together again

we the generation that founded the state of israel are a fucked-up generation really there's a singer yonatan gefen's son i think who screams that we're a fucked up generation and every time i hear him i get furious fuck you what the hell are you talking about a fucked up generation you had everything handed to you our parents had dreams and left us the hard work of realising them sewage electricity plumbing build die earn money to support our children their dreams and their trips and their long treks in south america who even had time to feel who even wanted to talk about pain when i came back from that inferno people didn't want to hear they'd change the subject start singing let it be let it be i'd start talking about the inferno let it be let it be both feet on the ground that's my generation the generation before it dreamed and the one after it dreams and that's my generation the founding generation both feet on the ground slowly slowly slowly sinking

every once in a while i'd dream that i was sinking into a swamp feet knees waist help and nurik with her nurikian instincts would feel how i was sinking and in her sleep would extend a real hand to my side of the bed and pull me up

during the years when she didn't want me i'd see her on mt scopus standing and talking with another girl or worse with another guy she had long hair then and there would be stabbing pains near my diaphragm the kind you feel after a fast run because she was with someone else and at the same time i had the quiet knowledge that in the end we'd be together it's hard to explain i'd been with many other women during the 5 years i waited for her but i never forgot the first time we walked together it was on agron street after a james dean movie we went with friends but they scattered in different directions and we kept walking beside each other just the two of us in the cold jerusalem night and we talked and talked and the entire time i had the feeling that we were walking home now that was the feeling that we were walking towards our shared future

but how can i put myself back together i asked her yesterday you say put the pieces back together but you don't tell me how and she said you're the one who always says that in crisis situations you have to be creative you have to change direction true but what direction what what what is the new direction i asked and she said that's something that has to come from you it's as if you are both the chick and the egg enclosing it how i hate it when you speak in metaphors i said and she laughed and said you remember that you left the factory because you wanted to be on your own so this is exactly the same thing you're standing on the same spot again okay i said i didn't have a choice then when i came back from the inferno i wasn't capable of letting anyone tell me what to do i wasn't being spoiled or arrogant i just felt that i'd end up hitting my bosses if i stayed there take a day or two off to pull yourself together that's what they said when i came back like napoleon who'd tell his terrified soldiers stand on your feet or I'll cut them off and that's why i left i just didn't have a choice then nurik but this is a different story why is it different nurik said maybe you really don't have a choice now either mentsch

they believe that the sun was born in that lake and at 5 in the morning when i go up on the roof to see the rays of the sun break through the spaces between the mountains and slide down the quinoa terraces i believe it along with them and i believe in manco capac and mama ocllo the adam and eve of the incas i don't know what the secret of their affection for the letter 'c' is but they knew the secret of the potion so they deserve respect and after all one god makes no more sense than many gods and maybe even less after the sun rises i go back to sleep in my bed and wake around midday eat trucha carvilla which is a very tasty trout a real delicacy and then i sit down on my dr gav back rest on a chair at the computer with the hebrew letters and write without stopping i mustn't stop i mustn't look down every now and then someone says something to me but i don't answer there's nothing to say i've spoken and spoken and spoken presentation after presentation after presentation a thousand dollars and sometimes even more for 50 minutes of charisma now i'm silent also because i'm afraid of what might come out of my mouth god forbid if i open it maybe sobs maybe horrific screams so i'm silent

i don't talk to my children either i know i should but i can't nurik berates me at night but i can't so at least write an email so they don't think that something has happened to you she says in a tone that she knows i can't refuse so i wrote one short email but every word was dug out of me with a supreme effort i still don't have anything to tell them i can't even say don't worry about your father because i myself are worried and don't know how much i am theirs at the moment and don't know how this storm will end and how many houses will still be standing when it passes when dori was little we went to a fairground in tel aviv and he wanted to go on the roller coaster with me I told him that i couldn't because i have motion sickness and he didn't understand didn't believe didn't want to believe and demanded that i go on it with him anyway children shouldn't see their parents weak and sick i wish i hadn't seen my father after he became ill and couldn't play anymore not that it's the same thing maybe i should admit that i'm sick all the klezmorim from their ship came to his funeral even pessia who plays the clarinet in the philharmonic and they played three pieces in his memory one of them was hatikvah by naftali herz imbar arranged for wind instruments and i kept looking for lily the whole time i wondered which of all the women there was the one whose name hovered in the air of our home like a wasp but she hadn't come or hadn't dared to approach me

yedidiya the driver was worried because he hadn't filed his tax returns and kept saying that the deadline had passed or would pass soon and late filers had to pay a very big fine and he didn't believe they'd go easy on him because of the war he didn't talk about his children and he had four of them he didn't talk about his wife and he had a good one every other day she sent him a package with underwear and butter biscuits that melted in your mouth but yedidiya just kept talking about income tax income tax income tax until elida the loader told him that he wished he'd get hit by an artillery shell maybe that would shut him up elida had already been wounded in the six day war a minor injury a few stitches over his right eyebrow but he believed that it was like an inoculation he also believed in the holy one may his name be blessed and in arik sharon and in brigitte bardot whose picture hung right in front of his eyes to remind him why it was worth staying alive and there was also rafi the gunner he and i became really good friends very quickly the kind of friends that only soldiers who don't know whether they'll see the morning can be rafi the gunner we said that when it was all over we'd go to see james bond together that was more than 30 years ago for more than 30 years i haven't thought about my crew and suddenly all at once

there was a pit a real pit that they threw all their shellshock victims into just like joseph in the bible but not because of jealousy like with joseph but because of embarrassment and maybe they also thought in their heart of hearts that it was catching people think that mental problems are contagious then when i went to see the regiment doctor and told him that i hadn't slept at all since what happened happened and i thought i had a piece of shrapnel stuck in my body he sent me there without an escort to this very day I don't know why there was no escort the pit was at the far end of camp behind the latrines surrounded by barbed wire and when i lifted the cover i saw ghosts and closed it immediately the way you close the cover of a boiling pot after you check how the rice is doing here i am nurik also deteriorating into metaphors when it's too hard to look into the pit and the truth is that i ran away i just took off i hitched a ride home there were a lot of accidents on the way drivers had been speeding to get away from the inferno and their vehicles overturned on curves people who'd managed to avoid all the artillery shells died in stupid road accidents in the sinai but the man who took me drove slowly they won't start without us he said his wife had given birth to a baby girl during the war and he wanted to see her so he kept himself in check and put classical music on the radio to keep himself even more in check and we entered eilat to the sound of beethoven's fifth which to this day i can't bear to hear in the evening i climb to the top of the hill here and eat in the imperio amara restaurant steaks on a bed of quinoa hoping that no israelis sit down next to me that one of them doesn't recognise me from the financial newpaper that some mother my age who decided to join her daughter on a girls' holiday won't come in i have no epidermis now and that israeli pain is too heavy a load for me please god sit some australians down next to me they exude such great naivety happiness that has no wound in its heart you can even sit americans here they're phony but anything's better than that israeli pain first intifada second intifada operation defensive shield it doesn't matter they all have the same terrible fear in their eyes about what's going to happen if we're not

in the middle of lake titicaca there's a small island a really small island all weeds and mud no larger than 100 square metres and standing on those weeds are no more than 23 straw huts all belonging to the aymara tribe no more than 100 people but even on that island there's a business war going on two souvenir stands one across from the other at a distance of 20 metres competing for tourists' money each one is owned by a different family each one badmouthing the other's stand his merchandise is old his merchandise is damaged one tries to lure the tourists with woven rugs in colours as brilliant as the other's and the other offers free lemonade to every buyer one hangs a sign in english and the other in german and even so it's obvious to everyone that no knives will be pulled here not surrounded by those turquoise expanses not to mention a tank that couldn't get here anyway and if somehow it did it would sink slowly squashing the straw till it turned into brown water that would drown all the crew members except the commander who'd remain alive of course

anything but tanks my father said to me anything but tanks people in tanks burn to death so do me a favour anything but tanks menny and i thought what does he know this father with his old-world harmonica what does he know about tanks and went to tanks on purpose tanks i went to tanks to prove to him that I might not be able to play an instrument but i could fight

rafi loved tuna as much tuna as possible apart from tuna there was one thing that rafi loved and that was tuna salad he had a stock of tuna in his kitbag and a pocketknife that also had a tin opener and a fork so he was able to eat tuna all the time with his pocketknife and elida used to tell him that he stank up the air and rafi would say stinky but kosher and yedidiya would mutter income tax will rip me a new one i have to go home menny maybe you can talk to the company commander and toss out the words self-employed it's not like a salaried employee no one will compensate me later for all the days i'm not at work and rafi would finish everything in the tin down to the last crumb of tuna and crush it and put it into a little bag he used to come out with these sayings like being clever means seeing which way the wind is blowing and knowing who farts i remember a tin of tuna right next to me after the inferno i remember the fish pictured on the tin looking at me with eyes that said let it be let it be now it's just you and me

sometimes i used to see rafi on the street once near heleni hamalka street when i walked out of the kol israel radio offices where I'd been interviewed on the financial hour i said logical, clear things and the presenter nodded as if we were on tv but he was wearing flipflops and the soundman was eating tuna from a tin and when i finished speaking and the presenter said thank you very much dr menny peleg for opening our eyes i didn't correct him and say that i wasn't a dr because deep down i believed that i deserved the title and i went out into heleni hamalka street which has something otherworldly about it and started walking up towards the russian compound and passed a woman in a thin chiffon dress who looked like the street's namesake queen helena and she gave me an inviting smile but i'm nurik's for ever so i just smiled back and then i saw rafi he had slightly thinning blond hair that he never combed and a bouncy step as if he were walking on very springy trainers at the time i thought i wasn't really seeing him now i'm not sure but in any case he vanished near the jail vanished before I could tell him that

you don't know how much you've been straining until you relax you don't know how insistent you've been until you give up you don't know how much you've loved until you're separated you don't know how thirsty you've been until you drink

and once i saw him when i was with tse'ela he was standing next to the talitha kumi monument leaning on the stone and i pulled tse'ela towards the pedestrian area and she said daddy but you said you'd buy me and i pulled her harder until she squealed i thought he was a hologram but i didn't want him to see me i didn't want him to see me with my daughter because it would hurt him he wanted a daughter so much one night after elida and yedidiya fell asleep he told me that he wanted a daughter with white sandals and a long braid but for the time being that whole love business hasn't been working out too well for him either he wants the woman and she doesn't want him or she wants him and he takes off or they're as nutty as fruit-cakes like naomi who went to london claiming that her art was more important to her than anything else right now or haviva who was allergic to his sperm i'm not joking who ever heard of being allergic to sperm don't worry my friend in the end that stuff works out somehow i told him confidently and handed him another cigarette what did i know i didn't know that

no friends since then the owner of the hostel here is a nice man my age judging from his stooped back even though it's hard to know with them they don't have grey hair he says hello how are you i think he's looking for a lost rib too yesterday he asked me if I wanted to smoke a havana cigar with him on the balcony i said thank you but maybe tomorrow i'm careful so careful of course there have been acquaintances over the years and sometimes clients wanted to go out for a drink with me to ease the loneliness of the long distance runner to tell a few jokes about three people who jump out of a plane or to try and find out if you cheat on your wife too maybe even in the same cheap motel room to gossip about business competitors i don't cheat i don't want to i'm incapable of it not now and not when she was alive not as long as her memory is with me and whenever we stood up to leave the clients would say that we had to do it again as if they were recreating a scene they'd heard in an american film such have been my friendships since the inferno clip my coupon and i'll clip yours and when people from the regiment called i'd signal to nurik with my fingers to say that i wasn't home and i didn't turn up when they made that memorial film with that psychologist what's his name adrian levine i sent a cheque but didn't participate in the end they gave up and stopped calling some of them and some of my clients came to nurik's curtailed shiva they sat close to me as if we were in a tank again as if the carpet were the tank track below us but i was so used to being an advisor that i couldn't unburden myself to any of them

write i tell my clients write in order to define your vision and goals to yourselves write your objectives and sub-objectives write down the obstacles and sub-obstacles and they follow me with wide-open eyes the way people follow a messiah and i never said write because if you don't

a year after i came back from the inferno rafi's younger sister called and said in a small voice we're producing a book about rafi and i thought i mean we thought you might be able to write something in his memory i know that you were close he talked about you in his letters he called you a kindred spirit and i thought i mean we thought that you might be able to write something it doesn't have to be long just a few lines i know you're a busy man what do you think i didn't say anything for so long that she said hello

look i said after her hello and took deep breaths between the words i don't know if i can and she said i understand but her voice was so small that i said i'll try and she said no pressure take my phone number and if you manage to write something call me and later i sat in front of a blank page for a few days with a fountain pen in my hand and nothing came just some lines circling around themselves that the pen drew without my noticing and now 30 years later

all my conversations with rafi are coming back to me it's incredible as if the supermarket bag has torn and all the tomatoes of memory are scattering on the floor but not exactly in the same order that they were taken off the shelf i did all the shopping nurik didn't have patience for minor things like that so i know something about supermarket bags for 30 years i hadn't heard rafi's voice saying buddy just because your father didn't make it as a musician doesn't mean that you can't try to do something you want there's no connection between the two things just the opposite you can learn from his mistakes look it's a fact that you don't cheat on your wife like he did even though lots of women would want you i noticed how the commander's assistant looks at you swallows you up with her eyes believe me buddy they give bottles of wine to people who don't have openers or buddy look at how you play backgammon you always make the safer play you never gamble never trust the world to catch you you can't get anywhere in life that way you know what i take it back you can get there but you can't enjoy it or give me me a smoke buddy you think maybe there's a war going on right now on one of those stars up there you think there's another planet with aliens stupid enough to invent a machine like a tank or buddy listen if anything happens to me i want you to promise me that there'll be a lot of hot chicks at my funeral i want women with black dresses and long legs cyring over me sorry that they didn't jump at the chance to sleep with me when they still could oh no menny take it from me you're wrong it's the other way around talking like this doesn't bring you bad luck it brings bad luck to the bad luck didn't they teach you in that economics of yours that a minus plus a minus equals a plus

i don't know whether there were hot chicks at rafi's funeral i wasn't at his funeral or at yedidiya's or elida's i couldn't bring myself to go i was already at the door i was already in the car i was already on the way but i was positive that the families would blame me why in the world would they blame you they're grateful nurik would say but the words didn't penetrate they passed by my ear like the whistle of an artillery shell nothing helped not even the medal i never wore because i never put on a uniform again but i milked it for all it was worth when it came to business menny peleg specialist in crisis situations winner of the medal of valour menny peleg ironed shirts effective humour independent thinking groundbreaking thinking menny peleg marketing man of the week of the month of the year will take you and your business a step forward he'll turn your dream into a brand name he'll analyse the hell out of the market for you point out the weaknesses yes yes gentlemen business is a living organism and a living organism cannot function well when one of its parts

if my clients could see me now good god this morning i took a quick look in the hostel's cracked mirror and i was horrified i look like those people who pester you for money when you've stopped your car at a red light i look like a monk with the jerusalem syndrome like theodor herzl sick at heart sick in mind sick with longing

i'm an island now an island of a person surrounded by a sea of panic and sometimes boats sail back and forth on that sea to and from the inferno carrying shrapnel okay the shaman warned me i can't say he didn't warn me that the potion would not always summon up nurik there's still a white sail on the horizon opposite a heavy black cloud all that we ask for – may it be and if holiday candles flicker in the evening windows all that we seek may it be may it be please may it be all that we ask for, may it be

Nessia

Looks at Dori from the door of the hostel's computer room as he reads his father's diary. His shoulders droop lower and lower, and suddenly he looks like an old historian bent over a new document that contradicts all his previous research, which was the basis for his fame.

Or like a lonely child, perhaps a lonely child who climbed a tree and now can't get down, perhaps a lonely child whose art class was cancelled and he returns home too early and discovers something he shouldn't.

She feels so sorry for him, and she floats ten centimetres above the floor of the room so as not to disturb him, and places a hand on his and kisses the back of his neck. He keeps reading and puts a hand on hers, and she feels the entire past and the entire future flow from his hand to hers, all of it flows from him to her until she almost bursts with

Menny

take a sharp right i told yedidiya and then came the shooting
and now 30 years later for the first time i dare to admit that
maybe i meant left but in the heat of the battle

when he was a boy dori couldn't tell the difference between
right and left i tried everything i bought him a watch i told
him that the hand with the watch on it was his left hand i tied
a red string to his wrist i told him that the hand with the string
was his right hand if you're in the sitting room the front door
is on your left the door to your classroom is on the right your
literature teacher's wandering eye faces left but he didn't get
it he'd always get confused and nurik would say quietly leave
the child alone and i'd say a person has to be able to distinguish
between left and right otherwise

tse'ela has already sent me an email but i'm not tempted to
fall into the trap i want the blue lake now i want the boats that
sail to the past and back i knew that my daughter's husband
was an idiot i knew but i thought that no one would ever be
good enough for her and i thought you're jealous menny because
he's taking her away from you take a step back for once don't
be a commander let her make her own mistakes and look at
what a big mistake she made one that could have been predicted
from the beginning but this time i won't save her definitely
not this time i have to save myself

it was 5 o'clock in the afternoon when i came home from
the inferno shouting was coming from ben eliyahu's apartment
again i stopped and wiped my shoes on the doormat i breathed

in the smell of home coming at me from under the door and only then did i knock i could have opened it i had a key but i knocked in case nurik was with her lover and only then did i go inside what lover what was i thinking there was only concern for me in her eyes dori was on the floor at her feet the sight of me terrified him and he crawled to his room and cried nurik went after him to calm him down and tse'elonet hugged me with her small arms and said daddy what did you bring me from the war now it occurs to me that maybe we really should go to the duty-free shop on the way to and from wars a duty-free zone for combat soldiers after all in the bible the word for blood also means money in any case i didn't know what to do nurik was in the other room calming dori down so i looked for some halvah in my pockets maybe there was some left over from the battle rations but there was nothing left the fire consumed it all to this day i don't touch halvah so i lied to her and said that the presents were locked in this big bag called a kitbag and i couldn't unpack it till tomorrow yes kitbag is a funny word tse'elonet and when i woke up the next day there was a moment in bed when i felt as if i could decide whether to get up and return to life or stay asleep for ever i felt that if i kept my eyes closed that's what would happen but i got up and went down to jaffa street with the shrapnel in my body and the 45 liras in my pocket that i'd earned for my soldier for hire services and bought tse'ela a huge lego set and a toy car for dori and was shocked to see that as usual prices were sky high and when no one was looking i shoved the presents into my kitbag and before dinner that night we opened the kitbag still stained with mud and blood as if it were father christmas's sack and dori cried and cried because he wanted lego too

twice in 30 years that's all twice in 30 years the rest of the time i rode my bike fast because if you ride fast you don't fall the first time was on the way to the sinai i had no fears about it i was more worried about doron ashkenazi who was a PE teacher and kept eyeing nurik and once she said that you can tell from his body that he's an athlete i never thought about the fact that i was going to the sinai or what would happen i thought about doron ashkenazi screwing nurit athletically in a tent while i was snorkelling with the kids it was clear to me that i'd kill him if it happened and then we reached the border and suddenly my heart was pounding suddenly i was sweating suddenly i bolted from the car towards the food truck and nurik followed me and said i'm with you it doesn't really matter the sinai or eilat and i thanked my lucky stars that i had such a generous wife who i would never deserve and i said wait my love it'll pass in a minute but it didn't and we drove to the sheraton plaza hotel without doron ashkenazi and nurik asked me that night after the kids had gone to sleep if i wanted to talk about it and i said that i wanted to keep quiet about it the second time was 10 years ago we went to the cinema to see fearless with jeff bridges in the film he's one of the survivors of a plane crash and everyone thinks he's a hero because he saved a few other passengers but he couldn't get past it for the entire film he and a hispanic woman survivor try to figure out why they want to die and sitting behind us in the cinema was a couple dori's age who were kissing and giggling throughout i asked them to be quiet i hate asking people to be quiet it reminds me that i'm getting old but i asked them anyway because there was something sacred about the film and they were desecrating it but they kept giggling and chattering and all of a sudden i got up and turned around and grabbed the boy by the collar and told him to shut his mouth or i'd shut it for him and the girl said let him go you're crazy and i repeated the same words shut your mouth or i'll shut it for you and the boy turned deep red and a commotion began in the cinema torches and ushers and nurik said let's go and grabbed my arm and took me to the snack bar to have an apple cider and said don't worry mentsch we'll see the end of the film on video and i said don't tell the children okay and she said you know maybe you should deal with this and i shouted i don't want to deal with this

and the third time was at el loco's place but it's different from the other two times because this time i'm not suppressing my anger this time i'm letting it live i'm letting the shrapnel sail through my body letting the memories come letting them be written i don't have nurik i don't have the strength to fight them anymore

there's a purpose for everything elida used to say nothing is accidental for example the fact that i was wounded in the six day war that's the work of the almighty who wanted to teach me a lesson to prepare me for this war elida would swear by the almighty day and night i swear by the almighty that i'll relieve you in a minute i swear by the almighty that i didn't eat your tuna i swear by the almighty that i'm not the one who farted and stank out the whole tank if he hadn't been such a total idiot elida could have been a great commander he had absolute confidence that everything would end up all right not only that he'd live but that we'd all live but i was the commander i never took off my watch kept everything inside took on everyone's anxieties spoke in a steady voice the most important thing is to maintain a steady voice and also to set an example to sleep less eat less than everyone give each solder in the tank the right to at least one whim yedidiya hid a package that someone's mother from his home town wanted him to give to her son and even though there was pretty clear evidence that the son was killed in the first bombing and even though we were very hungry he wouldn't open the package and elida who used to whisper his fears in soft french at night to brigitte bardot but he wouldn't tell us what he said to her and rafi would provide subtitles for us oh brigitte everything happens for a reason oh brigitte show me the concha oh brigitte i have a baguette for you the likes of which you've never seen before if it hadn't been for the watch that was stolen in ottavalo i wouldn't have known i was alive the second hand kept moving and i knew that i was alive if it weren't for the second hand i'd have thought that they the three of them were alive and dragging my body to shelter and not the other way around medal my arse valour my arse a mixed up soldier with a back broken from the jump his ears full of sand sand on his eyelids sand under his nails seeing the turret overturn thinking maybe everything that happened was his fault because he said right and not left and only the second hand tells him to keep moving keep moving

the picture of brigitte bardot burned up in the inferno too a few years ago i saw a documentary film about her she lives a secluded life in the south of france and speaks only to animals she's given up on people maybe rightly so she's still beautiful and feline but looks completely mad

as if you're not writing for the walls menny peleg as if you're not struggling with the devil as if you don't look totally crazy with that beard

last night after i took the potion nurik appeared to me again and said: shave

i first encountered the potion in guatemala in chichicastenango or for short chichi there's a large market there twice a week on thursday and sunday green masks sets of indian dishes small witch bottles painted gourds at the foot of the church that has incense burning on its steps and flowers in honour of the mayan gods that's how it is here the locals continue their ancient rituals sometimes even right inside the church for them the sun god is jesus and the moon goddess is mary and written in small letters in a separate frame in the guide it says that a short walk of a kilometre from the church in a clearing in the forest on mt pascual abaj there's a shrine with a neckless statue where you can sometimes meet up with a local shaman he treats the farmers who make a pilgrimage to him there's an expression his legs carried him i always thought that was bullshit but in this case my legs must have carried me right at the start from israel from the funeral from the curtailed shiva my legs must have carried me to that shaman a peddler was walking beside me on the path his heavy pack was tied by a rope to his forehead and he walked so bent over that all you could see were his legs when we reached a crossroad we parted ways he to his family and i to my longing i to the shaman from pascual abaj who was treating a local woman when i arrived meaning that he put his hands on her forehead rattled bunches of leaves around her and created wind with a feathered wing over to the side was a kind of altar with stones and flowers and incense there was no one queuing up after the woman so i went over to him and before i could say anything the shaman already knew why i'd come and said in spanish señor not now señor will come please after the sun goes down

after the sun went down there was no one but us in the forest clearing the shaman asked me to come close to him he rattled sage leaves around me and then spread a piece of cloth under me and i knew that i had to sit down he poured a dark liquid into two deep clay bowls and gestured for me to do as he did and drink it all down in one swallow it tasted godawful more bitter than wormwood at first i didn't feel anything i mean i didn't feel different from myself i just listened to the sounds the forest makes at night i listened to the trees breathing oompa oompa and to the ground breathing hoom hoom and then i had terrible stomach pains and i vomited my guts out what a great expression that is i vomited my guts out this time it was especially accurate because after i vomited up my guts the emptiness inside me was filled with something else the ground embraced me like a sea and the trees began to speak to me in hebrew and clouds took on the shapes of crabs that crab-walked in the heavens and tigers that tiger-walked in the heavens and monkeys that leaped from cloud to cloud and then leaped to the moon which was suddenly very close to me i could actually climb on to the moon so i stood up and climbed on to it i walked among the craters careful not to be joseph and looked for nurik but she wasn't there she only appeared a certain dreamtime later and she was totally nurik and i told her i was sorry to bother her and she smiled and said it was fine and i said i just don't know where to go without you and she said but you're already going and i said but where where i keep moving but what is the point you are the point and she was silent and smiled and was suddenly a seductive acrobat hanging on the large minute hand of my watch and then she disappeared i hoped she'd come back that she'd talk to me but until sunrise all i had in my mouth were the sounds and tastes of fruit even though i hadn't eaten anything and at sunrise the birds chirped and i knew how to distinguish between the chirps the way i never could before and i heard the conversations between the chirps like i never had before and i saw the gorgeous quetzal bird which had eluded me for the entire trip blue green sitting on a branch and the shaman woke me and washed my face and gave me bread where did he get bread from and fruit maybe he picked the fruit off the hebrew-speaking trees and he sprayed me with water from a bottle that had agua de florida written on it and said to me your dead wife has a beautiful soul and i asked him i had to ask him will i see her again mr shaman and he said it depends on you but he waved a finger in warning the potion won't always lead you to her the potion is an internal mirror and sometimes it shows you other places and i said okay i'm ready to pay any price to

shave?! i said to nurik last night that's all you want to tell me? you have nothing more healing? soon there won't be any more little bags of potion i took from el loco and only the writing keeps my head above water because where can i go without you then she said to shave and then we can dance this way you're too prickly rafi had a long pointy red beard like the jew in nazi propaganda films i told him to shave because if a fire broke out it would grab his beard and he said sir this beard reminds me that i finished regular army service and if i run my hand over it i feel smart for a few seconds almost like a philosopher and i can see this whole war from a distance as if i'm looking down on it from above from an air balloon see that once again the human race is trying to solve problems in a way that creates more problems and that helps me move away a bit to think so with your permission sir i'll leave it for a while longer and if all ends well i promise to shave it off and we'll go to see james bond like we said and after the film we'll go to your house for dinner don't worry i won't embarrass you in front of your nurik if it all ends well i'll stop smoking i'll shave and wear a white shirt and everything in her honour he always said if all ends well and i'd correct him when it all ends and he'd insist that a philosopher has to be sceptical

and sometimes on route one near the airport a plane flies low overhead and my body wants to take cover but i can control it except for once when i was driving with a client he was at the wheel and saying he was sure that management was for him and a plane flew too close and i couldn't silence the scream migs! migs! that went off in my head i dropped down into the space under the glove compartment and put my hands on the back of my neck and the client asked what's wrong menny and i waited for a few seconds until the noise of the plane had faded and took a deep breath and said my pen fell i'm looking for my pen that fell

nurik passed away at 1.26 in the oncology ward of hadassah ein kerem hospital she took advantage of the one second i closed my eyes i knew that as long as i stayed awake she wouldn't dare she didn't have the heart to leave me i didn't burst into sobs i didn't take her hand and cry no no no no i wasn't jacques brel ne me quitte pas ne me quitte pas i just covered her with the hospital blanket and called tse'ela and said mum and didn't know what to say after that mum is gone mum died mum passed away mum is no longer with us her candle is extinguished her fluorescent light went out i'd never called her mum like those couples who call each other mum and dad i always called her only nurik so she wouldn't forget that before we had the children there was just the two of us and i asked tse'ela to tell dori and over the next few days i made all the burial arrangements as if it was another task to be checked off my list death announcements check burial permit check headstone check but that hissing had already begun inside me like the volcano near antigua the name escapes me and when the townspeople hear the first hissing sounds they know that they have to run yedidiya and elida and rafi began to demand satisfaction at the funeral i suddenly saw them standing with everyone else at the grave burnt around the edges like the birthday cards tse'ela used to make for her school friends and i wailed in a horrendous unfamiliar voice for nurik and for them and on the sixth day of the seven days of mourning i said let's pass on tomorrow and on the seventh day the hissing grew so strong that like the people in the town near volcan del fuego that's the name of the volcano i had to run away so i got into the car in the morning and drove till nightfall without stopping from jerusalem to eilat to the golan heights and stopped only for petrol but the entire country was filled with death after death after death and i could find no peace anywhere there was no reason to live everywhere held an unbearable reminder of nurik like the volume getting louder and louder till it reaches the point where you can't hear any more like el loco like menachem begin who said i can no longer

tell me what's good i'd ask her sometimes on the terrible days and she'd lie down beside me in bed and turn off the light and say into my ear the children are good and the evening breeze blowing in through the kitchen window is good and the hummus in pinati is good and scotland is good we still haven't been there but i know it's good and our touching is very good i love the way you touch me and the comedy sketches on saturday morning radio are good and the fact that the children let us sleep late on saturday morning is good and getting a haircut is good you really love getting a haircut and shaving is good and dates are good not dried dates fresh dates are good and she would go on like that putting weights on the good side of the scale until i touched her hand and said thank you and during those last weeks in the hospital i lay beside her on the bed and asked her if she wanted me to tell her what was good and she said no and i said maybe just a bit and she said sing a song into my ear and i said which one and she said any one you want and i said but i sing out of tune and she said i don't care mentsch so i moved closer to her ear and sang chava alberstein's i shall talk to you from memory let me talk to you and let me walk in your shadow to be with you there is strength in me there is strength in me don't pity me don't keep your thorns from pricking my legs i sang to her till she touched my hand and said enough

what do you think mr peleg they asked me at the museum we're considering issuing a memorial book for nurik we're thinking about combining items about her with works from the museum that she loved we're thinking about calling it nurit's golden age what do i think what do i think what do i think i think you should do whatever you want but we wanted you to be involved i'm sorry i can't may i ask why because it's too soon for me the thing is mr peleg that if we want it to be ready for the first anniversary of her death maybe we should

look nurik i shaved for you i said last night and she finally arrived after i'd been waiting for her for 3 nights in a row on the roof of the hostel i was beginning to think that the potion wasn't working that my brain had developed antibodies she was wearing the clothes she used to wear to go folk dancing a long green skirt a red blouse with a modest neckline and white trainers and she said the couples dance is starting soon do you

want to join in of course i said and as i moved close to her i
added you know you look younger every time yes she smiled
maybe in the end i'll be ready to be born and so we danced on
the roof of the hostel the moon above, the lake below, possibility
in the air there was no music there was no may it be may it
be may it be and there was no official dance teacher and we
didn't dance the steps we were supposed to dance no yemenite
steps and no crossovers and more than anything i felt that it
was our second and final farewell dance because every love
story has two endings at least so i moved my feet very very
slowly took very very small steps so our story wouldn't end too
quickly and she moved slowly too and intertwined her fingers
with mine and pressed her cheek to mine and a minute before
fading right before she detached herself from me she whispered
in my ear: Baron Hirsch, Mentsch. That's what she whispered.
Not 'I have to go now' not 'I'll never forget you, my love'. Just
Baron Hirsch, Mentsch. Baron Hirsch.

Inbar

Asks Dori if he wants something to drink.

No, thank you, he says. And then — his eyes still on the computer
— well, maybe yes.

Coffee? Tea?

Tea.

She doesn't ask how many sugars he wants, to avoid
disturbing him again, and goes into the hostel kitchen.

Alfredo's there, sitting on a chair. His arms are folded on his
chest, his small pot belly bulging from under them. His head is

tilted forward, butting the air. How is he? he asks. The flirtatious spark has vanished from his eyes, replaced by sincere concern.

Still reading, she says.

Is *muy difícil*, what he is going through now, he says. Clients fall apart in my hands at this stage, like dry earth. I had a mother, from Sweden. We were looking for her daughter together for two weeks. In the end we found someone who danced with her at a party in Antigua, Guatemala. He told her how her daughter behaved. What she put up her nose. Who she left the club with. The mother just didn't want to believe it. The guy knew that her daughter had a birthmark shaped like a sea horse near her belly button, and that crazy woman still didn't believe him, and she wouldn't let us follow the information he gave us. Two weeks we wasted because of her. Two weeks! And in the end it turned out that everything he said was true. That's nothing. I once had a minister from Nevada. When I showed him a picture of his son with whores-with-a-prick in São Paulo, he said: He's not my son any more. Turned around and went home. That's how it is. The closer someone is to you, the harder it is to accept that he has changed.

Inbar nods. The kettle has boiled, meaning that she can –

Take this, Alfredo takes a teabag out of his pocket. It's something special, it'll calm him down.

Inbar pours the water over Alfredo's teabag, holding the kettle very high the way Shula, Eitan's mother, does, and then adds a teaspoon and a half of sugar and mixes. Very slowly. She wants to make Dori the best tea in the world.

The truth is, Alfredo says, that a son looking for his father, a father who changes on him – that is something I never had.

I think it's even harder, Inbar says. Parents are supposed to stop changing before they have children, aren't they?

Alfredo scratches the very narrow space between his thick, dark eyebrows: How should I know? He moves closer to her, extends his large hand as if to place it on her shoulder, then changes his mind, puts his hand back on his hips and says: You will read the diary too, Señorita Inbar, okay? And if there's something not good there, if his father plans to put himself in danger, *por ejemplo*, you will tell me. And . . . help Mr Dori, eh? Usually, when it comes to these things, I am the one who talks with the clients. Make them a good meal. Hug them, if they need it. But Mister Dori . . . I don't know. I think he'd rather have you now.

She nods and puts the cup of tea on a small saucer.

Bring him a biscuit too, he says and takes another small bag out of his pocket just as she's about to leave the kitchen. A biscuit is always good.

She opens the bag, puts the biscuit on the saucer, thanks Alfredo from the bottom of her *corazón* and hurries back to the room.

*

Thank you, Dori says when she puts the saucer on the table.

My pleasure, she says. And immediately regrets the word (what pleasure? You think the guy is enjoying himself?).

I'll be finished soon, he says, and turns to her. I'd like you to read it too.

Are you sure? It's not too personal?

I'm sure, he says and turns back to the screen.

Menny

According to the Inca faith, a bearded white god (before I shaved at Nurik's request, I looked a little like him) first appeared here, on this holy rock, the puma rock. He pulled the sun out of the water, thereby driving away the darkness and confusion that had been in the universe until then. Then he created the Inca Adam and Eve, Manco Cápac and his sister-wife Mama Ocllo. And that's how their Genesis begins.

I've climbed up there for three days now, every evening, waiting for 'Baron Hirsch' to explain it to me.

What am I supposed to learn from this forgotten story of a farm established in Argentina for East European Jews?

On the Internet, I found photographs of Baron Hirsch's farms, then and now, in various places throughout Argentina. One of them showed a building with faded bricks and a ramshackle roof that looked very familiar to me. Too familiar. At first I didn't understand from where, and then I remembered that on one of my potion journeys, when I was searching for Nurik, I saw that farm. That is, I saw myself walking along its paths. But I still don't understand: why did Nurik send me there, to the past?

I've regained the ability to put a full stop, thank God. The turquoise water and the chirping of the birds and the sheer beauty of the sloping terraces and the writing have deadened my need to shout. The great storm, I think, has passed. But it's been replaced by a kind of blandness. Dull and unpleasant. Life without love.

It wasn't until the fourth day that a boat crossed the lake below me, drawing an arrow, that I finally saw it: Nurik hadn't sent me to the past, but to the future.

It doesn't matter what Baron Hirsch intended to do with those farms; it matters what I can do with them.

Today, on 20 April 2006, at five o'clock in the morning, it began. The volcanic eruption of ideas. Feverish. It's happened to me at work, but never with such intensity. Notepad in hand, I walk among the Inca ruins that are scattered on the island and envisage: objectives, courses of action, structure. There are many people around me on the island. Maybe later I'll need them. Now I formulate guiding principles for myself. I don't actually formulate them. They are revealed to me as if they'd always existed in my mind. I see the place I'll set up on Baron Hirsch's farm, down to the last detail. I don't imagine it, I see it. I see it the way I saw Nurik with the help of the potion. I know what colour the toilet will be and how the paths will be laid out and where I'll send the people after their training and how many beds there'll be in each room, as if I've always known it. I write down every detail that appears before me, and at night copy everything to a new document, separate from this diary. And organise it. My fingers run across the keyboard without stopping. I'm filled with power. I finally understand the illness and know what the medicine is. I'm the old Menny Peleg. No. I'm a different Menny Peleg, Menny Peleg who has received a call. Like a taxi driver who receives a call with the exact address he must reach as quickly as possible. So I hurry. I don't take the potion any more. I don't hear MiGs any more. I don't want to die any more.

*

Today, 22 April 2006, the name of the place flickered before me. Suddenly, I just knew it. And I also knew that at the entrance to it, on the plain wooden gate, I'll write in huge letters the words that Herzl wanted to be written on the gates of his Jewish state: 'Man, you are my brother'.

Dori

The man who wrote this diary knows many intimate details of my father's life – Dori thought while Inbar was reading – but he's not at all like him . . .

What exactly did you expect? he argued with himself. El Loco told you explicitly. Yes, but I thought this was just an episode. A single attack, after which he'd go back to being my father.

And what if *this* is your father? – he shuddered – and the person you thought was your father has always been just a fake, Jacob disguised as Esau.

*

Did you check to see whether there's another file? That it isn't hidden inside a different file? Inbar asked after she finished reading the diary.

I checked all the files – Dori shook his head too many times, as if he couldn't stop the movement – and there's nothing. He must have taken the file with the 'vision' with him.

Are you okay? she said with concern. You look pale. Really?

Let's go outside, she said, and get some air.

*

They went out to the wooden balcony that overlooked the lake. It was cold. Rivulets streamed down over crevices. A procession of alpacas passed them, their backs loaded with twigs. Their shepherds brought up the rear. A young boy and girl. Brother and sister? Lovers? The procession of alpacas was followed by a procession of donkeys, their backs loaded with straw. On this island, they were always transporting something to somewhere. The cold wind wrinkled the surface of the lake. It's like fingerprints, Inbar thought, and the thought wandered from her to Dori without a word being spoken.

My father was in Yom Kippur too, she said after long moments of silence. But from what I understood, he wasn't at

382

the front. Even though the . . . 'inferno' never reached him, he joined the protest movement after the war. He set up a tent in front of the Knesset, and Motti Ashkenazi, who led the movement, stayed in it with him for a few weeks.

My father didn't even do that! Dori blurted out. He didn't stay in any tent, didn't carry any protest signs. And thirty years later he suddenly remembers to be post-traumatic?

Maybe . . . maybe it's just the first time since then that he's had the time to stop and think, Inbar said.

I don't know. What is all that shit, 'medicine', 'illness', 'vision'. Who does he think he is? The Messiah?

Dori stood up abruptly and began pacing around the hostel balcony like a detective trying to solve a riddle. Several riddles. The riddle of his father's metamorphosis. The riddle of that place he wants to establish. The riddle of his own feelings: Why, instead of being concerned about his father, is he so angry, so enraged. After all, that diary should upset him. The person who wrote it is deeply disturbed. The person who wrote it might be swallowed up in his emotional hurricane and never come out of it. The person who wrote it left it behind as a road sign that asks, pleads: Follow me, dear reader. Find me. Save me from myself.

So why is it that all Dori wants to do is shout at him?

*

I have no air, he says, stops and puts his hand on his chest. I keep inhaling but no oxygen gets inside. There's no oxygen here. Do you feel like that too?

Sit down, Dori, she says, putting her hand on his back. We're at an altitude of 4,000 metres. And you really don't want to get a case of altitude sickness now.

*

It's funny, Inbar said after he sat down. And recovered slightly.

What's funny?

That only this morning, sitting on the steps, we talked about Baron Hirsch.

He took a deep breath and said, yes, that's really spooky. As if my father's idea stayed here in the hostel after he left and it's been floating around in the air until the right person for it came along, someone whose mind it could enter.

And then it saw us going up the steps of the island and . . .

Exactly.

After a thick silence, rife with possibilities, Inbar said: There's a school in Haifa that I was supposed to go to. My whole primary school class went there. And I went to a different school that my mother thought would be better for me, and my entire life took a different direction from my primary school classmates'. A while ago, I was asked to give a lecture about radio to the children studying communications at that school. Walking down the corridors there, I had the weird feeling that even though I didn't go to that school, even though I was only *supposed* to go there, it played a part in my life. Do you understand?

Help me, he said.

Maybe there's a kind of collective unconscious that remembers the road not taken. Maybe that's why everything on this continent seems so familiar to you. Maybe that's why the . . . why your dad's emotional upheaval brought him to Argentina, the same country we were talking about on the steps. I don't know. Maybe I'm just babbling because I don't really know what to say about the diary even now that I've read it, except that I don't have the feeling that your father wants to hurt himself—

You don't have to say anything, he said. He suddenly had a powerful urge to put his head on her shoulder, the way she'd put hers on his, to rest a while from the strain of the search, from the strain of trying not to be hopeless about the search, of trying not to be frightened by his father's diary, of trying not to be indifferent to that diary, of trying not to settle accounts with his father for past offences, of trying not to shout at Alfredo, of trying not to give in to his homesickness, of trying not to give in to the fading of his homesickness, of trying not to think about his mother too much, of trying not to think about Netta too much, of trying not to think about the money being poured into this journey every day – five months' salary gone already – of trying to understand Spanish, of trying to breathe without oxygen, of trying not to rest his head on Inbar's shoulder because resting his head on a woman's shoulder makes him vulnerable, too vulnerable, and the minute he does it, the cold fire creeping upwards might reach the critical point and he won't be able to take it any more.

Just the fact that you're with me, he finally said, I mean . . . it would be a lot harder for me if I were on my own now.

I'll stay with you to Argentina too, she said and hugged herself. I mean, if you want me to.

And he said: I don't know. Then added quickly: First I have to see whether I want to go there at all.

And she said: What do you mean, want? You have to go. Based on that diary, it's not clear that your father is completely . . . balanced. Anyway, after all this effort, surely you can't go back without seeing him? Without even talking to him?

And he said: I've been here for almost three weeks already. That's a lot of money. And a lot of time. And they need me at home.

*

That night, he borrowed Alfredo's phone, called Roni from his room and told her the latest developments at length – and cut Inbar out of all the pictures he drew for her, like a Soviet clerk tearing out encyclopaedia pages that the Kremlin didn't want the public to know about. Roni also thought that he had to go to Argentina. From what you're saying about the diary, she said, it's obvious that your father has flipped out. But what about Netta? he asked, and Roni said: Netta's fine. And he said: how's it going at nursery? And Roni said: great. The teacher says he's going through a very good period and there's no problem when I leave him there in the morning. He stopped hanging on the fence and this week, two friends came over to play with him. Two days in a row.

You're joking? Dori said.

Absolutely not.

But how do you explain it? What do you think happened?

Either something in him matured or . . . the psychologist was right and something about your relationship with him was holding him back.

What? The psychologist never said anything like that!

Psychologists don't say explicit things. If they did, the sessions would be cut short and they'd make less money.

I didn't . . . I didn't pick up on anything like what you're saying.

Sometimes people only hear what they want to hear, you know. What do you think she meant when she wondered whether you want Netta to have a better childhood than you did so much that you lean too far in the opposite direction?

He didn't know what to say. Yes, the comment she's mentioning had been made in therapy, but even back then, something inside him had rebelled against the transparent interpretation. After some more small talk, they hung up because 'it's very expensive, Dori.'

Only later, only after passages from his father's diary have spun around in his mind all night, mixing with childhood memories, the memory of his parents' love, Roni's coldness on the phone, and the warm simplicity of Inbar's offer to join the search, did the answer become clear to him. Like an Impressionist painting, which you can only really see when you move away

386

from it, or like when you drive in pouring rain and then pass under a bridge and it's suddenly absolutely quiet and you can hear your innermost thoughts . . .

Yes, maybe he had suffocated Netta with too much love. But it wasn't because he was trying to be different from his father. Not *only* that, at any rate.

So why? he heard Roni asking in his head.

Because with you, there is no exchange of love, I haven't been receiving it or giving it for a long time, he replied to himself, his voice shaking even though the conversation was only in his mind. The channels between us are blocked, Roni, so according to the law of connected love, like the law of connected vessels, it all flows towards Netta.

*

That's how it is, Udi said. There's nothing we can do about it.

They were sitting in a new bar that had opened on the ruins of Café Moment, which had been destroyed by a terrorist's bomb. Udi had called at midday and said he was going to a convention in the Jerusalem Convention Centre, and after that, in the evening, they could have a drink together.

Yeah, why not, Dori said.

They arranged to meet at nine.

Nine o'clock Udi time? Dori asked, to be sure.

Udi laughed his huge laugh, the one that always carried over everybody's head during lunch breaks at school, and said yes.

He arrived at 9.30, with that open, confident walk of his, but when they hugged, Dori felt a small belly pressing against him. A belly! Udi Merom, the team captain. First place in the 600 metre race. The school record holder in both the long jump and the high jump.

I'm so glad you could make it, man, he said.

Me too, Dori said.

Whisky, neat, Udi said to the barman. And while he waited for his drink he checked out the other customers.

There are no decent women in Jerusalem, he noted. But it's better that way. That's not our territory any more, hey? Galit'll call in a minute, he added. When she does, I'll give you the phone and you can say hello, okay? So she knows I'm with you.

Yeah, fine, Dori said.

We had this thing a few months ago, Udi said, lowering his voice and leaning slightly forward. But it's between us, okay?

Of course.

She read an email I got from a woman. And really, there was nothing going on between us, man. Just a little harmless flirtation, you know.

Dori nodded in understanding. Even though he didn't understand, because he wasn't a flirt.

But she just didn't believe me, you know?

Dori nodded to show that he knew, even though he wasn't sure that he himself believed him. He'd seen Udi get into hot water for lying too many times because of his need to be loved by everyone.

She was pissed off with me anyway, he went on, even before that. So you can imagine what kind of explosion there was. I was already thinking this is it, she's taking the girls and leaving. And you know how crazy I am about my girls. To cut a long story short, I've been sleeping in the living room for two months now. And Galit keeps saying to me: I don't know if I can trust you any more. I don't know if I can trust you any more! And it was just an email! Can you believe it? And her mother's ill now too. Juvenile diabetes. A seventy-year-old woman. All of a sudden, just like that, out of the blue. And then me, with all the pressure at work, and the mortgage that's bleeding us dry —

Udi Merom complained. He complained for an hour and a half, and Dori didn't know what to say. Nor was he sure that Udi wanted advice or if he just wanted to get it off his chest. And in the background, cover versions of the '80s hits they used to listen to were playing, sounding now like one long, monotonous song.

But that's life, Udi summed up and took a sip of his whisky. Nothing we can do about it. It's that kind of decade. We raise the kids. Take care of our parents. Have bad sex once every two weeks. Don't try to get back on our feet, because we just get shot down again. Walk down a long corridor without looking right or left, without thinking too much, till the corridor ends. Don't tell me it isn't like that with you and Roni too.

Dori sipped his malt beer and didn't say anything. This crowded intimacy with Udi, after they hadn't seen each other for a whole year, was too much for him. And also the consolation that Udi offered, the universal 'that's life', didn't work for him. That wasn't 'life' for his parents or for him and Roni. Well, there were some similarities, but there was still a strong firmly soldered bond –

They'd just signed up for a ten-session cookery course given by a well-known chef who, Roni said, had a regular slot on a morning TV show. Dori didn't have a good feeling about it, but Roni claimed that they 'never do anything together but look after Netta, and that just comes between us'. He wasn't sure that was what drove them apart, and he didn't feel comfortable signing up for the gluttons' workshop when his mother was ill, and he wasn't happy that the classes were in Tel Aviv, a city in which he always felt like a complete stranger . . .

But Roni secured her point: she's getting it from work free, and not to go would be a real waste – even though she had a very good salary, the word 'free' still worked on her like magic. So he dragged himself along with her – no, that's not accurate: he went with her because he loved her and with the knowledge that there was something in her claim that he wasn't open enough to new things, and in the hope that the course, called 'The Taste of Love', would be good for them.

At the first class, in a luxurious and melancholy hotel, the chef, clad in a white apron, a white shirt and red shoes, regaled them with his philosophy on the inherent difference between food and cuisine, told them that cooking for oneself is much more than pleasure, it is a statement, an ideology, a way of life that puts the personal before the industrial, the sensual before the ascetic, the creative before the banal. The participants — nine couples who looked frighteningly alike; two of the women were even wearing the same dress — listened open-mouthed to the speech as they sat around the large, stainless steel island, and Roni said later, as they merged into the ubiquitous traffic jam on the road out of Tel Aviv, fascinating, wasn't it? Ummm. Actually I found it a little over the top, he said, I mean, in the end, it's only food. But that's exactly what he said — Roni fired up like a gas range — that there's no such thing as just food. That food is everything. I don't know, maybe after we start really cooking I'll get into it more, he said hopefully. But in the sessions that followed, each of which was devoted to preparing a different, creative meal, and to a teriyaki-soaked competition between the couples to see how well they'd prepared the peculiar dishes, the situation only worsened. More and more new concepts were tossed into the frying pan: *concasse* — a special technique for cutting tomatoes, upon which the success of the dish depends; *mandolina* — something related to onions (he didn't understand what, because as soon as the chef uttered the word, he pictured Zvi Mandolina from Grandpa Pima's klezmorim); nano-grating — done to especially small nuts. And also cheese. Or do you do something else to cheese? Between one concept and the next, the chef tried to sell them, under the table, items that he used: Atlantic sea salt for fifty shekels (fifty shekels! for salt!); three kinds of professional knife for various kinds of cutting, because 'what works for cutting a large beef filet does not work for slicing tissue-thin carpaccio'; silicon pans — forget Pyrex, only silicon would do. And more and more. At some point, he stopped paying attention to Roni's small purchases and the recipes and focused his attention on observing the chef. The more his fellow participants oohed and aahed over him, the more ridiculous he seemed to Dori, with the French accent he put on when he pronounced the names of the dishes, with his endless reminiscences of his very brief attendance at Le Cordon Bleu, with his tendency to put his hand under his apron and stroke his chest hair, with his insistence on giving their rather prosaic work profound significance: 'Patience is the key word, both in preparing the fish stock and in love.' 'It is important to know how to compromise in life. But also how not to compromise. In the quality of ingredients, for example.' As he spoke and instructed and commented, Dori would picture him, as he was, in his chef's clothes, washing the dishes himself instead of the silent Thai girl who cleaned the place during every class, or sitting in the first row of a driver re-education course. And he enjoyed deliberately sabotaging the dishes that he and Roni prepared during the lesson, adding a bit too much salt, a bit too much wasabi, a lot more cream, causing the chef to sniff the results with dissatisfaction. He also enjoyed making Roni, who loved winning everything, however much she tried to hide it, flush all the way down to her lovely neck and rebuke him later, in the traffic jam at the entrance to Jerusalem, saying that he was acting like an unruly student, and how did he expect to teach well if he himself had no curiosity and no desire to be exposed to new things? It's not a matter of curiosity, he said. Then what is it? she said angrily. I just can't avoid the historical context. What historical context are you going on about? she demanded. Throughout human history, he said – and hated himself for lecturing her, but couldn't stop – peoples and societies in crisis, on the verge of destruction, have been characterised by their pursuit of the decadent. So I can't help asking myself whether this entire course, and this whole obsession with food in Israel over the last few years isn't a kind of 'eat, drink and be merry, for tomorrow we die'.

Oh Dori, Roni said.

Oh what?

Don't you get tired sometimes?

Of what?

Of being you. Don't you feel like forgetting sometimes? And just living life? The answer to her question was already on the tip of his tongue — they'd had this conversation many times before — but something in her tone this time shut him up. Choked his throat. She spoke to him the way he spoke to the students he'd tried everything with, to no avail. She spoke to him as if she'd already given up and now the time had come for unadulterated, subtle irony. And that frightened him so much that instead of saying that 'the present is just a thin shell', as he truly believed, he said, maybe you're right. And he also said: I'll try harder. What's the next session about? Desserts? I promise you that our dessert will be the tastiest one there. We'll blow them all out of the water, Roni. Our brûlée will knock their socks off. Our caramel will be finger-licking good.

A few hours before the next meeting, his mother's condition deteriorated even further and his father asked him to come to the hospital.

It's okay, you can go to the class, he told Roni.

Are you mad? she said. What are you talking about?

*

You're so lucky to have a mother like her, Roni said after they'd met for the first time. Someone you can learn from. Someone you can love as a person, not just because she's your mother.

She's impressive, your new girlfriend, his mother said after that meeting. You need real character to grow up in a kibbutz and turn out to be such an individualist.

When he and Roni separated, she was upset and called his mother, who reassured her: Patience. He'll come back. And it won't take him more than a day or two.

When they got married, several months after the separation, his mother stood on the lawn in front of the kibbutz dining hall and read the badly rhymed poem she'd written for them, much of it dedicated to her daughter-in-law:

> Do not let her beauty mislead
> For Roni's beauty is much more than skin deep
> It shows in her every action and deed
> A clear conscience and a sharp mind has she
> Quick to act and quick to see
> Though she's not a great drummer, Shlomo Barr will agree
> She learned to play on Dori's heartstrings, one-two-three
> So it is with joy and love, dear Roni
> That we welcome you into our family.

Their idyllic relationship began to show cracks when Netta was born. His mother thought Roni was wrong to take on such a demanding job at that particular time. Roni thought that Dori's mother wasn't exactly the model of a woman who sacrificed her career on the altar of motherhood, so she shouldn't judge others, and told her — because of the two women's uncompromising directness, these things were spoken out loud and not whispered behind their backs — that family is a unit, and since Dori has much more free time than his father had had, she can allow herself to be away from home more. And that is certainly preferable to being bitter and frustrated and taking it out on the baby. But it isn't just that, Roni'le — his mother said, formulating clearly what Dori himself was still circling around — the place where you work, the aggressiveness of the business world. It will seep into you. It's already seeping into you.

It's a living, Roni replied. I don't want Netta to be like me, going into the world from the kibbutz with a pair of All Star trainers, I want him to have everything he wants in life, even if . . . his father chose to earn a teacher's salary.

But what about you? his mother persisted. You're missing out on your child's most beautiful years! Dori, do me a favour – Roni's patience finally wore out – tell your mother to get off my back.

She's angry because she knows I'm right, was his mother's reply.

That's what you always say to Tse'ela, he protested.

Tse'ela also gets angry when she knows I'm right, she said.

Nonetheless, she promised to be quiet. And so, for several months, the two major figures in his life maintained a balance of fear: genuine smiles were replaced by artificial ones, and soul-searching conversations were replaced by idle talk.

Then his mother became ill, and the caution between them was put aside.

Roni's such a good person, Tse'ela said enviously. Look how many hours she spends at Mum's bedside, how much she cares about her.

Yes, Dori nodded. The absence of Tse'ela's husband Avram at the hospital really put Roni in a positive light. And, to be honest, he didn't have a bad word to say about his wife. He just had a vague feeling, the echo of a feeling, that he expected more from her. More what? He couldn't say.

Right after the shortened shiva, Roni went back to her normal working life. She put in even more time to make up for the hours she'd taken off when his mother was in hospital. The laptop entered their bed for the first time, and she'd work on it till her eyes closed. And again, Dori found it hard to complain. It was the right, the accepted thing to do. The strong flow of life pulled you along with it. And if you came right down to it, it was his mother, not hers. The fact that Roni didn't take on his pain – that she put up a wall between them, which said we're two separate people, and this sorrow is yours – that was fine, because someone had to provide a balance.

But logic notwithstanding, he felt abandoned. Even if he couldn't put the feeling into words. Even if he suspected that he himself was doing the abandoning. Even if there might be another reason for the abandonment between them that he was unaware of. And so his thoughts grew muddled and kept him from getting a handle on what was going on. After all, he'd always been better at deciphering the past than understanding the here-and-now, at observing what was outside, not what was inside –

*

About two months after his mother died, the pangs began.

He'd settle down in the sitting room after Roni went to bed, promising her that he'd be with her soon, and turn on the TV to watch the sports news. The programme was usually half over when he turned it on, so he'd wait for the repeat to see the first items, the ones he'd missed. Sometimes, on especially hungry days, he didn't turn it off even when the ones he'd already seen came on, and he watched them all over again, even though he knew very well that he was only trying to postpone the moment when he'd turn it off and the pangs of longing would begin. At first, he confused them with hunger pangs, and he'd make himself large night-time meals taken from the recipes in the folder from the cooking course – maybe sirloin would deaden the pangs, maybe pasta would ease them – but the pangs continued, mainly in his stomach, pangs of undefined longing, longing for the sake of longing, longing that playing the drums used to dissolve before he sold them. One in the morning, 1.30, 2, 2.30, each time he'd set a different hour for himself to get up and join Roni in bed, and each time, he'd sit down at the computer and log on to her email, searching in vain for anything that would verify his suspicion that she'd cheated on him in Barcelona, then he would read the news, read historical titbits on the feminist-history site Herstory, which his mother liked, then read the small number of emails she'd sent him over the last few years, and his throat would fill with a kind of wolf-howl he wanted to hurl at the moon. His eyes closed with exhaustion as he sat in front of the computer, but the longing, ever awake, would send him to Netta's room at dawn. He'd always made fun of those scenes in American movies where the father returns late at night from work, goes to the children's room and looks at them sleeping. He'd pasted the sticker, 'I want to see my children awake' on his heart before he became a father, and yet, when all the anchors were gone, he'd wander from the computer room to the smallest room in the house, where toys were scattered on the floor, to clutch on to some kind of certainty. In the arch of all the doubts, there was still the keystone that held it all together: that child. That child loved and needed him. And he'd be rock solid for him, free of undefined longing.

There, in Netta's room, listening to his breathing, the pangs would grow still. Slowly. Until the next night.

How many such nights had there been? While it was going on, he didn't pay attention to how they were accumulating. Each night was independent of the others. Only now, from the distance of the journey, did he realise that there had been many, very many nights like that. In fact, for many weeks, he'd felt the longing without knowing what it was he longed for.

*

It wasn't until the middle of the night, when he got out of bed in the hostel to go to the bathroom, that he noticed the note that had been pushed under his door.

Hi Dori,

I have no idea what you've decided. But anyway, on second thoughts, I'm not sure it's a good idea to continue together.

I'm heading back to the coast after breakfast to carry on my trip from there.

It was a (rare) pleasure to meet you.

Inbar

Inbar

Wrote six versions of the note, each shorter than the previous one. And each time, felt she was putting too much on the table when in fact she wasn't sure what the other side wanted or, even worse, what she wanted. Between the fifth and sixth versions, she called Eitan. He was warm and loving and generous, like Eitan. And her body responded to him from the place it always responded to him: her chest. Dori, on the other hand, with his smell, his sad shoulders, his prominent Adam's apple, his erudition, his Hebrew, his perceptive Jerusalemness, his concern for his father and several other things she couldn't put her finger on – Dori made her itch in a totally different place. A much more dangerous one. High up in her throat, near the base of her tongue. The place where madness lay, waiting to erupt. It had taken her so long to find balance after Yoavi, she thought. It had taken her so long to start eating again. To laugh. To listen to music. So there was no justification for pulling the rug from under herself for another Hoffman. And also: it had taken her so long to begin writing to find her voice, that it would be a shame for all of that to melt away now in the flame of a hopeless love. She had a shower to wash away the itch. Then she took a pair of clean pants out of a shopping bag she once got in her local greengrocer's. Written on it, of all the things in the world, was: A Taste of our Forbidden Fruit.

Now, Inbar, now's the time for the full stop, she told herself. Now, before it's too late—

And the sixth and final note, she pushed under his door.

397

Nessia

Appeared from behind Inbar's shoulder while she was writing and throwing away notes.

What are you grinning at? Inbar said angrily.

'The Wall must fall when the meteor of love arrives.'

What?

Don't you remember? That's what it said on the Wall gallery in Berlin: 'The Wall must fall when the meteor of love arrives.'

Forget it.

The Wall must fall . . .

Enough!

When the meteor of l-o-o-ve arrives.

Dori

Tossed and turned in bed for two hours, and at dawn fell asleep for a few minutes, during which he had a very brief dream, a kind of moving picture: *Inbar and he are walking down Itamar Ben Avi Street in Jerusalem, vertical to the ground, when suddenly, she places her head on his chest as if they're lying down, horizontal to the ground. And they continue to walk together in that position, lying down in direct*

opposition to all the laws of logic and gravity, and it's perfectly
natural for them. Then Robespierre comes towards them,
holding a toy guillotine, shouting: Long live the revolution,
long live the revolution!

In the morning, he lay in wait for her at the door to the
hostel. The lake still slept. Haze still covered the mountain
summits, and he hugged himself and listened to the birds
conversing in a language different from the language of birds
in Israel.

When she arrived, the large rucksack on her back making
her look smaller, he put his hands together and said: I'm
going to Argentina. Maybe you'll change your mind and come
along?

Inbar

Doesn't know how to answer.

He didn't demand: Come!

He pleaded: Maybe you'll change your mind?

And it was that desperation of his that cracked her confidence
in the decision she'd made in the night. For a moment he looked
to her like a little boy, Marco in search of his mother.

That is, his father. And he needed all the help he could
get.

Are you sure it's a good idea? she asked.

I . . . yes . . . look . . . maybe you're afraid that . . . But I
belong to the conservative party of . . . so I think it would be
a shame to give up on . . . after all, you've become part of —
you're already involved. And even though there sometimes is

. . . so you have nothing to . . . because I have a son . . . he's my keystone . . . so . . . do you understand?

More or less.

Good. Because I myself didn't completely understand what I just said.

She laughed. Not because of what he said, but because the area around his Adam's apple flushed as he spoke.

Say thank you, she thought. He put the full stop for you.

And she placed her bag on the ground.

*

Alfredo was late coming down to the lobby, so they went up to his room and knocked on the door. He opened it, wearing a red silk robe, and sprawled on the bed behind him, covered by a sheet, were two young girls. The unbearable odour of his body – as if he sprayed himself with sweat-scented deodorant – made her take a step backwards.

Si, por favor – he looked at her with mocking eyes, as if to say, look at what you're missing – how can I help you?

It's late. We have to get going, Dori said.

So get going, Alfredo said.

What do you mean? What about you?

Read our contract, Mister Dorrrri. I am really sorry. But I do not enter Argentina.

There was no clause like that in the contract, Alfredo.

I am very sorry, but there was. Seven-D. You are invited to check if you do not believe me.

Alfredo

And I really did want to stay with him till the end, till he found his father. After all, I did not take this job for no reason. When Se'ela called me the first time, I said to myself, Alfredo Gonzales, you have here a chance, and really, it is too bad that it is ending like this because all the broken pieces of the vase were glued together nicely after Dori told me what was written in the diary: his father's meetings with his dead wife, the *kilombo* he made on El Loco's farm, picking Titicaca, of all places, where the sun was born, as the place to write his diary, cutting himself off from his children, the one email he did send them – everything led like an arrow to a man who wanted to, who had to start his life all over again. *Mierda*. It would have been good to find someone alive for a change, after all the bodies I had this year. With clothes, without clothes. With worms, without worms. It makes no difference. A corpse is always shit. And here I don't think there will be one. From what I saw, people who have something to live for, even if that something is completely imaginary, they do not tend to die. It would have been interesting to see the place where Mister Dori's father wants to build something on a farm from a hundred years ago. Only a crazy man could think of such an idea, but Bolívar was also a crazy man, and Che was crazy too, and without crazy people like them, humanity, not just the earth, would move in circles.

Except is a shame it is in Argentina. If it was in Alaska, or Australia, or the Fiji Islands I would be happy to go with them.

And pay for it out of my own pocket. Really. Only because I care about Mr Dori and Señorita Inbar and Se'ela.

But not in Argentina.

There is someone there who I will kill if I see him. I cannot call that someone 'father', because he does not deserve that title. A man who beat and abandoned and never sent a single peso to his wife – who made potatoes for her children at lunchtime and potatoes in the evening and potatoes with rice on Sunday evening – such a man does not deserve that title. A man who never asked if his children are sick, who didn't come to the funeral of Alonso, his first-born son, and never gave them pocket money or took them to a football game or hugged them or even beat them with his belt, like a normal father, such a man does not deserve that title.

I know that he's in Buenos Aires, that man. My sources report all his movements to me. He is old now, they say. He even has a cane. But I do not care. It is only in Hollywood movies that everyone forgives everyone in the end. In real life, there are things that even water cannot soften. And if I see him now, there is a very good chance that I will take his cane out of his hand and beat his head in with it until the police come. And jail in Argentina is not jail in Bolivia. You only leave there in a coffin. So it is better for me not to take the risk. I would have gone to any other place with Mr Dori. And, in the end, I would also have fucked the señorita. In the end, she would understand that from the history teacher, she will get nothing, and she would come to me. Who cares if I am a consolation prize. The main thing is to be between her legs. To squeeze her *culita* with my hands. But what can I do, to Argentina I will not go. And I never speak about the man who is there. Even my informants who follow him for me do not know who he is. How do I put it? Better to kill the past than to kill the person. So I put clause 7D in every contract I make. And also clause 7A, which guarantees that if clause 7D is implemented, the client is entitled to a fifty-per cent refund of what he spent on the search, and to the close assistance of my informants in Argentina.

A swindler I'm not, eh? Sometimes I go overboard. Especially with beautiful women. But a swindler I'm not. That is what I said to Mister Dori. And he got angry. Like a tornado. I thought he would go crazy like his father and yell at me, 'MiGs, MiGs'. You're a piece of shit, he said. You knew the entire time where my father was, but you dragged me to all those places so you could make more money. And now you don't feel like going on to Argentina, so you just leave.

That is not true, Mister Dori, I tried to explain to him, and kept my eyes on the señorita. Maybe she could calm him down. You must believe me when I say that I am sorry, I cannot go with you.

So tell me why! he banged his fist on the door. I want to hear an explanation. Not a clause in the contract.

This is the music that the gods have decided to play this time, and I must dance to it.

Don't bullshit me, he said. I deserve to hear a reason. I am paying you money.

Money? Look at the contract and you will see that you are paying me fifty per cent less if the search goes to Argentina. Besides, my people will pick you up as soon as you get there. And another besides – just so you leave with a good feeling, the two plane tickets to Argentina, yours and Inbar's, are on me.

I don't need any favours from you, he said. But his voice was already less angry. That's people for you. Even if they have blue blood, when you give them a discount, they soften up a little. And when you give them a big discount, they soften up a lot. Let us shake hands, amigo, I said. My hand hung in the air for a few seconds until he reached out slowly, grudgingly. And his grip was weak. Hey, I said, I will miss you. Who will find my sunglasses for me, eh? He did not smile. Instead of being angry at me — I wanted to say — be angry at the person you really should be angry at. And fuck. You really need to start fucking right away. Anyone can see from looking at your body that you are not fucking enough. And stop being as serious as death. It is a shame to spend your life like that, boy. Like a father I wanted to speak to him. But how do I know how a father speaks.

The señorita kissed me on the cheek and said, *gracias por todo*. Very nice of her. Maybe if I had found someone like her, someone classy, at the right time, I would have stopped and had children with her. But I am good at finding lost people, not love. And now it's too late. I cannot stop moving.

After they went, I ordered another two whores to come to my bed, and I still could not drive away the sadness. Usually I feel like this when I find bodies, but if I enjoy a little *vida loca* with the whores, it passes. This time, I do not know why, the sadness did not pass. That Mister Dori and Señorita Inbar and Se'ela, who never stops talking, they have come into my heart. I never let that happen with clients so it won't interfere with the search. Maybe I am getting old. Maybe I need to adopt the orphan boy who is always going up and down the stairs from the hill to the dock, and stop moving. And maybe not. Maybe the whores on this island are just not classy.

After the last one left with her pantyhose in her hand, I called my man in Buenos Aires.

Listen, Victorcito — I said to him — I want you to wait for them at the airport. For the señorita, buy a few bags of Bamba. I don't care how you find them. And for Mister Dori, buy a coat, but a good coat, eh? Rainproof and windproof. Whatever it costs. He is walking around with a little *jacketito*, and I do not want him to catch pneumonia. Then take them to eat at Amora's Asado. Yes, I know it is expensive, Che. I will reimburse you. Do not worry. Whatever they ask for — do it. Whatever they need — get it for them. And do not try anything stupid with the señorita, eh? I am warning you, Victorcito. If I hear that you touched her even with the nail on your little finger I will cut off your left ball. *Y mas importante,* when they reach the farm, I want you to call me and describe what is going on there. The place his father is setting up, what it looks like. The meeting between him and Mister Dori, how it was. And do not, under any circumstances, call me two hours later, Victorcito. Call me immediately. On the spot. Or else I will cut off your right ball. *Entiendes?*

Lily

The moment they had all dreamed of, the moment they finally reached their new homeland and set foot for the first time on the holy ground — which was all soft sand — that moment had come, and strangely enough, the only thing she remembers about it now is the young boy who shouted, my tefillin! my tefillin!

Come with us, the men waiting on the beach told them. But he insisted in Polish, which they did not understand: My tefillin! A gift from my father! They fell into the water! And they urged him in Hebrew, which he didn't understand: Come on, the British are on their way. When they saw that he wouldn't move, they grabbed him by his wet clothes and dragged him with them, to keep him from endangering the rest of us.

*

Before Catriel, the commander who had been sent to them by the Haganah decided to run the ship aground on the Tel Aviv coast, he had tried to do it at Jaffa. During that attempt, two people were shot and killed by gunfire from a British coastguard boat. Dr Schwartz and Zvi Bichler. When she thinks about that now, a shudder runs across her back, as if a drop of ice water had fallen on her. A short machine-gun burst from the boat, two fallen bodies. Two widows. Three orphans. As if someone – a kind of clown of fate, a fellow with a bow-tie and a highly developed sense of humour that she sometimes imagines – had decided to show them that this land they were approaching was a land not only of milk and honey but also of blood. And to give them a chance, an absolutely last chance, to choose.

That was rubbish, of course. At that point, they no longer had a choice: though the ship had retreated several kilometres after they heard the shots, it was only waiting for the right moment to try and approach the beach again. All the passengers were standing or lying on the deck, tense, grieving, burnt by the sun. Two circles of people surrounded the new widows, trying to console them. To defend them. To keep them from jumping to their death out of grief.

At two in the afternoon, a small ship approached them and began transmitting a series of Morse code signals to the communications room. Pima, who was standing beside her, translated the coded message for her: The Germans have invaded Poland. The Luftwaffe is bombing Warsaw. War has broken out.

And then he put his hand on her shoulder.

That was the first time he'd dared to touch her in the light of day, on the deck. She removed his hand and moved slightly away. Daytime Lily did not like to be touched. Daytime Lily was faithful to Natan and yearned to see him with every fibre of her being.

Night-time Lily was another story.

At eight that evening, the ship turned on its lights, raised its anchor and headed towards Tel Aviv.

Some of the women took out make-up and mirrors and began to beautify themselves for the Promised Land. Some of the men took out razors and shaved. She and Pima were too exhausted to join in: they'd spent hours together preparing the passengers' last newsletter, which included the life stories of the two dead men, a brief mention of the news about the war that had broken out in Europe, and their expectation – so they decided to write after discussing it – that it would be 'very short, according to those in the know'.

They decided to hang the newsletter on the base of a mast because no one was going down to the sleeping quarters now. But even so, not many readers noticed it. It was apparently not the right time to contemplate the bitter fate of others.

Commander Catriel announced that the ship would run aground in a few minutes, and asked the passengers to run to the opposite side of the ship if it listed too far to one side, in order to rebalance it. A short time later, the ship stopped a few hundred metres from the shore. It swayed a bit, then steadied itself. The propeller blades dug into the sandy sea floor until they grew still. The lights of their new land had never been so close. You could reach out and touch them. Small boats (later, she would learn that they were called surfboats) were sent out to them from the shore, and ladders were dangled from the deck.

Run, Pima told her. Run with Esther and get into one of the first boats.

What about you?

I'm staying with Pessia. He's hiding in the sleeping quarters. Doesn't want to get off the ship because of what happened the last time. I'll wait until everyone is off, and then I'll carry him on my shoulders. I don't want to hold everybody up now. Especially you. Run. Before the British make it to the beach.

And she ran. Without hugging him, without even kissing his cheek — someone might see, someone might suspect. And she jumped into a boat with Esther. It pitched in the waves for a minute, no longer, then they were ordered to jump into the water. With our clothes on? With your clothes on. With our suitcases? With your suitcases. There is no choice. Look, another precise moment dredged up from the depths of the years: the moment her feet touched the sea floor. Esther's feet, she remembers, touched it first because her legs were longer. And Esther reached out and pulled her forward. A few more waves hit her, pushing her forward, eastward, and then she felt it: land.

Wave after wave drove them to the shore as if they were pieces of wet timber. The men standing on the sand pushed and shouted them along. For a moment, she thought she would stop to translate the words of the confused young fellow who had dropped his tefillin; for a moment she looked around for Natan, knowing it didn't make sense that he should be waiting for her on the beach, but she still hoped — and then a strong hand grabbed her arm and pulled her forward to a shed that stood further inland on the beach. The Hilton Hotel is there now — or is it the Dan? She's not sure about things related to the present — but back then, there was a shed made of tin sheets joined together. Arms reached out to her from inside the shed with a warmth she would later learn to call 'Israeli'. Moving brusquely, women helped them take off their wet clothes and handed them dry ones. The trousers they gave her were too short for her taste, and the blouse was a man's shirt, but she didn't complain. They were offered a cup of tea. How many sugars do you take in your tea, comrade? one of the women asked her, and she looked at Esther in amazement. It had been so long since she'd heard a question like that.

*

Suddenly, the phone rings. It's very late. People don't call her at such hours these days. Grams, a pleasant voice says, it's Inbar. Hello Inbar, she says. But quite a few seconds go by till her brain manages to remember that this is her granddaughter. Inbar! she says again, this time affectionately. Where are you? Are you back?

Not yet.

Come back, my *tsipke feuer*.

Soon, Grams.

Soon plus soon adds up to a long time in the end.

I dreamed about Pima last night, Grandma. It's the second time I've dreamed about him.

Which Pima?

Your Pima. What other Pima do you know?

But where . . . You don't even know . . . How did he look in your dream?

Tall, with a huge mane of hair and long legs. Kind of handsome.

Are you joking? Pima was ugly, bald and not tall at all.

But he played the violin, didn't he?

The harmonica. Sometimes the trumpet.

In my dream, he played the violin. It was in the square in front of Beit Hakronot, and when he finished, you walked around with your red hat and collected money. Dori and I gave you money.

She tries to remember who Dori was. Inbar is talking to her as if she's supposed to know him. So she probably is supposed to know him. But dammit, she can't picture him in her mind.

I won't have it! she says.

What?

Who gave you permission to take my Pima into your dreams?

Inbar laughs.

She tries to picture her, but can't place her granddaughter in a setting. She has no idea how she looks there, in South America.

Grams, Inbar says, do you know that I love you?

Well come home then. It's not healthy for a Jewish girl to be in exile for so long. Exile is punishment, isn't it? It's not good for a person to be without a home, and it's not good for a home to be without a person. And it's not good for a granddaughter to be without a grandmother. Or a grandmother to be without a granddaughter.

I'll be back soon, Grams. I have a mission to complete here.

A mission? What are you, one of the child detectives in *Casamba*? All right. Do you need money for a return ticket?

No.

That's good, because I don't have it anyway. Are you eating well?

Yes.

Dressing warm enough? Brushing your teeth? Cleaning your ears? Not talking to strangers unless they're handsome?

*

In the morning, she no longer remembers the details of her conversation with Inbar. That's how it's been recently, new facts fall out of her like hair, leaving only a general sense of things: Haim from the shop is worried about something unrelated to her; her best friend Gita is losing her mind; the Prime Minister is a big liar; Inbar's in love.

*

She didn't know what happened to Pima. The first passengers off the ship, like her, managed to blend into the large crowd waiting on the beach and slip away from the British. Throughout the night, after a brief stay in the sheds, they were dispersed to private homes. She and Esther — they insisted on staying together — were sent to a small apartment on Mazeh Street in

Tel Aviv, and the family that lived there invited the girls to join them for a supper of tomato soup with rice, fishcakes, cabbage salad, and pudding. The food was similar to what they were used to at home, but seemed to contain some kind of local saltiness. After supper, they were told they could wash, and in the shower, unbelievably, there was soap! And the towels smelled clean! There were scales! (She'd lost ten kilos on the journey.) Afterwards, beds were pulled out for them! Real beds! With sheets! True, the beds were crowded tightly on the balcony, and Zionist mosquitoes buzzed around them all night, and the iron springs in Esther's bed squeaked every time she moved and kept them awake, but in the morning, when they placed their feet on the floor, it didn't move up and down. And awaiting them on the kitchen table were two glasses of fresh orange juice. With thick slices of black bread. The lady of the house said a short blessing and placed two bowls on the table, next to the bread. One held jam and the other, rendered chicken fat.

Lily and Esther nodded thanks, their mouths too full to speak.

Do you know that war broke out in Europe yesterday? the lady of the house asked.

We know, Esther said.

People say that it will reach here in the end. Next week, the British will start handing out gas masks. I imagine that you will both have to—

Excuse me, Lily interrupted her. She knew that news of the war was supposed to upset her, but at that moment, something else entirely was on her mind. Do you know by any chance what happened to the people who landed on the beach after us?

Let's check the newspaper, their hostess said, and spread it on the table.

'Holocaust!' a headline shouted from its frame at the bottom of the first page. Lily didn't know the word and tried to work out what it meant from the context: 'Are your teeth falling out? Are abscesses erupting on your gums? Start using Ginozi toothpaste today, and prevent a holocaust in your mouth.'

They finally found the article they were looking for on page six. The last boatload of illegal immigrants from the ship that landed on the Tel Aviv coast last night, the reporter wrote tersely, have been captured and sent to a detention camp in Sarafand.

*

No one could tell her with certainty that Pima was being detained in Sarafand. But she assumed that if he had somehow managed to evade the British soldiers, who'd been waiting on the beach, he would appear at the funerals of Dr Schwartz and Zvi Bichler, for which no date had yet been fixed.

Before the funerals, she walked around the city with Esther, her emotions in turmoil. Here she was, finally in Eretz Yisrael, but instead of looking around, like Esther, at the wonders of her new homeland, she was searching for a bald man with a prominent Adam's apple and a too-large nose.

Look, Esther stopped in front of a public bulletin board, there's a cinema here!

They stopped and read the names of the films: *My Heart Calls to You*, *Lovesick*, *My Uncle and I*.

And a travel agency too! Esther pulled her along, almost tearing her arm out of its socket.

A cardboard sign hanging on the door of the agency said: 'Visit France, the land of beauty. Luxuriate in the warm baths. Relax in the mountains. Partake in the joy of life.'

Do you believe it? Esther enthused, a Jewish travel agency! Shall we travel to France, Mademoiselle Lily? A pharmacy! Esther cried at the sight of the next shop. And then, with the same unflagging wonder: An estate agent's! A shoemaker! A tailor! A kiosk!

The kiosk sold cigarettes with Hebrew names: *Aluf, Atid.* Maybe, she thought, she'd buy a packet and take it to Pima, in Sarafand. If he's in Sarafand, she reminded herself. You don't even know.

What's wrong? Esther asked. Why so quiet today?

Am I usually a chatterbox? she replied.

No, but your face is pale, as if we were still on the ship, rocking in the waves –

Esther had unwound the bun she usually wore on the top of her head and undone the top button of her blouse. Her very short, khaki shorts set off her long legs. Workers winked at her from every direction, and she smiled back at them, touching the top of her head in embarrassment, as if the bun were still there.

I'm waiting for Natan – Lily spoke the truth and lied at the same time – I'm afraid he hasn't heard the news that the ship's arrived.

She couldn't tell her friend about Pima. She had stolen to his bed behind the curtain under cover of darkness, and left it at dawn, and what they did – they did surreptitiously. Half asleep. All in the dark as if they were in a dream, and she was afraid that if she spoke about those nights, if she put them into words, the memories would fade and everything would become real. Too real.

Come on, Esther tugged at her arm, two fellows I met this morning invited us to dinner at their little house in the Montefiore quarter.

Another time, Lily said. I want to go to the beach now, to see our ship.

Our ship? Oy. I think that just looking at it would make me feel sick, Esther said with a laugh.

So we'll meet back at the apartment? Lily said.

No problem, comrade, Esther said, and that 'no problem', a phrase so typical of their new homeland, rolled off her tongue naturally, effortlessly.

*

Their ship had listed to one side, and boats were circling it, unloading what they could and bringing it to the beach.

Just like a widow's friends who break into her room after she dies to loot her jewellery, Lily thought. Gloom descended upon her. Their large, strong ship was now irreparably damaged. The starboard side had a tear in it, like the tears in the clothes of mourners, and it didn't look as if it would ever carry illegal immigrants again. She thought again about her father and sisters, left behind in Poland. What were they doing now? Some of their neighbours had prepared escape routes, in case the war came. But her father had been optimistic by nature. He continued to open his shop at eight on the dot. And close it at two. And open it again from four until 7.15. When they sprayed grafitti in black paint on the windows, he went outside, chuckled, and said, well, it's a good thing this is a hardware shop. Then went back inside, took a rag from the bottom shelf and turpentine from the top shelf, went out again and rubbed out the writing in four strong, determined strokes, then another slower, more pensive one.

Had she known then, standing there on the beach, that she would never see him again? It's not clear. She wanted, with all her might, to believe they would meet again. After all, people who should know had said that 'the war is expected to be short'.

Her gaze came to rest on a black strip on the sand that looked to her like the beginning of a tarball. But no — it was tefillin. The ones that boy had lost yesterday. She pulled them out of the sand and wound the strap around her arm. In Warsaw, it never would have occurred to her, as a woman, to do that.

But here, she wound it around her arm without a second thought and walked towards the sheds, where yesterday she'd received a cup of tea with one and half spoons of sugar in it, to ask what to do with her discovery. The first shed was locked, and standing at the second one were two very suntanned fellows ironing trousers on a wooden board they'd stretched between two piles of bricks. They told her to take the tefillin to the exhibition hall in the port, and even drew her a small map on a paper napkin. That's where all the belongings pulled out of the water had been put and could be reclaimed. They were very friendly, but even so, she felt such a foreigner that it hurt, so she hurried away. She walked along the busy streets, following the map they'd drawn for her, her shoes kicking up sand with each step, her eyes searching for Pima – she both wanted and didn't want to find him. Buses passed her, traffic lights greeted her, a poster advertised a play called *Breach of Trust*, and another advertised the upcoming Maccabiah games. People carried umbrellas – not because of rain, but because of the blazing sun, which beat down on her head, the back of her neck, her back, but she kept walking even though she felt that the pulse pounding inside her wasn't hers, the tremulous breaths weren't hers, the steps she took weren't hers. An ambulance with a Star of David on its side passed her, and for a moment she had the urge to signal it to stop and take her to the hospital. She stopped at a kiosk to buy a cold lemonade. They had been allotted ten *grushim* a day, and she didn't want to waste it so quickly, but she was unbearably thirsty. Grafitti on a wall opposite the kiosk said: BRITISH BASTARDS GET OUT. There were signs in Hebrew everywhere. Signs in Hebrew! She was supposed to be thrilled by that, but even after she'd added an internal exclamation mark to strengthen the effect, she felt hardly a stir.

After a long while – her feet were red from the effort – she reached the exhibition hall. It was filled with the hustle and bustle of scores of people, and whenever she asked someone to please make a note of at least the name of the ship that had carried the tefillin from Poland, they shrugged and referred her to someone else. In the end, she gave up on writing down the ship's name and placed the tefillin carefully between a single brown shoe and a book by Ahad Ha'am, whose pages had not yet completely dried, and left.

*

On the way out, she bumped into a group of comrades from her training camp. Lily Freud, how are you? they said cheerfully. I feel as if I've been dreaming, she replied, lying, yet not lying. They offered to drive her to the apartment on Mazeh Street where she was staying, and after a moment of weighing up their unbearable cheerfulness against the difficulty of walking, she joined them. They sang at the top of their voices all the way there, and she moved her lips and looked out of the window. Who knows, maybe he's there, oh my God, maybe he's there. A carriage drawn by a horse that had dropped dead from the heat blocked the traffic on the street for quite a while. I could have walked, she thought, and while she could avert her gaze from the sight of the dead horse lying on its back, there was no way she could keep the nauseating stench from assailing her nostrils. When they came to the corner of Mazeh Street she asked them to stop, insisting that she didn't want them to drive her to the door of the building. They were surprised at her insistence, but let her get out. We'll see you tonight at Beit Brenner; there's a lecture on administering first aid during air raids and then some folk dancing, they said. And she wondered what Beit Brenner was and how all of them already knew about it and she didn't.

A sudden gust of wind came from beneath her, lifting, then dropping her. A fan, she thought, and began walking, that's what they should distribute to every new immigrant arriving in this city.

A man was standing at the entrance to the building she was heading for. She saw him from a distance and shaded her eyes from the sun to see him better. He waved hello with his entire arm, and began walking towards her in a strange gait that, in seconds, turned into a run.

*

You both sleep here and I'll go back to Montefiore, Esther said to them. You must want to be alone together.

That's very nice of you, Lily's friend, he said.

My name's Esther, she said.

And I'm Natan, he said and extended his hand.

I know, she smiled and shook it.

The sound of peddlers hawking their wares came through the window. As usual these last few days, for every word Lily understood, there were two she didn't.

So tell me, Esther, how was it with those fellows from Montefiore? Lily asked in an attempt to postpone for as long as possible the moment she'd be alone with Natan.

They don't have a bit of culture, those *vilde hayas*, those boors, Esther said, her forehead reddening. But there's something . . . nice about that too.

What did you eat there?

What did we eat? Esther wondered – her friend had never taken an interest in details like that – bread and black olives. Nothing special.

On the kibbutz, Natan said, the fruit and vegetables are fresh. You pick them in the morning, and in the evening they're on your plate. Tomatoes, marrows, cucumbers, peppers . . .

Lily looked at him as he spoke. He was better looking than she remembered. A long, fresh scratch on his arm emphasised

417

his newly developed muscles. His cheeks were a good colour, and all the little spots on his forehead had disappeared without a trace. His eyes, which caressed her as he spoke, were untainted by any spark of guilt. Which meant that there'd be no balancing out of sins here.

Oranges, plums, grapes – he went on listing with shining eyes – melons and watermelons, only in season, of course—

So . . . when are you going to the kibbutz? Esther interrupted gently.

Tomorrow at dawn, Natan said.

Not tomorrow! Lily said – her voice rougher than she intended – and Natan stared at her and scratched his ear with his little finger, the way he used to back in Poland when he was embarrassed.

Not tomorrow, Natan, she repeated in a more subdued voice. Tomorrow is the funeral of the men who were killed on the ship.

*

She didn't see him at the funeral: no matter how hard she looked, she didn't see him either in front of her or behind her. Nor was he on either side of her, and his klezmer orchestra did not appear; not a single note was played. All the mourners heard were long speeches and more long speeches, in Hebrew, which most of them didn't understand. There was chaos in the cemetery, bedlam, with everyone squeezing together, and the men took advantage of that to press up against the women. She asked Natan to protect her, to stand between her and the sweaty mob, and he wound his arms around her and said, yes, it takes time to get used to this, I mean, to the lack of personal, private space here. Everything is communal, and everyone crowds together under one small roof, and she nodded slowly, reluctantly. Another speaker who was to read his eulogy from notes walked resolutely up to the podium, and she continued to cast her eyes into the crowd as if she were casting a fishing rod into the sea, but instead of catching Pima on her hook, she caught Esther. Her hair was loose, its ends already burnt blond by the sun. She was surrounded by her group of admirers from the Montefiore quarter, where she'd spent the night, but as soon as she saw Lily and Natan she waved excitedly and made her way through the strait of shoulders until she reached them. Hello, Natan, she said, her forehead reddening. I have to speak to your dear girlfriend, is that all right? And before Natan could reply, she dragged Lily by the arm around to the back of the grey bus with the iron screens, which at first had made the new immigrants extremely anxious. They'd thought it was a British police vehicle waiting to take them away, and they didn't relax until the old-timers explained that the bus belonged to the cooperative Histadrut trade union, which had put the screens on it to keep grenades thrown by Arab terrorists from landing inside.

He's in Sarafand, in prison, Esther said. He's fine. Waiting for a certificate.

But how—

One of my boys in Montefiore has connections in the Haganah, and I asked him to find out.

But how did you know that I—

Oh really, you don't have to be Freud to know.

Thank you, she said, and hugged her friend and kissed her on both cheeks. Then she moved slightly away from her and stroked her long hair. It looks nice this way, Esther, she said. Eretz Yisrael suits you.

A smart person – Esther said, glowing at her – once told me that this is our chance for a fresh start! A chance for people, for couples, to have different kinds of relationships. Every generation repeats the previous generation's mistakes, that person told me, and our generation says – enough! Let us be creative. So, as a beginning . . . I decided to go to Weiss's salon and give myself a new look!

Lily smiled weakly.

And it's so nice for you to be with your Natan. Esther kept trying to cheer her up. I can see how much he loves you.

Lily nodded.

And the bald one – don't be fooled by him. He'll find himself new prey in no time at all.

Lily nodded slowly.

Come on, Esther said, grabbing her hand, let's go back, and she led the way through the crowd to Natan – handed her to him as if she were returning lost property – then flew off back to her suitors. Another speaker walked up to the podium. The sixth one. The sun was at its zenith, burning up any possibility of feeling genuine sadness.

How long will this go on? she asked Natan.

It's hard to say.

So let's go.

But I thought—

Come on, we'll leave for the kibbutz now.

*

She had one final moment of choice (actually it was the one before the final one, why hide it), a moment when she could have chosen a different path. Another bus was parked in front of the one that would take them to Natan's kibbutz, and in front of it – the work of the devil, the one with the bow-tie – another bus with a sign on its window that said: Sarafand. When Natan climbed on to the roof of the kibbutz bus to secure her suitcase on it, the engine of the Sarafand bus came to life. To keep herself from boarding it, she closed her eyes and summoned up the image that always filled her with a sense of security, adding several up-to-date details: she and Natan are in their new home on the kibbutz. It's surrounded by greenery, a small stream burbles beside it, and the inside of the house is painted in bright colours. Natan, wearing shorts and a vest, brings one of his wonderful omelettes from the kitchen, along with a glass of fresh orange juice, and the sun shines through the window. She sits cross-legged on a thin mat and beside her, dozing on a bed of soft blankets, is their little baby girl, whose name she already knows.

When she opened her eyes, the bus to Sarafand had driven off.

Natan finished tying her suitcase to the roof of the bus and they boarded and sat down close to each other on the seat behind the driver. She enjoyed his body, which wasn't sweating despite the intense heat (Pima sweated all night). She enjoyed the touch of the white shirt he'd worn for the funeral, the one that reminded her of the shirt he'd worn on their first evening together in Warsaw. She enjoyed the fact that he could decipher her secret Morse code message and give her the gift of silence during the first hour of their trip (Pima was incapable of keeping quiet). And then she enjoyed his picturesque explanations – which were detailed without being pompous – of the new land that was being revealed to her, kilometre after kilometre, fragrance after fragrance, through the window: Those are orchards, those are irrigation pipes, those are combines. That's a moshav, that's a village, that's a collective farm, that's a kibbutz. There are many differences between them, you probably remember that, but they all share the passion to make a fresh start.

He talks just like David Litvak in *Altneuland*, Lily thought. With the same, confident pride of the old-timers in this land. And I am an ignorant foreigner, like Dr Friedrich.

The bus coughed going uphill, and for a moment she thought it would roll backwards. But it coughed once again and continued climbing, until they saw a chessboard field spread out in a green valley below them.

A gust of wind carried an unfamiliar, pungent odour, which she would later learn to recognise as the smell of sage.

The Jezreel Valley, Natan said, and swung his arm widely, as if the entire valley were his possession.

She held his arm and planted small kisses along the length of the scratch on it. There are a lot of thorns here in summer, he explained, a bit embarrassed, either by the scratch, or her kisses, or the fact that he was talking so much. And she kept kissing until she reached his wrist – that, she knew, was one of the places he loved to be touched.

With a two-day delay, she felt a tiny bit of the joy she'd expected to feel when she'd imagined their meeting. With a two-day delay, she also felt a tiny bit of the excitement she'd expected to feel here when she participated in the activities of the youth movement in Warsaw, heard overlong lectures on realising the dream and tried to picture her life in her new home-land. And now those two joys – she said to herself as the bus crossed the valley – were one and the same. Natan was her new life and her new life was Natan. All the rest was pure illusion.

When they'd been on the bus for almost four hours (the trip took six hours back then!) her head dropped on to his shoulder and she fell asleep. In her dream, her head dropped on to Pima's shoulder. And that gave her pleasure. The strong swaying of the bus woke her, and her head was on Natan's shoulder. And that gave her pleasure too. A few minutes later, exhaustion overcame her and again, Pima was in her dream. They came to a British police barricade, and once more her eyes opened to see Natan. And so, during her first trip through the country, a partition plan was established that would be part of her life until Hana was five and there was a knock at the door of their home in Haifa: Natan – in her life, and Pima – in her dreams.

Inbar and Dori

They'd already been on the road for three days. First they had to sail from the Island of the Sun to the town of Copacabana on the shore of Lake Titicaca, then take a direct bus from there to La Paz, and at the airport, they'd board a flight to Buenos Aires.

Alfredo estimated that the entire trip shouldn't take them more than a day.

If nothing went wrong.

The first thing to go wrong was the boat, which suddenly began to fill with water – the sun had cracked the sides, the boy sailing the boat explained – and they had to return to the island to wait for another boat to leave. By the time the other boat left, they'd missed the gringos' punctual bus and had to wait for the locals' bus, which left four hours later and made countless stops. Travelling with them on the Titicaca-La Paz-via-Altiplano bus were three chickens, a small pig and two parakeets in a cage. Three people sat in seats for two and ate food they'd brought along, using their fingers. Every once in a while, a boy boarded the bus and tried to sell corn, or lychees, or Fanta in plastic bags. Flat. It was very cramped, and Inbar squeezed up against Dori so that people wouldn't squeeze up against her. Her trousers brushed lightly against his. Her breath mixed slightly with his. She occasionally looked at him. But averted her gaze when he looked back at her.

Makes you miss Israeli buses, he said just to say something. And she laughed in relief, yes.

I feel — he slid in on her laughter — like someone who's had his cataract removed. Only now do I see how sterile the trip in Alfredo's trailer was.

You'll miss that sterility, she said. And as if to prove her point, the bus stopped a few minutes later at a police barricade. Two policemen got on, asked for the tourists' passports, kept them for a long time, and finally returned them all, except for Dori's. In Spanish, which was so fluent that it amazed Dori, Inbar managed to explain to the head of the police unit that there was a problem, and they got off the bus, took their backpacks off the roof and went to look for the passport. After a few long moments of anxiety — that is, he was anxious, and Inbar not in the slightest — the passport was finally found in the bottom drawer of the desk in the police shed beside the barricade, but by then their bus had left. A few minutes later, the policemen also left the scene, racing away on their motorbikes as if escaping from someone, leaving Dori and Inbar behind in a cloud of uncertainty.

The nowhere they found themselves in grew dark.

A herd of alpacas crossed the hill facing them, but there was no shepherd to be seen on the horizon. The wind blew up clouds of dust like tornadoes which dissipated before they could gather any real momentum. The only thing visible on the entire plain was a single house. They walked towards it because they didn't have a better destination. But as they approached, they saw that it wasn't a house, but the single, standing wall of a ruin.

They walked back to the road. A few minutes later, a car stopped and the driver offered them a lift.

Wait, Dori said, and grabbed Inbar's arm. Look at the guy in the back seat. Isn't that a gun under his shirt?

To be honest—

Say no thank you, he told her.

No, gracias, she said to the driver. Who didn't move. The man sitting in the back gave them a dirty look.

Donde! Donde from here! Dori waved his arms and shouted the wrong Spanish word at them. But the driver understood the threatening tone that went with the waving arms, and drove off.

*

The sun sets, but the moon doesn't rise. Two people in the heart of Altiplano, not knowing which way to go. The woman thinks it's a good thing that the man is with her, otherwise it would all be a bit scary. The man is frightened. There was a time when a situation like this wouldn't have bothered him. Just the opposite: something cold and calculating would grow inside him in moments of danger. But ever since his son's birth, moments like this arouse the if-something-happens-to-me-my-child-will-be-fatherless terror in him.

Donde from here?!! Inbar suddenly repeats the words that Dori shouted and she laughs loudly into the night.

What's wrong with that? Wait . . . what exactly does *donde* mean? Dori asks.

Where! Where from here! That's what you yelled at him. Where from here, man!

*

They finally hitched a lift on an oil tanker truck whose driver looked trustworthy enough. He dropped them off in a nearby village, where they hoped to catch a bus. But after they got out of the truck, they discovered that not a single bus stopped in that village. More accurately, for the first few minutes, Inbar wasn't able to communicate with anyone – it turned out that the local residents spoke only an unfamiliar, consonant-laden language – and half an hour passed before they managed to find a young girl who spoke Spanish. She explained that the only way out of the village was in private vans, which don't travel at night because of the gangs on the roads. They're not Peruvians, she added, they're Colombians and Brazilians. Why don't the police deal with it? The girl smiled bitterly. The police work with them for a percentage. The police take gringos off the buses to 'check them' and leave them in the middle of nowhere so the gangs can offer them a lift and rob them.

I see . . . so, where can we find a safe place to spend the night here? Inbar asked. The girl pointed to a wooden house that stood on the outskirts of the village, on the top of a hill dotted with dry bushes. That's the village hostel? Inbar asked. There's no hostel here, the girl explained. That's Don Angel's house. He's our shaman. And sometimes he takes people in. If it suits him.

They headed for the wooden house, passing beds of potatoes and corn, and a brook with a makeshift bridge of wooden boards over it. Careful, it's slippery, Inbar said and held Dori's hand until they reached the other side. It was growing darker now, a freezing wind began to blow through the gaps in their clothes. They tightened the straps of their backpacks on their stomachs and walked faster before total darkness fell.

When they began to climb the hill, Dori stopped and put a hand on his chest, and Inbar waited for him to get some oxygen into his lungs.

Just a bit further, she told him. We're really close now.

*

A short man wearing a green jumper and jeans with a small tear at the knee was standing in front of the house. *Ola*, he said as they approached, and gave them a broad, tranquil smile, as if he'd been waiting a long time for them. If he'd said, '*Ola*, Inbar, *ola*, Dori,' they wouldn't have been surprised. With a small but unmistakable gesture of his hand, he invited them in. When he turned, they saw a long thick braid down his back, and Inbar suppressed an urge to touch it, to unbraid it.

The inside of the house did not seem particularly suited to guests. Children, younger than expected, ran through the rooms, which were separated only by cloth dividers. Hammocks were spread through the house. Steam rose from a small pan that stood on two millstones. In the corner of the room was a musical instrument that Dori had never seen before: a sort of harp with a single string. A woman walked past the harp, then disappeared into the shadows.

I am glad you came, the short man said in fluent but heavily accented English. Not many guests come to our small village. I am Don Angel. And you?

This is a shaman? Inbar wondered. Where are his coloured feathers? Where is his furrowed face?

I'm Dori and . . . this is Inbar, Dori said.

Come and sit down. The shaman pointed to a low wooden table with two clay plates on it. Your food is ready.

Dori and Inbar exchanged looks. This whole business was very strange, but armed gangs and bitter cold awaited them outside, and there was something about Don Angel that inspired trust. What else could they do?

They took off their bags and sat down. They ate fish. And shrivelled black potatoes. And a grain reminiscent of quinoa. Don Angel sat with them. He didn't eat or speak. In the silence, only the sounds of their chewing, the croaking of frogs and chirping of crickets that came from outside were heard.

When they finished, Inbar could no longer bear the silence and began to tell their story. The bus. The police. The passport. The oil tanker truck.

Don Angel listened calmly, as if he'd known the story in advance. It is good that the road brought you here, he said when she finished speaking. And smiled again.

Suddenly, the front door opened and a woman, a baby and the wind burst into the house.

You will have to excuse me, Don Angel said to Inbar and

Dori with a serenity that was in sharp contrast to the woman's hysteria. He stood up, rubbed his chest with two quick movements of the back of his hand, and turned to her. She spoke to him in that consonant-filled language. She was worried about the baby, that's why she'd come — they could understand that from the way she moved her hands and the way the baby looked. Its eyes were closed, its chest rose and fell slowly, as if it were having a hard time breathing, and its pug nose, which reminded Dori a little of Netta's, was blocked. With unhurried movements, Don Angel spread a piece of cloth on the wooden floor, took the baby from the woman naturally, as if it were his, removed the red woollen hat that covered its head and laid it, face up, on the cloth. Then he waved a feathered wing close to the baby's face, rattled a bunch of leaves close to its nose and sprinkled it with some drops from a bottle of transparent liquid labelled Agua de Florida. Dori needed a few seconds to remember why this series of actions seemed familiar, and then it came to him: his father's diary. That's exactly what the shaman from Pascual Abaj did before he gave his father the potion to drink. The baby didn't respond. If something like that happened to Netta, Dori thought, he would never allow . . . How could this hocus-pocus help anyone? Why didn't they take him to a normal hospital?

Don Angel was unfazed. He put his hand very close to the baby's face, uttered a series of noises that sounded like the hooting of an owl, and then took a drink from the bottle of Agua de Florida and spat it out through his teeth, like a sprinkler, three or four spurts into the air above the baby's throat.

In the end, he and the mother counted in that strange, consonant-filled language: one, two, three, four.

At four, the baby began to cough. And opened its eyes.

*

428

After that, while the baby was crawling on the floor, Don Angel had a long talk with the woman. She tried to explain something to him and he tried to understand. Then he tried to explain something to her and she tried to understand. Then he took two small pieces of paper out of his shirt pocket, put some powder on them, took out a piece of string, estimated its length, as if trying to be exact, and used it to tie the pieces of paper together, then handed the small package to the woman. Who again tried to explain something to him.

Every once in a while, they heard a Spanish word in the flood of noises, and Inbar tried as hard as she could to extract some meaning, to put together a story. As soon as the woman put the baby's woollen hat on its head and left, she asked Don Angel, what was wrong with the baby? And added, I hope it's okay for me to ask.

It is perfectly okay, Don Angel said with a smile. That is your nature, to be daring. And then he was silent.

What a load of shit, Dori thought. He met her five minutes ago, and he thinks he knows her nature already?

Don Angel went over to the millstones and removed the small pan. Then he took small glasses from a shelf and slowly filled them with the maté, South American herbal tea, which had already been offered to Dori at various stops on his journey.

He couldn't stand maté. And the maté that Don Angel gave them was expecially revolting. As bitter as wormwood. He wondered whether a request for sugar would be a desecration, and took a small sip out of politeness.

When something like that happens to a baby, Don Angel replied to Inbar's question as if it had been asked a second, not a minute ago, it often has something to do with the relationship between the parents. Especially when it is an only child. That triangle, mother–father–child . . . all triangles . . . their geometry is . . . complicated. Often, when the angles are too sharp, especially if the side that connects the parents is not stable, too much weight is placed on the child. As he spoke these words, his eyes rested on Dori's.

So what did you advise her to do? What can be done in a situation like that? Dori heard himself ask.

First, I asked her if everything is okay between her and her husband. And after she told me what she told me, I tied together the two pieces of paper with the tobacco and told her to put them under her pillow tonight, and said I would perform a ceremony with them tomorrow.

A ceremony?

That will bring them closer.

Dori shifted uncomfortably on his chair. The shaman gave him a look which implied that he knew him, as if he had the ability to read not only his thoughts, but also his memories. That seemed totally crazy to Dori, and made him angry.

Since when have you had back pains, Dori? he asked. With that look again.

What? How do you know I have back pains?

From the way you move on your chair, I can see that you're in pain. May I?

Dori felt like saying: No, you may not. You and your friends messed up my father's head, so don't touch me, if you don't mind. But that 'may I?' was so matter-of-fact and unassuming.

Can you please stand up? he asked. Dori stood up. Don Angel placed his hands on his lower back and kept them there for a long moment, quietly whistling a tune that sounded suspiciously like an Israeli pop song called 'Something Small and Good'.

You don't have support, he finally said.

Dori moved away slightly and thought: Wow. Illuminating stuff.

Excuse me, Don Angel corrected himself. It is not that you do not have support; you do. You just cannot see it yet. The way we cannot see our backs. That is the way you do not see that you have support. But do not worry – he looked at Inbar from the corner of his eye – you are on the right path. You are making all the right mistakes.

Right mistakes, Dori said, I don't know. I think my back is bad because I've been sitting on planes and buses for two weeks.

Maybe, Don Angel smiled. An irritating smile.

One of his children came into the room. Barefoot. His eyes were very slanted, almost like Japanese eyes. He asked his father something, received an answer, tried to argue, received the same answer and left. Children are children are children.

Don Angel sipped his maté and added: In any case, I advise you to consider using a Dr Gav.

What?! Dori blurted. You've met my father? Why didn't you say anything?

Don Angel continued to sip comfortably and said: Unfortunately, I have never met your father.

So where did you hear about . . . Dr Gav?

The Internet. A wonderful invention. Every time I am in La Paz, I go on to the Internet and look for medical innovations. Most pharmaceutical company drugs do more harm than good, but sometimes there is something interesting. I ordered a Dr Gav from Israel a month ago. It has not arrived yet. As soon as it does, we will build others like it for some of the village elders.

Inbar laughed. The shaman laughed too. A full, rolling laugh.

Come, he said, you have had a long day. Your hammocks are ready for you.

Just a second, Inbar said. She'd been quiet until then, following the interaction between Dori and Don Angel with a mixture of tension, mockery and surprise, feeling it would be inappropriate for her to intervene.

From what I understand, she said, you – I mean shamans – can help create a connection to . . . the souls of people who . . . have died.

This is not the time, Don Angel said.

I just wanted to ask, I didn't mean . . .

Don Angel became serious. You don't need help to connect to your dead, Señorita Inbar. On the contrary — your dead is trapped inside your stone, and maybe it is time to release him. And besides . . . that is not my expertise. I have already told you, my expertise is bringing people closer.

Okay, fine, sure, Inbar backed down.

Come, it is late, I will show you where you will sleep, Don Angel said. And led them to the room where the children slept.

Inbar

Standing at the entrance to the next world was a small shed with a sign on it that said INFORMATION. *She bent down to the window and asked the man behind the desk where she could find Yoavi. The man, who looked not unlike Hoffman, referred her to the Musicians' Quarter, 19 Pure Souls Street. Then she knocked on the door and Yoavi opened it. He avoided her hug and said, I'm glad you came, Sis, we're missing a few words. Suddenly, John Lennon, Paul McCartney and Kurt Cobain were there, and they all played together, and she gave them words in all languages. She was really good, and Paul McCartney said to Yoavi, lucky you to have such a talented sister. And Kurt Cobain said, talented and beautiful. Then they put down their instruments and invited her to eat an artichoke with them. The artichoke was huge, the size of a watermelon, and they ate it leaf after leaf. Down to the heart. She really enjoyed eating an artichoke with Yoavi and his new friends. But then Don Angel came to call her, took her hand in a way that made it clear that she had to go. Okay, so bye, she said to them. See you in heaven, they replied, and Yoavi leaned over and whispered in that voice of his, sorry I can't hug you, Sis, I want to, I want to so much, but I just can't.*

Inbar and Dori

They said goodbye to Don Angel in front of his house, the place where he'd stood the night before when he'd seemed to be waiting for them. He packed them some food for the road, chosen from all the gifts the woman whose baby he'd treated had brought him at dawn: fruit, vegetables, and a savoury pastry.

It was freezing. Even colder than at night. Dori rubbed his hands together. Inbar hugged herself and remembered her dream. Don Angel laughed for no reason. Dori remembered an article he'd read about the Dalai Lama's visit to Israel, which said that he'd laughed the entire time. Inbar wondered whether Don Angel knew that the Hebrew word *inbar* referred to a precious stone, amber, that had dead insects inside it, and that's why he'd said what he said about the dead person inside her.

Nothing was said. Not by people, anyway (birds were chirping their opinions in dozens of different voices).

The van that Don Angel had arranged to take them to the main road finally arrived, surrounded in fumes.

Be on your way, Inbar and Dori, Don Angel said and pushed them gently with his hand. People are waiting for you.

*

A little before La Paz, the bus let them off at a spot where they could take a taxi directly to the airport. They'd already missed their flight to Buenos Aires, but hoped they'd be able to get a ticket for a different flight. No problem at all, the man at the Aerolinas counter said, but ticket exchanges can only be made at the airline office, which is in town. They protested, and he sympathised as he showed them its location on a map.

A short time after they left the airport, La Paz appeared all at once, winding around itself. Channel after channel descending into a broad wadi, but instead of water, houses flowed through them. They were built on such a dramatic slope that it wasn't clear why they didn't break away from the ground and fall into the wadi. No ships sailed in the wadi, only minibuses, dozens of minibuses, one of which took Inbar and Dori to the airline office. But the office was locked – true, with only a ridiculous bicycle chain, but locked all the same. Inbar asked some questions in the bakery next door and learned that the office closed early on Saturday and didn't reopen until Monday morning.

I brought us some of these, to make the bitter pill salty, Inbar said and handed Dori a white paper bag.

What's this? he asked when he pulled an alien-looking pastry out of the bag.

Saltinas, she said. They're amazing. Trust me.

They had nowhere to sit, so they collapsed on to the pavement in front of the closed office, their backs against the window – shoulder to shoulder, elbow to elbow, knee to knee – and gorged themselves on *saltinas*.

They really are good, he said.

I told you, she said. And chuckled: It was worth missing the flight, hey?

If I were here alone, he thought, I'd blame myself for missing the plane and wallow in the feeling of failure for a long time.

If I were here alone, she thought, I wouldn't be here. This section of La Paz doesn't look very appealing.

A minibus with its door half open passed them, and a boy, half his body inside it and half outside, shouted at them to get on: *Rodriguez! Cementerio! Cinquenta centavos!*

Not yet, Dori thought. I want to stay here like this a little while longer. Let the minibus move, not us.

Not yet, Inbar thought. I want to stay here like this a little while longer. Let the world keep moving on its axis, not us. She rested her head on Dori's shoulder. Not in her sleep. Deliberately.

So what do we do? she asked after they didn't get on any of the three more minibuses that drove past. Her breath warmed his neck.

If this is the music that the gods are playing for us, he said, we'll dance to it.

Which means?

Vamos, he said, and a young, prehistoric Dori shook itself awake in him, we'll drop our bags in the first hostel we find and go for a walk around La Paz.

*

And suddenly, on the way to the hostel, he began to dance in the middle of the street. They'd come to a stall selling CDs, and he almost tore off his rucksack and began to move to the music that was coming through the loudspeakers. At first, he danced alone, but then he took off her rucksack, grabbed her hand and twirled her around – no . . . I don't . . . she tried to object . . . know how to dance. So what? He twirled her again, we don't know anyone here, and anyway – he dipped her in a quick movement and then pulled her to him slowly, not right up against him, but close – Señorita Inbarita, there's no such thing as knowing how to dance, there's only wanting to dance. But . . . she tried to protest again, but nevertheless let him twirl her around a little more and then a little more, until the song ended, and also her daring. There was an ice cream place next to the CD stall, and they pulled slowly away from each other, picked up their bags and walked over to it. They deliberately chose the strangest flavours – passion flower, kiwi, lychee, watermelon – and ate tiny amounts with the tiny spoons, and laughed when they realised that the watermelon ice cream tasted like water. They continued walking towards a newspaper stand and tried to read the main headline together – she bragged that she already knew enough Spanish to translate for him, but couldn't really do it. Out of the ten words in the headline, there were only four that she knew, but he didn't make a big deal out of it, and instead invented headlines that would suit the photo – a man in a suit wearing a miner's hat. 'We have no choice but to make painful concessions,' and 'Bolivia condemns Israel,' always a sure thing. She laughed, and he pointed to a long line of people walking behind a coffin and said, look, a funeral. Let's join it. Are you serious? she wanted to say, but he'd already taken her hand. They walked to the edge of the crowd and sang the extremely catchy mourning songs along with the others. They eulogised the deceased to each other in Hebrew – what a wonderful person, a fine person, always ready to help, always paid his union dues on time. A few minutes later, when the line of people was approaching a steep rise, they looked at each other, and without a word left the group and went to get pastries, because, as Dori said, after a funeral you have to have a pastry or it doesn't count, and all the time she was thinking, I knew it, I knew it, I knew he was like this too.

*

That night, she told him about her brother.

They were sitting in a terrible restaurant near the witches' market that, for some reason, Lonely Planet recommended (it's his fault! Inbar pointed to the picture of one of the writers that appeared in the front. Michael Dexter? That's not a *mochilero*'s name! And look at that ironed shirt. With buttons!!! I bet you he sat in his house in Brooklyn and made up the chapter on La Paz.

The place was quite dark, and even the candles in the middle of the table couldn't erase the smell of the darkness. Hammers, saws, knives and frying pans hung on the walls in no discernible order. A water filter without water stood to the right of the bar, with cases of Coca-Cola, which contained Sprite, lined up under it. There were only six tables in the small restaurant, and the only other people were a couple of American pensioners who were planning next day's trip on a large map they'd spread over their plates. The waiter, who was also the maître d' who'd greeted them at the door, took their order and went to the kitchen to cook it.

Sentimental music played in the background. 'I want to live with you, I want to be with you, I want to live with you, I want to be with you,' Inbar translated the words to herself.

Their knees touched under the small table. It wasn't deliberate, but neither of them moved their chair back.

They ate thin, hard, oxygen-starved steak, with Bolivian salad *sin lechuga* – without lettuce – because, Inbar warned him from her own experience, lettuce has more bacteria than any other green vegetable.

You know, Dori dared to say, I tell you so much about my family, and you don't tell me anything about yours.

What's to tell? she shot back at him. A younger brother who committed suicide in the army. I mean, *apparently* committed suicide. But *definitely* dead. A father who left everything and went to Australia. And at the age of sixty, had a baby boy with another woman. A nervous, beautiful mother who lives in Berlin with a wealthy German, but is actually still sitting shiva for her son. And me. The firstborn. Who hasn't cried about her brother even once. Not at the funeral and not during the shiva. Just your average family, right?

A barefoot boy with a tray of lighters stopped at their table, and they bought two. Just so he'd leave them alone.

When did it happen? he asked in a measured voice after the boy had moved on to the next table. Your brother, I mean.

Five years ago, she said.

So he's the dead person inside the *inbar*, he thought.

And she added, as she turned her lighter on and off: Anyone who says that time heals – is lying. For example, it hurts more now than it did the first year. I've never missed him as much I have the last two weeks.

It's the same with me, about my mother, he said, and added (quickly to make it clear that she wouldn't be able to shift this conversation on to him), you know, Alfredo actually had a theory that a journey does two things: it opens your appetite and it opens your memory.

Smart man, Alfredo, she said, and stuck her fork into the tiny pieces of salad remaining on her plate.

Dori didn't touch his food. Tell me, how old was your brother when he . . .

Nineteen. A soldier.

Of course, he thought, cross with himself. She told you that it happened when he was in the army. So why are you asking her how old he was?

The kids travelling here she said, if he were alive . . . he could be one of them. We might even have travelled together.

Were you . . . I mean . . . brothers and sisters are supposed to . . . but . . .

Were we close? He was a mummy's boy and I was a daddy's girl, but somehow, the fact that we belonged to different coalitions at home never kept us from loving each other very much. I mean, I at least loved him very much.

I'm sure that he——

You can't be sure about anything, Dori, she said, restrained anger in her voice. You see, I was sure I understood my brother. But after what happened . . . I began thinking that maybe I didn't see him at all because he was too close, or that . . . or that he put a scarecrow in front of me while his real self went somewhere else. How can I know?

Dori, feeling slightly rebuked, didn't say anything, and thought: Really, how can anyone know anything about anybody?

I'd really love a cigarette now, Inbar said, and turned on the lighter again.

You smoke?

No, but there are moments when you just feel like having a cigarette, aren't there?

Yeah, Dori said. And thought, that's something Roni also says sometimes. And thought, in fact, they're not such opposites. And thought, but the way I bond with them is totally different.

Eat something, Inbar said, pointing to his plate. You haven't eaten a thing.

Because I'm listening to you, he said.

You can't eat and listen at the same time?

Not when the conversation is important to me.

I don't know how I ended up in this conversation at all. I don't usually talk about my brother.

Why not?

I'm afraid people won't understand me. That they won't understand me the way I want them to. That they'll be taken aback.

Taken aback?

Yes, that they'll start talking to me in a serious voice, that they'll stop being natural around me. Feel sorry for me. Swear to me that's not what's going to happen now.

He put his hand on the menu as if it were the Bible, and said, I swear.

Now eat, she ordered him. Your steak is getting cold.

He cut himself a very small piece and put it into his mouth.

You eat funny, she said, did you know that?

Me?

Yes, I've noticed it before. First you cut everything very neatly. And then you just dive in and attack your food.

And that's funny?

Very. We'd make songs together, she said, her eyes fixed on her lighter. Yoavi and I.

Make songs?

He'd play and I'd give him words. We started doing it when we were kids, I'd make up all kinds of stupid poems about kids who lived near us who we didn't like. Then we became more sophisticated about the subjects we chose.

What did he play?

Guitar. Other instruments too, but mainly guitar. He had picks everywhere. In his shirt and trouser pockets, behind his ear, in his sleeve. He had a huge stereo in his room that was always on. He had really weird taste in music. Very eclectic. Sometimes I'd sit in my room and try to guess what he'd listen to next on the other side of the wall, and I never could. He could put on Beethoven after the Beatles, and it just flowed naturally. When he had a girlfriend at school, you could tell what stage their relationship was at from the music he put on. He'd ask for my advice about that girlfriend. He was worried about their sex, not worried – tormented, because . . . because . . .

For a moment she seemed to change her mind, in the midst of the flow of words. Her eyes glistened and she choked up.

What's wrong? Dori asked cautiously.

I suddenly realised that what he told me was private. True, it doesn't really matter any more, because he's not . . . But somehow, he is . . .

Dori nodded. So you don't have to—

Anyway, she went on, still slightly choked up, during the

summer holiday that girlfriend dumped him for someone else. We, the family, didn't pay much attention. Maybe because he himself didn't make a big deal of it. But who knows. Who knows. You see, that's what destroyed us later. Maybe that was what . . . maybe we should have . . . maybe if we had . . . if I had . . . because I was the only one he talked to about things like that. If I had . . . at the time . . . then . . . I should stop, Inbar said, before I start to . . .

No, Dori said. And looked straight into her eyes. Don't stop.

But you have enough on your mind. You don't need me to dump my stuff on you too, she said.

That has nothing to do with it, he said. I can – I *want* to listen to you.

She didn't cry again that evening, but the simplicity with which he said, 'I want to listen' made her tell him much more than she intended: she even told him a bit about Hoffman, and how preoccupied she'd been with whether he'd show up at the shiva or not, but she didn't go into the really embarrassing details. Nonetheless, that was a story she'd never told anyone: not her father, not her mother, not Eitan.

And he understood. Without judging her. She kept waiting for a spark of disapproval to appear in his eyes, but it simply didn't. Instead, his gaze stroked her hair. Really. His hand still held his fork, but his eyes moved gently down from the top of her head to the ends of her hair, again and again. She felt caressed, and yearned to reciprocate his generosity. Then she said, I think I've come with you because of Yoavi. On the search. At least, that's one of the reasons.

What do you mean? he asked, even though he did, in fact, understand.

Because with Yoavi, there was nothing I could . . . but your father – it's still not too late to save your father.

I hope you're right, he said, his tone grim. I very much hope so. In any case, I'm glad you came with me.

The truth is that you didn't really give me a choice, she said with a laugh. You begged me.

I begged you?

May-be you'll change your m-i-ind and c-o-ome with me? she gave an exaggerated imitation of the way he'd put his hands together in supplication.

And he lowered his gaze and smiled, as if admitting guilt.

Inbar

The waiter-cook-busboy cleared their table, and she felt as if her heart were a large magnet that wanted to be drawn out of her and was banging on the inside of her body in frustration.

All the way from the restaurant to the hostel, they leaned towards each other, like two glasses of wine about to clink, and they did actually bump into each other by mistake several times. Shoulder to shoulder, hip to hip. And once, his elbow sent electricity through her right breast. He said he was sorry, and she thought about how much she loved his old-fashioned gallantry, the fact that he apologised and led the way for her on the street and in the bus, and that if there was a jug of water on their table in a restaurant, he poured her a glass first. You could tell that he'd had comprehensive training in couplehood. He knew when to be concave and when to be convex with a woman, and that was really what it was all about. And she also liked that he never said a bad word about his wife. Hoffman had always been complaining about his wife, and that lowered him in her estimation. And she loved the fact that Dori had so much knowledge but, unlike her mother, had no need to show it off all the time. And the fact that he couldn't lie – she liked that too. Even though they'd known each other only a little over a week, she knew for sure that Dori would never lie to her. And he had such a good smell. Not aftershave. The natural smell of his body (when she rests her head on his shoulder, she turns her nose towards his neck and inhales). And she was curious about the contradiction between the two languages his body spoke: when he walked, he was completely open, and when he sat, he was completely closed. Together, it was as if he were a hidden oilfield that had been waiting a long time to be drilled so it could gush out. Or as if he hadn't been watered for a long time. Or, without any of those metaphors, as if he hadn't been properly loved for a long time.

All the way from the restaurant to the hostel, he half danced in the middle of the street, and she walked close to the pavement, close to the stalls selling *choclo con queso* – and all the way to the hostel, they were covered by a mosquito net, the kind that isolates good couples from the stings of the world. That was how she felt, in any case. If she'd been absolutely sure that he felt the net too, maybe (after all, there was still Eitan, still Hoffman, Hoffman, Hoffman) she (not only Nessia) would have gone to his room and loved him properly that night.

At the radio station, she'd had an assistant producer named Revital who believed that any man who didn't want her had to be gay. And that's exactly how she walked, spoke, dressed. It had always been much more fragile with Inbar. She needed compliments. But Dori never gave any compliments at all. Never said anything nice to her. And when they reached the hostel, he said goodnight with a small wave, close to his chest, and hurried off to his room without giving her a hug or even a peck on the cheek, as if she hadn't just let him into her dark room.

*

But that was still forgivable. His behaviour the next day, however, was not.

In the morning, she suggested that they go to eat at the hostel-restaurant Sabres, in the centre of town. She remembered hearing that it was the unofficial gathering place for all the Israeli *mochileros* in South America. Yes, I know, she said when she saw his annoyed expression, I'm not in the mood for all that Israeliness either, but since we're already stuck in La Paz, maybe we can pick up some more information about your father.

Of course, he said, with a disappointment she couldn't figure out. I'll go up to my room and get his pictures.

*

At first glance (and at the second), Sabras reminded her of a pub in Haifa she used to go to: the damp, glass-covered wooden tables, the long benches, the menus trapped between the glass and the table. Orange and blue curtains along the length of the walls and windows separated Israeli autonomy from the Bolivian street. In a corner of the room, as befitted Israeli autonomy, was a memorial with a candle, not in memory of a soldier, for a change, but of a traveller named Daniel Ruppin, who was killed on Death Road. The walls were decorated with typical tourist pictures – three-quarters of them showing sunsets and sunrises – and stuck among them were computer printouts with news from Israel alongside optimistic stickers: Only Love Brings Love, Thinking Good Things Brings Good Things, There's No Despair in the World, His Death is a Mandate for Peace. The background music was Israeli pop in Latin rhythms a bit too appropriate to the place, and the background to the background music was the sound of pots clanging in the kitchen. The large, central room, which served as a restaurant, led to other, smaller rooms: an Internet room with nine computers, all of them in use; a library of books to exchange (excellent,

Inbar thought, I can finally swap the Holocaust books I can't bring myself to read); and a room with recommendations for tourists, containing coloured folders arranged by country.

Hebrew was everywhere. Now and then, there were words in different languages, like a lone olive on a slice of pizza, but the Israeliness she'd tried to avoid until she met Dori dominated the place. And to her surprise, she found it comforting. Like a compliment. At least three or four Hebrew-speakers filled every corner of Sabras – the guys wearing an outlandish combination of shorts, Teva sandals and heavy Indian sweaters, and the girls, like the pioneers of yesteryear, in simple trousers and sweat-shirts, each with the addition of a personal, feminine, modern touch: pink alpaca wool culottes; a thin, wine-coloured scarf; a hair ribbon; large earrings; a thin, gold ankle chain.

One of them, whose hair was braided into dozens of small plaits, went up to Dori. Mr Peleg! she said loudly, which caused several heads to turn in their direction, what are *you* doing here?

Holiday, Dori smiled at her, a new smile that Inbar hadn't seen before. I deserve one every once in while, don't I, Gal Nisimov?

What? You remember my name? I don't believe it!

Not only do I remember your name, but also your term paper, Gal, 'History Repeats Itself: Patterns of Decline into a War That Neither Side Wants,' yes?

Yes! the girl said, delighted. I want you to know, Mr Peleg – she played with her braids – that on this trip, I keep remembering things you taught us. My friends are sick of hearing about you. 'Mr Peleg said this', 'Mr Peleg said that'. Like that whole thing about critical thinking? Perfect for South America. Because it's so easy to fall in love with nature here, and not notice the less beautiful things. You can't believe what goes on in the wealthy neighbourhood here. Rehavia's a slum in compar-ison. And on the other hand, on this street where Sabras is, people sleep in banana leaves.

Dori nodded in agreement. A slight, but clear movement of his chin.

And also what you always told us, that there's no such thing as only one history? It says in Lonely Planet that the Spanish ruled here for four hundred years, but for the locals, no one really rules them because they maintain their culture secretly.

Very good, Dori said with a smile of satisfaction, I see that you already have a subject for your university seminar paper.

Really? You think I can do that? I mean, that I can get a degree in history?

I have no doubt that you can, Gal, Dori said.

So – the girl batted her lashes – you're really travelling and stuff here?

Actually, we're looking for someone here, Inbar interrupted.

Where? Here? In Sabras? the girl asked without taking her eyes off Dori.

No, Dori got back to business. Not just here. We're looking for my father. He . . . he's travelling . . . in South America . . . We lost contact with him . . . And we're trying to locate him.

Isn't that something, the girl said, her voice rising in a question. Her glance lingered on Inbar, as if she were trying to evaluate this new discovery: aah, so is this my teacher's wife?

Do you have pictures of your father? she finally asked Dori. I can check it out with the guys.

He took out the pictures, and the three of them walked from table to table (the way you do at your wedding, Inbar thought), and though everyone was very friendly, the only one who claimed to know Dori's father remembered a second later that he was really thinking of a German guy, the owner of the bakery in Nicaragua where he used to eat breakfast.

The best thing to do, Gal advised them, is to wait for Haimon and Dafna.

Haimon and Dafna?

The owners of Sabras. They should be back in about half an hour.

*

Half an hour turned into half a day. She didn't mind, but Dori was extremely irritable – he kept looking at his watch and pinching his Adam's apple. She didn't understand why he was being like this: after all, their flight to Argentina wasn't until the next day. Nor did she understand why he was so distant with her when they'd been so close the day before. She just didn't know him well enough to know what to make of it.

They ordered *milanesa de pollo* – a huge, paper-thin breaded chicken cutlet – so they wouldn't be taking up room in the restaurant for no reason. At first, they sat alone at a long table, ate in silence and looked around at the beehive buzzing with honey and pats on the back. That naturalness, she said to Dori, the warm, direct way Israelis relate to one another is our greatest achievement, greater than the drying out of the swamps, greater than the technology industry. He didn't say anything. He didn't even nod. Just like his father, she thought, remembering something he'd told her about his childhood. You talk to him and he doesn't answer. It really is unbearable. Should I mention it? But how would he react? There are so many things she doesn't know about him. Was he this serious in bed too? Did he sleep on his stomach or his back? Did he use mouthwash or just toothpaste? Did he get upset only when the Bolivian police lost his passport or did other things stress him out too? When you got down to the level of his egotism, the kind we all have, even Mother Teresa, what did you find there? What kind of annoying little egotistic things had he managed to conceal from the world?

Three sharwals asked if they could sit at their table. Amir, Tamir and Guy. Medical students from Beersheva. Smart. Funny.

Quick-witted. Amir and Tamir had decided to travel for a while before starting their residencies. Guy was travelling so he could decide whether he even wanted to start, because he suddenly wasn't sure: Did he really want to be a doctor, or was he doing it just to please his father? Pretty fucked up, eh? he said, staring into her eyes. It happens in the best families, she blurted out, a remark that Adrian always used on the programme. Yes, it does, he nodded enthusiastically, as if she'd said something rare and brilliant, and she encouraged his flirtation with an instinctive, involuntary smile.

Dori didn't participate in the conversation. He looked past them. And that pissed her off. So what if they were waiting for Haimon and Dafna? In the meantime, he could enjoy himself. What's his problem? Was listening to them talk about their trip beneath him?

So, are you here on your honeymoon? Guy asked, shifting his gaze from one to the other.

She waited a few seconds before replying, giving Dori the chance to jump in. She wanted him to say something clever that they could smile about later, when they were alone. But he remained silent.

No, she finally answered. We're not . . . I mean, we met here on the trip.

How about that, Guy said, sounding pleased.

*

When Haimon and Dafna finally arrived, she considered staying at the table with Guy and not getting up to go with Dori. But when he stood up, he hesitated for a moment, as if he'd lost something, then gave her that maybe-you'll-change-your-mind-and-come-along look again.

Haimon, wearing a grey poncho, recognised Dori's father the minute he put on his glasses. He has this Dr Gav thing, right, guys? he asked them, as if he were talking to a whole group of people, not just two.

Yes, Dori said.

So it's him. He has this kind of Herzl beard now. But it's him. He gave a lecture here three or four months ago.

A lecture?

I didn't hear it, because I had to leave to receive a shipment of hummus. But Dafna told me later. You should ask her, guys. She's at home with the kids. It's at the back. Where the blue door is. Behind the white curtain. You don't have to knock, just go in.

Dori knocked on the door anyway, and when there was no response, he pushed it gently. The smell was the first thing that signalled the transition from restaurant to home: the smell of damp wood was replaced by the smell of wet wipes. Instead of frying oil — massage oil. In the middle of the living room, Dafna, who was much younger than her husband, was massaging an apple-cheeked baby girl who was lying on a small mattress. With long, strong strokes, she oiled the baby's feet and legs.

It really relaxes her, I always do it after her bath, she said to Inbar and Dori as if continuing an earlier conversation.

What kind of oil is that? Almond? Dori asked and knelt easily beside the baby. Dafna poured some liquid into her palm and handed him the bottle. He looked at it and nodded knowledgeably.

And what's this little beauty's name? he asked (Inbar didn't think the baby was even pretty, let alone beautiful).

Iris.

Iris, what a lovely name. It sounds good in Spanish too, doesn't it?

All three of our kids have names that sound good in Spanish too: Sol, Daniel, and now Iris.

Inbar felt how easily this maternal conversation came to Dori, and anything *she* might say would only ruin it. So she didn't say anything. Simply looked around. The sitting room they'd entered was a crazy mishmash of 'Israeli' furnishings – a Kandinsky poster, a row of coat hooks on the wall, straw furniture from the Druze village of Daliyat al-Carmel, and items from the Bolivian street, like a brightly coloured wall rug, and a pretty scary collection of carnival masks.

How long have you been here, in Bolivia? Dori asked.

Almost fifteen years.

And why Bolivia, of all places?

I have family here. They escaped from the Germans in the '30s and set up a light fixture company here. In '88, after we were evacuated from Nueba and didn't know what to do with ourselves, they invited us to come here to have a break and work for the company. So we went back and forth for a few years. Until once we came and didn't—

The baby screamed, and Dafna stopped speaking in the middle of her sentence.

You simply stayed? Dori tried to keep the conversation going.

It wasn't so simple. It's never simple, Dafna sighed and took a nappy out of a packet. Don't get me wrong, we miss it a lot, she continued as she lifted the baby's legs, but life in Israel . . . is a little too stressful for us.

So meanwhile, you opened yourselves a small embassy here.

That's not too far from the truth, Dafna said. They closed part of the embassy here two years ago, and today we do some of the things they used to: we help with issuing *laissez passer* documents for people who've lost their passports; we're a centre for parcels and other mail from Israel. Sometimes, kids end up without money, so we give them some. Sometimes they pay it back. Sometimes not.

She finished dressing the baby and picked her up. Dori took out his pictures and said: I understand that my father was here.

Dafna examined the pictures, then studied Dori, then opened her mouth to say something. And didn't say it.

What? Dori asked. Tell me. This last month, I've heard everything you could possibly imagine about him. Nothing can shock me any more.

It's nothing especially shocking, Dafna said. He just wasn't honest with me. He said that he wanted to give the guys here a lecture on creativity, and he showed me all his business cards. So I let him, even though we usually try not to give all kinds of second-rate gurus a stage. He just looked to me like . . . a serious person. It was the day after the Seder night – did you know that people come here from all over South America on the Seder night? There were a lot of people here, maybe sixty or seventy. We also do Memorial Day. Independence Day. The anniversary of Rabin's assassination. Excuse me a minute, she's a little hungry.

Dafna unbuttoned her blouse, took out a beautiful, perfect breast, and put the nipple in the baby's mouth. Inbar couldn't take her eyes off the sight. She had seen mothers feeding babies in the park next to her house, but she had always looked away.

In short – Dafna continued, her voice slightly hoarser – he really did start talking about creativity in crisis situations. He gave a few examples of advice he'd given to various companies. I think one of them was a kibbutz on the verge of financial collapse because their shoe factory closed and, thanks to his advice, they shifted their whole orientation to education, to setting up nurseries in the kibbutz that would attract other people from the area.

Dori nodded as if he were familiar with that example.

Now you must know that your father is good at working an audience. Before he opened his mouth, they were a little sceptical because of the way he looked, with the beard and everything, but the minute he started speaking, there was total silence in the room. When he finished giving examples from the business world, he talked about himself. And then even my Iris was quiet and stared at him. He said that almost a year ago his wife – I mean your mother – passed away. He said that she was the love of his life and 'the root of his soul', and that he fell into a deep crisis when she died. So deep that his whole life and all that he'd achieved suddenly seemed pointless. He sank deeper and deeper and didn't know how to pull himself out of it. Until he realised that he had to do exactly what he advised others to do: stop trying to get out of the crisis and start seeing it as an opportunity. That's how he made the decision to travel to South America.

At that point, all eyes were fixed on him. And then, instead of continuing to speak about himself or his trip, he started talking about them, the people in the room. He said that their journey to South America was also a courageous step. He said, you could've just continued along the usual army-university-mortage route, but instead you chose to be brave and step off it. To explore other things. To ask questions.

They must have loved hearing that, Dori said in a slightly mocking tone.

Yes. Dafna finished feeding the baby and straightened her clothes. That was the bait, she said, but then came the hook. He said, you know what your problem is? That you don't really use the trip to tell a new story about your lives. In another month or two you'll go back to Israel, and everything you learned here goes into the shredder. Someone will put a stop to your momentum, and that someone will be no other than you yourself.

And there's another problem, he told them – I remember this part really well because he mentioned the restaurant – you're travelling in South America, right? But you're not really learning to know it. It's just an excuse for you to see each other in Sabras. To hide behind the curtain, inside what is familiar to you. So that, God forbid, you won't be exposed to something different that will shake your basic beliefs or open a wound you've been trying hard to close, because that's just too dangerous.

452

That's all well and good, Dori said, but what did he recommend they should do?

That's exactly what I wanted to shout at him: so what do you suggest? But your father, like I said, is a fantastic lecturer. So he asked the question himself, and answered it with one word: Neuland.

What?

That was more or less everyone's reaction. And then he paused, you know, for the drama, and said Neuland again, and started talking about Herzl's vision and about the gap between that vision and the way it's been realised in Israel, and said that this is a crisis, but definitely an opportunity too. That's where I got a bit lost, I must admit. Herzl reminds me of history homework, and now he wasn't speaking like he had in the first part of his lecture, which was very structured. Now he jumped around from one point to another in a pretty associative way. As if he was speaking in a dream. Some people in the audience didn't understand what he was doing either, and about a quarter of them left. Then this kind of, you know, uncomfortable mumbling started. Like I said, your father is an experienced lecturer, so he sensed the discomfort and announced that the limited time Dafna had allotted him – I didn't limit anything, by the way – was up, unfortunately, so he'd have to get to the point. He said he was on his way to Argentina, where he was going to start a new pioneering project, the first of its kind. He couldn't really expand on it in the time frame he'd been given, but anyone who was interested, who was attracted by the opportunity to make real changes in himself and society, was invited to talk to him personally for more details. And that was it. He sat down on his Dr Gav and took a sip from his bottle of water. And waited.

And people went up to him?

Not many. Maybe five or six. Most of them went back to playing cards and planning their trips. But the ones who did talk to him left with him the next day — as far as I know — for Argentina.

The baby made a few chirps of complaint, and Dafna apologised, saying that they couldn't talk any more because Iris wanted her afternoon nap.

The baby's right, Dori said, and picked up the small mattress for her. Sometimes, he said, I think that if all adults had siestas, there'd be no more wars in the world.

You . . . you're much nicer than your father, you know? Dafna said, and a different kind of spark ignited in her eyes.

Dori didn't answer, and Inbar wondered whether he really wasn't aware of the fact that Dafna was flirting with him now, or was he just pretending?

The man you met, he said at last, isn't exactly my father. I mean, he's my father. But he's different. Something happened to him on this trip.

The baby began to emit sounds of distress now. Yes, that's the impression I got, Dafna said. Look, she said, rocking the baby gently, I don't want to upset you, but I think it's . . . very good that you're looking for him, and — she shifted her gaze between Inbar and Dori — I'll be happy to help you further down the road if you need it.

*

When they returned to the restaurant, the three doctors were still sitting at the table, and Guy looked at her, waiting.

Dori gave them a quick glance and said, I'm going back to the hostel.

His tone was aloof, so she said: I think I'll stay here.

No problem, he said, as if he were really saying: What is there between us anyway? No past, no commitment, no nothing. Do what you want.

There is a problem, she wanted to tell him. There's a problem

454

when you get close to a woman, press up against her body when you dance with her, and then give her the cold shoulder. There's a problem when you ask a woman to join you on a journey and then treat her as if she's an annoyance. There's a problem when you have a band of white skin on your ring finger. There's a problem when sometimes you act as if that band of white skin isn't there. There's a problem when everything is dwarfed by what's happening to your father. There's a problem when I'm the one who got you important information today, but you treat me as if I did something wrong. There are many problems, she wanted to tell him, but felt it would be stupid to do so. That everything between them was stupid. As if she hadn't learned anything from what happened with Hoffman and was still running headfirst into a glass wall with her eyes open.

So goodbye, he said, and bit his lip.

Damn all that lip-biting. I wish that everything inside him that wants to burst out would just burst out, she thought. And said: Bye.

Dori

Suddenly, in the middle of the cutlet, he was seized by a jealous rage against that Guy, with the wire-framed glasses and the long hair and the loose, striped trousers, who could, who was permitted, who had no wife and child. The jealousy was so unbearable that he just wanted to get out of there before it erupted in front of everyone, spurted out of his mouth like yellow lava. But he remained sitting at the table with them, faithful to the search for his father, faithful to his image as a teacher, faithful to the source, and slowly filled with complaints against Inbar, complaints and criticism. He squinted and saw, or tried to see, everything unattractive about her: how she bit her nails, not exactly her nails, but the dry skin around them; and her too-jumpy knee; and the fact that in every conversation with her you had to peel away her defences all over again, till you reached the real her, and even then, you're not sure you're actually there. And he didn't like the way she dressed, yes, the colours she chose were loud, and he didn't like the fact that every time they met people she became extroverted and tried too hard. Like with this group of medical students sitting with her now. Suddenly, she's laughing out loud. Suddenly she's interested in neurology. And she keeps touching that Guy's hand, the one with the wire-framed glasses, and he's coming on to her. The bastard. And he lights her cigarette. And only yesterday she said she didn't smoke.

Yesterday, after she told him about her brother, he had begun to feel those stabs of longing familiar to him from the many nights he'd spent watching sports news, but this time, there was nothing mysterious about the longing. This time, it had a clear object.

You're completely confused, he tried to convince himself: you and Inbar are simply becoming closer. It's natural for people on a journey who spend so much time together. Besides, he repeated the mantra, you are a member of the conservative party of people who have only one great love in their life.

But the longing continued to eat away at him all night. So much time had passed since his longing had had an object. How frightening it could be. After all, for him, unlike his former friends, it was all or nothing. Even when he was single, he could never fuck and forget. Either he was totally indifferent or the cold, crawling fire inside him reached the critical point and he ignited, and then he was like oil gushing from a well – he started behaving like an idiot and spun scenarios in his mind, shaved twice a day because his stubble grew faster, ate too little or too much, lost balls when he played basketball, was moved by sentimental songs, forgot important dates in history, like that of the Wannsee Conference or when World War I broke out, wanted to jump off every high place he found himself in, not so he could die, but so he could spread his wings –

Close to four in the morning, for the first time since they'd met in Tumbes, he allowed himself to fantasise about Inbar. Only once, he cautioned himself. But the minute he pulled his finger out of the dam he couldn't stop the flood, and the most frightening thing was that the best part, the most satisfying part of the fantasy wasn't the fuck itself, but what came afterwards: the close proximity of two bodies, naked and unashamed. The languid moments when words, if they were spoken at all, were softer.

He tried to inject good moments with Roni into his veins. As an inoculation. Here she is, leaning over to kiss him for the first time, in her apartment in Beit HaKerem. Here they are, making love in a secluded place, on the bank of the stream below her kibbutz. Here he is, asking (he always had to know the history): So tell me, am I the first guy you brought here? And she replies: Don't be silly, I'm a kibbutznik. A few seconds later, she sits on him, naked, wet leaves in her hair, and says: But you're the first one I ever loved. Here she is, surprising him on his first day at school with a turkey pastrami sandwich and a sour pickle, and she drives him to the gate of the car park and says: You'll be the best teacher in the world. He asks: How do you know? She puts her hand on his chest, half caressing, half pushing him towards the future, and says: I just know. Here he is, walking in the shopping centre near the hospital, a plastic bracelet on his wrist, passing a man with one leg who's eating a Big Mac in McDonald's, and he stops to buy a beer and a chocolate bar, then begins to walk back to the hospital – no, he doesn't walk back, he floats three centimetres above the ground, because of his beautiful baby boy, because of the brave woman who gave birth to him, the woman with whom he's forged a new bond, that's how he feels, during that long, wonderful and terrible night of the birth — at the ninth hour, she squeezes his hand hard and suddenly yells out to a god she doesn't believe in, and he whispers in her ear, I love you, I'm here, I love you, and then the midwife says, I see his head, here he comes—

And what about after the birth? He tries to find good moments that are fresh, not from the past. But all the images breathed their last on the way to his consciousness, and in their place came others that he had frozen in the corners of his memory a long time ago. And now this lengthening journey has defrosted them. Here they are, the three of them, having supper a few weeks ago, and Roni tells him about Danny Koris from university, who's just gone to do his post-doctoral research in Connecticut, and she says, you know what the really crazy thing about that is? That he's much less talented than you. And he says, so what? And she says, nothing. And he reminds her, forcing himself not to raise his voice, not when their son is there, that he *chose* not to be an academic because he wanted to have an impact, to touch the beating heart of life and not observe it through the thick glasses of a scholar. And he adds, there's something annoying about the way you keep raising this over and over again. How would you feel if I kept putting down what you do? And she says, but you do put down what I do, you don't have to say it out loud for me to know. You think my job is to market crap. And you think you're better than me. You think you're better than everyone. And he says, that's not true, but let's not have this conversation around Netta. After the boy fell asleep, finally fell asleep, after three trips to the loo, two of which were false alarms, he asks her if she wants some tea, the way an Indian offers a peace pipe to a white man he's in a dispute with. Then, as they sip, he tells her that the main thing is for her to be happy with what she does. That's what's important. And the truth is that he's very proud of her for knowing how to stand up for what she wants, and for the way she treats her employees. Sometimes, he hears how she talks to them and thinks that he'd like to be one of them. That's not a good idea, she says, I'd sexually harass you all the time, she says, and adds: The nephew of one of my department managers is a student of yours, and he praises you to the skies. He says you're a role model for them. But what do *you* think? he thought. Why is it that any nice thing you say about me is a quote from other people? But he didn't say it, to avoid damaging their joint effort to disguise the ugly truth, which had been spoken earlier during their argument, to blur it into other things, which were also true, in their way. Then they begin to talk about Netta, sharing with each other his clever remarks, his magic, the hurts he suffered, analysing every detail of what he does as if he were a Chinese emperor, at the least.

But that — he said to himself now — is the antibody, that is the shared moment you're looking for in the present. Netta is the beautiful, ongoing moment that you and Roni share now. Netta, who holds your hand and hers, three, four . . . and jump. Netta, who runs to both of you on Friday, the only day you pick him up from nursery together. Netta, who whispers secrets in your ear loudly enough for his mummy to hear too. Netta, who turns the page of a book before you finish reading it. Netta, who refuses to put shampoo on his hair. Refuses to put on his pyjamas. Refuses to believe that there are no monsters in his room and asks you to lie down beside him until they leave through the window. Netta, who finally lifted the embargo and agreed to talk to you on the phone a few nights ago: So where are you now, Daddy? Where is Bolivia on the globe? Is there another little boy there? I thought maybe that's why you haven't come back. When are you coming back? If you don't come back soon, maybe I'll get so big you won't recognise me. Yes, I sleep

459

in bed with Mummy. It's great. And she lets me drink Sprite. Only after we take out the bubbles. It's very good. Like juice. We ordered pizza for my birthday. You said you'd come to my party. But you didn't come. We ordered pizza yesterday too. We didn't eat all of it. Should I save you a piece?

You belong to that child and his mother, Dori said to himself, you are so intertwined with them that you couldn't leave them even if you wanted to. And yet, the longing for Inbar keeps eating away at him in small, present bites. He opened his Lonely Planet, and contrary to his habit of first reading the entire historical survey of every place he planned to visit, he went straight to the section on city tours and found a short route called Moon Valley, which included a walk among the white, serrated stone columns, whose chalky shapes changed every year. Want to come to the moon with me, Inbar? he'll ask. And then, when they're walking side by side among the columns, he can say things he hasn't said to her yet – he won't pour out too much, but he'll at least tell her that meeting her has been very special for him, and it's also shaken him a little . . . yes, that's the phrase he'll use – when was the last time he created such a detailed scenario in his mind of a future date with a woman? Maybe school – and maybe her response will teach him something about what she wants from him, because that's not completely clear to him either. Yes, maybe if they get away from the crowded city and leave the search behind for a few hours, he can solve the enigma, demystify it.

But before he could push the well-organised plan to a corner of his mind – those scenarios, even at school, never worked out as intended – she suggested that they go to the Israeli restaurant to try and find more information about his father. A great idea, he said. And was disappointed that she'd chosen to spend the day in the company of other people, and was immediately disappointed by his disappointment. After all, he hadn't come here to have an affair, but to find his father. Who might at this very moment be in a pit, waiting for someone to rescue him.

For the first few seconds in the restaurant, a postcard that Herzl wrote to his family from the beach in Ostend flashed through his mind: *'Although there are many Viennese and Budapest Jews on the beach, the rest of the holidaymakers are very pleasant.'*

Yes, there were too many Israelis in the small area of Sabras. The girls made him feel old. And how noisy they all were! Loud laughter, fragmented shouts. Then came the smell: cigarettes, sweat and hummus. A group of people was crowded in front of a noticeboard that had a piece of paper pinned on it: an update from the Israeli news site: Soldier kidnapped by the Hamas. He looked away. His own missing person was enough for him. A girl suddenly broke away from the crowd and came straight over to him. Hi, he said, recognising her – a former student of his. A smart girl. Curious. There were two friends, his internal search engine reported to him, Gal and Sigal, who sat in the front row, right-hand side, and used to play with each other's hair during class. Gal Nisimov, yes, that's her name. He remembered, as she warmed his heart by telling him how the things she'd learned in his class had enriched her thoughts on her trip, that the title of her final paper had been 'History Repeats Itself', and how she had been able, rather brilliantly, to identify patterns of being dragged into war that repeat themselves over and over throughout history.

He spoke to the girl warmly, but briefly, and tried to balance his desire to reciprocate her affection against his desire to be alone with Inbar. But then Inbar herself – who gave her permission? – told her about their search for his father, and within a minute he found himself walking with them between the plates of food, showing pictures of his father, like the boy with the lighters who'd come to their table the day before – that's how he felt, asking for a handout. Nonetheless, he hoped someone would recognise his father and give them information, shed light on the upsetting things in his diary.

Wait for Haimon and Dafna, they all said, so he sat down with Inbar and ordered a breaded chicken cutlet, even though he had no appetitite, as usual when he was on the verge of being ignited. Suddenly, he had no words. Suddenly, after admitting to himself that if it weren't for the circumstances, he'd want Inbar, everything became too charged and all he could think of saying sounded too loaded with meaning. And the presence of his student, who was sitting too close and staring at them, made it even more difficult for him, so he shut up, and Inbar, for her part, nodded enthusiastically when the trio of young medical students asked if they could sit at their table. They began an animated conversation, which also made him feel that he'd lost all his social skills, that the only thing he knew how to do was lecture – look at the way he'd given a lecture to his former student – and he simply had no idea how to just join in a conversation. So he folded his arms on his chest and pretended to listen, not to notice how that Guy with his wire-framed glasses was flirting with Inbar – he knew he had no right to be jealous, but it made him crazy, that and the Israeli, Latin-rhythm pop CD no one had bothered to change all morning – the words were boring a hole in his brain.

It was a good thing that Haimon and Dafna finally arrived. Another round of that CD and he would have smashed either the stereo or Guy's glasses.

After a brief conversation with Haimon, he and Inbar went to the house that was separated from the restaurant by only a door, and there, with Dafna, he had the only kind of conversation he'd felt comfortable with for the last few years: a mothers' conversation. In the middle of it, when Dafna took out her breast to feed the baby, he felt slightly attracted to her too. As if the moment he allowed himself to fantasise about Inbar, a code of behaviour had been broken. But it was only a spark of attraction, and it was extinguished when Dafna began describing his father's lecture.

The examples she gave were familiar to him from conversations he'd only paid partial attention to over the years. And the fact that his father was charismatic wasn't news to him. When Dafna asked whether he knew that his father was great with an audience, he nodded, and an old image popped into his mind: During break time at primary school, he goes outside and discovers that none of his friends are in the playground. Or at the fountain or the snack bar. The sound of voices leads him to the school gate, and there he sees his father, surrounded by dozens of children listening to him blow a pretend-trumpet with the help of an inch of grass he'd stretched between his fingers.

But the zeal in his eyes at the end of the lecture, the zeal of a messiah that Dafna described − that wasn't like him. Not in the slightest. His father was no Shabbatai Zvi. Just the opposite. He'd always been as cool and solid as a rock. And as mild as water. Even when playing basketball, he hated the elbowing under the basket and liked to run the game from further back on the court. He never raised his voice, never smashed his fist into the wall in anger. Once, at traffic lights, when another driver got out of his car, stomped over to him, pulled open his door and shouted at him, you son-of-a-bitch, you cut me off, get out of the car if you call yourself a man, his father looked at him calmly and said, I'm sorry, sir, I apologise if I bothered you, it wasn't on purpose, believe me. Then he reached out, closed the door and drove off, leaving the hothead standing on the road in shock.

The more Dafna recounted what happened at the lecture, the more embarrassed Dori felt. He'd always been proud of his father, proud and envious, and had wondered if he himself could ever be such a rock. For the last few weeks, he'd wondered and worried – would he even recognise him when they met? Because it sounded as if he'd completely lost it. What if, after the whole journey, his father looked at him as if he didn't recognise him, or tried to drag him into the madness that seemed to have overtaken him? Neuland? What the fuck is Neuland?

I don't want to upset you, Dafna interrupted his thoughts, but I think it's a good thing that you're looking for him. Leave me your details. If I hear anything, I'll get in touch right away. A year ago, we had a tourist your father's age here who had a heart attack at the Rosario Hotel. It's three blocks from here. His room was on the fourth floor, and he collapsed on the third floor. There are only two hospitals here, and at both of them they know that if an Israeli is admitted to the hospital, they get in touch with me right away. Again, I don't want to upset you. Physically, your father looks fine. But we should keep in touch and update each other, okay?

He thanked Dafna and they went back to the restaurant. The three doctors were still sitting at the table, and he couldn't deal with their freedom. I'm going back to the hostel, he told Inbar. Are you coming? No, she shook her head. I'm staying.

On the way to the hostel, he trod the smooth, worn stones that lined the narrow path between the official shops and the makeshift roadside stalls. Night had fallen on the city, extinguishing the colours, and everything suddenly looked seedy and sad and hopeless. All the smiles were toothless, all the glasses cracked, all the shoes scuffed, all the poles bent, all the umbrellas torn, all the shamans were charlatans, all the magic a sham, all the oranges were squeezed out, all the candles doused, all the Israelis were bargaining, all the shoeshine boys would be shoeshine boys for ever, they wouldn't conquer the world, and all the women peddlers were wretched, utterly wretched . . .

Wearing Charlie Chaplin hats, pots of chicken soup at their

side, they offered him a potion that would bring him success in business, knock-off T-shirts, and purple sabra fruit. *Señor, por favor, Señor,* and he apologised to them in Hebrew, by mistake, and then in Spanish, *desculpe,* or *pardon,* he wasn't sure what the right word was, so he said them both, and thought that if he were just a tourist, he'd definitely buy a few presents for Netta now, but he wasn't just a tourist, he was on a mission that seemed to be slipping farther and farther out of his grasp with each passing day.

At the last stall, right below the hostel, he saw a brightly coloured fabric notebook cover and thought: That matches the colours of Inbar's cap, it could protect her notebook from the cold and rain. *Cuanta costa?* he asked the woman selling it. She took out a pocket calculator and punched in the numbers for him, seventy bolivianos. He gave her a hundred and didn't take the change: *gracias, Señor, gracias,* she called after him. As he shoved the notebook cover under his arm he suddenly felt a fear that bordered on certainty that he had no one to give that gift to, that Inbar would go with that sharwalled Guy to his hostel and sleep with him, and then she'd travel with him and his cool pals, and who could blame her, considering the alternative: a married man who couldn't really enjoy the trip because he was so concerned about his father, and the only thing he had to offer her was confusion.

*

In the hostel, he logged on to <u>findfather@gmail.com</u> and found an email from Noya. The subject was: is your father a guru?

   Hi Dori – she wrote –
   Things got sort of messy with me. Tuval drank too much one night and made an embarrassing confession. So embarrassing that I can't even repeat it. Anyway, he and Irad had a fight

later on, and we decided to break up the threesome and give each other some space. But that's not why I'm writing to you. The thing is that after we split, I hooked up with a gang of Dutch kids (they're so tall!) and one of them, who just came back from Argentina, talked about this farm of Israelis he went to a month ago. They call the place Neuland, and it's run by an older Israeli guy. Something about the way he described the older guy sounded familiar, so I took out the picture you gave me and showed it to him and . . . bingo! That older guy is your father, except that he has a beard now. The Dutch guy took off from Neuland after one night because 'the energy there was weird' – that's what he said. But I have to qualify (I've always wanted to use that pretentious phrase) and say that from the off, even before he smokes, the Dutch guy, Lars, is stoned, and he's so tall that maybe the clouds hide the world from him. When I asked him for more details about the weird energy and exactly where in Argentina the farm is located, he said he didn't remember, but even so – I thought you'd want to know (maybe you already do?).

I don't know if you're at all interested, but I'm not going back home for the time being. I cancelled my registration for a Master's in international relations. I cancelled my return ticket. I think that after this trip, I want to go and study in Europe. How can you study international relations in a country that's in conflict with the whole world? I might even stay in Europe after I get my degree. What's to keep me in Israel? I have no kids. And no family (we never got to talk about that). Anti-Semitism? Really, that's about as scary as boo! Holocaust? That was a long time ago. In another century.

I don't know. Maybe I'm just talking. I tend to do that, in case you hadn't noticed. Maybe I'm just confused because of the thing with Tuval and I'm turning it into an ideology.

Anyway, I'm heading for Colombia. And from there, I'm planning to go to Guatemala. Even though this trip has taught

me not to plan too much. I heard that the underground in
Colombia kidnaps tourists (if that happens and you find your
father in the meantime, will you come and save me?).

Yours,
Noya

*

In his personal email box, he found a message from a student who wanted to ask him a brief question about the work he'd set for the summer break. He never failed students, and instead asked those who'd received a low final grade to write a paper on a subject of their choice to be handed in at the end of July. This student had decided to write about the Golden Age in Spain and wanted to ask where he could find material, because there wasn't enough in the school library.

Dori sent him to the library in his mother's museum, and wrote him a long reply, enjoying the feeling that, after weeks of walking day after day along an unfamiliar, misleading path, he was finally doing something he knew how to do. Something he was skilled at and could do with quiet assurance.

By the time he finished replying, he was feeling calmer, and when he looked up from the screen and saw Inbar and her cap walk into the hostel, he was glad to see her. And no less glad she hadn't come back with Guy.

There was an empty chair next to him, but she remained standing, her arms folded across her breasts.

I bought this for you, he said, handing her the brightly coloured cover.

Thanks, she said coldly.

It's for your notebook.

I figured.

I've had new information about my father, he said after a few empty seconds. Want to read it?

467

She sat down. And moved her legs away from his.

It's from a girl I met on the flight to Quito, he said in a slightly apologetic tone, as if she were his girlfriend and he had to explain why a girl who wasn't her had written to him.

Okay, she said when she finished reading. This fits perfectly with what Alfredo told me.

Alfredo? When did you talk to him?

After you left Sabras, he called and told me that, according to his sources, two months ago someone matching your father's description withdrew a large sum of money from the bank in Mosesville in Argentina, and a few days later he paid cash for an old farm and some land in the deserted area between Mosesville and the next town, Palacios. Two towns, by the way, that really were Baron Hirsch's colonies.

So, what did he do with the land after he bought it?

That's just it. Alfredo promised that his people in Argentina are working on it now. And by the time we land in Buenos Aires there'll be more information on it.

To be honest, I didn't expect Alfredo to continue working for us. I was sure he—

He cares about you, Dori.

Let's not get carried away.

Tell me, she flared up, making him think for a moment that she planned to slap him, why is it so hard for you to accept that people care about you?

He was silent, and bent his head to the keyboard. If only he could turn the H on its belly, he thought, and place it between them, like a bridge.

Anyway – she said after a silence as long as the exile of the Jews – I think there's a chance your journey is about to end. It looks like your father has settled down in one place.

Come with me to see him? he asked, because he noticed that she wasn't using the plural, and he put his hand on hers, which rested on her knee. I'm pretty scared about seeing him. I don't know exactly what I'm going to find.

She pulled her hand away, put it in her lap and said nothing.

I'm sorry about today, he said. I was wrong. It's just that this whole business with my father, and these weeks away from home, and meeting . . . you – sometimes, all the strings get knotted together and I don't know where to begin to unravel them. But I want to make it clear, I want you to come with me very much.

Nothing could stop her. She smiled for the first time. She still didn't look at him, but she smiled. Yes, you're infuriating, she added. But I'm too curious to stop now. And I want to succeed, just once, in saving someone.

She moved her head towards him. Their faces were very close now.

He heard that hum of desire inside him, the hum that preceded a kiss.

But before he could fully understand its meaning and lean towards her, or stop himself from leaning towards her, she stood up abruptly, and said, see you tomorrow morning.

*

He kissed her on the flight to Buenos Aires. On the head.

At first, she kept her distance from him, signalling that she still bore a grudge. But after take-off, she fell asleep, her head lolled against his shoulder, and he kissed her hair. And waited impatiently for her to wake up. To talk. He missed her talking. Their talking. She was actually re-teaching him how to hold a conversation. And she was interesting. You could tell that she wasn't a child any more and already knew something about the world and people. But on the other hand, she didn't think she knew everything. It was refreshing to be with a woman who was searching, whose ideas and opinions were not already set in stone. There were cracks in her that let in the light. It was refreshing to be with someone so alert. And funny. Who could even be contented sometimes. Roni, for example, could be happy sometimes, but not contented. Her inner self was too tough for contentment. Inbar's inner self, or so he thought, was different. So was the way she threw herself into the search for his father, with all her heart, without thinking twice. Sometimes he thought she cared about finding him more than he did. And that made him feel good, having her on his side. It had been a long time since he'd felt that someone was on his side. And a long time since a woman had looked at him like that. There had been yearning looks from girls in his class, yes, but they didn't count, because the podium raised him up. Inbar, on the other hand, just thought he was terrific. Without any podiums to raise him up. And how liberating it is when a woman thinks you're terrific. Suddenly, your steps become lighter. It had been a long time since he'd felt so light with a woman.

Maybe he'd never felt so light with a woman. In films, the other woman always excites you more than your wife. With Inbar, strangely enough, he felt the opposite: with her, he could relax, because things flowed naturally. It piqued his curiosity to know that she had her own secret world. That she wrote. That she opened her notebook, filled a few pages and closed it. And while she was at it, you'd better not disturb her. Only when she'd finished did he allow himself to ask: a travel journal? And she said, not exactly. I've wanted to write for a long time, and didn't do anything about it. Now suddenly, on this journey, a character has been born. So I write her. I have no idea whether anything will come of it, but I'm writing.

Once, during one of the bus rest stops, she left the notebook when she went to the bathroom, and he was almost tempted to open it.

Now, on the plane, he kissed her head again, the way you kiss a little girl and said to himself: It's okay, you're just kissing her head. Then he stroked her hair and said to himself: It's okay, you're just stroking her hair. Then, his arm kept moving and he slowly stroked her arm, down to her elbow and back. He raised the ends of her hair to his nose, getting high on the smell, and said to himself: It's okay, you're just touching her arm and smelling her hair, you're still not cancelling your membership of the party . . .

And the entire time, she breathed the deep breaths of sleep you can't fake, but when she woke up, as they descended for landing, she looked at him differently, as if the part of her consciousness that did not go to sleep had figured something out. Then she took the notebook out of the cloth cover he'd bought for her and began to write, hiding the words from him with her hand.

Nessia

Doesn't reject anything out of hand. After all, we regret our 'nos' more than our 'yeses'.

She's willing to believe that trees have souls, that the world was created in six days, that the phone call she's waiting for will come. She's willing to believe people who have already lied to her, and the legend of the Wandering Jew, who's been walking around for two thousand years with nails in his feet and hasn't died.

But this business of sex in an aeroplane bathroom is suspect because even if you manage to squeeze in there, what about all the people waiting outside, bladder after bladder after bladder?

She prefers a washing machine (on the spin cycle).

A carpentry shop (just so she could say she's been screwing among the screws)

A Finnish sauna (in Sweden).

One of Baron Hirsch's farms (in 1912, among the hay bales, at sunset. She's wearing a Little-House-on-the-Prairie dress, and Señor Dori, the last Jewish gaucho, undoes the front buttons. Slowly).

Inbar and Dori

Maybe you'd like to rest first? Victorcito asked them. He was a very skinny man with a puzzled, almost frightened look in his eyes, the look of a man who's just come home and to find that he's been burgled. No, they replied, almost in unison. Not even a shower? Victorcito opened his eyes even more. Señor Alfredo booked two rooms for you, at his expense, at the Buenos Aires Hilton. Dori looked at Inbar. That's not necessary, she said. So at least let me take you to the Amora restaurant. Alfredo will cut off my balls if I tell him I didn't take you to a restaurant. And it's a long trip to Santa Fe, where the farms are.

Listen, amigo, Dori said, putting his hand on the man's shoulder. We've been held up long enough. I want you to take us to my father now. And if that doesn't work for you, we'll go alone.

No hay problema, Mister Dori, no problem, Victorcito said quickly and led them to his car: a banged-up, white Fiat Punto that looked so much like the white Punto Dori and Roni had

had at university that for a minute Dori suspected that it was
the same car, which had somehow found its circuitous way there
from Jerusalem.

Roni

More coffee. And more coffee. She has no time to be tired. She
has to finish everything by 3.30. How can she finish everything
by 3.30? When Dori was here, she'd stay till 6, that is, till 6.25.
But 6 sounded more maternal. And if it's 6.25, it could be
rounded up to 6.30 without sounding like a lie. She hasn't been
rounding up for two weeks now. She turns off her computer at
3.30, and if one of the product managers wants to talk to her,
she asks him to walk to the lift with her. They're like children,
her product managers. She thought she'd take advantage of this
period to delegate authority, but they hang on to her apron
strings and ask for her opinion, when in fact they want her to
decide for them, because they don't have the courage to make
mistakes. When she was a product manager, she wasn't like
that. Maybe it's her fault for not training them properly. But
who has the time to think about that? Results. You have to get
results. A process is nice, but only if it's short and leads to
profits. Sales. And now she has to achieve all that by 3.30. And
at 3.35, put the Mazda in drive, because she mustn't be late at
the nursery. Not that Idit, the teacher, would leave Netta on
the street. But the look on her face the only time she was late
– the entire staff there thinks she's a terrible mother even if
she comes on time. Because Dori always brings Netta and picks
him up. Are you new here? one mother asked her, even though

she knew very well that she was Netta's mother. No, she tried to keep her voice steady. I'm Netta's mother. It's just that his father usually comes . . . And now he's out of the country. A business trip, yes. Teacher exchange programme. It's like a student exchange programme, but shorter. A week. I mean two weeks. Does she need any help? No, thank you.

She's still reluctant to suggest a play date, even though there's been a breakthrough this week, or maybe because of it: she doesn't want to ruin it with a refusal. And also — it was actually good being at home with Netta. Just the two of them. For the first few days, he cried because she, not his father, came to pick him up, and she made a supreme effort not to be hurt. Then he slowly began to send out feelers of happiness. They slept in the same bed at night. His body didn't take up much room, and it smelled good, like his father's. Now and then, he shoved his foot straight into her face, but she accepted that with love. The mornings, on the other hand, were difficult. He was used to Dori's leisurely pace, and she wanted to hurry things along and get to the office. Come on, Netta. Trousers. Top. Teeth. By myself? You can put the toothpaste on the brush by yourself next time. Why are you crying now? Do you think that's worth crying about? Okay, here. I washed the toothpaste off the brush and now you can put it on yourself. Where are your sandals? Here. They're not comfortable? Sorry, they're the ones you have to wear. Let's go, Netta. Come on. I'm late. We can't talk to Daddy now. It's the middle of the night there, I've already explained that to you. Why? Because the earth moves. We'll look it up on the computer later, if you want. Maybe it'll have a better explanation. Yes, we'll call Daddy when we come back from nursery. But this time, you must actually talk to him, okay? He feels sad when you don't say anything, okay my love? How handsome you are. I can't believe such a handsome boy came out of me. Yes, you were in my stomach. Eight months. You really wanted to come out, so you were a month early. No, daddies can't be pregnant. Their stomachs aren't built for it. Why? When we look up the earth on the computer, we'll look that up too, okay? Pick you up? But you're a big boy. You don't need to be carried. Okay, all right, I'll pick you up. We just need to leave.

They call Alfredo's phone when they come home from nursery. No answer. She calls again because Netta's waiting anxiously and she doesn't want to disappoint him. This time, Alfredo answers. He always sounds as if he's in the middle of a fuck, panting slightly, and a little sleepy. Hello, Missiz Dori. How are you? Okay, she says tersely. Is Dori with you? What do you mean, on the way to Argentina? You haven't gone with him? What clause in the contract? What are you talking about? Okay, I get it. I'll consult with my lawyers tomorrow and we'll see what they think about that clause. So what if you have contacts in Argentina. The agreement says that you accompany him personally. Tse'ela knows about this? I'll make sure she does. Don't tell me that I must understand. You left my husband alone instead of going with him. What is there to understand here? With a friend? What friend? He never mentioned any friend when we talked. Israeli? So what good is that? He's a foreigner just like Dori. Okay, listen, if you speak to Dori, tell him that we're looking for him. His son wants to talk to him, okay? And about that clause in the contract, be prepared for a call from my lawyers tomorrow.

Daddy can't talk now, she tells Netta, and before he can burst into tears, suggests: Do you want to go to the playground? He's still scowling, so she adds: With your new scooter? Now a small smile begins to bud. The day before yesterday, she bought him a scooter and told him it was a present his father sent from South America. She has to let Dori know before Netta says anything to him about it, so there's no screw-up. She has to get a bag ready. A bottle of water. A change of clothes in case he has an accident. There's been a regression over the last two weeks. She wonders why. She has to call her mother and ask her to come on Wednesday because she has a directors meeting at five. And update her on the regression. She has to turn on the dishwasher before they leave the house. What do women with two children do? Maybe if they had two children it would finally feel like a family and not like a triangle without a base. Besides, they have to have another baby so that Netta won't be on his own. Have to do this. Have to do that. Have to. Have. It makes her want to scream. And sometimes she does. She goes up to the roof of the office building where she works, leans her entire body on the railing and lets out a long, liberating scream. She tried to do it yesterday too, but no sound came out. She stood there among the huge flowerpots for a long time and waited for it to come naturally, from inside her, and in the end she went back to the office because she had to go back. Have to again. It isn't until Netta is on the seesaw that, between pushes, she has time to contemplate her conversation with Alfredo. Contemplate isn't the right word. Parents don't have time for more than brief flashes of thought that don't crystallise into insights. Dori went alone. With a friend. Doesn't call. What friend? Friend in English can be female. Dori wouldn't do that. And if he did, is it really such a big deal? Yes, it's a big deal. No, it's not. Anyone who grows up on a kibbutz can't think that such things are a big deal. After all, everyone knew that my father was fucking Nati Ganot's mother, who was fucking little Are'le's father, who was fucking my mother behind the barn when everyone was at the Shavuot ceremony, thereby closing the circle. Anyway, Dori wouldn't do that. And what if he did? The trip's been too long for Netta anyway. If she'd known it would go on for so long . . .

Bullshit. Even if she'd known, she would've told him to go. After all, it's his father. Who would've believed it about his father. So focused. So in control. He always kept a respectful distance from her, but the few times they did talk, she was impressed by his sharp analysis of business situations. And now, what? She wants Dori to find him and come back from his odyssey. For Netta, mainly. For her, the space that has opened between them is actually good. It hasn't been easy with Dori since his mother died. He keeps expecting something from her that she can't give. And he's always disappointed. Even in their phone conversations now – the same expectation. That's why she was relieved when Alfredo said Dori wasn't there. Is it normal for her to feel relief? Does she even love him any more? When she saw him ten years ago drumming in the workshop, all she wanted was to sleep with him. And move on. But the sex with him was so surprising. She didn't think anyone could show her anything new, what with all the experience she'd had on the kibbutz. But Dori taught her that foreplay doesn't have to be boring. And in the morning, he'd spent a lot of time making her omelettes. With extras. Which she devoured in half a minute. And she continued to enjoy them, extra after extra, for quite a while. His pace, it made her laugh. It opened her heart to him in a way she hadn't thought possible. On the days he had a busier timetable than hers, she'd wait for him in the Rehavia apartment, under the heavy duvet, wearing only pants, so he'd have something to take off. She didn't read, didn't watch TV, didn't go over the notes she made in class. She just listened to music and waited for him with uncharacteristic serenity, with the quiet knowledge that he'd be there soon and would take off everything but his pants, and get under the covers and press up against her from behind.

But all that was a long time ago. A really long time ago. She's moved on these last few years. And he's still under the covers. Such a . . . Jerusalemite.

They had a lecturer at the university who wrote on the board: 'Love = mutual dependence that respects the other's independence.'

As if you could define love and all it encompassed. Body. Time. There. Here. Give. Take. Go. Come. Those were the words that suited a couple's relationship in this decade of child-rearing. Dori always plays a CD by Danny Robas in the car when he takes Netta to nursery. She thinks he's past it, but Dori likes him. Netta sings the lyrics of one song: *I come home from the night, turn on the light in the stairwell*. He's so adorable. Why doesn't the whole world see it? How long can this boy seesaw? Isn't it practically autistic? Do you want to go on the slide, Netta? Okay, no is no. The Hamas abducted a soldier yesterday. Near Gaza. There was a picture in the paper. A little boy's face. Netta will go into the army too. Maybe a miracle will happen and by then he'll have some small medical problem. Nothing major. Something that will lower his profile. No way. Dori would never let him stay out of the army. Sometimes she doesn't understand him. He won't go on the March of the Living in Poland with his students because it 'fosters their sense of victimisation', and 'they should be sent on a ten-minute bus ride to my mother's museum to foster their pride in the amazing creativity of the Golden Age in Spain'. On the other hand, he shows up like a good little soldier every time he's called to reserve duty. Not because of his buddies. Truth is, he can't really stand the other guys on reserve duty with him. He goes because 'it's part of living in this country'. Maybe that's what she should say when people ask her. That Dori's doing reserve duty, instead of the teacher exchange lie. I hope there's a prisoner exchange to get back that abducted soldier and we hand over as many prisoners as it takes. That face of his. Five unanswered calls. Five! What am I going to do with those product managers? She's running a school. No, a nursery school.

Netta's finally ready to get off the seesaw. He rides his scooter for a while, falls suddenly and screams as if he's going to die. She makes a face as she hangs up on her employee and runs over to him. Her bra is too tight. Nothing happened. Everything's fine. No blood. Now he doesn't want the scooter any more. He wants to go home. At home, supper. A shower. Teeth. A story. Another story. Cover me. Again, cover me. Doesn't fall asleep. Sings those lyrics again: *Over the heads of people, our glances meet.* The comforting smell of his body. Then he falls asleep, thank God. She has a shower she doesn't enjoy because she has the nagging feeling that she's forgotten to do something. When she gets out of the shower, she remembers and calls her mother. Wednesday's okay for her. You're amazing, Mum, she says. Why weren't you like this when I was a child, she doesn't say. Why, when I was young, did you always have this look in your eye, as if you wanted to be somewhere else?

I have the feeling that a war's about to break out, her mother says now, like an expert on a panel. But you always have that feeling, she says. You'll see, her mother insists. You'll see that this time, I'm right. He's wetting himself again, she says. She doesn't have to say who. Well it's no wonder, her mother says. When is Dorinka coming back? Don't know. Now he's on his way to Argentina, Odysseus. Seems that his father's craziness took him all the way there. Who would've believed it about Menny Peleg? her mother says. Such a nice-looking man. Okay, Mum, she cuts her off, see you Wednesday?

She opens her laptop. Takes it to bed. Replies to emails. The ad agency supervisor is trying his luck again. 'It was hard to concentrate at the last meeting,' he writes. Pain in the arse. After all, she made it clear to him in Barcelona: Once. No more. It happened a few months after Dori's mother died. Every night, she put on her most revealing negligee and said to Dori: Come to bed. But he'd say: Soon. And kept watching the sports news. Then the replay of the sports news. Then she went to Barcelona on a short business trip. And those Europeans drink wine all the time. Before meetings, during meetings, after meetings. And she was premenstrual. So she said to that supervisor who walked her to her hotel room and leaned his elbow on her door, trapping her with his hungry look: Once. And he said, sure, of course. Men will agree to whatever terms you set a minute before, and every few weeks since then, he's checked to see how she is. Testing the water, maybe she's amenable. And she replies as curtly as possible, without offending him. Because on the one hand, she doesn't and never did have a drop of feeling for him, and on the other, they work together. Just before she falls asleep, she writes a short email to Dori.

Hi Dor,
I heard that you left Alfredo and are on the way to Argentina.
Call when you can. Netta wants to talk to you. He misses you.

Then she changes *he misses* to *we miss.*

Maybe it's a white lie. At the moment, in any case, she's too tired to want to think about it. Her eyelids droop. Before Netta, it took time for her to fall asleep. Now she can drop off any time, anywhere. Before Netta, she used to dream. Now there are no dreams. That is, it could very well be that she dreams about a waterfall gushing from a high rock like a skirt of water. She's caught between the waterfall and the rock, and under cover of the tumultuous flow she screams the scream she couldn't get out on the roof of her office building – but in the morning, she doesn't remember any of it.

Neuland

Dori

A BIG CITY, BUENOS AIRES. IT TAKES THEM AN HOUR and half to get out of it. Traffic light after traffic light after traffic light after toll booth at the entrance to the motorway. And on the sides of the roads – a branch of Ikea, second-hand car dealers, and hotels with names like Kiss Me and Paradise, the kind you're sure you can rent by the hour.

At one of the traffic lights, he sees a sign with an arrow pointing to Garibaldi Street, and says to Inbar, this is where we kidnapped Eichmann.

I knew it! Inbar says happily, I knew the whole story about your father was a cover and that you're really a Mossad agent!

Yes – he plays the game – Isser called and told me that we have to push up zero hour by thirty minutes, and I told him, Isser, the car. But he didn't want to hear it. Bring him to me alive or alive, he yelled at me. So I put my gun in my sock and went – enough. Hey, did you really think I was a Mossad agent?

Yes, don't ask. I had a whole fantasy about it.

Sorry to ruin it for you. Teaching is much less sexy, I know.

Not really. What's sexy is the passion. And any man who's passionate about what he does—

Inbar

Surprised (but not very) by the word sexy when he says it. Why sexy? Okay, he's the one who said it first. He started, she thinks. But says nothing. And moves slightly towards the window and says to herself: Hoffman or no Hoffman, I have to sleep with him and that's all there is to it.

Then she turns her gaze to the hoardings outside and tries to understand what they're trying to sell her in Spanish. As she does that, she thinks about an idea for a short story: a Nazi who flees to Buenos Aires after the war, finds work with a local Jew, till the Nazi's son falls in love with the daughter of the—

She takes out her journal and writes.

A little while later, she looks up from the page. They're passing through wide expanses of fields. Flat. Monotonous. Soporific. This isn't Neuland, it's No Man's Land, she thinks. Victorcito's car radio is playing a tango, and she pictures herself and Dori dancing a tango. Although she has no idea how to, she likes pressing up against him, cheek to cheek, breast to chest. Like in La Paz. That was sexy. Okay, enough of that word. She looks over at him. His eyes are open and he's humming voicelessly. An unsexy habit of his. If they were a couple, it would probably annoy her at some point. What is he thinking now? An irritating question. She won't ask him. But she still wants to know what he's thinking. Judging from the cloud that crosses his eyes and the fact that his body is no longer leaning towards her, he's probably thinking about his family. Maybe if she concentrates, she can read his mind. It works sometimes, when you spend a lot of time together.

Dori

Driving on the road/Early winter, not cold/The scenery hurries past/Or am I the one going so fast—

Dori Radio plays Danny Robas. His eyes are fixed on the window. His body has grown used to the swaying and rocking of the car, to the different way you breathe when you're on the road, and his glance turns inward: he hasn't spoken to Roni and Netta for three days now, and he doesn't miss them. That is, he does miss them. But not wildly. His thoughts about home are dim. Blurry. Yes. There's something very wrong between him and Roni. More accurately, there's something wrong in the Roni–Netta–Dori triangle. This trip has made him realise that. Or acknowledge it. But strangely enough, he has no desire to fix it. Maybe he does have the desire, but it's blunted. All the desires related to home have been blunted the last few days. While everything that's happening with Inbar is . . . sharp.

Like the erection he gets when she says 'sexy'. Engorged with blood. Stabbing the front of his trousers. He shifts position to be more comfortable, tries to see if she's noticed it. Wants her to notice it. Wants her. Here and now. In the back seat. To kiss her lips and run his hand through that hair and slowly lay her down on the seat and unbutton her shirt and unbutton her trousers and discover that everything between them is only this kind of attraction. That would be much simpler. But she's writing. He gives her a long look. She's so serious when she writes. She looks up from the page and their eyes meet

485

momentarily, but then he shifts his gaze to Victorcito and sees, to his horror, that his narrow head is drooping on to the wheel.

Hey! he shouts.

He's falling asleep! he shouts at Inbar. Tell him to stop!

They stop at a roadside shop. It's very cold outside. The sky is clear and cold. There are saddles, horse bridles and horseshoes inside. And accessories for drinking maté. Victorcito explains to Inbar, who explains to Dori: This is the maté gourd, and this is the *bombisha*, the metal straw you drink the maté with. And this is the *termo*, where you can get hot water if you just want to refresh your maté. And these are the plants you use to make the various flavours of maté. What would you like?

Coffee, Dori says. And Inbar coughs to keep from laughing.

*

It happens down the road. It happens when the wheat fields turn into wheat fields that turn into cornfields that turn into soybean fields and the silence in the car has grown relaxed. It happens right after Dori thinks — Baron Hirsch was right. The unimaginable breadth of Argentina calls you to settle it. It happens when his eyelids begin to droop and his forehead relaxes —

He lets his head fall on to Inbar's shoulder.

It's not that he doesn't know what he's doing.

It's not that he doesn't know that from this point on, he won't be able to play dumb.

But he no longer has the strength, he simply doesn't have the strength to fight it.

Nessia

Doesn't enjoy watching nature through a car window. You don't need to see nature, she's learned on her journeys. You need to feel it.

To drink in the air, for example, and feel how it's dotted with sun. To kiss the wound on a tree. To walk between the raindrops, not metaphorically, but really to walk in the pouring rain and try not to let a drop fall on you. To throw a stone into a puddle and see the waves it makes grow wider and wider. To release all the animals from their cages in the zoo.

Including the cheetahs.

And only after you've done that can you move on to the next stage, in which you understand that everything resembles everything else. For example, tree branches and people's arms. And everything fits in with everything else. For example, nakai emerging uninjured from between a shark's teeth.

And in a world like that, all you can do is try to fit in, try to always do only what comes from inside you, so if a man rests his head on your shoulder during a drive, you stroke the back of his neck, caress his shoulder, comfort him, the hell with everything, with endless gentleness.

Lily

She still sometimes hears Natan walking around the house. She still hears him dragging his left foot a bit, and then stepping forward on his right foot, the strong one. She still sometimes makes food for two by mistake. Forgets that she only needs one egg. And that there's no one to eat such a large amount of sweet carrots. She doesn't set the table for him, of course not. Doesn't put a plate, a knife and fork, or the tall, narrow glass he liked to drink water from on the table in front of his chair. She's not senile, even though, for the last few days, she has dead moments, like the car radio has when you drive under a bridge.

Sometimes she listens to the news and imagines what Natan would say. He always had something to say. And it was always original and interesting. Sometimes the commentators would say exactly what he'd said a minute earlier, and then the tip of his nose would turn red with satisfaction . . .

Since his death, the news hasn't really interested her. And maybe that's why she notices the tendency common to all the leading newsreaders: turn people into heroes, raise them up so that later, they can—

In general, she's been watching much less television since Natan died. Watching TV together was nice. Watching TV on her own makes her feel lonely. And also, there used to be an Australian series, oh, what was it called? She can't remember what it was about, damn it. Only the name of the character she liked: Emily. An attractive woman. With a good figure. She reminded her a lot of Esther, with her beautiful legs. Maybe that's why she liked her so much. In the series, Emily was one of three sisters who lived in Melbourne. The other two were bad and stupid, but she was clever and full of common sense. And she always wore a ponytail and beautiful earrings. Then, all of a sudden, in the middle of the third season, she died. Something must have happened to the actress who played her, there's no other explanation. The other sisters said that Emily had plastic surgery and there were complications – but why would such a lovely woman have plastic surgery? What did she have that needed to be fixed? At any rate, her death came as a surprise. It was too much like the way death comes in real life.

Alone in the living room, she cried during the episode when Emily died. She cried about many things. Spirals within spirals within spirals of longing for what was gone. And ever since, she hasn't been able – doesn't want – to become attached to characters in TV series, and if she doesn't become attached, then—

Sometimes she smells Natan around her. In the living room. In the bedroom. And sometimes—

He smelled like an orchard. Even after they left the kibbutz, even after they'd lived in Haifa for four years, even after all his friends already smelled of old age, Natan still smelled like an orchard.

They left the kibbutz three months after they arrived there. Because of her. She didn't want to be there, and he wanted her to be happy. When you're a couple, he said, one can't be miserable without the other being miserable too.

He didn't speak much, her Natan, but he always spoke logically. And he always tried to listen to her because he knew that discussing things was important to her.

And she tried for his sake. Took an interest in football and made stew with noodles, the way his mother used to make it, and wore a miniskirt when miniskirts were in fashion, even though she didn't have the legs for it.

And she tried as hard as she could to forget Pima.

But why did she want to leave the kibbutz? Suddenly, she can't remember. That's how it's been for the last few days, even when she's sitting in her memory chair, everything is full of holes, like lace.

And when Hana called yesterday to make sure Inbar was in her will, she didn't recognise her voice – she thought it was someone conducting a telephone survey and said she was busy, and Hana was hurt. Of course she was hurt. Feeling hurt is chronic with her. Whatever she does hurts that child, who is already an educated, successful woman.

She was jealous of Hana. Because she did look good in a miniskirt. She was jealous because of her daughter. There's no way to make that sound all right.

But how old was Hana when she let her wear a miniskirt? A network of holes, that's what her memory is, a network of holes.

Maybe today she'll turn the fan to the third speed and not the second. The planet is warming, they said on the news. The glaciers are melting. The sea is rising. Maybe in July, the second speed isn't enough any more.

Yes, like this. It's good.

Every time she pictured the house she would have with Natan on the kibbutz, she pictured it slightly different. Once she added a chimney. Once a tiled roof. Once she planted lilacs in the garden. And then she and her imagination decided that chrysanthemums would be more appropriate to the climate in Eretz Yisrael. Sometimes the house had three rooms and sometimes two, with a large balcony. When their ship was approaching the shore of her new country, she decided to add a dividing wall between the sitting room and the baby's room, and right before they landed on the beach, she decided, on second thoughts, to remove it . . .

But in all those imaginings, she never pictured someone else besides them living in it.

I have to warn you about something, Natan said as the bus neared the gate of the kibbutz.

I know, she said. That's why I only brought simple clothes with me. All the clothes belong to everyone anyway, so—

That's not what I mean, Lily.

*

Her name was Gordonia. Everyone called her Alberta, but she insisted on being called Gordonia. And she was the condition that the kibbutz had given Natan. You want to live with your girlfriend from the training camp? Fine. But you'll have to add a third comrade. For a while.

The minute she walked into the little house, even before she saw their room-mate, Lily smelled the smell that would identify her. The smell of sperm.

After the smell came Gordonia herself: stable boots and a man's shirt that hung down to her muscular thighs. Welcome, Señora Lily! She crushed her in an embrace and then held her by the waist, moving slightly away to study her, and said: You're real. We were beginning to think that Natan had made you up. *Pero* – she stuck a finger into her shoulder as if checking her – even though there'll be a few very disappointed girls here, you definitely exist.

I forgot to introduce myself – Gordonia Steerin! She reached out and crushed Lily's hand in hers. I'm your third wheel. The thorn in your side. The mud on the floor. The sounds that don't let you sleep at night. The hair in the bathtub. I apologise in advance for everything. I would have preferred a place of my own, I had a place of my own in Argentina, but this is a kibbutz. Everyone together, eh? By the way, there are some *empanadas* I made this morning in the cupboard. You must be hungry after the trip. I'm sorry, but I can't stay with you. I have to get going. Weapons training starts in a few minutes. *Un beso* — she brought two fingers to her lips and blew them a kiss—

Chau!

Gordonia was born in Mosesville, one of the first settlements established by 'Baron Hirsch's Jews' in Argentina. Her family, she told Lily over a cup of maté she brewed for the two of them, had come to Argentina after the Kishinev pogroms. Her best childhood friends were horses. And ducks. When she was fourteen, she lost her virginity to a local gaucho. Not Jewish. When she was fifteen, another gaucho, who sat down next to her in the Kadima cinema, taught her what she'd be happy to teach Lily too, if she wanted: how to have three orgasms, one after the other, a few seconds apart. When she was seventeen, her family, like many of the families who lived on Baron Hirsch's agricultural farms, moved to Buenos Aires. At eighteen, after meeting a delegate from the kibbutz movement, whose skin had the wildly delicious taste of oranges, she woke up to Zionism. Why did you move to the city?! she berated her family. The Jewish people cannot rise again if they do not work the land! And the only land worth working is the land of Zion!

One moonless night, she ran off to Palestine with the delegate. By ship. He was sure they'd get married — but marriage was not for her. So what did you do with the poor fellow when you arrived in the country? Lily asked. What do you mean? she asked, surprised by the question. I left him crying on the beach in Jaffa. Someone has to keep the sea salty, no? Then I got on a bus to the kibbutz. How did I know to come here and not somewhere else? I had no idea. I went from one place to the other, looking for one that had a decent stable. And that's how I got to this godforsaken place. I have to go now. The tour is waiting for me. *Un beso*, Lily, *chau!* I won't be back till tonight, so if you and Natan want a little . . . *pasarlo bien* . . . After all, he waited *mucho tiempo* for you!

*

Every day, Gordonia rode with the Guards, a carbine slung across her right shoulder. Her sharp features and thick shirt made it difficult to see that she was a woman.

She also worked in the cow barn. And the chicken coop. And the orchard. She was quite familiar with all the work from her time on the Baron Hirsch farm in Mosesville. She worked hard. Proudly. Passionately, and came back to Natan and Lily's little house every evening. Smelling of the stable. And of sperm.

She spent her nights, on the other side of the thin wall, with the guards. A different one each time. Lily tried to close her ears, but couldn't help seeing the lizards run out of her room through the cracks when it began, and hear her cries of *Dios! Dios! Dios!* Three times in a row, a few seconds apart.

Lily herself hadn't had even one *Dios!* since she came to the kibbutz. That was because they didn't have a drop of privacy, she complained to Natan. But the truth was more bitter. That kibbutz, the place she'd been so anxious to go to since the training camp, depressed her. She failed utterly at all the jobs she was expected to excel at. The amount of milk produced when she worked in the barn was so pathetic that the comrade in charge suspected that she was lying and keeping a secret store of milk for herself. In the chicken coop, her very presence drove the chickens outside. In the kitchen, glasses and plates slipped out of her hands and broke. And on guard duty, she fell asleep on the phone right before the Hagana inspector arrived.

She felt like Samson after his hair was cut: all the qualities that had made her Lily Freud, committee head and big fish in a small pond back there, were of no value in the kibbutz. No one cared that she loved to read. And knew how to write well. Just the opposite: after she tried to talk to the kibbutz girls about books, they all thought she was a snob.

They gossip about you, Natan said. And the moment he told her what the gossip was, she felt surrounded by it whenever she walked down the kibbutz paths or sat in the dining hall or was in the laundry or the children's house. Gossip gossip gossip, snatches of conversation, looks. One Friday morning, a blouse she'd brought in her suitcase had completed its round of all the girls and miraculously came back to her. A bit faded, but hers. She put it on, wound her arm through Natan's, straightened her back, and raised her head high. I might not know how to milk a cow, but at least I look good, she thought. Then she heard, or thought she heard, a girl coming towards them say, Natan's girlfriend is a show-off, and another one whispered, bourgeoisie. She confronted her, say it out loud, why are you muttering, say it out loud, and the girl, embarrassed, said, I was only saying, I want some tea. I'm thirsty, and Lily said, you're lying, you're a liar. Natan said, Lily, stop, Lily, it's not her fault, then took her arm and led her back to their room. There, the lizards scuttled off through the cracks and Gordonia shouted *Dios! Dios! Dios!*, then came out of her room with a girl – oh no! – and Lily missed home. But there was a war going on there, and who knew what would happen to her father and her sisters. Why, after the letter he wrote describing the way his karakul hat was stolen right off his head, had the letters stopped coming? But that was something else nobody talked about here . . .

Where's your head? Rama, who was in charge of the kitchen, asked her one day when another glass dropped out of her hand and shattered on the floor.

There, in Warsaw, she blurted out the truth. My father and my sisters, I haven't heard a word from them for months.

You think you're the only one, comrade Lily?

No, but—

*

Esther was the one who helped her make the final decision. She took the first bus to visit Lily as soon as she received her letter.

I was worried about you, she said. And now I see that I had good reason. Look at you. Pale. Skinny. Even your breasts have fallen.

Really?

No. But you look like a dried tomato. What have they done to you here?

Come to Haifa, she said after hearing the details from her friend. Someone has just moved out of the room on the floor below mine. It's tiny, but you'll have it to yourselves. No third wheel.

As if to give added strength to her words, Gordonia burst into the room – *Ola*, Lily – kicked off her boots as she walked, and then noticed the guest and asked, who are you?

Esther, Esther replied.

Esther?! I have heard *mucho* about you. (Lily couldn't remember ever having told anyone on the kibbutz, except Natan, about Esther.) Nice to meet you. I'm Gordonia Steerin! The third wheel. The thorn in the side. The fly in Lily and Natan's soup. She walked over to Esther, smiling broadly, crushed her in a hug and then stroked her leg to where her shorts ended, and said: Pshhh . . . Such nice legs, Estherika. I'd kill for legs like that. You came to cheer up our Lily a little? *Buenistimo*. She really has been a little sour since she got here. Maybe you'll explain to her that sourness doesn't go well with the climate here in Palestine.

*

That night, Lily spoke to Natan. And he – as Esther predicted – agreed. Your happiness, he said, is my happiness. And Haifa is a beautiful city. You can see the sea from everywhere.

But we dreamed of the kibbutz for so many years, Natan – she was a bit frightened by his quick consent. We dreamed of establishing so many new things. Better things. To have a different kind of relationship between people. Not urban. Not bourgeois. Egalitarian.

So we dreamed, Natan said. Dreams exist mainly so we can endure reality.

I'm so lucky, she told him as the bus moved away from the kibbutz, to have you in reality. And she was ashamed that the first thought that came into her mind as they approached the Carmel was: Haifa is a big city, and many people live in it. Maybe I'll bump into Pima here.

*

Gordonia – she remembered now, surprised by the sadness she felt – was killed in the War of Independence. A stupid death. Friendly fire. A few months after she died, the kibbutz called. It turned out that she had left a signed letter for her. For me? Lily wondered. Are you Lily Bloom? If so, there's a letter here for you, the operator said with post-war impatience. If you don't come to get it within a week, it'll be thrown away.

She went. It seems that Gordonia left many letters before she went off to battle. As if she had known. The one meant for her contained precise instructions on how to reach three orgasms in a row, and there was one more sentence at the end: *I hope you take this as compensation for my crude behaviour. Yours, your third wheel.*

At the memorial that was set up in her honour on the riverbank, a sign read: IN MEMORY OF A WOMAN OF VALOUR, GORDONIA (ALBERTA) STEERIN (1922, ARGENTINA – 1948, ISRAEL).

*

Inbar calls at night. When you wake Lily up in the middle of the night, the holes in the lace of her memory are larger.

I'm in Argentina, Inbar says.

Gordonia, she says, weren't you killed in the War of Independence?

This is Inbar, Inbar says. Who's Gordonia?

Ah, Inbari! Why don't you come to visit me more often?

I'm in Argentina, Grandma. Did you forget?

How could I forget if I didn't remember? What are you doing in Argentina?

I'm on my way to a place called Neuland.

Altneuland?

No. Neu-land.

Inbar?

Yes, Grandma?

You're bothering me in the middle of my dream. Can you call later in the morning?

Of course. I was just worried about you because Mum says that—

You can't worry from far away, dear. Worrying from far away is like kissing through a sheet. Or like buying Israel bonds. You want to worry about me? Then come home.

Inbar and Dori

In the back seat, after Inbar finishes speaking to her grandmother, they move closer together again, shoulder to shoulder, shirt fabric rubbing against shirt fabric. It's been eight hours already, the time it takes to cross Israel from Kibbutz Dan in the north to Eilat in the south. They drive through endless, green, forested plains occasionally crossed by a river with such a slight incline that it's impossible to say in which direction the water is flowing. There are fishermen with poles along the river. And cows. Many cows. Black cows with white spots, white cows with black spots, standing as still as statues. It feels as if everything has been still here for thousands of years. Nonetheless, as they drive farther away from Buenos Aires, they can feel a slow, gradual change: the countryside becomes poorer, the road becomes patchy, the cows are skinnier, the birds perch on electric wires that look taut but sink in the middle like hammocks. A sign offers 'A Home for Life', a prefabricated house that moves with you from place to place. Another rusty sign advertises a hotel, which is not there. Maybe it was there once, but it closed. Football goalposts suggest that there was grass there once, but now there are only scattered weeds. The entire countryside is becoming more random, sagging, spirits sagging, old roof tiles sagging, memories sagging.

Until the first sign announcing Mosesville appears. Only ten more kilometres.

Are you excited? Inbar asks, and places her hand on his. And leaves it there.

I don't know, Dori says. I still can't believe that we're really going to see my father. I have the feeling that as soon as we get there, we'll find out that he's just left for somewhere else.

Desculpa . . . Señores . . . We . . . have to stop in Mosesville for a few minutes, Victorcito said in a choked voice.

Por que stop?! they say almost in unison.

To pick up a señorita who lives here. She will take us to Neuland, *si?* Victorcito apologises. In the rearview mirror they see his eyes filled with alarm. The farm is not in the town, he explains, but in the fields between it and the next town, Palasios. And the road . . . it is *un poquito* complicated. And I do not know it well. This way it will be more *seguro, Señores. Por favor.*

498

At the main entrance to Mosesville stands the statue of a ship that looks like the ones that brought the illegal immigrants to Israel. Inbar translates the sign below it for Dori: 'In Celebration of the Centennial Year of the First Jewish Colony in Argentina.'

*

If the streets of Tel Aviv look like runways with everything speeding to take off, then the streets of Mosesville look as if everything has already landed. That is, it bears a slight resemblance to a landing pad. Wide, lazy and very quiet. Even Victorcito slows down, as if matching his speed to the pace of the town, and slides right and left amid the glances of the inhabitants, who watch them with the eyes of small places where everyone knows everyone else, and every visitor is an attraction.

They finally stop in front of a beautiful building, old and almost ruined, but well plastered, with a large sign in Hebrew on the top: *Kadima* (Onward).

Stay where you are, I'm going to call our liaison, Victorcito says. *Momentito*, and I'll be back.

We're alone, we can kiss, Inbar thinks. But Dori's entire being is focused on what's outside, so in solidarity, she looks too: through the car windows they see a synagogue, a butcher's shop, a shoemaker's, the office of 'The Jewish Cooperative Founded by Baron Hirsch', two dark-skinned boys riding bikes, a group of old men drinking beer, a restaurant.

Just like a *shtetl-ito*, Dori says in surprise. Inbar rolls the Yiddish word with the Spanish suffix around on her tongue. It tastes good.

At that very moment, a young señorita bursts into the car like the wind. She sits on her knees in the passenger seat, her back to the windscreen and her flushed face towards them.

Cecilia-Aharona

Greetings and welcome to you, my friends from Eretz Yisrael. It is with great joy that I welcome you here to Mosesville, which is the Jerusalem of Argentina, and show the way to Neuland. My name is Aharona. And my name is also Cecilia. *Bueno*, call me whichever name makes you feel more comfortable. And you? Inbar and . . . Dori? Did you know, Dori, that you look very much like Menny Peleg? He is your father? What is it you discuss? I mean, what do you talk about? You must forgive me. My Hebrew is a bit amusing. Hebrew from a seminary. We here in Mosesville learn Hebrew in a seminary. And we have no place where to rehearse it. A terrible shame. That is why I much desire to travel to the Holy Land. But my family does not agree in it. I am eighteen in December and they do not wish me to go and die in the Israel army like Rosita-Vardina, my aunt, may she rest in peace. *Bueno*. Remove all worry from your heart. In two weeks will be the Bible quiz of Argentina, and the first three places will go to Jerusalem of Gold. Even my family cannot stop me if I win the quiz as the representative of the province of Santa Fe, and thus will I fulfil my dream and perhaps also defect to Eretz Yisrael and find there pure love like yours, my friends. In the meantime, I will be a helpmeet to all the Israelis who want to go to Neuland and do not know how. Thus, I can also rehearse my Hebrew. *Bueno*, I have talked about myself for so long that I did not discuss to you about our Mosesville. We are now this minute arriving at the intersection of Benjamin Ze'ev Herzl Street and Baron Hirsch street. Herzl and Baron Hirsch met twice: the first time Herzl tried to convince the Baron that the safe haven for the Jews should be in Eretz Yisrael, but *bueno*, the style of Herzl's speech did not please the Baron and he deported him from his office and decided: Argentina is the destined land. The second time, Herzl and Baron Hirsch met here in Mosesville. At this intersection. Or is it 'on' this intersection. I have trouble remembering the right prepositions. *Bueno*, the first settlers of Mosesville came from Europe. From Russia and Poland. At this time, as you can see, we have *mucho* non-Jews here and only three hundred Jews. How do we tell it here? The day our town has more years than Jews, we can close it. It is with a smile. But seriously, we here in Mosesville are very proud of our history. After all, if not for us, where would the Jews of Europe have escaped after Kristallnacht? We have here in our possession in Mosesville a museum, *si*. And a hall of culture with the name Kadima. And four synagogues. I have in my possession the keys to all of them, if you have a desire to see them. I understand. Yes, of course, I understand. You are interested to go to Neuland and the history is already known to you. Señor Dori is a teacher of history? Why did you not say that before? And I talked and talked, and I don't know what I am talking about. A terrible shame. If so, what arouses your pleasure, my friends? You just want to reach your destination quickly? Bueno, *a la escuerda*, Victorcito, we shall turn left here to this lower path. Do not worry, whatever happens will happens, or there will be nothing. I mean, our trip will be rocky, but brief. No more than fifteen minutes. We here are very happy about Neuland, which has brought only blessings to our small town: every Monday, Sarah the heroine of Neuland, comes and makes a very huge purchase at the butcher's shop and the fruit and vegetable shop, and a few fellows from Neuland help her to carry the crates. In the afternoon, all the Neulanders come to help the farmers in the area — anyone who desires it. Only last night, a doctor from Neuland gave a boy from San Cristóbal the medicine that we cannot get here and saved him from grave danger. My girlfriends in Palacios suddenly began to speak fluent English. A fellow from Neuland, who went to their village, taught them. And Don Rodriguez does not stop telling everyone how the young people of Neuland helped him with his cornfield after the great storm. What do they do on their farm, you ask? Turn your head and see, on our right are cypress tress and on the left casuarina trees and eucalyptus trees, and *palomas*, I mean pigeons, are on every branch, just like in Israel, the land of milk and honey. And we have sabras here. Like you do. Look, do you see the spikes? *A la derecha*, Victorcito. *Y una vez mas a la derecha.* Where were we? You desire to know what is happening inside Neuland? Well, I am unable to help, because I am not yet eighteen and you cannot enter the gates of Neuland before you are eighteen. So I can only say what I can say, *si?* Hold tight because now there is a big pit. *Bueno*, all the fields that we view on our way are soy fields. Once there were *vacos* here. Cows. Once I used to whistle like this, with my fingers, and fifty cows would turn their heads. Now it is all soybeans. The land of milk and honey and soybeans. That is with a smile. The Chinese love soybeans, so they buy *mucho*. From Neuland? There will be much soybeans in the end. Your father bought a dozen *hectares* from Hugo Yacobi. And right after the purchase, he began to renovate everything with the *chalutzim* who came with him. First they made a huge purchase from the building constructor. Then they made a small castle out of Hugo's *casa*. They brought tents. Paved lanes. A pride to see. How do I know? You can see it through the fence. Without going inside. Slowly, more people began to come, and now, at least once a week, a wanderer arrives. And whenever a wanderer gets off the bus in the central square of our town, they send him to me immediately, because everyone knows that I desire to rehearse my Hebrew and desire to know people from Eretz

Yisrael. *Dios*! How could I forget. I brought you knishes for the road. How can it be that you do not know what a knish is? It is Jewish food. My Grandma Paula made these. Here, taste it. That is not poison inside, it is potatoes. Tasty, yes? I told you. Take more. There is more than enough. *Bueno*, finally you are quiet a little and I can speak. That is with a smile. Eat. Eat. It is good for the Jews. The building on our right was a synagogue. Not any more now. There is a synagogue in your father's Neuland too. They are renovating it now. Would you be so kind as to tell me, my friends, if it is true that in Eretz Yisrael every fifth house is a synagogue? No? You don't say! *Bueno*, we are coming to Neuland. It is right there, behind the cypress trees. You cannot see it yet. Only when you are very close. Your father, Señor Dori, chose a place especially because you cannot see it by accident, from the road. For the *privdad. Cómo se dice privdad* in Hebrew? Never mind. Your father is . . . he is head and shoulders above other persons. Once he came out to me with maté after I brought them another *mochilero* and spoke to me, Cecilia. I spoke to him, you can also call me Aharona, whichever one gives you more comfort. So he spoke to me, Cecilia-Aharona, I would like to thank you for the help you have given us the last few weeks. So I spoke to him, the pleasure, it is all mine. And then he offered me to drink maté with him, which for us in Argentina is a sign of enormous respect. And he looked at me deep into my *alma*, my soul, and then I understood why everyone is enchanted by him. Without entering Neuland even one time, I understood. Because anyone who can look into your soul, you are ready to do many things for him.

Bueno, aqui no mas, Victorcito. You can see the gate to Neuland before you. On it are seven stars, a reminder of the flag that Herzl wanted to present to the Jewish state. Seven stars symbolise the seven hours of work that a labourer puts in, and sends a universal message of an equal burden of work for all. And on the other hand, if you are so kind as to notice, you can see that the boards of the fence that surrounds Neuland form the shape of the *Estrella de David* – the Star of David. You see it, yes? Look, my key-ring is also the Star of David. *Bueno*, I talk and talk, and you can see it all by yourselves and you desire to enter.

Entonces, Señor Dori, Señorita Inbar. How do we say it here: *Buena suerte*. Which means, good luck. If you need me, I am in Mosesville, 32 Estado Israel Street. And next Independence Day, turn on your TV at noon and it is possible, with God's help, that you will see me there. Aharona Steerin. The Argentinian representative in the Bible Quiz.

Chau. Here, we say goodbye with a kiss on the cheek *Un beso*.

Si, like that. Exactly. You need to shave very urgently, Señor Dori. His beard does not bother you when you kiss with him, Señorita Inbar?

Bueno, see you later, *muchachos*. *Vamos*, Victorcito?

Inbar

I'll wait outside for a few more minutes, Victorcito told Inbar. If you don't come out, I'll report to Alfredo that you have found who you have been looking for, and I'll go. Here is my number if you need a lift back to Buenos Aires. I'll stay in the area for a few more days.

Muy bien, Victorcito. *Muchas gracias*, she said, and gave a tip to him and to the desirous Cecilia-Aharona. Dori was too tense about seeing his father to pay attention to goodbyes.

*

They approached the entrance gate, which was topped by an arch that had NEULAND written on it. Beneath it were the words, 'Man, you are my brother' in three languages: Hebrew, English and Spanish. The only sounds they heard were the chirping of birds and a monotonous banging they could not identify, in the distance.

The gate opened and a familiar-looking guy (from where . . . from where . . . from the flight to Lima?) greeted them with a broad smile. Welcome to Neuland, he said, and then hugged them both, embracing her slightly longer than Dori, and added: Men, you are my brothers!

I'm David, he introduced himself, and there are some questions I have to ask before you come in. Don't worry. It won't take more than a few minutes. There are no mobile phones or other communication devices in Neuland, so I need to know if you happen to be carrying a mobile phone, a camera or a tape recorder.

Dori shook his head, and Inbar said that she had a mobile, but the batteries were dead and she didn't have an Argentinian adaptor.

You'll have to leave it with me, David said.

But I just told you that—

Those are the rules. Is there anything else you want to declare?

She and Dori exchanged quick glances of surprise. No, Dori said. We have nothing else we want to declare.

Drugs of any kind? You should know that you can only take drugs in Neuland if they're going to be used in ceremonies—

No, we don't have any drugs, Dori interrupted him.

Great. So my last question is, what is the purpose of your visit? You don't have to answer. This is a question we ask for our own, internal reasons.

A meeting.

With whom, if I may ask? Again, you don't have to answer—

Menny Peleg.

Mr Neuland? Did you make an appointment? Because he doesn't usually—

He's my father, Dori blurted. Do you think I need to make an appointment with him?

Mr Neuland is your father? What an honour! You don't have to get angry, man! Neuland is anger- and violence-free.

You don't say, Dori hissed.

Look — Inbar touched Dori's shoulder before the situation escalated. Dori has been searching for his father for a few weeks now. All he wants is to talk to him and see if he's okay.

No problem, no problem, David said. Then he looked at his watch and added: But you'll have to wait a while because Mr Neuland is envisioning now.

Envisioning?

Yes, in every society, someone has to think about the future. And in Neuland, he's the one who takes the burden upon himself so we can be free to live in the present. He finishes envisioning at four. Then they'll tell him that you're here. Meanwhile, I'll give you a small map and a few information pages. You can walk around freely. Dori, man, I apologise from the bottom of my heart if the entrance process made you uncomfortable. Maybe it's my fault. Sometimes I forget how hard it is to make the switch from the world to Neuland. I hope you find it in your heart to forgive me, man.

*

You can fall in love with places too. A place can bring a long-dormant joy to life inside you. And that's what happened to Inbar when she and Dori walked through the entrance gate and saw Neuland: a blast of beauty smashed straight into her heart. A long, wide avenue lined with tall, unfamiliar trees led to the old farmhouse, which looked amazingly like the house she'd always imagined she'd live in when she was a famous writer: climbing plants that nearly obscured the arched front gate. The wide, white steps. The large windows. A small attic where she could put the large desk with her old typewriter on it.

She turned to Dori, to share her excitement with him, but he was scanning the place with a spotter's eyes, trying to locate threats.

Branching away to the right and left of the avenue that led to the dream house were lanes of tightly packed earth: each of them called to her to discover where it led, and they had a certain symmetry – not the rigid kind seen, for example, in the Bahai Gardens in Haifa, but a harmonious, balanced symmetry. And another, blatant difference between Neuland and the Bahai Gardens was immediately apparent: young people, wearing heavy sweaters and woollen hats, filled the lanes, and the place bustled with vibrant, joyous life, which didn't stop when they appeared. Every now and then someone passed them on the avenue (with a wheelbarrow full of gravel, with construction boards, with a smile), said hello and went on his way. And there was one guy wearing boots who stopped for a moment and stared at Dori as if trying to figure something out. Yes, what? Dori asked him in a voice she didn't recognise, and the guy shook his head and said, it's all good, man, cool it. It's all good. And went on about his business.

But apart from that one occurrence, Neuland took no notice of their entrance. People were sitting on colourful benches in pairs, talking. A small group was eating around a long table, and another group was making the banging noise that Inbar had heard at the gate: they were playing paddleball in a round clearing with a piece of cloth stretched across just three poles above them to provide shade. The fourth pole, Inbar saw, was missing. And a closer look made it clear that many things were still missing in Neuland. The pool at the end of one of the lanes was empty and looked more like an open wound than a swimming pool. A lane on the left ended abruptly, as if someone had run out of earth. And the new top floor of the farmhouse looked more like an idea than the actual storey of a house. Nevertheless, despite the unfinishedness of the place, Inbar felt that it was somehow comfortable in its own skin.

Comfortable and a bit familiar. Like the character in Kurosawa's *Dreams* who enters a Van Gogh painting and begins to walk in it, she thinks. The place is new to me, but not foreign.

A few moments later, a girl came up to them, introduced herself as Sarah, welcomed them, and offered to give them a tour of the farm. She was wearing a checked, button-down shirt that might have been considered masculine, were it not for the slender build of the person wearing it, and a cute cowboy hat with abundant black hair bursting out from under it and flowing down to cover her shoulders.

Thank you, but there's no need for a tour, Dori rejected her offer. We're only here for a meeting.

Meeting?

With my father, Menny Peleg.

He's your father?! – a spark of awe flashed in Sarah's eyes. Now that you mention it, you really do look a little bit alike. Has David already told you that till four, Mr Neuland is envisioning and can't be disturbed?

Yes, we had the . . . pleasure of meeting David, Dori said.

I hope he didn't frighten you, Sarah said with a smile. He's a bit wounded . . . but he's harmless. There are some people here who . . . I mean that's part of the idea of the place.

Can you take us to my father now? Dori asked.

I can, Sarah said. But as I said, till four . . . Look – she looked at the sun as if it were a clock – the truth is that in any case, the break ends soon. So I think that we'll pass on the formal tour and I'll just walk you to the visitors' lodgings, so you can drop off your bags before the meeting, okay?

Dori gave a slight, distracted nod, and they began to walk along the central thoroughfare. It's called Herzl Avenue, Sarah said. Those trees are – wow, I'm really rubbish at tree names – ah, yes. *Paraiso*. Paradise trees. And that building across from us is our community centre. The first Jews to come to Argentina under Baron Hirsch's patronage lived there—

We know the history, Dori interrupted her.

You're right, Sarah said. We said without a tour.

They continued to walk, and passed the play area again. Tell me, Dori asked as if he were cross-examining their guide, is paddleball a part of the *idea* of the place?

Yes, Sarah said generously, with a laugh, ignoring his tone. Paddleball is our 'national sport' here in Neuland. How does Mr Neuland . . . your father put it? Not everything in our source country is bad. Paddleball, for example, is a great game that promotes cooperation and non-violence—

But at that moment, one of the players smashed a ball with violent force straight into the stomach of his partner, a guy with a wild mane of hair, who fell to the ground with exaggerated slowness, like a cowboy hit by a bullet in a western who now has to die in stages, until the final credits begin to roll. What's happening, Sarah-heroine-of-Neuland? the cowboy asked after his death. Aren't you going to play with me today?

Can't you see that I have guests, Jamili?

Don't believe a word she says, Jamili said to both Dori and Inbar, but smiled only at her. Just kidding. Don't believe people who tell you not to believe.

Wow, Jamili, Sarah said, stepping into his line of vision, what a cool remark. Where's that creativity when we're trying to put together our charter?

I can't concentrate when you're in the same room as me, Sarah.

Oh man – Sarah rolled her eyes – you never stop, do you? Go back, Jamili, go back to your game.

Jamili tossed Inbar a final smile, then threw the ball to his partner.

Sarah continued walking, and they followed. Tik, the ball hit the paddle behind them. Tik-tak-tik-tak.

Doesn't that noise drive you mad? Inbar asked.

You're not the only one to bring that up, Sarah said. Some

of our members are getting together to raise the subject of the noise at our next general meeting. On the other hand, paddleball seems to help our wounded members.

What exactly does 'wounded' mean? Inbar asked. You used the word about David too.

Sorry, Sarah apologised. We have our own language here, and sometimes I forget that other people don't know it. If you read the information pages you received, you'll see that Neuland is described as a 'community therapeutic space'. The basic principle of . . . your father's vision — also because of his own personal experience — is that life in the source country, in Israel, is an ongoing trauma. And everyone who comes from there is wounded to some degree or another.

Everyone?

We try to distinguish here between the first generation of wounded and the second. And there are distinctions within that separation. We have people, like David, who you met at the gate, whose wound is more visible, as opposed to people like Jamili, whose wound bleeds internally. And we try to treat all of them.

How? How do you do that? Inbar asked, and thought: My Yoavi wound, is it first generation or second? Visible or bleeding internally?

By living a totally different lifestyle than the one in the source country, Sarah explained, and by holding special ceremonies every Thursday in the main tent.

What happens in those ceremonies? Dori asked. David told us something at the entrance about . . . drugs?

I'm not authorised to talk to guests about the ceremonies, Sarah said, her eyes suddenly going blank and the movement of her hands, which had been relaxed and soft, now became abrupt. It's something — she made a closed circle with her hands — that we'd rather keep confidential. You should probably ask your father about it when you see him. But come with me, the main tent is near the guest lodgings, and I can show it to you, okay?

They turned left into another lane. A woman with a rounded stomach passed them and greeted Sarah: Hi, my sister.

Hi, Ofri, Sarah smiled at her, how do you feel?

Better than in the morning. But pregnancy is pregnancy, you know.

What month are you in? Inbar asked, surprising herself. Since when has she been interested in pregnancies?

Seventh, Ofri turned to her, and then shifted her glance to Dori — and puzzlement showed in her eyes. You know, I mean . . . You look so much like . . .

This is his son, Sarah said.

I didn't know he had a son, Ofri said in surprise.

He also has a daughter and three grandchildren, Dori said.

Dori came here to see him, Sarah explained, and Ofri's voice was suddenly filled with apprehension as she asked: Do you know that he envisions till four and can't be disturbed?

Yes, I've heard about that, Dori said.

Good, she said. I'll get going now. Standing too long hurts.

That's going to be Neuland's first baby! Sarah said when Ofri was gone. We're all very excited about it. Its father, she went on in the low, gossipy voice typical of small communities, was killed in a terrorist attack in the source country.

The lane they were walking on curved, and they curved along with it until they reached a large tent.

It looks like a circus tent, Dori said.

You know what? Sarah said, I think your father really did buy it from a bankrupt circus in Buenos Aires. But I'm not sure. In any case, this is where we have our general meetings.

This is a real kibbutz you have here, Dori said, his voice clearly mocking. General meetings of the members. Celebrating the birth of the first child. Now I bet you'll tell me that on Shavuot you have a first-fruits ceremony.

You're not the first person to say that, Sarah said, but the kibbutzim belong to the past. And we look to the future.

Which means?

It's hard to explain in a sentence or two. If we'd taken the tour—

Give me an example.

Did you see those brightly coloured benches when you came in? People have 'personal vision' meetings there. Neuland is a cooperative society, like the one described in *Altneuland*, but we take it a step further and believe that true cooperation can only work if it allows every person to realise their personal aspirations. In general, we try, in hothouse conditions, to implement some of the principles Herzl set forth and the source country diverged from, but there's no way we can ignore the fact that more than a century has gone by since Herzl's book was written, and we have to make adjustments.

Adjustments?

That's what your father is trying to do during the time he can't be disturbed: to envision Neuland, not Altneuland.

A-a-hh, Dori said, and added nothing, and Inbar thought, okay, he's not finding all this talk interesting now that his father is so close, but even so, only out of politeness, he could—

You're probably anxious to see your father, Sarah said. Later, after you two meet – she shifted her gaze to Inbar – it would be great if you'd join us for a communal meal. By the way, does either of you play an instrument?

I do, Dori admitted through clenched lips.

Terrific, so you can join the klezmer jam session after dinner. It's customary here for our guests to contribute their talent in any way they'd like instead of paying for their lodgings. You too, she said to Inbar, can think about what you'd like to contribute.

Gladly, Inbar said. When people were generous with her, she always felt a desire to reciprocate. And she liked this Sarah more every minute. Heroically she swallowed the scepticism Dori shot at her, and when she answered him, she'd been careful to look at both of them, so Inbar wouldn't feel left out of the conversation. The look she gave them was alert but not nervous, penetrating but non-judgemental. And her carriage – her carriage was fantastic, like a dancer's, the kind Inbar had always wanted to have. Shoulders open. Back straight. A spine. Yes, a spine, that's what all the girls she'd met in the hostels didn't have.

Okay, Sarah said, there are a lot more things you haven't seen: the entire agricultural area, for example. I'm sure that not all of it is clear to you yet. And that's fine. Neuland came into being to disturb people and arouse their doubts. And honestly, it's not all completely clear to us yet either. The founders only came here two and a half months ago, and there are many things we're still trying to figure out. In any case – she looked into Inbar's eyes – read the information on the pages David gave you and let the place sink in. I'll open the lodgings for you now so you have time to get organised before the meeting. Sound good?

*

The 'guest lodgings' were seven straw huts arranged in an arch, like Herzl's seven yellow stars. Sarah opened the squeaky tin doors of two huts, and when she'd showed them where the woollen blankets were, 'because it's cold as ice here at night', she parted from Inbar with a long kiss on the cheek, and from Dori with a quick handshake, then touched her hat lightly in goodbye, like a cowgirl, and left with that perfect posture of hers.

They hesitated briefly before entering the huts, and Dori rubbed his face as if he were about to suggest something to her. If he asks me into his hut now, she thought, then probably . . . what?

But Dori was all business, and suggested that they sort themselves out and meet outside in ten minutes. She wasn't hurt. It was natural for him to be tense about a meeting with a father who wrote that diary. And also – the kind of journey she and Dori had taken together accelerates the getting-to-know-each-other process, and just as she already knew that he needed to go to the toilet almost immediately after drinking a Coke, she also knew that there were moments when he withdrew. And that it didn't always have something to do with her.

In her hut there was one mattress on the floor with a naked light bulb dangling above it. Hebrew texts with Spanish translations in colourful frames hung like mobiles from various places in the room: the poets Amihai, Rachel and Zelda, as well as a quote from Herzl that hung directly above the pillow: 'Dream and deed are not as different as many think. All the deeds of men were once dreams, and all man's deeds will one day become a dream.' Nice, Inbar thought, and took off her shoes. Her sore feet met a soft carpet whose unravelling threads were a clear sign that it was hand woven, and she thought that this was the first time since she'd left Israel that her feet felt at home and her toes allowed themselves to really spread out. There was a small chair in a corner of the hut, the kind they used to have in schools, except that this one had a grey Dr Gav backrest. Right beside it stood a square table with only one drawer.

She opened the drawer to put her money belt in it—

And recognised a very familiar drawing on the bottom of it: a violin, and next to it, the words, THE WANDERING JEW.

Below the words, written in black ink, was the familiar list of cities and dates, with one addition: Neuland 2006. She touched the ink, and her fingertip came away lightly stained with black.

Fresh ink. Which meant that he was close. Her Wandering Jew.

Who knows, she thought, and took the information page out of her pocket, maybe she'd finally meet him. Here, of all places.

Neuland – Information for Visitors

People, Brothers,

Welcome to Neuland – a communal therapeutic space based on the principles of Benjamin Ze'ev Herzl. To make your stay with us not only enjoyable but also meaningful, here are some details you should know about the place.

The Neuland farm was established in April 2006 by a small, pioneering group headed by Mr Menny Neuland (Peleg), to be a centre of value-based activities for Israelis travelling in South America. Nevertheless, as part of Neuland's universalist view, it is open to all peoples who abide by our basic values:

Non-violence – physical, verbal and emotional. This is to ensure that Neuland can be a purifying experience for those who come here from Israel or other areas of trauma in the world.

Progressive equality – with regard to rights and obligations, but not personal property. This is to ensure that Neuland can provide an alternative to the capitalist model, as well as to the communist-kibbutz model.

Giving – Every member of Neuland must do community work in the local villages. This is in keeping with Herzl's vision, which saw the Jewish people as agents of progress and enlightenment in the world.

Openness to the 'other' – 'From man have we come, and to man shall we return,' and others are our only salvation. Therefore, the members of Neuland are as open to strangers and visitors as they are to each other.

Enlightenment – Neuland encourages its members and visitors to learn and study, in the belief that only knowledge of the past and information about the present can allow us to dream about the future.

An important point! Neuland was not established to be a substitute for Altneuland, which is the State of Israel. Our goal, at the moment, is to challenge, to place a mirror, to bring people closer together, to be a miniature 'shadow state', if you will, to remind the State of Israel what it was supposed to be. And what it can be.

Another important point! Neuland is not a utopia. It exists in the real world, and as such it is filled with contradictions, defects and problems. In many areas, we are still searching for the golden mean, and we would be happy to hear any illuminating comments you might have at the end of your visit. A map is attached to make it easier for you to find your way around. We hope your visit to Neuland will be a stirring experience.

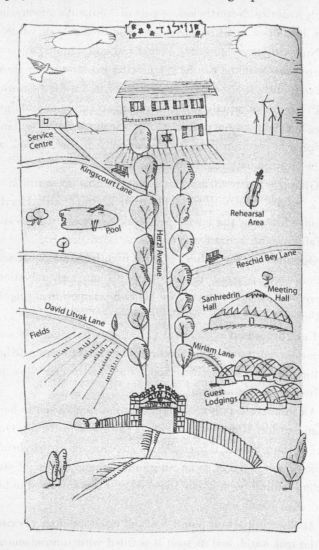

Inbar

A community of clouds assembled in the sky to decide whether to drop rain or not, and she began to walk beside Dori towards the old farmhouse. On one side of the lane, a group of young people were setting up a wind turbine. All the blades were in place, and now they were trying to lift it and set it down on a raised surface. They couldn't manage it. Instead of remaining upright, the turbine collapsed on them and they collapsed on each other. When they stood up, two men blamed each other for the collapse, and for a moment, it looked as if a fight was about to break out. But a third man intervened, got between them and spread his arms to the sides, like a dash. Another group, further down the lane, was spreading honey from jars into a wooden mould of English letters, and Inbar approached them curiously. What . . . what are you doing? she asked a girl with cropped hair who was filling the letter T. Don't you know Shlomo Barr's song? the girl answered with a question, without stopping her work. Song? Shlomo Barr? Inbar didn't understand. *'And they write on a wooden board, with honey from A to Z,'* she heard Dori sing behind her. *'And say to him, lick it up, habibi,'* the girl completed the verse. But . . . what . . . who . . . ? Inbar didn't understand. The kids in the villages around here, the girl explained as she delicately completed the wings of the T, one after the other, we teach them English. And we thought this would be a tastier way for them to learn. What a great idea! Inbar said admiringly, wanting to spread some honey herself. Learn. Lick. And then, when they continued walking, she pinched Dori's arm lightly and said: Come on, admit it — it's a great idea.

He didn't admit it. He didn't speak at all on the way to the farmhouse. They walked along the lane, passing groups of workers (one was carving toys, another painting a chessboard on a piece of cardboard), and Inbar wondered if her Wandering Jew was among them. Actually, she thought, she had no way of knowing, she'd never have a way of knowing, unless she caught him red-handed, drawing a violin.

The lane came to an end at Herzl Avenue. Branches formed a canopy above them, speaking to each other, brushing against each other. Unfamiliar flowers in breathtaking colours blossomed in large, elaborate flowerpots that lined the street. 'And once again my heart expanded like a white cascade,' she recalled a line of the poem by Zelda that hung in the bathroom of her hut, and her heart expanded. She thought about telling Dori about the poem, but decided that it wasn't the right moment. She remembered Cecilia-Aharona's funny misuse of the word 'defect' when she said she wanted to 'defect to Israel and find there pure love' like theirs. Hers and Dori's.

Someone had poured bright white gravel at the front door to the farmhouse, and their shoes made satisfying crunching noises when they stepped on it. Wheels of an old plough, rusted at the edges, hung on either side of the door. They walked past them and entered the house—

And were stopped by David.

How are you, brothers? He gave Inbar a long hug and shook Dori's hand suspiciously.

You don't have to stay at the entrance gate? Inbar asked.

Only the morning shift, he explained. From noon on, I'm here, at the entrance to Mr Neuland's office.

We're on our way to see him, Dori said and tried to walk past him.

You'll have to wait, David said, blocking the way.

It's four o'clock, Dori said, getting angry.

Three minutes to four. But why are you standing? Sit down. And at four, I'll tell him you're here.

They sat down.

Like Saturday mornings, Dori hissed.

What's like Saturday mornings?

The closed door. Once every few Saturdays, he'd lock his door, to work. And we weren't allowed to disturb him.

She pictured Dori as a little boy, standing outside the door, and she felt so sorry for him. What . . . And you all accepted that, submissively? she asked.

I did. Because I preferred being with my mother anyway. But my sister would stand at the door and wail. I just can't believe that we're really sitting here and waiting for the guru to let us in. It drives me mad.

And he didn't come out to her, to your sister?

In the end, he did. In the end, she'd wear him down and he'd come out to calm her. That was the only way to get love from my father: be weak. And shout 'help' very loudly. And Tse'ela – she was a champ at doing that. So, is it four yet?

Two more minutes.

Fuck it.

The walls of the entrance hall were covered in framed, faded black-and-white photos of Old World Jews standing in the middle of a fallow field. Beside a plough. Beside a horse. Wearing clothes unsuited to horse riding. The Jews that Baron Hirsch brought here, she remembered. They didn't look happy; but didn't look sad either. Maybe embarrassed.

Dori's knee was jiggling nervously, and she put her hand on it, to slow it down. That helped a little. The knee kept jiggling, but more slowly.

Can you see what's written on the guru's door? he asked after a brief silence.

She squinted and tried to read the words. Read it to me, she said, and pressed his knee gently. I can't see it from here.

And he read out the lines from a Shmulik Kraus song: '*So narrow was I that I had to spread my wings and fly, to a place like Mount Nevo where all things are clear from high in the sky.*'

*

At exactly four, Neuland time, David walked reverently to the office door. But before he could open it, it opened from inside and Dori's father stood in the doorway.

Inbar's first thought was: Wow, he looks just like Dori.

He took a few steps forward, towards the hall, and only then did he see them.

Dori'nu! He froze. What are you doing here?!

Dori

His father hugged him. He didn't pat his shoulders. He didn't pat his back. He really and truly hugged him. Dori had yearned for such a hug for so many years, but now he was the one to move away first. He had too many questions to allow himself to enjoy it.

They studied each other. From the tips of their toes to their Adam's apples.

What a surprise, what a surprise, his father mumbled. It wasn't clear from his tone whether it was a good surprise or a bad one for him.

Dori said nothing. A cocktail of anger and relief bubbled in his throat.

Where did you come here from? his father asked.

Buenos Aires, he replied.

So you must be very tired, his father said sympathetically. Have they already showed you the guest lodgings?

Yes, he said. Sarah showed us.

A very fine girl, Sarah, his father said.

There was a brief silence. Dori thought that his father looked ridiculous with that Herzl beard, shot through with grey.

Where are your manners, Dori'nu — his father nodded towards Inbar. Aren't you going to introduce me to the young lady?

I'm Inbar, Inbar said before he could open his mouth.

Menny, his father said, reaching out for a handshake. He stared deeply into her eyes as if he wanted to find something there, and then smiled, as if he'd found it.

I joined Dori's search in Peru, Inbar said, and since then—

Search? What are you searching for, son? his father asked, and judging by the look in his eye, he wasn't joking or feigning ignorance.

You, Dad, Dori said.

Me?

Tse'ela was terribly worried about you. You disappeared. You stopped sending emails. And the ones you sent were very strange. Also, the stories I heard from people who met you on the road were . . . worrying.

But—

Not to mention your diary.

My diary?

The one you left in the computer, on the Island of the Sun. His father suppressed a sigh, like a politician confronted with a dark episode in his past. And like a politician being confronted with a dark episode in his past — he changed the subject.

How long have you been on the road, son? he asked.

Three weeks.

Wow! That's quite a while.

You could have saved us the time if you'd taken the trouble to update us on what's happening, Dad.

I couldn't. If you read the diary, you know that I was in no condition to—

One phone call, Dad. That's all you needed to make.

His father scratched his beard. Somewhat embarrassed. Not a lot. But, he said, why did you have to come all the way here yourself, son? I imagine you can hire a team . . .

You didn't take out rescue insurance before you left, Dad. And without it, hiring a team is incredibly expensive. Besides, we wanted to keep it quiet, so your clients wouldn't think you'd gone off the deep end before we knew whether that was true or not. You see, we were thinking about you while you couldn't even bother to pick up a phone.

His father took a long, deep breath, familiar to Dori from his childhood. He breathed like that when he and Tse'ela were too slow getting organised in the morning. Or when they argued with each other. Or when Dori didn't understand something in geometry, even after he'd explained it for the third time.

Dori'nu, he said now, I'm so happy that you, both of you, are here. And we'll have plenty of time to talk about everything that needs talking about. You must be hungry, no? Our communal meal is in the evening, but let's go to the community kitchen together and make you both sandwiches.

Inbar

It's always fascinating to meet the parent of someone you know. A bit like peeking into the kitchen and seeing what your meal will consist of. After she met Eitan's father, for example, she understood where his designing talent came from. He was an accountant, Eitan's father, but the way he spread the tablecloth on the table in one precise movement, and the way he placed the sections of the weekend paper he'd finished reading on a separate pile from those he hadn't read yet – were a blueprint of the future Eitan. And once, when Revital's mother – Revital was Inbar's co-worker, the one who thought that any man who didn't want her had to be gay – arrived on her very high heels to take their apartment key from her daughter, you could see where Revital's conceit came from. Sometimes it worked the opposite way: years after she scratched Hoffman's Honda, his son came to the station to deliver a package. Even though he'd grown up and wore a messenger's overalls, she recognised him immediately from the time she'd stalked his family on Fridays, from the Maoz Aviv café. After a few minutes of a failed attempt to have a conversation with him, she decided that either the kid took after his mother or his father's pomposity had, in the mysterious way parents affect their children, made him shy.

Now she looked at Dori and his father. She chose not to take part in the conversation they were having, so she could observe.

Dori's father was a handsome man. More handsome than in

Dori's pictures. More handsome than Paul Newman.

He had large blue eyes, and the turquoise poncho he wore made them even bluer. His beard was long, but not too long, and clearly well groomed. His Adam's apple was prominent, just like Dori's. When they stood face to face, after their hug, it looked as if their Adam's apples were about to touch. When Dori mentioned the diary, he swallowed, and his Adam's apple moved up and down as if it had a life of its own.

He put his hands on his hips, like Dori. Folded them on his chest like Dori. Used them to emphasise his words, like Dori: an arm spread wide for 'we'll have enough time'; a small, firm karate chop in the air for 'you must be hungry'.

After less then five minutes in his company, she also understood where Dori had got his old-fashioned manners.

He opened the door for her after saying, 'May I?' and let her pass. In the kitchen, he made her a sandwich, following her instructions precisely: a thin tomato slice, two long, thin pickle slices. No onion. No mayonnaise. No asking what the hell she was doing with his married son. As with Dori, his chivalry never crossed the line into condescension. Years of working for male bosses had taught her to recognise when that line was crossed: the appearance of the word 'doll' at the beginning of a sentence, for example. Or of the phrase, 'Let me do it!' before she had to do something technical that was as simple as could be, like restarting a computer. No. There was nothing condescending about the chivalry of the Peleg-Neuland family. A sincere desire to help: maybe that was the best way to define it.

And the entire time – while he was making the sandwiches, when he washed the plates and put them in the Ikea drying rack that, incredibly, had reached even here, and when the three of them walked beneath the star-strewn sky to the communal dinner in the meeting tent and he offered her his poncho because 'Neuland's seasons are opposite to the ones in Israel, so July is cold here' — that entire time, she tried to see the broken, confused man who wrote the diary. And couldn't.

*

In the tent, he sat down on the special chair — a chair with a Dr Gav back support — reserved for him at the head of the table, and invited her and Dori to sit on either side of him. The members of the community came in slowly, and there were many more than she'd seen on the tour with Sarah. At least thirty. Maybe more. Most were young, but there were also a few grey heads. Most of them looked Israeli, but there were at least two fair-skinned men with Viking build. There were a few more men than women, but only a few, and they were all dressed in simple, but clean clothes. She tried to see which of them had 'visible wounds' and couldn't really tell: everyone looked happy — as if their minds were comfortable in their bodies. She looked around for Sarah, and when she saw her, invited her with her eyes to come and sit next to her. Sarah came over, with that lovely walk of hers, and touched her arm affectionately. Some of the members approached Dori's father and consulted him about problems they'd come up against during their afternoon activities in the villages. One of the men said that the local English teacher felt threatened by the fact that they had begun teaching English to the village children. You should hear him speak, he said. Full of mistakes. A girl, apparently a doctor, told him that a mother whose son she'd treated wanted to give her a gift that she didn't want to accept; but she didn't want to offend her either.

Dori's father replied to each one briefly and to the point, and set up private meetings with them for six the next morning. He was impatient, but not impolite. After he'd spoken to all who wanted his advice, he cleared his throat.

525

Good evening, friends, he began, and told them his son had arrived on a surprise visit, so – he apologised in advance – for the next few days, he wouldn't have as much time for private meetings. Then he asked those present to think deeply in preparation for their upcoming group discussion about the request of some of their religiously observant members to make the kitchen kosher. He finished with a reminder that in the evening, right after dinner, the Neuland klezmorim would be performing in the meeting tent.

He then repeated everything in English for the non-Hebrew-speakers, and a few seconds after he finished – as if a signal had been given – the members burst into a rousing rendition of 'Hatikvah'.

That is, the local version of 'Hatikvah'.

They'd made some changes to the original text: instead of 'looking towards Zion' they sang 'looking towards the universe'; and instead of 'to be a free people in our land, the land of Zion and Jerusalem' they sang 'to be a free people living as we choose, in respect and serenity'.

Dori raised his eyebrows at her when the song was over to see whether she shared his puzzlement. The anthem thing is weird the first few times, Sarah whispered in her ear but then you understand.

*

The meal itself was wonderful (or maybe she was just very hungry). Tomato soup with herbs was the first course, *asado* with a side dish of knishes was the main course, and for dessert – a fresh fruit salad of bananas, oranges and apples. Two pitchers, one of water and the other of a sweet juice she didn't recognise but was embarrassed to ask about, were placed in the middle of the table, and people poured for themselves. Salt and pepper shakers were passed from hand to hand, sometimes over heads. Those who wanted more food asked for it, and got it. It was all very ordinary. Very familiar. But also strange in a way that Inbar couldn't put her finger on. It was like the first few hours in the Sinai, she thought: when you're sitting in the main hut and feel as if everyone around you is acting in sync with an internal music that you still haven't heard because you've only just arrived.

The food here is wonderful, don't you think? Sarah asked her proudly, and Inbar nodded in agreement.

Dori, on her left, barely touched his food. He was pale, and even his prominent Adam's apple had sunk into his neck that night.

Aren't you hungry, she asked, concerned, and pressed her leg against his under the table.

I'm still taking it all in, he replied.

*

He didn't want to hear the klezmorim at first either, but then Sarah climbed on to the makeshift wooden stage and whispered something to the clarinet player, who then whispered to Jamili, the paddleball cowboy, who was now playing the violin. Without stopping his bowing, he announced to the audience that they had a musician there that evening who 'doesn't know that in Neuland you don't refuse an invitation'. Then he got the audience to join in the call, Do-ri, Do-ri – and Dori had no choice but to acquiesce. He climbed on to the vegetable crates that led to the stage and took his place among the musicians.

At first, he drummed hesitantly with his hand, and Inbar thought he was trying harder not to bother anyone than to play, but as the show went on, he loosened up, and she saw that, apart from his body language when he sat, and his body language when he walked, he had a third body language – when he played music – and that was the coolest language of all.

She watched his hands, the way they fisted and opened, depending on the sound he wanted to produce, how they softened or hardened, depending on the force he wanted to exert on the stretched leather of the drum, and, feeling a surge of heat between her legs, imagined what it would be like if those hands were to touch her skin, move under her shirt, inside her pants, over her bottom. Yes, what did she have to fear? That she'd get too attached to him? Who was she kidding? After all, she'd felt attached to him for a long time, and for a long time had wanted him all to herself. All to herself. All to herself. The rhythm of the klezmorim's renditions of Israeli pop songs grew faster, more energetic. Jamili strummed the violin as if it were a guitar, Dori pounded away at the drums, and the audience began to dance. Sarah grabbed her hand and tried to pull her over to join them, but she refused, and, embarrassed, pressed up against the wall of the tent.

Music is a marvellous thing, said Dori's father, who'd come to stand beside her.

She nodded without looking at him.

I think, he said, that it's the greatest cultural achievement of the source country. All the inner pressures that poison the society there have made its music brilliant. And you know why?

She couldn't think of an appropriate response and felt as if she were failing an exam.

Because people listen to each other, he replied to his own question. Musicians have to cooperate in order to create something together that is greater than each of them separately. That's why music is a really important part of life here in Neuland. So that we can use it to develop ways of listening to each other.

Inbar nodded. But even though she wanted to say something that would impress him, she was tongue-tied. As if the few hours she'd spent in Neuland had been enough to infect her with the reverence that all the members felt towards Dori's father.

Dori'nu's grandfather was a musician, he said, and pointed to his son, who was rocking wildly over the drums. He always wanted *me* to play. But, unfortunately, I was a dismal failure at it.

I know, she blurted. From your diary, she hurried to explain.

You read it too? he asked.

Yes — she felt her foot going deeper into her mouth — Dori asked me to. He wanted me to tell him what I thought. I'm sorry if—

It's okay. Anyone who leaves his diary behind like that, on a computer, might have wanted someone to read it. At least — he added with an unhappy smile — he loses the right to complain.

She was silent, embarrassed to the roots of her hair, and pretended to be focused on the music.

So you and Dori'nu met in Peru? Dori's father asked.

Yes, she replied, lowering her glance to her shoes.

And then you joined him on the search . . . for me?

Yes.

'And you know that he's married and has a child' — she was one hundred per cent, no, two hundred per cent sure that's what he was about to say—

But he simply grazed her back with his hand, the way her father always did, and said, it's very nice that you joined him. Not many women can identify so strongly with someone else's search. And added — removing his hand from her back — it's good that you're here with us, Inbar.

*

It rained after the performance, the kind of light rain that, in Israel, makes everyone run for shelter; the kind that, outside Israel, people hardly notice.

Inbar, Dori and his father stood at the corner of two lanes near the tent.

And stood.

And stood.

When people are about to part from each other, there's always a slight hesitation. This time, the hesitation went on and on. Inbar shifted her weight from one foot to the other for a long time, inhaled the good smell of wet earth and waited for something to develop between father and son.

It's still hard for me to sleep on my own . . . without Mum, you know? Dori's father finally said.

Dori nodded deeply, as if to say: It's hard for me without her too.

His father said, during the day, I'm too busy to think, but at night . . .

Dori nodded deeply, as if to say: Me too.

His father wiped a raindrop, or a tear, off his eyelash and asked: Will you come to my office tomorrow morning?

Dori replied – a tinge of sarcasm in his voice – I don't want to disturb your 'envisioning', Mr Neuland.

His father said – in a clean voice – tomorrow I want to envision you, son.

After a brief silence, he said goodnight. And added to Inbar: If you need anything in your hut, Inbar, another blanket, for instance, there's someone on night duty in the service centre.

Thank you, she said. And didn't know what to add after the thank-you: Menny? Dori's father? Mr Neuland?

Then they went their separate ways – they to the guest lodgings and he to the farmhouse. When she turned to look back, she saw him walking slowly, his poncho trailing behind him and his shoulders stooped, sad, just like his son's had been when she'd seen him for the first time, in Ben-Gurion Airport, bent over the photographs.

What a day, she said as she and Dori approached their huts. Can you believe that last night we were still in La Paz? It's great to see you play, she added, and when he didn't answer, she asked, are you okay? And reached out daringly to stroke his cheek. I don't know, he said, and rubbed his hands together as if he were cold. And said again, I don't know. This place seems weird to me. That business of 'Mr Neuland' is weird. Everyone here seems to be completely off the wall, but they all look happy, don't they?

Yes, she said, they do. And enthusiastic.

I still don't know about what, he said.

Neither do I. But this is only our first day here, you know. When you read a book, for example, it takes a while to get into it.

So, he said, maybe they're perfectly fine and I'm nuts? Is that what you're saying? Dori spread his arms in bewilderment. He looked to her like a little boy again.

Do you want to come in and . . . talk about it? she asked, pointing to her hut.

He curled a lock of her hair around his finger for a moment too long, then brought it to his nose. And let go of it.

I want to, Señorita Inbar, of course I do. Maybe I want to too much . . . I mean . . . You and I, we're a lot more than just travelling companions . . . And that's exactly why . . . it's a lot more . . . he said, but didn't move. Do you understand?

Yes, she said.Then said again, yes. And turned to go into her hut because she was so embarrassed. Damn it, now that she finally—

Tell me – he grabbed her arm, a little too strongly – would it be all right if I call you every once in a while in the night?

What?

I've had this strange feeling since dinner. As if they put some of that cactus concentrate my father drank with the shaman into our juice. I don't know. I tried to tell you earlier. There's something about this place . . . the anthem . . . the names of the lanes . . . the way my father acts . . . There were moments during the performance this evening when I wasn't completely sure whether I was in a real place or hallucinating.

What does that mean?

531

Forget it. I haven't slept for forty-eight hours. Maybe I'm just talking shit.

Okay.

But still, if I call you, will you answer me?

Yes.

Thanks, he said. And kissed her cheek. Close to her lips. Then turned and went to his hut.

*

Ten minutes later, she heard a shout: Inbar!

I'm here!

Thanks!

Towards morning, he shouted again: Inbar!

Here!

Thanks!

And she thought, shit, I love him.

Dori

Didn't fall asleep till almost dawn, and in his dream Inbar was an astronautics teaching assistant, explaining to a university class that, statistically, it is more reasonable to assume that there is life on other planets than to assume that there is life only on earth. He was a student in her course who went up to her at the end of the lecture and, without saying a word, laid her down on the desk as if they weren't in a hall full of people, moved her hair gently away from her face and kissed her on the mouth – tasting her more than kissing her, and she tasted wonderful – and then

532

he was suddenly sent off to the Yom Kippur War, where General Gorodish, with his thick-framed glasses, screamed that he was a traitor, a disgrace to his family, and told him to start walking towards the Suez Canal. He walked through a vast desert, with no water in his canteen, and sang a Danny Robas song to himself to stave off the loneliness, *I come home from the night, turn on the light in the stairwell, reach up for the key*, but at some point, while he was walking, his voice faded away and his lips were so dry that they cracked, and blood spilled from them instead of words. He knew that he had to find an oasis, he couldn't go on any longer, he had to disobey Gorodish's order and get something to eat or he would be forced to drink his own blood, which had already begun to drip into his mouth and had a sweet, strange taste—

When he woke up, he still had the taste of blood in his mouth, and for a moment, he wasn't sure where he was and couldn't remember what this hut was or what that table was or what the poems hanging on the walls were. But even though the feeling lasted only a few seconds, after which he managed to place himself – Neuland, Argentina, July 2006 – there was something disturbing about it, and he got up and washed his face and called out: Inbar!

A few seconds later, he called out again: Inbar!

Only then did he notice that a note had been pushed under his door.

Good morning, Dori'nu, she wrote. *I hope you finally managed to fall asleep. I'm dying to understand what's going on here, so I'm going for a short walk on the farm. Anyway, I think you and your father need some time together, no? See you soon. Yours, Inbar.*

How considerate of her, he thought. She's really wonderful. And he thought, he's not exactly my father, that man she thinks I need to spend time with. Nonetheless, he got dressed and brushed the taste of blood off his teeth and shaved down to the last bit of stubble so that, God forbid, he wouldn't grow a ridiculous Herzl beard too, and left for the farmhouse.

The sky was filled with heavy clouds, and the strong wind

carried an unpleasant smell — what is it? sulphur? — and tossed the hair of the members who were working outside, and the hair of the pregnant woman who was walking towards him. When she reached him, she hugged him as if they were old friends, and asked: Do you have children? He stammered, what . . . how do you . . . why . . . No one here has children, she said, so I have no one to talk to about it, and I thought that maybe you . . . Yes, he admitted, I have a son, and she hugged him again and said, that's wonderful, I'm not alone. And walked off with her huge belly, without adding another word.

Two guys wearing boots stopped him further down the muddy lane, and they too forced a hug on him. When did you leave Israel? they asked, almost in a whisper. Three weeks ago, he said. So tell us, they whispered, do you have any idea who won the football championship this year? Beitar Jerusalem, he said. And the cup? Also Beitar, he said, but why are you whispering? You know why, they said without clarifying. No, I don't know why, he said. And they laughed too loudly and carried on walking. I am an island of a person surrounded by a sea of panic, he recalled a sentence from his father's diary, and passed two girls conversing animatedly on one of the personal envisioning benches. A word drifted over to him, along with the smell of sulphur, on the wind: wings. Wings, one of the girls said, and the other nodded in understanding. To him, not her. Why? He nodded back and continued walking towards the farmhouse, as a suspicion again began to rise up in him: Were they really talking about wings? Maybe he'd imagined the word. Maybe he was imagining that sulphur smell. Maybe he'd imagined Inbar's invitation to come into her hut last night, and his refusal as well. What an idiot I am for not accepting it, he thought, and looked around for Inbar, to take back his refusal, to take it back with her under the blankets. But she wasn't in any of the lanes, or at the farmhouse, and it was the wounded David, not she, who welcomed him there. Man, he said, you played the hell out of those drums last night! and led him to his father, who was waiting at the entrance to his office as if he'd known exactly when he'd arrive. He was wearing a white poncho instead of the blue one he'd had on the day before. He gave him a long hug, and Dori froze inside it, thinking: Since when has my father been a hugger? His father, as if he'd heard Dori's thought, said, I learn a lot from the children here. About the importance of touching, for example, in the therapeutic process. And Dori thought, what is he actually saying — that I'm sick? And thought, maybe I really did catch something yesterday, and that's why I have this weird feeling, as if the motion sickness has passed from him to me. Come in, child, he said, and Dori walked inside, really feeling like a child. It's incredible, he thought, how quickly a person shrinks in his parents' presence. Would you like something to drink? his father asked. Do you have a phone here? he asked. Let's call Tse'ela, Dad, and tell her that you're alive. And Netta. So he can hear his grandfather's voice. He misses you.

Sorry, his father said leaning back on his grey Dr Gav, Neuland is a telephone-free area.

Completely?

Completely. Will you have some maté, Dori'nu? It's — he pointed to the large pitcher in the corner of the room — the Feldmans' old samovar. Hugo Yacobi got it from them when he bought the house. They brought it with them from Russia. I got the samovar from them free of charge, so you'll get it free of charge too. He also left me a telegraph key, and this long stick. Pick it up, go on, pick it up. What are you afraid of? They used it to drive away swarms of locusts. Locusts are a real plague in Argentina, Dori. Not biblical. In 1947—

Tell me, he interrupted his father and handed back the stick, aren't you curious enough about your grandson to speak to him? To your daughter? Aren't you interested in what's happening with them?

It's not a matter of curiosity, Dori. His father returned the stick to its place on the wall.

Right, it's a matter of parenthood, Dori thought. Mum, for example, would never behave like this. He felt a spear of anger hurtling through his body and dispersing the confusion he'd been mired in since the morning. Tse'ela's in a bad way, he told his father. The business with Aviram is getting messy. The kids are torn between them. Do you know how much she wants to talk to you?

His father's eyes wandered restlessly around the room, and Dori hoped that the worrying information about his favourite child might finally awaken the father he knew.

Your sister's life isn't healthy, he finally said. I wrote and told her that she needs to go on a journey in order to break out of the closed circle she's spinning around in. That's all I can do. My hands are full, with everything we're doing here.

But she's your daughter, Dad! Don't you care what happens to her?

I received a call, Dori. And when you receive a call, you have to answer it.

He remembered the phrase, 'I received a call' from the diary. He hadn't understood it then either.

And when Herzl, our prophet, received his call, he gave himself up to it totally, his father said and stroked his beard.

Dori was silent. This is not how he'd imagined his meeting with his father would go. Not at all.

His father was silent in return, an infuriatingly relaxed silence.

Tell me — Dori still tried to find some common ground — aren't you interested in what happened to Hapoel? I mean, you left the country in February. You have no idea how the basketball season ended.

So really, how could it have ended? His father gave a deceptive smile, the original Menny Peleg's smile — they probably lost the championship to Maccabi by three games in the finals. Maybe they stole the cup. As usual.

Dori would have loved to have been able to say to his father, 'That's just it, no,' and pull the rug out from under the arrogant prophecy. But he was right.

Wait a minute – he remembered his practical request, as yet unanswered – don't you even have an emergency phone here? What happens if someone gets ill?

We have a mobile clinic staffed by two doctors. They treat people mainly with natural substances made from indigenous plants. But they also have the necessary conventional equipment.

But what . . . what's so bad about telephones, Dad?

They have an adverse effect on intimacy. Concentration. And also discretion.

But what do you have to hide? Do you know what I thought when that David interrogated us at the entrance? That you're training a small army here, like in *Apocalpyse Now*.

It's just the opposite, Dori. The exact opposite. This place is meant, among other things, to allow former soldiers who . . . have been emotionally damaged . . . or members of the second generation of damaged people . . . to work out their trauma in an appropriate therapeutic space, so that what happened to me won't happen to them, and all the pain won't explode out of them years later.

And does this therapy include giving them the drug you wrote about in your diary?

Only someone who's never tasted that potion can call it a drug.

Oh excuse me, really, excuse me. So what do you call it?

His father closed his eyes. Was he insulted? Was he thinking up an answer? Dori didn't know. The father he knew never responded by keeping his eyes closed for a long time.

It's a door – he finally opened his eyes – a door to the world of dreams. To the unconscious. To compassion, to attentiveness, and to the calls the world is sending out to you. The door that the Indians discovered years ago, domesticated and used in moderation, just as we try to do in our healing ceremonies.

So Neuland is actually a farm for treating post-trauma in . . . let's say, unconventional ways?

Neuland is more than that, Dori. Much more than that. Come along, you'll see. He stood up and opened an iron door that separated his office from a small balcony. A cold wind, bearing that sulphur smell, burst into the room, and Dori followed his father out. The morning clouds had dispersed, leaving only one hanging over the world like the large rock in René Magritte's Castle of the Pyrenees. The expanse spread before them was vast. Boundless. The spotter in him reported that it was free of hostile elements. He and his father leaned forward on the railing, which was painted turquoise, and although the paint wasn't really fresh, it was slightly sticky to the touch. It's natural paint, his father said proudly: contains no poisons or chemicals.

Dori nodded, pretending admiration. He'd had no idea that there was such a thing as 'natural paint'.

Those are our agricultural lands, his father said, reaching out as if to say: 'Some day, son, all this will be yours.' We intend to start growing soybeans here, he promised. Very soon. Soybeans are in great demand now all over the world. You see those ruins on the right? That's where the synagogue once stood. We're just finishing the restoration plans now, in the hope that by next summer we'll be able to reopen it. Meanwhile, the team writing our charter is trying to decide what kind of synagogue it will be. What kind of Judaism we want here. As you can imagine, it's . . . not easy. Behind the synagogue – you can't see it from here – we've started building a basketball court. If you'd come a few months later, we could have played one-on-one. And that's not everything. While we were digging the court, we accidentally discovered a hot water spring. They call it *aguas termales* here. We still haven't decided what to do with it. Maybe we'll sell the land with the spring to fund the rest of our activities.

Maybe we'll operate a spa ourselves. Look to the right. Can you see the steam rising from the ground?

Yes, I can see it. Doesn't the smell bother you?

What smell?

Of sulphur.

You smell sulphur? He sniffed the air. I don't.

Dori looked to the left, to Neuland, which was bustling with young people. Even though it was break time and the ground was muddy, many of them were working. Building, drilling, hammering, laying bricks. There were two new wind turbines next to the original one, which was standing upright now, and another was being hauled up at that very moment. Behind the turbine crew, two more people were busy working, one putting together some colourful boards with an iron chain hanging above them, and the other sawing a round, wooden surface that looked like the base of a merry-go-round. They're building a playground, his father replied before Dori could ask. Benyamin, Neuland's first baby, is going to be born soon, and everyone here is very excitied about it.

Dori tried to find Inbar among the teams of workers. How long had it been since he'd seen her? Not long. And he missed her already. Very much. His Inbar hurt him, he thought, remembering Netta's phrase about Roni when she was away and he missed her. Why was he so slow, why did he always understand things like this so late? The next time she invited him into her hut—

Aren't those kids beautiful? his father said. For three months, I just looked at them. After all, before I . . . before I drank the potions, I spent a few months just travelling around like everyone else. When you're an older traveller, you have almost no one to be friends with, so most of the time, I observed. Either nature or young people. At first, I watched youngsters from all over the world, and slowly, I began focusing on Israelis. There was something mesmerising about them. So much energy. And so little joy. I saw each one's wound. I didn't imagine it, I saw it. The precise spot where the shrapnel had entered. Most of them wanted to look away from their wound, but some actually talked about it. Shared it with their fellow travellers. Their generation is much more open. And I'd sit at the next table, listening, admiring them, but at the same time . . . not understanding.

Not understanding what?

How young people could be so defeated. Why they gave up so easily, in advance, on the possibility that they could make changes when they went back home. I think that that's when I first had the idea that they needed to experience something significant before they went back to the war of survival. Something that would release the enormous amount of energy bottled up inside them.

Bottled-up energy? What exactly does that mean, Dad?

Okay, I'll try to explain it another way. A young person travels to a different country. The distance allows him to understand things about himself and the place he came from, and he makes himself all sorts of promises. How he'll turn his life around. How the future will be different from the past. But when he's back in Israel, all his promises melt away in the heat, are shredded by the humdrum details of daily life. That's what gave me the idea that they needed a hothouse where they could actually effect the changes they'd promised themselves they'd make, both on the personal and the social level, before they boarded the plane home. At that stage, I still didn't know what form the hothouse would take. I still hadn't received the call.

The call? I have no idea what you're talking about, Dad.

Sorry, that's the language we use here in Neuland. I've already forgotten that it's not clear to everyone. You read my diary, didn't you? Look, I don't know what you managed to understand from it. It was so . . . turbulent.

I managed to understand that your journey made you remember Yom Kippur.

That's true, his father said, turning away from the railing and taking him back inside. He moved a chair over to Dori and said in a different tone of voice, here, sit down.

They sat down beside one another, the edges of his father's poncho almost touching his knee.

Reading it must have been strange for you, his father said.

Yes, because I never . . .

Neither did I . . . His father sighed. And added nothing. He simply stared into space.

The father he knew couldn't stand silences. Or pauses. Or staring into space.

All my . . . beliefs were proven false after your mother died, he finally said. Everything I thought before, about myself, about the meaning of life, about the country I was born in, suddenly seemed to have no bearing. That was very frightening. But at the same time, I felt as if there were no point in fighting it, that I had to allow myself to fall apart so that I could have a chance of putting myself back together again. Can you understand that?

Yes, I can understand that. Even though . . . Dori said. Then remained silent.

Even though what?

Dori looked over at the telegraph key in the corner of the room and thought, if it worked, I could telegraph Tse'ela now: *I found Dad. Stop. But not exactly the Dad you know. Stop. He had a soul-searching conversation with me. Stop. Which is what I always wanted. Stop. But now it mostly annoys me. End.*

Even though . . . what, Dori'nu? his father asked again.

Even though I still don't . . . still don't . . . allow myself to fall apart, he finally answered. And couldn't help adding a bit of sarcasm to his voice.

It's not good, Dori, to keep everything inside, his father said, and put an arm round his shoulder (his father! put an arm

547

round his shoulder!). Do you remember how she used to kill jokes? he suddenly asked.

I do, yes (his mother could take the best joke and ruin it, by saying the punchline right at the beginning, or forgetting it altogether. Sometimes she mixed up the punchlines of two different jokes she'd been told the same day. She could say something like: 'And then the rabbit said, the tree didn't fall far from the apple,' and wait silently for everyone to laugh).

And the cheese? Do you remember the smell of the cheese?

Of course (his mother was obsessed with smelly cheese. She had an entire shelf in the fridge filled with smelly cheese from all over the world).

And how, when you were upset about something in the army, she'd calm you down with stories about the Inquisition? She'd tell you about the people who were sent to be oarsman on warships, and spent a whole year in the hold without ever going on deck. You see, Dori, she'd say, there are worse punishments than holding a pair of binoculars—

That's enough, Dad. Dori could feel his entire body objecting strongly to these memories, furious about the transparent attempt—

Why is it enough, Dori? I begin every day here with weeping. Just so you know. I sit and cry over your mother for half an hour, and begin my day happy.

That's you, Dad. I'm different. I have a different rhythm. I'm still not ready for all the—

You know what, said his father – that is, the open, attentive man his father had become, or was pretending to be. You're right, Dori'nu. Do it at your own pace.

Inbar

The most visibly striking thing was their enthusiasm. What does enthusiasm look like? Lots of blood in their lips, lots of gesticulation, the way they sat leaning forward like sprinters about to take off. Nine people leaning forward around a round table, eyes flashing at each other. Ideas were thrown into the air, mated there and gave birth to new ideas. A gourd of maté with a metal *bombisha* was passed from person to person, not in any order, but randomly, to anyone who wanted it, and whoever got the gourd gave a quick suck and passed it right on. She sat slightly to the side – as much as you can sit to the side of a round table – and listened to their language, which sounded like Hebrew but included expressions like 'the deeply wounded', 'source country', 'to Neulandise'. For the first few minutes, she thought there was no way she'd understand what they were talking about, that they were in a narrative completely different from her own, but slowly the pieces began to fit together and the picture of what they were talking about began to become clear to her. Two clauses of their charter seemed to be causing the greatest disagreement: one had to do with the role, if any, that Judaism would play in the daily life of Neuland; and the other – Jamili defined it, to the laughter of the others, as the 'Who is a Neulander' clause – dealt with the question of who could be accepted as a member of Neuland and how to decide between the desire to be open to people of all nationalities and the desire to give Neuland a particular character that would preserve the connection with the 'source country', which was Altneuland.

Sarah conducted the heated discussion. Using her eyes as a baton, she deflected those trying to dominate, and saved the timid from their silence. Occasionally, when she thought the discussion was becoming too personal, she channelled it back to its original purpose with a word or two. And sometimes, when they reached a dead end, Jamili came to her aid: Wow, I could really do with some cottage cheese now, he said in the middle of one silence. But Neuland-style cottage cheese — Sarah waved her finger in mock seriousness — where all the curds are equal! And each one is tolerant of the others! someone else added. They all laughed, and added things of their own that they missed from the source country: cappuccino, Shabbat overnight stew, *kubbeh* soup, Atzir falafel from Hadar Yosef.

They know how to laugh at themselves, Inbar thought. That's a good sign. She wanted to add her grandmother's sweet carrots to their list. But the other participants had already wiped the saliva from their lips and were arguing with each other again.

She hadn't taken part in a discussion about principles for years — not since her youth movement days, in fact. Inbar zoned out of the words flying around her. I've never tried to define what I believe in. And I'm not the only one. Everyone around me — they're all sceptics, all suffering from a quiet, dark despair. They all abstain in advance, all bow their heads in advance, curl up into their castles, stay locked into 'that's just the way it is', convinced there's no way out.

And what do you think, Sarah asked her.

Sorry . . . she blushed. I was thinking about other things . . . About what?

About Judaism and its place in what we're trying to do here.

I'm not sure I completely understand what you're trying to do here, she admitted, and Sarah smiled at her sympathetically, encouragingly. But, she continued, if you're planning to start everything from the beginning — Sarah nodded in confirmation — then maybe Judaism's something worth starting again.

Which means? Sarah asked.

Which means that in your discussion you talk about the symbols of Judaism as they exist today in Israel . . . excuse me, in the source country. It's true that you're Jewish, whether you want to be or not. But you can actually reinvent Judaism to suit you.

Invent a new stream of Judaism?

Why not? There are three streams today. So why not four?

The Jamilis, Jamili suggested. And when the laughter died down, they went back to discussing and analysing what she'd suggested, and getting tangled in the complications. Then they cut up a huge salad of fresh vegetables, ate it from wooden bowls, and went back to their arguing, joking, suggesting compromises, quoting from Jewish sources, from *Alteneuland*, from popular Israeli songs. All of it had the sort of inner fire she hadn't felt burning inside her for a long time, neither at work nor at home, an inner fire she disdained and envied at the same time.

When the group dispersed, only she and Sarah remained in the room. The air still vibrated with the sparks of new ideas.

So what do you think, Sarah asked, touching her arm affectionately.

It was strange and interesting, Inbar said truthfully.

If you decide to stay here — Sarah looked at her brightly — I'd be happy for you to join our think tank.

Stay? To be honest, I hadn't considered that possibility.

Most of the people who sat in this room with us today came here by accident, stayed for the experience, and then at some point became infected by the germ, and asked for an acceptance interview with Mr Neuland.

Were there people who weren't accepted?

Not many.

How many is not many?

Three, Sarah admitted. One overturned a table in the middle of a charter team discussion. It was pretty scary, because he turned it over on to me. I said something that made him angry. The second one was a girl who spent every day sitting alone on the envisioning benches, pricking herself with her nails. So he thought she'd be better off going back to her parents in the source country to get her head straight. And the third was a stoned Dutch guy who had no idea where he was and tried to sell hash to the people here.

Tell me, Inbar asked, Mr . . . Neuland has to approve everything you decided today about the charter? Because if he's the envisioner of this place then I don't really understand why—

It comes from two directions. There are ideas that we bring to him, and there are questions he asks us to raise.

But he has the last word?

Wrong. The Sanhedrin does.

The Sanhedrin?

Our general assembly. We're not a cult, Inbar, even though I imagine it could seem like that to outsiders. You need to understand that we don't worship Mr Neuland, we really don't. We just respect him very much. He envisioned this place the way Herzl envisioned the Jewish State, and that's why he has a special status. But there were people who opposed Herzl too, you know. And he made some decisions that weren't approved.

Who conducts the ceremonies on Thursdays?

He does – Sarah pulled her hair back into a tight ponytail – but I'm not . . . authorised to talk about the ceremonies.

Why does there always have to be a secret in all these closed communities? Inbar thought. To add an aura of mystery, to give members the feeling that they know something that outsiders don't. And even though the manipulation is transparent, she admitted to herself, she'd like to participate in one of those ceremonies. Just on the off chance that it might help her see Yoavi.

Never mind the ceremonies – Sarah undid the ponytail and let her hair flow freely again – they're a bonus, not the heart of what we do here. I think it's a lot more important for you to take part in our afternoon activities in the villages. That's what grabs me most about Neuland. Because it really means that we stop being the persecuted Jews of the Holocaust and start being 'a light unto the nations', as Herzl envisioned. Do you know the blessing we say on Friday nights? 'You have chosen us *together with* all the nations.'

Instead of 'of all the nations'? Nice.

So you'll join us later?

I'd love to. How does it work?

Do you know how to ride a horse?

No.

You should learn when you can. It's great. Meanwhile, talk to the guy in charge of scheduling, and he'll find you and Dori seats in one of the vans that transport the people who don't ride.

The guy in charge, where can I find him?

Do you have a map?

Inbar took out the map she'd folded and put into her trouser pocket. Sarah opened it and moved her finger along it as she explained: Turn right on Kingscourt Lane, go past the tomato beds and the service centre, and there he is, on the left of the klezmer rehearsal area.

Inbar's gaze was caught by the drawing that indicated the rehearsal area. Instead of a guitar, which she would have expected, or musical notes, there was a drawing of a violin. A violin that looked very familiar. From many walls.

Do you have any idea who drew this map? she asked excitedly.

Why?

No reason. I've never seen one like it. It's really a small work of art.

Yes – Sarah sighed – Jamili is very talented. Wounded as hell, but talented.

*

547

Stepping outside, they were greeted by a strong wind that rocked the hammocks hanging between trees. On Herzl Avenue, a few members were hanging fruit-shaped, coloured lights on branches. Long ladders had been placed against the trunks, and Inbar thought it looked like reverse fruit-picking. And she also thought: There's something thrilling about their enthusiasm, as fantastical as it might be, that crumbles your objections and melts your indifference. Another few days here, and who knows, maybe I too—

This is where the electricity for the lights will come from. Sarah pointed to the three new turbines that were spinning quickly, as if someone were doing it by hand. It's a lot better than the rattling of the generator, right?

Sarah! Someone came up to them and announced excitedly, we have visitors! Three of them, two men and a woman, and . . . you won't believe it, they say they're from Lebanon.

Lebanese? Light flashed in Sarah's eyes as she spoke. Are you sure?

That's what they said.

If it's true – that's wonderful! Sarah turned to Inbar. Mr Neuland envisioned that it would happen some time. He said it would be one of our greatest tests. The way we treat people who are not us, he said, that was one of the source country's greatest failures. And it's because we're extraterritorial that we can do it better. Listen, I think I have to go to the gate—

Of course, Inbar said, and added: Thanks.

You're welcome. Sarah smiled in embarrassment that was in direct contradiction to her confident posture. I really would be happy if you decided to stay in Neuland. I really miss having a best friend.

So do I, Inbar said, trying to reciprocate Sarah's kindness. And she thought: If I had a best friend, maybe I wouldn't invite a married man into my hut. But said: If I don't stay, we can see each other when you come back to the source country—

If I go back to the source country, Sarah said. I still haven't decided.

There's talk about some of us going back and renting an apartment together in Jerusalem where we'll Neulandise. I mean, make changes there. But it's complicated for me in the source country. My younger brother . . . was killed in the army in the Golan Heights a year ago.

The Golan Heights?

A tank fired at him during an exercise.

I . . . I'm sorry for your loss. I mean, I can imagine what you went through.

Wherever I went after that, I could see holograms of him. They looked so real that I'd reach out to touch him – I'd stand in the middle of the street touching the air. Can you picture it? This is the only place where it doesn't happen. After he was killed, I couldn't feel anything. Not love. Not hate. Not happiness. Not even sadness. It was as if lots of black clouds were sitting on my chest. Only here, in Neuland, did something open up. A little. So I don't know when I'll go back. When I feel like less of a danger to myself, probably.

Menny and Dori

They sat beside each other for a while, silent with the memory of the woman they both had loved. Dori suddenly recalled – his tears taking him by surprise – one night in the hospital. Everyone else had already left, and only the two of them remained sitting on the plastic chairs beside her bed. Her eyes were closed, but she opened them suddenly and looked at her son and his father, smiled that lovely smile of hers, and said, you've become so alike that for a minute, I thought I was beginning to see double.

Let's go, his father said now, I want to show you something.

He stood up abruptly and headed for another part of the farmhouse. He stood straighter and walked faster than he had in Israel, and Dori, whose back still ached, felt like a small child trying to keep up with a grown-up. The story of this farmhouse is special, his father said as they walked along corridors, and without waiting, without checking to see whether his son really wanted to hear the special story, he went on: They arrived here in 1932, the Yacobi family, when it was still possible to leave Germany. Do you understand? In the '30s, Baron Hirsch's settlement in Argentina, which failed at first, became a safe place for absorbing all the Jews of Europe who were wise enough to escape in time. Which was exactly what Baron Hirsch had planned. And the wonderful thing about it was that, in a short time, the Yacobis themselves became the bridgehead of the bridgehead. From '38 onwards, this farm took in Jews who fled Germany after Kristallnacht. This is where they spent their first night, where Mrs Yacobi gave them a hot meal and a pair of cowboy boots before they moved to one of the Jewish settlements in the area. Look, we're here –

His father opened a door, and Dori saw a room that had been turned into a small library filled with shelves lined with books.

His father was silent for a few seconds, to let the image sink in, and then said: When they left the 'absorption centre,' they'd leave the senior Yacobi a book as a gift. And so, as the refugees passed through here, his library grew to become the largest one in the area. This is a treasure house of Jewish creativity, Dori, especially in German, but also in Yiddish, Russian, Hebrew and Spanish.

He took a book off a shelf. Do you know this one? And showed him the cover, which said: *Los Gauchos Judíos*.

Alberto Gerchunoff?

Yes. Through vignettes taken from the daily life of the Jews here, he documented their attempts to settle the land, his father said, riffling through the pages until he found the one he was looking for. This is in Spanish, he said, so I'll try to translate for you.

'And so, when Rabbi Tzadok Kahan talked about the migration, I was so overjoyed that I forgot Jerusalem and remembered the words of Yehuda Halevi: Zion lies wherever peace and serenity hold sway.'

His father held out the book, but Dori didn't take it. As far as I remember, he said, Zion lies in a very specific place.

Oh, Dori'nu, you missed the point.

So explain it to me, he said, and thought: I'm a father myself now, so I wish he'd stop calling me Dori'nu.

A country cannot exist only to survive, Dori'nu. The original reason for the establishment of Israel was to gather all the Jews of the Diaspora in a place where they would not be persecuted. But that *was* the purpose, past tense. A country needs a vision. A country without a vision is like a family without love. And if there's no love, why preserve the family?

So? What does all this have to do with Neuland? Dori was beginning to lose patience. It pissed him off that his father had gone back to talking to him the way a guru talks to his followers, and it pissed him off even more that a man who shows not even a drop of interest in his own family was using the family as a metaphor—

Neuland will be a reminder, he said. A reminder of the Athens that the State of Israel was supposed to be if it hadn't turned into Sparta.

But why in Argentina? Why not establish something like this in Israel?

It's impossible, Dori. Any organisation you set up in the source country will encroach on someone else's territory, and that's why it would immediately be labelled as being 'against' something, and it would have enemies. Anyway — his father continued before Dori could get an objection in — these young people travelling in South America are at exactly the right time in their life to gamble on something new. How did Herzl put it? Great enterprises require a bit of despair.

So you want to establish the Neuland Diaspora with them? You know what Mum would say about it, that even the Golden Age ended with . . .

The expulsion from Spain. I know. If it's easier for you, you can think of us as *Futuro*, Herzl's visionary ship of wise men, or as the Sanhedrin of Yavne, which Ben Zakkai established when he fled from the besieged Jerusalem. A different Judaism, more spiritual, and free of the heavy burden of the siege, was born there after the Temple was destroyed.

But—

After all, you're the one who refuses to go with your students on the March of the Living in Poland, aren't you? You're the one who claims that those marches instil only fear and suspicion. So what we're trying to do here is just the opposite, to invite young people on a journey of enlightenment and openness.

His father put the book back on the shelf, and Dori said, okay, enlightenment and openness are all well and good, but how do they fit in with the interrogation that your crazy guy David put us through at the gate before he confiscated Inbar's phone?

It's all right, son — his father said, and pulled another book off the shelf — it's natural for you not to understand everything yet. After all, people took a long time to digest Herzl's vision too. And he predicted that as well, by the way. Look at what he wrote in his epilogue to *Altneuland*: 'You will have to make your way through hostility and misrepresentation, as through a dark, evil forest. But if you meet kindly people, my child, greet them in the name of your father.' And that's what happened to me, he added. I was lucky, and I met the kindly people who are here with me now.

But why does the information page say 'for the moment'? Might Neuland want to be something else one day? Is Neuland's small plan only your cover for a large Neuland plan?

His father closed his eyes and was silent for a long moment, too long a moment, during which Dori felt like taking the locust-beating stick off the wall and hitting him with it, to make him answer. So he'd speak to him the way he had when they were in the office.

Finally, his father opened his eyes, looked at his watch and said: The break is over. You and Inbar can go with the volunteers to one of the villages and call home from there.

The Wandering Jew

Can I have the racket? Inbar asked the guy who was playing with Jamili, then picked up the ball, which had fallen on to the ground, and batted it hard over to him. Jamili smashed it right back to her, at exactly the right height, and they volleyed the ball back and forth a few times without letting it fall. Not bad for a visitor, he complimented her as they played. Where are you from in the source country?

Haifa, she said, hitting a low ball over to him. And you?

Different places – he leaped forward and managed to keep the ball from touching the ground.

What does that mean – she hit the ball back – what are you, the Wandering Jew?

He froze – and the ball whizzed past him.

Sorry, he said and walked over so close to her that they couldn't play. What did you say?

You heard me. The Wandering Jew. The Wandering Jew Tour.

I have no idea what you're talking about.

The violin drawing on the map, Jamili. Otherwise, I would never have caught on to you.

Why are you shouting? he asked, lowering his voice to a whisper. Come on, let's go somewhere we can talk.

They put their rackets on the ground, and he led her behind one of the wind turbines.

I don't usually like to talk about it, he said, playing with his chest hair. People misinterpret me.

Inbar walked confidently along a familiar path. Types like him were the bread and butter of the radio programme she produced. They were naturally hesitant at first. They'd hidden their inner worlds for so long that they'd grown used to it. But she knew from experience that all they needed to start talking was one question that would signal to them that, during their conversation, the questioner was willing to play by the rules of that inner world.

It really wasn't very nice of you to refuse to let Jesus drink, she said, trying to provoke him. At the end of the day, you deserved the curse he put on you.

What does Jesus have to do with it? he burst out. Since when does Jesus put curses on people? Listen carefully: it was senseless violence, the destruction of the Second Temple, that's where it began. We're left with only the Western Wall. And good luck trying to live in a house that has only one wall. Even the guest huts in Neuland have three walls. So I started wandering. Appearing and disappearing. Changing cover names. What do you mean, how? Like in a time tunnel. Just without the tunnel. Tossed into a time period. Sometimes a good one and sometimes a shitty one. It's a lot easier to fall into Woodstock than Treblinka, even though, for your information, there were some bad moments in Woodstock too. Do you know that two people died in Woodstock because of a battle with forks? You have to play the record back to hear them screaming when they were being stabbed. They hide that from the public to keep the image intact. An image is a very important thing. My image, for example, is problematic. Have you seen what I look like in the Scandinavian pamphlets? Hideously ugly. Not that I'm Marlon Brando, but I'm not as ugly as those anti-Semites paint me either, you have to admit. Only once, in the fourteenth century, in Toledo, did I manage to sleep with the woman who was supposed to paint me. A kind of artist, you know. She really liked the whole wandering business. No commitments, none of that I-love-you stuff, no herbal tea. Pure lust. On the kitchen table. While her husband was sleeping. And later, her portrait of me was so flattering that they executed her a few months later, for committing adultery. Or practising magic. When men want a beautiful woman and she turns them down, they find a way to get revenge. Even though there's been some progress on that. With the perspective of two thousand years, I can tell you that the status of women has improved, but there's still a long way to go. In any case, when I heard about her death, I was already in Paris. I cried a river. Why are you surprised? Just because I wander doesn't mean I don't get attached to people. That's who I am – a wanderer who gets attached. I get attached and wander on. Who do you think walked through the Luxembourg Gardens with Herzl when he envisioned the Jewish State? Re-a-lly? You think one person could have come up with all of that alone, in two weeks? And Herzl, of all people? Who didn't know a thing about Judaism or wandering till he met me? And who, in your opinion, thought up the line about taking Manhattan and taking Berlin? Leonard Cohen? That's what everyone thinks. But ask them to explain what that line means – and you'll get silence. The truth is that I tossed out that line to him in the '70s. In a bar in Manhattan. At two in the morning. Look around you, my friend, he said, doesn't everyone here look Jewish? And I gave him the line. I mean, you can give a country to a wandering people, but you can't take the urge to wander out of them. Don't look at me like that. If you don't believe me, go to that bar in Manhattan — I don't remember the name — on the corner of Seventh and Broadway. Go into the men's toilets and you'll see my signature. With the violin drawing. And by the way, you can also find my signature in the Nablus Casbah. After Manhattan, I had a few horrible weeks in Franco's interrogation dungeon in Barcelona, and just when I thought it couldn't get worse than that, I was thrown into the second Intifada. A medic in the paratroopers. What a nightmare. I did things there that a Jew shouldn't do. I'm telling you, if I hadn't had a little perspective, I would've lost my mind. No, please, no, don't look at me like that, as if you've finally solved the riddle. Don't say to yourself, that's where it all started. Because it's not true. It all started with senseless violence. And the destruction of the Second Temple. Just like I told you. I've been on the road ever since. Giving senseless love to Gentile women. Edison — who do you think switched on the light over his head? And Bell? And Galileo Galilei? In all modesty, without me, humanity would still be stuck in the Middle Ages. You think I'm exaggerating? What a shame. I thought you were different. This is exactly why I don't like to tell my story to people. Because this is the reaction I get. They grab me by the head, as if I were a carrot, and try to pull me out of the ground so they can find my psychological roots. Bullshit. If I have roots, they're historical, not psychological. And historical roots are planted so deep in the ground that not even Bugs Bunny and all his friends can pull them out. And, to this day, the only person who understands that is Menny Peleg. They call him Mr Neuland here, the idiots. That reminds me too much of the week I spent with David Koresh's pals in Texas. So I just call him Mr Menny. He has no problem with that. From the minute he saw me, he knew that he'd have to bend the rules somewhat. When I told him about my history, he said it sounded to him like I'd travelled a long way before I arrived here. So I said to him, long is not the word, and he said he couldn't promise me that I'd feel at home here, because he knew it wasn't in my nature to feel at home. But he hoped that Neuland would be one of the more meaningful stops on my journey. Yeah, I said, why not? And that's how my acceptance interview ended. Later, Sarah saw that that I'd written 'drawing' in the talents clause of the application I filled out, so she asked me to draw a map for visitors. There was practically nothing here yet then. Just ideas. And goodwill. In all my wanderings, I'd never come across so many people with goodwill. So I drew the place the way Menny said it would be. I even added a swimming pool, though there was no plan for one, because I thought it would be a nice gesture to the kibbutz. I've lived on a kibbutz too, yes. Ein Harod. But it was at the time when it split into two ideological camps, and I didn't know which to choose, because I didn't understand what the big difference was between them. Everyone told me to take a stand, take a stand. How can you not take a stand? So I was pretty glad to be thrown out of there to a canal in Amsterdam. Anyway, the imaginary map of Neuland that I drew is becoming real, as you can see. We're even starting to dig the pool.

Impressive, you say? Worrying, I think. Why worrying? Because Menny told me, told all of us, that the whole idea of the place is not to be a new territory, but a wandering shadow camp. A diaspora Sanhedrin to be re-established in a new place every time. I have a bad feeling that meanwhile, the cactus has gone to his head and he's changed his mind and wants to establish a kind of permanent mini-country. And that, I have to tell you, is not at all to my liking. I already have a country. True, after what happened in Nablus, I don't see any way that I can live in it in the near future. But what is it I always say? A home is not a place you live in; it's a place you know you can go back to if you want. And you don't need more than one place like that. So what am I planning to do now? I think I'll be thrown out of Neuland in another week or so into another time period. Would you like to come with me? I don't invite just anyone. But, well, there's something about you. Or maybe it's more accurate to say: there's someone about you. I've been picking up your soundwaves ever since we started to talk. I mean, ever since I started chewing your ear off. It's just that it's been a long time since I met a girl who made me want to wander with her. Don't blush. I'm not talking about you, Inbar. I'm talking about the girl inside you. You know, the one who doesn't answer to anyone. Tell me, just between us, what do you call her? I promise not to tell anyone. Nessia? So maybe you can set Nessia free and let her come with me? I think that if she holds my hand really hard, she'll be able to go from place to place with me and, like me, she'll never die. I'm not sure it'll work. But it's worth a try, no?

Dori

She was waiting for him when he came out of the farmhouse, and when he saw her, he went straight over and gave her a long, lingering hug which, at some point, turned into something like two prize fighters in a clench. I missed you, he said. Inbar said nothing.

Sorry about yesterday, he said.

The loss is all yours, she said, smiling into his neck.

I was all over the place because of my father. Throughout this whole thing, I was sure I was coming to rescue him . . .

Yes, she said, slowly breaking away from his embrace, but he actually seems . . . fine to me.

That's just it, he said: sometimes he seems fine and sometimes he seems like he's gone off the deep end.

They walked along Herzl Avenue, and only now did he notice that they were moving towards the exit. The sun came out from behind the clouds for a moment, glittering on the leaves of a paradise tree. Three people hurried past them, speaking a foreign, but familiar language. The Lebanese! Inbar remembered, and thought that if they didn't have their *mochilas* on their backs, it meant that Sarah had persuaded them to stay.

Where are we going, by the way? Dori asked, giving her his hand.

To do some work in the villages. I like the idea of being a bit of a light unto the nations. Will you come too? she asked.

I don't know, he said, I'm not sure I can connect to . . .

For me, she asked.

Okay, he agreed.

I have to admit that your father is pretty . . . charming, she said cautiously.

Women always get excited about him, he said.

I didn't mean that way, she said. You're better-looking than he is, by the way.

Really?

Yes. Anyway, what I meant to say is that I think that being here is good for him and that his intentions are good.

The road to hell is paved with those, you know.

I wouldn't say this place is hell.

This place has the smell of hell.

Smell?

Sulphur. Can't you smell it?

Now that you mention it . . . a little.

Well, finally someone else smells it. I was beginning to think I was imagining it.

I don't know . . . Dori, I have the feeling there are things here that I don't understand. But we've only been here for a day and a half, and I think they're still trying to figure out a lot of things for themselves.

Are there any things here that you *do* understand? He dropped her hand. Maybe you can explain to me how it's possible for this place to be based on 'Herzl's principles' when Herzl's main point was that the Jews need territory of their own? To live according to Herzl's principles in Argentina is like living according to Lenin's principles, minus the bit about equality.

What I understand is that . . . your father wants to make a change in the source country, as he calls it, but he doesn't think that the change can come from inside, so he has to offer an alternative that will upset and challenge people by the very fact of its existence. Look at how it's upset you.

Yes, but—

And the idea is that later this 'shadow country' will feed the source country. Sarah, for instance, is planning to go back to Israel and Neulandise —

Now you're starting to talk like them!

She wants to make a change. What difference does it make what you call it. She wants to go back to Israel and set up a community that'll try to implement what she learned here.

Did she tell you *when* she plans to go back?

No.

Of course not. She's probably waiting for permission from the envisioner. After all, he's the one who 'sees the future for her'.

It's not really like that . . . but you're right, there are some weird things in Neuland, Dori. The way they talk about your father. Those secret healing ceremonies. And there are a few real characters here. I just spoke to one of them during the break . . . never mind . . . In any case, I think I'm a little too sceptical to really join them. But I'd stay here for a week or two, for the experience. At heart, they're good people. And it's always good to air the rules you live by, to imagine a different story, to take a short walk along . . . the road not taken, you know.

Inbar

In the end, she didn't stay in Neuland for a week or two. Not even for a day or two. Because when they reached the gate, Victorcito and the van were waiting for them. I'm glad you came, he said. That *hijo de puta* – he pointed to David – has kept me outside for an hour and won't let me in. I have an important message from Alfredo to give you, Mister Dori.

Message?

They are looking for you urgently from Israel.

What happened? Dori was terrified by Victorcito's terrified expression.

Tell him, Victorcito said to Inbar, that I brought him a phone so he can call.

They've been trying to get in touch with you from home, she said, and Dori took the phone and tried to call. And got the engaged tone.

Should I wait for you? Sarah tugged at the reins and stopped the beautiful, muscular horse beside them. The beautiful, muscular horse fixed his right eye on Inbar as if he too were waiting for a reply.

No, Inbar said. Go on. We'll catch up later.

After ten nerve-racking minutes, someone in Israel answered Dori. She only heard one side of the conversation and tried to deduce what the other side was saying.

What did they want? What?! When?! Did you tell them I was out of the country? There are a lot of people who . . . ? Was Netta awake when they came? Shit. Shit. Is he at home now? Is there a shelter at the nursery? Tell him I love him and I'm coming home tomorrow – the day after, at the latest. Yes and no. Yes – I found my father. It's a long story. But he's here. And he's alive. Okay. Okay. Of course. On the first plane. Bye.

What happened? she asked, and put a hand on his shoulder. War, he said, and handed her the phone.

*

She called Grandma Lily. But instead of her deep, hoarse hello, she heard her mother's high, nasal hello.

Inbari, where are you? We've been searching high and low for you. I just finished talking to the embassy hotline in Buenos Aires. What? A rocket hit Grandma's building. So I took the first plane here. She's in a bad way. I'm packing a few things for her and we're going to Eitan's. Your Eitan, Inbar. He called and told us we should come to your place. Out of the range of the rockets. No. Physically, she's fine, but she's in a state of shock. Never mind, Inbari. Come back as soon as you can. We have enough to worry about as it is.

Dori, Inbar and Menny

We have to tell my father, Dori said.

Inbar explained the situation to Victorcito and asked him to wait a few more minutes for them.

What happened, brothers? David asked them at the gate. Why didn't you go to the villages? War broke out in Israel, Inbar said, and David said in a quiet, measured voice, as if she'd told him

562

that the sun rises in the morning, ah yes, that was envisioned. Mr Neuland told us it would happen this week. Or next week, at the latest. What?! Dori shouted. And David, who was a bit in awe of him, took a step back and said, yes, brothers, he envisioned that there would be war and told us that we wouldn't have to be involved, that what we do here in Neuland is no less important. Okay, get out of the way, you lunatic, Dori said, walked past him and ran with Inbar along the avenue of paradise trees to the farmhouse, where they burst into his father's office.

His father looked up comfortably from the book he was reading – his feet rested on a stool – and asked: So, did you make your 'urgent' calls?

War, Dori told him, still panting from the run. On the Lebanese border. They're shooting rockets on Haifa.

Well, his father sighed, that's no surprise. They have to start a war every once in while to divert attention from the fact that there is no vision.

How do you know who started the war, Dori said angrily. I only just told you about it!

His father was silent, stroking his poncho lightly. Will you have some maté, he asked, pointing to the samovar in the corner of the room. I was just about to make some for myself.

Is it true what David said at the gate? Dori asked, ignoring his father's invitation.

What did he say, his father asked casually, as he poured hot water into the maté cup, put a sugar cube in his mouth and sucked the liquid through the *bombisha*.

That you told them not to go to this war because what they're doing here is more important.

I didn't tell them what to do. I can only share with them the information I received when I was envisioning.

Which was?

That this is an unnecessary war that won't change a thing, and there's no point in participating in it.

563

How do you know, Dad? Have you gone completely crazy? Do you hear yourself? Who are you to decide whether there's a point or not? What are you, a prophet? A messiah? You know, if we were in Israel, I could report you to the authorities and they'd institutionalise you.

So it's a good thing we're not in Israel, his father said, his voice slightly mocking, his feet still resting on the stool.

Of course it's a good thing we're not in Israel. The easiest thing is to treat the symptoms and not the disease. The easiest thing is to sit here and talk about a vision without getting your hands dirty.

That's only one way of looking at it, Dori'nu.

And what's the other way?

That there's no way of defining a new vision if you're still slogging around in the same bog. That there are situations in which we have to climb Mount Nevo if we want to see far and wide.

What Mount Nevo are you talking about? You're in Mosesville, a crummy little town in Argentina, which was part of Baron Hirsch's crummy little project, which failed. F-a-i-l-e-d!

Mr Neuland . . . Dori's dad – Inbar entered the conversation for the first time – I think you're doing something unfair. Some of the kids here admire you. Whatever you tell them is written on stone as far as they're concerned. I think you should give Dori a chance to offer them a different view.

Dori's father put a new sugar cube into his mouth, sipped from his cup of maté, rubbed his beard, and a few seconds later, said –

Certainly, no problem, certainly. You're right. Dori, you can present your arguments to everyone at the next general meeting of the Sanhedrin on Friday.

But that's four days away, Dori said, we won't be here.

His father rubbed his hands together as if to say: what can I do? Then he looked at Inbar and said: I actually thought it was good that you came. Together. Where are you rushing off to? How long have you been here? Two days? Sit down. Have some maté. Stay with me a little while longer. Get to know the place — and *your* potential — a little more deeply.

I've been here long enough — Dori burst out — to know that you need help. And I'll tell you something else: If Mum were here, she would be ashamed of you. The drugs were bad enough. But not to give a damn about your daughter and your grandchildren, who are in danger? Rockets might be falling on them as we speak, and you sit here and drink your maté as if you didn't have a care in the world. Mum would never forgive you for that.

But your mother is the one who sent me here, Dori'nu. She appeared to me in a vision—

Visions?! They're not visions, Dad, they're drug-induced hallucinations—

I've already explained to you, Dori, that the potion is not a drug. It's a door to a clearer vision of the world of the soul.

Clearer? You've gone off the deep end, Dad. And the problem is that you're dragging other people down with you—

That's only your take on it, Dori'nu.

Forget it — Dori waved his arm angrily, hopelessly — there's nothing to talk about. Let's go, Inbar.

Inbar, dear — Menny ignored Dori and turned to her — of course you're invited to stay here if you want to. We still haven't talked about your wound. And our Sarah feels strongly that you could help us a great deal here, as part of the community.

Thank you, Inbar said. I also feel that you could help me a great deal, but . . . I'm needed at home.

A blast of thunder shook the window, and the birdsong they'd heard constantly since they arrived in Neuland grew silent.

*

Dori's father, wearing his poncho, came out to see them in the pouring rain just as they'd finished loading their bags into Victorcito's van. He was holding a small object, which he handed to Dori: a pan pipe.

Take it, he told him. This is the gift that Netta asked me for, isn't it.

Dori nodded in surprise.

I'm sorry you're going . . . like this, son, his father said. Despite everything, I'm glad you came. Kiss everyone for me. Tell Tse'elonit that I'm fine. There hasn't been a war in this region for two hundred years, so she doesn't have to worry about me. She should worry about herself and the children. Tell Netta that his grandpa is doing everything he can so he can grow up in a better place. And . . . tell Danny Klein that if he doesn't bring a first-class player to the team, he'll never win the championship. Well look at that, you're beginning to smile. You're so serious, my son. Everything's so bottled up inside you. You have to let yourself fall apart a little. That's the only way you can make yourself whole again.

Don't let him be too serious, Inbar, he said to her, then bent down and kissed her on both cheeks. He even smelled a little like Dori.

She got into the van, anxious to feel the warmth of the heater, and again wondered how he could have been so friendly to her for those two days when he knew that Dori had a wife and a child. And she thought: He acts as if he'd envisioned me, as if I were Neuland.

*

She saw them through the window, Dori and his father, standing facing each other for a few more seconds in the light of the streetlamp, in the lashing wind, as if, in another minute, they'd hug.

Finally, there was a brief, almost hostile handshake. Dori turned and got into the van. His father turned and headed back into Neuland, the sign 'Man, you are my brother' lighting his way, his stooped, sad shoulders rocking from side to side.

Inbar and Dori

They had one more moment of choice, at the airport in Buenos Aires.

Alfredo had arranged plane tickets for them. One phone call on the road from Victorcito, and he'd pulled a few strings to get them adjoining seats.

There was no commotion near the El Al counter. People weren't crowding around the attendants pleading to return to war-torn Israel. But there was an air of suppressed tension. In so many Israelis all at once. In the chirping of their phones. In the sweat stains under their arms. In the deep worry lines between their eyebrows.

Wounded, she said to Dori. Just like your father said.

Wounded, he had to agree.

After passport control, they split up to buy presents in the duty-free shop. He bought make-up and toiletries for Roni and lots of chocolate and toys for Netta. She bought toiletries for Eitan and lots of chocolates and toys for Reuven (even though she wasn't sure they'd come from Australia now that there was war).

He went to the loos and saw in the mirror that he had less grey hair, and thought, this can't be, there's no such thing as hair getting darker.

She went to the loos and saw in the mirror that she had spots on her face, the kind she used to get as a teenager, before she started sleeping with boys, and thought, it's incredible that we didn't sleep together in the end.

He called home and asked to speak to Netta. I'll be home soon, he told him, I'll be home soon. I have a present from Grandpa for you.

She took out her phone to call Eitan, and held it to her heart for a long time before she finally just sent him a message.

She met up with Dori again at the gate. They were each carrying sealed bags.

Shall we board? he asked.

I like to wait till the last minute, she said. And sat down. You can get on if you want.

He sat down next to her, put his bags on the ground between his legs and took her hand.

Together they watched the long, crowded line of passengers grow smaller. Until only the two of them were left sitting there.

Inbar – he stood up – you'll miss your flight.

I know, she said with a smile, and remained seated. She opened her arms and wondered if he knew it was a reference to *Before Sunset*, if he knew that in the film Julie Delpy is the one who says to Ethan Hawke, married with a child, that he'll miss his flight home, and he was the one who said I know and spread his arms across the back of the sofa in her apartment in Paris.

Come on. Dori held out his hand to her.

She took it and pulled him lightly towards her.

For a brief moment, they pulled each other in opposite directions, until she gave in and stood up. And went with him.

Nessia

She remained in Neuland and waited for the Wandering Jew, Jamili, to ride back from the villages on his horse.

Hi, Ness, he said when he saw her. Hi, she replied, and they rode to his room and took off each other's boots and lay down

And had sex

And had sex

And had sex

Because how much of that sexual tension could they stand.

After the post-coital cigarette, he asked: Will you ride with me, even without a horse? And she said: Of course. Then he pointed out: I haven't said where. She smiled and said: I don't care.

They stopped speaking in rhyme, then packed and moved forward to a different place in a different time. A couple of Jews, wandering.

Inbar and Dori

Didn't speak much during the long flight. After take-off, over Buenos Aires, they were still intertwined. Hands, fingers. Then the flight attendants handed out yesterday's newspapers with pictures of the war. Inbar recognised a few of the destroyed buildings in Haifa. She knew them well, and it gave her the chills. Dori looked at the long convoys of reservists moving north, and calculated how much time he could allow himself to stay at home before he reported to his unit. He at least needed to see Netta, whom he suddenly adored so much that it hurt. He had to hug him, play Taki with him, make up for staying away so long, for enjoying the break from him, for feeling more relaxed without him. But maybe he should go directly to his unit to avoid making it even worse for him with another departure. Fuck it. Who knows what the right thing to do is? This parenthood thing was so complicated, and he'd taken three weeks' unpaid leave from it.

Unaware that they were doing it, he and Inbar had disentwined their hands, lowered the armrest that separated their seats and sunk into their own worries. Then the film was shown – *Saving Private Ryan*, of all the films in the world, as if the war at home wasn't enough. They took off their earphones a few minutes after the screening began. She fell asleep on his shoulder. That, yes. And he turned his head to hers. But more out of the exhaustion of an amusement park operator at the end of a day than out of a desire for closeness.

When he fell asleep over the Atlantic, he had a nightmare: A miniature olive tree was growing on the left side of Netta's chest and he didn't know what to do. After all, you can't let a child go to nursery like that, with a miniature olive tree stuck in his chest. But on the other hand, if he wrenched the tree out of his small chest, who could guarantee that his skin and his heart wouldn't come out with it? In panic, he rifled the medicine chest for a cure to treat miniature olive trees growing on chests, and couldn't find one, damn it, he couldn't find one . . .

*

Eitan would be waiting for her outside, Inbar told him after they collected their luggage from the carousel at Ben Gurion. In their family, there's no such thing as someone going home from the airport on their own.

So should we say goodbye now? he asked.

People on both sides of them were walking towards the exit, one hand on their trolley, the other holding a phone. On both sides of them, battalions of shoes streamed forward, and they, like in that first café in Tumbes, were stuck in the middle. Like an island.

Yes, let's say goodbye now, she said with a nod. Then she stood on tiptoe and gave him a quick kiss on the mouth.

I had to, she said. And he, slightly surprised at first, pulled himself together, slipped his hands under her arms, held her by the waist, pulled her towards him and kissed her again, a longer kiss this time. She ran her fingers through his hair and they moved together, holding whatever could be held so they wouldn't fall — neck, waist, legs — opening their eyes and closing them again to dive into another kiss, tongue crashing against tongue, tongue winding around tongue, hands clutching flesh, in the middle of the airport. After so many opportunitites to do this privately, it happened in the middle of the airport, in front of all the policemen and passengers. They trembled from their tail bones to the tips of their hair, at the same second, and stopped for a moment to breathe. Everything was so new, like a new country. He stroked her hair, moved a few locks to his nose and sniffed. She kissed his Adam's apple, then planted small kisses down to the bottom of his neck, then back up to his ears. You do know that . . . don't you? she pants, and he nods, I know. Then they just stand there, pressed up against each other, pressed so close together that all the parts of their body are touching, transmitting all the things they hadn't been able to say throughout the entire distance they'd travelled together to Neuland. The last passengers, the ones whose suitcases hadn't appeared, had already reported to the lost property desk, and they were still pressed together, hearts beating against one another, until some rough-voiced money changer shouted at them from his stall, what's with you two anyway, don't you have a home?!

*

They move away from each other. Slowly. Heads, necks, then stomach and pelvis.

They hold hands a bit longer, fingers a bit longer — and then they too fall.

And they stand facing each other. Without touching. Trembling all over.

I don't even have your phone number or email address, she says.

A muscle of withdrawal twitches in his cheek. And before he can say it, she says: Maybe it's better that way.

He reconciles himself to it — why give ourselves pain — and adds: You go out first. I'll wait here a little while longer. And he gives her a brief kiss that is already sending her away.

She turns away from him, clutches her trolley so she won't fall, and walks alone towards the exit on the green customs line, the one for people who have nothing to declare. And cries. Finally cries for the first time in five years, the first time since Yoavi, and not a few random tears that drip from her eyes to her cheeks, but a real cascade, an Iguazu of tears. Some of them fall on to her bags, some on to the linoleum floor, and some into her mouth, and she drinks them as she walks slowly past the customs officers to the arrivals hall and to Eitán, who's standing there, as expected, with a heart-shaped balloon, at the front of all the people waiting. The moment her tear-filled eyes meet his bright ones, he runs over and hugs her with one hand because the other is holding the balloon, and says: Don't cry, sweetie. You're home. Everything will be fine now.

Grandma Lily

And then, one morning, when Hana was five, Pima crossed the line that separated dream from reality, and knocked on their door. Hana was at nursery school. Natan was working in the Dead Sea Industries at the time and came home once every two weeks. She was the age Inbar is now, thirty, maybe a bit more.

What was she wearing that day? Had she had a premonition that made her dab perfume on her neck that morning?

She's sitting on her memory chair now, facing the window at a certain angle, and the fan is turned up to the second speed, not the first or third. She has a glass of tea in her hand, the normal kind, not any of those new brands with the ridiculous names.

She wants to get the details of that morning exactly right. That morning, she suddenly realises, is the reason for making this entire journey. All the memories from the ship and the kibbutz that she's immersed herself in over the last few weeks were only steps meant to lead her to that morning. After all, that morning, more than any other moment, was the crossroads of her life.

She takes a small sip of tea and closes her eyes. And then there's a knock at the door. For a second or two, she's confused – was that really a knock at the door or am I just remembering?

But then the knock turns into stronger, louder knocks that turn into pounding, and then – all the walls of the house shake. The portrait of her that Natan painted falls to the floor and the glass shatters. Reluctantly, she gets up from her memory chair, sweeps up the broken glass, and throws it into the dustbin. She turns on the TV as she works. 'A rocket attack on Haifa' is written across the red strip on the bottom of the screen. Then the phone calls begin, and the neighbours come to take her to the shelter, which smells like wet animal fur. Then Hana calls to say that she's getting on a plane, and where's Inbar? Then Hana lands in her apartment, without her Nazi. Bruto? Bruno? And where's Inbar? Then Hana talks to someone named Eitan on the phone. Suddenly, she doesn't remember who Eitan is. Hana says they'll go to stay with him until it's safe. Then Inbar calls and says she's coming back too, and she's too ashamed to ask Hana where Inbar is, because she's supposed to know that. As they're about to go down to the car, she says to Hana, I want to take that chair, and points to her memory chair. Hana says, there's no room in the car. Then another rocket lands nearby, tearing her eardrum. She feels as if her memories are dripping out, getting lost, through that tear, and she insists – without the chair, she knows, she won't be able to go back to that crucial morning – and Hana says okay, she has no time to argue with her because any minute now, another rocket might land. So they push the chair into the back seat, one of the legs thrust forward between them, and drive down the mountain, crawling along in the huge traffic jam of cars escaping the city.

Altneuland

Dori

SINCE HE CAME BACK, HE'S BEEN AN OUTSIDER IN HIS life.

One Dori does everything he did before he left. But another Dori observes it all from the sidelines. Which makes him suddenly notice many things.

How beautiful Roni is, for example. Not your ordinary beautiful, but head-turning beautiful. And how unhappy she is with him. How even her rare smiles have a line of bitterness. And how they no longer talk. That is, they talk, but the path of their conversations always moves towards a clash.

Exactly like her parents, who came from the kibbutz to stay with them when the war started, and have taken over the apartment. He's always thought they were tough with each other, but now he sees that there is a certain difference between them: her father is tough with her mother, but loves her. Her mother is tough with her father, and doesn't love him.

What is love? Hard to say. The desire to do the best for another person? He loves Netta with all his heart. Since he's been home, the time he spends with him is the only time he doesn't feel like an outsider. So why is it that the best thing he's ever done for him was to go away?

There's no denying it, something about the boy's exhausting neediness has faded. And something in his eyes is shining. He spends every morning with him now. He doesn't take him to nursery until one o'clock, and before that they're in 'Daddy Camp', as Netta calls it. They play memory games, make up stories together, go to the market and the Biblical Zoo. Netta has finally grown out of drinking formula, so he can eat hummus with him, and Dori can teach him how to use the pitta bread to pick up the hummus like a spoon, with a twist of the wrist. He orders grape juice and a straw for Netta so that the piece dipped in hummus can slip down his throat. Then he sits on a bench with him, arms spread to the sides, and make up riddles. What's the opposite of far? Near. What's the opposite of bad? Good. What doesn't belong in this list: sitting room, bathroom, bedroom, street?

And in all the time they've spent together, the boy hasn't had a meltdown. Neither does he cling to him. He's drawn a line between them that Dori has never been able to draw himself. Or maybe hasn't wanted to draw.

But perhaps that isn't it at all, perhaps something else has brought about the change in him, something that even the Dori observing from the sidelines can't see.

*

When he comes home after dropping off Netta at nursery — without any heartbreaking sobs; the child just walks inside and says, it's okay, Daddy, you can go — Iska, Roni's mother, is waiting for him at the door to remind him of his list of chores for the day: do the laundry, fold the laundry, make a large salad for dinner. And the radio's on constantly, so they can make sure that no rockets have been fired on Jerusalem.

I don't think that'll happen, he says. There are too many holy places here.

You never know, Iska says firmly.

Then she complains about the way he's folding the laundry — not like that! — and shows him how it's done. Sleeve, sleeve, fold, fold. Sleeve, sleeve, fold, fold, she sings in her deep voice, and he stifles a smile.

So, I hear that your father's a bit bonkers, she says as she keeps folding.

Bonkers? I don't know. Maybe he just . . . changed.

Changed? she says with a chuckle, spraying a bit of saliva. People our age don't change. Look at Ephraim. For fifty years, he's been having an afternoon nap. Goes to sleep at 1.30 and gets up at three. Like a clock. And he does the same thing here. What do you say about that?

Dori doesn't know what to say about that.

It's a shame, Iska says, a handsome man like your father.

It's not exactly a shame, Dori thinks, it's more complicated than that. What he's trying to do there is naïve, naïve and sometimes puzzling, but at least he's trying to do *something*. He wants to explain Neuland, and his father in Neuland, to Isaka, but for the last few weeks every time he's tried to explain Neuland to people he's come up against questioning, almost admonishing glances: There's a war on. We have to win it. Do we really need to hear about South America now?

He hasn't even really told Roni about Neuland.

His first night back in Israel, they made love, and while they were doing it, he couldn't stop thinking about Avivit, of all the women in the world, Avivit, his youth group leader from school. That wasn't something he liked doing – sleeping with one woman and thinking about another. During sex, his screen is usually clear of thoughts, and this time he tried to go through the motions too, but suddenly he had a momentary vision of the clubhouse on Hankin Street, where Avivit had asked him to come to organise a timetable for the summer camp. When he arrived, there was no one else there, and she said, I saw what you sprayed on the outside wall, LOVE HAS NO RULES. I'm sorry, he said, I'll clean it up tomorrow. You're completely mad, Dori, she said, then put her hand under his shirt and touched his stomach . . .

As he kissed Roni's stomach, Grandpa Pima came into his

head too, and said, it's not good to live with one woman when you have another one in your heart—

Then Roni grabbed him by the hair, which had grown long on the trip, pulled him up, took him by the chin, as if he were a rebellious child, and said – what's going on? Is everything okay? Are you here? He avoided her penetrating green eyes and said, yes, just a bit worried about reporting to the unit tomorrow. Tomorrow is tomorrow, she said, and bit him under the Adam's apple, on the spot only she knew about, and he abandoned himself to her. Despite everything, something here still clearly worked on him. Despite everything, she was so deeply imprinted on so many places in his soul—

When they'd come, with their usual time gap, they lay beside each other and she told him at length about how wonderful it had been for her to be with Netta while he was away, and how good it was that the other children wanted to play with him – and he asked her if she wanted to hear about Neuland.

Yes, she said, but not now. I'm exhausted. Tomorrow, okay?

The next day, he waited for her to ask, and thought, maybe telling her will bridge this gap between us. But she didn't ask. Nor did she ask on the days that followed. At first, it puzzled him. Then it angered him. And then, it sent him to the computer to torment himself with emails to Inbar, emails that grew longer and longer.

*

After putting away the clean laundry according to Iska's instructions, he turns on the computer, hoping and not hoping to see inbarbenbinisti in his inbox again.

Seeing her name in his inbox fills him with joy that has a kernel of sadness. Seeing her name in his inbox fills him with yearning that has a kernel of fear. Seeing her name in his inbox, he feels the taste of her in his mouth, when they kissed at the airport.

But he hasn't seen her name in his inbox for more than a week now. She's not writing to him. They agreed on that in the last email. *We don't write, but we meet after the war, near the Western Wall.* But since when does she stick to agreements? And who can he talk to about Neuland, if not her?

One day, he breaks down, and writes to her: *Funny. I only want the war to end so we can finally see each other again.* And hesitates before sending it. He has so much to lose. Everything he has, in fact. So he decides not to decide, but to wait for night-time, when everyone goes to bed and his mind is clear.

Lily

Pima knocked on the door at 10.35 in the morning. Now, after Inbar has left the room and the tea is on the side table and she's in Eitan's apartment, far from the range of the rockets, she manages to raise the image of the clock from the depths of her memory: the small hand is between ten and eleven. The long hand is pointing to seven. And then – a knock at the door.

It was a few months after the war had ended, and the survivors had drifted out of the camps and the forests and made their way to the shores of Israel. Or the shores of Cyprus, and from there to the shores of Israel. At that point, she already knew almost for certain that her entire family tree had been felled during the first months of the war, and doubt had stopped eating away at her insides. Nonetheless, when she walked down the street, her heart would pound at the sight of short, stout men who reminded her of her father, and at the sight of women whose profiles reminded her of her sisters. And every time there was a knock at the door, she went to answer it, filled with a baseless, illogical hope that a miracle had occurred, and on the other side of it—

(Not only Lily. There were thousands like her – not suntanned sabras or pale survivors, but a kind of cross-breed of people, a mixture that didn't even have a name, because what could you call them: second-hand survivors?)

She looked through the peephole. Pima.

Standing there was Pima, from the other past.

For six years, she'd only seen him in her dreams. And here he was, in the flesh. In those six years, she'd given birth to her daughter and called her Hana, after her little sister. She and Natan had bought their first apartment, in Haifa. Three days a week, she worked for the council as an advisor to families in crisis. She'd gone back to being a little bit of Lily Freud, just from 8.30 to 12.30, so she could take Hana home from nursery.

She could pretend that she was at work now, she thought. And the *musicant* would go away.

He knocked again. This time, with a bit of musicality: tam-ta tam-ta, ta ta ta ta tam.

Let me in, he said. I know you're there, Lily. I can smell you through the door.

The nerve of him, she thought, he always had a lot of nerve. And opened the door.

He's grown ugly. That was her first thought. Back then he hadn't been very handsome, but now he was even less so. And he was balder than before, if such a thing were possible. And his forehead was full of wrinkles.

You're more beautiful than I remembered, he said, and brushed her cheek with his hand, making her blush.

And you less so, she thought.

Aren't you going to invite me in, he said with a laugh. Give me something to drink? I see you left your manners in Poland, Lily.

No one had teased her like that, not for six years. Natan wasn't given to teasing, Hana still hadn't developed her teasing skills, and at work, all her colleagues were humourless.

How many sugars? she asked as she went to the kitchen to make him coffee. He followed her, his glance burning her bottom, just as it had back then, on the ship.

Three teaspoons, please.

Three?

Life is short, he said.

They waited in silence for the kettle to whistle. She – staring down at her shoes, he – staring at her.

Would you like me to show you around the apartment? she asked. Anything to stop standing there awkwardly.

Why not, he said with a smile, why not.

She showed him the bathroom. Her and Natan's bedroom, the bed unmade. The window that overlooked Haifa bay. The spare room. Our little girl sleeps there. We open that for her, she said, pointing to a folding bed.

He smiled.

You know that we have a daughter? she asked.

I do, he said, still smiling.

Why is he constantly smiling, she thought angrily. No one had made her this angry in six years.

I have a son, he said. The same age as your Hana. Almost five.

The whistle of the kettle brought them back to the kitchen. How does he know how old Hana is? She shuddered.

She poured him coffee, accidentally spilling some on the table. She wiped it up quickly with a cloth, trying to draw confidence from the precise movements: She has a home. Swish. She has a husband and a child. Swish. No one can unsettle her now. Swish swish.

So what brings you here? She asked him the question she always asked her clients.

I was in the neighbourhood, so I thought I'd come and

see you, that's all. We have a performance in Haifa tonight – he went on to give her the details when he saw the scepticism in her eyes——

You still play, she asked.

Yes.

You can make a living from it?

No.

So how *do* you make a living?

I don't. This is a country that throws its musicians to the wolves.

Pima averted his gaze for a moment, and she took the opportunity to observe him. Under his smiles, something had slumped. His shoulders slumped, his nose slumped, even his Adam's apple was less defiant, as if it had sunk in shame into his neck.

Against her will, she felt her heart come undone at the sight of how dejected he was, and a thin thread reached out from her to him.

I'm thinking of leaving, he said.

Leaving? What do you mean, leaving?

To go to America. Artists have a future there. Everything is going up in flames here, Lily. Remember Aharon? The one who drummed with forks? He joined the Brigade, was killed in El Alamein. And Giora, the violinist? Who used to raise his foot when he bowed? Killed by sniper bullets in Birya. And it's not going to get better, Lily. It's just going to get worse. They don't want us here, our neighbours. We'll have to face them with drawn swords for ever, and anyone who always has a sword in his hand can't play music, or write, or love.

Lily was silent. She didn't know what to say.

We should have gone to Uganda, he went on. Or Argentina. Or we just should have kept wandering from place to place. That way, we wouldn't arouse such hatred. Instead, we insisted on this bad old country where everything is burned by the blazing sun.

Where too many eyes of too many religions are focused on us. Where the acoustics are, let's face it, unbearable. How can a sound reach your ears properly when there's so much tension in the air?

So you came to say goodbye to me before you left, she interrupted his speech — is that why you came, Pima?

No, he said. I came to take you with me.

Hana

The nights are silent. Yossi, his wife and their child have gone back to Australia. Her mother goes to sleep. Eitan's mother goes to sleep. Eitan's teenage brothers laugh together on the closed balcony until he goes out and silences them with a cross word, then comes back to join her in front of the TV. Together, they watch scenes of the war in silence. He knows her views (territory is death). She knows his views (territory is life). And neither one is interested in opening an internal front. So she sits with her bad ear closest to him and they don't speak. Every once in a while, there's a picture of a boy in uniform, and the words, 'the funeral will take place tomorrow', and her heart bleeds with longing for Yoavi. She lets the longing flow freely for a few minutes because she's already learned that there's no point in fighting the first, powerful wave. Only later does she remind herself that she's here, in this ghetto called the State of Israel, for a limited time only. She has a nice house and nice furnishings and a nice man in another, saner place.

After the final news broadcast, and before the final, final broadcast, Eitan goes to his room. He has to get up for work tomorrow. Although there's been a drop in orders from the central area of the country, he explained to her, in the north, people need to replace their broken light fittings, and they seem to be upgrading while they're at it. He gives them a good deal. Of course he does. A special price for northern residents. We're all brothers, after all. This time it's them, and the next time, the rockets might rain down on us.

On the way to the bedroom, he pauses at the computer, where Inbar's sitting. Are you coming to bed? he asks her every night.

In a minute, she tells him. Every night. Without raising her eyes from the screen.

Should I make you some coffee? she asks Inbar after he's gone to the bedroom and closed the door behind him.

Only if you have some too, she replies.

She adds an Oreo cookie to the saucer – one, the way her little girl likes it – and places the coffee and cookie carefully on the desk, far enough away from the keyboard.

Are you still writing what you started to write on the trip? she asks one night, unable to restrain herself.

You might say so, her daughter answers, and smiles, hiding something.

There was a time when she persisted until she found out what she wanted to know. Maybe she might even have peeked at the screen. Not now. A new, silent understanding has grown between them. Not closeness, just understanding. And she doesn't want to ruin it. So instead, she turns on her own computer, writes to Bruno about how much she misses him and reads about how much he misses her.

If you don't come back, I'll come to you.

I'll come back, she promises. *This place reminds me of too many things I want to forget.*

It's strange eating alone, he writes.

It's strange sleeping alone, she writes.

So come home, my Hana, now. I'll send you a plane ticket, he writes.

But my mother, she writes.

When they finish emailing, she opens her dissertation and rereads the chapter on the Wandering Jew, which is already finished, and thinks: Maybe I should write an addendum about the Jews who cause other people to wander. After all, when we finally stopped wandering, we drove others out of their villages. Destroyed their homes with non-smart bombs.

That's another dissertation, she tells herself, and goes back to work on the last few lines she wrote in a café:

I believe that the legend of the Wandering Jew existed, exists, and will continue to exist, not only as a result of the historical rift between Judaism and Christianity, or the anti-Semitism that is so deeply rooted in European culture, but as a result of human longing – a longing underpinned by fear, of course – to leave the permanent residence and move to another, better place, to believe that the repetitious, daily routine is not the only possibility. Can it be that the Jews' tendency to wander in order to 'escape the famine' is really stronger? Or have they been compelled to fulfil time and time again the human desire to wander, even though they have tired of it? This dissertation—

Esther! her mother calls her. Even though she already knows that when her mother calls out Esther, she means her, there's still something hurtful about it. What's wrong, Ma? She goes to her room, annoyed by the interruption. Can you bring me a cup of tea? her mother asks. It's two o'clock in the morning, Ma, not teatime. Okay, her mother says, then I'll make it myself. No, Ma, she pleads. The last time Lily went to 'make it herself' she left the apartment and got lost in the streets of the city. Two kind-hearted young men – one painfully resembled Yoavi – found a notebook with phone numbers that she had on her and called.

She'll make her some tea. She won't be able to concentrate on writing now anyway. The apartment breathes soundlessly.

Even Inbar has turned off her computer and gone to sleep. Only Air Force planes thundering their way north, and she and her old mother are awake.

She brings the tea to her bed. Her hand is steady, to keep from spilling the hot liquid.

You know, Esther — her mother says — in the end, he came to see me.

She doesn't have to ask who.

He knocked on the door of the apartment we had in Neveh Sha'anan, Esther, you know, the one with the dried-up garden, and asked me to go to America with him. You heard me. Without the children, he said to me. Just you and me. And I told him, with all due respect, I won't leave my daughter. If you'd come before Hana, maybe I would have agreed to listen to you. But that little girl is my homeland. That's what I told him, Esther.

I'm not Esther, and it's too late now, Ma, she says, tears spilling. She puts her hand on her mother's trembling hand. We'll tell each other our dreams tomorrow morning, okay?

That's not a dream, Esther, her mother protests weakly. But her eyes are already closed.

Lily

She laughed, like Sarah did when the angels came to tell her she would give birth to a son.

Yesterday, she couldn't remember how she'd responded to Pima's offer to take her to America with him. There was a sudden power cut in her brain, and all the details flowed out of her like water through a fork. This morning, she asked Inbar to turn the fan up to the fourth speed. After all, this was Tel Aviv. In July. And slowly, the details returned, and along with them, the memory of her laughter.

Why are you laughing, Lily, Pima had asked her then, a tinge of disappointment in his voice.

Because . . . how can I say this delicately . . . you're a little late, Pima. Even if I wanted to go to America with you – and I'm not saying I do – I have a little girl. I can't leave her here.

But she's daddy's little girl in any case.

What do you mean? How do you know that?

I've been watching you. I left home a week ago. When we argue, my wife always says, go, go to your Lily if you want to. So I left. I took only a small bag with me. And my harmonica. I've rented an apartment in Hadar, and every morning I climb up here and watch you. That little girl's duet with her father. And there's a dissonance between you and her. In the threesome, you're the one who's left out.

Lily was silent. Somewhere beneath her efforts at self-persuasion, she knew that everything he said was true.

When the angel came down from the heavens and announced which people would be paired off, Lily – Pima continued, encouraged by her silence – he announced our names together. And instead of listening to him, we've been torturing ourselves. For six years.

So where were you six years ago, Pima – her voice cracked – why haven't you come till now?

Because I was young and stupid then. I thought that what we had was something that happens every day.

*

And that was her absolutely final moment of choice.

Pima leaned back in his chair as if to say: Look, I've put

my offer on the table, and now you have to decide what to do with it.

She knew he wouldn't ask her again. But she also knew how much courage he needed — anyone needed — to put himself on the line like this. So many people want to leave, escape, flee, ask the forbidden question, take apart and put together, delete and start fresh —

Very few actually do.

Part of her wanted to say yes. Of course. Part of her screamed to be one of the few who dare. But the cuckoo burst out of the clock and announced: Twelve. In half an hour, she had to pick up Hana. And Natan was at the Dead Sea. If she didn't pick her up, or was late, the child would stand and wait alone at the gate.

I can't, she finally told Pima. She could have said: I don't want to. But she chose to say: I can't. And maybe we're inclined to exaggerate the distance between those two no's.

That little girl, she said to Pima, is my homeland. She drives me mad, it's true. But that doesn't mean she's not my homeland. I carried her in my womb. You men can't understand that. How can I explain it to you? Too much time has passed, Pima. Too many things tie me to this place. And I've already passed the point of no return.

Pima's shoulders sagged. Castles crumbled in his eyes, then collapsed. His chin doubled all at once. His Adam's apple disappeared as if it had never existed.

She remembered how he'd once stood on the deck, dog-tired after a terrible storm, and accused the sea of anti-Semitism.

And once again, as it had been then, her heart unravelled for him, thread by thread.

She looked at the clock again. Twenty-five more minutes.

Nonetheless, she smiled, stroked his cheek and said, if you've already taken the trouble to come all the way here . . .

She stood up. And unbuttoned her blouse. And thought

– even dreams need to be fed by reality sometimes, or else they fade – moved closer to him, till they were a breath away from each other, and said: We have twenty-five minutes, *musicant*. Are you still as quick as you used to be?

Inbar

Her grandmother, taking advantage of the fact that all the residents of the apartment had gathered to watch Nasrallah give another speech on TV, opened the door surreptitiously and went out to the street. It took them half an hour, maybe more, to realise that her room was empty. After they discovered, to their horror, that she wasn't anywhere in the immediate vicinity of the building, they split up – without plan or order – to search (where's Alfredo when you need him? Inbar thought).

Eitan's brothers set off southward. Eitan rode his bike east, towards the Hatikva quarter. Her mother headed for the sea, and she again checked out the relatively close area. Shoken Street. Herzl. Salame. And northwards.

The only passers-by were local foreign workers, Nepalis, Senegalese, all very young. Too young. Have you by any chance seen an old lady? she asked them in Hebrew. Then in English. Then in Spanish. *Una abuela vieja*, she said, the language of her journey rolling off her tongue.

Sí, they replied, they had. She was going in this direction. That direction. No, this way. No, that way.

Maybe – Inbar began to suspect – there are dozens of refugee grandmothers wandering around the city at any given time?

Then, to be more specific, she added: She's short. A full head of grey hair. She's wearing a dress and white trainers. We're very concerned about her because she may not remember the way home.

Now the passers-by were less sure that they'd seen her.

If I don't find her in another couple of minutes, she thought, I'll call Dori. I helped him find his father, so he can help me find my grandmother.

Early evening. She can hear news of the war blaring from the windows of the houses. And also: an argument between father and son, an electric drill, a pop song and, again, news of the war. 'One hundred and seventy new immigrants have arrived in Israel since the war began.' Incredible. How bad does it have to get here for immigration to stop? 'A sheep named Lilush crossed the border into Lebanon and hasn't come back.' Poor thing. A Katyusha probably landed on her. 'A resident of Nahariya fleeing a rocket attack fell and broke his back.' Did they write those rhymes in advance? 'A million dollar donation from the American Jews for building shelters.' Thanks a lot, really.

For a few weeks now, Inbar has barely left the building, which has become a shelter, and now her steps, hesitant at first, become firmer and more urgent as she walks. She peers into front gardens. Maybe her grandmother misses the Carmel so much that she's resting under a tree. Maybe she had an irresistible urge to urinate as she did once, when they were on a bus going from Haifa to Jerusalem and she demanded, unembarrassed, that the driver stop at the side of the road, where she got off, crouched, and peed behind a bus stop.

Her mother calls: Have you found her? Not yet. You'll let me know if you do?

Dori will come, she thinks. Of course he'll come if I call him. It'll take him an hour, an hour and a quarter to get here from Jerusalem. Will he kiss me when he sees me? On the cheek? On the mouth? Will I have the courage to reach out and straighten his hair? And what if he doesn't come, she asks herself sadly, if he finds an excuse: My son. I have to take my son to nursery, have to pick up my son from nursery, have to take my son to the doctor because he has a fever. What then? And why doesn't he write to me? I loved reading his emails so much. True, we decided not to write any more, and to meet after the war, but I was sure he wouldn't be able to hold out.

She passes a building site. The fence around it is covered with red posters advertising a performance of Depeche Mode. The posters are still there, even though the gig was cancelled. 'Dear Traffic Warden,' a note on the windscreen of a blue Mitsubishi says, 'I ran away from Haifa last night and am staying here with my friends. Please be kind.' An ambulance passes, siren wailing. Hey wait, maybe her grandmother's inside that ambulance? Maybe her old heart couldn't take the effort of walking and she collapsed in the middle of the street?

Not yet, Grandma, not yet. Tears well up (since the dam burst in the airport, she cries once a day. At least). Don't disappear on me now, I'm not ready to say goodbye to you yet. There's something I have to tell you. Don't disappear on me now, Grams. Without you . . . please . . . without you . . . I love . . . without you, how can I turn the question marks inside me into exclamation points . . .

Dori

All the fathers except him and Arnon Strozman are holding video cameras. Arnon Strozman's ex-wife hasn't spoken to him since their divorce, and she comes to events at the nursery with her tall boyfriend, who holds the video camera and films the boy as if he's his son and not Arnon Strozman's. Even though the boy barely looks in his direction, Arnon Strozman continues to come to all the events dressed like a groom on his wedding day, and he always stands slightly to the side, a bit separate from everyone. Without a camera.

Today he's standing next to Dori, who isn't holding a video camera because he doesn't like taking pictures. He doesn't like to feel a barrier between him and Netta. And he doesn't want any barriers, especially now, because as it is, he's been feeling cut off from him since his return. How nice of you, Roni hisses at him in the sarcastic tone she's adopted these last few days, how really nice of you to land me with the camera. It wouldn't be a tragedy not to film this, he wants to say. But remains silent. They argued at home, before they left. And they argued in the car, on the way. The words he was able to take almost in his stride at home, now became harder to bear. Maybe she felt the same. Anyway, he doesn't want another argument; certainly not in front of all the other parents.

The best-looking boy in the class is dancing now. And singing. And taking part in all the activities. This is the first time that the best-looking boy in the class has participated in all the activities. In the past, he used to press up against his father's legs, frightened, rejecting with a stubborn shake of his head every one of the teacher's and parents' attempts to coax him into joining the party.

Now he's dancing. A spin, applause, a spin, applause. And he even smiles at a freckled girl as he dances. Dori is amazed that he's like this, that the invisible barricade that had blocked him for so long is gone, but he also knows that maybe he himself was the invisible barricade that has been removed.

I'd like all the children to sit down now, the teacher says, we want to give out your end-of-year certificates. Netta suddenly breaks away from the group of children and runs over to him.

At least, that's what he thinks at first. But no – he runs to Roni. A huggie, he announces and jumps on her, saying the word in the diminutive form to reassure and send the message: This is just a short pit stop and he'll go back to being a good boy in a minute. Roni hands him the camera so she can hug Netta back, and he takes it – he has no choice – and looks through the eyepiece like all the other fathers. He sees his son go back to the group of children and sit down in the seat the freckled girl saved for him. Then he sees him get up when the teacher calls his name – close-up! Roni says. Press the green button for a close-up! – and he sees him walk lightly, confidently back to his seat, truly a different child, holding his certificate proudly, oozing health from every pore, looking over at his mother.

Roni drives. He looks through Netta's drawings. As they were leaving, they were given a folder of all the work Netta has done during the year, arranged chronologically. This is wonderful. Really wonderful, he says with sincere admiration. I can see how you progressed from one drawing to the next. And the colours – wow! How do you know which colours to use?

There are colours that look good next to each other and colours that don't.

Did the teacher tell you that?

No.

So who did?

No one. I feel it myself when the colours go together.

In one of the last pictures, there's a drawing entitled My Family. Did you see this? he asks Roni. Yes. He did it when you were away, she says.

In the family that Netta drew, there's a father and mother in the middle, and two children, one on either side of them. A child next to each parent.

Who's this family? he asks Netta cautiously, not wanting to analyse him. It's our family, he replies confidently. And who's this other boy? Dori asks. Netta doesn't answer. He opens and closes the electric windows. Is it your brother? Would you like to have a brother? No, Netta says, that's Netta. You? Yes, me. But this is you too, here, isn't it, on Mummy's right? Yes, that's

Netta too, he says. So why do you need another Netta? he asks. I don't know. Can I have another marshmallow, Daddy?

Whatever Mummy thinks, he says.

Whatever Daddy thinks, Roni says.

At home, they discover that Dori mistakenly pressed the wrong button on the camera and stopped the filming, so there was no record of Netta receiving his certificate, which drove Roni completely mad, but didn't have the slightest effect on him. What difference does it make? he asks her, it's burned into our memories anyway. She gives a long, loveless sigh, the way her mother always does with her father, and says, forget it, you don't understand. We don't understand each other any more.

Inbar

Finds her grandmother in a café in the Florentine quarter, behind a very clean window, the kind you don't see so you bang into headfirst. She's sitting at a table that faces the street. Her wrinkles are illuminated by the candle in the middle of the table. There's a glass of steaming liquid and a piece of what looks like cheesecake in front of her.

Inbar sends a calming text to everyone: Found Grandma. In a café. Looks fine. I'll sit with her for a while then bring her home.

She wipes away her tears with her sleeve, then goes inside.

Tsipke feuer, her grandmother says, smiling at her. How did you know I was here?

I didn't. We've been looking for you. We were worried about you.

Why should you worry about me? Soldiers are fighting in

Lebanon and you're worried about me? I can't listen to anything about that Nasrallah any more. That scum of the earth. So I went out for some air. This is quite a city you have here. Ugly as sin, but interesting. Sit down for a while, Inbar'ele. Why are you standing? A person should not drink alone.

She sits down.

Meet Julia, she says, pointing at the waitress. A lovely girl. Came to Israel from Belarus when she was seven. Studying psychology at the university. Wants to specialise in family counselling. She's paying for university herself. You must try their cheesecake, Inbar'ele. It's wonderful. And there's a discount for people from the north. Would you like me to order you a piece?

No thanks, Inbar says. I don't eat cake at this time of day.

That stupid diet again? Inbar'ele, you have a very good figure. The kind a woman should have. It's only those pretty boy designers who don't like that kind of woman. That's why they make clothes you can't wear.

Well, maybe I'll have a hot chocolate, Inbar says to the waitress. Two-thirds water and one-third milk. When the waitress is out of earshot, Inbar scolds her grandmother lovingly: Grams, you can't just leave the house without telling anyone. We almost called the police.

Yes, I know you're right, her grandmother says, stabbing her cake with a fork. But a person needs a change of scenery every once in a while. Even if she's old!

Her hot chocolate arrives. She drinks it and studies her grandmother. And then, as if her grandmother were the optical illusion that can be seen as both an old lady and a young girl, depending on your focus, she suddenly sees her as a twenty-one-year-old, on the train from Warsaw to the port of Constanţa. With her small, bursting suitcase. The first traveller in the family. If she hadn't had the courage to get up and leave, there wouldn't have been any other journeys. There wouldn't have been a home to leave.

So how is your lover, her grandmother asks after she finishes gathering the last of the cake crumbs with the tip of her finger.

What do you mean? You see him all the time. You're staying in his house—

Not Eitan, no. The one you write all those letters to on the computer. While you're typing, your neck gets all red.

*

Excited by her grandmother's ability to read her, she takes a deep breath and tells her about Dori. Everything. Where they met. How she joined him on his search. How their souls became intertwined. Even though they were both involved with other people. And he has a son. She had been sure it was because of the trip. That it would end when the trip was over. But that turned out not to be true. She tells her all the details, including the caramel taste of his lips at Ben Gurion airport. This is the first time she has told someone about Dori, and it makes it all more real. And more painful.

Her grandmother doesn't ask anything while she's speaking. She just listens, the thinnest of smiles on her lips.

And I still haven't told you the craziest thing, Grandma. He's Pima's grandson. His father is Pima's son. The Pima who was on the ship with you.

What Pima? her grandmother asks, her eyes vacant.

Pima, Inbar says in surprise. Pima from your dreams.

Her grandmother shakes her head.

Pima, with the bald head, Inbar says, pleading now. The *musicant*, Grandma. The one who was with you on the ship.

Sorry, her grandmother wrings her hands, I have no idea who you're talking about. Then she withdraws, as if withering, into herself. That's how it's been recently, it comes and goes, she says in apology and embarrassment, and touches her temples. That's how it's been recently, it comes and goes, she repeats, as if she's

598

forgotten that she just said exactly the same thing. Then she says, my father stood there with his karakul hat. He was short even with the hat on, short and nice-looking my father was, and I didn't go out to him. My father stood outside the hotel all night. I'm not sure he had an umbrella, and the rain there is not like here. The rain there is angry, and I didn't go out . . .

After a delay as long as the Diaspora, she adds in a trembling voice, there are short circuits in my brain, Inbari. Maybe you'll take your grandmother to be mended?

Florentine is full of people who fix things: shoemakers, carpenters, glaziers. Inbar strokes her grandmother's arm silently and thinks, we need one with a sign over his shop door that says 'Restores Lost Memories'.

Her mother calls. Everybody's waiting for them at home. When are they coming back?

Soon, Inbar promises. Soon.

The tables in the café fill up with people who can still remember. More and more candles are lit. The entire place suddenly looks like a house in mourning. And the candles like memorial candles.

The waitress comes to ask if everything's all right. Yes, she tells her. Though it isn't.

Her grandmother closes her eyes.

Are you tired, Grandma, she asks. Do you want to go?

The man you love, you said he has a son? She suddenly opens her eyes. As if all at once, the electricity has returned.

Yes, Inbar replies. Yes, he has a son. Four years old.

And he's close to his son? Because there are men who—

He's very close to him.

That's too bad for your heart. That man is only good as a third wheel, Inbari.

Third wheel?

It's what they called the third person they added to couples' apartments on the kibbutz.

So what does that mean? I don't understand.

Stay with him, Inbari. In your thoughts. In your imagination. In your dreams. Those are life too, not only what happens in reality, but also what could have happened.

But—

You think you're so special, *tsipke feuer*? Look around. Everyone sitting here in this café is also sitting in a different place now, in his mind, with someone else. Sitting beside every couple you see here is a third person that one of them is imagining. That one of them has to imagine in order to keep on sitting here. This Tel Aviv of yours — how could you stand it if you didn't imagine a different city, a more beautiful one, all the time? And what about our country? So many Jews living in one place, but in their minds, they have another place they came from and another place they want to run away to tomorrow. And that's a good thing, *tsipke feuer*, because imagining and thinking about wandering is the only way they can give up real wandering. And stay here.

But it's so hard . . . staying here, giving up, Inbar said, sighing a grandmother's sigh.

Staying is what takes courage. And you're not really giving up, Inbari. That's what I'm trying to tell you.

But I can't be satisfied with what you're telling me to do, Grandma. Imagining a kiss is not like a kiss. And I want a real kiss. From him. Lots of kisses. I want him, Grandma. Like I've never wanted anyone, ever.

Her grandmother is silent.

Inbar's eyes fill with anger. Why doesn't it ever work out, why is everything she wants always behind bars, why why why why why is it that every time she tries to correct a mistake she makes a bigger one.

She asks for the bill, pays and signs the receipt. She presses down too hard with the pen, and the paper tears. Dammit.

They leave the café and try to cross the street.

Bicycles pass them, then a rickshaw, then a car, before they can cross.

Write to him, her grandmother says.

What?

Write to that man of yours. You always wanted to write, didn't you?

*

Walking home, arm in arm with her grandmother, she's already composing the email she'll send Dori.

Everything is clear to her now — beginning, middle and end. She even chooses a nice quote to add, 'Somehow, I should have parted from you', from a Cortázar story whose characters are a man and woman who become involved with each other through the graffiti they draw on the walls of buildings in the city, 'and at the same time, ask you to continue. I should have left something for you before I returned to my den, of which nothing remains now but a hole to hide in until the end of the darkest darkness, and in it, remember so many things, and sometimes, as I imagine your life, I picture you making drawings, going out at night to make more drawings'.

And under the Cortázar quote — she decides as they cross Salame Street — she'll write From Inbar, with love. Because if she doesn't admit it now, then when?

And she'll sign it with a full stop (there is always a moment, she believes, when it is possible to put a full stop).

But when she opens her laptop that night, after the commotion made by all the war refugees who fill her house has died down, she sees that he's beat her to it.

He wants them to meet. After the war. To go to the Western Wall together and put a note in it.

He says that he can't stop thinking about her, and maybe if they really did see each other — only once, no more — it would help them release each other. And finally put an end to the journey.

*

She answers him, hesitating for a long while before she clicks the mouse: life and death hanging by a Send.

After all, she can bring Nessia back from her wanderings and send *her* to Jerusalem 'to finally put an end to the journey', so Dori can drive *her* crazy. Yes, she could easily send Nessia to Jerusalem in her place, and accompany her in her imagination until she reaches the WELCOME TO JERUSALEM sign at the entrance to the city, and from there, past the Convention Center to the Old City. All of that without moving from her chair. Without risking a broken heart. And yet, her finger clicks the mouse: Send.

> To: Dori
> From: Inbar
> We'll meet at five, after the war. At the Jaffa Gate. I'll be standing next to the bagel vendor, holding a book by Julio Cortázar.
>
> Send me your phone number and I'll send you mine, just to be on the safe side.
>
> Yours, Señorita Inbar.

602

Inbar and Dori.
Epilogue and Prologue

Death stands there in the background, but don't be afraid.
Hold the watch down with one hand, take the stem in two
fingers, and rotate it smoothly. Now another instalment of
time opens.

'Instructions on How to Wind a Watch', Julio Cortázar

Inbar

WHEN SHE WAS A GIRL, SHE USED TO PLAY A GAME
with herself on the road to Jerusalem: she tried to guess which
bend in the road would lead to the WELCOME TO JERUSALEM sign
at the entrance to the city. She always lost, always guessed one
or two bends before the real one. Since then, they've added a
traffic light next to Sakharov Gardens, and there's a new exit
off to the right, which takes you directly to French Hill. She
continues straight, betting on the bend just after the lights. But
she's wrong again, because it turns out that there's one more
bend before the WELCOME TO JERUSALEM. Once, her birthday fell
on a rare snowy day in November, and all the letters of the
sign were covered in white. It's summer now, but the air coming
through the window she opens is cool, and the Convention
Center traffic lights turn green for her, one after the other, and
the radio news broadcaster says that Lilush the sheep has come
home to Kibbutz Misgav Am after she'd gone missing on
the first day of the war. I never thought we'd see her again,
Nehama the shepherdess says. Then they report that Kibbutz
Manara has gone back to apple-picking, and describe the gradual
return of the troops and the lines of people asking for passports
at the Polish embassy —

*

Will there be somewhere to park at the Jaffa Gate? Inbar
wonders, and as if he'd heard her — on the same private

wavelength the two of them seem to have been broadcasting on since their return – Dori calls – his voice, it's his voice – and asks if she needs directions. Sort of, she says, trying not to sound too excited. They were just going to put notes in the Western Wall together, that's all. I know how to get there, but I don't know where to park, she says, and he explains – you can really tell that he's a teacher – turn left in Rehavia, and after you pass Terra Sancta and Independence Park, go straight on at the lights, towards the Wall, and then you'll see paid parking on the left. Great, she says, keeping herself from saying, I've missed you, keeping herself from telling him that she's broken up with Eitan. If you get lost, call me, he says, I'm here at the Gate already. Thank you, she says, and thinks, forget the thank you, take off your clothes. She follows his directions, parks and climbs a lot of steps from the car park, crosses the bridge over the river of cars, and sees him standing next to the bagel stand, wearing jeans, a red T-shirt and a new haircut. He gives her a little wave, and she stops herself from running to him, why should she run, after all, we're here to *really* liberate each other, that's what he said, so she walks normally, her steps liberated, liberating, but her toes stretch out towards him in her shoes, go! her big toe shouts, just a few more metres –

They hug briefly, disappointingly, and she thinks, this isn't Neuland, people know him here, that's the reason for this hug. Then she says in a too sprightly voice, you cut your hair, and reaches out daringly – why does she always have to be daring – and touches his head. Yes, he says. It suits you, she says, and he blushes and says, you too . . . I mean . . . that's the hat you wore when . . . I mean . . . you look good too. She pulls her shirt down slightly to deepen the neckline, and says, yes, Jerusalem does that to me. It's a beautiful day, he says. During the war, the air here was totally stagnant, and today, the wind started blowing at four. In Tel Aviv, the air's still stifling, she says, and thinks, since when do we talk about the weather? We never talked about the weather when we were there. Shall we start walking? he said, his voice slightly impatient, as if they were on a mission, and maybe that's how he thought of this meeting of theirs, another chore to tick off his list. Or maybe this is just how he is, not only when he's searching for his father, but always, terrifyingly goal-oriented. That's David's Tower, he says, pointing to the right. Yes, Dori, she says, I know, and he blushes again and says, of course . . . I just . . . I guide tours here sometimes, so I can chatter away about the things we pass here, and disguise the fact that I'm very excited to see you.

Okay, she laughs in relief, go for it.

They begin walking, and they're the old Dori and Inbar again. He tells her about David's luxurious palace, about the Armenian Quarter, and how the Wall was built. She listens to the melody of his voice more than to the actual content, only occasionally absorbing a word or two.

Wait, he says and stops. I haven't asked how your grandmother is. Not good, she tells him. We're moving her into a home tomorrow. Her house in Haifa was hit by a Grad, and it'll take time to rebuild it. And I can't have her in my place in Tel Aviv because I'm leaving it. Why, he asks. I broke up with Eitan, she says, and adds: yesterday. He takes a deep breath, as if he's just heard bad news, and asks, so where are you staying? For the time being, in the sitting room, she says, on the sofa. But I'm looking. Then, slightly embarrassed, because she hadn't planned to show all her cards so quickly, and for free, she adds: Let's keep walking. We still have a note to put in the Wall today, don't we?

They continue walking down to the Holy Basin, and coming up towards them are Palestinians in faded shirts, tourists with shining eyes, monks in ascetic robes, and ultra-Orthodox men with curly side locks. One of them, a young man, presses up against the wall so she can pass without, heaven forbid, brushing against him, and she has an urge to reach out and touch him, to say, *don't be afraid, the world is a narrow bridge, a very narrow bridge, and the main thing to remember is not to be afraid at all, but to take a flying leap off it when you have to* . . .

Come over here, there's a good observation point, Dori says, and the way he touches her back feels so good, the first touch. She follows him up the iron steps and stands on tiptoe. Through the cracks in the wall, they can see the Dome of the Rock, the Augusta Victoria Hospital, and the Hyatt Hotel, where Rehavam Ze'evi was murdered, of course she remembers, and there are the excavations, and down below, the Arab village of Silwan, where, before the Intifada, you could visit the Shiloah Pool. Yes, she says, she once went there through the tunnel with a torch. Who knows, he says, maybe we passed each other on the same day without knowing it, and she says, could be, and thinks, at least then, you were available.

And he, perhaps noticing her clouded expression, places his hand gently on her waist for a brief second and says, shall we move on? And they go back down the iron steps to the narrow street that leads to the Western Wall. A shoemaker who looks too young to be a shoemaker gestures for them to come into his shop, as if it were a fish restaurant, and only after they walk away from him does she realise that she knows him from somewhere, that young shoemaker. His eyes, his unkempt hair, wait a minute—

Jamili! she says out loud. And Dori says, what? That shoemaker, she says, that's the guy from Neuland! Dori says in surprise, how . . . what . . . but agrees to go back with her. But the shoemaker is no longer there, and the shop is locked with bars. Only Nessia, so Inbar imagines, is standing outside and saying, it's time, hold me close, make us one. So she embraces her and presses her to her heart and says to Dori, let's go, I must have been imagining—

Dori laughs, maybe you have a case of the Jerusalem Syndrome, and tells her about that fixation — it's actually included in the psychologists' book of mental illnesses, he says. Some of the people who come to Jerusalem for the first time go completely crazy. They start thinking that they're the Messiah. Sometimes you can see them on the streets, shaking a plastic cup. And the truth is that even though he was born here, he can understand it. There's something overwhelming about Jerusalem. I know, she says, this city always overwhelms me with love.

She immediately berates herself, Inbar Benbenisti, calm down with all this love business, and they keep walking, close to each other, almost but not quite touching, and after this bend . . .

We'll see the Western Wall, with all the grey, dry bushes protruding from between the stones. Even though she's been there many times, this is the first time she's able to picture it as a wall that's part of a whole building, one wall of a larger temple, so she asks Dori to remind her exactly how the Second Temple was destroyed. As they walk down the curving street leading to the Wall, he tells her about Titus' huge army rushing towards this place with their horses and torches. To this day, there's no consensus among historians about whether Titus was the one who gave the order to burn the Temple, or whether the torch-bearer threw his torch in the heat of battle.

Now they're standing at the entrance to the large area in front of the Wall, which has a barred gate along its entire length. They have to separate because there are different security checkpoints for men and women.

What's a separation of a few seconds for us, compared to a month, she thinks. Nonetheless, she's anxious to be back with him – her check is over before his, so she's the one waiting for him and can watch him walk towards her and remember the first time she met him on the roof in Tumbes.

Look, he says, rejoining her and drawing her attention to a plaque with a quote from Isaiah written on it, 'For my house shall be called a house of prayer for all peoples.' She's a bit surprised — so the Temple wasn't only for us? she asks. That's the thing with Judaism. Sometimes it opens up to the whole world, and sometimes it closes itself off to the world, shifting direction each time. By the way, she asks, have you heard anything from your father? He sighs and says, my sister's going to see him with the children in the holidays. He sent her plane tickets. I warned her that she wasn't going to see the father she knows, but she says she doesn't care, she needs to get away after this war—

Wow — she blurts out — look at all those people!

They're standing at the entrance to the open square in front of the Wall, and below them is a carpet of yellow hats and red umbrellas, cluster after cluster of tourists with cameras, and soldiers standing in groups of three.

A fair-skinned girl approaches and asks them to take a picture of her and her boyfriend. He's black. They put their arms around each other and smile broadly. She takes the picture and thinks, they must have had to overcome all kinds of obstacles in order to be together. Thank you, the girl says, and she gives her back the camera and asks Dori, is it always like this here, all these people?

Not this many.

Maybe it's because the war's over, and they've all come out of their holes.

Could be.

He takes a black yarmulke out of the pocket of his jeans, puts it on his head and says, it's Grandpa Pima's, and she says, Pima from the dreams. Yes, he smiles, and she walks to the men's entrance with him. He takes a folded note out of his pocket and says, look, nothing happened to it in the wash. A miracle, she says, then asks, have you read it? Of course not, he says, horrified by the idea, it's private! And she thinks, there's no way, no way, he's such a good, well-behaved little boy. And, as if picking up on her sudden despair, he strokes her cheek slowly, the third touch, and says, the first one finished waits for the other, okay? Okay, she says, and knows that, as usual, she'll be the one waiting for him.

He puts the note back into his pocket and walks away. She stands there for a few seconds, wondering where to take herself before she finally enters the women's section, despite its insulting smallness, and looks at the crowd of dark stockings and hats. There are so many women there with notes to put in the Wall that it's impossible to get close to it. Okay, she says to herself, as you're here, you might as well write something. But she doesn't have a pen, and even if she did, who would she write her request to . . .

There is no God, Grandma Lily always used to say. And if there was one, he died in the Holocaust. So what is there instead, Grandma? The clown of fate. What's a clown of fate, Grandma? A fellow with a well-developed sense of humour. And what does he look like? He wears a bow-tie. What colour bow-tie? I don't know, Inbari. What are all these questions today?

The girl who asked Inbar to take a picture of her and her black boyfriend earlier walks past her. Excuse me, she calls after her and asks if she has a pen and paper. Thanks. Just a minute, she says, takes a deep breath of mountain air, and with her heart burning —

To the fellow with the bow-tie

Listen. I don't like your sense of humour. I didn't find anything funny about your letting my little brother die. It took me five years and a journey to get over it. And I think that it's time for some compensation.

So here's how it is. I will not have my grandmother suffer. Either she gets well or she dies quickly. Don't let it take years for her to fade away. She doesn't deserve that. And I want that man. Yes, the one who's in the men's section now. His name's Dori Peleg. He has a prominent Adam's apple and a few strands

of grey in his hair and he smells wonderful and he's a bit
sad and I love him and I don't care that he has a wife. I want
him to love me back and I want us to be together and make
children together.

    For your consideration,
    Inbar Benbenisti

Dori

Put on tefillin, someone on his left offers him, join the minyan, someone on his right asks. But he walks straight ahead, to the Wall. A man wearing a bicycle helmet instead of a yarmulke leans it against the stones as if he were a soldier in the Six Day War. Dori stands beside him, takes out the note given to him by the grocer in Ecuador and looks for a space between the stones that isn't too full. He tries to shove the note in three times, but it falls back into his hand each time. It's really crowded today, hey? the bike rider says, and suggests that he walk over to the roofed section, there might be more room there.

Dori nods and walks past a group of people praying around a bar mitzvah boy, and a group simply praying, and a group of Givati soldiers, and a group of Golani soldiers.

His headmaster called him last night, to say that he's going back to the army, and made Dori an offer he couldn't refuse; financially speaking, that is. And also, he said in a tone bristling with self-importance, we have to fix all the things that went wrong during the war because in the Middle East, anyone who shows weakness ends up in the sea. Why had the man chosen him, of all people, to fire his clichés at, Dori wonders, why did that petty tyrant of a lieutenant-colonel feel the need to call him and not someone else? The answer to that question came towards the end of the conversation: The thing is that they need me at headquarters urgently, he explained, and the entire offer depends on whether I can be available within a few months. So I thought that my replacement should come from inside the school, which would shorten the transition period. There will be other formal procedures, you know. The administration has to approve. But don't worry. I'll take you across that bridge when we get to it.

You won't believe the offer I just got, he said to Roni when he'd hung up. But she didn't get excited at all. How much of a difference will it really make in your salary? she said. You'll just work harder and still earn so little. But this is a chance to make a real change, he almost shouted. To implement everything I believe in here, not in Argentina! She shrugged, opened her computer and hid behind it, and he couldn't take it any more. He strode over, pushed the screen forward and said, tell me, what's been wrong with you since I got back? Why are you like this? Don't ask, Dori, she said. And as if he were his father, as if he were Begin, he said, I can't do this any more, I need an answer. This isn't a good time for questions like that, she said, and I'm not sure you want to hear the answer. But I do. In a cold voice, she said, I'm not the only one who's acting like this, it's both of us, and it's not just since you came back. It started a long time before that. Our lives are moving in very different directions. Anyway, our threesome with Netta doesn't really work. So . . . what . . . what do we do? he asked — because as usual, she beat him to the punch, easily putting into words what he hadn't been able to say to himself all this time, and he knew her well enough to know that she already had a practical solution. She looked up from the computer and said, what do we do? What everyone does. He knelt down beside her and asked, what does everyone do, Roni? I have no idea, so tell me, please, I beg you. She stroked his head without affection and said, another child –

He tries to make his way through the narrow, roofed part of the Western Wall. Here too, the crowd of beseechers is large, and he has to wait until a spot near the stones becomes free. In a small, almost invisible alcove between the columns in front of the stones, a few yeshiva students are sitting on black plastic chairs, listening to a Gemara lesson being given by their rabbi, and even though Dori is dying to find the right resting place for his note between the stones and get back to Inbar, he's always been drawn to learning, so he moves nearer for a few seconds, leans on the supporting wall and listens to the young, alert-eyed rabbi chanting a very melodic description of Yochanan ben Zakkai's escape fom Jerusalem in a coffin, before the destruction of the Temple: 'And they took him out and carried him until sunset when they came to Vespasian the Roman. They opened the coffin and he stood before him. Vespasian said to him: You are Rabbi Yochanan ben Zakkai. What shall I give you? And Yochanan said: I ask of you nothing other than the city of Yavne, there I will teach my pupils and hold prayers.' And here – the young rabbi says, looking up from the page, at him, Dori thinks – our sages are divided. Some ask: Why didn't Ben Zakkai ask Vespasian for Jerusalem? Why didn't he take advantage of the opportunity to ease the sufferings of the besieged? And others claim: Because Ben Zakkai asked for the safety of Yavne and its sages, he was able to establish a new Judaism there, the roots of modern day Judaism. Some ask: Is it possible that Ben Zakkai escaped from the city too soon, and that was why, before his death, he wept and told his students that he was not sure whether he would enter the Garden of Eden or Hell? Still others argue: Ben Zakkai knew in his heart that the loss of Jerusalem was inevitable and, with the help of the Almighty, established in Yavne the foundations for the rehabilitation of a people who seemed to have died—

Dori moves away because he's had enough, and walks along the stones of the Wall until he finds a path among the people and a narrow gap between two stones. He thrusts the note inside, lingers a few more seconds to make sure that the request made by Jesus, the grocer from Ecuador, doesn't fall on to the ground, then leaves the roofed section for the open area, for the light, and beyond the stand of cardboard yarmulkes, he sees Inbar waiting for him.

She doesn't see him watching her. She's looking in a different direction, and moves a few locks of her hair to her nose and sniffs—

How is it that you can fall in love with a woman because of a single gesture she makes?

It isn't until he reaches her that she turns to him, and he puts his hand on hers, and she says, the yarmulke. He takes it off and puts it in his pocket. The sun sends its absolutely final rays towards the international centre of the Fire of the Torah, and towards the six stars of the Yizkor sculpture under it. As they make their way through the security gate, he spreads his fingers so she can fit hers between them, and he doesn't care if anyone he knows sees them. What difference does it make now? They walk out of the Old City through the Dung Gate and stop on the edge of the abyss, near the *kunafa* pastry stall. And there they stand for aeons and aeons. Silently. Their shoulders touching.

Do you see the sea? she finally asks him.

What sea? he says, turning to face her.

The Sea of Jerusalem, she says, pressing his hand lightly.

He looks forward again, and at first doesn't understand what she's talking about. He doesn't see any sea, only a stand of *darbuka* drums and a taxi with two wheels on the pavement.

But slowly, it happens . . .

An evening breeze begins to blow in the world, waves of wandering, waves of return, waves of alienation, waves of closeness — and the waves grow higher before his eyes, like shock waves after a very large explosion, rising one after the other from the depths of the Judaean Desert, reaching their zenith on the hills surrounding the city, breaking where Dori and Inbar's shoes meet the ground, leaving behind a thin foam of opportunity.

Then they recede, folding back into one another, only to begin all over again.

Acknowledgements

Writing is also a journey, most of which you make alone.

But with this book – perhaps more than ever before – I was fortunate to have the help of many people who joined me for a while and contributed generously of their knowledge.

Thank you to those who were partners in planning and carrying out the research in South America: Yoav Adler, Yuval Hollander, Dorit Morali, Bat Sheva Fisher, Gachi Kremer and Eva Rosenthal.

A special thank you to Enrico Grinberg, who accompanied me personally during the trip and became a friend (and one friend is an entire world).

Thank you to Frank Domhan, Leah Hersher (Berlin Tours) and Keren Presente for the days in Berlin.

Thank you to Homaya Amar, who opened the doors to shamanism for me.

Thank you to Micha Odenheimer and Yishai Levy Binyamini, through whom I learned about the admirable activities of the Tevel B'tzedek (The Earth in Justice) NPO.

Thank you to Yoram ben Yehuda, Shmulik Calderon and Yossi Rofaizen, who opened my eyes to everything about the Yom Kippur War and the way in which it continues to reverberate in the lives of the soldiers who fought in it.

Thank you to the Hagana Archives for helping me to locate the personal diaries of those who sailed aboard the Tiger Hill. The story of the Tiger Hill, which was the last ship of illegal immigrants to arrive on the shores of this country before the outbreak of the Second World War, was the inspiration for the story of Lily's journey to Eretz Israel.

Thank you to Pola Barzam, Tal Davidovitch, Prof. Galit Hazan-Rokem, Meirav Londers, Hilik Magnus, Tal Nitzan, Amnon Sadovsky, Ilanit Frank-Hakim, Franca Crystal, Doron Rachmani and Dalit Rishpi-Tor, for making me wiser, each one in his own field of expertise.

Thank you to my first readers, who were exposed to early versions of the book – Shimon Adaf, Yael Gover, Oshrit Gur, Orit Gidali, Meital Mor, Yoram Meltzer, Moshe Azuz and Lior Sternberg. Without their honest and astute comments, I would never have got here.

Thank you to Hila Bloom, the best editor in the universe.

And thank you to Anat, my wife, my love and my partner on the true journey. The journey of life.

Altneuland, 2008–2011.